P. V. NARASIMHA RAO

# The
# INSIDER

VIKING

VIKING

Penguin Books India (P) Ltd., 210 Chiranjiv Tower, 43 Nehru Place, New Delhi 110 019, India
Penguin Books Ltd., 27 Wrights Lane, London W8 5TZ, UK
Penguin Books USA Inc., 375 Hudson Street, New York, NY 10014, USA
Penguin Books Australia Ltd., Ringwood, Victoria, Australia
Penguin Books Canada Ltd., 10 Alcorn Avenue, Suite 300, Toronto, Ontario M4V 3B2, Canada
Penguin Books (NZ) Ltd., 182-190 Wairau Road, Auckland 10, New Zealand

First published in Viking by Penguin Books India (P) Ltd. 1998

10 9 8 7 6 5 4 3 2

Typeset in Sabon by Digital Technologies and Printing Solutions, New Delhi

Printed and bound in India by Ajanta Offset and Packagings Ltd., New Delhi

Grateful acknowledgement is made to the following for copyright permission:

Atlantic Publishers and Distributors, New Delhi, for permission to quote from Bhagat Singh's correspondence with his father, excerpted from *Revolutionaries and the British Raj*, 1988: © S.R. Bakshi

Sterling Publishers Private Limited, New Delhi, for permission to quote from the diary of Jahanara Imam, excerpted from *Of Blood and Fire: The Untold Story of Bangladesh's War of Independence* (translated by Mustafizur Rehman), 1989: © Jahanara Imam

Asia Publishing House, Bombay, for permission to quote from *The Discovery of India*, 1961: © Jawaharlal Nehru

While every effort has been made to trace copyright holders and obtain permission, this has not been possible in all cases; any omissions brought to our attention will be remedied in future editions.

This humble work of his follower
is respectfully dedicated to
the Revered Leader
**the late Swami Ramananda Tirtha,**
head of Sri Ramtirth Ashram, and
leader and liberator of the people
of the former Native State of Hyderabad,
who agonized over **'The Land Problem'** all his life

Frail in body, enfeebled by incarceration,
having long denied himself the life of the householder,
this Sanyasi stood for the people and for Democracy,
and declared to the mighty and oppressive Nizam—
**'I shall break, but not bend!'**

# Acknowledgements

I am grateful to:

First and foremost, the scores of friends, colleagues and other persons who are fictionalized in this book as characters in the story. They have generously lent their flesh and blood, their tempers and idiosyncrasies, and their remarkable human characteristics. Real identities have been suitably disguised wherever necessary.

My literary guru, the late Shri Garlapati Raghava Reddy, for the profound inspiration he gave me to study the Indian literary tradition, and for inculcating in me the urge towards self-expression.

My scholarly cousin, the late P. Sadasiva Rao, who goaded me to write, write and write—despite my compulsive tendency to slide into political preoccupations.

Ms. A. Chhaya Devi, noted Telugu writer, who read some initial drafts and offered valuable advice.

Ms. Kalyani Shankar, well-known journalist, who scrutinized the text, helped in several ways to facilitate its publication, and above all, suggested the title of the book.

# A Note from the Author

This novel first began to take shape over twenty years ago as a sort of autobiography. I committed an unfinished draft to paper, and then other matters prevented me from completing it. An early draft, under another title, was leaked to the media by someone I had entrusted it to, in a complete breach of confidence. Since then the novel has been almost entirely rewritten and I am now satisfied with its shape and form and content.

This is not a regular autobiography, nor is it entirely a work of fiction wherein the writer has the freedom to create characters and improvise situations at will. It is, however, a tale of Indian politics in two volumes, spanning half a century, in which I have tried to mesh historical reality with the lives of several fictional and semi-fictional characters and situations to maintain narrative continuity and sustain the reader's interest. The central character, whose experiences are often derived from my own, participates in the final phase of India's freedom struggle, and continues through the regimes of eight Prime Ministers of independent India, before assuming that office himself. Having worked at the heart of the political process through much of his life, the story he tells has about it the truth (albeit fictionalized) of the insider.

The story, however, is necessarily confined to the experience and observation of just *one* insider, and does by no means claim to be a comprehensive or representative account of the vast and variegated subject it deals with.

This narrative extends till 1973, when Indira Gandhi was at the zenith of power and popularity. The far-reaching changes in national thinking, aspirations and socio-political formations thereafter are dealt with in the sequel to this book, which I intend to present in a few months' time.

New Delhi
January 1998

# Part I

Part I

1

THEY NAMED HIM ANAND, ON THE ELEVENTH DAY AFTER HIS
birth, according to custom.

Soon after he was born, the first thing he became aware of was
an object whose soft tip was thrust into his mouth whenever he
cried. He began sucking his mother's breast, right away as if he
had learnt that skill while still in the womb. As the days passed,
he began to respond to his environment. He learnt to recognize his
mother's voice, he liked the touch of her soft lips on his cheek. All
this was very agreeable. But when others crowded around him—
with their prickly stubbled chins and bad breath—he protested,
his loud wails drowning out the sounds of their endearments.

Little sharp teeth emerged from his gums when he was a few
months old. The first use he made of the teeth was to bite his
mother's breasts hard whenever he was being fed. Mother cried
out in pain and he would burst into laughter. Biting was fun; then
it became a habit. Something needed to be done—and was done.
One day, the breast tasted terribly bitter in his mouth. He pulled
his mouth away, tried in vain to spit the bitterness out and
screamed at the top of his voice. Now it was Mother's turn to

laugh. Some women from the neighbourhood who happened to be present also giggled at his discomfiture. They had all used the same recipe to wean their children from the breast. The recipe was simple. Apply a paste of neem leaves around the nipples and the baby wouldn't look at the breast ever again.

He enjoyed the massage and the hot bath Mother gave him every morning. She would sit on the floor, fold her sari up to the thighs and stretch her bare legs out in front of her. She would place him across her thighs, now on his face, now on his back, and rub sesamum oil all over his body; she would also put a few drops in his ears, eyes, a bit in the nostrils. She would then bathe him in water that was heated just right. He would feel like a rubber doll in her hands, while blood raced through his supple body. He liked all this, but loathed the oil when it entered his eyes and gave him a burning sensation. Then all hell would break loose. He would howl and kick Mother's belly and breasts viciously.

After the bath, Mother would put him into his cradle and expose him briefly to fragrant 'sambrani' smoke. Amazingly, he would slide into an untroubled sleep at once.

But sometimes, when he was in deep sleep, his face would inexplicably screw up, as if he was in great misery; on other occasions his countenance would light up with joy. What he was experiencing in his subconscious state, as most babies do, was a connection with the deepest mysteries of human existence, racing back through time and space. For all anyone knew, his grieving could have been for the misery of mankind—past, present and future. He may have been witnessing in his mind's eye the horrors of war, the atom bomb, the blood of Mahatma Gandhi, Indira Gandhi and Rajiv Gandhi, felled by assassins, mingling with the dust of Bharat.

Again, when he was beaming and gurgling contentedly in his sleep, perhaps he dreamt that he was the greatest individual in the Universe. Or perhaps he imagined himself consorting with legendary beauties like Shachi Devi, Indra's consort and the most beautiful woman in Indian mythology. Whatever caused his dreams, it worried Mother. Greatly agitated, she called in a *bhoot vaid*, an exorcist, to rid her infant son of whatever demons were troubling him. The dreams disappeared as naturally as they came, but the *bhoot vaid* got both cash and credit in the process.

About the same time, Mother began to feed him soft-cooked cereal, adding a little salt. First he looked at it with disdain and spat it out; but hunger prevailed. The food began to taste tolerable, then good. He cried for more, but Mother wouldn't oblige. She increased his intake gradually, so he wouldn't get indigestion.

In time, to his family's delight, he began to toddle. Nothing in the house stayed any longer where it belonged. The right shoe remained at the front door while the left travelled all the way to the other end of the house and into the backyard. Sometimes things disappeared altogether mysteriously. The mystery kept thickening until one day someone chanced to see a brass utensil fly like a missile into the well outside the house. Divers were commissioned to scour the bottom of the well and a variety of things long since given up as lost were retrieved.

At this time he encountered the most traumatic experience of his early childhood—the fortnightly dose of castor oil administered to him. Castor oil was a must for children. Mother insisted on it, as her mother had—for generations. The village *vaid* had a long lecture, complete with Sanskrit slokas, in praise of castor oil and its efficacy where children were concerned. It was an unimpeachable principle of ayurveda, he asserted, that the stomach was the repository of all potential ailments. Keep the bowels clean and live a hundred years, was his dictum. And always begin with babies, he would enjoin, rearranging his soiled clothes that smelled of medicines.

Anand couldn't tell time or count the passage of days, but with some kind of animal instinct, he knew the exact day when the castor oil was due. All in the family would brace themselves for that major operation. He would try to give them the slip and a search would start—under the beds, in the closet, behind the bushes in the backyard . . . He would discover new spots each time. On one desperate occasion, he shut himself up in a big wooden box. He would have suffocated to death, had the bustling and ubiquitous ayah not rescued him just in time.

They would eventually find the little fellow—after searching for an hour or so. When they converged on him, he would still make a last-ditch attempt to escape. When he discovered that his efforts to elude his tormentors were futile, he would kick, bite, howl, spit, struggle, grapple, wail, grit his teeth, keep his mouth tightly shut . . . Eventually, he would be overpowered and his stubborn mouth would be opened with a spoon. He knew he could neither bite it nor spit it out. With his hands and feet securely held, the hated castor oil would slip into his gullet smoothly. He knew he could do nothing to stop it. However, adequate recompense would come instantly when Mother pushed a pinch of sugar in his mouth. He would swallow it, with the philosophical resignation of one who takes the good along with the not-so-good.

As the weeks rolled by, the noises he made were slowly moulded into intelligible words. He didn't know what they meant, indeed he had no idea why anything should mean anything, or what was meant by meaning. Soon he came to relate the sounds he uttered to individual people. 'Amma' was Mother, and no other. And so on. And he too came to respond to a given combination of sounds—called a name, as he learned later. His name. His own. His alone. He came to pronounce it himself, bit by bit, error by error. Ana . . . Anad . . . And finally, Anand. Thus labelled, he stood out, distinct from the rest of humankind: ANAND.

*

As his confidence grew, Anand ventured out of the house and discovered a magical world. The cattle-shed, in particular, fascinated him. Every evening he would watch the cows come into the shed. They emerged from out of the dust-screen raised by their hooves. The jingle of bells tied round the necks of some of them heralded their arrival.

Mother wouldn't let Anand go anywhere near the cows—particularly the sharp-horned ones who kept a vigilant and protective eye on their infant calves. Even the adults were afraid of them, but Anand was still unaware of fear; all he felt was wonder. He would approach the cows stealthily, while Mother was away in the kitchen, or was late in returning from the temple. Quite remarkably, he came to no harm. One of the cows even licked him on the head affectionately once, before the ayah raised an alarm and took Anand away.

The most enjoyable time for Anand was in the morning, when the cows went out to graze and the calves remained in the shed. He talked to the calves in a language no other humans knew, yet the calves seemed to understand perfectly. Neither he nor they had yet been contaminated by grammar and syntax; there was no scope for misinterpretation. Mother, however, found this new-found friendship a nuisance, for Anand would return all covered with dung. She would have to catch him on the run—which was a job in itself—and give him a thorough scrubbing. She would then warn him sternly not to approach the cattle-shed again. But, of course, he knew Mother did not understand this friendship, so he would ignore her and go back to the cattle-shed at the first opportunity. When the ayah tried to prevent him he would yell at her and the calves would support him with a chorus of resentful moos.

Soon, to his chagrin, he was no longer the cynosure of all eyes, for a baby sister was born and laid claim to primacy in the family. But if Mother was busy with his sister, there were others to fuss over him. There was an uncle who humoured him all the time. He would often take Anand out on his evening walks on the tank bund outside the village. Anand would carry Uncle's stick, taller than himself, and put it to a variety of uses. It would become a horse as he sat astride it, with his hand holding its end like a bridle. He would use it as a gun, to fire at birds that flew by, simulating the sound of the shots by a deep aspiration of his lips. He would threaten passers-by, by pointing the 'gun' at them. They would all pretend to be terrified, much to his delight.

If Uncle was wonderful, Father somehow inspired fear. Anand did not know why, but he instinctively treated Father with respect, because he seemed a little stern.

The difference between Mother and Father was so clear, so palpable. He could run into Mother's arms at will, as of right; she was much more sympathetic whenever he wailed or threw a tantrum, and was always fussing over him. Where Father was concerned, he would wait for a signal before seeking the refuge of his arms. Father was loving, but not indulgent; his affection was less evident. Perhaps for that very reason, it was so much more welcome whenever he showed it. There were some compensating features, however. Father would hold him by his tiny wrists, toss him straight up into the air and while he shouted with joy and abandon, catch him neatly on his way down. He would tickle him in the ribs, ruffle his hair, pinch his chubby cheeks and do a myriad other tricks, which nobody else could do. The best of these was when Father lay on his back, lifted his legs at right angles and made a platform with his upturned soles. He would hoist Anand atop the platform, face down, and balance his little body there. Sometimes he would do this on just one foot and Anand would shriek with delight and delicious terror. He revelled in all these acrobatics—until hunger reminded him of Mother.

Father was muscular and sturdy. When young, he had wielded a lathi proficiently when there were scuffles, and sometimes regular riots, between the farmers of his village and those of the neighbouring ones over land and other causes. That was how the farmers of his village—and those of the others—had come to respect him as one who could provide leadership when needed. Those were times when the official settlement of village lands had not been initiated by the government of Afrozabad State. As a result, the boundaries of village lands were generally drawn as per historical tradition, conciliation, or when these did not work, by muscle power. In any event, even when conciliation succeeded, some skirmishes did take place to begin with, as if each side was trying to measure the other's strength and determination. Only when one village proved its superiority was there peace. After proving his mettle, Father settled down as village officer, the local symbol of authority.

For Anand, Father was also a teacher. Every night, after dinner, he would stretch himself on his favourite cot in the courtyard, or inside the house in the winter months. Then, he would place Anand on his chest and recite verses from the *Bhagavata* in a long chain, in the very order they appeared in the epic, beginning with the invocation to the gods. Anand never knew how long the recitation continued or how many verses his father recited, for he would invariably fall asleep midway through the proceedings.

In a few weeks' time, Anand began to recite the verses. Father would accompany him for a while and then trail off. Anand would go on, depending on his own memory. When he faltered, Father would come to the rescue. Then Anand began to falter less and less. His phenomenal memory became apparent before he was four. When the village *imdadi* teacher began his *aksharabhyasa* (initiation into the alphabet), Anand astonished him by reeling off verses like a pundit.

By the time Anand was five, he had learned all that the little village school could teach him. There was nothing more he could learn there. The state government had taken care to see that thousands like Anand got stuck at the third standard and lapsed into illiteracy. Denying the masses education was the government's way of keeping them under control. Father realized this, of course, having himself been a victim. He could recite hundreds of verses from the epics and the classics, but all that had been his own efforts to educate himself. He did not know a word of Persian, the official language of the state. He knew how humiliating that had been for him, and so decided to cram Anand with 'modern' education.

As a first step towards this end, Father decided to send Anand to his younger brother's village, twenty miles away, where there was a primary school.

# 2

IT WAS APRIL. ANAND WAS TO LEAVE IN JUNE, AFTER THE SUMMER vacation. Mother was crestfallen but tried to look cheerful. Anand did not know what he was in for. He was enjoying himself as usual.

It was a middle-class family—middle middle-class, to be more precise. The class that invariably gets the beating, being at once sensitive and vulnerable. The upper class, the elite, was close to the ruling aristocracy. They had different norms—rather, no norms at all, so they could ignore all the dictates of society with unconcern and indulge in anything they wished. They were a thin crust at the top and were extremely influential. They looked conspicuous, with their fez caps and other features of attire and attitude—called *lawazimaat*—that were typical of feudalism. Then there were the pseudo-feudals, who tried very hard to be accepted as part of the Haakim's (ruler's) coterie. The more they aped the feudals, the more they looked ridiculous. Yet they hung around the aristocracy with pathetic tenacity.

At the other end of the spectrum came the lowly ones, vast in numbers but completely without power or prosperity. They were just nondescript. They counted for nothing, wanted nothing beyond being allowed to live. A full meal once in a while, a copious drink of toddy in the evening, an occasional patronizing gesture from the 'lords', even in the midst of a heap of insults and kicks—this was their lot. Indeed, they were so conditioned to their plight that they did not feel the insults acutely. You could say they were happy in their own way—their own brutalized way.

The middle class fell between these two extremes. Sensitive to the point of touchiness, yet dumb and powerless, their lot was to burn within. The aristocracy derided them, the lower classes loathed them. They were culturally distinct from the masses, being literate and in some cases refined as well. They stood out in the life of the village. And some of them, the village officers for instance, were hated symbols of the king's authority. They often served as promoters of tyranny and conduits of corruption; they were themselves petty tyrants and corrupt to the core. All this only served to alienate them even more from the villagers they oppressed.

Most of the time they merely did the dirty jobs of the government, so the people often saw them as part of the government. Everyone in authority stepped on them, yet no one took notice of them. Consequently, they represented no one. Theirs was an isolated existence, squeezed from both sides. They lived on the spot and took the blame. The higher-ups were far away from the scene, and largely immune.

Anand's village was called Anantgiri. When Anand was a child, Anantgiri's population was about two thousand. The village had a few ancient landmarks which no one ever cared much about. The only monuments the villagers paid attention to were a semi-dilapidated *burj* about two centuries old, a Shiva temple and an imposing Hanuman statue that towered majestically over the village. A two-foot wide, seven-foot high slab of stone with an inscription in an unknown script stood close by. The statue signified that long ago the village had adopted Veer Hanuman as its protector god who, in turn, was believed to have kept the village free from *pisachas*, the evil spirits. Some people, especially women from this and other neighbouring villages, diagnosed as afflicted by some *pisacha*, still came and worshipped Hanuman for a given

11

period (usually forty days) and went back satisfied, having been successfully exorcized. Nothing was beyond the great Hanuman, the son of the wind god, they said. The villagers showed their deep faith and gratitude by getting Hanuman anointed with fresh sindoor paste at their own expense whenever it was time to do so according to the shastras as interpreted by the local pundits.

Old people said that in their childhood they had seen the surrounding scrub forest almost abutting the village. They related stories of how panthers and wolves entered their houses and cattle-sheds and carried young calves away. All that had changed during the last seventy or eighty years, they reminisced. Now, the scrub had receded three to four miles away from the village. Trees were no longer considered sacred as of yore, although some symbolic ceremony of worshipping them was still observed. Elders remembered how, in the old days, intruders from other villages who felled trees in Anantgiri illicitly were invariably caught and thoroughly thrashed. But now some good-for-nothing fellows from this very village join the thieves. Who will save the village and its properties today, they asked. And in reply, said, No one, with a deep sigh. Bad days have come—was the final conclusion everyone seemed to have come to. Anand remembered listening to this refrain from the time he was a child.

The village was situated in the major native state of India, Afrozabad. The state had a chequered history. It began with the last Mughal emperor's Subedar (commissioner) Nasir Jah declaring himself independent of the weakened Mughal empire. His new dynasty continued to rule the state for a century and a half. The tenth Nasir Jah's regime coincided with the concluding quarter century of India's freedom struggle. There was a widespread superstition connected with this dynasty. The founder of the dynasty, it was believed, had visited a local saint soon after declaring his independence. The saint had blessed his dynasty with uninterrupted rule for ten generations. From all accounts, the saint's prophecy had come true; the dynasty had indeed continued for ten generations. Now, if the other half of the prophecy was to be fulfilled, the present king, who happened to be the tenth descendant, would be the last to rule the state. With the Indian

12

independence movement gaining momentum, there was a strong prospect of all the native states merging with the Indian Union. For decades and decades, the feudal regime in the state had committed unspeakable atrocities against the people. Loot, murder, rape, arson, collective fines in almost every village on mere suspicion of disloyalty—every conceivable crime was perpetrated in an unending orgy hatched by the king's henchmen to terrorize the people and put down the slightest sign of democratic aspiration. The oppression of the king's regime became intolerable, particularly when the king began to feel insecure because of the new desire for freedom sweeping the country. When no one came to their rescue, a sense of extreme dejection came over the people. All that they were left with was the saint's prophecy. They kept recounting it in whispers—hopeful whispers—with lips, however, tightly sealed.

Mahatma Gandhi had exploded on the political scene with his civil disobedience movement in British India. A new feeling of elation and expectancy, a new spirit of service and sacrifice was evident everywhere in the country. It was a time of high patriotic fervour.

However, all this had only a muted impact on the native states since almost all their rulers were wholly subservient to the British. The ruler of Afrozabad, in particular, had a special dispensation to insulate his kingdom from outside influences—or so he imagined. There was practically no communication between the state and the rest of India. Rail passengers travelling by any route across the state were not permitted to break journey within the state. There was no radio anywhere in the villages; no newspaper ever reached there. The state was, for all practical purposes, as isolated as the remotest atoll in the middle of the ocean.

Anand grew up in this milieu. Where no political expression was permitted, cultural preoccupation became dominant, of necessity. In point of fact, the native states themselves were artificial and arbitrary entities carved out of culturally homogeneous areas of the country to serve various political and imperial exigencies. So the kings imposed political blackouts on their subjects, but all their efforts to suppress the centuries-old cultural ties between the people of the states and those outside in British India failed miserably.

Afrozabad had shut out the languages of the masses from the higher echelons of the administration. They were also out of fashion among the intellectual elite who employed derisive epithets to describe the vernacular tongues and ignored the rich literatures in these languages. According to the elite, such languages were crude. Uncivilized. Tortuous. Incapable of becoming the vehicles of administration or of scientific expression. This caused deep resentment and alienation among the people, and they came to love their languages all the more. Language became an unbreakable bond between the people of the state and those outside, more than ever before.

Scholars, artists, saints and savants had a grudging but comparatively free access to the state. Theatrical troupes, mainly staging mythological plays, were a common sight in towns and villages. Humming popular tunes from the plays and playing host to actors and actresses—particularly the latter—became a status symbol with the minor feudals in the countryside. The air was full of the *Ramayana*, the *Mahabharata* and the myriad themes of puranic lore. Well-known artistes from the adjacent areas in British India performed these plays in improvised theatres. The local audiences were very fond of them. They bought tickets ranging from one anna to a rupee. Besides these, Hari Katha recitals and the performances of various local troupes were most popular. In the case of local performers from neighbouring villages, there were no tickets. The plays were staged in the open, so the season started after the cessation of rains, from October. The time coincided with the harvest. Grain was plentiful, and the whole village paid the performing artistes in kind. The village traders paid them in the first instance; the village then partly reimbursed the traders, each farmer giving a percentage of his land revenue. To this arrangement, all but the indigent contributed, while the whole village—the rich and poor alike—enjoyed the nightly entertainment. Culture had thus become a very important prop in the lives of the people. And gradually, political themes from the epics, introduced allegorically, began to allude to contemporary subjects in many ways, depending on the subtlety and competence of the writers and artistes.

Little Anand immersed himself in the epics. The poems Father recited night after night brought about Anand's identification with something beyond the visible and tangible world. He began to see Rama, Krishna, Prahlad, Dhruva and a host of mythological characters as familiar friends. His fertile imagination conjured up situations in which he found himself in their company as naturally as with the calves in his cattle-shed. Without realizing it, he developed an amazing capacity to live in the skins of other characters and become sensitive to their emotions. This helped him, he realized later, to suspend his ego and tap into his empathetic nature with ease.

Quite naturally, Hanuman became Anand's hero. At five, he saw no one else as great. An admixture of the fun provided by the monkey and the great deeds accomplished by the son of the wind god, as he heard Hanuman described, left no doubt in Anand's mind. He fancied himself as Hanuman. He became Hanuman—no fancy as far as *he* was concerned. A piece of rope tied round his waist, with one end projecting in the rear like a tail, turned him into Hanuman. A paste of red kumkum applied on the mouth and a cardboard crown as shown in Hanuman's pictures, which Mother fabricated with skill, completed the make-up. When Anand jumped from a one-foot high stool, he felt, quite seriously, that he was jumping across the ocean. The family found it hilarious. Even Father looked impressed. Anand's bosom swelled with pride.

In a matter of days his identification with Hanuman was almost total. If he was Hanuman, he couldn't remain Anand. The logic was simple. As he went through life, he found that less and less of his self determined his actions—an unusual trait that eventually distinguished him from many others.

When a troupe from a nearby village staged a play depicting Hanuman's great exploits in all their vividness, Anand was in raptures. While much older boys went to sleep within an hour or two after the show began, he sat bolt upright without a wink of sleep, fascinated by the all-night show.

The next morning, Mother found him absorbed in deep thought. She wanted to ensure that he slept, to make up for the previous night; but he had other ideas. Hanuman had possessed him. What haunted him was the image of Hanuman setting on fire the box-like bamboo structure covered with sheets of paper, representing Lanka, in the previous night's show. He admired the structure going up in lovely flames. If he was Hanuman, he must accomplish something equally remarkable, he decided. And he *was* Hanuman, of course.

As the morning hours ticked by, Anand kept planning diligently. After a thorough survey, he thought his uncle's thatched hut would serve as a good Lanka—as good as any. The roof was low and, in any event, there was a wooden cot under the eaves. Lanka was within his reach when he stood on the cot.

Setting fire, however, was a tougher proposition. His parents never let him go anywhere near fire. There was Father's standing threat to spank him if he ever did so. Father's shirt pocket usually had a matchbox, but Anand had never touched it. He had often wondered how the flame emerged out of nowhere when Father struck a stick. That day, however, his interest was more practical; he had no time to wonder. He had to find a matchbox quickly, and initiate himself into the art of stick-striking. He was sure the flame would oblige. And he would accomplish the burning of Lanka.

But where on earth could he find a matchbox? . . . Where? It came like a flash, like the flame from the matchstick he had admired so often. He remembered that Mother kept a matchbox in the pooja alcove close to the kitchen. There were a few idols and photographs of gods, prominent among them Balaji of Tirupati. Anand knew a little about the godly alcove. Only a little, since neither he nor anyone else with the usual clothes on, were allowed to touch anything in it. That was the family custom. Mother alone, after her bath every morning, would do the pooja. Then she offered food to God; no one ate before that. *Naivedya* had an immutable priority, strictly enforced.

Anand attended pooja with religious regularity; religion to him meant the sweet prasad at the end of the worship. His first

16

impression of God was sweet. Sweet and desirable. Just before the prasad, Mother performed the aarti, the camphor flame presented to the deities and then shown to the devotees. Anand rather liked the scent of burning camphor. Aarti and prasad made a nice combination.

So *that* was where he could find a matchbox! Reminded of it, he was pleased with himself—and with God . . . Yet he had to work out the logistics of retrieving the matchbox. First, secrecy. It had to be a solo performance, a one-child conspiracy, with no accomplices. Mother should know nothing, of course; so he had only limited time for the operation.

Next, the 'how' of it. How could he touch anything in the pooja alcove with his clothes on? That would be sacrilege. Even theft had to be committed with purity. He didn't know it was theft anyway, or what theft was.

It was about eleven, the time when Mother went to fetch drinking water from the large step-well outside the village. The well in the backyard of the house had brackish water. So did all the wells in the village.

He was in the courtyard, pretending to be playing innocently when Mother stepped out of the house carrying a brass pail. The moment she was out of sight, Anand dashed into the backyard, took off his clothes and poured a few tumblers of water on his body—an apology for a bath. Thus rendered pure, he entered the kitchen, stark naked, and approached the pooja alcove in a fever of excitement and awe. He was on the first expedition of pilferage of his life—stealing straight from God.

He retrieved the matchbox and instinctively paid obeisance with folded hands to the group of deities. Then he darted out of the kitchen, gripping the matchbox tightly, while the gods watched him with amusement.

Now for Uncle's hut. For Lanka. For a re-enactment of Hanuman's most wonderful feat.

Approaching the wooden cot he looked around. No one in sight. Good, he reassured himself. Then he realized that he had never struck a match before. He had watched Father and many others minutely enough. Yet, that was mere observation. So different from participation, as he could see now.

He took out a stick, held it between thumb and forefinger and looked at it, mystified at the blackish sulphur cap that would produce the flame. Then, rather clumsily but as closely following Father's action as he could, he struck the match . . . and dropped it instantly with a suppressed shriek. The flame had burnt his last two fingers. Not much, but enough to scare him . . .

He pondered over that first experience of burning his fingers. Then he struck another match and then another, each time learning to position his fingers and adjust the angle of the matchstick. After a few sticks lay scattered on the floor, he got it right. He had learnt fast.

Now for the real thing. He should hurry up; he didn't have all day. Mother would be returning any minute. He didn't want to leave the task half done.

He stood on the cot and stretched his hand up. The palm-leaf eaves were just within his reach. The ends of the dry leaves felt crisp and brittle under his touch. Perfect.

He struck the matchstick, making no mistake—of grip, angle or jerk. The lovely flame appeared before him, at his service, like the genie in Aladdin's lamp. At his bidding, the genie kissed the eaves. The rest followed.

He jumped down, ran out of the hut and watched the flame rising. It was beautiful, he thought. Lanka began to burn magnificently. The sight was a lot better than last night's, he concluded proudly. He was lost in admiration.

Just then, he heard a loud cry. The washerwoman, who had come to collect the soiled clothing of the family, rushed across the courtyard and into the street, screaming like a lunatic. Within seconds, a dozen or so men converged on the hut. Anand saw Father directing the fire-fighting operations . . . It was then that fear gripped him. Fear such as he had never known before. He didn't know why, but suddenly he felt that he shouldn't have done it. That was his first stab of repentance . . . Shouldn't have . . . Shouldn't have . . . Shouldn't have . . . But he had done it! What now?

No one took notice of him; no one knew what had

happened—yet. But he, Anand, knew; and when he caught a glimpse of Father, that settled it.

He slipped out of the house. Didn't know where to go. Just felt that he must disappear. After running for what seemed like hours, he thought he had gone very far, to the other end of the earth, never to return. Never to see Mother. As it was, he was only on the outskirts of the village, in the scorching sun. Contrary to what he wished to believe, everyone in the street had seen him sprinting naked, crying aloud. With some amusement they let him run as far as he could. Then an elderly man collected him in his arms and brought him back home, while he still twisted and turned and sobbed louder and louder.

Thankfully, he didn't have to see Father that day. Only Mother, who hugged her truant son and smothered him with kisses.

Lanka was saved.

# 3

AS THE *MRIGASIRA* SHOWERS IN JUNE WRAPPED THE VILLAGE IN rain-scented breezes, the date of Anand's departure to the other village, called Sheogaon, approached. He came to know about it only a few days in advance. What frightened him was his impending separation from Mother. He burst into tears at the slightest thought of that eventuality.

Brisk preparations were on. People began to brace Anand up for the ordeal. Someone gave long and tempting descriptions of Sheogaon. The school, the playground, the wonderful time children had on the slide and the swings. Then they mentioned the three teachers, not just one as in this village. He would be taught Persian, the rarefied language of the aristocracy. Every Friday would be a holiday, besides festivals like Id, Dassehra, Dipawali, etc. Of particular interest was the ten-day vacation for Muharram, when Anand could come back home to be with Mother. Which, Anand reasoned, confirmed that at other times he was to be away from her. In addition, there would be a holiday whenever a baby was born in the king's family. For instance, the sixty-year-old king

(God save him!) had married a beautiful girl of sixteen only last year. He (or, as some put it significantly, that latest wife of his) had been blessed with a son only a week back. There was public rejoicing all over the state. The authorities distributed sweets to all school children. The children naturally wished and prayed, 'May God bless the numerous wives of the good old king with many more children—in fact, a child every day!' Again, a death in the royal family brought a school holiday too. So the children wished for more and more deaths in the king's household. All in all, the effort was to convince Anand that school at Sheogaon was just a string of holidays to be enjoyed!

Then followed a description of Uncle Maruti, his wife Manorama Devi, and their son Raju and daughter Kamla, with whom Anand would be living. Very good people, someone said. Very, very good, another chimed in. Extremely nice and kind and loving, elaborated a third. What wonderful company!—they all exclaimed in a rather artificial chorus. The chorus didn't impress Anand. He looked at Mother for comfort, with tearful eyes.

Mother looked sad; she did not participate in the collective effort to brainwash Anand. She was preoccupied, a little absorbed in herself. One could also detect a faint red tint in the white of her eyes; yet no one had seen her cry. She would give Anand an extra hug, as if to compensate for what both of them would miss. He felt a lump rise in his throat too and tears spilled down his face. The uncle he was to stay with was none other than Father's younger brother adopted into another branch of the same family, resident at Sheogaon. Anand would thus live virtually as a member of his own family. Staying with close relations for education was a common practice in those days when schools were very few. No payment was expected; some grain or vegetables were voluntarily sent on some occasions. There was no paying guest system; in fact, any payment as quid pro quo was never accepted.

In order to spare Anand further grief, there was no overt mention of his departure as such. However, they had a long debate on who should accompany him on his first visit 'abroad'. Uncle Maruti came to escort him to Sheogaon personally. If Mother were to accompany Anand, she could not, as per established custom, ride in the same cart as the uncle. A married middle-class lady in the countryside could ride in a vehicle only with her husband, father or brother—no one else. No one, especially on her husband's side of the family . . . So they would need two bullock carts if Mother went along. They also reasoned that Anand would adjust better to his new surroundings if the trauma of separation took place at home and at one time, rather than in a strange place. They decided that Mother would remain at home.

The bullock cart was ready. They started early in the morning, with Father in the driver's seat, Anand next to him and Uncle in the rear. Mother had made Anand's favourite dishes and fed him well. She chattered away without letting him see the flood of tears that welled up again and again in her eyes. She knew Anand loved the bullock cart and dwelt upon that topic all the time. Her talk at last lured him into sitting next to Father in the cart, looking excitedly at the bullocks about to step forward. He didn't realize that while the bullocks moved with the bells round their necks jingling rhythmically, Mother had gone out of sight. He suddenly found himself sandwiched between Father and Uncle. Black depression overtook him within minutes when the new reality dawned on him.

Again, within minutes, Father deflected his attention by companionable conversation, telling him all about the bullocks, their names, characteristics and specialities. The wealth of detail distracted Anand, at least for the moment. And he was really excited when Father made him sit in his lap, gave him the whip and began teaching him to drive. Despite Father's protective arm round him, Anand imagined he was driving the cart all by himself. The action kept him temporarily diverted from thoughts of Mother.

They arrived at their destination by noon. Uncle's son, Raju, and daughter, Kamla, at once whisked Anand away to join them in a game of *gulli danda*. Auntie, Anand thought, was a bit forbidding, both in appearance and demeanour. He dismissed the thought somehow and got absorbed in play. Again, it was diversion, not reconciliation . . . However, when they sat down to their first meal in the new home, the fact of Mother's absence devastated Anand. He broke down completely, ate next to nothing. Father sat with him till late in the night until Anand somehow fell into a fitful sleep.

*(For years and years later in his life, whenever he saw school-going children in the city, he would recall this occasion and remind himself that he had never quite reconciled himself to leaving Mother, nor to eating anything other than what she fed him. The scar remained on his psyche, a sense of sudden loss nothing else could compensate for. He had become motherless at five; that's how he saw it—nothing less.)*

After that first meal under Uncle's roof, Anand became surprisingly cooperative, even docile. No tantrums, no fuss of any kind. It was a relief to everyone. They admired Anand for his good sense. To Anand, however, it felt very different. He developed a peculiar stoicism and nothing seemed to matter to him any more. His soul, as it were, went mechanical. He did not mind; rather, did not care.

Father left after a few days, Anand did not quite notice when. The natural resilience of youth asserted itself and he became part of the new scenario he had been plunged into. The three teachers in the school and their timetable of lessons, etc. provided a new experience. School started with a prayer for the long life of the king, their benign sovereign. He was great. He was noble. He was benevolent. They all bowed before him in deferential allegiance, the prayer said. Amen . . . Anand recited the full text of the prayer on the second day, astonishing teachers and pupils alike. Many boys liked him; some who probably found him overly intelligent, did not. Within a short time, his innate talent manifested itself and he began to enjoy himself and the life of the school.

They taught the mother tongue in the first two grades only, half-heartedly. There was no future for those who were confined to using the local language. A pupil could fail in it and still get promoted to the next higher class. Only Persian, the coveted language of the elite, was crucial; it held the key to the future. There were a few Muslim boys in the school. Two of the three teachers were Muslims too. Anand was mingling with boys of another faith for the first time, but it didn't make the slightest difference to him or to them.

Muharram was at hand. Whatever the Muslim mullahs said, people in the village took it as just another festival. They made elaborate preparations weeks in advance. Like all other festivals, the vast Hindu population observed Muharram, along with the handful of Muslims in the village. They called it the festival of the 'pirs' (reverends or ancestors) in this state. A pir consisted of a pole surrounded by a cylindrical bamboo frame wrapped around by a colourful cloth inlaid with *zari* work. They called it *dhatti*. Rich individuals, often Hindus, presented *dhattis* to the pirs. It was a token of gratitude to the pirs who, they believed, had fulfilled wishes they had made earlier. They called the wish *mannat*. There was no religious distinction among those who made it, just as there was none among the common wishes of all human beings. It was part of the common faith, or superstition—depending on how you looked at it.

From the *Ramayana* to Muharram was no doubt a broad jump, but Anand found it easy enough. If he could become Hanuman, he could also transform himself into a pir worshipper. There was a belief that when some persons carried pirs, the pirs 'possessed' them and they became unconscious of the outside world. In such a state of trance, they could walk over burning coals, stand on one foot for days, run at fantastic speeds; in fact, accomplish any feat impossible for normal human beings. Many individuals were prone to these trances and some indeed remained 'possessed' for the entire ten-day period of the Muharram ceremonies. Only after they bade the pirs *al-widaa* (farewell) on the last day would the state of trance abate, bit by bit. It was an especially absorbing· occasion for the village urchins who enjoyed every moment of the long vacation. Either they followed the pirs wherever they were carried, or themselves improvised small pirs with whatever sticks and pieces of cloth they could lay their hands on, to celebrate their own mini-Muharram—trances and all.

Anand experimented with the trance-like state. He stood on one foot for what seemed to him an eternity—about five minutes.

It was a record among all his companions. It made him a hero among the boys and the girls of the village—a coveted distinction indeed.

Something very different, however, unfolded within him—the capacity to lose himself in other beings. Transmigration of self, as it were. He didn't know it at the time, of course. And he didn't care. Indeed, he didn't care for anything any more, with Mother no longer close by. The self was at large, trackless.

Mercifully, no one mooted a proposal to walk on burning coals.

*

After the excitement of Muharram, life fell into a fairly consistent pattern for Anand. School, play, all-round achievement, approbation, moments of elation—albeit with a diffused sense of deprivation. But Anand suffered no bouts of agony, felt no sudden pangs, when he remembered Mother. Indeed, he hardly remembered her as a physical presence any more. Yet her absence affected him subconsciously and sawed away a part of him, as it were, making him less than whole—much less.

However, life did go on. At the age of six, with his boundless energy, it couldn't be otherwise. Anand was too full of talent and positive volition to keep out of the mainstream. He became someone special in the village, a prodigy. Several theories on what he would become later in life were current among the village elders. A sub-inspector of police (Amin Sahib, as they called him), maybe. Even a tehsildar, God willing. Beyond that, neither the aspiration nor the imagination of the village could extend. Anand knew nothing of this speculation. He couldn't even fancy a choice, since he didn't quite understand what one's future meant. And again, he didn't care. He lived, heart and soul, in the present.

Soon, he outstripped the class; later, the school. The poems he had learnt from Father made him sound a bit more scholarly than the teachers, but he didn't parade his learning. In any event, reciting poems in the mother tongue was not a mark of attainment at the time. It was Persian, the beautiful, flowery and effective tongue that set the standards of excellence. It also spelt authority.

It compelled everyone's attention. It sounded grand also because the bulk of the people in the countryside did not understand it. Persian was royal—at any rate the ignorant people thought so.

Anand took to Persian immediately. The Persian teacher's ancestors had lived in the state for several generations. Yet, he prided himself on the belief—never quite established—that some distant ancestor of his originally hailed from Lucknow. That was another status symbol in those times—hailing from Lucknow or somewhere in what was then the United Provinces. It gave one the right to look down upon the natives, Hindus and Muslims alike—they called them Mulkis. The teacher lost no opportunity to make the point that 'these Mulkis' (locals) could never master Persian the way those of Lucknawi origin could.

In Anand's case, however, he had to admit, rather grudgingly, that the lad was an exception. His flair for the language was quite commendable. Unable to reconcile this undeniable fact with his pet theory, the teacher even improvised a hypothesis that Anand's distant ancestors must have migrated from Lucknow. Nothing else, he asserted, could explain his talent. He would rather change Anand's genealogy than relax his own linguistic dogma even in one exceptional case . . . This teacher was a classic example of the immigrant Muslims, real or supposed, from northern India, whose fanatical brand of religious and linguistic exclusivism was to play a devastating role in the affairs of the state towards the close of the monarchical era.

At home, Anand got a mixed response. Uncle was a poet of sorts in the mother tongue, but had never had the benefit of any formal education. He adopted Anand as his own favourite exhibit. He was proud of his young charge, and saw in the little fellow all that he had himself wanted to achieve but could not. When the sub-inspector of police, the revenue inspector and, once, even the tehsildar of the area were on a visit to the village, he called on them at his uncle's insistence. They all had a good word to say about Anand. Uncle felt happy. He wrote long letters to Father, in praise of Anand. Messengers carried the letters from village to village. There were no postal facilities anywhere in the villages at the time.

Coming to Auntie, however, Anand found her a curious bundle

26

of affection and apathy. Sickly and irritable, she did not appreciate having another child in the family to attend to. She was an indifferent cook and no one relished the food in the house. She drudged day and night as much as any other housewife, but got no praise for it. Her own children grumbled all the time. Still, the woman was kind-hearted. She fussed over everything and everyone in the house, including Anand.

Auntie's attitude to Anand had a slight tinge of envy. She found him promising, in contrast to her own troublesome brats, Raju and Kamla, who were noisy, obstinate and uncouth. Yet, there was something happy-go-lucky about these two that attracted attention. They mouthed the obscene phraseology picked up from the adults in the village. They savoured every word without knowing what it meant. At their age it could only be smut for smut's sake. And when their horrified mother protested, they roared with laughter and repeated more and more of the same vocabulary . . . They were extremely fond of Anand, probably because he was so different. The attraction between opposites, maybe.

Anand got initiated, unwittingly, into a different world by his boisterous cousins. He was going on seven now. One morning he found them squatting in the backyard together, urinating in the open. This was not strange; you could see scores of men—and women—answering the call of nature in the open in any village in India. Besides, there were no public latrines or private toilets. The only way to ensure some privacy was to confine the proceedings to your own backyard, if you happened to have one. And children, before puberty, usually treated the voiding of bowels as a communal activity.

It was usual for boys and girls of Anand's age in the villages to go about with the upper or lower part of the body naked. Normally, the bottom part was bare, except when in school. Children considered covering the lower half unnecessary anyway. The few school-going children in that age group jettisoned their clothes below the waist the moment they returned home. There was no self-consciousness, no sense of shame or of sex . . . And in any event, a vast majority could not afford both a shirt and a loincloth. While the adults, especially men, retained the lower piece and went topless, children made do with the shirt alone, leaving the lower region in perfect freedom. Only adult women clothed both the halves, often with tatters.

That day in the backyard, Anand saw Raju and Kamla engaged in an elaborate examination of each other's genitals. Seeing Anand, they readily invited him to join the scrutiny. He saw no harm in doing so, and watched as Kamla opened her legs and showed him what he had never paid any attention to before. Apart from a sense of novelty, he felt nothing worth mentioning.

When he woke up the next morning, he felt something hard and erect in his groin. He remembered that he had felt it many times before, but never so palpably as now. It was perhaps because of the detailed scrutiny of Kamla's anatomy of the previous day. Meanwhile, his attention was diverted and he found, to his amazement, that nothing hard remained in the region any more. For the first time he discovered that this was the only part of his body capable of such variations in size and stiffness. Why was that so? The query crossed his mind in a flash but he had no explanation ... Meanwhile, he had to get ready for school, and forgot all about the matter.

Something came over Anand suddenly, giving him a vague feeling that he must keep the member with the variable size concealed—why, he could not figure out, beyond the reason that the grown-ups did so. He also noticed the obvious difference between himself and cousin sister Kamla at just one point in their otherwise identical bodies—why, again, he did not know. He mulled it over, found it getting curiouser, and gave up temporarily.

His perplexity, however, was not to abate yet. Life had embroiled him fully and completely. It began to enmesh him in the jigsaw of observation, discovery and knowledge. It compelled his own thinking and imagination to operate, unaided by promptings from any intimate person such as Mother. The cousins were generous and friendly, but being dimwits themselves, they could in no way satisfy his intellectual curiosity and craving. And it was not all merely intellectual, come to think of it!

More shocks of mystery were in store for him. He had, by and by, become fully conscious of the existence of the two sexes—and their differences. He did not, of course, perceive them as male and female, nor did he know what they meant; he merely saw them as two different types of the same species. What was the point of this, he asked himself again and again. Why must his little cousin sister Kamla, whom he had come to like, be without the organ with the changing size? Would it grow later, maybe? In that case, why should she have to wait, poor thing? . . . All this made no sense, he had to admit to himself . . . And most shocking, no one seemed to mind this gap. He didn't propose to share these thoughts with anyone himself; he sensed an unspoken taboo. He complied with it unquestioningly. Consequently, he found himself in an abnormal situation—now resigned, now defiant, but always disturbed. He felt humiliated by the mystery. It was an affront to his powers of comprehension. He demanded explanations—of whom, he could not say. He got none, naturally.

They had no separate bedrooms in the house. Uncle and Auntie did use one small and dingy room rather exclusively, but they too slept very often in separate beds next to each other in the common living portion of the house. The children slept, sometimes in small cots and sometimes on the floor, a few feet away in the same area. Anand found his sleep disturbed time and again by Uncle's loud snores, Auntie's coughing bouts and the shrill cries of his cousins in sleep. Then there were the cats chasing mice and knocking things over all night. When the servant who milked the cows knocked punctually at five in the morning, Anand invariably leapt to his feet and opened the door. All the others either continued to snore or, if awake, felt too lazy to get up. This had become the routine and no one complained of disturbed sleep. Poor and middle-class families share sleep too, like beds and blankets.

One night, at what time he couldn't guess, something suddenly woke Anand. He instinctively felt there was something unusual. He opened his eyes once, looked in a particular direction, closed his eyes, opened them again, half closed them and kept looking. Why he did not bring himself to sit up and stare at the scene, or to close his eyes and go back to sleep, was impossible to explain. All that he realized was that even if he closed his eyes, he wouldn't be able to sleep. Also, he didn't feel like closing his eyes, even if he could sleep. Consequently, he witnessed the scene with eyes closed enough to seem asleep and open enough to see everything—the scene was so disturbing . . . His body tensed for no apparent reason, but he kept his eyes riveted on Auntie's bed. There she lay, moaning and coughing, with Uncle straddling her. Anand could not see clearly enough in the dim light; all he could make out was that Uncle was battering Auntie with his body . . . That confused the boy completely. He concluded, quite logically, that this was the culmination of umpteen quarrels between wife and husband, that had of late become a daily feature. He had been witness to a particularly violent one that very afternoon . . . How cruel of Uncle, he mused, to have chosen the dead of night to punish poor Auntie—so helpless, not even able to shout, apparently! . . . He found it increasingly difficult to contain himself. Should he not raise an alarm to save Auntie's life? After all, she had been nice to him in her own way . . . Meanwhile, he could see Uncle's head bend over Auntie's, with his hands on her chest, close to her throat . . . Anand was now certain that Uncle was strangling her . . . That decided him. He was about to shout when he saw Uncle dismount abruptly, leave Auntie's bed and get back into his own. O God, he has killed her already, Anand said to himself . . . However, the next moment he saw Auntie rise from her bed, rearrange her sari, open the door and go into the backyard, walking quite normally and calmly. There were no signs of violence or physical damage that Anand could see . . . He suppressed his scream in the last split second, glad to be able to do so. He did not know what to do, nor what to make of what he had witnessed. One thing he was sure of: that scene would remain etched in his memory for ever and ever—why, he did not know.

Strangely, once the scene came to an end, he fell asleep quite effortlessly, without realizing when.

THE YEARS PASSED, REPLETE WITH EXCITEMENT, EUPHORIA, achievement. Anand's innate genius flourished. There was nothing more his primary school could teach him. It was time to move on. The school had opened up his mind, taught him to be conscious of, and receptive to, the outside world.

Mother came to visit him every now and then. He went back to his village for vacations. Yet, nothing was the same as before. Father spoke of examinations, marks, further studies and prospects. Anand responded readily, naturally; he had matured quickly and was swift and competent. In the process, however, he had become a stranger to Mother, a stranger to his own old self. Mother, of course, tried hard to find in him the earlier qualities—and perhaps did; she was not sure. The cows and the calves, the cats and the urchins, his uncle's hut and the winding muddy lanes in the village: Anand found that everyone and everything looked different. They had undergone a deterioration of growth—*his* growth. He just didn't belong any more. The village meant nothing special any longer; it was to him just a speck in the wide world. Almost.

The change in his perceptions, however, had not come overnight; it had stolen over him, almost imperceptibly. Separation from Mother was always an ordeal. While leaving her Anand cried and cried each time, until the bullock cart was out of the village and the bullocks settled into their rhythmic run. Then they slowly cast their irresistible spell on him and made the heaviness of his heart more bearable. The dust raised by their hoofs obscured his sadness, as it were. The animals served him in their own faithful, inarticulate way.

As his innate curiosity and intelligence asserted themselves, the pull of the world outside somehow provided a kind of countervailing focus to his yearning for Mother. When he was nine, a map he saw on the wall in the headmaster's room made him realize, for the first time, that the world was much wider than the villages he knew. There was a taluk, a district, and finally the State of Afrozabad. A king ruled the state. Anand and the rest of the school prayed every morning for his long life. The teachers, of course, restricted their teaching to the context of the state—it was the boundary of their universe.

Then Anand chanced on an atlas and a globe, again in the headmaster's room. He became curious. A few more visits to the room completed the revelation. There was much more beyond the State of Afrozabad, as he could see in the map of Hindustan in the atlas, printed in different beautiful colours . . . That was Anand's discovery of India. He felt elated as he stared at the vastness that was Hindustan.

Other discoveries followed, each bringing wonder. One day someone came to the village on a bicycle. Anand could not believe his own eyes. How could the thing move forward without falling over sideways, he wondered. A bunch of urchins sprinted after the cyclist until they were out of breath and gave up; Anand was the last of them. The cyclist was very pleased with the boy's tenacity. He seated Anand on the horizontal bar and gave him a short ride. Anand got a thrill he had never known before; he felt he was flying.

Much more sensational, however, was his first ride by bus. Uncle and Auntie were to attend a wedding in Gulshanpur, the district headquarters, twenty-five miles away. They readied the bullock cart, as usual, for an eight-hour journey; but just a day prior to their departure, one of the bullocks came down with the foot-and-mouth disease. They had to abandon the bullock cart. Uncle wanted to cancel the visit too, because money was tight. A careful calculation followed: Uncle, Auntie, their two children and Anand, whom they could not possibly leave behind. (Why not, they argued at one stage, but eventually concluded they couldn't, rather shouldn't. What will his parents think if they come to know, was the consideration that tilted the scales) . . . Well, that made a total of five passengers to travel by bus. Not quite five, really, since they would buy only two full tickets, the remaining being half tickets for the children. Even so, the fares to and fro came to over three rupees—frightfully expensive, Uncle declared. Besides, when you visited a town, you had to spend money right and left. It evaporated before you knew what was happening . . . No, forget the wedding, he decided reluctantly.

Raju and Kamla, however, kicked up a big rumpus. They raged and they remonstrated, they screamed and they sulked, until late into the night . . . As usual, Auntie was the first to soften. Finding the ground slipping from under his feet, Uncle gave in too, but not without a dig at her. 'I know *you* want to do some shopping yourself, to make my purse lighter!' he jeered. Auntie made a face; but she was glad, finding her husband reconciled. Anand, of course, remained a mute spectator throughout. Inside, however, he was bursting with excitement.

To go to the bus stop, they borrowed a bullock cart. They did not hire bullock carts in those days; the very idea of hiring for money was repugnant. The practice of lend-and-borrow was prevalent instead among those who owned bullock carts. Walking twenty miles at one stretch was nothing extraordinary; it became a habit in early childhood for the lower classes. For the village elite, however, a bullock cart was a must. It was also a status symbol.

The bus stop was about five miles from the village, situated on the only road in the district. It was a concrete road; the stones were firmly embedded in some patches and loosely strewn in others, making shallow pits. The constant attack by the iron-banded wheels of passing bullock carts, laden and unladen, had smoothened the concrete stones that lay fractured in shimmering colours under slanting rays of afternoon sun.

Anand and his cousins got busy exploring the road, the bus stand and the other passengers who stood among their boxes and neatly stacked bedrolls. They made friends with the other children and thoroughly enjoyed themselves. The elders waited for the bus, nervously aware that they would have to scramble for seats, and even for a place to stand.

Presently, they heard a loud rumble, like mild thunder. Then came a long honk that sounded like a donkey's bray. In a few moments the long-awaited bus appeared, emitting angry puffs of steam from the mouth of the radiator. The lid of the radiator danced loosely in the ascending steam and made its own hissing music. Anand kept staring at the monster, scared and fascinated; he had seen nothing this huge in his entire life. The bus drove past them and stopped about fifty yards ahead, as the mechanical brakes brought it slowly to a squealing halt.

There was a general stampede; men, women and children raced behind the bus through the thick cloud of dust over the road. Minutes later Anand found himself standing inside the bus, sandwiched between Uncle and Auntie. Raju and Kamla clung to him, whining and whimpering . . . It was an exhilarating moment for him; he forgot the chaos and suffocating crush. He had suddenly found himself in the belly of a gigantic cart that moved by itself, without bullocks or other animals drawing it—which would have been utterly unthinkable had he not seen it with his own eyes that very moment! The one person he admired most at that breathless moment was the bus driver . . . Hanuman was being quietly replaced in Anand's pantheon.

Later, there was a long discussion among the cousins on how the bus possibly moved. Raju had no doubt that ten or fifteen bullocks, hidden under the bus, carried it forward. Kamla was sceptical about this theory. Anand thought it rank nonsense but said so in different words. The debate remained inconclusive.

The children found their stay in the town wonderful. For one thing, there was no school. Here was complete freedom to do what they liked. Again, given the atmosphere of the wedding, the possibility of parents spanking them was minimal. Taking advantage of the situation, the cousins asserted themselves tempestuously once again and bullied Uncle and Auntie to take them to yet another unknown wonder—the silent movie. Their temporary friends at the bus stop had told them all about the movie. Some of them had boasted of having actually seen it themselves. Uncle first objected, on grounds of expense. Auntie was silent but did not agree with the objection. The kids, sensing an ally in her, redoubled their efforts. Uncle's resolve began to weaken since neither he nor Auntie had seen a movie so far, although neither admitted this. In the end, they decided to go to the movie, but the adults pretended (even grumbled, with characteristic adult hypocrisy) that the entire expenditure of about ten annas was 'wasted' only for the sake of the children!

They occupied the cheapest seats, priced at two *annas* each. The stink of human sweat and biri smoke filled the theatre since there was no restriction on smoking inside. The screen was a tattered sheet. But none of this mattered to them, or to others watching the show. Suddenly, the lights went off and ghostly images began to flicker on the screen. The hero of the movie was Master Vithal, a dashing luminary of the silent film world. Anand lost himself in the movie. He became the hero who jumped over mountains and towers, swam across torrential rivers, vanquished hundreds of armed men single-handedly and, most important, rescued the heroine. The last part enthralled him the most. For the first time he conceived of a heroine—*his* heroine . . . For the first time, he thought he could perform such impossible feats for a special woman, *his* woman, his heroine. For the first time, again, this new and fascinating status of the heroine dawned on him, vague but unmistakable.

Comments on the movie were many and varied. Auntie thought people enacted a real drama somewhere behind and shadow-played it on the screen. Uncle disagreed and thought they must have photographed it earlier. Raju and Kamla were more interested in the operational part. The following day they regaled everyone by enacting a fencing bout, imitating a scene from the movie, with swords made of neem twigs cut from the tree in front of their host's house. Will the shadows also talk one day, wondered Anand. 'Never! That's impossible,' said Uncle with authoritative finality.

The town of Gulshanpur was a new world. Anand examined it carefully, since he was to come here to study after the summer vacation. He was both happy and not so happy with it. It was so different. He had not put on a shoe or a slipper so far. Children ran barefoot in the village; the soles of their feet toughened early. They could run on rough or rocky ground and walk in slush with equal ease. And when a thorn pricked the sole and its broken tip got stuck in the flesh, they took it out, within minutes, with another thorn . . . Here in the town, Anand found almost everyone wearing shoes or chappals. He also noticed that everyone wore too many garments, one over the other, which made them sweat in the summer and smell awful. In particular, he found the garish strip of cloth called a necktie ridiculous and superfluous. Guests at the wedding who were in town for the first time made several hilarious comments about it. One old village elder said it looked like the rope they used for dragging a stubborn buffalo calf! . . . Yet, the wearer of that coloured strip plainly commanded respect for no reason Anand or his companions could think of.

The wedding was a noisy affair. It was an occasion of rejoicing primarily for the guests—rather, only for the guests. For the bride's parents it was a real ordeal. They had to arrange and pay for everything—the entertainment of the guests, a cash dowry for the groom, procurement of gold ornaments for the bride, gifts for the in-laws, which the latter demanded as of right. It was an endless and back-breaking list of obligations, hallowed by custom. The wedding was a long process extending over five days. Indeed, many relatives on the bride's side arrived several days ahead of the wedding and stayed on for several days, or weeks, after it was over. Then there were the big and small quarrels that broke out on the imaginary grievances of the groom's side. All these made a daughter's wedding very arduous for a middle-class householder. Much depended on how good and considerate the groom's parents were. At times, pressurized by the guests who came from their side, they also had to join in the fray, aggravating the already tense atmosphere.

Anand concentrated on the bride and the groom. They were his age, more or less; the bride was ten, the groom twelve. There was general criticism that the bride was two years too old for marriage. The Hindu scriptures enjoined a girl's marriage before the age of eight—or so the orthodox elders asserted.

Anand made friends with the young couple at once. Their common interest lay in the band playing outside the house. They couldn't care less what happened inside—the quarrels, the chanting of *mantras*, and the *homa*, the sacred fire that emitted a lot of smoke and caused discomfort to the couple seated in front of it. Yet they couldn't move away, since they were literally captive until the ceremonies were over.

The next morning, as he stood with his relatives at the bus stop on their way home, Anand remembered the excitement of the past few days. He had made friends with the bride and the groom and was sorry to part with them. For a moment, he wondered what marriage meant, and whom he would marry. She would be beautiful, like the heroine in the movie—of that much he was certain. But beyond that, he could not think of any other attribute, since he knew so little about the event called marriage and where it fitted in one's life.

In all the hustle and bustle, little did he know that while the marriage was on, someone had spotted him as a possible bridegroom and that he was not very far from being clamped in those fetters himself.

# 5

EVEN AS HE REVELLED IN THE MYRIAD ACTIVITIES OF THE SCHOOL and threw himself enthusiastically into his studies, Anand couldn't but be aware of a subtle change in his social environment, the first signs of the sectarianism that would in time ravage the tranquil face of India. By and by, Muslims in the village found themselves in embarrassing situations. When a village-born young Muslim working in the town came home on leave, he brought with him attitudes quite alien to the village. They were compelling, nevertheless. Since the king was a Muslim, this was a Muslim kingdom, they argued. Going further, they asserted that the logic of a Muslim kingdom was that every Muslim in the state was a part of the institution of kingship, a king in miniature. They propounded the theory called *An-al-Malik* (I am King), that epitomized the status of Muslims in the state. It percolated down to the villagers, albeit in a slightly different, rustic version. This new-found status led to Muslims asserting an identity based primarily on religion. However, Muslims had identified themselves with life as it was lived in the villages for centuries. They found the new identity perplexing and at times irritating. Some, however, found it tempting . . . Someone with religious authority told them that Islam did not favour Muslims associating with Hindu festivals based on idolatry. This was indeed a bitter pill to swallow. It was very difficult for Muslims not to participate in Dassehra and other festivals; but after this edict, they had no choice. They were fast losing the nerve to refuse this imposed choice and to pursue common traditions.

Then came the conversions to Islam, sponsored by, or under, official authority. Villages had indeed seen numerous conversions for centuries, but much more naturally. The retired Muslim head constable in Anantgiri had a Muslim wife. In addition, he had taken a Hindu woman as wife by nikah (Muslim marriage). The nikah changed the woman's name; the eight children she bore him were all Muslims. And so it happened in thousands of cases. The woman's in-laws and other relations, however, neither became Muslims themselves nor severed relations with her. Life flowed on as usual; the nikah, and the consequent birth of Muslim children drew no particular comment from anyone.

The recent conversions, however, metamorphosed a fully adult Mallikarjun into Mohammed Ali overnight. He also acquired a new aggressive swagger in the bargain. No conviction or faith was involved—only inducements from the state. This disturbed everybody, for there was no obvious reason for the change in behaviour.

Anand found it all mystifying. For some time past he had noticed that only Hindus participated in Hindu festivals. Muslim elders either made a casual appearance and disappeared, or found some compelling reason to be away from the village. Something was giving way from within, as it were. Still, life as a whole did not manifest too much strain on the surface. Associations that went back for generations still asserted themselves.

Anand did not know where to draw the line between Hindu and Muslim. He thought, with simple logic, that it was merely an accident of birth and no more. He had both Hindu and Muslim friends and found nothing to distinguish one group from the other

. . . However, he began to find some insights as he looked around. Like many precocious children, he was able to cut through the facades that adults often use to mask the truth. He began to understand the forces at work.

He was on his way to school one morning when his friend Karim waylaid him and invited him to witness his four-year-old brother Rahim's circumcision ceremony. Anand knew nothing about what this was, of course. After making a half-hearted excuse of being late for school he let himself be dragged to Karim's house. It was evidently a festive occasion. Some elders gathered in the courtyard sat on creaky cots or on the chabutra. They smoked biris or cigars and chatted amusedly. One person among them, whom they called Afzal Chacha, seemed to be a stranger, possibly from the city; he was smoking a cigarette, holding one end between the second and middle fingers of his closed fist and blowing on the top of the fist. The posture seemed to give him a special dignity, not usually manifested by the rustic biri smokers. He was bespectacled and wore a wristwatch, which no one else in the group did. His fez looked conspicuous among the village turbans.

Going inside the house Anand saw young Rahim with a big lump of gur (jaggery) in his hand. The lump was so big that no mother would ordinarily let her four-year-old son eat it at one go, except as a special bribe. In a few minutes its purpose became clear, for the village barber, seated close to the boy, took out a razor, bared the foreskin of the youngster's penis and expertly cut it away. As blood spilled out, Rahim shrieked in terror and pain. Anand felt utterly confused. He got up and rushed away. None of his friends—Hindu or Muslim—could tell him what that scene meant.

This was too much, he thought. In the first place, some children, like his cousin sister, were born without 'it'. And now, some who had 'it' were supposed to keep licking a lump of jaggery while the barber cut part of 'it' off mercilessly. He couldn't understand at all . . . Perhaps he now knew of *one* distinctive feature of a Muslim. Just one . . . But who knows? Frankly, no one was sure that the barber's razor would spare him if he was not a Muslim. After all, it was perhaps done later among non-Muslims! Each argument on the subject filled him with peculiar foreboding.

*

Soon the village became absorbed in other festivities. Janmashtami, the birth anniversary of Lord Krishna, was approaching. Anand had been taking part in the celebrations for the past three years, ever since he had turned six. He and his friend Karim were the most active participants, indeed the leaders of the celebration activities. This year the village elders had drawn up a specially ambitious programme extending over eighteen days and culminating in a day-long ceremony on Janmashtami proper. They commissioned a famous singer-pundit with a tremendous voice, to recite one of the eighteen skandhas (cantos) of the *Bhagavata* epic each evening. Then followed an enactment of Krishna Leela (Krishna's miraculous feats) on the concluding day, in which a large number of the villagers—men, women and children—would participate. The village had not had a programme of this nature and duration for many years, so everyone was looking forward to it. People were to come from many adjoining villages. The village elders made elaborate arrangements to feed all visitors throughout the period of the celebrations. Free of cost, of course.

The air was full of music. It was amazing to see scores of adults and children of the village appear suddenly from nowhere and dance gracefully to the beat of the *mridanga*. These people seldom appeared in the village in normal times. The adults stayed and worked in their fields round the year. The children, never put to school, also worked with their parents, mostly tending cattle. They had the trees and the shrubs and the birds and the standing crops and the beasts of burden as their audience each day. They drew inspiration from their own capacity to forget themselves and merge in an unknown, all-inclusive, all-pervading spirit that they could not describe.

The school-going children were surprised to find themselves out-sung and out-danced by this unfamiliar crowd of untrained performers from the forest and the field. Over the eighteen-day festival, the artistic talent of the village sprouted everywhere. It transcended class and caste and radiated the ecstasy of devotion to the most perfect among Vishnu's incarnations. Occasional August showers and a downpour or two during the period added thrill and delight to the proceedings. When dark clouds shadowed the village, the pundit raised his voice, as if to tune it to the intermittent thunder by bursting into *megh* or *malhar* ragas. At the first splutter of heavy raindrops, he would switch to a description of Krishna raising the Govardhan mountain to shelter the inhabitants of Gokul. Children recognized the description instantly and danced in unison, each with left hand raised and its little finger stretched skyward, as if to balance the huge hill on its tip. It was a different world . . .

By the end of the first week there was a virtual explosion of performances centred on Krishna. Old women burst out spontaneously into a torrent of half-forgotten songs that they had learnt from *their* mothers and grandmothers sixty years ago. Then came the younger and still younger ones—until folklore adapted itself to span three generations effortlessly, while the Krishna legend remained fresh as ever. No one had written the songs, no one recorded them. They flowed through a collective memory, subtly altered in each generation as they were passed along. They sounded more beautiful in each successive version. There was no single authentic text; each village had its own distinctive treasure. Scores of children appeared as Krishna, complete with flute in hand and crown flaunting a peacock feather. They were of all ages and complexions, from fair, slim young Anand to swarthy men of fifty and over. Their enthusiasm was infectious. The village girls celebrated also, made up as gopis (milkmaids described in the *Bhagavata*). They broke into spontaneous dances that no one had ever taught them. In those days no one ever taught the villagers anything anyway. Yet the persistent instinct of generations prevailed, and cultural traditions, affirmed year after year, bound the community.

At last dawned the eighteenth day, the day of the grand finale to the celebrations. The village was beautifully done up to resemble Brindavan where Krishna had spent his childhood years, according to the *Bhagavata*. The performers improvised the scenes as described in the epic. The artisans of the village did a fine job. All lanes and by-lanes presented a riot of flowers and colours. Mango leaves hung from strings tied across the streets, interspersed with a variety of flowers from field and forest. Anand had not seen most of these flowers before. In front of every house, water had been sprinkled to keep the dust down and beautiful patterns of rangoli adorned the doorway. At the climax of the Krishna Leela, they would enact the scene of Krishna and his friends on the rampage. The entire village assembled in the main chowk. Earthen pails containing milk, curds and butter hung from crossbars about fifteen feet high. Krishna's horde was to scale that height and steal the milk and butter, to the ecstatic delight of thousands of spectators. All the milk available in the village was reserved for this spectacular occasion. Besides, many neighbouring villages contributed liberally. The boys were to drink some of the milk, the rest was literally to flow in the streets, symbolizing prosperity.

Anand, of course, was voted for Krishna's role. He was made up with great authenticity. He looked exactly like the original hero from the *Bhagavata* text as described by the pundit. The make-up of the face alone took one full hour; a blue vegetable dye transformed him into the young Lord. After his make-up, he proceeded, along with other boys similarly made up, to Karim's house. There was no time to lose. Karim had promised to come in time for the make-up but had obviously overslept. The lazy dog, one of the boys muttered angrily . . . There was no trace of Karim at the house either. Instead, they found Afzal Chacha, the uncle from the city. Afzal coughed a few times and said enigmatically, 'I don't know where Karim has gone. And anyway, why do you want him? It's *your* festival, isn't it? So Hindus only should celebrate it . . . ' The boys were dumbfounded. They returned to the chowk, crestfallen.

Later, precariously perched on top of the pyramid made by a hundred other boys, as described in the epic, Anand reached for the pail of milk and tumbled it. The milk had gone sour.

*

The fact of the milk going sour was discussed and re-discussed in the village. The spectators felt a tinge of regret. But some of those who had come from other villages took the incident lightly. 'Why should any Muslim boy be given a part in this celebration at all, in the first instance?' they demanded. 'That's how the Hindus are so meek, trying to placate the Muslims all the time. This nonsense should stop forthwith!' The village elders, for whom any common celebration was a question of prestige, pure and simple, had never entertained any such ideas before. Embarrassed no end, they quickly wound up the grand finale and managed to dissipate the tension.

As Anand's primary education came to an end, he had to get admission in the high school at Gulshanpur, the district headquarters. He had no difficulty since everyone, including the headmaster of the primary school, helped him.

Anand was overjoyed and looked forward to the new school. At the same time, he felt sad at leaving Uncle's home and in particular Raju and Kamla, with whom he had had such an affectionate relationship. He sensed that he was about to lose touch forever with a time and a place that had contributed significantly to his self-discovery.

IT WAS THE SECOND YEAR OF HIS HIGH SCHOOL STUDIES. ANAND'S brilliance as a student was already becoming well known in Gulshanpur. Gulshanpur could be called a town because it housed the district headquarters, represented by a cluster of government buildings, reasonably wide roads, a large number of police vehicles and police personnel, a few hotels vying with one another in blaring popular songs through very loud loudspeakers—and all that went with this bustle. Otherwise it was nothing more than a biggish village. The village-like part of the town was equally busy and noisy, with vendors, male and female, loaded with big baskets, loudly calling their wares in sing-song chants. The lanes resounded with their musical and not-so-musical cries. Illiterate women from the adjoining villages, who sold milk to individual families, had their accounts accurately indicated on the walls of the houses they supplied, in neat, straight rows of fingerprints or perpendicular lines drawn with charcoal. It was amazing how no one, not even children, thought of making any alterations in these authentic public accounts and how mutual confidence settled everything without any dispute whatsoever.

During the years that Anand stayed in town, he was witness to several new developments. While carrying milk on the vendors' heads continued, some enterprising *gwalas* (milk vendors) bought some Murrah buffaloes and started a novel way of selling milk. They took the buffaloes, with their impressively large udders and sturdy calves, to each customer's house, milked them in the customer's presence and sold the milk to him, thus introducing a new concept of home delivery. The traditional milk vendors (some of whom could not afford to buy the Murrah) would never agree to this practice—of exhibiting the buffalo, particularly its large udder, to thousands of eyes in public. They were sure that the evil eye would strike the buffaloes and they would go dry. The new method impressed some customers, but many would not give up the good old practice of buying from the milkmaid and paying her as computed in the wall account. Besides, the milkmaid, going from house to house, volunteered a bit of gossip from the village, free of cost.

Another new phenomenon that emerged almost overnight was the free tea stalls at the main chowk in the town. No one had known of tea in the town or village till then; in fact very few liked it, even when they were given it for free, in the beginning. The only morning drink in vogue was milk for those who could afford it, and in the summer months, a cool sherbet made from mangoes. Soon after tea was introduced, the tea companies seemed to be losing ground; but they made up slowly by employing publicity material such as coloured posters of semi-nude women, having absolutely no connection with the tea or its quality. These semi-nude female pictures, invading for the first time the claustrophobic ambience of burqas and low-pulled ghunghats, took the town by storm. Hordes of men gathered in front of the pictures and sometimes even caused traffic jams on the narrow roads. The gap between tradition and what the tea-poster girls suddenly exposed the town to, created a culture shock for some days.

Then the companies coined a curious slogan—*garmiyon mey*

*garm chai thandak pahunchati hai*! (in the hot season, hot tea will keep you cool!) It was unbelievable, of course, but the sheer audacity attracted some customers, reinforced by the free supply of tea which seemed to be for all time. You paid nothing, did nothing, just kept drinking tea all your life! So what could you lose?

Within about six months, thousands of fashionable people (no one understood the connection) became tea addicts before they realized what had happened. Then, within a few days, all the free tea stalls disappeared as mysteriously as they had appeared, leaving a compelling addiction behind. Instead of the stalls, small kiosks appeared, with packets of tea leaf, tea dust etc. *for sale*, in different sizes. The largest size seemed to cost proportionately much less when compared to a smaller one, implying, of course, that you would drink tea for a longer period! The message was: the longer you drank tea, the cheaper it would be for you! Addiction thus meant economy. And tea gradually entered every household in town and village alike.

The Hindu-Muslim configuration had always had a higher profile in towns than in villages. It was essentially of urban origin and seeped down to the village. Anand observed its manifestation almost as an inseparable part of life in the town. Besides, it had become rapidly magnified as compared to what it had been earlier. For one thing, several dilapidated mosques in the town began undergoing repairs and acquired a sudden facelift. Construction proceeded on a war footing. Anand sometimes heard questions such as, 'Where is all the money coming from?' First in whispers and then aloud. There was, of course, no reply. So the question was repeated more emphatically.

Then came several Hindu religious institutions, equally suddenly, with a similar mystery about where the money came from. They mushroomed rapidly, but did not function freely or prominently, not in the beginning. Yet it was only a question of time before the rhetoric on both sides became equally shrill and the utterances irrational. On one side was the *An-al-Malik* slogan, affirming that the king's power extended to everyone born into the religion into which the king was born. In reply came the counter-claim of the numerical majority in the state: how could ten per cent of the population claim primacy over ninety? That's why the state must have a democratic government with the king acting only as a Constitutional head, if at all. How can one out of the five-hundred-odd native states have a different dispensation? It was all so absurd! After all, the majority in a state must have a major role and position. It was only just that the long-standing injustice in this state be ended forthwith!

Public meetings and rallies became more frequent and more vituperative. A vicious smear campaign and scathing condemnation were carried on day in and day out. The atmosphere reeked of mutual hate; disinformation crossed all limits of decency. There was a never-ending competition in crowd-gathering; people were brought in large numbers from villages. What they understood at the end of the day was that every Hindu citizen was every Muslim citizen's enemy—and vice versa. However, even at the height of the madness, people in general did not believe this nonsense. They were influenced, but still retained the age-old, innate desire to live together in peace. Even so, the onslaught of communal fanaticism proved more and more difficult to resist. One noteworthy feature of this communal avalanche was that most leaders from both sides came from outside the state. They visited places, vomited venom for an hour or two, and disappeared.

Anand's life spun into confusion—studies in school punctured by a very different cacophony outside. Some incident, spontaneous or contrived, mostly contrived, gave rise to tension every day. Students of the high school normally did not wish to be embroiled in the incident, but events were contrived so that they somehow got involved. Slogans like 'Naara-e-Takbeer—Allah-o-Akbar!' and 'Bajrang Bali ki Jai!' rent the air any time of the night or day. There was no riot yet, but the situation was not very far from it. The tension was palpable, tempers were on edge.

While Anand enjoyed his scholastic reputation, he became acutely aware of the estrangement between Hindus and Muslims. The one paraded numbers and the other flaunted governmental power. Without realizing how, Anand was often caught in the communal crossfire. Hindus ascribed his brilliance almost entirely to his being a Hindu. Muslims grudgingly acknowledged that he was brilliant *despite* being a Hindu. No one tried to see him as himself. This was the case with thousands of people who, in their humdrum existence, had no need to think in terms of being Hindu or Muslim. They hardly ever had to stand up and be counted—until recently, until being Hindu or Muslim became good or bad in itself. In spite of these absurd and uncompromising attitudes, Anand was happy, since he had earned a place of some prominence in the society he lived in.

There was one Girls' Middle School in the town—exclusively for girls, that is. It had a fleet of spacious bullock carts for transporting the girls to and from their homes. Purdah being strictly observed, each school cart had a curtain in front and another at the back. Since there was no direct visual contact, all assessment of the beauties inside the carts depended on the imagination of the schoolboys who chased the carts regularly. Anand was one of them. Whenever he happened to be walking behind a Girls' School cart, the girls inside huddled together to peep stealthily at him through the rear curtain and greeted him with admiring giggles. He felt flattered and a bit flustered. And somehow those laudatory signals seemed to give rise to an unknown and indefinable sense of elation in him; why and how, he just could not figure out then. It was happiness, but not just happiness; there was some other component. A definite change was coming over him, perhaps a bit before its time, as often happens with prodigies.

He was not old enough to understand or analyse his future, but when he thought of any of the marriage ceremonies he attended by the dozen—particularly in the marriage season chosen as auspicious by the pundits—he was, as it were, beset with the question, 'What next?' There was no immediate answer, and like everyone else he went on to attend the next wedding. And the next . . . Then he would ask himself where the bride and the groom were from; how had they met in the first place, since they belonged to different places?

What would happen to them? What would they do after the pomp and the noise of the wedding subsided? What was the meaning of the bride being described as beautiful, lovely or average? Was anyone interested in the bride's beauty? And why only the bride's? And what did they mean by beautiful? What did beauty consist of, basically? These and many such questions appeared and disappeared in his mind. Answers, in bits and pieces, came from friends, relatives, and mostly from boys with similarly fragmented knowledge. Boys, however, never questioned girls about such things; they were prevented by an unspoken taboo. Anand surmised that there would be similar questions and answers in the minds of the girls.

By this circuitous route, Anand gradually formulated the concept of the 'future'—his or anyone else's. It wasn't quite clear; perhaps ambiguity was one of its main characteristics. Suppose it had been clearly known, in advance, he speculated, how would that be? Then he began planning what he wanted his own future to be . . . He thought and thought, but couldn't decide on anything! How strange, he reflected again and again.

His mind, however, was made up. How, he could not figure out (in fact, he could see the impossibility of it all), but he decided that he alone had to be the architect of the very special destiny he sensed for himself. He wouldn't agree to anyone else even helping him; alone he would fashion everything. He would be superior to anyone he was able to imagine right then! He would do something for the country, in fact, for the whole world, for humanity at large, which no one had even spelt out so far in words. His achievement would touch the skies, there would be no limit . . . But what would it be? He didn't know yet, of course!

And yes, his wife. She had to be his own vision. Anand spent days visualizing his ideal wife. The more he thought, the more complicated the vision became. Yet, his hypothetical wife seemed to be the very centre of what was cumulatively called the future. When he couldn't visualize a wife, how could he visualize his future? But no . . . he came back to the starting point. He convinced himself that in his future, everything in general, and his wife in particular, had to be *his* own personal, exclusive choice. She had to correspond to his ideal. He would not compromise on that . . . his wife. But when he proceeded to envision her, he found the task beyond his intellect. And suddenly his imagination forged the concept of a persona that would inhere in him better than anyone else—as his other half. That presence, or absence, would be his most profound emotional treasure and he would live with it for ever . . . He wouldn't accept anything less, anything else.

Curiously, when he came to know within a few days of this experience that he was to be married shortly, he was disappointed but *not* shocked, the way he thought he would be. Indeed, by fashioning his other half, such as he willed and made it, he had already exhausted the right of his own choice and was left with no further choice, he concluded. His inner self remained unaffected, he told himself with a touch of assumed satisfaction. His other half remained as real as he had taken pains to make her. Over time, it became a part of his thought process—that everything is only half, it has *another half*—as an entity, as a proposition, as an argument, as a fantasy and, of course, as an indelible truth—all in one. For him, therefore, nothing had changed.

Whether this was an intellectual alibi resorted to by a helpless but thinking individual, or a genuine feeling in an extraordinarily gifted young person who was still groping to spell out his ambition, it was difficult to say. Adolescence and high intelligence seemed to create a confusing question mark. How would an individualistic, almost arrogant youngster feel when told that all choices given *him* in *his* life had already been exercised *for* him by someone else? And provided for? That is what tradition does for you. Are you happy, you ask a thousand young men and women. 'Yes!' is the loud response from many. 'No!' Anand cried louder, alone or with a few . . . It was a most basic question for him. It struck at the very root of his life. It was as though someone else was destined to lead his life and he was to pretend that it was his, Anand's! The absurdity of the situation stunned him. For the rest, he had nothing whatever to say on the merit of the decision itself; there was no difficulty on that score.

He went to his village for the summer vacation, to find arrangements for his wedding going on in full swing. Being the groom's house, this was not the venue of the wedding. The ceremony would take place at the bride's place, in another village.

Yet the groom's house wore a festive look too. In any event, the groom's relatives had already arrived in full force and were enjoying themselves. They also braced themselves for the many quarrels without which no wedding is complete.

The match had been arranged with absolute objectivity and worldly wisdom. There was to be a wedding: whose, was at best a secondary question. People were always married; they never took the step independently. It was an event in the family. Nothing was to happen to the bride or the groom on their level, at that point. They were mere cogs in the social wheel, the wheel that perpetuated the family. By begetting their progeny, in turn, they were duty-bound to contribute to the sublime state described as *sadgati*, after death, to the line of ancestors in which they would be part of an eternal chain. The central idea, Anand concluded, was to live for the ancestors, not for oneself—an absolutely impersonal attitude. It smashed individual ego, reduced the 'I' from a defined line to a microscopic point. The mandate was unequivocal: *aputrasya gatirnasti* (no son, no salvation).

The families were distantly related. Beyond this, Anand did not know, nor was it necessary for him to know, anything. You were given a wife or a husband, just as you were given eyes, ears, a nose; only, the spouse came some time after birth. In both cases, things were beyond your control. Among some castes, babies were married while in the cradle, apparently to locate marriage as close to birth as practicable. That was the hallowed pattern. Thousands fitted themselves into it without demur.

Back in the town after the vacation, whenever he found himself behind a Girls' School cart, he lingered on the wayside and let it go far far ahead, out of sight.

*

Anand's future, which he had imagined as better than anything imaginable, became increasingly convoluted. His adolescent ambition kept itself unfettered. His achievements as a student—as a scholar and intellectual—somehow did not permit him to set his sights on anything in particular. A peculiar self-confidence, bordering on arrogance, possessed him—he felt there was nothing he could not achieve.

After his wedding, however, events followed in quick succession. For the first time, his ambition seemed to have got a real jolt. His potential for achievement suddenly dipped; it circumscribed itself, without his volition. He might or might not become this or that; but he could no longer aspire to a future of his choice. This was the real measure of the difference. He had not identified it before his marriage; he had wanted to be free to do so whenever he chose. The marriage deprived him of that crucial choice—the choice of the time to make the choice. Now, he saw that it did not matter; in fact, nothing mattered. Life could follow any line; so long as it was not *his* line—which, in fact, he had not chosen—it could be *any* line.

These thoughts, however, took their time to crystallize in his mind. Meanwhile, he remained part—an active part—of the scene around him. The concept of democracy attracted him, as it attracted thousands of young minds. He did not know, however, that the government of the king equated democracy with treason and obtained intelligence reports about each student and teacher on that basis.

*

It was the annual prize distribution function of the school. The vice-principal reeled off a long list of prizes that Master Anand had bagged:

General Merit Prize, for standing first in the annual
     examination
The Principal's Special Prize for English
The Executive Engineer's Special Prize for Mathematics
     and Science
Special Prize for proficiency in classical language.

The principal beamed with happiness. The director of public instruction, who had graced the occasion to give away the prizes, was highly impressed.

Introducing his star pupil to the audience, the principal said,

'Ladies and gentlemen, I present to you this very talented student who has won almost all the merit prizes since he was admitted to this school. We are proud of him and wish him still greater achievements in his future career. And now, Master Anand . . .'

A thousand eyes converged on the dais as Anand, puny and nimble-footed, ran up the steps and stood at attention. His large eyes, darting from the director to the principal to the audience, stood out in his thin face.

The director looked at the boy indulgently and gave him a smiling nod bordering on affection. He was a large man with a large palm, in which he held Anand's agile hand and said, 'Well, scholar, brought a *tonga* to carry your prizes? Congratulations! Keep it up . . .'

There were ripples of appreciative laughter from the audience. Anand felt somewhat embarrassed, but very happy. The director began, 'Ladies and gentlemen, I am so happy to meet Master Anand. I hope he will be another Ramanujam. The gracious government of our benevolent monarch will render full assistance to him and anyone like him, to attain the highest that God made him capable of. Our benevolent monarch supplements God's will. He is the wisest of rulers. I wish and pray that Master Anand may blossom into a top intellectual of this great kingdom of Afrozabad and a most loyal subject of our benign sovereign . . .'

This was the first formal speech Anand had heard, containing references to the sovereign, loyalty, subject etc. In that small town, people had begun to bandy these expressions about with such flamboyance and flourish only recently. So far they had understood the notion of the ruler and the ruled; that was a traditional concept. So was the attitude of the people to it. If one was born among the ruled and not a ruler, well, that was that. How could one be born as one wished to? Loyalty too, whatever it meant, was not a point of discussion or exhortation; it was taken for granted. Why then, he wondered, is this high-up from the state capital belabouring these issues? Was it part of the change that he, Anand, had noticed over the years?

The following day he went to the principal with a serious expression on his face. 'Come in, Anand,' the principal said. 'What is bothering you?'

'Oh, it's nothing, nothing at all, sir,' Anand said haltingly, more than dropping a hint that there *was* something.

The principal loved Anand like his own son—perhaps better because his son had turned alcoholic and homosexual. His family hailed from Lucknow and had a close relationship with a well-known nationalist Muslim leader. Now, having migrated to this princely state, he couldn't even refer to that relationship. Exigencies of service ruled that out. The principal was a fair and just man. Of late, however, he had been finding it increasingly difficult to look on both communities impartially.

'I know there *is* something. Out with it, let's solve it.'

Under the spell of the principal's sympathy, Anand opened up. 'Nothing very much, sir,' he began timidly. 'I was wondering why the DPI talked so much about loyalty to the king yesterday at the meeting . . . Did he suspect someone's loyalty? And what exactly does loyalty mean, sir?'

The principal reflected silently for a long time. What happens to many brilliant boys in adolescence has happened to Anand, he said to himself. It is the impact of an ever-probing intellect. From now on it will stop at nothing, bring no solace to the poor lad. It will either lift him to the skies or, what's more likely, hurl him into deep trouble. There can be no compromise, the principal ruminated.

'Was that a stupid question, sir?' asked Anand.

'No, it wasn't stupid,' the principal said slowly. 'It was dangerous . . . yes . . . dangerous is the word . . .'

'Oh, I'm sorry, sir. Please let the question remain unasked and unanswered . . .'

'I guess so. Loyalty, I think, is essentially an unquestioning attitude.'

'That is, a blind and unthinking attitude?'

'Well, unquestioning is not necessarily unthinking; yet in the long run, it's easier not to think and not to question than to think and still not to question . . . Isn't it?'

'Yes, sir, but is it possible to stop thinking, deliberately?'

'You have a point there, my boy. To a thinking being, thinking comes naturally, involuntarily . . . He can't help it.'

'Following the same analogy, sir, can't there be a questioning being? I mean one who can't help questioning?'

'Why, yes, indeed. You seem to be evidently one such . . .'

'Then does it follow that I am disloyal?'

The principal winced at the question. Anand had led him, slowly and logically, into a tight corner. Suddenly he flared up; he had no other way out. 'You and your logic!' he shouted. 'Now quit this useless hair-splitting and go back to your class . . . I've no time for nonsense!'

Anand looked into the principal's troubled face and withdrew, shaking his head in utter incredulity.

He also noted that his question on loyalty remained unanswered.

AFTER HIS MARRIAGE, A STRANGE BUT STRONG SENSE OF AN ambiguous, unspoken taboo began to dominate Anand's psyche. The vehicle of his free choice had suddenly been put back on the rails of family tradition, and the steering wheel he held suddenly became superfluous. But once he had come to terms with this reality, he felt freer, bolder, clearer in thought and word. He felt he was hurtling towards action—what action, he did not know yet, and did not care.

His childhood obsession with driving the bullock cart had intensified over the years. He enjoyed it immensely and knew many delicate points in that art. There were two kinds of bullocks in the village. First, those meant to plough and to haul loads. Wet or dry, they went on and on ploughing perseveringly, six to eight hours at a stretch, normally from cock-crow on. If overnight rain had waterlogged the land, they started after an early meal, at about nine. Anand marvelled at the intelligence and diligence of the load-hauling bullocks who negotiated all the tricky bends in the village lanes accurately and brought the laden carts safely into the farmer's courtyard, without so much as brushing against a wall or a corner. When another cart came along from the opposite direction, the bullocks manoeuvered their cart close and parallel to the wall and arched their own bodies sideways so as to let the other cart pass. They managed these subtle moves by themselves, without the driver who often followed far behind, harassed and fretting over something or the other, swearing at someone or the other, as he exhaled thick clouds of smoke from his cheroot filled with country tobacco wrapped in tendu or palas leaf.

The other kind were the *sawari* bullocks meant for quick transportation, their speed touching about eight miles an hour—for the first hour or so, or so the owners claimed. They were given special training and were maintained meticulously. They were looked upon as status symbols in the countryside. Fantastic stories circulated about the high performance of the *sawari* bullocks of this or that farmer, this or that landlord. That a particular pair had sprinted parallel to a running train for over a mile; that another pair had not allowed a Road Transport bus to overtake it for half an hour; that a third pair had trotted the ninety-mile distance from the district headquarters to the state capital in one night when the owner missed the last available train, etc., etc.

Anand was very fond of his *sawari* pair, Rama and Bhima—almost identical in build, height, colour and even in the curvature of their crescent-shaped horns. Such a perfectly matched combination was very rare. When there was one, superstition had it that it would be short-lived. Something would happen to one of the bullocks—death, deformity or damage—and the pair would break up. Anand, of course, did not believe in this nonsense. He had learnt quite a bit from Father about the high-speed variety of bullocks, their distinctive characteristics, maintenance, training, sicknesses and the like. For instance, by just watching a bullock run for half a mile, he could decide at once whether it was useful for quick transportation duties. If it had the tendency to drag along or rub one of its hooves against the ground or knock one hoof against the other leg while running, it could not be used for transportation. Otherwise, over a distance of ten or twenty miles, its hoof would get filed off and lead to bleeding from inside the foot, and permanent damage. Then there was the style of running to consider. If it had an element of gallop, in which the entire body gets lifted off the ground, it would never do. The bullock would be exhausted too soon. The fast-moving bullock's run should be steady, easy, breath-saving, uniform, rhythmic and swift. Anand recalled with pride many instances when Father had fully endorsed his judgement.

Musing thus, he drove the bullock cart that afternoon on his way to the village. He sang the while, as if enchanting the bullocks into a musical run. He had, like Father, developed a special touch that set Rama and Bhima on an easy trot. Many other drivers tried prodding and beating, which only evoked a half-hearted response, if that.

Anand sang, drove and thought—all at once. Touching Bhima, he recalled with an inward chuckle that the rogue had been the dandiest bull in the village, sniffing and pining for cows in heat. The cows would seek him out too and approach him with uplifted tails. However, with his castration some six months earlier, Bhima had suddenly become steadfast, hard-working, responsible, dignified and intelligent. He had literally sobered by the day and blossomed into a perfect bullock, by any standard.

The memory of Bhima's exploits as a bull made Anand think of himself. For a boy of sixteen he was remarkably well informed about the eternal attraction between men and women. He had read a lot about sex, secretly of course, with his native scholastic avidity. He knew more about the subject than many older boys with actual experience. Yet it was all in theory, a kind of unapplied science . . . The moment the thought about himself crossed his mind, he made a determined effort to erase it. He forced himself to think of something—anything—else. He had been practising this feat of deflection for some time—since his wedding, to be exact.

He was not to be spared so easily, though. Gangi, the local butcher's daughter, accosted him one evening at the turn of the lane leading to his friend's house, where he often went to play chess. Gangi had remained in the seventh standard for three years in a row, then left school and lost all interest in learning. Instead, she developed an unflagging passion for men—below the belt, to be precise. She was going on eighteen, with a voluptuous and full-blown anatomy in which the concaves and convexes blended perfectly. She had a rather pudgy face, dotted with pimples. Many believed that the pimples were due to unfulfilled sexual desire. Youthful lust flowed from each movement of her shapely form.

She came directly to the point. Catching Anand's hand, she said, 'Come to my house; there's no one there now . . .' Her other hand rested under his chin.

'Whatever for?' Anand asked, taken aback.

'Can't you understand, silly?' she snapped, somewhat mockingly. 'Want to crush you between my thighs!'

This sudden outburst of amorous aggression unnerved Anand completely. Gangi's hold on his hand tightened and the pressure on his chin increased with every moment. With flaming eyes she approached his face in a determined bid to plant a kiss on his lips. Anand thought furiously, drawing upon all his intelligence to devise an escape from that ridiculous and revolting situation in the middle of the public lane. With one determined jerk he freed himself from her grip and remarked in a jovial tone, 'Gone mad? Find a tree trunk, girl!' And before anything further could happen, he quickly strolled away, while she chafed and cursed and made faces at his retreating back.

Well, it was not fair to blame her either, for she had also heard so much about the young prodigy and saw him often visiting her lane. She had become infatuated with him in her own fashion. She was through with the common run of human stallions and was looking for someone different. She longed for this delicate, innocent and brilliant boy, three years younger, who had not yet taken the plunge, as she could clearly see. She wanted him all for herself and perhaps hoped to devote herself to him, to protect and love him in an impossible mother-cum-mistress relationship.

Now, while driving to his village, Anand reflected on that anticlimactic episode. His cart, meanwhile, entered a wayside hamlet and Rama and Bhima slowed to a brisk walk to pull through the narrow lane. Just a few yards more and the cart would emerge at the other end of the lane. At that point, Anand heard a

60

loud, rasping yell, 'Hey, you fool! What d'you think you're doing? Stop that damn cart and go back! . . . Stop, I tell you . . . Stop at once!'

Jolted out of his reverie, Anand looked ahead. There stood another cart, a few yards in front. It had just entered the lane from the opposite direction. The driver was a hefty individual with upturned mustache and a beard to match. On his head rested a tall fez with a longish tuft of thin black silken tassels (called a *phunna* locally) on top, which flew in all directions when he nodded his head.

'Stop that cart and go back!' he shouted again.

'How can I, sir?' said Anand. 'I'm only a few yards from the end of the lane and the cart can't turn . . .'

'Then unyoke the bullocks and back out!'

'That would take too long, sir,' Anand pleaded. 'Instead, you could back up a few paces and let me pass. That would be so much easier . . .'

At this point, the patel (headman) of the hamlet materialized from nowhere. He recognized Anand and said, 'Oh, that you, Anand? Don't you see Girdawar sahib (revenue inspector) is in the other cart? How can *his* cart go back? He is the government's man, see? . . .'

Anand's attitude hardened at this unwarranted show of authority. 'There's no government prestige involved here,' he said simply. 'It's a matter of convenience . . .'

The revenue inspector at once saw how absurd his position was. Flaunting authority was futile, he realized. The bully in him gave in, but not without giving vent to his pent-up venom. 'I know what you young brats are all up to!' he shouted. 'I know you're plotting against Ala-Hazrat and his benign government! I know all Hindus have become members of Gandhi's Congress and want to overthrow the king! You're defying the sovereign's authority at every step; it's treason, treason all the way!'

'Enough!' Anand cut in. 'Enough of these accusations, Girdawar sahib! Please mind your tongue . . .'

Ala-Hazrat's representative raved on. 'I'll show you, I'll show all the Hindu traitors!' Still shouting, he headed for the Hindu patel's house where a sumptuous meal awaited him.

When Anand reached the village, he found that reports of his exchange with the revenue inspector had preceded him, in a grossly distorted form. Father was in a terrific rage. 'How can you hope to get a job in this government if you take it into your head to behave defiantly? A revenue inspector may be small fry by himself. Still, government is government and you had no business to challenge him the way you did! You got the whole family in trouble!'

'But Father,' Anand protested heatedly. 'I didn't say anything rude to him; it was all his fault . . .'

'I know that, son,' Father said, cooling down a little. 'And I believe you. Still, what are we before the mighty government? If it's the revenue inspector's word against yours, whom will they believe, you think? Here we are, your elders, saving our skins for decades for your sake. And you want to throw everything to the winds! Frankly, I don't know how you're going to survive . . .'

In that moment, Anand decided, in a flash, that he would never, never, seek employment with the government of the princely state. The decision gave him immense relief. But he kept it to himself.

'Listen, son,' Father began in a conciliatory tone. 'Our scriptures say that the king is the incarnation of God. That may or may not be true, but what is undeniable is that the king is always right and when you differ with him, you are always wrong. The king develops a logic of his own—that one who is not with him is *against* him. This is the reality, and I don't think anyone can change it, least of all a non-entity like you. You had better go back to the town tomorrow and resume your studies. Avoid further brushes with the government.'

That was good, solid, sensible advice, as far as it went. However, it did not matter now; Anand was never going to be a government employee. What would he do? He hadn't the faintest idea. He had made just one half of a decision.

The other half, however, was not long in coming. Packed back to town unceremoniously within twenty-four hours of his arrival, Anand fretted. Mother looked quizzically at him, as at an offender. He did, however, find in her face the mute melancholy he had come to observe whenever it was time for him to leave. As for the others, their stares seemed to say, 'Serves you right!'

A host of confusing thoughts crowded his mind as he drove back. He had stepped on a live wire, as it were. The shock was inescapable. The government is no joke, he thought he heard the trees and the bushes and the streams cry out. He began to believe the whole world was out to hold him guilty. With no justification whatever, he asserted to himself, rather helplessly yet doggedly.

He was passing along a track through the paddy fields of a jagir village. About fifty women were transplanting paddy seedlings. They sang a rural song of love in a chorus. Anand knew that jagir village well. It had many features that other villages, including his own, did not possess. It had straight lanes (widened into streets, in fact), houses built in a row, perfect discipline among the inhabitants, instant and complete obedience to the jagirdar's orders. Peace and tranquillity reigned, although some scoffers called it the peace of the grave. No one could remember any case or dispute, civil or criminal, having ever crossed the precincts of the village. Nothing went to court or a government office. The jagirdar's manager wielded all powers—civil, criminal, revenue. He was the lawgiver; he was the law.

Just as Anand's cart reached the spot, the women's song stopped abruptly. The jagir manager held one of them by her long hair. He slapped her on the cheeks again and again, spewing the foulest abuse. The woman shrieked and sobbed. The other women stood like statues and looked on with pale and expressionless faces. When the manager roared at them, they all bent forward and resumed their work at once. The manager continued his beating and swearing.

Reminded of Father's stern advice to keep out of trouble, Anand wanted to proceed on his journey, but something impelled him to stop. He jumped out of the cart and shouted to the manager to stop being a brute. Shocked and incredulous, the manager did stop the beating. For a moment he was overpowered by a superior force—Anand's moral force. Only for a moment, though.

The incident was astounding. The woman, it turned out, had a two-month-old baby at home, wailing to be breast-fed. She had asked for permission to go home for a half hour. The manager would have none of it; instead, he had sneered in a biting tone, 'Milk shooting up your breasts, eh? How about squeezing the breasts and sending the milk to the brat? Relief to mother and child both, ha ha ha!' . . . Over this there had been an altercation, resulting in the scene Anand had just witnessed. Addressing Anand, the manager raved, 'You don't know these wretches, Anand! They're always looking for excuses to get away from work—the shirking hags! Now for breastfeeding, now to look after an old mother-in-law, now to spread their legs to a waiting paramour, though they won't admit it. Believe me, discipline has become a thing of the past. You see, I'm getting on in years, having served the jagirdar sahib for four decades and kept this damned village always under his thumb. Now I get the feeling that the dirty devils are getting out of hand. Don't know just what they're up to, the scoundrels . . . Treason, I imagine. Everybody seems to be plotting against the government. And these impudent women are getting the cue too . . .'

The manager ranted on. He looked every inch a devout Hindu, a Vaishnav. His forehead was almost completely covered by two broad white vertical bands that neatly flanked a thin red line in the middle. His arms, belly and chest flaunted similar 'one hundred and eleven'-like marks prominently all over. This faithful servant, after four decades of loyal service maintaining discipline in the jagir, saw intolerable indiscipline in a woman begging leave to breastfeed a hungry wailing baby . . .

His agile brain began to dissect the paradoxes he observed everywhere. A Muslim principal loves a Hindu pupil for his brilliance. A Muslim revenue inspector's insufferable arrogance gets wholehearted support from a Hindu patel. A Hindu manager serves a Muslim jagirdar for forty years, beating and humiliating Hindu women with impunity. A Hindu father teaches his son the philosophy of surrender to the vagaries of the Muslim king's maladministration . . . ! It was all so bewildering. The more Anand reflected, the clearer it seemed to him that there was no Hindu-Muslim confrontation, as such, at any point . . . Then what was the shouting in the name of Hindu and Muslim about? He thought a little deeper and suddenly things seemed clearer.

In a flash, he made his other decision. He would not, repeat *not*, submit to this anti-people Hindu-Muslim combination that perpetuated kingship. He would be one with those who wanted to end that institution—Hindu or Muslim, he couldn't care less.

A rebel was born.

For about a month there was nothing to disturb his routine. Then all of a sudden, all hell seemed to break loose around him . . .

Anand had been a regular user of the school library for years. He would sit there for hours on end, thumbing through books, rummaging through racks, exploring lists and ploughing through catalogues. Each time he left the library, the librarian would find dozens of books strewn on the floor. Several racks and shelves would be in complete disorder. The librarian was an elderly person, with unalterable notions about the divinity of kingship and a strong hatred for every attempt to destabilize it. He was planning to write a book on the blessings of the British empire and was counting on Anand to help him sift and collate the material, read proofs and help in the publication. He and Anand hit it off admirably—for some time.

However, the librarian had, of late, noticed what he considered some disquieting tendencies in Anand. For one thing, he found that Anand had stopped reading books on literature and mathematics and had begun to explore the obscure corner containing books classified as 'political'. The librarian thought these books to be 'not quite desirable for promising students'. They were not too many, to be sure; but how big a spark do you need, the librarian asked, to set fire to a whole city? He had objected to the very proposal of buying those books for the library. The principal had overruled him, saying one could not insulate a whole generation of students from the winds blowing everywhere in the country. The librarian complied with the principal's decision, but never agreed with his dangerous liberalism. He continued to argue that liberalism was only one step from radicalism and one more from treason. He had read somewhere, and believed firmly, that revolutions are born in the minds of men—men, he pointed out, like Anand. Men with brilliant intellect coupled with unflinching character. You could not control such men except, in some cases, through their self-interest. But if a person was above self-interest too, he became a dreadful menace to the establishment. You couldn't do a thing against him. After noticing the change in Anand, the librarian had warned the principal in a 'Didn't I tell you?' tone. Then he had proceeded to do a bit of reporting on his own to the higher authorities. He knew this was irregular, but he felt strongly about the matter and did what he thought right.

Then came the crucial showdown.

The principal paced nervously in his office. Anand stood in a corner, looking innocent and, in contrast to the principal, cool and collected. The door opened and the librarian walked in, stiff and stern, in the style of a prosecutor.

'What books has he been reading?' the principal asked him.

'Jawaharlal Nehru's *Autobiography*, Jawaharlal Nehru's *Letters from a Father to a Daughter*, and —'

'Jawaharlal Nehru's *Glimpses of World History . . .*' added Anand, completing the charge-sheet.

'The government is of the firm view that this is dangerous literature, especially for Anand who is a merit scholar and expects government patronage . . .' the librarian presented the case for the prosecution.

'Why did you choose these books?' the principal almost shouted at Anand.

'Because I like them, sir . . .'

'The DPI is extremely disappointed in you. He wants me to warn you and get an undertaking that you won't read such books again,' the principal added.

'But sir, I don't see anything . . .' protested Anand.

'Never mind what *you* see or don't see,' snapped the principal. 'The DPI feels that such literature undermines the loyalty of His Royal Highness the king's subjects.'

'It is dangerous literature . . .' interjected the librarian.

'Please let *me* handle this,' screamed the principal, betraying an excessive irritation out of all proportion to the librarian's provocation. He knew about the secret reports the librarian had been sending to the DPI.

The librarian withdrew, evidently in a huff. The principal didn't seem to care. He looked at Anand with a troubled expression. 'I knew all along that you would come to grief,' he said resignedly, and added, almost as an afterthought, 'for no fault of yours, though . . .'

'What are you talking about, sir?' asked Anand. 'Why would I come to grief? What have I done? I don't understand . . .'

'Neither do I,' echoed the principal. 'I only know that you have entered the list of the disloyal—officially.'

'I did nothing disloyal, sir. What has loyalty got to do with reading Jawaharlal Nehru's works? Why are these gentlemen planting the idea of disloyalty in our heads? What is the background of all this anyway?'

'Now, now, you are already talking the language of . . .'

'I'm sorry, sir, I didn't mean it that way,' Anand continued. 'This is sheer persecution, isn't it? Can't I read the books I like? I repeat, I feel ennobled when I read Nehru's books. I sometimes wonder if the letters he wrote to his daughter were for me too, and thousands like me. He is in jail right now, isn't he?'

'Why do you want to know where he is? . . . Look, Anand, don't ask me why, but let me tell you again, they have marked you as disloyal, a potential rebel. All I can say is, God help you!'

In that moment Anand made the third significant decision of his life: he would join the rebellion against the king, when the time came . . . He still wondered about Jawaharlal's letters to his daughter . . . they were definitely for him too, he concluded.

One thing was clear to him: He did not understand personal loyalty. He would be loyal to an idea, an idea he believed in. The insistence on *personal* loyalty—perhaps the corollary of personal rule—was anathema to him. Logically, therefore, he cherished democracy. He vaguely believed that it was the antithesis of kingship and did not compel personal loyalty. His simple, schoolboy logic did not pause to ask whether democracy would be really different in this respect and whether the he-who-is-not-with-me-is-against-me attitude would not confront

him after freedom came, whenever it came. He just believed so . . .
And the rebel grew.

# 8

EVERY NOW AND AGAIN, THE SCHOOL HAD A CULTURAL EVENING
when visiting artistes would entertain the student body and
teaching staff. One evening a troupe of qawwali singers were slated
to perform. As they were very good and very famous, Anand sat
in the front row, although he generally preferred to sit in the very
last row, especially if he anticipated a poor performance that
deserved heckling. The sound system in the school, running on car
batteries that were often half charged, went dead now and then or
spat out multifarious beastly sounds, reminding the audience of
the inmates of the Afrozabad zoo to which every young students'
group on excursion was invariably taken. That evening, however,
the sound system worked perfectly and the qawwali songs sung by
the troupe from the state capital captivated the students, teachers
and parents—for a full two hours. No one remembered such a
wonderful performance having taken place in the town before.

Qawwali music consists exclusively of the mystic outpourings
of saints or of the great devotional poets, depicting God as a
beloved and weaving various themes of love around that divine

entity. However, Ghulam Aziz Qawwal, the leader of this troupe, had made some special innovations in his repertoire of qawwalis. About half of them dealt with a description of the great blessings of the Nasir Jahi princely dynasty over the decades, and how the subjects of the kingdom had always lived in peace and prosperity. Unlike *qasidas* (odes), qawwalis as such did not lend themselves to the praise of mundane kingdoms and kings. But since the king had granted a munificent jagir to Ghulam Aziz Qawwal, the grantee had made this unusual departure from tradition. Several well-known musicologists and theologians considered it a blasphemy and grumbled, but royal patronage justified—at least glossed over—everything. Ghulam Aziz Qawwal went from strength to strength as the pampered performer of the state administration. He paid 'official' visits to schools and colleges and did a good deal of propaganda regarding the benign king's countless services to the people—using qawwali music to considerable effect in the process.

Like the other boys, Anand lost himself in the music—deliberately not letting the catalogue of princely virtues disturb his concentration. He enjoyed it as much as he had enjoyed bhajans and *Bhagavata* recitals in his childhood. Differences of phrase and thought seemed to vanish in the infinite manifestations of those seven notes. Absorbed in aesthetic rapture, Anand felt his spirits soar.

Just then, a stranger gently tapped on his shoulder. He had evidently come along with the qawwali troupe and seemed to be part of it, as indicated by his clothes and long hair. He seemed about four years older than Anand, with a short, Lenin-like beard that made his face look narrow and long. His eyes were intent and penetrating, but did not compel attention. Anand thought the man might be a poet; he had heard many jokes about the greatness of a poet being measured by the length of his hair! He could not have imagined that the man was a revolutionary—at that time he had no idea what the word really meant.

The stranger had noticed Anand's absolute absorption in the music, so he waited a long time before tapping his shoulder. 'Good evening,' he greeted. 'Are you Anand?'

'Yes,' Anand responded, quite surprised.

'Don't be surprised,' the stranger said. 'I have heard about you from my uncle, who happens to be the DPI of the state. I am a student in Lucknow University. I've come to Afrozabad for a short visit. My name is Hafeez . . .'

'I am glad to make your acquaintance, Hafeez Bhai,' Anand said effusively, shaking his hand. 'But how did you come into this qawwal outfit?'

'That's what I am keen to tell you, but first enjoy the music; it's really absorbing you, I can see.'

Anand returned to the music gratefully.

After the programme was over, Hafeez quietly handed over a largish envelope full of booklets containing many more qawwalis. 'I'm sure you'll like each one of them immensely,' he said aloud. Then, steering him away from the crowd, he whispered to Anand, 'There are some different poems too; you will like them even better!'

Anand passed a restless night. The poems Hafeez had given him were pure dynamite. Each line echoed the spirit of sacrifice—inspiring one to lay down one's life at the altar of the motherland's freedom. 'DESTROY AFTER READING!' was the urgent instruction at the end of each poem.

The whole night he thought obsessively about the encounter, but could not quite understand the inscrutable young Hafeez. Was he a fugitive who had gone 'underground' and was travelling incognito from place to place? Was he recruiting young persons to his cadre—whatever it was? And what was it in fact? How could he be the nephew of the most loyal of the king's functionaries, the DPI, of all people? Did that official have an inkling of Hafeez's activity? Many sleepless hours later, the actors and the drama continued to mystify him. But he obeyed Hafeez instinctively and destroyed the dangerous poems, all the while repeating them to himself. He would remember them all his life. He only prayed that he would not mumble them in his sleep!

71

The next day, a Friday, Ghulam Aziz Qawwal and his troupe were to hold a huge public qawwali recital in the large courtyard of the main dargah (called the Mian ki Dargah locally). People of all religions began to pour in three hours in advance and soon the courtyard overflowed on three sides, leaving the dargah itself clear on the fourth, illuminated by several dazzling rings of petromax lights.

Anand arrived very early and found a vantage point in a corner not far from the dais on which the qawwali performers were seated, arranging their musical instruments. He had come for two reasons: he was keen on the music, of course, but was equally keen on meeting Hafeez.

Again and again he craned his neck and cast his gaze as far as he could, close to the dais and around; there was no trace of Hafeez. The recital was drawing to a close and the audience made that typical, collective, heaving movement that heralds its rising; still it didn't actually rise. In that fleeting moment, Anand suddenly saw a young man push his way through the throng. Approaching Anand with some difficulty, he panted, 'Sorry, your friend left for Afrozabad this morning urgently. He has sent you another packet of qawwalis. He said these are the latest from the great Ustad.' And he gave a closed bag to Anand. 'I shall see you tomorrow,' he said matter-of-factly.

It sounded like a normal conversation between two individuals who were well acquainted. Anand had the presence of mind to play it likewise and said, 'Thank you, bhaiya, I'll wait till tomorrow.'

Anand could hardly wait to reach his hostel room. Since he had read and memorized the poems Hafeez gave him, he had been thirsting for more . . . and more. That was why he had looked for Hafeez at the dargah; he had to know much more from him. A whole new vista of emotion and action seemed to open up before him; it was his, was made for him, as it were, spontaneously tailored to fit him . . . But now, without Hafeez, the bag in his hand was the best luck he could expect. Wending his way through the thick crowd, he suddenly remembered his school librarian who had kicked up such a fuss over—just imagine!—Jawaharlal Nehru's writings. Wouldn't he, Anand mused with an inner chuckle, have dropped down stone dead if he had been exposed to one of these incendiary poems?

The past two days had brought about an unimaginable transformation in Anand. A new star had appeared in his firmament: the star of sacrifice, of whatever the motherland wanted, required. Just anything—no limits, no bars, no regrets. He realized he had grown secretive and conspiratorial in the past two days. The bag he carried could contain a bomb, a gun, a most destructive weapon or device. Who knew what he would need in the future? He had to fight the king's regime, set the people of Afrozabad free. He was no longer a student imbibing Jawaharlal Nehru's lofty ideas. He was past that stage, most certainly. He was now a freedom fighter, a young crusader.

His dinner was waiting for him in his room, kept in a thali covered by another thali. Everyone else had retired. Rhythmic snores of different pitch and length resonated from the other beds in the room. Now that he was awake, he wondered how he was at all able to sleep so well through that loud cacophony of snores! In any event, to sleep that night was out of the question; not because of the snores, but because he couldn't wait to devour the qawwalis in the bag. As for his dinner, he left it alone; his appetite had vanished, for no understandable reason.

Quietly he slipped out of the room with his hurricane lantern, kept dimmed when not in use. He carried a wooden chair to a far corner of the hostel courtyard, brought another for the lantern and set it comfortably in front—a familiar scene in the students' hostel when the rooms were sultry and the courtyard pleasant. He increased the flame, opened the bag and began reading the papers. Strangely, there was not a single qawwali. It was a bundle of newspaper cuttings and other papers containing all the details of the trial of Bhagat Singh and his comrades Rajguru and Sukhdev. There were copies of letters, notes, a number of intensely patriotic poems and other extremely provocative material which was evidently in secret circulation. Even in the midst of the most distressing and humiliating atmosphere in the country, there was a rousing and ennobling message of hope and courage in the poems and other literature.

73

Anand read on and on. The inspiring future depicted in the poems made him read them again and again, not only to memorize, but to savour the euphoric and reckless spirit they infused into his being.

These soul-stirring odes reverberated through hundreds of spontaneous congregations of youth and students all over the country (barring some native states like Afrozabad, where it was dormant, but no less intense).

As Anand read on, tears came into his eyes:

*Kabhi woh din bhi ayega*
*Ki jab azad ham hongey*
*Yeh apni hi zamin hogi*
*Yeh apna aasman hoga;*
*Shahidon ki mazaron par*
*Lagengey har baras mele*
*Watan par marne walon ka*
*Yehi baqi nishan hoga!*

That day shall also dawn,
When we shall be free;
This land will be ours,
To us the sky shall belong;
At the tombs of martyrs
Fairs shall be held every year
Of those who die for the motherland
This shall be the only sign!

The other patriotic song which had entered millions of minds was the following:

*Sarfaroshi ki tamanna ab hamare dil mey hai,*
*Dekhna hai zor kitna bazoo-e-qatil mey hai;*
*Waqt ane de bata denge tujhe ey aasman*
*Hum abhi se kya batayen kya hamare dil mey hai!*

Our hearts are filled with the desire to sacrifice ourselves,
We have to test the strength of the murderer's arm;

74

Let the time arrive—we will show you, O heaven—
Why should we at this moment reveal what is in our hearts!

There were still many papers to read. Anand could not stop weeping. Overwhelmed with indescribable emotion, he was, at that moment, willing to give up his life for the country.

One document in particular held his attention—the letter which an annoyed Bhagat Singh had written to his father who had made legal arrangements for Bhagat Singh's defence, to save him from the gallows. In September 1930, when it became clear that Bhagat Singh would be given the death sentence, his father Sardar Kishen Singh took recourse to some legal devices. Bhagat Singh, in principle, was totally against offering any defence in his case. He had declined the offer of government defence counsel as had several of his comrades. He was angered by his father's efforts, and wrote to him:

> I was astonished to learn that you had submitted a petition to the members of the Special Tribunal in connection with my defence. This intelligence proved to be too severe a blow to be borne with equanimity. It has upset the whole equilibrium of my mind. I have not been able to understand how you could think it proper to submit such a petition at this stage and in these circumstances. In spite of all the sentiments and feeling of a father, I don't think you were at all entitled to make such a move on my behalf without even consulting me. You know that in the political field my views have always differed with those of yours. I have always been acting independently, without having cared for your approval or disapproval.
>
> I hope you can recall to yourself that since the very beginning you have been trying to convince me to fight my case very seriously and to defend myself properly. But you also know that I have always been opposed to it. I never had any desire to defend myself, and never did I seriously think about it, whether it was a mere vague ideology or that I had arguments to justify my opinion is a different question and that cannot be discussed here . . .
>
> Father, I am quite perplexed. I fear that I might overlook the ordinary principles of etiquette, and my language may become a

little bit harsh while criticizing or rather censuring this move on your part. Let me be candid. I feel as though I have been stabbed in the back. Had any other person done it, I would have considered it to be nothing short of treachery. But, in your case, let me say that it has been a weakness—a weakness of the worst type.

This was the time when everybody's mettle was being tested. Let me say, father, you have failed. I know you are as sincere a patriot as anyone can be. I know you have devoted your life to the cause of Indian independence, but why at this moment have you displayed such weakness? I cannot understand.

In the end, I would like to inform you and my other friends and all the people interested in my case, that I have not approved of your move, I am still not in favour of offering any defence. Even if the Court had accepted that petition submitted by some of my co-accused regarding defence etc., I would not have defended myself. My application submitted to the Tribunal regarding my interview during the hunger strike was misinterpreted and it was published in the press that I was going to offer defence, though in reality I was never willing to offer any defence. I hold the same opinion as before. My friends in the Borstal Jail will be taking it as a treachery and betrayal on my part. I shall not even get an opportunity to clear my position before them.

I want that the public should know all the details about this application and, therefore, I request you to publish this letter.

Anand read this document very carefully. As he folded the papers and put them carefully away, he wondered if he would, some day, have to write a similar letter to his father!

*

'Throw cold water on his face! Wake him up! Shake him up! What does he mean sleeping so late, like Kumbhakarna?'

A group of boys carrying a bucket of cold water surrounded Anand's bed, shouting. That was enough. Anand at once leapt to his feet and shouted back, 'Why are you fellows after me today? You know I am an early riser, unlike many of you!'

'Then why the hell are you still sleeping today? Did you forget there is a Test match at Lords beginning at ten?'

'Oh, sorry, sorry, I forgot the match,' Anand pleaded contritely. 'Just give me half an hour and I shall be there before the toss. Okay?'

The boys were duly satisfied and left, singing some qawwali bits from the previous night's concert outrageously out of tune. Anand's first reflex was to look for the bag of papers he had kept under the pillow. It was there, and had also escaped inundation from the threatening bucket of water. So far, so good.

Now, to Lords. The cricket enthusiasts of the school, under the guidance of a young teacher who had played for his university about ten or twelve years earlier, had adopted names from England for their own cricket outfit. They used three grounds in all. The largest, which also had the football and hockey fields in it, was named Lords; its cricket pitch was long enough to accommodate stumps on both sides. The other two grounds, situated in distant corners, were named Manchester and the Oval, and had a half pitch that could take stumps on one side only; that did not deter the boys from playing matches because on the other side they were able to stick one stump to mark the bowling line.

At Lords that day, they expected a 'mini Ashes' kind of match between two locally reputed teams; they were known as permanent 'cricket foes'. Anand was not considered good enough for a place in the cricket team; his forte was hockey. In cricket he sometimes served as umpire since both teams trusted him. But most of the time he served as an errand boy and a morale booster for his school team. Sometimes his suggestions on tactics in the match were taken seriously.

Punctually at ten minutes to ten, Anand reached Lords and reported to his school team. 'We've won the toss, but the pitch is wet,' the captain told him. There had been a drizzle in the early morning hours and this was to be expected. The captain wanted to put the other team in to bat first. The fielders trooped out into the field within a few minutes and the match commenced with everyone in high spirits, Anand's team hoping to skittle the rival team out for a low tally.

Anand had nothing else to do in his team's corner and quietly

drifted out of the ground to the adjacent public road. There was a
tea stall near by and he headed towards it. But before reaching the
stall, he suddenly saw a dark young boy seated on a culvert staring
at him rather intently. Anand stopped and stared back. He was
sure he had seen the other boy somewhere before. They stared at
each other briefly, then the other boy left the culvert and came to
him, stretching out his hand. 'Namaste,' he said, 'I met you at the
dargah last night.'

They shook hands warmly, then went up to the culvert and sat
down. There was no one else there.

'My name is Sudershan; very few people know me here. Hafeez
has sent me to talk to you. How did you like the poems?'

'They're about to change my life. I have simply no words to tell
you how I feel . . . '

'Don't tell me, I know . . . Only, think and decide. I don't know
how Hafeez spotted you. Perhaps he knows that the state
government spotted you first. That's where his uncle—not uncle
really, but a distant relation's friend, the DPI—became his
informer, in a way. I shall contact you through someone after a
fortnight. You will get more literature through suitable channels;
be careful. Meanwhile, study hard for your public examination.
You'll be moving to Afrozabad from June next, I presume?'

'Yes, depending on how I fare. Anyhow, my father will decide
finally . . .'

'I understand. Now I shall leave you to your match.'

'You mean, my "Ashes"?'

'Could be; in any event that's the prospect for us as of now.
Goodbye.'

And Sudershan disappeared.

*

Time raced by and brought Anand and his fellow students to the
threshold of the public examination. As the crucial week
approached, two things happened. One, more and more hurricane
lanterns burned throughout the sweltering night in the hostel
courtyard, with students in their undergarments in various

postures—sitting, reclining, lying flat on their backs, sideways, on their bellies with chins resting on pillows—absorbing as much text as they could, mainly through 'made easy' notes. Secondly, there was a wave of faith in God among the students. The normal import of coconuts into the town seemed to need considerable augmentation. All the temples and mosques, particularly the dargahs, and the two churches in town gave a glimpse of how devout a needy person becomes, regardless of age and avocation.

One yatra, however, remained to be performed, and the coming Friday was chosen for it. There was no question of any student sitting for any examination in Gulshanpur without having a darshan of the great deity Someshwar Swamy, at the most sacred temple of the area, about twelve miles from town. Again, students of all religions visited the deity; since they appeared at a common examination, they thought it logical to pray at a common shrine. Of course, the same was true of the great dargah in the town where the qawwali recital had been held some days earlier. Whatever might happen, no student worth his salt was willing to forego the divine advantage believed to accrue from God, in whatever name and form.

Around one thousand students set out on bicycles that Friday on the twelve-mile ride to the Someshwar temple. It was, in addition to the prospect of receiving darshan, an enjoyable trip. Each of them carried some food, to eat on the way at a well-known picnic spot where there was a *pucca* well with sweet, clear water lifted into an overhead reservoir by a diesel engine. That day the engine had to be kept running for a really long time and the boys as well as the passers-by marvelled at the enormous power of the springs in the well, as a result of which it could maintain its water level for many hours at a stretch. Since no other well anywhere in the vicinity had such flow, this well was believed to have derived its power from Lord Someshwar Swamy. Indeed, the story went that Lord Someshwar appeared in the landowner's dream and pointed out a particular spot on his land, ordaining that the well sunk there would possess remarkable recuperative powers and sweet healing water, especially if he made it freely available to all pilgrims on their way to and from the temple. The owner had gratefully sunk the well in that precise spot, and the water turned out accordingly . . . Even the indifferent snacks the boys carried with them tasted wonderful, accompanied by the sweet water. They set out on the rest of the pilgrimage with redoubled zeal.

Just as Anand began to eat the food he had brought, another boy his age called him by name and introduced himself. 'I am Brahmaraj, sent by Sudershan. Thank God I've found you at last. It's perhaps safer this way, you are alone among so many unknown pilgrims.'

'Glad to meet you, Brahma,' responded Anand as to an old friend. The password 'Sudershan' worked magic and they immediately felt a conspiratorial excitement and camaraderie. 'I didn't know you would be away on this expedition to placate Someshwar Swamy just on the day I arrived at your hostel. I met your housekeeper Pankaj and chatted a while. Nice old fellow, he seems to dote on you—like his own son, he told me. I gave him a thick envelope stamped "On His Highness the Royal Government's Service". That's the best way of transmitting secret papers which no one will waste his time snooping into. Pankaj promised to deliver the envelope to you personally, and to no one else. Was I right to trust him?' Brahmaraj asked hesitantly.

'Absolutely, no problem,' asserted Anand. 'Pankaj comes from a distant tribal area. He is childless and has virtually adopted me as his son. He is my guardian, in a way. His honesty is proverbial in the hostel. Since he came, about two years back, not a single theft has been reported by any inmate . . . But tell me, did you have anything to eat? We have to be going soon.'

'No, I brought nothing with me, and I am famished.'

'Then let's go to the canteen near that huge banyan tree so you can eat something.'

While Brahma devoured a plateful of bhujias, Anand finished his own food. As they ate, Brahma whispered, 'There is some more revolutionary stuff in that government envelope. You will find copies of thirty-eight proscribed poems, written in different hands. I can assure you, no young man can resist their emotional impact; they are terrific.'

'I'm dying to read them!' responded Anand.

Later, they cycled together at a leisurely pace, talking casually. 'I don't know why,' began Brahmaraj, 'but both Hafeez and the DPI seem to be keen to capture you—for different purposes, of course. I agree one hundred per cent with Hafeez that an armed struggle alone, along with untold sacrifices, can save the people of this kingdom. The Khadimaan (the king's private militia) movement is spreading by the day. The government and the king feign ignorance, but everyone knows the king is squarely behind it. Mahatma Gandhi and his followers in British India are talking of non-violence and satyagraha; I for one can't understand their language. In any event, those concepts are irrelevant to our situation here. So tell me, what have you decided? Hafeez wants to know. He wants to introduce you to his comrades in Cawnpore. Sudershan is very restless. That's why I had to become a pilgrim today, even without any examination to sit for!'

'You are right; the DPI sent word to my father through the district collector, promising a handsome scholarship for my college studies. But my heart and soul are in the movement. On my own, I have decided not to seek government employment. I also decided to serve in the anti-monarchy movement. I can't figure out the rest, beyond this . . .'

After a minute of silence, Brahmaraj changed the subject and asked Anand, 'Can you recognize this banyan tree during night time?'

'Why not?' replied Anand. 'It is close to the eighth milestone on the road to the Someshwar Temple.'

'Good that you know this,' commented Brahmaraj, 'you may have to come here at certain appointed hours, mostly around twilight.'

'That should be no problem,' said Anand. 'I'll carry something to eat and bring something extra in case of an emergency guest . . .'

'Your main task will be to devour this last remnant of monarchy, the kingdom of Afrozabad!'

They joined the flow of pilgrim traffic towards the temple, quietly and smoothly.

\*

After the expedition, Anand got into the habit of visiting the huge
banyan tree on the road to the temple, following which he would
go to another place about five miles into the hills which looked
quite innocuous from a distance. No bicycle was taken beyond the
banyan tree; those who met there just walked the rest of the
distance in the shroud of twilight. About a dozen young men would
gather there; of them Anand knew only Brahmaraj. They held
discussions about the various armed struggles in different countries
and the tactics adopted and the victories won. They seemed to have
developed a poor opinion about non-violence and satyagraha.
They had no means of holding training in firearms there; no
facilities were available. 'You will get trained when you pass your
examination and enter the university at Afrozabad next June,'
Brahmaraj told Anand. Full of revolutionary fire, the young
idealist curbed his impatience and attended each meeting regularly.

*

When he went to his village after the public examination, Anand
found almost everyone staring at him. He was completely
perplexed. Unable to stand the suspense, he went to Mother and
asked what the reason could be. She looked him up and down and
exclaimed, 'Do you realize how tall you have grown in the past six
or eight months? It's unbelievable! God save you from evil eyes!'

When he walked through the lanes to his favourite swimming
well outside the village, he sensed many young women staring at
him from their doorsteps. Two years earlier they used to freely
meet him as childhood friends, but now . . . God! How different
he looked—different and manly! He too noticed a change in the
girls, that went far beyond the physical; for one thing, they were
all married and several of them would soon be leaving to live with
their husbands. He could neither approach them as he used to do
earlier, nor even summon enough courage to talk from a distance.
The sense of approaching adulthood and insistent sexuality coiled
around them like barbed wire. How much innocence they had
lost—lost for ever!

Life at Afrozabad was scholastically rewarding and politically hectic. Anand took his training seriously; he made it appear as part of the University Training Corps. In any event, several movements were going on simultaneously and clashes between the agitators and the Khadimaan were reported regularly; no special notice was taken of any particular individual's activities. The widespread atmosphere of resistance spread rapidly, and the newspapers outside the kingdom were full of incidents detailing the atrocities of the Khadimaan and the sufferings of the ordinary people.

Meanwhile, the whole of British India was rocked by the 'Quit India' movement and Anand strongly felt drawn to it. He and Sudershan crossed the state border into the adjacent state and savoured the spirit of the 'Do or Die' call given by Mahatma Gandhi. They participated in the movement to the extent they could, with the limited contacts they could make, with some local friends of Hafeez's. Eventually, however, they returned, to concentrate on Afrozabad—for several years after the 'Quit India' movement had concluded and brought independence for India.

Then Anand was told that the main resistance party in Afrozabad had decided to carry on a state-wide satyagraha movement and a parallel armed struggle, in view of the exigencies of the kingdom's political situation. One unanimous demand summed up the revolutionary mission: depose the king and merge the kingdom with the Indian Union.

# 9

SUDDEN AND UNFAMILIAR, THE RAPID CRACK OF RIFLE FIRE PIERCED the noiseless dark. Jolted violently out of their sleep, the villagers cowered inside their huts. They had no means of telling the time for no one had a watch or clock in that little hamlet of a thousand inhabitants in one of the most far-flung districts of the state. The intermittent hoot of an owl added a deep sense of desolation to the night. For some time past, the owl had roosted on a tree somewhere on the outskirts of the village. Its presence gave the villagers strange premonitions, but despite their efforts they couldn't drive it away. They were sure the owl was a supernatural harbinger of disaster. And now, just as they had feared, their destruction was at hand. They had often heard the village priest mention *Kaal Ratri*—the night that would mark the end of the universe. This is that night, sure enough, they thought, and shut their eyes tighter, hoping to escape the horrific sight of the world's annihilation.

The village was called Veerapur and abutted onto thick tropical jungle, the Reserve Forest of the state. For weeks now, it had been suffering the depredations of the Khadimaan hordes, the state police, the petty officials of the forest department and the local feudal lords, who had taken advantage of its isolation and its lack of defences to wreak havoc upon it. On several nights in succession, the Khadimaan had descended upon the village and carried away sheep, goats, chicken and grain, all without payment, of course. Then the state police had plundered what remained. The young women of the village were hustled away for what one sub-inspector, with a cruel humour symbolic of the regime, called 'investigation'. When the policemen were through with this procedure, the girls were returned to the village, dishevelled and bruised. Without exception, they had been raped. The next lot of predators were the forest guards and the foresters, uncrowned rulers of the area, each a monarch in his own right for whom nothing was unavailable in the village. For, if the village fell from the foresters' grace, no villager, man or woman, could so much as step into the Reserve Forest, even to relieve themselves.

In the last week, not a day had passed without the Khadimaan gangs and police parties visiting the village. There was a rumour that some 'underground elements' were hiding in the nearby Reserve Forest and the police believed that the residents of this village gave food and shelter to the rebels. None of the villagers knew anything about this, but the police presence grew, and more sheep, goats and grain disappeared from the village and more and more girls came back from the jungle with their clothes in tatters and blood trickling down their legs. The people, in their ignominy and desperation, hoped for the coming of *Kaal Ratri* with all their heart, for it seemed that only an apocalypse could bring their agony to an end.

Soon after the shots rang out that night, dim lights began to flicker in the dark; a dozen police constables ran down the street in their heavy, flatfooted way, torches and hurricane lanterns bobbing in their hands. They broke down the flimsy doors of selected huts and herded about forty men and women into the field at the centre of the village. Dazed and uncomprehending, the villagers blinked in the glare of the police lanterns as a torrent of abuse rained down on them. Soon, the words were accompanied by kicks and the villagers began to drop where they stood, writhing in pain. A sub-inspector with a luxuriant moustache and bloodshot eyes was in charge. He would grunt in appreciation as an especially thundering blow landed, but was otherwise silent. In his shadow stood the village patel, cowering in fear. Abruptly, the sub-inspector turned away from the brutal beating and slapped the patel hard.

'*Be-iman* scoundrel, where is that wretched terrorist?' he yelled.

The patel whimpered.

'Surrender him, or we'll flay you and burn the whole village,' the sub-inspector raved. As he barked at the old man, he remembered the infuriated visage of his immediate superior, a circle inspector who had said, 'If you do not come back here with that terrorist dog and his gang, alive or dead, your career is over. That much I can promise you.'

'Sahib, *mai-baap*, none of the people here know anything about those rascals. Nobody has seen them. If anyone sees their leader or any of his gang, we'll kill them ourselves and bring them to you, piece by piece . . .'

The patel's incoherent babbling seemed not to have registered on the policeman, for abruptly he called over someone who seemed to be his immediate assistant, and whispered something in his ear. His men immediately spread out and began to search the village; every now and again they would drag some unsuspecting villager from his hut and beat him mercilessly.


Anand was perched precariously on an old mud wall. He had climbed up to escape the probing torches of the police, but his hiding place was not very satisfactory. Although he was fairly well concealed by the grass and weeds that had taken root on top of the wall, the slightest slip could send him hurtling down into the clutches of the police. The wall was possibly a hundred years old, built no doubt by some petty chieftain to keep out robbers, wild beasts and other predators. It had crumbled, except for a short length which stood intact, still defying time. Its wide base had become thinner by the year and holes had appeared in it, through which cats, bandicoots and sometimes small urchins could pass easily. It was surprising that the wall still stood, with that battered, disintegrated base and no foundation—like an old civilization whose vitals had been eroded for centuries, yet whose external attributes managed to endure.

Anand could not see where the wall ended. He had scaled it in a single spurt, propelled by the rush of adrenalin that only mortal danger can bring. He pressed closer to the wall so that the dry prickly grass hid him completely. To his agitated spirit this lowly vegetation was like a celestial gift; it had certainly saved him from immediate discovery. As he watched the determined progress of the police posse through the village, the wounds he had sustained during his flight through the forest—cuts, scrapes, bruises—made themselves felt. He shut his mind to the pain, and willed himself to remain completely still.

Anand and four others, Sudershan, Brahmaraj, Ranga and Hari, had attacked a police outpost about six miles away the previous night, and had captured six .303 bolt action rifles and several muzzle loaders. The raid had been very successful in that none of them had been wounded, and they had captured the weapons they needed so desperately. However, the police had not been caught totally unprepared, with the result that they were able to give chase to the escaping revolutionaries.

'Nobody anywhere, *sarkar*,' the head constable reported, his pot belly, from which a whole and unmutilated goat could have jumped out, heaving. He reeked of the toddy he had drunk along with the other policemen, at the patel's house, before initiating the search.

'Where did you look, you shirking drunkards?' roared the officer.

'Everywhere, *sarkar*,' mumbled the head constable, saluting his boss as smartly as he could, given his hideous condition.

'Do you think I'm an idiot?' his superior bellowed. 'Even a blind man can see just how much you've searched. You fellows have just been strutting around! Now listen: if you don't find that dog immediately, every one of you is going to be begging on the streets next week. Go, start searching before I get really angry!'

The head constable lumbered off with his men, and more villagers were dragged from their houses and beaten and abused. The *shup-shup-shup* of canes landing on emaciated human bodies filled the night.

Anand tensed and his hand tightened on the gun he held. From where he lay, it would be easy to spray bullets into every policeman on the street. He knew that the others, who were hiding elsewhere in the village, must also feel the same way, but he prayed that no one would do anything foolish. Too many innocent villagers would be caught in the crossfire and would die . . . Meanwhile, the sub-inspector's torch shone on the mud wall and he yelled to a constable: 'Eh, Rahim, see that wall? Climb it and see if there's anyone there. Quick, you donkey!'

The constable approached the wall. He shone his torch up and down it, looking for footholds. It had drizzled earlier in the night and the wall was wet and slippery. It wouldn't be easy to scale; the constable stood at its foot and fidgeted.

Anand froze when he heard the sub-inspector's order. Noiselessly, he swung around to where he would be able to bring the gun into firing position easily. He would shoot the sub-inspector first, he decided, and then the head constable, and every other policeman he could find, the moment he was discovered.

The constable walked the length of the wall, the beam of his torch flitting restlessly back and forth, then suddenly he jumped back yelling, 'Snake! Snake!'

Confusion reigned and the policeman ran from the wall as though there were a hundred venomous snakes at his heels. His panic infected the policemen closest to him and they began to run as well. The sub-inspector roared, 'Stop, you cowards, you fools, you good-for-nothing donkeys!' The policemen stopped, a little sheepishly. The officer stared at the patel questioningly. 'Yes, *huzoor*,' the latter explained. 'The wall is full of snakes—and cobras at that. I'm sixty-two, but I have never seen any one climbing it so far. *Sarkar*, if the thief ever gets there, I assure you the cobras will finish him off and your bullets will be saved for other sons-of-whores . . .'

Aha! My reptile friends!—Anand said to himself. Come, let's play. My pious mother pours lots of milk in your pits on Naag Panchami day. Let's see how you repay that. Let's see if you too believe in repaying milk with venom—like the king does to his hapless subjects . . .

The police posse dispersed in different directions, to the accompaniment of whistles, flourishes of torches and loud curses. Within minutes the harassed villagers disappeared into their huts, and the street was deserted.

Anand lay still, his eyes and ears straining for any sign of activity in the street. He hoped his four companions had managed to slip away to join the rest of the group in the forest. As their hiding place was relatively far from the police search, it would be easier for them.

He decided to look for an escape route. Dropping as noiselessly as he could to the ground, he crept to the end of the lane, gun at the ready. Dogs barked in the distance but everything around him was quiet. He could hear the police posse crashing around, and decided it would be best if he lay low until they disappeared. Light seeping through the cracks in the closed door of a small hut a few yards away attracted his attention; he decided to seek shelter. The villagers were not hostile to the revolutionaries, though they did not actively support them for fear of reprisal by the police. But he would have to hope this villager would help him, as he could hear the policemen returning.

He approached the hut gingerly and knocked gently on the ramshackle door. There was no response. Cautiously, he pushed the door and it opened; it seemed to have no bolt inside. He opened it slightly and slipped in, closing it behind him. There was no cry of alarm, and he sagged against the wall in relief. A wick lamp giving off a characteristic whiff of castor oil burned in a corner. He suddenly remembered the castor-oil lamps he had studied by as a child. He wondered what his parents would say if they could see him now, just a hair's breadth away from capture, torture, possibly death. They had hoped he would be a good student, get a comfortable government job, lift them out of their middle-class rural existence. Not even in their wildest dreams could they have imagined that their eldest son would plunge into a battle with the mighty king of Afrozabad, the faithful ally of the British empire.

The excitement of recent events, his injury, his exhaustion, and the promise of a safe haven suddenly overwhelmed Anand and he slumped to the floor in a dead faint. When he came to, he found himself stretched on the floor, his face tingling under the touch of cold water. For a few seconds his mind was blank, then he realized where he was. His first reflex was to feel for his gun. It lay by him, loaded. Reassured, he turned his gaze towards the door. He found the cracks between the wooden planks neatly covered by a black cloth—probably a sari or a thick blanket. A large stone mortar was placed against the door. Close to it was a hefty pestle. The last thing he noticed as consciousness ebbed from him again was a dim shape hovering over him.

As he struggled into a waking state, he saw an old woman bending over him with obvious concern. Her furrowed face creased into a smile as he came around. He was at once drawn to that strange, ugly, rustic and ancient presence. She began to whisper conspiratorially.

'How do you feel?'

'Much better.'

'Are your wounds aching?'

'Yes, a bit.'

'I have some *jowar* gruel. Eat.'

'I'm not hungry.'

'Nonsense. You must eat now.'

'I will, just a little later, thanks.'

'What are thanks?'

He was at a loss to explain the expression, for it was obvious it was unfamiliar to the old woman. Yet he felt that if there was one occasion on which an expression of gratitude, in some manner, was essential, it was now. He thought for a short while and said, smiling, 'You're like my grandmother.'

'Good, I like that. I am your grandmother, don't forget that!'

She pointed to something in a corner of the hut. The cloth-wrapped bundle heaved gently and he realized he was looking at someone who was obviously fast asleep. 'That's my granddaughter Rami,' the old woman said. 'My son and his wife died of cholera. I'm alone now with my granddaughter. But now I have a new grandson,' she added, looking at Anand with pride.

Meanwhile, disturbed by the voices, Rami stirred under the blanket and looked around. The old woman gave her a silent signal. Rami showed no sign of alarm at Anand's presence and he muttered a silent prayer of thanks.

'Why have you come here?'

'I am a member of the party, a volunteer.'

'What's that?'

Another barrier of incomprehension stood between them. She knew nothing about any party, nor did she understand what a volunteer meant. How ironical that these villagers had to endure such incessant hardship without even understanding what it was all for, or what the revolutionaries were trying to do!

Again he tried to explain, 'I'm a sepoy . . . do you know who a sepoy is?'

'Yes, yes, a sepoy goes and fights . . . so that's why you have a gun! There is a sepoy in the village. He gets money from the *sarkar* every month. Fought forty years back, he says . . .'

'That's right . . . I'm a sepoy too. I fight against the king.'

'King? Who's the king? Why fight him? Why should a young boy fight anyway?'

'He is a bad king. So we all have to fight him.'

'But how can someone so young fight a king alone?'

'Oh, I'm not alone. There are many leaders behind us. Big leaders . . .'

'So, where are your leaders? Why does a young boy have to face the *sarkar*'s bullets? Why don't the elders do that? Don't they have any shame?'

She has hit the nail right on the head, he thought, as he struggled to find answers to his rescuer's relentless barrage of questions. Strangely the illiterate old woman shot off questions as though she were aware of the opportunism of older leaders who pushed youngsters to the fore whenever sacrifice was required!

He was jolted out of his reverie by shouts in the street. The old woman drew the sari aside slightly and peered out through the crack in the door. The next moment she rushed across to the lamp and snuffed it out, leaving the hut completely dark. She then virtually rolled the youth, gun and all, to where the girl lay half awake.

Someone knocked thunderously on the door. Then it was impatiently kicked open and two policemen peered in. Immediately the old woman set up a loud wailing; its suddenness and intensity shocked the police into silence. Without pausing to catch her breath, she switched from wailing to a torrent of abuse directed at the policemen. Their faces, lit by their torches, still looked dazed. Moving quickly in the darkness of the hut, she covered the two young people with whatever clothes she possessed, all the while spewing invective.

'What devils are you that you can break into the house of a poor, god-fearing woman? I have nothing, no money, no food, no gold. Thieves, fools, good-for-nothing rascals, go to the patel's house if you want gold and money. He's a devil just like you, his wife is covered with gold from head to toe. Go rob her if you have the guts, you . . .'

With movements as quick as a young dancer's, she rolled up a sari to resemble a loincloth and swathed Anand's lower body, hiding his trousers. She tied another cloth around his head like a turban. Finally, she whispered to her granddaughter to clasp Anand in a tight embrace. The policemen had recovered from the shock by now and one of them flashed his torch in her direction and shouted, 'You vile spawn of a donkey! Light a lamp before I break your back!'

The old woman responded with a derisive laugh. 'As if a poor woman like me can afford to keep a light burning all night! Wait till I find a matchbox, you devils!'

The constable's torch settled on the old woman and he gave a start. As she stood there, breathing heavily, she looked like some vengeful mythological demon, her stringy hair hanging loose about her gnarled and wrinkled face. She wielded a broomstick menacingly in one hand. The constable said roughly, 'Have you seen a young man with a gun?'

The old woman shouted, 'What young man? What gun? What

are you talking about? Is this a whorehouse for young men to come to at night? Do I look like a whore? That's my granddaughter and her husband sleeping there and there's no one else in the hut. How dare you call us whores? Why not ask your wife and daughter if they are whores? . . . Oh, oh, I see now. You want an excuse to drag my granddaughter into the forest and rape her? You beasts, blackguards, did our king ask you to do this to poor people? A curse be on your heads! Yelladei, Malladei, Maradei, Pochadei, Durgadei, Maisadei; may the curse of all the goddesses be on you devils! Go rape your own daughters and sisters . . . Let me see who touches my girl! I'll kill him and her and myself . . . Mahakali's curse on you bastards! May dead bodies come out of your houses! May your wives become widows! May lightning strike you! Watch out, watch out . . . you devils!'

More policemen peered through the doorway, attracted by the tumult. Stunned by the old woman's frenzied defiance, they stood around uncertainly. Just then the sub-inspector and the patel arrived. The officer took in the situation at a glance, and concluded that there was no point in wasting time on the old woman. Aloud, he said, 'All right, all right . . . Now don't you scream like that and wake up the whole village, you dirty old hag! Go to sleep now . . . If I hear you making any noise I'll shoot you!'

He moved off, taking his men along. Anand, who had lain as rigid as a corpse, every nerve and sinew taut as the storm exploded so near him, closed his eyes which were brimming with tears of gratitude and relief. The girl in his embrace was so tense, she clung to him as stiffly as a wooden doll even when he sat up and tried to disentangle himself from her terrified grip. Watching them, the old woman's face cracked into a smile.

# 10

'WHILE THE WORLD SLEEPS, INDIA AWAKES TO FREEDOM,' DECLARED Jawaharlal Nehru at the stroke of midnight on 14 August 1947. However, as the rest of the country rejoiced, Anand and hundreds like him were still deeply engaged in the people's struggle in the state. They passed sleepless nights—some in jails, others in the depths of the forests. The guerrilla fighters in Afrozabad found this night of freedom particularly ironic. It was extraordinary that while the British imperial power was ceremonially departing, one of its chief vassals should be declaring his own independence. What had happened one and a half centuries earlier was threatening to repeat itself. The tenth Nasir Jah expressed his intention to emulate his first dynastic forbear and make his state independent of India and invest it with all the attributes of sovereignty. Among several grandiose plans was one in which the king proposed to buy an important part of the east coast to secure an outlet to the sea for his emerging sovereign country. There were dreams of taking back, in whatever manner possible, all the areas which the earlier Nasirjahi kings had ceded to the British Indian government, and before that to the East India Company. Nasir Jah was laying the foundations of another empire methodically and firmly. And to all appearances, his dream seemed on the verge of becoming a reality.

More than five hundred native states posed a problem to the integrity of independent India. The Chamber of Princes—an association of the rulers of the native states or princely kingdoms which had been allowed a measure of independence and autonomy by the British—had suddenly come to life and become aggressively vocal, with the open encouragement of the departing British power. It had become very active under the tutelage of the ambitious Nawab of Bhopal, in a bid to create a third India. It was altogether a depressing scenario, especially after the trauma of Partition that had torn the subcontinent into two amid much bloodshed and grief. And now, nothing less than a second Partition stared the country in the face, with another one-third of India almost poised to tear itself asunder.

As newly-independent India convulsed in the throes of birth, the future of Afrozabad State was uncertain. The valiant young men and women who had fought the king and his cohorts for several years now, could only hope that the new government of India would take steps to emancipate them. The careers of a whole generation of students had been in the doldrums, their lives caught between studies and agitations. As many of their countrymen woke to freedom, these young men and women found themselves in fetid prisons, or in thick forests among snakes and wild beasts. It was a time of stunning paradoxes and treacherous ambiguities.

On the morning of 15 August, Anand and his comrades were cooped up in a thatched hut deep in the Reserve Forest. Snatches of information came haltingly from their lone battery-powered radio. The battery had to be recharged every few hours with a charger, which in turn was fuelled by kerosene oil purchased and brought at great personal risk. The radio was their only window to the outside world and they took great pains to ensure it was in good working order.

Today their mood was cheerful. They had improvised a national flag by putting together a white band of cloth, and a red one in lieu of saffron. Since they couldn't find a green cloth, they joined it to a band made of three teak leaves stitched together, end to end. Sudershan, the innovative member of the group, drew the Asoka Chakra in the middle of the white band with a piece of charcoal. They hoisted this unique flag on a fairly tall teak tree and saluted it with undisguised emotion as it fluttered majestically in the forest breeze, teak leaves and all.

There were nine of them in the group—all highly educated, highly motivated. Sudershan was one of Anand's closest colleagues, urban in origin and upbringing, yet completely involved in the group's underground activities that entailed untold hardship and risk. He had jumped into the struggle when he was in the final year of the MBBS, with no political ambition whatever. He merely wanted to see the people of the state through to freedom and integration with India. He would then return to college to obtain his medical degree and settle down as a practitioner. He was the no-nonsense type, pragmatic, responsible, upright. He was Anand's sincere friend, one who admired him and quite often criticized him unflinchingly for one thing or another, confronting the doubts and fears that arose from the latter's self-inflicted psychological complexes and sensitivity.

Brahmam—also called Brahmaraj—was the arms and explosives expert of the group. He was the son of a highly skilled blacksmith who lived in a narrow by-lane of the old section of the state capital. Brahmam's father also repaired rifles and revolvers. His calling had no political overtones; the elite owners of automatic weapons knew him as a competent artisan. While most of the guns he repaired were licenced, some unlicenced weapons too had begun to slip in and out of his house in recent years, through Brahmam. He didn't ask his son too many questions, since he couldn't read the licences anyway. Besides, as Brahmam knew, it wasn't just that his father was illiterate; he deliberately avoided asking questions about gun licences. Repairs and overhauls went on quietly, efficiently. Brahmam had completed his M.Sc. in chemistry years ago. Then he jumped into the struggle against the king. He had no special reason other than that no patriotic and self-respecting young man could keep aloof from the resistance movement any longer. The spirit of revolt was all-pervasive.

So was the case with the others in the group. They had no self-interest or narrow aspirations and did not even know whether they would live to see the state liberated.

'There is hope now,' said Sudershan after their improvised flag-hoisting ceremony. The others agreed. But within a few days came the news that the state government had entered into a 'Provisional Agreement' with the Government of India. That meant a long delay before any change could come about in the status of Afrozabad. Dark August clouds above and impassable slush below became the physical as well as the political climate for the inhabitants of the state.

The people had to wage an intense struggle for fourteen months after India's independence, amid horrendous scenes of murder, rape, plunder and devastation by the Khadimaan organization led by the fanatical and maniacal leader Rahim Alvi. The depredations of the Khadimaan gangs spread far and wide; their atrocities exceeded anything seen anywhere in British India during the entire period of the freedom struggle. The Provisional Agreement was primarily meant to give the Central government some breathing space to cope with the myriad problems immediately following the country's partition. However, the king and the Khadimaan leaders interpreted it as a sign of weakness of the Central leadership. As a result, the Khadimaan's appetite for loot increased a hundredfold. Thousands of harassed families fled their homes to take refuge in the adjoining areas outside Afrozabad. Thousands of others offered satyagraha, courted arrest and organized demonstrations protesting the excesses. The government itself arrested a large number of unconcerned and innocent citizens and incarcerated them for no specific reason, except to terrorize the common people.

As the nation's worst misfortune yet came Mahatma Gandhi's assassination. It left everyone emotionally paralysed for a long time. Apart from their grief at the nation's bereavement, Anand and his friends grew depressed as they saw the chances of the state's emancipation recede into further uncertainty. There was nothing they could do but continue to fight—and hope.

At long last, the Union government realized that the king's runaway ambition was getting the better of him. Also, he soon became the captive of the Khadimaan organization, the monster whose birth and ascendancy he had earlier connived at, as a counter-blast against the Centre. It was time to act.

Yet, there was continued delay for one reason or another, adding to the tribulations of Afrozabad's population. The Khadimaan hordes harassed and plundered innocent citizens, ostensibly because they were engaging in 'treasonable' activity. In actual fact, many innocents were accused of treason by local thugs who wanted to have them arrested so they could occupy their valuable property. Those who took refuge in the neighbouring states of the Indian Union were treated well in the beginning, but in course of time unscrupulous shopkeepers and businessmen began to exploit them. For instance, the refugees from Afrozabad had to pay highly inflated house rents. Prices of essential commodities spiralled up, for no discernible reason other than the influx of needy people from a neighbouring area. Matters went to absurd lengths when exorbitant 'refugee prices' came into vogue. The rising prices also affected the local inhabitants who, in turn, blamed the refugees from Afrozabad for their woes. Hostile feelings intensified between the refugees and the locals.

The Khadimaan movement spread rapidly, right down to the villages. Unfortunately, it mainly involved the Muslims. Some Hindu feudals were also associated with it, but their number was not large. Many feudals, both Hindu and Muslim, heartily approved of the organization and the concept of an independent Afrozabad State; but the Hindus among them played a more subtle game. They protested their loyalty to the king from the housetops, but, in fact, kept their options open. They proved to be adept in the game of riding two horses at the same time. Some intellectuals from the adjoining states of British India, whom the state government cultivated personally, became enthusiastic votaries of the proposed sovereign and independent State of Afrozabad. They wrote books and treatises and propagated the concept, trying to prove that independent Afrozabad would be far more prosperous than any state of British India. For the moment, however, those authors alone prospered fabulously while the people suffered.

With every passing day, with every incident of rape, loot and arson by the Khadimaan, the climate of despair thickened. Anand and hundreds like him fought bravely, but could never hope to match the arms brought in clandestinely by the British gun-runner Henry Callon and distributed liberally to the Khadimaan. Anand saw several of his comrades killed in encounters, overpowered by superior weapons. He found himself in mortal danger many times but survived each time. Death seemed to have its random pick, as well as random rejection—with no reason for either.

One morning, Governor-General Rajagopalachari remarked in Delhi, 'As Governor-General, I tell you not to worry about Afrozabad. . .' That statement apparently came after a long silence and was noted in all quarters. Though not quite explicit, it revived hope everywhere. Anand and his comrades intensified their acts of resistance for several weeks, as if in a new spurt of inspiration and faith. They fought successfully against the king's police in several pockets of the Reserve Forest, and their morale rose.

This spell too did not last very long. The government began to set up new outposts by the dozen and the resistance groups soon found themselves outnumbered by police with superior weapons and unlimited ammunition. Poor and illiterate villagers still gave the 'terrorists' food and shelter. Some village elders carried coded messages on scraps of paper, carefully concealed in cheroots made of *palas* leaves. They did everything to help the young rebels. Yet they knew it was an utterly unequal fight and counted the days restlessly, awaiting the promised deliverance at the hands of the Central government. Meanwhile, police atrocities and indiscriminate and excessive collective fines broke their morale, bit by bit. Under pressure and inducement, some villagers began to furnish information to the police about the hideouts of resistance groups in the Reserve Forest . . . All in all, time was on the king's side and as nothing happened on the political front after the Provisional Agreement, the anti-monarchy agitation began to show fatigue. For the armed young men, the only choice was between victory and death. There was no middle course.

It was then that Anand and his comrades decided to do

'something big', something that would ensure that they went down, if that was to be, literally with all guns blazing. The group had some crack shots, among them Anand, and an arch manoeuvrer in Sudershan. When it came to sheer daring, nothing was beyond Anand; his capacity to savour peril increased in direct proportion to the peril. He had, as it were, cultivated a relationship with Death. His actions were never foolhardy; yet they evidenced a disdain for death that at once distinguished him from the others. When there was grave danger, Anand would be the one to lead; that was the rule. The regular leader of the group, however, was Sudershan, who understood Anand's phenomenal spirit. In his heart of hearts, he did not expect his dearest friend, Anand, to outlive the struggle. Whenever the thought crossed his mind, he became unusually sad.

The action proposed was a lightning raid on a very important police outpost, followed by the capture of a large cache of arms and ammunition. The cache included some modern weapons that Henry Callon had brought from Italy. They had arrived at this outpost just a few days earlier. That was the special attraction which made them decide upon the raid.

The rebels planned each move meticulously. The group would start from its hideout at about midnight and carry out the raid between two and three in the morning. This was the ideal time when the late sleepers and early risers would both be out of the way. The previous evening, a village shepherd had brought them a huge basket of custard apples from the weekly bazaar a few miles away. The basket was now topped by two layers of custard apples, with thirty hand grenades stacked neatly at the bottom. Anand was to be in charge of the basket. As he carefully packed the grenades and then the fruit, he was reminded of his mother, who carefully picked out the best custard apples for him—they were his favourite fruit and as a child he had always taken great delight in chewing the thick sweet pulp and spitting out the shiny black pips under her indulgent eye. He remembered competing with other children to see who could spit the pips furthest. He hadn't seen his mother or anyone else from his family for over a year now, and he was suddenly gripped by a deep sorrow. Were they all right, he wondered, were they even alive? He shook the mood off with a strenuous effort of will. This was no time to get sentimental.

The other members of the little group occupied themselves with a variety of tasks, cleaning their weapons, cooking the evening meal, clearing the camp. Some of them stared vacantly into space. Sudershan was resting, his eyes shut. The tension was palpable. They would have been even more anxious had they been aware of a mishap that was to cost them dear. The group had an informer in the police camp they were to raid. This man who served as cook and dishwasher looked every inch a timid idiot and the police inmates of the camp trusted him for his good cooking as well as his half-wit appearance. He did not know a word of the language the policemen spoke among themselves; that was an additional safety factor. At the slightest frown from any policeman, he would fall at his feet crying, 'hajoor, hajoor!' and tremble from head to foot, to the great amusement of the onlookers.

In reality, however, he was from a village that Hari, one of the revolutionaries, hailed from. They were boyhood friends and the job at the camp was managed between them, by a circuitous method that involved many risks. Ramu the cook merged admirably with the police camp and at the same time found a hundred ways to convey information to Hari, with no one whatever suspecting them. Ramu also knew the language the policemen spoke, but never, never let it be known; his restraint was superb. That was how he got wind of a plan to send out a police patrol that very night in the direction of the group's hideout; it was an unexpected new decision, and at the first opportunity he got, Ramu ran into the forest to alert the young men. Unfortunately, at that late hour, he stepped on a cobra and was bitten; shortly afterwards he died on the spot in great agony. The group remained unwarned.

They set out, single file, shortly after midnight. Scarcely half an hour later they ran into the police patrol. Both groups were taken completely unawares; the policemen recovered first and opened fire and the group had no time to take cover. They scattered, but not before Sudershan was hit in the thigh. He fell to the ground, bleeding profusely. Anand seized him and somehow pulled him to cover. The police party spread out and began searching the forest. Watching them fan out, Anand clamped his hand over Sudershan's mouth to stifle his groans. He was determined not to leave his friend, but if he stayed there much longer, discovery was certain.

Whispering to Sudershan to be as quiet as possible, he removed a grenade from his bag, removed the pin and hurled it some distance away. The forest lit up with the flash of the explosion, and the advancing policemen turned in its direction. Anand ran a short distance and hurled another grenade to the left of the first one. The police party split up, believing the enemy was attacking on two fronts. He hurled the rest of the grenades, one after the other, in a short arc; the police fired blindly in the direction of the explosions and their fire was answered by the group. Anand crawled to where he had left Sudershan, and began to drag him back to the hideout. He hoped the others would remember to retreat in an orderly fashion to the camp, without drawing attention to it. The police posse, confused by the grenade spread, thought it safe to return to their camp; Anand had left that direction free from grenade hits. By morning, everyone in the rebel party had returned safely; apart from Sudershan, only one other fighter had been injured—a bullet had torn a furrow through his arm.

They learned of the informer's death the next day and decided not to risk attacking the armed camp. Over the next few weeks, Anand's group had some success in sniping at and killing some policemen, but the police presence was too strong and pervasive for these marginal successes to have much impact. Elsewhere in the state, the success of the other groups was mixed, but it was obvious that they were fighting a losing battle. Even so, the impact of their raids caused real panic in the Khadimaan ranks. The state government felt somewhat threatened.

Rumours grew about the wavering in the Central government's tacit support to the freedom fighters; the confusion was assiduously fostered by the state government. The state's Prime Minister, Hashim Ali, and other ministers were reported to have deeply impressed Jawaharlal Nehru by their intellectual sophistication and extremely polite manners at several interviews with him. An equally persistent rumour had it that the sycophantic approach of the ministers had produced the opposite effect on Sardar Patel, the home minister. Prime Minister Nehru had described these ministers as *sharif*, while the worldly-wise Sardar had denounced them as 'scoundrels'. No one knew the truth and the rumours grew in volume and vehemence. In actual fact, the Prime Minister and home minister were so preoccupied with more pressing issues, such as the fate of Kashmir, that they had little time to focus on the king of Afrozabad; yet they were only looking for the appropriate moment for action. Their perceived indifference, however, goaded the Khadimaan and the state government to further defiance.

When the Central government finally moved, it did so decisively. It was obvious that the action would have to be perfectly executed, for it could easily spin out of control. From Sardar Patel's point of view, the state resembled an exquisite jamawar shawl trapped in a malignantly thorny bush. If you pulled it hard, it would come free, torn and tattered. If you did nothing, the thorns would pierce deeper and deeper into the cloth and damage it permanently. To free the shawl without ripping it to shreds, each thorn would have to be carefully prised from the delicate material. In the end, the Sardar executed the Central government's plan to perfection. Around the middle of September, the army went into the state. The action was completed in four days. The Khadimaan were silenced. Although some of them held out, blew up bridges, carried out random killings and even tried to break into the jails to kill political prisoners, they were soon captured. The state's army surrendered on the fifth day. Within days, all traces of the Khadimaan movement disappeared. Its ferocious cadres from the countryside merged with the rural populace once more. Several state leaders, including Prime Minister Hashim Ali, made their escape to Pakistan. There were few reprisals once victory was assured, the predominant feeling being one of relief. The people were anxious to rebuild their lives, they had no time for futile retaliation. A military government took over the state administration. One interesting episode was that several minor feudals (some majors too) who were ardent Khadimaan supporters appeared overnight in lily-white Gandhi caps.

After causing such havoc, the king escaped lightly—he was appointed the Raj Pramukh of Afrozabad State, an integral part of the Union of India.

Many of the young men who had joined the anti-monarchy movement—those who survived it, that is—now went back to their studies or professions. Anand found he had no real preference where his own future was concerned. Academics held no attraction for him; nor did public life in a post-freedom era in which the remnants of a feudal order were still strong. He knew he had to fight the old system now, if his public life was to be worth anything. But the feudal core was older and had stronger roots than the short-lived Khadimaan movement or even the symbolic apex of the movement, the king. And he also realized that the fight had to be peaceful and constitutional—on a front where the feudals were far more formidable than raw visionaries like himself. It would be extremely difficult to replace the existing order completely. And to reform it meaningfully seemed even harder than establishing a substitute of some kind.

Those who understood this dilemma compromised with the feudal order in a variety of ways. Their sights were on the coming democratic set-up in which the status quo would, hopefully for its protagonists and beneficiaries, perpetuate itself. There would, of course, be marginal variations and a tremendous awakening among the people; no one could stop that. That certainly would be a silver lining. But when Anand thought of his party leaders at the local level, he had no doubt about the future scheme of things . . . The scenario was, by any token, far from inspiring. But could he give up? And what then? . . . He had no vested interest to save or safeguard. No life of peace and contentment to cherish. No material gains to make him circumspect in any manner. Besides, his friends such as Sudershan felt strongly that he should remain in public life—for whatever it was worth. 'We staked our lives for something—whatever it was,' they asserted. 'It's good to see someone hold the fort for the dreamers, whatever the results . . .'

Most important, public life afforded Anand an alibi, a

pretext—for what, he often asked himself. For not doing what he would otherwise have to do? For refusing to be bogged down by a mundane existence that would simply drive him mad? For not plunging into a rat race in which he would be a hopeless misfit? For not participating in a life of material aggrandisement for which he had no motivation, as a result of which he would probably not fare as well? This last factor was too painful to contemplate. He had been an unqualified success and a prodigy in all the fields he had been involved in, right from childhood. Many had come to believe, wrongly of course, that he could not fail, whatever he did. And precisely because of this belief, the spectre of failure somehow became ingrained in him, perhaps imperceptibly in the beginning . . . After days of endless rumination, he came to the conclusion that no matter which path he took, it finally did not matter one way or another, because of the sustained, stoic detachment he had cultivated as an integral part of his mentality and a way of coping with the relentless pressures of a cynical, antagonistic world.

Then, when he gave himself over to reflection, the great attraction of public life seemed to be its expanding frontiers, its flexible horizons. It was a realm of infinite possibility, a task that was never concluded, a challenge that never abated. And he chose it precisely for these intimidating characteristics, its endlessness.

He decided to stay—rather just stayed—in public life.

His state party's armed struggle programme came to an end with the Central government's action and the integration of Afrozabad State into the Indian Union. The new Indian Constitution took effect in the state on 26 January 1950. So, if he had to remain in public life, Anand had to be a participant in a multi-party democracy. Political parties had already mushroomed, and it was difficult to distinguish them from one another—except perhaps through their leaders. Important leaders such as Jaya Prakash Narayan, Asoka Mehta, Ram Manohar Lohia etc. founded a separate party, mainly to fulfil the need for an effective Opposition in a multi-party democracy. The Communists were already active in several fields; Anand had rubbed shoulders with them in the students' movement. They decided to participate in the democratic process. But the Telangana movement was still fresh in the people's memory; it did not quite fit in with the new system. The Communist Party did not quite abjure violence while entering the democratic process. For them, this was more in the nature of an experiment rather than a matter of conviction; they joined the democratic process to derive all possible advantage from the incumbent system without having much faith in it—not for the time being, at any rate.

Leaders in Anand's party in the state were all praise for him, although they knew he could not be fitted into a mould. When the state party merged with the All India party, Anand had to familiarize himself with all the subtle nuances of the game of democracy. He found it difficult in the beginning, but adapted himself to it with some effort. Still, he could not take political life either as a 'game' or as a regular profession. For many others, he found that it was one of these two. But to him, political power was a serious and puzzling matter in which a person's success was measured—at any rate ought to be measured—not on the basis of his effort or personal achievement, but on what happens to the vast mass of people.

The announcement of the first general elections triggered unprecedented activity all over the country. The ruling party, in particular, found itself subjected to unending pulls and pressures due to a sudden surfeit of candidates asking for tickets for the Lok Sabha as well as the state legislative assemblies. It was obvious even to any casual observer that the gravitational pull for many of these individuals was power alone; few seemed to be aware of the responsibility devolving on them, and still fewer were ready for it.

# 11

THE COUNTRY WAS GALVANIZED INTO FRENZIED ACTIVITY WHEN the general elections were announced towards the end of 1951 under the new Constitution. Looking back far into history, no comparable event had occurred in India. There had been elections of course—to panchayats, to district boards, to legislative assemblies, under the aegis of provincial autonomy—all with limited franchise of various kinds. Indeed, historians describe the holding of elections of some kind—and, therefore, the existence of a democratic system—in ancient India. Nevertheless, general elections throughout India with universal adult franchise, under a sovereign independent Constitution, had a significance that was unmatched in the nation's history.

This very first election in free India gave Anand his first taste of defeat. The people whom he had served for years with obsessive devotion abandoned him. His defeat was quite unexpected. He was one of the best campaigners in the party and was in constant demand throughout the election period, particularly in constituencies where his party was not very strong. The clarity of his logic, the range of his ideas and the felicity of his expression won over a variety of audiences, extending from urban sophisticates to utter illiterates. He could effortlessly feel the pulse of a crowd and become one with it. He did very well at places where the audiences had heckled and humiliated many senior leaders. As the campaign intensified, Anand drove hundreds of miles from meeting to meeting, barely pausing to sleep, eat, and bathe. He would often take the wheel during long night drives. As he drove, he would sing and lose himself in the rhythm of the road. The jeep would hum along for hours, almost musically, in the quiet of the night. And in perfect tune with the vehicle, Anand would sing, his voice rising to frequent crescendos of exhilaration. The jeep was his sole companion, confidante and co-conspirator. His friends packed inside like chickens in a basket were mere listeners, permitted only to exist on the periphery of his cathartic emotion. Absorbed in his rapture, at some moments he almost resented them as intrusive. Yet he made each of them feel important, for which they were grateful and adored him all the more.

His efforts helped several other candidates win, which made his own defeat rather odd and ironical. The magic of the secret ballot made it impossible to say accurately why the people who had listened to him with such empathy had abandoned him at the crucial moment. A wind had swept the region against his party. Its genesis was difficult to understand at the time. It wasn't illogical, yet not quite logical either. It was, in essence, a part of life, political life as it existed at the time. The people had never ceased to love Anand and his party; only, they didn't vote for him. It was not surprising that in that first election an overwhelming majority of poor illiterate voters voted for the first time. Looking back on the possible psychological make-up of that voting, Anand later asked himself, 'Did you not ignore the fact that those totally ignorant voters might not have quite understood the nexus between loving you as an activist-benefactor on the one hand, and voting for you on the other? Is it not conceivable that they found a sudden and compulsive incentive just at the time of voting that tempted them to vote for the other party? How would they realize that not voting for you, Anand, was such a serious matter for them? Did they understand the consequences of not voting for you? Could you even explain the implication clearly to them in those last two days when the new incentive was let loose suddenly and secretly and you and your workers were still talking about Mahatma Gandhi and Nehru's policies?' Something entirely different came over them at the moment of voting. A fancy for the new. The temptation of five acres of land and a milch cow for every single vote cast for the other party was dangled in front of them in the last two days of the campaign. Who made the promise? To whom? When? Where? Nobody knew, nor cared, nor paused to think—until after the poll. Also, fear was subtly induced among the common people that if the other party lost in the election, it would once again take to arms and violent activities. Yes, once again there would be nocturnal raids on the villagers as they slept, fires in haystacks, cutting throats in public, the shooting of 'marked' persons in the presence of their kith and kin . . . 'You remember all these things that happened not so long ago, surely? Do you want them to begin all over again? . . . No? . . . Then cast your votes for the other party.' It was a fail-safe method to 'convince' the voter. Only, it was a distorted version of democracy. Again, no one knew about these tactics until after the poll.

Each voter, it appeared, had decided to grab the five acres and the cow all by himself, to the exclusion of everyone else. Each one behaved as though the offer had come to him alone; so he allowed just himself to be the exception while foolishly believing that everyone else would vote for Anand, and as a result, he would win, being the favourite candidate.

They waited a few days for the promised land and the cow, and when these did not arrive, realized they had been tricked. They then went to Anand in droves vying with one another to prove their loyalty and to reassure him that some others had betrayed him, not they. This was the refrain of every group that met him. They told him stories of bribery and coercion and even told him subtly that if he had only spent some money 'in other ways', his victory would have been certain. No candidate could win an election entirely by merit, or by brandishing posters of Mahatma Gandhi and Jawaharlal Nehru, great as they were, they implied.

For a first election, they had learnt remarkably fast.

They felt greatly relieved when Anand said that the election was now behind them; they might as well stop referring to it. They were thankful to him for this amnesty and promptly returned to their petty requests and recommendations, pestering him as they had done before the poll, as if nothing at all had happened. Often, however, they showered praise on him to his face and condemned him behind his back. What a spineless fool, they exclaimed, to forget his humiliation and run to serve those who had forsaken him barely a week back! . . . Must have an extraordinarily thick skin indeed! . . . He will, someone commented caustically, continue to help everyone foolishly until someone else trounces him in the next election! He's made that way.

Anand was taken aback by their venality but didn't let it show. He had actually earned the wrath of his family by selling off part of the ancestral property to finance his campaign; and now he had nothing to show for it. But he wasn't going to hold the villagers responsible for his defeat, and said as much to them. In addition to the votes he had lost, he also lost the support of many of his friends and well-wishers. Indeed, the only thing he gained was their derision; they castigated him for ignoring their advice on how to 'manage' votes. His response to his defeat only served to further infuriate them. When the results were announced and fellow politicians came to console him, he merely said, 'How does it matter?' This indifferent response puzzled them, and deprived them of the opportunity to shower their false sympathy on him. Indeed, his calm at his defeat was almost an affront—how could he take an election so lightly? They had no chance to say, 'Didn't we tell you?' Above all, a lost election was indeed a serious matter and when he made light of it, they concluded that it was either a pose or an insult to them—or both. It wasn't any particular wickedness on their part; they were his friends all right. But the fall of the brilliant one, friend or foe, gives rise to a subtle, indescribable ripple of joy in many human hearts. And this is especially evident in the political field . . . So Anand's friends called him arrogant, unrepentant, hypocritical, insincere and even wicked—behind his back, of course. Again, there was no real enmity in all this; it was a sort of logic according to which he had to be what they thought he was. But he refused to beat his breast when they expected him to. It was, to say the least, abnormal behaviour. Therefore, inexcusable.

If his supporters were disappointed and angry with him, his family was sullen and disapproving. His relatives had never really approved of his abandoning his traditional profession to acquire an education. They had fumed at his refusal to listen to their advice and opinions and were overjoyed (secretly, of course) that he had now tasted humiliation. He had, at no time, cared much for them anyway; they could never bear to see anyone prosper at levels that were beyond them. As Anand had risen in his field, so had their hatred for him. It was middle-class snobbery, in which several motivations mingled. Fear. Jealousy. Sneaking admiration. Simulated nonchalance. And plain hypocrisy.

His family was deluged with visitors who insinuated, in their refined language, of course, how useless Anand was, and how he had let them down time and time again. How could he have ignored the sacrifice they had made to send him to school and college? First, he had fought against the king's regime, and now he had made a complete fool of himself in electoral politics. Indeed, what was the point in standing for elections when any idiot could see that he would definitely lose? No money, no major caste backing, none of the paraphernalia so vital in elections; how did he ever think he would win? And having lost, why was he saying that it didn't matter? And thus it continued, day after day. It amounted to nothing, even as criticism; the fact was, they just didn't like him.

To Veena, her husband's political involvements were a constant source of anxiety. She knew vaguely that years ago Anand had been involved in some dangerous activity against the king—with guns and bombs. After that chapter was over, he had become engrossed in politics, which she liked even less. Particularly, when it led to his selling family property. That was the limit. Perhaps she just wanted Anand to settle down in the village like everyone else, to look after his land, raise children and be a normal family man. There was nothing wrong in her wish, but nobody, least of all

Veena, was absolutely sure that this was indeed what Anand was cut out for. She only became confused and gradually found herself close to those who were unsympathetic to Anand.

There is something terrible about the unarticulated tension in a Hindu family. It releases an unending drip of poison into the fabric of life—day by day, drop by small drop. There is hardly any argument, any ventilation of grievances, yet life becomes deeply affected. Nothing happens. Men and women adopt a fossilized attitude, a culture of death—variously called ancient, wise, great, enduring, traditional—you name it. The slightest urge to resist is instantly and ruthlessly suppressed. Revolt and perish. Or conform and die in quiet, inane dignity. That's the choice, if you can call it one.

Despite his stoic and calm exterior, Anand was inwardly demoralized by his defeat. Where had he gone wrong? Was this the future pattern of the democratic process in the country? At best a wave; at worst a gamble. How could he fit into this? His deriding relatives were perhaps right, he surmised. Should he, then, leave public life alone? Should he return to—to what?

Anand decided to plough a lonely furrow. Neither total conformism nor total rebellion. Conformism was out of the question; he knew he could never manage it. Rebellion was equally untenable, since family commitments were inescapable. Being the eldest male child of the family, he had to shoulder a heavy responsibility. Two younger brothers—one of whom was still in his teens—were to be taken care of. It was a kind of detached involvement. He adopted this attitude without knowing where it would lead, yet was certain that he couldn't do otherwise. It was, he thought, the price he was paying for being different.

He suffered silently under the shadow of his electoral defeat, but public life had its own demands that would not wait, and Anand slowly began to immerse himself in his work once again.

For four long and eventful years after the first election, Anand worked feverishly and proved his mettle at all levels, from the village to the state. The freedom struggle against the monarchy in Afrozabad had not been as long-drawn as the national struggle against the British rule. As a result, it had not thrown up a multi-generational leadership at the political party level in any great numbers. There were, of course, several senior leaders who drew inspiration from Mahatma Gandhi and Jawaharlal Nehru; but these state leaders generally operated mainly from the capital. Anand's was indeed the first generation that originated in the rural areas and reached leadership positions comparatively quickly.

When elections were announced in 1952, there was no legacy of 'sitting members' in the state. Thus Anand became involved in all party programmes and became one of the main draftsmen of party documents and statements. In the years after the first general election, Anand campaigned for the party in several by-elections and helped it edge the other party out convincingly. The tall promises made at election time by that party never materialized; the false land-and-cow promise had brought its credibility tumbling down—more or less permanently in this state, as it turned out. The prospects of Anand's party began to look up distinctly; the people had second thoughts about how they had voted in the first election. Their perspective had altered significantly by the time the second general election approached.

# 12

THE WORD 'TICKET' IS COMMON TO EVERY LANGUAGE IN INDIA.
But there are tickets and tickets. And those actively involved in the
political process interpret a ticket as permission to contest an
election as candidate of a given political party. The candidate, if
elected, sits in the legislative assembly, or any other body for which
he contests, as the representative of that party. The system being
one of multi-party democracy, parties are its primary building
blocks, although individuals are also permitted to contest as
independents. Naturally, the scramble for party tickets is intense,
and is often accompanied by inducements, both monetary and less
visible, by candidates hoping to be selected. The attractions of a
prized ticket are obvious—fighting an election on the ticket of the
most popular party virtually guarantees the seat, barring
last-minute reverses, of course.

In the months preceding the second general election, Anand
witnessed the 'ticket fever'—some ingenious word-coiner called it
'ticketaria'. A radical change had taken place in the party set-up
in the state, with several leaders who had been in the forefront

114

during the first general election having been either sidelined or cast into oblivion. Given the lack of an entrenched and experienced leadership in the state, the selection of suitable candidates for the party had become a free-for-all, with personal connections assuming greater importance than merit. It became important to know the right people and get into their good books, if success was to be achieved. And 'who knows whom' came to assume a special connotation for women applicants—particularly those who were young, good-looking, and keen on the ticket.

All of which Aruna happened to be. Although she was plain and rather dark, she had a captivating presence. She had very good reasons to enter politics, but Anand learnt of these much later. When she first decided to seek an assembly ticket, Aruna had found herself whirled into the 'who knows whom' cycle, much to her shock. A member of the selection committee was very keen to 'know' her. Finding himself rebuffed, he was determined to see that she was denied the ticket. Any other woman under the circumstances would perhaps have returned to her kitchen, or alternatively, met the leader's demand. Not Aruna. She decided on a third course of action. It was thus that she walked into Anand's drawing-room one morning.

She introduced herself tersely: she was from a family of freedom fighters, her husband worked for the government, and she herself had a graduate degree in social work. She had been an activist for civil rights while in college, and was deeply interested in spiritual matters. She now wanted to enter politics because of her interest in public service. She was an applicant for the party ticket to contest for the legislative assembly. Would Anand help her secure the ticket, please?

Anand was a bit surprised at her tone; very correct, very direct, very persuasive. He had been looking intently at her while she spoke, and thought her dark complexion set off her features admirably. When she had entered the room, dressed in a pale pink sari, he had taken her for a young college teacher or maybe the wife of a well-to-do businessman. The idea that she might want to enter politics had not occurred to him. This was also a novelty in a native state where most of the time one stared at burqas . . . He

115

came out of his reverie when he realized she had stopped speaking. Getting to the point, he said, 'Madam, I'm not at all sure you've come to the right person. I'm not a member of the selection committee, nor do I have a major say in party matters. Who advised you to approach me, anyway?'

'Everyone in general, no one in particular,' Aruna replied.

'That's interesting,' Anand said. 'But if I helped you in general, too, and told no one in particular, I'm afraid you'd get nowhere . . .'

'Oh, yes, there is someone in particular you could talk to . . .'

'Then, madam, please name him . . . or her . . . or it!'

His pleasant manner and obvious attempt at humour broke the ice and her face relaxed in a smile. She said, 'If only it had been a she or an it, I would have had no trouble. As it happens, it is a he and the name is Raghav . . .'

'Oh, but that's impossible, Deviji. He's the last person I'd be able to help you with. We've been at daggers drawn, sort of, for quite some time. He is a member of the selection committee, all right, but he'll never listen to me. You'd better approach him yourself and . . .'

'I have.'

'Oh, you have? What did he say?'

'Shall I tell you?'

'That's up to you; but I can assure you I am not a gossip!'

'He wants me to sleep with him,' she spat out after a brief pause, lowering her gaze.

He was surprised and impressed by her candour. This was no ordinary woman, he thought to himself as he tried to compose a suitable response to what she had just said. He was aware, of course, of the lecherous character of some partymen, but he was still a newcomer to this aspect of politics and idealistic enough to feel scandalized by what he heard.

Arriving at a decision, he picked up the phone and called up Raghav. He spoke sharply to the man and received an equally harsh response. 'What the hell is your interest in her?' Raghav asked acidly.

'I am not interested,' replied Anand. 'Yet I do happen to know

116

what kind of interest you have shown. And that does credit neither to you, nor to our image. I hope you'll keep that in mind!'

Raghav banged the phone down and Anand, who was annoyed by now, replaced his own receiver with a stern look on his face. 'Please go back and let him be,' he told Aruna. 'The party still doesn't lack leaders who go by merit. Keep up your effort; I hope you will succeed.'

She thanked him and left.

The next visitor arrived and Anand forgot all about Aruna. When the final list of candidates was announced, he was pleasantly surprised to see her name on it. He didn't know how she had managed it, especially as he was sure Raghav had not had his way with her. However, other matters pushed her out of his mind immediately. He began drawing up his own campaign plan, since the election was just a couple of months away. This time around he was determined to win; he couldn't endure a second defeat.

It was at that juncture that he was told to contest as the party candidate from another constituency, Srirampur. His state leaders did not allot him his home constituency of Rahimabad, in which his village and his uncle's village were situated. When he tried to protest, he was told that the party high command had decided to allot him a difficult constituency in which the party had lost its security deposit in the 1952 elections—because, by common consent, he was the only candidate who could win that seat for the party! 'Srirampur or nothing!' asserted Raghav at the meeting of the selection committee. 'After all, Anand is from the same district and is very popular everywhere. I can vouch for his victory. It is his duty to get this tough seat for the party . . .' It was clear that Raghav wanted to get his own back on Anand. It was impossible for the other members to bring pressure to bear on Raghav, since their own favourite candidates had been accommodated with Raghav's consent, and they could not afford to displease him with regard to one seat. And so it was decided.

Anand had to work much harder in the new constituency. He was known there, of course, having visited it in connection with dozens of public functions for several years. He also had a large number of friends there. Yet, he was now being foisted on the constituency from outside, and there was bound to be some resentment among local leaders who naturally had expected one amongst themselves to be considered by the party high command. Indeed, this was Raghav's hope and calculation—that the enraged local leaders would conspire against Anand and effectively obstruct and destroy his efforts.

Srirampur constituency was mainly in the Reserve Forest and was inhabited by very poor and backward people, many of them tribals. There were practically no roads, and the black soil made the whole area slushy and impassable for eight months in the year. Nothing could reach those distant villages during those months. There were times when the poor people had to boil and eat the bark of trees, and gnaw tubers to keep from starving. In every respect it was a complete contrast to Anand's home constituency. No one could believe that both areas were situated in the same district . . . Anand, however, understood the new situation at once and adapted himself to it. Within a few days he came to like the people of the constituency for their guileless simplicity, again, in contrast to his home constituency. His anxiety abated and he began to feel confident he could win.

He started his campaign with a massive mass contact programme in which he made hundreds of acquaintances, through personal encounters and public meetings. He had a message from his party to all—men, women, children. Especially children, who developed a special liking for him and followed him with loud cheers and supportive slogans wherever he went. Befriending the village children at election time was half the battle won; it was really no effort where he was concerned, for he enjoyed the company of children himself.

The people of the constituency had been thoroughly duped by the other party's land-and-cow promise in the 1952 election. They were completely disillusioned by their sitting MLA who hardly showed his face anywhere in the constituency, since he could produce neither land nor cows to redeem his pledge. From that standpoint, Anand had an advantage when he shifted his candidacy to Srirampur. But the handicaps were formidable too. There were villages in the far recesses of the Reserve Forest where no signs of civilization were visible. The king's government had never noticed these impoverished subjects for decades on end; and after Independence, the political leaders had been too busy with their intrigues and power games to look at those distant pockets where the people's existence remained at a subhuman level.

Anand visited all the far-flung villages during the campaign. He was surprised at the intense curiosity with which the villagers looked at the jeep he was driving. Then he realized that none of them had seen a jeep, or any other automobile for that matter, which was why they were engrossed in inspecting it as if it was a strange animal. No one seemed to know anything about the elections. They knew nothing about the preceding elections either, because no one had visited those villages during that campaign.

In one such village, Anand called out to an elderly person who wore a tattered loin cloth and looked rather ill. He asked him if he wanted anything. The man said, 'No, nothing!' Anand found it hard to suppress his emotion; his eyes brimmed with tears. Not even the wealthiest, and most powerful, nor the most popular person could have given that reply—I want nothing! He told them then and there that for the next five years he would make it a point to visit those villages very frequently and see that all their primary needs were fulfilled. For several days after that he made sure to visit the most remote villages in the constituency in order to see for himself what he, as legislator, would have to do in that challenging constituency.

One morning, while campaigning in a village on the fringes of his constituency, he heard a story that surprised him. According to the villagers, three days previously another candidate belonging to Anand's party had passed through the village. This person's group had held a hurried public meeting and made forceful speeches in favour of Anand's candidature. They were on their way to another area for campaigning, they had said.

An elderly woman spoke up. 'Hajoor,' she said to Anand, 'they brought a good kirtan group and all of us were thrilled by their performance.' Then suddenly remembering, she said, enthusiastically, 'There was one nice woman leader in the group, hajoor, who told us many good things about your party. Her eyes,

119

face and voice held us all spellbound. She seemed highly learned and drove the car herself. Still, when she spoke, she made us feel that she's our own daughter. And *hajoor*,' and here her eyes brightened up, 'she just talked and talked and talked about you!' A faint smile flitted across her wrinkled face—or so Anand fancied. Then she confronted him with a straight question. 'But *hajoor*,' she said, 'you know her, certainly, don't you?'

'I'm afraid I can't say for sure,' he said haltingly, while the sharp memory he took so much pride in made a furious effort to place her. And even as he spoke, he suddenly realized that what he had said wasn't quite true. For a moment he stared at the old woman uncomprehendingly, then the pieces fitted together. Of course, it had to be, what was her name, yes, Aru . . . yes, Aruna! Aruna it was . . .

The episode remained a pleasant memory for a while and then slipped from his mind as the campaign became very tough in the final run-up to the polling day. Some of his own partymen began to instigate sections of the people not to vote for their own party. For one thing they said Anand wasn't going to win, since senior leaders didn't want him to win. 'I'm telling you on their authority,' asserted one of them who was fairly reliable and rich. The story circulated in whispers and was enhanced in late night meetings, where it was further reinforced by money and liquor. Eventually, however, the saboteurs had to give up, since Anand's campaign had already made his position impregnable by then . . .

Anand returned to Afrozabad to await the results. Once he was declared elected, he began to follow the fortunes of other candidates. He realized that he was particularly concerned about one result—Aruna's. When she was declared elected by a narrow margin of a few hundred votes, he was strangely exhilarated.

On the day of the swearing-in, the marbled lobbies of the assembly were filled with the flushed, excited faces of the victorious candidates. Old friends hugged each other, and first-time MLAs looked around in incomprehension. Anand had won for the first time, but he was well-known in party circles; he was embraced and congratulated by partymen and friends. Suddenly he spotted Aruna standing in a corner of the lobby, looking on amusedly at the all-male hugging-cum-backslapping-cum-shouting-cum-bragging. She was one of the three women MLAs and stood out in the throng of khadi-clad men. Anand went up to her and congratulated her. He chatted for a couple of minutes, then, remembering, thanked her for her support during the campaign. She smiled and said, 'Oh, that visit? That was nothing. I was simply passing through the area.' She sounded casual, and a bit reluctantly he responded as casually.

After the rigours of the campaign, Anand decided it would be a good idea to relax in his village for a short while. He hadn't spent more than a couple of days at a stretch at home for a long time, so he wanted to stay for some days with his mother and brothers. His sister was married to a farmer in a nearby village and he wanted to visit her as well. Besides, it was months since he had seen his wife.

After a fortnight or so, however, he began to grow restless. He tried to interest himself in his farm and such matters, but they did not hold his attention. He had, in fact, outgrown the family and the farm long ago. And now that his responsibility suddenly extended to his constituency and in general to the whole state, his mind began to push him towards that new task every moment. It was indeed a curious turn of attitude. Normally, his new position should have made him give some priority to his family and property affairs, so badly neglected for years and in a really bad condition at the moment. However, not only did this not happen but Anand also developed a trepidation about attending to domestic matters, lest the people should perceive selfishness as his very first visible activity after being elected to serve others. The village and the family were part of his responsibility, of course; yet the people had a special eye for the priorities of an elected person. Their vote had, in a way, saddled him with a code of conduct which he would find extremely difficult and irksome. He was yet to step into those no-win situations, but it was merely a question of time, a short time.

Perhaps it could, but then again maybe it could not. As he watched his mother carry out her daily pooja, it struck him that the answer to his dilemma could lie in a contemplation of the infinite. Never very religious, especially after he had entered college and been caught up in the excitement of the struggle against tyranny, he now decided to try and recapture his lost religiosity.

He visited Balaji's shrine in Tirupati and stood at the threshold of the sanctum sanctorum, in front of the magnificent idol. But when he was about to petition the Lord for guidance in his personal and spiritual quest, he heard the priest reel off the names of the maharajas who had donated gold and diamond necklaces to the Almighty. Anand's head began to reel too and he quickly left the temple . . . His visits to many other shrines proved equally barren. It seemed he would not find the fulfilment he longed for in God—especially in God's shrines. He had no interest in the formal, fussy kind of devotion in which faith is choked by ritual. It appeared that God had been reduced to the position of a provider of services and fulfiller of a host of banal wishes—good health, wealth, success in examinations, destruction of enemies. Wholly disenchanted, Anand began to realize at last that the fulfilment he sought would have to originate within himself, as he negotiated the things that challenged his imagination and intelligence to the limit. Things that would provoke and stimulate his idealism, his will to demonstrate that intense idealism and dogged devotion to a cause need not depend on the crutches of evil to succeed; things born of his fervent desire to make a mark upon the world and transcend the pettiness and ordinariness of routine and demoralizing cynicism; things that would catalyze the expansion of his spirit into a pervasive empathy with the joys and sorrows of the people—fully invoking his childhood propensity to transmigrate into the figure of Hanuman, or anyone other than himself . . . And no matter where his mind and imagination wandered, he always returned to the one activity that most engrossed and engaged him—public service through the fascinating institution of politics.

# Part II

# 13

THE CLINK OF GLASSES AND THE MURMUR OF RELAXED
conversation filled a comfortable nook in Afrozabad's Press Club.
It was a relatively recent institution; there had been nothing like
the press during the king's regime. A few newspapers—called rags,
in common parlance—used to be published, primarily to eulogize
the achievements of the monarchy and the monarch. One young
man, who courageously printed a weekly that espoused democratic
aspirations, had been murdered in cold blood by some unknown
assailants. It was clarified through the whispering gallery that he
was killed not because he advocated democracy, but because he
did so despite being a Muslim in a Muslim kingdom. All
newspapers published from outside the state did not get automatic
entry into the state; there was a long blacklist which was constantly
added to, almost every day. Despite the king's antipathy towards
the press, the Press Club was situated in a palace he had donated.
The magnificent building impressed visitors—and that was the
only thing that mattered to his benevolent Highness.

After Independence, however, the power of the press increased and the people, for the first time, had access to uncensored information. And, adding to the good fortune of the press, their exclusive Press Club wasn't taken away from them.

The cosy corner, that evening, was occupied by two journalists seated comfortably, with glasses of their chosen liquor sparkling in front of them. 'Now, my friend, what's the hottest news of the day from Delhi?' asked the local correspondent, after a few drinks were downed.

'Call it the night, my dear fellow! Politics is essentially a nocturnal activity, isn't it? Look at the subdued light in the room and the total darkness outside. How symbolic!'

'No excursion into philosophy, please. Do have another drink and give me some good inside stuff. Okay?'

'Okay,' replied the tipsy special correspondent of the national daily *Great India Times*, published simultaneously from twenty different centres. He had descended on the state capital from New Delhi the previous day to interview the chief minister and various ministers of his cabinet. Now, halfway through his work, he was trying to impress the local press corps. He had spent the early part of the evening fulminating against just about everyone he could think of. He had reeled off a long list of God Almighty's faults in creating this mess called the world; in particular, the land mass called India that is Bharat. He was plied with drinks by various members of the Press Club and grew more and more incoherent. Losing interest in his vacuous disquisition, most of the journalists wandered off except for the local correspondent of the *Great India Times,* an ambitious young man who hoped to extract something about New Delhi's conspiratorial cliques that would create a stir in the local media.

'So you've no news from Delhi, no inside stuff on our state politics?' he asked bluntly, when it was evident that the special correspondent would ramble on forever.

The man from New Delhi, who had been slouching in his armchair, shifted indignantly. 'No news? No information? What d'you mean, no news?' he shot back. 'New Delhi is always full of news and you know it. The point is, there's so much to choose from. Do you think only your chief minister is earth-shaking news?'

'Even so, he is news today, isn't he?' the young reporter remonstrated.

'Well, yes,' the other conceded. 'Doesn't add up to much, though. The powers in Delhi see Mahendranath as an arrogant and uncouth bully whose days are numbered. I have it on the highest authority of the Central Hall of Parliament that he has long since fallen from grace, especially because he dreams about making his debut at the national level.'

'National level? That sounds interesting,' mused the local reporter. 'You mean he is to leave state politics and migrate to the Centre?'

'Why? Are you surprised?' The special correspondent sounded less drunk now, and more focused on the conversation.

'Because that's utterly unbelievable, I tell you.'

'Who wants you to believe anything anyway?' asked the special correspondent. His bulbous eyes glared at the young man in front of him as he took a long pull from his glass.

The young reporter was quick to retreat, since there was no point in alienating the other man. 'I don't mean to doubt your version at all,' he said. 'What I'm wondering about is, how would Mahendranath fit in at the Centre? He has no background of Central politics. He is a totally home-grown politician and is known to be against the Centre.'

'Central Hall gossip has it that he has changed his attitude for diplomatic reasons and intends to take the whole of India by storm one day . . .'

'*Wah, wah*, that sounds like a scoop,' said the young reporter eagerly. 'I'll check on that. As far as state-level rumour goes, our chief is happily busy here with his girlfriends and wouldn't like to move out of the state, unless there are countervailing inducements elsewhere. And it would be really surprising if he decides to desert the scores of women he amuses himself with, and the casual one-night stands that would take this total into three digits!'

The New Delhi journalist guffawed, then said bombastically,

'New Delhi's dossier on Mahendranath says that all linguistic groups are adequately represented in that pretty crowd. Now, leaving this evergreen topic aside, the more urgent subject is the rift between him and Chaudhury, which has given a shake-up to the state political scene and has made the party high command sit up and take notice! Meanwhile, both leaders are engaged in a fight to the finish, in which Chaudhury happens to be New Delhi's hot favourite.'

'When are you meeting Chaudhury? Shall I fix up an appointment?' asked the young reporter casually. If he could figure out the real reason for the special correspondent's visit, it could mean a big story.

'I don't know; I've to meet a host of ministers and leaders here; thanks for your offer, but don't worry, I'll manage,' drawled the special correspondent equally casually. He did not want to refer in specific terms to the appointment fixed for him to meet Chaudhury the following day. That, in fact, was the sole purpose of his current visit to the state capital. All other engagements were mere camouflage. He wanted to meet Chaudhury because the second floor of his new house in New Delhi's Friends Colony had remained incomplete too long, thanks to rapid cost over-runs in the recent past and his wife's insistence on frequent changes in design. Had she been another man's wife, the correspondent would have directed his vitriolic pen against the ficklemindedness of 'some' housewives who continually added to their husbands' financial woes . . . As it was, she was his second wife—the one person in the whole universe whom the correspondent's journalistic genius dared not touch. The incomplete second floor had become an object of ridicule among professional peers and rivals. So the correspondent had perforce to approach useful and ambitious characters like Chaudhury, to improve his own situation. If the interview went well and he could publish a flattering profile of Chaudhury in his newspaper, the second floor would see the light of day soon . . . This perfect plan was, of course, to be executed with great finesse, particularly because the special corespondent had, of late, acquired a special reputation as a determined crusader against corruption. So, the local reporter, who was proving to be an inquisitive nuisance, had to be kept off the track. Which wasn't easy. It became, in effect, a battle between two competing journalistic instincts to sniff out a trail. Both seemed to be succeeding.

He began to talk once again of Central politics. The local reporter seemed to sense that there was nothing more he was going to get out of the Delhi man, and prepared to leave. As he got up, he asked: 'When do you think Mahendranath is going to find a niche at the national level, if that's what's going to happen?'

'Depends,' answered the special correspondent, slowly and deliberately, masking his ignorance with a reflective mien, aided by the flush of liquor. He looked every inch the political seer he wasn't.

'Depends on what?' persisted the local lad.

'On this and that,' mused the sage from New Delhi. 'I'm not sure that any of the power coteries at the Centre are keen to promote Mahendranath. The move is to dislodge him from his present position, if you ask me. To provide himself with a fallback option, he's trying to find a place for himself at the Centre.'

The man from Delhi was close to the truth but he had only stumbled onto it by the longest of routes and one of those unintended coincidences that just happen for no reason. Mahendranath was indeed trying to move to the Centre. The stand-off between the chief minister and the Centre was not a new phenomenon. It epitomized an ever-present equation in the Indian political context, umpteen Mahendranaths dotting the length and breadth of the country, always, in a variety of conflicting situations. The nation was still too close to the feudal era to be able to usher in any radical change. An inability to modify traditions and adapt to the new attitudes of a free and democratic nation quickly was understandable; but there was also such impatience that, inevitably, this failure led to the vociferous complaint that nothing had really changed. Chieftains appeared in the new garb of chief ministers. Imperial authority seemed to have merely turned into Central authority. Both kinds of changes seemed superficial; the substance remained the same, by and large.

Neither the democratic nor the federal principle had taken root to supplant the feudal ethos that had prevailed for centuries. If you enquired of an old man in some remote village about government, he would probably reply, 'How could there be a Raj without a Raja?' That was a typical reflex in the native states, although British India worshipped authority no less. Someone else, maybe an illiterate woman, would probably say that the 'Chakravarti' (emperor) still reigned in Delhi, while the king reigned over the state, or region—she didn't know which, and didn't care. When a minister visited a village, any old man or woman could surmise that since the 'mantri' had come, the 'raja' wasn't far behind. The designation itself invariably reminded one of the age-old association. We thought we only chose the words from our ancient lore; but the words also devolved along with their corresponding concepts. Thus the concept of kingship and allegiance to a monarch was ingrained in the collective consciousness.

There was a remarkably uniform perception of authority and power among the majority of the country's inhabitants, especially those who lived outside the cities. And into this political milieu came and went presidents, prime ministers, chief ministers and, further down, sarpanches of the panchayats at the village level. They reigned with varying degrees of benevolence or despotism: yet what they did was to reign. Democracy in action at best consisted of the question 'Who should reign?' The essence of democracy as people governing themselves had not taken root—yet.

Mahendranath fitted into this milieu perfectly. He had all the attributes of a medieval king—iron-handed administration, cruelty, sadism, egocentrism, intolerance, arbitrariness, aggressiveness, ruthlessness, sexual licence as of right. And an utter contempt for the people except, of course, at election time. He was also like a medieval chieftain—such as the first Nasir Jah—whose attitude towards the Central authority was never really cooperative or cordial. Worse, there was no apparent reason for the unarticulated, yet obvious hostility; it was defiance for its own sake. He appeared on the verge of revolt all the time; yet he never actually revolted, since there was nothing to revolt against, really.

Many interpretations of his attitude were circulated—now by

friends, now by foes. Some said that he suffered from a terrible inferiority complex, being only 'moderately educated'—to wit, a non-matriculate. Others asserted that he found himself out of depth in Jawaharlal Nehru's presence. Still others opined that he was really jealous of Jawaharlal Nehru; even if far-fetched, this view persisted, fuelled by some of Mahendranath's sycophants. They did assert that he was in no way inferior to Panditji—as though a comparison were at issue. All in all, many said that Mahendranath was an extremely difficult person to get on with. Many detested him; almost everyone feared him in the state.

Yet, despite his distaste for Central authority, no chief minister could do without interaction with New Delhi. Fortunately for Mahendranath—maybe unfortunately, as it turned out— Chaudhury, his efficient minister of industry and faithful second-in-command, always managed to keep Mahendranath's Delhi connection well oiled, greased and in good working order. Chaudhury did all the dirty work, allowing Mahendranath to project himself as the clean colossus at the state level. In the process, Chaudhury's own contacts and popularity grew apace.

Chaudhury was one of those politicians with no particular ideology other than power. He did not believe in any of the 'isms' bandied about in statements and resolutions. In a country of half-naked illiterates living in sub-human conditions, what is the relevance of any ideology, he often asked. Is a drinking-water well socialist or communist? Does a village road have to carry the stamp of a political party? It's all so much nonsense, he asserted. We wanted to rule our own country, so we made the British quit. That doesn't mean we have to reject British techniques of administration. Rule with a firm hand and to hell with ideology!

How had it happened, then, that such a man had formally joined a political party, way back in the forties? The answer was simple, though he himself never mentioned it. A distant cousin and rival had joined another party and had become an 'OBE' (Obedient to the British Empire) within a few years. When his cousin reached that dizzy height, the young and equally ambitious Chaudhury decided to go one better and joined the anti-British agitation. Anti-British really meant anti-cousin to him at the time. He joined

131

the party and lectured about its greatness day and night. When Independence was finally achieved, Chaudhury found himself at a point from where just another hop would catapult him into state power. His destiny was so equal and so opposite to his cousin's that had the latter become an anti-British leader, Chaudhury would most certainly have become an 'OBE'. One chose to exploit the British emperor; the other, Mahatma Gandhi.

Chaudhury was a firm believer in money and tactics. They had served him, literally, as so many rungs of the political ladder—until the first general election, when he was rejected by the very people who had readily accepted his money, enjoyed themselves on his copious supplies of whatever they demanded for a full month, and then elected a fellow with no money, no social standing, nothing. The voters thought Manohar, the other fellow, a good young man; that was all. The betrayal enraged Chaudhury. If this is the extent to which these voters can go in downright treachery, he raved, democracy is sure to drive the country to ruin.

For three years, he reeled under the humiliation of his defeat. He tried to console himself with repeated spells of drinking, womanizing, and gambling in distant Nainital. Strangely, he learned his new political philosophy from one of the many high-society prostitutes with whom he slept now and then. One night while they lay in bed, satiated after a bout of drinking and frenzied sex, she became unaccountably wistful. She looked at herself in the mirror and discovered, as if for the the first time, that her breasts had begun to sag and that there were dark rings under her eyes. She suddenly turned to Chaudhury and asked him, 'Why were you attracted to me, darling?'

'Your appearance, of course,' said Chaudhury, a bit surprised.

'Do you like my make-up?'

'I adore it; I know no one else who is so perfectly made-up.'

'Oh, come on, I want the truth, not your usual flattery . . . Still, you said something very true, whether you meant it or not! What the world takes seriously is your make-up, not *you*!'

That very moment, while he stroked her breasts affectionately, a profound truth struck him. Appearance, make-up, not the real you; that was what politics was all about. After that night, his

political understanding changed completely. Gone was the sense
of humiliation at his electoral defeat. He wondered regretfully why
he had brooded over it like a fool for three long years. He was now
ready to enter the fray and test this newly-acquired insight, as well
as the skill of deftly switching social and personal masks as and
when the context required.

Earlier that evening at the local club, Chaudhury had
pooh-poohed the 'socialistic pattern of society' which was to be
the subject matter of a historic resolution of his party at a session
near Madras in a week's time. He had quoted with hearty
approbation someone's gibe that socialism is a system that makes
all people equally poor. 'I wonder how many heads and feet you
would have to cut off if the principle of equality of height were to
apply to the ladies and gentlemen standing right here, on the dance
floor,' he had said.

That witty comment had caused ripples of laughter. In short,
the whole club, with Chaudhury as the star performer, had
dismissed socialism as a dangerous doctrine utterly unsuited to our
great country's genius—whatever that was.

Within a few hours of that remark came the unexpected
epiphany as he fondled the prostitute's sagging breasts. Chaudhury
understood the fundamentals of the socialistic pattern of society
from her careless remark, just as Isaac Newton had discovered the
principle of gravity from the random fall of an apple. By the time
he reached Madras the following week, Chaudhury had become
an aggressive socialist, having mastered a 'made-easy' booklet on
socialism during his train journey. At the meeting of the Subjects
Committee of his party, he moved an amendment to the official
resolution. The resolution, he roared, did not go far enough. He
wanted socialism 'here and now', instead of the circumlocutory
(according to him) socialistic pattern of society that was being
mooted. What was the use, he asked, if the pattern alone became
socialist, while the content continued to be capitalist, as the
resolution implied? We are still unable to understand the
aspirations of the people, he emphasized forcefully, repeatedly
glancing at Jawaharlal Nehru, who sat, alert and cross-legged, on
the dais. Eventually, when Jawaharlalji intervened in the debate,

he looked at Chaudhury indulgently. Whereupon Chaudhury gracefully withdrew his radical amendment, but not before the great leader had thrown another glance at him that Chaudhury felt was nothing if not significant.

After that intoxicating success, Chaudhury became an expert in the nauseating art of political make-up. He learned how to mouth his party's ideology ritually and endlessly, without believing a word of it. It worked very well and, moreover, he found that there were several like him. None of them cared about values, ethics, standards or beliefs. Many had—or thought they had—hoodwinked Gandhi by wearing short dhotis just reaching the knees and leaving the upper half of their bodies in shirtless simplicity. In private, they were corrupt and lascivious. Chaudhury was amazed at the kind of luxury in which some 'socialist' leaders lived in the city, their ill-gotten wealth derived from highly exploitative businesses and other unsavoury sources. Their speeches and writings on socialism, however, were published, read and appreciated. Taking the cue from these successful hypocrites, Chaudhury went on to complete his own transformation from honest feudalism to hollow socialism within a decade and a half. He achieved phenomenal political success on the way.

Thousands of political activists were overjoyed by the Madras resolution. It initiated a new epoch in the political thinking of the party. Jawaharlal had introduced in the party his faith in the socialist ideal, which alone, as he said often, suited India. Many thought this ought to have been done immediately after Independence in the interest of clarity and thrust. Some of them had floated a new party some years ago, but when it came to voting, the people stuck to Jawaharlal in the 1952 general election. His charisma carried the day, whatever the ideological underpinnings. Later, when Jawaharlal Nehru thought it was time to adopt the socialist objective, several leaders who had become entrenched in important positions in his party and government during the intervening years became—rather had to become—socialists of convenience overnight, like Chaudhury. This was part of the setback which hit the socialist ideal in India. Along with the numerous genuine young activists, there appeared more than a sprinkling of spurious time-servers.

Behind the socialistic veneer, however, Chaudhury's political philosophy was exquisitely simple and logical, a masterful exercise in sophistry. Political power is the only means by which you can serve the poor in an underdeveloped country like India, he said. So you have to be in power continuously, for the sake of the poor. If you happen to get rich en route, that is only incidental. And logically, therefore, whatever you do to gain or retain power is legitimate, since it is meant for the poor.

As a young man, Chaudhury had been impressed by the story of King Dasaratha in the *Ramayana*. When Dasaratha felt he was too old to rule, he decided to install Rama, his eldest son, on the throne and go into voluntary retirement . . . Later in life, Chaudhury was even more impressed by the example of the Mughal emperor Aurangzeb. Aurangzeb became impatient when his father Shah Jahan continued to rule too long in his old age; so he threw the aged monarch into prison to accelerate his own accession to the throne. This, thought Chaudhury, was the more practical way. It was certainly the core of the modern political system. You see, he argued, power really resides in one person, be he emperor, king, President, Prime Minister or chief minister. The essence of power cannot be shared. It's you *or* me, never you *and* me. What appears as sharing is only an optical illusion of the political kind. So, the only way to attain power is to usurp it. It all became crystal clear once he was able to silence his scruples. His scheming mind did the rest.

He had perfected the Aurangzeb technique through hours of cold-blooded introspection. He had also run several risks in the process, during which only his own consuming ambition had sustained him. He had lost several times in party elections, mainly due to his closest followers applying Aurangzeb's technique against him. Eventually, however, he was able, slowly and painstakingly, to insinuate himself into a position of authority, becoming the right-hand man of Mahendranath—the ruthless, ferocious, direct, honest, vicious, uncouth, carnally insatiable and strangely popular chief minister. Chaudhury continued as Number Two in Mahendranath's cabinet for four long years. Finally, the

Aurangzeb in him, chafing at his second-fiddle status, gave him sleepless nights and made him chart out a devious route to self-advancement.

Mahendranath and Chaudhury were good friends, as long as the friendship lasted, though it was too good to last very long. Basically, they fell out because of Mahendranath's arrogance and Chaudhury's ambition. What manifested itself, however, was a series of accusations and counter-accusations to camouflage the real clash . . . And the inevitable parting of ways came about. The leader and the operator fell out, finally and irrevocably. All attempts at reconciliation failed.

Soon Mahendranath had another ring of counsellors, well-wishers and ardent hangers-on. Their foremost mission, with every passing day, was to make his hatred of Chaudhury more and more implacable, his confrontation with the Central leadership more and more pronounced. In this new strategem lay the vested interest of the new ring. They improvised on the basis of a fairly controversial issue. They made Mahendranath the champion of the federal principle. There had been too much servility to the Centre so far, they argued. This was bad for the Centre, bad for the states, very bad for the people. After all, they asserted, the Centre and the states were creatures of the same Constitution. So there should be no question of the Centre bullying, dominating or dictating to the states. Why should the chief minister curry favour with the Prime Minister? And why should the chief minister—this chief minister at any rate—not become the Prime Minister eventually? How could he ever develop his political personality if he was to play a subordinate role all the time? . . . Mahendranath himself may not have any such ambitions, they said; yet it was not a question of his ambition, it was a question of the nation's interest. And, of course, a question of high democratic principle.

Whether Mahendranath had any ambition at the national level was not quite clear. In any event, his followers subtly as well as overtly manipulated his thinking, so that the aspiration to become Prime Minister began to seem a natural part of his political instincts. Left to himself, he would perhaps have made friends with the Central leadership and furiously told his federalist votaries to go to hell. Yet such an eventuality was nullified by his 'well-wishers'; they told him the route of conciliation with Delhi was closed to him because Chaudhury was clearly the favoured player there. It was in this way that the banner of federalism perforce came into Mahendranath's hands. In the bargain, some who sincerely felt the need to defend the federal principle became Mahendranath's vociferous followers, since they also needed a leader of some stature. It was mutual convenience all round.

Federalism was all very well; but what about the party hierarchy? Ah, that was a problem, admitted the Constitutional pundits. It is the monolithic party apparatus that rides roughshod over everyone and compels unquestioned obedience from all state leaders, they lamented. They wanted Mahendranath to lead the revolt on the party front as well. There was no one else who had the guts. He never depended on the Centre for his political position, thank God, they asserted. He was self-made and self-propelled, every inch of him. And by his great rebellion he would cover himself with glory and blaze a new trail in Indian politics, the sycophants concluded euphorically.

Catapulted into this strange company by Chaudhury's desertion, Mahendranath would still have made his peace with the Centre and jettisoned the federal banner. All he needed to do was secure the services of just one other Delhi operator even half as good as Chaudhury. However, that was not to be—not immediately, at any rate. So he had to bear the cross of the federal principle, like many other leaders on whom the mantle of leadership falls unexpectedly and unpredictably—more by the conspiracy of circumstances than by personal volition. With his back to the wall, he had to cast himself in the ill-fitting role of a crusader for state autonomy, spurred by lofty as well as crafty motives. And more than anything, Chaudhury's closeness to the Central leadership, partly true but mostly played up, became an intolerable irritant to Mahendranath.

'How they play one state leader against another and make both run to Delhi all the time like dogs!'—he told a journalist 'friend' bitterly, in a moment of misplaced confidence. Salivating at the prospect of a juicy story, the journalist was under no obligation to keep Mahendranath's remark secret. Chaudhury's lobby promptly picked it up and the Central Hall of Parliament reverberated with thick rumours that Mahendranath would be eased out any day now.

The Central leadership had neither permanent friends nor permanent foes in the states. It only had a stock of permanent tools. No two of them were alike and no one agreed with the rest, ever. Each gloated over his own 'pull' in Delhi and ran the others down for having 'fallen from grace'. They furnished regular reports to the Centre about each other's nefarious activities, exaggerated out of all proportion. Each of them waxed eloquent about the supposed CBI investigations ordered against the others. They could provide graphic details of the number of dossiers neatly stacked on the Prime Minister's table against this chief minister or that. As a result, all lobbies, pro or anti anyone—no matter who—reinforced the belief that the party's Central command was all-powerful and that any state leader falling out of step would find himself out of the saddle.

While many senior legislators had seen many such dramas in the past, newcomers were getting their first taste of intrigue and mystery. Anand found, to his dismay, that the interests of the people figured nowhere in the high-voltage political drama that had engulfed the state.

All were trapped in it, some directly, others vicariously.

# 14

IN HIS FIRST TWO YEARS AS LEGISLATOR, ANAND REMAINED AT A judicious distance from the battle of his two party titans. Determined to be of service to the people who had voted him to the legislature, he would spend weeks on end in his constituency, travelling extensively to the distant villages in the area. He had vowed to take up the challenge of social transformation in an extremely difficult area—perhaps the most backward in the state—and he tried to do the best he could for his constituents. But many others had a different attitude. With the exception of a handful of first-time legislators, Aruna among them, the rest threw themselves into the fight between Mahendranath and Chaudhury. It would only be a matter of time before he too was forced to take sides, Anand knew, but he decided to wait as long as he could. His friends in the party mocked him and called him a do-gooder, a man who didn't know the ABC of politics, a second-hand Gandhi. Some called him utterly unrealistic, while still others commented, 'He isn't all that innocent, brother. The young fox is merely biding his time, keeping all his options open! He has also gathered a fair number of fence-sitters like himself and will choose the proper time to strike. Don't underestimate him. And don't forget that in the group game, sometimes the last to join earns the greatest value because he is the one who scores the goal eventually!' Anand stuck to his resolve, though often frustrated by the pressure exerted by his scheming colleagues. Meanwhile, reports began pouring into New Delhi that Mahendranath was in full revolt against the party high command. Chaudhury's henchmen grossly distorted and exaggerated them, but no one noticed this at the time. It was the worst political mutiny in recent years, the reports asserted. Mahendranath had attended—indeed, organized—a conclave of several important leaders at a secret place to hatch a plot against the Central leadership. No one could elaborate further, since no one knew anything about the plot. No one was sure if there *was* a plot. Possibly there had been none at all. Yet, the critics described the plot with the authenticity of eye-witnesses. They nodded their heads knowingly and asserted that Central Intelligence had procured a secretly tape-recorded verbatim account of the conclave. The tape had reached the Prime Minister within a few hours of the proceedings, they said, as if they had carried it to Delhi themselves.

It was astonishing how, according to politicians, anything happening anywhere, any time, reached the Prime Minister within hours (when they wanted to make it more dramatic, they said minutes). In effect, what they meant to say was that the PM was watching all the goings-on at the state level closely and waiting for the right moment to ease errant chief ministers out. It was a modern variant of the 'Samrat' dealing with defiant chieftains.

There were also reports that Mahendranath had made a public speech in which he cast aspersions against the Centre. His speech was analysed and re-analysed in the Central Hall of Parliament. Innumerable political microscopes scrutinized it again and again. They declared, almost unanimously, that the speech reflected a dangerous trend of subversion that was a threat to the unity and integrity of India. There were, however, widely differing versions of his speech in the newspapers, and it was unfortunate for

Mahendranath that the Central Hall experts had chosen the one most unfavourable to him. They did not know that this particular version had been filed by the special correspondent whose special attachment to Chaudhury had resulted in the completion of the second floor of his new house in Friends Colony. The experts also missed the significant fact that Mahendranath's real grouse was against the Central leadership's pro-Chaudhury attitude, rather than the leadership itself. All in all, Mahendranath's anti-Centre image was confirmed indelibly. Nothing could possibly change it now.

No one knew what the Prime Minister thought. Those who thought they knew believed that in the PM's view Mahendranath was a real problem, a significant threat. How do you cope with such a menacing character, they asked. Contrary to current belief, it was not possible to remove a chief minister at will. The Central leadership was helpless for some time, although everyone generally believed that nothing was beyond its power. It was embarrassing for the Centre to encourage a tirade against any chief minister directly. If he were from the same party, it would be demoralizing. If he belonged to another party, he would cry wolf in advance, to protect himself. And Mahendranath had some supporters too among vocal MPs in the Central Hall—those who hated Chaudhury for their own reasons.

As the days passed, the party high command seemed to have found a novel way to deal with Mahendranath. They began to give rather disproportionate importance to him, in a variety of ways, as never before. They paid tributes to Mahendranath's qualities of head and heart—perhaps what they meant was muscle. The attitude mystified even keen political observers.

Many saw it as a typical Delhi operation.

Just then Chaudhury arrived in New Delhi, ostensibly to hold discussions with the Planning Commission. In point of fact, it turned out to be planning during the day and meticulous political plotting during the nights. Dinners, discussions, deliberations, intrigues. Despite all provocation, Chaudhury had refused to resign from Mahendranath's cabinet. He decided to destroy him from within. He had drunk the poison of daily humiliation like a delectable beverage. If he burned with rage inside, his face never showed it. During the three days of planning and plotting in Delhi, he made several statements praising Mahendranath. He called him 'my chief minister and leader', and made it appear that he was fully reconciled with his superior. This contradictory attitude engendered more confusion all round, as intended. It was too good to be true; yet no one could say it was false. The mystery baffled everyone, even seasoned speculators in the all-knowing Central Hall of Parliament. Chaudhury returned to the state capital, looking mightily satisfied.

Nothing happened for some months. The party high command continued to pamper Mahendranath. They invited him to functions in other states. They lionized him everywhere as a leader of 'national' eminence—adulation that massaged his ego and prevented his ambition from going adverse.

Mahendranath's common sense and rustic instinct had always made him wary of flatterers. But the psychological boost he received during his foray into other parts of India promptly overwhelmed his common sense. He now felt himself growing in stature by the minute. His cautious approach to sycophancy disappeared. His appetite for flattery became insatiable. No one in his immediate circle, however, knew about his new-found thirst for praise, so no one praised him to the skies, at least not in the beginning. Angered at this, he began to insult one and all openly. Even though he was known to possess a volatile and unpredictable nature, his recent irritability took his well-wishers by surprise; they could not figure out what had come over him.

Given his educational background, Mahendranath was not at all erudite, nor of any intellectual stature. Lacking the finesse of his opponents, he was completely deceived by their false praise. Uncharacteristically, he believed every word of this empty hyperbole. He began to wonder why he had not discovered all those qualities in himself earlier. Sometimes he attributed this to his own excessive humility, but that did not quite satisfy him. He concluded, in his myopic pride, that everyone else had downplayed his intellectual prowess. It was all so illogical, but he was in no mood to look at the matter with any semblance of clear reason.

What he thought was true, must be true, was in fact true. There was no argument regarding this. It was, again, the well-known trait of an all-powerful king—megalomania.

The spotlight of the public gaze mercilessly illuminates and magnifies all the faults and frailties of politicians in power. Thus, while Mahendranath strode the length and breadth of the state—and sometimes outside—in his ill-fitting role of a political-cum-intellectual colossus, perceptive individuals laughed in their sleeves at the comic figure he presented. Perhaps Mahendranath did not deserve to be seen as a pathetic buffoon; yet this is how he was mostly regarded, especially after the fiasco of his birthday celebrations.

Mahendranath did not know his real birthday. His mother had never been specific about it. His father had died in a local riot when Mahendranath was very young. His uncle had some approximate date entered in the school register. Mahendranath never said anything about his birthday himself.

After he became chief minister, some sycophants began to talk about celebrating his birthday. Power, they thought, entitled him to a proper, formal birthday; so they chose it after long and thorough deliberation. The day, if you have to select one, must be convenient for a public festival, his followers reasoned. The season must be right—neither too hot nor too cold. The state legislature must normally be in session, so the legislators could be present in the capital without extra payment of TA and DA. Most important, all the astrological aspects were thoroughly scrutinized. The planets themselves could not have chosen a more auspicious day!

Coming to the *modus operandi*, the newspapers widely publicized, in the first instance, that all these years Mahendranath had never thought of anything like a birthday celebration. Indeed he had never cared to verify his birthday since his mother could never be sure whether it was the fortnight of the rising moon or the waning moon. A relative, the papers reported, had entered an approximate date in the school register, which became Mahendranath's recorded birthday. This was another proof of Mahendranath's humility, and it was praised for some time. Then, one fine morning a box item appeared in the newspapers that

Mahendranath's 'real' birthday had just come to light—'by sheer accident', they said. The date was inscribed in a bundle of moth-eaten papers left by his deceased father in the attic of his near-dilapidated house in the village.

This caused a mild sensation. Mahendranath's followers hailed the event. Newsmen plied Mahendranath with a few silly questions; but he shrugged the whole thing off as of no consequence. That, of course, was further proof of his humility. Immediately, astrologers—in fact, a 'panel' of astrologers—went to work and the 'truth', as revealed by the stars, was disclosed. Bit by suspenseful bit, this 'truth' appeared for several days in a series of articles on the centre page of a widely-circulated English daily, as well as in its local language versions. While readers lapped up the articles, politicians and political pundits who proclaimed that they had no belief whatsoever in astrology, read them more than once, each time more carefully, though secretly . . . Oh, what a wonderful time and date of birth! said everyone . . . Absolutely unblemished. The 'subject' was destined to attain Himalayan heights . . . No, corrected the first flatterer, the sky was the limit, really. Naturally, since the 'subject' was none other than Mahendranath, their popular chief minister, their great leader! . . . After all, how could the stars be wrong? . . . How fortunate that his date and time of birth, which would go down as perennial proof of the infallibility of the science of astrology, were discovered . . . at long last!

So spontaneous was the discovery—some cynics called it an invention, in hushed tones for obvious reasons—and so tumultous its reception that Chaudhury's followers nearly lost their nerve. Why should they, with their eyes and ears open, defy the incontrovertible stars? They consulted their own astrologers and set up a rival panel to see if there were any flaws in the configuration of Mahendranath's natal planets. But alas, there were none. His horoscope was perfect. Impeccable.

Chaudhury was calmly watching the new drama unfold. From the very beginning he had smelt a rat in this brand new birth story. He was absolutely certain that no horoscope could be as perfect as Mahendranath's unless experts had fabricated it, working backwards. Like the perfect evidence tendered by a well-tutored false witness. He started his own probe and found out, sure enough, that the horoscope was indeed an invention. He even bought over one astrologer from Mahendranath's panel who confessed to the intrigue in full. When one or two of Chaudhury's lieutenants came to know of this, they proposed that the farce be exposed at once. Chaudhury, however, vehemently disagreed; when they looked at him quizzically, he said, 'No one will believe your story at this juncture . . .' When they asked him what they should do, he said firmly, 'Nothing . . . Let the planets run their course . . . Let Mahendranath's ego bloat and bloat. Just wait and see what happens . . .'

'To be more exact, what Chaudhury will cause to happen,' one follower said ingratiatingly.

'Have it your way, if you wish,' Chaudhury remarked with deliberate guile. He knew inwardly that this enigmatic comment would boost the morale of his henchmen no end.

Mahendranath's recent visits to other parts of India and his projection as a 'national' leader softened him in many ways. He agreed, for the first time (after initially dismissing the idea in a fury) to the proposal that his next birthday, just a couple of months away, be celebrated in a 'fitting' manner. As to what 'fitting' meant exactly, it was for his loyal followers to decide. Where some of them were concerned, it challenged the outer limits of their imagination. Yes, nothing less, because they were Mahendranath's new-found supporters. They had filled the gap created by Chaudhury's betrayal and desertion. They craved for a means to demonstrate their loyalty, with the zeal of new converts. In the process they also wanted to show that Chaudhury's defection had made no difference whatever to Mahendranath's political stature or muscle. They explained to him in detail what they considered the political benefits of his birthday celebrations. It would be a truly stupendous show. Leaders from all over the country would congregate. His personality would be projected sky-high. This grand event would be so impressive that his position would become impregnable. And then . . . from chief minister to . . . Prime . . . well, it wouldn't be a very wide or difficult jump, they hinted with ear-to-ear smiles. Mahendranath, however, did not show much enthusiasm; in fact, he initially discouraged the idea. But his sycophants persisted, keeping their plans deliberately ambiguous and tentative, thereby holding Mahendranath's attention and finally forcing his consent.

As the war hotted up and the final parting of ways between Mahendranath and Chaudhury drew closer, the allegiances of the legislators swung from one side to the other. Those who had been together through thick and thin for years suddenly found themselves on opposite sides of the fence. Some who were not even on talking terms hugged one another with unbelievable affection. The fence-sitters had glorious opportunities for some time. The managers of both camps kept chasing them with a variety of inducements. However, the force and pace of polarization soon proved irresistible. It pulled the vacillators into definite camps. Everyone chose the group that suited their individual interests. That was all there was to it; no principles of any kind were applied. Everything seemed possible; the most absurd and unlikely hypothetical affiliations suddenly became concrete realities as options were juggled with fascinating rapidity and precision.

Chaudhury was still in Mahendranath's cabinet, so his followers adopted an attitude of abundant caution. In the initial stages of the drama of separation, they tried to bring about a rapprochement. They had no altruistic motive: they simply wanted to avoid the complicated task of choosing between two equally unattractive and dangerous options. They found, however, that the rift was complete and absolute. It was also bound up with what was vaguely referred to, but never explained, as 'Central' politics. They also realized that the chief minister's position was indivisible, it wasn't for sharing . . . It had to be Mahendranath or Chaudhury. There could be no compromise.

The local press rushed into a frenzy of scoops and learned projections. Cartoonists worked overtime. Sales of newspapers— including those, rather specially those, referred to as 'rags'—skyrocketed. The capital was plunged into hysteria. None of this really mattered to the common man; but an illusion was skilfully created that nothing else mattered to him!

There were divisions in the press too. Rather, the press divided itself along the lines of enlightened self-interest. If the English version of a paper was aggressively for Mahendranath, the language version eulogized Chaudhury no end. Some audacious columnist wrote that while the pessimists were all on Mahendranath's side, the optimists had opted for Chaudhury. It wasn't that simple, really; yet somehow this journalistic maxim stuck so well that it almost became a generalized belief. The line-up did largely conform to the formula. Those who had only short-term objectives flocked round Mahendranath—the current chief minister. They were superannuated legislators who had lost all hope of contesting or winning the next election. For them, a ministerial berth was now or never. Then there were ministers who had to save their skins from some 'scandal' or the other. There were contractors who would incur heavy losses unless the chief minister decided their cases at once. There were officers who were about to retire and whose prayers for extension or reappointment were pending with the chief minister. And, of course, there was the usual crowd of flunkeys and time-servers who always managed to be close to the chief minister—any chief minister who was in office, that is. In addition, there were many others who, for reasons of caste loyalty or gratitude for favours received, adhered steadfastly to Mahendranath . . . And lastly, there were some who honestly believed that Mahendranath, for all his faults and angularities, was a better chief minister than Chaudhury could ever be. Simply put, they considered Mahendranath basically honest and Chaudhury, dishonest.

On the other side were young first-term legislators who knew they could not yet aspire to ministerial berths. They considered the future chief minister a better bet for their prospects. There were also some ministers whom Mahendranath had treated, time and again, like dogs; he loathed them and had shown it in no uncertain fashion. Officers who would retire after two or three years expected their own extension or reappointment cases to go to Chaudhury, and began to support him to the hilt. Some MPs who knew of Chaudhury's influence with the party high command saw that their own prospects at the Centre hinged on Chaudhury's goodwill. They made a beeline to his door. Here too the time-servers remained as busy and active as their tribe generally is. And finally, some legislators honestly thought that Chaudhury, for all his schemes and his corrupt disposition, would make a better chief minister because of his flexibility, amiability and better understanding of people's problems.

The most active elements in the drama were, however, the non-participating political busybodies, press hounds and hundreds of unemployed riff-raff. They just wanted the melodrama to intensify so that they could continue to be entertained; they felt a bit irritated that nothing was happening—at least not the sensational developments they enjoyed. They were looking for a change, any change, for better or for worse, change for change's sake. They would even have welcomed an air crash with Mahendranath or Chaudhury or both on board; there would be a double obituary coupled with endless speculation in the media for days and days on all aspects of the succession struggle. No one expressed these noble sentiments, however, in so many words.

There was a third category operating on Mahendranath's side, diametrically opposed to his other supporters. The most prominent among these was Shekhar—young, energetic, machiavellian, intelligent, ambitious, soft-spoken and unscrupulous, and an untiring organizer. He was indeed a replica of Chaudhury and had been the latter's close associate earlier, being from the same district. How and why he switched to Mahendranath's side so promptly after the split was a matter of endless gossip in political circles. One theory was that it was a case of genuine defection for enlightened self-interest. You see, they said, with Chaudhury in power, what can poor Shekhar expect to become? His claims for political office will always remain subordinate to Chaudhury's. It is an immutable law of power politics that Numbers One and Two are always ranged on opposite sides. That is how they maintain the delicate balance of power. By defecting to Mahendranath's side, Shekhar has attained a place equal to Chaudhury's, hasn't he? Clever bastard. He is now in a more secure position than most of the loyal seniors in Mahendranath's outfit. Ha ha ha! The fruit of defection is sweet

indeed, my dear friend! . . . One of these days he'll become deputy
chief minister, mark my words!

There was another theory, which had its own supporters . . .
Didn't you notice that until recently, Shekhar was running to New
Delhi to perform Chaudhury's errands? Didn't you mark the
highly significant fact that soon after Chaudhury's recent visit to
Delhi, Shekhar switched his loyalties to Mahendranath? And
wasn't he also present in Delhi at the time of Chaudhury's visit,
participating in the plottings that went on? . . . What do all these
coincidences signify? Well . . . if you still don't see the light, let me
tell you in plain language. This Shekhar fellow is Chaudhury's
plant in Mahendranath's camp. He will surely upstage
Mahendranath in a manner no one will be able to guess. He's so
insidious, like a thin sheet of water spreading unnoticed under a
mat. He's going to be Mahendranath's undoing, and I'm willing
to bet my last naya paisa that my prophecy will turn out to be
accurate.

This was the rumbling among Mahendranath's faithfuls who
found themselves eclipsed by Shekhar's volte-face. No one,
however, could brand Shekhar as a traitor openly, so complete was
the expression of his new-found loyalty to Mahendranath and so
consummate his strategy of organizing all-round support for him.
No one could match him in any department of the game. The mere
faithfuls overtly brandished Mahendranath's torch; but when it
came to the crunch, they were no asset to him, only deadweights.
While the loyalists mumbled and grumbled, Shekhar was
ceaselessly active. He bullied, promised, ranted and
reasoned—now with tearful eyes, now with a tongue spitting
flame—to great effect. He bribed everyone who was bribable—in
other words, everyone. He even succeeded in winning over a few
pot-bellied moneybags by paying special attention to their
powdered, perfumed, willing wives.

He streamlined his strategy after consulting many politicians,
although the central idea was his own. He saw that when
Chaudhury parted company with Mahendranath, the latter
became weak in many respects. The media, almost solidly behind
Chaudhury, took every opportunity to embarrass Mahendranath.

They were exacting sweet revenge for the insults he had heaped on them, day in and day out, when he had been basking in official glory. Their sniping became intolerable and shook Mahendranath all the more. Mahendranath's mercurial temperament and carping tongue added fresh enemies to his list day after day. In his blind animus against Chaudhury, he overruled everything the latter wrote in the files and thus threw the administration into chaos. Every such decision promptly hit the headlines. The press, of course, was fully briefed by an 'unimpeachable source'. In other words, Chaudhury.

Following the political tumult caused by Mahendranath's unpopular decisions, protests became the order of the day. Again, professional agitators found the opportunity of a lifetime. They took revenge for each act of ruthless suppression they had endured at Mahendranath's hands. The state government found itself tottering on the brink of a volcano; it was only a question of time before the final eruption.

That, in short, was the time when Shekhar came along and joined forces with Mahendranath—as a godsend and saviour, as protective political armour. No sinking leader in recent history had been saved with such efficiency, observers said admiringly, predicting with confidence that Shekhar's meteoric rise would remain unmatched for a long time to come.

# 15

AS THE POLITICAL DRAMA UNFOLDED, ANAND AND ARUNA WERE naturally sucked into it, with varying degrees of involvement. They met off and on in the assembly, at meetings, during visits to the districts, and at public functions. They served on several House committees together and each made his or her presence felt. They lived about fifty yards apart in the legislators' hostel. Yet for almost three years, they meant nothing to each other outside the context of their duties as legislators. Anand had successfully smothered the faint flicker—of something, somewhere within himself—detected at the time of the last election and soon after.

However, a friendship of sorts that was wholly personal, yet neutral, had sprung up between the two, given their continued interaction over the years. It was close, good-humoured, cordial. They supported each other on some issues, vociferously opposed each other on others, worked the way each wished to—now together, now at cross-purposes. And they inevitably came to know each other better and more clearly. They had known a few personal details about each other—as long-term friends and acquaintances. That was all. For almost three years. Until a very casual incident suddenly brought about a change. One dull afternoon, Anand sat in the sixth row in the assembly chamber, listening and not listening to a desultory debate. Aruna was in the Chair, being one of the panel of chairpersons appointed by the Speaker. Another MLA, Deepak, a colleague of Anand's, came and sat by his side and nudged him in the ribs. Anand turned to him with a start and said, 'What is it, friend? What's bothering you?'

'Did you notice how beautiful she looks in that high chair?' Deepak murmured.

Involuntarily, Anand's eyes sought the occupant of the Chair. Till that moment he hadn't bothered to notice who it was. 'She's a married woman, you scoundrel,' he told the other man in mock anger, finding himself unable to say anything else.

'So what? How could an unmarried lass be elected to the assembly, our Constitution being what it is, unless she's an old maid whom marriage has passed by?'

At that moment Aruna looked in Anand's direction and their eyes locked. Meanwhile the deputy speaker came and occupied the Chair, relieving Aruna. She came directly to Anand and said in her usual chafing manner, ignoring Deepak totally, 'So what were you staring at, Mr Brilliant, like a hypnotist?'

'Staring at a lovely woman is not a penal offence, if I may enunciate the law!' Anand began, in the same tone. 'And when the staring, let's say, is committed within a chamber of the legislature, it is also protected by parliamentary privilege, I am sure. Besides, there's nothing in May's *Parliamentary Practice* to say that it is unparliamentary, such as snoring is! So staring could be done, as of right, a fundamental right directly deriving from Part III of the Constitution. Any objections?'

She laughed heartily and looked back, rather stared back, at him, as if to exercise the newly-minted fundamental right with a vengeance.

After a pause she said thoughtfully, 'You know, I've never heard you talk to me like this in the last three years . . .'

'I never thought I would,' he answered, almost contritely. 'I am sorry.'

'Oh no, I didn't mean to make you feel sorry,' she said with a smile. 'Not at all.'

Bathed in the radiance of that smile, Anand felt a blaze light up within him. It made him restless and feverish and he did not attend the assembly the next day. Toward evening, he was seated in an easy chair, eyes closed with fatigue, when Aruna came in quietly and placed her hand on his forehead. He opened his eyes and saw her. Looked again and saw her—in his quarters for the first time in three years.

They were alone. His burning hand rested on hers and applied that eloquent pressure from which a message emanates—loud and clear. She did not withdraw her hand, only looked around and murmured, 'Someone might come . . .'

They looked tenderly at each other. He smiled and said, 'I'll get well in a day.'

'Of course you will!' she almost sang, and left, leaving him exhausted but in a state he was unable to describe.

He recovered, but was more confused than ever. The vision of a plunge into some unknowable state gripped him. He shied away from it, stalled it, tried to ignore it, to circumvent it, to close his eyes and pretend that it didn't exist. For a full week he stayed out of town, absenting himself from several committed engagements during the assembly session. But when he came back, his confusion came back with him too.

Aruna did not approach him again, until they met at the meeting of a Joint Select Committee of which both were members. After exchanging the usual pleasantries, they became absorbed in the proceedings. About ten minutes before the meeting was to end, Anand quietly slipped out and made straight for the park next door. He lay full length in a quiet corner of the lush lawn and surrendered to the turbulence within himself.

'Am I disturbing you?' asked a voice which sounded as if it came from another planet. He saw Aruna through a film of tears. She had followed him unnoticed.

'No, not by coming here.'

'Have I disturbed you otherwise?'

'Well, if you frame the supplementary in those terms,' he said,

153

already assuming his usual bantering tone, 'I must say that the answer is in the affirmative . . .'

'Oh, don't talk like one of those stupid ministers!' she said and sat down with poise.

The jocular tone he adopted could no longer mask Anand's internal chaos. It was clear that his equilibrium was shaken.

Unlike on other occasions, they sat in silence, as in a temple where the presence of God descends silently upon the consciousness of believers.

It was getting dark; they rose to leave. Then she suddenly said, 'Look, why not come and have dinner with me? I'll cook something for you myself. About eight, shall we say?'

Surprised, Anand nodded assent. Then he left, finding nothing else to say.

He spent the next hour and a half torturing himself, endlessly repenting that he had agreed to her dinner. Then all of a sudden an overpowering anger rose in him—against himself. What fantastic nonsense was he allowing his mind to indulge in? What if he had accepted Aruna's dinner invitation? Why was he behaving so foolishly? What could possibly happen? So ran the arguments with which he tried to brace himself. They only added to his anger, and a premonition that it wasn't the fact of her invitation that made him nervous. It was something different, beyond his capacity to avert. And he didn't find in himself any strong wish to avert it either—no use lying to himself. Finally, he decided to accept whatever was in store, no matter what.

He had another engagement in a distant part of the city. He borrowed a friend's car, attended to that engagement and drove straight to Aruna's house at quarter past eight. The delay was deliberate, though he couldn't imagine what purpose it served! She was waiting for him—with two more guests, a couple who were her relatives. Anand was relieved—and disappointed. A furious monologue was about to erupt in him again, but he silenced it and engaged in polite conversation with the guests.

'Oh, what a nawab you are, Anand!' commented Aruna. 'To drive the fifty yards from your quarters to mine by car!'

'I am happy to be called a nawab, since we had a king not long ago,' answered Anand. 'Thanks anyway for the comment, I drove all the way from the old city.'

The presence of the other guests kept the conversation at an impersonal level. Anand discovered, or thought he discovered, a design in the presence of strangers. Inwardly he admired Aruna's strategy; at the same time, he felt like strangling her.

When it was time to leave, Aruna said to Anand, 'Before you become a minister and drive people crazy, why not drive our friends to their residence on the other side of the park?'

'With great pleasure, ma'am,' said Anand with a broad grin, as if she had done him a special favour.

Aruna's relatives tried to protest, but she talked them into accepting the lift. When Anand went out to fetch the car, she told them, 'Here is a rare specimen of humanity. No guile, no evil, yet he manages to survive in politics—in fact thrives—and that's the most amazing part of it!'

The car slid noiselessly in front of the door and they seated themselves—the men in front and the women at the back. Anand reversed and drove onto the main road. Within minutes they reached their destination. The couple alighted, bade good night and went in. Anand found himself alone in the car with Aruna, for the first time in his life. In a flash, he realized that he couldn't have devised such an opportunity—indeed, he couldn't even have thought of it. So Aruna—he trembled at that obvious inference . . . Or could it be a coincidence? Oh, for heaven's sake! Let things happen their way! And he gave up his frenzied brooding, for the time being at any rate.

'Return home?' he asked casually.

'No, you dud,' she said. 'Let's go to the nearest theatre, if you know the way.'

And the car sped on and entered the compound of an old theatre where a re-run of a nondescript Hindi film was showing. 'Last day' the noticeboard said. Anand parked the car and bought two tickets for the balcony while Aruna looked intently at the posters. There were a dozen or so movie-goers in the lobby and when Anand returned with the tickets, she walked quietly ahead of him and entered the balcony which, had less than the usual number of occupants. This was by no means unusual for the last show of a re-run . . . You think she planned this too, Anand asked himself. They chose a corner and sat down.

The movie was about some medieval queen ruling a semi-historical principality. Anand and Aruna knew nothing more; they hardly looked at the screen. They had almost the whole balcony to themselves for three hours, with a half-hour interval to boot. This prospect agitated and transported them. For once the marathon length of Indian films appeared a great virtue. They sat quietly, while inwardly exhilarated and a bit tense.

Half an hour passed. Some high-flown, hysterical dialogue, some shrill music, some swords being drawn—some such things went on, unnoticed . . . Then, on a sudden impulse Anand clasped Aruna's hands in his own, in undisguised emotion that welled up in him. He wanted those moments suspended in time forever. He wanted to forget everything else. He knew he would remember that moment of upheaval till his last breath.

She responded at once. A state of oneness swept over them, binding yet dissolving their beings. The clasp of their hands seemed unbreakable.

Each waited for the other to speak.

They talked very little. The stream of lurid melodramatic images flowed over the seats all around them, reel after reel.

'Why are you always so serious? Why do you seem to be unhappy?' she asked him gently, after a long silence.

'That's a long story,' he sighed, resting his head on her bosom.

'Just as I thought,' she said, pressing his head closer.

On the drive back they almost forgot themselves and the car nearly went off the road. 'Clear case of drunken driving!' she pointed out.

'I plead guilty!' he confessed at once. 'But I can't promise not to become a habitual offender!'

The following day, Anand was elated. He made a deliberate attempt not to curb his exhilaration—that would be excruciating, he felt. Now he had found a fellow-traveller. His vacillation vanished. He felt invincible.

That afternoon in the Assembly while Aruna was presiding over the deliberations, he summoned an attendant and sent a slip to Madam Chairperson—nothing unusual during the proceedings of the House. On the slip was written, 'What happened to the queen in the movie last night?' Aruna frowned, then smiled and scribbled on the same paper and sent it back, 'Shut up. Come to the park after the House adjourns.'

He obeyed her promptly. Again, they sat in silence for a long time. As the light faded from the sky, he lay with his head in her lap while she combed through his smooth hair with her fingers. He felt her fingers transmit a sweet new joy, as though urging his self's 'halfness' towards a modicum of the paradoxical fullness that it longed for.

Later, they sat up, apart. 'What were you doing for three years?' she asked.

'Doubting and debating . . .' he said haltingly.

'Oh, you conducted a legislature within yourself?'

'I suppose so, but I would rather call it the Lok Sabha, judging by the turbulence and the high level of the debate,' he commented, returning to his customary banter. 'There was no Speaker to give a ruling and the debate went on and on until . . . until . . . until no more arguments were left, either way.'

Dusk turned into dark and gave them a few moments of peace and privacy . . . Then they rose to leave. But before letting go of her, Anand held her again ardently for quite some time. 'How greedy you are!' she exclaimed. 'It's time to return to reality!'

'I owe you so much for these moments,' he admitted.

She became serious, just for a second, and said, 'You owe me nothing! But you have no idea what you owed yourself . . .'

They walked up to the main road, hand in hand. Before they stepped into the glow of street lights, she tapped him gently on the shoulder and said hesitantly, 'But is all this right . . .? I mean . . .'

'For heaven's sake, Aruna,' Anand burst out. 'Please don't start that again. I don't know about you and I've no claim; but I think this is a good thing that has happened to me. So take it or leave it, but don't argue.'

And he took a few quick strides and merged with the pedestrian traffic, leaving Aruna dumbfounded and alone.

# 16

ONCE SHEKHAR DECIDED ON A COURSE OF ACTION, HE FOLLOWED its dictates relentlessly. His first postulate was that Mahendranath's sagging image needed to be bolstered. There is nothing so demoralizing to the administration as the unpopular image of its leader, he asserted. Mahendranath had quite a few good qualities, but somehow only his unsavoury personal characteristics had received publicity so far. Worse, they were being magnified all the time. Shekhar argued forcefully that this trend must be reversed forthwith.

Therein lay the snag. Forthwith. Everyone knew that it was not possible to reverse trends in politics forthwith. Still, Shekhar's persuasive advocacy succeeded in glossing over the snag and all the chief minister's men supported the idea of an immediate image-building programme. When Mahendranath heard this, he felt something stirring restlessly within him. Perhaps his common sense warned him that the proposal simply wasn't right. But what were the alternatives? What would happen if the situation continued to drift? The prospect was appalling. In other words,

Mahendranath had no option but to act—and he had no option but to act as Shekhar suggested, for no one else had any worthwhile plan of action.

Life in general, and political life in particular, does not always present clear-cut, black-and-white choices. Thus, whatever Mahendranath's initial scruples, the urge for political survival promptly silenced them. Who can blame political beings if they think of their own survival interests first? . . . He still thought he wouldn't agree. But his followers did things in a manner that did not need his agreement. It was an exercise in subtlety and misrepresentation. They assured him that nothing they proposed to do was wrong in any way. And he was convinced, because he wanted to be.

But how did one go about building an image? Clearly, you needed an appropriate occasion, at least as a starting point. 'Any objections?' Shekhar queried at a meeting of Mahendranath-loyalists he had convened. There were none, of course. 'So think of a suitable occasion, natural or contrived. Natural if possible, contrived if necessary, that is. Agreed?' Well, yes, said the sluggish faces. 'Now, think of a suitable occasion and let's discuss it tomorrow, all right?' And the war council was adjourned to the following day.

The blank expressions remained blank at the next day's meeting too. The amazing tendency in political circles is to let one person do all the decision-making, while everyone else reserves the right to criticize it later, in case it goes wrong. And above all, this business of image-building involved some really dirty work. No one wanted to do it; yet no one dared oppose it either. Everyone would be quick to share the credit, if any. So everyone contributed his dumb presence at the conclaves of the war council. That much was considered safe . . . This attitude of the legislators suited Shekhar admirably. He proceeded to unfold his grand design. 'Listen, friends,' he began. 'We decided yesterday to build our great chief minister's image appropriately. Since there's no concrete plan ready, shall we disperse today and take some more time to think about it?'

No one spoke for a few moments. Then an octogenarian leader, who apparently didn't wish to be bothered again about the matter, said, 'Why delay the matter, Shekhar? I'm sure you must have thought of something. Why not discuss it and decide right now?'

'You're right, Maulana sahib, I have thought of something,' Shekhar responded. 'But it's still so vague and I haven't had time to figure it out clearly. Besides, don't you think some more time would really help?'

Shekhar did not want his irritable colleagues to gain the impression that he was hustling them. He kept up a veneer of 'vagueness' so no one could pick too many holes in his plan when he did choose to propound it. He was also confident that once they knew, even remotely, that he had a plan up his sleeve, no one else would bother to think of an alternative. It was so much easier to comment on something already on the table. Besides, being a newcomer to the group, he knew that the seniors were none too happy at what they considered his upstart prominence. If he tripped up he knew they would either finish him off or leave him to stew in his own juice. They hated him, yet they knew they needed him. They felt that he didn't 'belong'; yet, in the circumstances, they had to endure him. They would therefore let him have his way—all the way—rather than modify his plans and share responsibility. They decided to let him run his course, like typhoid fever. They didn't know how else to deal with him.

'Shall we disperse now and meet next Monday?' asked Shekhar.

'Shekhar,' drawled another ancient, 'I don't see any good in this postponement. If you feel like sharing your scheme with us, please do so now. We have a bitter battle to fight against a powerful opponent. Time is of the essence and you can't build political images overnight. We need not meet again, action may begin at once . . .'

All the others chorused endorsement. There was silence again for a few moments and everyone looked at Shekhar expectantly. Weighing every word, he began, 'What other occasion would be more suitable for image-building than our Leader's newly discovered birthday? We have just about a couple of months' time and if we work hard, we can turn it into a grand occasion. The task, as you can see, is to generate intense euphoria in the minds of the people regarding Mahendranath's personality. Fortunately, not much is known about his distant past, so we can fill it in with whatever colours we choose . . . We can project him through a brand new biography. Let everyone know him as *the* natural leader of the people, as a Yuga Purush come to save the world—in this case the state, maybe the country . . . And let no one dare trifle with him!'

No one spoke. None had the courage. They knew the birthdays of many leaders, dead and alive. They celebrated them on the due dates. But they never associated these directly with image-building. Most of the legislators wanted to put a few searching questions on the advisability of the proposal, but with no concrete alternative of their own, they thought they would sound hollow if they just raised objections. It would have meant, by implication, that they were not very keen to enhance their leader's image—or so they reasoned in panic. That inference, of course, would be terrible. Particularly if the Leader himself saw it that way, under the spell of this upstart Shekhar who was fast rising in Mahendranath's estimation as his most effective weapon in the battle against Chaudhury. No, no, they shouldn't oppose Shekhar's plan, even if they detested it . . .

Still, each was uneasy, genuinely uneasy about the plan, as if he had swallowed a fly. And Maulana spat it out somehow, unable to contain himself. 'I . . . I . . . I've no objection, as such,' he stuttered. 'Seems to be a good idea. But Shekhar, do you think Mahendranath will agree?'

Every face at the meeting, except Shekhar's, brightened at the question. 'He won't! He won't! Never!' they chorused with a new sense of relief, even exhilaration. As if the fly each had swallowed had turned into milk chocolate!

Shekhar's face twisted into a scowl. 'Of course he won't,' he responded testily. 'He's a great man and like all great men he's humble. He doesn't like the idea of image-building at all . . . But what of that?'

'What of what?' shot back Maulana. 'How can you go ahead with your project if he doesn't agree? We all know what a firm mind he has. Once he sets his face against anything, that's that, and no mistake. How d'you get over this real hurdle?'

'What kind of followers are you?' shouted Shekhar. 'Either you mean business or you don't. And if you don't, let Mahendranath damn well become a sanyasi and go to the Himalayas! . . . What idiotic nonsense is this? Don't you realize that Mahatma Gandhi's days are over? You don't have too many national leaders today, do you? And if you have to build up some, shouldn't you take some positive steps to that end? You aren't going to have another national liberation movement, are you? When we are constantly engrossed in factionalism, how is a national leadership to emerge? Will it drop from above, for the mere asking? . . . And what's wrong with image-building, which is nothing more than a little legitimate publicity and projection, come to think of it? Is it sinful to call a spade a spade? Aren't they doing it everywhere in the world all the time? They set up museums in the name of individuals, maintain personal archives, encourage researchers to delve deep into the lives and times of important leaders, to extol their personal characteristics, to describe how they sneezed and how many they slept with. They institute awards, foundations, fellowships, studies, chairs . . . you name it. If all this is not image-building, what's it, I'd like to know? . . . And here you are, loyal followers of a great man, senior politicians who genuinely want Mahendranath to burst on the national scene as a prospective Prime Minister, right? And you're making a massive fuss over a simple proposal to celebrate his birthday in a fitting manner! Shame on you!'

The harangue had the desired effect. Each participant felt, by implication, that unless he stepped up his own enthusiasm to match Shekhar's, and quickly too, others would somehow see him as lacking in loyalty to the Leader. Maulana promptly said, 'Enough of your lecture, Shekhar. So, granting your argument, what do you want us to do?'

'As Mahendranath's old and loyal followers, you have to get his consent for the birthday celebrations. You do just that, I'll do the rest. Fair is fair . . .' And Shekhar concluded the deliberations for the day, appearing quite satisfied but leaving everyone else in a quandary.

Maulana and the others just did not know how to convince Mahendranath about anything. They always took orders from him. The very idea of suggesting anything to him was alien to them. His gruffness was very unnerving, and their general passivity and imbecility had strengthened it. At last they summoned up the courage and cautiously, very cautiously, unfolded the birthday plan to him. He responded with fury, as expected, and said, 'What's there to celebrate in my birthday?' Then, as an afterthought, he added, 'Besides, I can't say why, but I don't like the idea. It smells wrong to me . . .'

They retreated, but brought it up again at Shekhar's insistence. This time, however, they felt, quite unaccountably, that the vehemence they found in Mahendranath's refusal did not warrant their giving up the effort. They probably divined that after all, Mahendranath would be willing—rather, he was willing—but again they could not figure out how to approach him. Only those who had observed Mahendranath for decades, through a variety of situations, could understand the nuances of his rhetoric. Maulana and the others now boldly increased the pressure on Mahendranath. And found, again to their utter surprise, that he was relenting—, or appeared to be—slowly, ever so slowly.

There was, however, a definite logic behind this acquiescence. Mahendranath did think that image-building was something immoral, unbecoming—and in any case it was not *his* cup of tea. Still, wasn't it unbecoming of his detractors, led by Chaudhury, to have launched a determined campaign of vilification against him? Wasn't it unbecoming to suborn a section of the press to denigrate him in a thousand ways? If the chief minister is always shown as the very devil, how can he run the administration? In a country where the king, or his substitute in the new system, is seen as the incarnation of God, what will this mud-slinging lead to? No, Mahendranath rationalized, he was doing nothing wrong by seeking legitimate publicity. It was only self-defence.

Shekhar had read his man correctly. His colleagues picked up the signal through their unfailing political radar. And once this happened, Shekhar accelerated the momentum for Mahendranath's birthday celebrations. No one said anything specific, but everyone knew everything that went on except Mahendranath himself, who remained in a state of dubious and partial understanding, thanks to the dexterity with which Shekhar managed the show.

A prestigious committee came into being, headed by an octogenarian leader. He had long since been interred in the pit of political oblivion, but he accepted this post for no discernible motive beyond a renewed craze for public notice. The committee called him only on formal occasions to preside over its meetings. The rest was Shekhar's exclusive domain, by virtue of his position as the committee's only secretary.

Then came the appeal for funds. The committee promptly opened a bank account in its own name, to be operated jointly by Shekhar and his confidante, Arvind Agarwal, nominated treasurer. They credited an amount that was neither too large nor too small. The accounts were maintained meticulously. However, this was more in the nature of a candidate's account of his election expenses, meant merely for technical compliance. The rest of the money came and went in a torrent of cash, with Shekhar as its sole regulatory valve.

The occasion proved a bonanza for all rich self-seekers. For the first time during Mahendranath's tenure, they got free access to him—rather to Shekhar—with money and gifts as their password. They prompted one another to act, like ants that pass on information about a lump of sugar and hasten in that direction with pinpoint accuracy. And with equally unfailing alacrity, the wealthy donors reported their gifts to a representative of the Central Bureau of Investigation. After all, Mahendranath had humiliated them so much and so often that this temporary thaw in their mutual relations did not endear him to their tribe by any means. They wanted him out with all their heart. The Bureau made a full inventory of the lavish gifts, item by item, under the special orders of none other than the Prime Minister—or so the reports went.

Shekhar and his cronies lost no time in mobilizing everybody and everything. Pomp and pageantry were to be the distinctive features of the occasion, reminiscent of the glittering scenes mounted by royalty which alone, it was pointed out, could make a lasting impact on the common man's mind. Since the cessation of kingship, the people had not witnessed a really impressive show. So Shekhar decided to make the celebrations an occasion to remember for decades. He took care to see, however, that Mahendranath did not go into all the minute details, nor had any idea of the massive scale of the celebrations. Not that it would have mattered, because by a combination of blind hatred, burgeoning self-esteem and the urge to survive—and to wreak vengeance against his detractors, notably Chaudhury—Mahendranath was now past the stage of compunction. Nothing suited Shekhar better. Indeed, nothing suited Chaudhury better.

The administration began to crack under the weight of the chief minister's birthday celebrations. First slowly and subtly, then blatantly, heads of departments were sucked into the vortex of the event. They wangled donations, made arrangements of various kinds, used government staff for purposes connected with the celebrations, regularized out-of-the-way decisions, did some arm-twisting, threatened and initiated punitive action under some pretext against those who did not cooperate—and so forth. One thing led to another, until the celebrations nearly became the government's sole activity for weeks on end. Their impact, conspicuous at the top, percolated down to the hinterland as well. Petty officials utilized the occasion to extract donations from one and all in the villages. This became effective publicity in its own way. People became aware of the chief minister's greatness by paying through their nose.

Shekhar's faction planned a mammoth procession along a twenty-kilometre route on the birthday. The transport commissioner operated his levers of power and hundreds of truck owners 'voluntarily' offered their vehicles, along with fuel, to carry the participants. Rich businessmen and government agencies erected beautiful arches all along the route, one every hundred metres, again 'voluntarily' and out of sheer admiration for the great chief minister. Local bosses of the film industry vied with one another in erecting gorgeous 'sets' at several places. They also converted the main rostrum, where Mahendranath was to be felicitated, into a dream world. Dealers in electrical goods, under 'persuasive' orders from the chairman of the State Electricity Board and his chief engineers, worked overtime to nullify the difference between night and day. They improved upon God's creation of the day-night cycle, and engineered a technicolour combination of perpetual luminosity. Fancy lamps and shades and gigantic chandeliers of foreign make, obtained from the palaces of several nawabs and maharajas, adorned Mahendranath's own house. The house was renovated and decorated at the expense of the public works contractors whose bills happened to be pending sanction of the superintending engineers . . . When Mahendranath protested against the ornate chandeliers that suddenly appeared at his residence, he was informed that the items were only borrowed for the celebrations and each one would be returned after the event.

Mahendranath could see his position being compromised at every step, but being in the midst of the most decisive battle of his political career, he couldn't withdraw. He kept silent for the moment, helpless, knowing that no costly material 'borrowed' for the celebrations would in fact be returned. If he threw it all out of his residence, his lieutenants would be only too glad to transfer every bit to their own. In any event, what was important was that his premises would glitter with fabulous decorations when thousands visited the house on the grand occasion of his birthday. For the rest, whoever believed that the king 'borrowed' anything from his subjects? He only appropriated it and the people gratefully gave him whatever caught his fancy. And so was the case with the chief minister—or would be, ruminated Mahendranath, utterly unable to stop Shekhar or reduce the monstrous dimensions of the forthcoming event. He had lost control of the situation completely.

As the actual day of the celebrations drew near, public opinion began to stir, bit by bit. This was nothing new. In ancient times, the emperor Rama took a suspicious washerman's comment about the royal consort Sita seriously, and sent her into exile. The modern sovereign Mahendranath, on the other hand, only became hardened with each critical comment regarding his birthday celebrations. He attributed the criticism squarely to Chaudhury's

166

machinations . . . Unlike the mythical land of Ramrajya, today's India was a much more complex entity where the old truisms no longer held good.

And what if one of Rama's opponents had bribed the washerman to make the malicious comment about Sita? Would that still be public opinion? And if the maligning had continued, wouldn't the sovereign be right in countering it with all his might? Such as more bribes, misuse of governmental power, political manipulation, intimidation and whatever else was needed . . . ? Shekhar and his colleagues hurled these unanswerable questions in everyone's face. Their conscience was clear. Their hands were clean. At least no more dirty than Chaudhury's, which was all that mattered . . . Or so they asserted.

Meanwhile, public opinion became more vociferous. Despite interested propaganda from both sides, the truth persisted, tunnelling its way into thousands of minds, like an earthworm. The more Mahendranath's henchmen tried to suppress it, the more it gained credibility.

The legislature was in session and rumour flourished everywhere. It travelled from mouth to mouth, becoming more and more distorted in the process, and finally reached every village in the state.

The celebrations became grist to the political mill. They provoked reactions of all kinds, worthy and unworthy. If I was in favour of the celebrations, you were automatically against them, since you were otherwise against me. And if someone else was against you, he would make common cause with me in support of the celebrations, even if he didn't know a thing about them and didn't care. It was at once a mesh of personal and impersonal motivations, which only added to the controversy. Whatever the argument, Mahendranath seemed to be the loser.

A few days before the main function, tension and excitement gripped the capital. The topic of Mahendranath's birthday seemed to monopolize the attention of the people, to the exclusion of everything else. It was again the age-old phenomenon: the interest of all subjects in whatever happened to royalty—the king's birthday, the anniversary of a sovereign's coronation, the birth of a prince, the nuptials of a princess, some jubilee of the ruler's regime, the illness of a baby in the palace, the exciting event of a tiger hunt by some members of the royal family . . . anything. Persons and designations changed, but the relationship between the ruler and the ruled persisted, albeit in a different form. And Shekhar's strategy succeeded in so far as it intensified this public interest.

The strategy failed, however, because it did not take into account the complex character of public opinion. It failed to realize that despite the old images, the allegiance to the chief minister was different from that owed to the king. Subconsciously, the people took the chief minister to be an ordinary mortal, unlike the king. So, while they witnessed the pomp and the colour with excitement, an undercurrent of disapproval slowly emerged. Some newspapers came out with strongly worded editorials criticizing the wasteful spectacle. The general public did not notice that the editors concerned were Chaudhury's friends. Then followed a series of investigative reports in the *Great India Times* that were picked up by other newspapers, about the lakhs of rupees collected for the celebrations and more lakhs that were diverted from legitimate government projects into the image-building exercise. Photographs—of letters, cheques, notes in files and a mass of similar material—filled the front pages of newspapers and provided a feast for the satirical pens of cartoonists everywhere.

In actual fact, none of the pageantry was funded by the public exchequer; virtually all of the money for expenses came from 'donations'. Yet no one would believe this. It appeared that the people's money was being squandered. Once articulated, the disapproval quickly spread. Students, in particular, ridiculed the whole show and created scenes everywhere. They arrived in vehicles arranged by no one knew who, and demonstrated vociferously in the legislators' hostel. When chased away by the police, they returned in larger numbers and created worse scenes. The contagion spread to street urchins, who had great fun throwing mud and dung on Mahendranath's multicoloured posters. They covered walls with obscene descriptions about his sexual exploits. Very few suspected that all this activity was being masterminded and funded by Chaudhury. Mahendranath, of course, did not know these details; his followers kept him in the dark, as usual. And the situation became very tense as the countdown to the inaugural day of the celebrations began.

Shekhar was well aware of these new rumblings. He knew that they were largely due to Chaudhury's manoeuvres but there was very little he could do (or for that matter wished to do!) to slow things down. Genuine doubts assailed Shekhar's own camp. Too many questions were being shot at him. What image of Mahendranath was Shekhar building, someone asked. And the obvious inference was: was he acting as a Trojan horse? . . . No one answered these questions. And like all unanswered questions, they assumed more and more significance. What really worried Shekhar was the terrible prospect of Mahendranath, in a moment of wrenching clarity, putting an end to the whole affair.

So he renewed his efforts on various fronts. He tried to enlist the support of several legislators. He drafted them into various sub-committees, enabled them to handle cash with no questions asked and to wield power and authority on behalf of the chief minister. In short, he involved them in all aspects of the programme, both right and wrong, just in case . . . The technique worked in many cases, failed in others, and definitely boomeranged in some. Such as Anand's.

Shekhar and Anand were well matched in many respects: both of them were articulate, and possessed youth, dynamism, intelligence, and tenacity of purpose. Yet they were poles apart in motivation and styles of operating, not to speak of conviction and ambition. Shekhar believed in ends. He was certain that all talk about pure means was so much nonsense. You attained a high position in life and the world credited you with all imaginable virtues. You failed and it condemned you, or derided you. The presumption was that you just didn't have the potential to succeed. So, he concluded, it was wise not to sermonize till you were safely on the Mount. That's where the flock heard you from, whatever your sermon contained. While on your ascent to the Mount, however, there was no need to live up to the sermon you were going to deliver; else you might never reach the top of the Mount

. . . Shekhar had tenaciously adhered to this philosophy, or non-philosophy. Soon he attained a position where politicians acknowledged him as a most efficient destroyer. He earned various nicknames—the political torpedo, *vakra buddhi* (crooked mind), funeral expert, third eye of Shiva, magician with the lethal touch, and so on. Despite this reputation—or precisely because of it—he was always in demand. No one trusted him, yet someone needed him all the time.

By contrast, Anand worked without any visible ambition. It was, in many ways, odd and unnatural. Even wrong and pointless, pointed out many of his well-wishers. Why does he shun ambition all the time? There's nothing wrong in being ambitious, they commented. They interpreted ambition in its conventional sense; so when Anand did not show the usual voracious appetite for political positions, they thought his detachment was a sham. They were unwilling to accept that ambition need not always manifest itself as a lust for personal power. They refused to believe that ambition could also consist of what one resolved to do—or thought should be done—for the people.

One evening Shekhar cornered Anand in the legislator's hostel and began needling him about his lack of ambition. 'I didn't say I thought ambition is wrong, did I?' countered Anand.

'Then why the hell do you run away from all situations? Why are you such an escapist?' shouted Shekhar, for once determined to have it out with Anand.

'Why are you after me today, Shekhar? How does my so-called non-ambition affect you?'

'Because lots of fools around here look to you for guidance,' yelled Shekhar. He enunciated each word savagely, expressing undisguised derision.

Theirs was a love-hate relationship. Together they could have worked miracles, since their talents were complementary. Except that they could never, ever, work together. Still, each had a certain regard for the other's potential.

'Look, friend,' Shekhar began in a conciliatory tone, 'I know you don't like me, but you can't wish me away. We are in a tight spot and I don't mind admitting that this celebration thing is getting out of hand. I don't know what to do next. The state is going to the dogs. These old parasites are thirsting for each other's blood, while both are running out of blood pretty fast. I frankly don't care what happens to Mahendranath or the other fellow Chaudhury. Personally, what I think this state needs is a fatal accident involving both. Regrettably, accidents cannot be made to order. We have to think of some other way . . .'

'Such as . . . ?' queried Anand.

'How in God's name should I know!' bellowed Shekhar. 'Fact is, there is nothing to choose between the two scoundrels. Together they destroyed every decent politician in the state. Now, they're themselves locked in a fight to the finish, again driving the state to ruin. None of us can stop the fight; indeed no one should, if you ask me. Take sides, I say, and never let the embers die down until they both turn to ashes!'

'How many others will turn to ashes in the process, any idea?' asked Anand.

'That's bound to happen too, I concede. That is the price society has to pay, I guess, to get rid of these devils thrown up by our perverse democracy . . .'

There was silence for some time. Anand was assimilating Shekhar's outburst. It was refreshingly bold—and depressingly cynical.

'Look, I'm going to be blunt with you!' said Shekhar after a pause. 'This is strictly between the two of us and I know you are discreet. You and I have a higher stake in this matter than many others; I'm sure you know what I mean . . . Can we, I ask you, come together just this once? Just on this solitary question? We could then go our separate ways if you wish. If we agree, I am sure there will be enough for both of us, politically. We'll have an assured future, as far as such a thing is at all possible on this slippery slope of politics . . . To be precise, both of us will be in the state cabinet. Any questions?'

'Just one,' Anand said, almost in a whisper. 'What is in it for the people?'

'How foolish can you get?' exploded Shekhar. 'This is pure power politics, my friend! What role do the people have in this dirty game? You want to know who is more of a socialist, Mahendranath or Chaudhury? Is that it?'

'You've made the issue sound absurd; yet in essence I think you have got my question right,' commented Anand.

'The answer is, simply, that both are enemies of socialism though they are equally impressive in mouthing it night and day. Mahendranath talks of nothing but the poor and the downtrodden. One of these days he might come out with the claim that he slept with a hundred women as a great socialist gesture! . . . I tell you, Anand, you're fooling yourself looking for the socialist ideal in these degenerates. Forget it, my friend, and come to your senses. Please realize that you have a very different issue to deal with here.'

'I concede that, Shekhar. I don't credit our state leadership with any socialist ideology either . . . But I still don't see your point.'

'The point is clear: we help destroy both the devils . . .'

'And then?'

'And then it would be a better world for the people, wouldn't you agree?'

'Would it?'

'Now, where is your logic? You agree that we should do away with the devils. Wouldn't that be an achievement in itself?'

'In itself, yes. Now, tell me, are Mahendranath and Chaudhury the very last devils you will be dealing with? How do you know a couple of younger devils won't take their place? And will you start all over again? All your life? Whose logic is defective, yours or mine?'

Shekhar felt a little uneasy. He thought Anand was being negative. We've got to do something about today's situation before we think of tomorrow's, and the day after's, he fumed. Why couldn't this fool of a dreamer understand this simple truth? Aloud, he asked, 'What, if I may ask, is your answer to the malady plaguing the state?'

'I'm afraid that is not the right question. All you seem to be worrying about is the situation at a particular point in time. That alone doesn't take you anywhere. Suppose . . . just suppose that both Mahendranath and Chaudhury somehow quit the scene. I would imagine that your programme would end abruptly. Wouldn't it?'

'Well, maybe it would, but what's the use supposing? You could suppose anything and still be exactly where you are . . .'

'I'm only trying to show the inadequacy of your thinking, Shekhar. As far as I can see, that won't do. I don't quite look upon political leaders as angels or devils. And when they are both devils, as you see them, I'd rather not throw my lot in with one or the other depending on my "affiliation". I wouldn't, of course, be neutral, doing nothing—make no mistake about that. I would rather judge even these devils from the people's angle. By what, with all their devilry, they manage to do for the people. In my view, this should also be something of a criterion. So, I prefer to reserve my judgement until a political choice appears. And meanwhile, I am in no hurry for positions of power.'

The last comment touched Shekhar to the quick. 'Do you mean to insinuate that I . . . ?' he began indignantly.

'I don't have to insinuate the obvious,' cut in Anand equally sharply. 'Do you mind if I am blunt too, for once, Shekhar? Are you really on a devil-killing expedition? Can you claim that honestly? When you admit that this is pure power politics, why do you bring in the people? Besides, why must you force an artificial division on an unwilling legislature party?'

'Wait a minute . . . Why do you say that?'

'You just said there is nothing to choose between Mahendranath and Chaudhury, didn't you? Then why do you pressurize everyone to choose? Now, listen, Shekhar. What I say may hurt you badly, but what you are doing has nothing to do with the war of the devils. It is merely an intelligent exercise in opportunism, whatever you may cloak it with.'

'Just what does that mean?'

'It means, in simple language, that you're exploiting the Mahendranath-Chaudhury rift to wangle a minister's position for yourself. Now, don't get upset, I don't blame you at all. You're doing exactly what many others would do. I simply object to your involving unwilling legislators. They are too simple to see through your guile. Don't be heartless.'

Anand's argument stunned Shekhar. Yet he knew objectively that there was no malice or hatred in Anand's bluntness. Indeed, he could see that his opponent's devastating clarity was rooted in compassion.

The dialogue had reached a dead end. Shekhar rose to leave. 'Very well, I know your views now,' he commented. 'Anyway, what do you make of this mess? Do you see any end to it?'

'We have been long enough in public life, haven't we?' Anand observed, as if asking himself. 'Haven't we seen again and again that the people have an uncanny way of stumbling onto the raw truth? Take your image-building project, for instance. It had no logic, although its flashy splendour did dazzle the people for a moment. It was a gimmick to deceive political circles here. You also wanted to impress on our Delhi bosses that they can't touch Mahendranath, or shouldn't, he is so immensely popular in the state. You started this game all by yourself. You played it close to your chest as long as it went well. When the returns began to diminish, you wanted to turn your solo performance into a patriotic movement. I know such brainwaves do succeed sometimes; this one didn't, unluckily for you. You've got yourself into a hell of a political jam and would do anything to come out of it. Am I wrong, Shekhar?'

'Your imagination is running riot,' retorted Shekhar in a surly tone. 'I can take care of myself very well, whatever I may have got into. No one need bail me out!'

'Don't take offence, Shekhar. I didn't mean to offend you. Mahendranath's birthday will come and go, but I'm afraid it will leave a bad taste in the mouth. So don't expect my cooperation in this venture. After this blows over, maybe we'll review the situation. After all, we live in a dynamic world, don't we?'

'So you prefer to keep your options open?' asked Shekhar, sounding rather casual. He had given up.

'Frankly, Shekhar, I don't see any option on this issue.'

'What will you tell your friends if they ask you?'

'I'm sure I'll know what to tell them—when they ask me. Look, I don't mean to rule out a choice between Mahendranath and Chaudhury for ever. It will come, but not on issues like birthday celebrations. All this shadow-boxing is of no use; we should work for a genuine, serious, issue-based political polarization.'

'Aren't you extremely naive to think that political polarization will ever work with two fellows who are equally impervious to ideology?'

'I don't agree with you, Shekhar. I'm sure circumstances will force a polarization.'

'God bless your dreams, and thanks for your input anyway,' Shekhar said sarcastically. He looked around, saw a couple of legislators from Mahendranath's group in the hallway and, without a word, left to join them.

# 17

ANAND WAS ANGRY. HE FELT HE HAD BEEN LED UP TO A DIZZY
height and had then been suddenly dropped, and told that he had
committed a terrible sin. Of course, he conceded, it wasn't Aruna's
fault. It was nobody's fault, or perhaps it was the fault of
both—which made it all the more exasperating.

For three days after he walked out on her in a huff, he went
underground—just to avoid Aruna, just to be defiant. When he
returned on the fourth day and entered the assembly chamber, he
found her in the Chair. She saw him and smiled—or so he thought.
As usual he tried to avoid staring at her. Within a half hour he left
the House and entered the library building. She followed soon
after. He sat, apparently immersed in a stout volume of Halsbury's
*Laws of England*. She too sat with an equally bulky volume of the
House of Commons debates, poring over its pages
assiduously—within whispering distance of him. In a few minutes,
the attempt to concentrate became a futile exercise. They began to
talk, all the while keeping their eyes glued to their books.

'Angry?'

'Think I should be happy?'

'I'm sorry about what I blurted out that evening . . . Just a typical female reflex, you know. Forget it.'

'What did you blurt out anyway?'

She smiled and said, 'Me? Nothing whatever . . . What are you talking about anyway?'

'Nothing . . . absolutely nothing . . .'

They sat in silence, scanning the pages of the gigantic volumes, obviously for something which wasn't there. Since both were studious legislators, they presented a common enough sight in the library and no one cast any inquisitive glances in their direction.

'Look,' she said suddenly, 'I've got to see a friend at Rajnagar tomorrow; I'd like to introduce you to him. It's important . . .'

'My friend's car is at your, sorry, our disposal, for as long as we want it,' said Anand with perfect anticipation. Indeed, he was about to suggest something similar himself.

'No, no, I didn't mean . . .'

'Of course you didn't; I did. So what time do I pick you up at your place?'

'No, not at my place.'

'Mine?'

'Yours? No, silly. Come to the fruit stall in the Mansoor Market. Nine o'clock sharp.'

'Done, Madam Chairperson.'

Next morning they drove through Rajnagar to the other end of the town. There was, of course, no friend's house to go to, and they were soon in the midst of rugged rocks and boulders, having left the town behind. She sat close to him. After a while she slipped her hand into his and left it there, withdrawing it only when he had to change gears. He drove along the rim of a lake and into the beautiful and wild countryside. He parked the car at a well-concealed point and from there they walked. They took off their chappals and strayed from road and footpath, roaming aimlessly through bushes, shrubs and ploughed fields, leaving footprints in the neat parallel furrows of soft soil that felt crisp and submissive under their feet. There was no habitation visible anywhere and Anand, looking around him and up above, was entranced as always by the vastness, timelessness and beauty of the

177

countryside. But this time, Aruna's presence made a difference. She did not disrupt his meditative ecstasy; in his innermost being he was still alone because he was with someone whom he had absorbed as part of himself. Each time their bodies met they fused like those of Shiva and Parvati in the deity's Ardhanarishwara manifestation. That exquisite icon had given Anand spiritual solace and aesthetic delight ever since his early adolescence. Indeed, it had led him to feel his own 'halfness' with a unique poignancy. All his life he had been drawn to the paradoxical figure of Shiva, the mighty cosmic dancer, lord of yogis, annihilator of the universe; yet this omnipotent power was incomplete without his consort, the incarnation of the female principle that energizes the universe.

As their senses ignited, their movements grew more ardent, intense. They revelled in long embraces, forgetting everything around them. Yet total solitude eluded them. They saw no one around in person, but heard and felt the presence of humans—now from the rhythmic sound of hammer and chisel pecking away on top of a boulder, now from the stray voices of labourers calling out to one another somewhere, now from the grunts of farmers urging on the bullocks yoked to their ploughs. Just when they thought they had at last reached a secluded spot, one of these sounds would disturb them again.

'What a pity!' exclaimed Aruna. 'Not one private spot in the wide world! . . . Humans everywhere . . . to disturb other humans! Not one spot to savour the silence, the peace . . .' Realizing her frustration, he clasped her to his bosom with a passion that overwhelmed her completely.

'Who's disturbing us?' he said, pulling her onto a bed of soft sand beside a tiny brook flowing close by. The day wore on and they abandoned themselves with no other thought. Feasting on their ecstasy, they became immune to hunger and thirst. Finally, as they found themselves absolutely serene, Anand broke the spell.

'We're not returning until after nightfall!' he announced.

'What happens to the assembly? What happens to your questions?' teased Aruna.

'I received full and complete answers to all my questions!' he said. 'And, in violation of all rules, not from a minister but from a chairperson!'

They moved at will, but then, their very aim was to be aimless for once, to forget that a world existed outside themselves. Suddenly he stopped, closed his eyes and said, 'God! Is such happiness at all possible?'

'Why do you ask?' she exclaimed, surprised at his spontaneous reference to divinity. It was for the first time in their acquaintance, as far as she could remember.

'Because I didn't know . . . and didn't hope to know,' he mused, framing her face between his palms and looking with a serene detachment into the depths of her eyes.

'There are many things we don't know, and will never know, and God is perhaps one of them,' she observed.

'No. I don't agree,' he said conclusively. 'I don't claim to know God; that's exclusively your department. Yet, I feel sometimes—as I do now, this moment—that God does have a way of making Himself felt by circumstantial evidence . . .'

'What's the evidence you specifically notice this time?'

'A certain chairperson who was to be in the assembly, hearing points of order right now!'

'You're crazy . . . just crazy . . . crazy and fanciful!' she said, rumpling his hair affectionately.

Gradually, as the day turned into night, they became pensive, as if savouring the twilight of ebbing emotion where pleasure and pathos blend their tumultous streams, where tears have no single, simple root or meaning. As if at the climax of happiness, pleasure is eroded and pain is exposed as its foundation. As if all creation originated as a manifestation of pain . . . Absorbed in the dimensions of bliss, the physical aspect became but an insignificant, if spontaneous, part of an infinitely deeper and all-persasive phenomenon. He had no words to describe it. His response to such situations had always been silence.

They walked deeper into the countryside; as the sun was about to set they came upon a huge boring rig, its long crane jutting at an angle like a raised finger pointing at the sky. The bit in the machine pounded the earth, somewhere deep down in its bosom.

The operator lightly touched the steel rope fastened to the bit, to ensure its perpendicular descent into the bore. Slightly embarrassed at the sight of the operator, Aruna tugged at Anand's sleeve and tried to steer him in another direction. But Anand patted her gently and said, 'Don't worry; no point in trying to avoid anyone now . . .' He advanced towards the machine in a casual manner, as if impelled by curiosity. He greeted the operator and began to put a number of relevant questions to him about the terrain, the water table, the presence or otherwise of sheet-rock, the depth at which they usually struck water, the rate of water recuperation, the firmness of the sides of the bore and whether it would need casing pipe throughout its depth, whether perforated casing pipe was readily available, and so on. Listening to jargon that only a farmer with some technical knowledge could understand, Aruna gazed at him admiringly.

'We had to do trial boring at six points on this land before we struck water at this one,' the operator explained. 'At all the other points, we struck sheet-rock and the effort was wasted . . .'

When Anand said goodbye to the operator and joined Aruna, he found her a bit pale, looking vacantly at the last arc of the setting sun, low down on the horizon.

'What is it, Aru?' he asked her gently.

'What's what?' she countered.

'Nothing,' he hastened to say. 'Don't tell me; let's go.'

'Wait,' she almost commanded, catching hold of his wrist. 'I must tell you; listen . . .'

Anand stopped, turned to her and waited. He brushed an errant strand of hair off her face lovingly.

'Explored six points . . . struck sheet-rock . . . and now struck water at the seventh . . .' Aruna was talking to herself, as if in a delirium without fever. Anand stood still, hardly breathing.

'Maybe there are similar . . .' her voice trailed off.

Then, without warning, she slumped in his open arms, sobbing uncontrollably.

'Now . . . now . . .' Anand said soothingly, patting her head, shoulders and back. He steadied her with some effort and wiped her flowing tears. He held her tightly until her hysterical sobs gradually subsided. 'Please control yourself, Aru, and don't talk.'

'But I must talk . . . I must . . .'

'No, not right now,' Anand said firmly. 'We're both emotionally overwrought and exhausted. Let's think only of the sweet and life-giving water that has been struck now. Okay?'

'Okay,' she agreed and smiled. Enchanted, he led her through the bushes carefully. The moon, almost full, appeared and dispelled the encroaching darkness. Bowed under a sudden weight of emotion, Anand and Aruna trudged back to where the car was parked. They were exhausted but supremely happy. Not for long, though. The real world intruded abruptly when Anand discovered that one of the rear wheels of the car had gone flat. He opened the boot and made a further discovery: no stepney, no tools. The car was not meant for use outside the city limits, particularly not on reckless romantic escapades.

While Aruna felt a little disconcerted and looked around nervously, Anand burst out laughing and gave her a huge hug. Her anxiety disappeared and she began to laugh too.

Stranded fifteen miles away from the town, in a desolate spot, hungry and thirsty, with no prospect of shelter or a lift, they felt unspeakably content, as if providentially released from the bonds that enmeshed them in a meaningless world. The October moon—like the *sharad-ritu* moon described in the Sanskrit classics—stunned them with its profligate silver.

'Ever walked fifteen miles?' she teased him, savouring the prospect that awaited them.

'Yes, I have. But that was drudgery—tedious, gloomy, tiring!'

'Now don't bluff,' she warned. 'Tell me the truth. You walked fifteen miles at one stretch? That is, walked on foot, as they say? Your own feet, not someone else's? Did you?'

'No,' Anand conceded haltingly, and just as a triumphant grin appeared on Aruna's face, added, 'not with an angel's hand held in mine!'

'Don't tease!' she exclaimed and kissed his neck. Anand locked the car and they began walking in the direction of the town, oblivious of everything save one another.

'You know, Aru,' he commented thoughtfully. 'When mankind

feels the way we are feeling now, the state will wither away, I imagine.'

'Bourgeois romanticism leading to Marxian consummation! How odd!' Aruna exclaimed and sat down on a culvert, laughing and opening her arms. He snuggled into them, like a weary traveller who enters an unexpected shelter. He pressed his cheeks between her firm yet soft, luscious breasts. She put her arms around his neck and pulled him close, entwining her fingers with his. Thus they remained ensconced—completely absorbed in that mutual transmigration of selves—they didn't notice for how long.

Presently, they heard the grating sound of wheels on the cement road. A bullock cart appeared, laden with paddy hay—probably of some short-term variety harvested in October. The spreading fragrance of the hay exuded an irresistible freshness, an intoxicating earthy smell, like a baby's mouth that smells of mother's milk. The bullocks walked at an easy pace and the mound of hay seemed to float horizontally in space. In that torrent of relentless moonlight, Anand began to feel as if he was hallucinating.

The cartman, amused at the predicament of the stranded couple, readily offered them a lift. After a few acrobatic attempts, Anand and Aruna hoisted themselves on top of the hay. 'Be careful and don't roll off!' cautioned the cartman good-naturedly, before raising his voice in a rustic song that echoed back from the rocks around.

'What a wonderful night!' exclaimed Anand, drawing her close. 'I assure you, the whole night is ours . . . this night of classic splendour, thank God . . . and thank the flat tyre!'

Aruna sighed and closed her eyes.

When the cartman called out to them on the outskirts of the town, he found them both peaceful and serene. When Anand paid him for the lift, he accepted the money hesitantly and said, 'Mine isn't a taxi cart, you know . . .'

'I know; but this is a gift, not a fare,' Anand replied.

The cartman lit a biri. Looking around in the haze, he found a tall arch across the road. 'What's that?' he asked. 'It wasn't there two days back when I passed this way.'

Anand looked at the arch, read the writing on it and explained the chief minister's birthday celebrations as best he could.

'Oh, that?' responded the cartman. 'That's the thing for which the Girdawar (revenue inspector) collected twenty rupees from me the other day? Tell me, what do I get out of whatever they want to celebrate?'

'Maybe there is some misunderstanding . . .' began Aruna.

'Nothing of the kind, Ammaji!' said the cartman. 'We have a new tribe of kings to loot us these days. If this is what we get, why not have the old king back, who was at least rich himself and didn't have to collect twenty rupees from poor farmers?'

He found their faces blank; they had nothing to say, feeling extremely guilty. Then he left them, concluding that they were an ignorant city-bred pair who didn't know a single fact about the woes of villagers.

'What do you think of the celebration?' Aruna asked Anand.

'Frankly, I refuse to think of it!' he replied.

# 18

MINISTER CHAUDHURY STROLLED IN THE SPACIOUS LAWN OF HIS official residence. Again and again he threw a battered football far into the flower-beds for his Alsatian to retrieve. The dog had almost become a football player, he thought approvingly, as it raced back to him with the ball in its mouth. Chaudhury enjoyed and admired its intelligent feats. Many years ago, he had begotten a child with a congenital deformity—due, reportedly, to the venereal diseases of his early youth. The child had died, and ever since he had doted on Alsatians and his wife Nalini Devi showered vicarious motherly affection on the children of relatives. Inwardly, she cursed her husband for her barren existence—the existence of a virtual widow with a husband, but she looked after him with the respectful love, or loving respect, characteristic of a Hindu wife.

Chaudhury, however, could not concentrate on the football game that day. The Alsatian did not enjoy retrieving the ball either; its master threw it with exasperating tentativeness. The dog sensed that something was wrong. Finally Chaudhury stopped throwing the ball altogether. With tongue lolling and ears twitching, the

Alsatian sniffed at the ball and stared at its master. Annoyed at the inscrutable illogic of human beings, it sauntered into the house.

Chaudhury paced about, while something nagged him inside like a shifting pain. His mind was restless as he reviewed his future in politics. He thought it was time he looked ahead, before the opportunities to entrench himself vanished and other aspirants' schemes overtook his. He had played along with Mahendranath for long, he thought, and the plan he had worked out with Delhi to flatter the chief minister until it went to his head was working very well. The disastrous birthday celebration was proof enough of that. Now was the time for the next step. From being the ostensibly loyal second-in-command to Mahendranath, it was time to stake his claim for the top job himself. But he would need to move with caution.

His first move was to enlist the support of the media who were only too willing to cooperate in lieu of past favours received. But they dare not denigrate Mahendranath openly, given his extreme vindictiveness; they usually reserved such shabby treatment for more gentlemanly politicians. Instead, they extolled Chaudhury's qualities of patience, sagacity, far-sightedness, refined behaviour, efficiency, insight into the people's problems and so on. Particularly glowing were the tributes paid to his spirit of self-abnegation for having drudged in the service of his (ungrateful) chief for so long. . .

As expected and planned, the encomiums paid to Chaudhury in the press infuriated Mahendranath. Also, as Chaudhury had anticipated, a large section of Mahendranath's supporters began to try and get the chief minister to dismiss his deputy before he was himself toppled. They said a political coup was in the offing. They commented that the machiavellian Chaudhury had even utilized women to lull him, Mahendranath, into complacency, perhaps to blackmail him. They warned that Mahendranath's reputation had already suffered a setback. They alleged that Chaudhury bribed the press right and left to get Mahendranath denigrated and himself extolled. And lastly, they asserted that unless Mahendranath woke up to these realities and made short shrift of

Chaudhury, he was sure to find himself out of power before he realized it.

One day, Chaudhury found his main portfolio taken away. The party executive was also reconstituted, to assign him a much lower position. During an informal chat with journalists that evening, the chief minister blandly declared that he was nobody's fool. Let nobody take him for granted. He knew how to show over-ambitious upstarts their place. In a brief aside with a senior correspondent who had shared many a thrill of the red light areas in the state capital way back in the forties, Mahendranath also whispered, 'No bitch can bowl me over, I assure you, Sharma! I offer no terms to any woman, other than pleasure in bed!' This, of course, was Sharma's version of the dialogue. Some believed it, others didn't.

There was some basis to the alleged boast, though. Sex was like a physical itch to Mahendranath. The urge to fornicate wasn't very different from the urge to urinate . . . All of which added up, rather unaccountably, to his reputation as a strict administrator never influenced by any woman. 'He knows,' they said, 'just what to do with any woman who comes to influence him—oblige her in bed to her heart's content, but never touch the official files she is interested in. He develops no attachment to any female beyond the duration of the sexual act. He treats them all with equal contempt and gets rid of them quick . . .'

But it wasn't that easy to fall out with an insider like Chaudhury. Once the rift was complete, everyone who was waiting to destroy Mahendranath took advantage of the opportunity of a lifetime. This invariably happens in the life of those in power, howsoever absolute the power may seem while it lasts.

Mahendranath had no idea of the extent to which the Delhi lobby backed Chaudhury. The years that Chaudhury had cultivated his contacts in the capital—both scoundrels and saints—ostensibly on behalf of his boss, were finally paying off. Mahendranath could never have managed to do what Chaudhury had done; the very sight of a dishonest or unreliable character sent him into tantrums. He basked in his own artificial purity, little realizing that someone else continually intercepted the muck and funnelled it away from him . . . So, the parting left Mahendranath high and dry. He found Delhi growing cold—cold and hostile. Those who had described him as an exemplary leader, an incorruptible individual and whatever else Chaudhury bade them say, now denounced him as arrogant, self-opinionated, defiant, dictatorial . . . and not quite loyal to the Prime Minister. The Central Hall of Parliament resounded with his denunciation now . . . Power has gone to his head, sure enough . . . He is dreaming of exploding on the national scene . . . How absurdly ambitious can you get in this blind rat race? And on what credentials! . . . Ever heard of any would-be Prime Minister so thoroughly woman-oriented? . . . How will he talk to female visitors, including highly placed foreign dignitaries . . . God! What a blind and rapacious desire to get ahead! As if merit is of no consequence! Well, it looks like Mahendranath's goose is cooked at last. There is no Chaudhury to do the dirty work for him in Delhi. Good old Chaudhury will show his real mettle now. Mark my words . . .

All of this vitriolic prophesying trickled into the outraged ears of Mahendranath; someone in Chaudhury's camp took care of that. The idea was to infuriate him all the more and make him rebel against the party high command. Mahendranath lost his remaining objectivity. He made erratic statements accusing the high command, directly or by implication. Where Chaudhury was concerned, of course, he threw caution to the winds and hurled vituperative allegations of all kinds. To which, Chaudhury's only comment was, 'No comment!' The contrast between the two was so striking, so glaring . . . The press projected Mahendranath's exit as just round the corner, a matter of days in fact.

What should he do now, ruminated Chaudhury, pacing back and forth across his lawns. The media pointed out, both editorially and in their centre-page articles, that the most effective way to deal with the chief minister's treatment of him was to resign and revolt. No leader would last long, they concluded, if this was the treatment he meted out to his senior colleagues.

The din of the media was truly cacophonic. They realized there was no truly sensational drama unless Chaudhury summoned up the courage to resign. Political reconciliations solved no problems, pointed out one able editor. He made it sound like an immutable natural principle. After a masterly analysis of the situation, a weekly magazine came up with the amazing theory that Chaudhury was, after all, to blame for the plight he found himself in. He had failed to realize, in time, that self-abnegation beyond a point turns out to be suicidal in politics. It would only look like weakness to bullies (like Mahendranath, the writer wanted to say, but didn't). The weekly also reminded everyone that its own visionary editorial column had all along been warning Chaudhury against this folly. Where and when it did not say, since the column had done nothing of the kind. The media almost made it appear that mankind's salvation lay in Chaudhury's immediate resignation from Mahendranath's cabinet.

Next came his friends. They were very angry. They had no face to show to the people, they lamented. Enough was enough and Chaudhury should quit at once, they insisted. Mahendranath wouldn't last a fortnight after Chaudhury went, they forecast with the sort of certainly that stems only from complete ignorance . . . The curiosity rose to such a pitch that one journalist even asked him pointedly if he had resigned already and if not, when was he going to do so? Faced with a question that made as much sense as if he had been asked 'When did you stop beating your wife?', Chaudhury did not reply. Which meant, as per the logic of the fourth estate, that he did not deny his resignation.

That was enough. The newspapers in the state put out banner headlines: 'CHAUDHURY QUITS!', 'CHAUDHURY ON WAR-PATH: QUITS!' etc., etc. in the morning papers. Only one of them had exercised some last-minute circumspection by wording the banner headline: 'CHAUDHURY'S RESIGNATION SUBMITTED?'

For the first time, Chaudhury realized that to a journalist, a compelling headline was much more valuable than the head of his best friend . . . But he would be able to use their insatiable appetite for sensational news.

The headlines had had one tangible effect that morning. Chaudhury's drawing room, normally overcrowded throughout the day, had a deserted look for quite a while. There were no cars parked outside, no swarming sycophants, no bustle. It reminded one of a graveyard without so much as a tombstone. All the cars were now honking in the lanes and by-lanes of the town, in the rooms and cafeteria of the legislators' hostel, at every conceivable point of rendezvous. They were searching desperately for the unknown replacement for Chaudhury. Political wheeler-dealers ran about carrying oversized garlands and huge bouquets, offering them to—rather forcing them on—those whom they considered hopefuls. They caused untold embarrassment to many legislators who themselves had no idea of what was happening. All in all, the forenoon witnessed scenes of tumultuous and multi-targeted felicitation. The sycophants garlanded the six or seven legislators whose names had appeared in newspaper speculations that morning. They disregarded the absurdity of running after so many fancied would-be claimants against a single uncertain vacancy. They were just not taking any chances; that was all.

Late in the afternoon, however, the atmosphere had begun to change, first slowly, then dramatically. The special correspondent of the *National Review* told the political corespondent of the *Enquirer* over the phone that in their enthusiasm to get the scoop across, they had forgotten to get Chaudhury's reported resignation confirmed from Raj Bhavan or the chief minister's office. Let them do it at least now, he said, just in case. That started another round of inquiries and the matter got curiouser and curiouser. Political circles naturally got wind of it and there was a concerted rush back to Chaudhury's residence. And even as he was strolling in the lawn, rather listlessly, his drawing room was again jampacked with journalists, friends and foes.

The special correspondents huddled together in the drawing room looked at once wise and foolish. There was enough indication from everywhere that their headlines had not been wide off the mark. Yet there was no official confirmation, as such. And for very good reasons, they observed, sipping the coffee Chaudhury's private secretary offered them. You see, they commented, these politicians are real crooks. They play every event in such an involved manner that each tries to blame the other. In the course of this loud-mouthed diatribe, the news value of the event evaporates—a catastrophe for the press. You don't know whether to go ahead with the headline or wait for confirmation (wait indefinitely and pick it up at third hand eventually, which no reporter worth his salt would be content to do). Hence the spate of headlines—rather premature, but inevitable under the circumstances. And in any case, when was the press ever penalized for a false headline?

In this case, all the journalists believed that Chaudhury's exit from Mahendranath's cabinet was a foregone conclusion. Events could not possibly take any other shape. All his followers, all editors sympathetic to him, all officials in their own restrained and diplomatic manner—almost everyone wanted him out, for his own sake as well as the state's. Even while they waited, the correspondents made mental drafts of the next morning's front page stories. Front page they had to be, of course.

Politicians who had made a beeline for six prospective ministers that morning now made an even more frantic dash to Chaudhury's residence. Their agitated minds oscillated between hope and confusion, between expectation and uncertainty . . . Had Chaudhury been despatched for good? The question nagged them . . . They were worried not because they wanted, or didn't want, Chaudhury to go or stay, but because they wanted to ensure that their own conduct was not out of step with the actual turn of events. And not knowing what turn events would take, they had perforce to hunt with the hounds and run with the hares.

Chaudhury made a quiet and unhurried entry into the drawing room. He smiled, lit a cigarette leisurely and emitted a long and loud belch. He greeted the waiting journalists cheerfully, a bit mockingly, some felt for a split second. He astounded others by his equanimity. He was clad in spotless white and exuded supreme confidence. When someone whispered this to the man sitting next to him, the latter hissed, 'Confidence, my foot! It's utter shamelessness!'

After the usual pleasantries the correspondents somehow found themselves asking the wrong questions. They had believed that Chaudhury would, for once, be in a furious mood. They expected his indignant outbursts to give them several convenient angles to shoot questions from. However, finding him so self-contained, they could not sustain the interrogation, could not even initiate it effectively. When they did start, it was a shaky start.

'What have you to say about the press reports of your resignation, sir?' asked a senior correspondent directly, after some oblique thrusts and feints that led nowhere.

'You were the ones who sent the reports, weren't you? So you should know better, obviously . . .' quipped Chaudhury.

'Has the governor accepted your resignation?' asked a clever one.

'How do you expect me to answer for the governor?' Chaudhury shot back.

Some political hangers-on who had gathered round the newsmen broke into laughter. They enjoyed Chaudhury's evasive and sarcastic replies, but were themselves no less confused. The elliptical dialogue gradually got on everybody's nerves. Chaudhury seemed to relish the suspense. He was in no hurry to come out with the truth. He knew which correspondent had contributed what speculation to that day's newspapers. They had produced an admixture of mock sympathy and affected wisdom, interspersed with a touch of ridicule. They were Chaudhury's friends, to be sure; they had profited too much from him to bear any animus towards him. Yet, while reporting on a prominent politician, they had to treat him with contempt. Any wayfarer is free to kick in the teeth a person in power; the fellow is so vulnerable. Some compared the politician to a prostitute's breasts which everyone has the right to fondle just as he likes. Without exception, the reporters treated the drama of political and personal motivations and counter-motivations that unfolded in the state like a clash between captive beasts, meant only for the entertainment of the world. *As if the whole gamut of government, ministers, chief ministers, power combinations, parties, manifestos, programmes, elections, successes, defeats, demonstrations, riots, firings, deaths . . . and a host of scenes involving the actions of thousands and the destinies of millions, was nothing more than cartoon material, to be laughed away and forgotten.*

Half an hour passed; still Chaudhury disclosed nothing. He took full advantage of the contradictions in the newspaper reports and pointed out their erroneous assumptions. As fiction, the reports were extremely interesting. As news, they were extremely unreliable. And Chaudhury, the correspondents found, had done his homework extremely well.

There was another round of tea and snacks and the atmosphere became somewhat relaxed. Everyone decided, within himself, to finally come to the point, abandoning the tangential, futile probes. They had got nowhere so far and none of them wanted his own relations with Chaudhury to be impaired over one speculative story. 'Sir,' said one very senior correspondent at last. 'You've dodged us enough and we've drawn a blank so far. You've always been good to us and we're grateful.'

'Except when you think I've resigned. Then I suddenly become an object of ridicule!' cut in Chaudhury.

That was Chaudhury's first serious sally of the evening. Still, he smiled and made it sound jovial. The mood, however, had altered, and the tension mounted again.

'I'm sorry, Mr Chaudhury,' began the correspondent, 'if you feel that we've been unfair to you. Keeping that matter aside to sort out later, may I ask whether you have resigned?'

'No!' shouted Chaudhury, thumping the table so hard it sounded like a bombshell—which indeed it was. His cigarette tin jumped, fell on its side and began rolling towards the edge of the table, where it was stopped by an alert hanger-on. And Chaudhury began, more deliberately, 'And I wouldn't tell you if I would indeed resign. You were obviously put on the wrong track by someone and thought you had got the scoop of your lives. I'm sorry for you, that's all I can say at the moment . . .'

There was a brief scratching of pencils on note pads—pencils that had remained suspended in mid-air for more than an hour. The interview ended abruptly and some of the infuriated correspondents almost wanted to plunge their sharpened pencils into Chaudhury's belly. There is no person more detestable to a newsman than a tight-lipped politician—a tribe which generally talks too much.

So Chaudhury had not resigned, after all! The shameless, cunning swine! He had sent everyone into a tizzy for two full days, the scheming scoundrel! Everyone was infuriated, including Mahendranath's close associates who had hoped for a heaven-sent resignation. To dismiss Chaudhury from the cabinet would have been politically impossible. It would have led to endless trouble both in the state and at the high command level. The rogue, they said, had so thoroughly bribed his way everywhere. Scratch anyone anywhere, and you would hear Chaudhury's money virtually barking at you. So the only way out was to somehow create conditions for his exit on grounds of self-respect . . . Brother, what a terrible mistake! Chaudhury and self-respect . . .? You might as well hope for the North and the South Pole coming together instead, sneered Mahendranath's lieutenants.

After the crucial press conference, one of Chaudhury's cronies approached him gingerly and said, 'You did something against everyone's expectations, boss! How come?'

'What can I do if you're such idiots and expect the impossible? Didn't you notice my drawing room and courtyard this morning when the news of my resignation hit the town like a tornado? Wouldn't many of my dear followers have deserted me completely if I had resigned? Do you think I'm going to hang myself so easily, just to oblige that bastard Mahendranath?'

'It's true that many legislators tried to get on the right side of the probables; but there are some principled fellows also in the party, sir. They have never behaved like weathercocks. I think you should cultivate them . . .'

'You mean those starry-eyed chaps like Anand?'

'Yes; they're quite a force, though they don't operate as a group.'

'I know, I know all about them. They just cannot be won over. And in any event, this is not the time to approach them.'

Chaudhury had indeed judged Anand and his idealistic friends correctly. He left them alone, but frequently praised them to third parties. That was his way of conveying his interest and affection.

Meanwhile, the battle was joined in right earnest. Mahendranath turned down every proposal that Chaudhury approved in the files. He overruled him with humiliating remarks. The skirmishes brought much amusement, and sometimes confusion, to the bureaucrats. While Mahendranath's final orders were gruff and overbearing, Chaudhury's endorsements were reasonable, well-worded, well-argued, balanced—but extremely inconvenient to Mahendranath. These recorded wrestling bouts gave rise to many jokes in the corridors of the state secretariat. For instance, some said that whenever Chaudhury, the cunning fox, wanted to get his own proposal approved by Mahendranath, he would first strongly argue against it! . . . There was also the rumour that he had managed several orders from the chief minister by this technique. In a few cases, however, acting on private information and a strange intuition of his own, Mahendranath had turned the tables against Chaudhury by agreeing with the latter's recorded view! . . . Thus the political fencing went on and on, with thrusts galore but no fatal wound on either side for a long time.

So, when news of Mahendranath's resignation broke one uneventful morning, no politician was willing to believe it. They had been fooled once by Chaudhury's ostensible resignation, so this time they were careful and ignored the news of the resignation with a shrug. The reporters were not sure either, but had to make the most of the news, such as it was. And Mahendranath was news, of course, one way or another. So the newspapers said variously that he had been removed, eased out, ousted, dismissed, sacked and so on. One particularly outspoken rag screamed, 'MAHENDRANATH KICKED OUT!' The state capital presented a stunned look for a full day. Then the truth seeped out bit by little bit. Finally, when reporters approached Mahendranath hesitantly and summoned up the courage to ask a direct question, he was humility itself. Someone remarked that Mahendranath's resignation had wrought a metamorphosis in him; he had never spoken so softly about any other subject.

It was the birthday celebrations that had finally done him in. Despite Shekhar's brave efforts, public opinion had exploded against the pomp and the pageantry. Mahendranath tried to withdraw at the last moment, but it was too late. His followers had made too many gaffes behind his back. There was no way he could extricate himself. Perhaps realizing this, he accepted the situation and began to defend it. How was it his fault, he asked, if the people in general and his followers in particular wanted to honour him on his birthday? What was so unusual in a birthday celebration? . . . The people in this state had got used to a certain grandeur since the princely regime. They simply couldn't accept anything on a beggarly scale. His birthday was only an excuse. They wanted a spectacle. They enjoyed themselves for a few days. How was that unpardonable? Why were some politicians making such a song and dance about it anyway, trying to vent their political spleen at the expense of the innocent public?

The arguments did not succeed. Lurid reports of the celebrations and the colossal waste of public funds cascaded into Delhi. It was asserted, for instance, that the Central Bureau of Investigation had produced a massive report on the celebrations. The report detailed, it was said, the money collected for the celebrations, the favours given in return for the contributions, the portions siphoned off by middlemen and—here came the fictional part—the cutbacks authorized by Mahendranath in favour of his favourite legislators and political followers. The party's reputation had plummeted to an unprecedented nadir in the process, the report pointed out. Or so Mahendranath's detractors said.

His opponents spread the wildest possible allegations about him. Mahendranath's followers were taken completely by surprise; they could get no clue to what had happened. And what happened depended on what you believed, as usual. The strongest rumour was that the Prime Minister had summoned Mahendranath by special aircraft late one night and confronted him with irrefutable evidence of his commissions and omissions. Mahendranath had to hand over his letter of resignation, written by hand, then and there. The Prime Minister sent the letter to the governor of the state the following morning. Another version had it that the PM did not send the letter, but told the governor about the resignation. A third version asserted with great authenticity that Mahendranath himself had flown to Delhi in the dead of night and sought an interview with the Prime Minister. This was promptly refused and he was asked, instead, to meet the PM's 'political secretary'. The secretary had confronted him with the evidence referred to in the CBI report and had asked Mahendranath to tender his resignation—again then and there . . . Well, the speculative tongues drawled, he is out now . . . for good.

No less assertive was the counter-rumour. Are you stupid to think that Mahendranath would cringe before anyone? What do you know of him anyway? Is there no end to this calumny? My God! Can you point out a more self-respecting politician in the whole of India today? A mere secretary reprimanding Mahendranath? Is that even conceivable? . . . Fact is, the high command was itself in a quandary and wanted to make up with Mahendranath somehow. For six months they had been inviting him to come to Delhi for discussions. As is well-known, he had refused to oblige and went about his tasks in the state. In fact he had given an ultimatum to the high command: either let him kick Chaudhury out of the cabinet, or allow Mahendranath himself to quit. Yet the high command had vacillated, trying for a reconciliation between Mahendranath and Chaudhury. To which Mahendranath had consistently said, 'No, thank you!' Finally, out of sheer disgust, he had flung his letter of resignation in the governor's face, without even informing the high command! He was in a rotten mood and wasn't willing to give the Delhi operators any more chance to procrastinate. And that is how the honest Mahendranath gave up his office, thereby setting a shining example to all politicians of all coming generations . . . In fact, brother, he had grown too big for state politics anyway, like an elephant passing through the eye of a needle. His place is at the national level. Now that he is free, you'll see him attain his full stature. He'll show you what a real colossus he is! Mark my words!

Goodness! What wishful thinking! To expect an irritable, authoritarian, uncouth sex maniac to lead the nation! What misfortune! Thank God the high command is strong enough to prevent this. Very few people know how the high command deals with defiant chief ministers. It gives them a long, long rope to hang themselves with. Then, at the crucial moment, it tightens the noose suddenly and mercilessly. Didn't it happen in states X and Y recently? Once toppled, does anyone remember the postal address of the outgoing chief ministers? . . . Such is the burial errant chief ministers receive at the hands of the high command. And mind you, the high command is always right and the other fellow always wrong! That's the law in the ruling party . . . The high command, you'll notice, is never partisan. It's never sold on anyone in particular. It only makes everyone feel happy and confident of its support. Until, of course, the incumbent begins to hang himself. The high command holds the scales even between warring factions of the party in the states, so delicately that when the moment of reckoning comes, the unwanted chief minister is eased out painlessly and the next favourite is installed with all democratic fanfare. And the procession goes on.

And the latest in the procession was Chaudhury. The high command sent an 'observer' to supervise the election of the legislature party's new leader. This 'observer' adopted special procedures at such 'elections'. Sometimes, the legislature party unanimously adopted a resolution requesting the Prime Minister to choose, or nominate (the phraseology was flexible at this point) the leader of the party. The resolution often contained a provision that the person so nominated was 'deemed' to have been 'duly' elected by the legislature party. On other occasions this cumbersome process was done away with and the 'observer' himself, or herself, would announce the successful candidate, very tactfully, of course. He would make a categorical statement to the press that the high command had no candidate in view, and that the election would be free and fair. Eventually, the person who emerged as the party's 'free choice' would be declared 'elected'.

Thus, the legislature party elected Chaudhury. The most ironic aspect of the election was that Mahendranath, the outgoing chief minister, unhesitatingly proposed Chaudhury's name. And Shekhar seconded it with gusto!

# 19

THE BATTLE FOR THE CHIEF MINISTERSHIP ENDED SO SUDDENLY that most of the legislators were swept into a vortex of confusion. They hardly knew who they should pledge their support to. To be fair to them, they were not hostile to the chief minister, any chief minister. Nor were all of them completely supportive, or wedded to the chief, any chief. They knew that every chief was a bird of passage. While some legislators were steadfastly loyal to Mahendranath and some others dead set against him, the majority were fundamentally neutral. Neutral but friendly. In some cases, you might say, not unfriendly. All these finer distinctions depended mainly on what each legislator wanted the chief minister to do for him. If it was some formal inauguration, the legislator was not overly eager to convert his neutrality into warm friendship. If he wanted funds for some project in the constituency, he would wear a smile of gratitude when he met the chief. Sometimes, the MLA wanted to secure a personal favour from the chief. It could be the appointment of a near relation to a post the incumbent did not quite deserve. It could be the nomination of the MLA himself as chairperson of a financially promising committee or corporation. In such cases, the MLA's loyalty and friendship with the chief minister knew no bounds, at least till the appointment was made. Which was why, during any political crisis, the chief minister's table overflowed with files dealing with nominations and appointments. The files were there for the legislators to see, but were not disposed of until the crisis blew over—whenever that happened.

In earlier days, when Mahendranath and Chaudhury were in one camp, legislators always went to the more accessible and affable Chaudhury. They asked for favours—particularly those that involved going a little out of the way or 'putting in a word to someone' in the administration. When the camp split, they were in a quandary and paid court at both ends. It was not opportunism, as some thought. Having had no hand in the parting of the giants, all they could do was keep both in good humour. If they didn't, they might be caught in the crossfire and find their future destroyed for good, for no fault of theirs. That was their real stake. Soon, however, the leader of each camp demanded a firm commitment. Then the shuttling became meaningless. Polarization became unavoidable. It was an unenviable situation.

Who were all these individuals on whom the destinies of millions in the state depended so palpably, and from amongst whom, within a day or two, Chaudhury, the new chief minister, would have to choose ministers for his overhauled cabinet? . . . It was a strange crowd—simple, complex, heterogeneous, spineless, variously motivated, united, divided and on the whole indefinable.

Chaudhury was familiar with each one of them, from the best-known to the mere hand-raiser. But now he had to do an intensive review of their profiles. Profiles, in political parlance, could mean a few good points, but mainly concerned the glaring faults that made each of them vulnerable, the Achilles heel that could be used to keep a minister in place, if ever it became necessary. There were also the social compulsions, the caste factor and its ramifications, apart from region, standing, experience, general reputation etc. Most important, of course, was loyalty to the chief minister through thick and thin—especially thin. And competence couldn't be ignored either, to the extent it gave the government some 'weight' in the eyes of the people. 'A few,' Chaudhury said to a journalist who was a confidante, 'just a few like that brainy young fellow who is keeping that pretty legislator Aruna happy . . .'

He went through the list, one by one . . .


The first candidate he considered was Rehman Khan.

Everyone believed that something unbelievable had happened when Rehman Khan won his assembly seat in the election. He won on the crest of a tremendous 'wave'. He was a tailor by profession, a sincere party activist popular in his home town. Yet, his name could never have carried the suffix 'MLA' in the ordinary course. Anyone predicting such an event a few weeks before the election would have been called an idiot. But Rehman Khan had pulled off the incredible feat. Subsequently, he often spoke forcefully in the assembly on the important issues of the day. When no one gave a damn, he relapsed into sullen cynicism within a couple of years of his election. After a while he no longer cared, one way or another. He let himself be pushed along, like many others from the weaker sections of society. They had been elected as a result of the 'wave', but soon found that they could neither influence the electorate nor the government. Suspended, inert, apathetic, with almost no future prospects, they were content merely to sit out their term and to perform their hand-raising duties regularly. They became temporarily important, however, at the time of elections to the Rajya Sabha or the state legislative council, when they were sucked inexorably into the wranglings of the affluent candidates. Some made a tidy sum in these indirect elections. Those who didn't were also tarred with the same brush. The presumption was that everyone in that company was dishonest.

Rehman Khan was in a terrible dilemma. Whenever there was an election or an important party decision, his colleagues took him for granted. Worse, they thought he was for quick sale, for less than a song. For one thing, they knew that Rehman Khan had no chance whatever of retaining his seat in the next election. He would be pitted against a multi-millionaire from a powerful caste. Everyone had thought that wealthy man to be invincible in the constituency. Yet Rehman Khan, the poor minority candidate, had trounced him in the last election because of the 'wave'. The 'wave' had now receded, thanks partly to the internal schisms in the ruling party and partly because such 'waves' don't last long anyway. To cap it all, the defeated multi-millionaire who had been expelled from the party for indiscipline had since been welcomed back to the 'fold' of the ruling party with much fanfare, to Rehman Khan's discomfiture. Rehman was now looked upon as a one-time MLA. It was concluded, logically, that he would make as much money as he could and return to his tailoring shop at the end of the term.

Chaudhury liked Rehman, but he had to weigh the matter carefully. On the one hand was Rehman, honest and good but weak and poor, and on the other, the multi-millionaire candidate who had walked into the party recently, with an army of musclemen crying for Rehman's scalp to avenge last election's defeat. He was certain that Rehman, if he received some support, would have to get the ticket at the next election, but would have no chance whatever of winning the seat. Besides, the multi-millionaire candidate was already bringing pressure to bear on Chaudhury against inducting Rehman into the ministry. All in all, it was a difficult choice; so Chaudhury rejected it, playing safe.

The next candidate he appraised was Sant Ram.

Sant Ram was a scheduled caste MLA who first came into the assembly after a bitter fight in the 1952 election. An old freedom fighter, he had defied the king's bullets more than once. Leaders had lauded his patriotism in glowing terms. They urged him to suffer more and more harassment at the hands of the police, but appropriated the credit of Sant Ram's effort themselves, in a variety of subtle ways. Sant Ram did not resent this. He had felt supremely happy to risk torture, imprisonment and death for the motherland. He had no desire for reward of any kind. When freedom came, he had danced and sung, sung and danced, with genuine joy and abandon. Tears had rolled down his cheeks, forming shining beads trapped in the rough and overgrown stubble on his chin.

On the eve of the 1952 general election, however, Sant Ram had been passed over in the selection of party candidates. The reason given was that since the election was an expensive affair, the party would lose the seat if an indigent person like Sant Ram got the ticket. The other hopeful for the ticket did not have such disadvantages, but no great history of sacrifice either. The matter had run into a tie and was taken to Prime Minister Jawaharlal Nehru for his personal attention. Glancing through the papers, Nehru had gone red in the face and had brushed aside all arguments against Sant Ram as 'fantastic nonsense'. And since then Sant Ram had remained an MLA. He had always been loyal to the party. They all knew about his personal rectitude, service to his constituents and general contentment with his lot. He had never intrigued to become, therefore never became, a minister. And never bore any grudge on that account.

Chaudhury thought Sant Ram would be a good asset to his cabinet; he would invest it with the stamp of service and sacrifice. Besides, Sant Ram had connections of sorts in Delhi. He regularly visited Jagjivan Ram and corresponded with him. Any Delhi connection was useful, though it was well known that when it came to the crunch, only one connection, the Prime Minister's, really counted.

Chaudhury scanned the other names on the sheet of paper before him and his eyes stopped at one—Bajrang Singh. Four months before the last general election, Mahendranath had not been aware that a person called Bajrang Singh existed. Yet, just before the election, he had not only made friends with Bajrang, but recommended him for the party ticket. And Bajrang Singh went on to become Bajrang Singh, MLA. It was a meteoric rise by any token.

The meteor had risen out of an agitation that rocked the state for more than a year—first against an increase in bus fares, and then in support of several other demands. The agitation had inconvenienced the people and the government alike. It entailed thousands of students engaging in highly exciting activities such as boycotting classes, shouting slogans, mounting black-flag demonstrations, playing hide and seek with the police, celebrating some 'protest day' or the other every other day, keeping away from examinations and demanding promotion, and so on and so forth. The meek and poor ones among them had intended to pass their exams and find jobs. However, the unruly gangs told them that no jobs were waiting for anyone anyway. So why be turncoats in a patriotic agitation and incur the displeasure of the musclemen? Everyone had given in and the agitation had gone on and on. It had promised to become a way of life.

At that point, the Prime Minister of India had graciously agreed to pay an official visit to the state. The harassed chief minister had felt at once relieved and doubly worried. His police force was adequate to cope with the official part of the arrangements. However, there was no star visible on the non-official horizon who could outshine the leaders of the agitation. It was then that the chief minister's scouts discovered Bajrang Singh. No one knew much about him beyond two facts—that he was one of the leaders of the agitation, and was ready and willing to defect to the government's side for a price. The deal was struck—by Chaudhury, of course, who was Chief Minister Mahendranath's main troubleshooter at the time. Bajrang gladdened the chief minister's heart and added an altogether new dimension to the situation.

About his personal life, no one knew much. He had studied solely in the 'University of Life'—in plain language, he was unlettered. He proudly publicized this fact to prove that what you called education was so much high-sounding nonsense. You didn't need to read a cartload of books to plan smuggling and bootlegging operations, to break open railway wagons waiting at sidings, to organize a gang of local toughs and keep them in fine fettle, just in case. And Bajrang had done all this for years with phenomenal success.

When the agitation erupted suddenly and fiercely, he had become, overnight, the champion of the great 'cause'—whatever it was. What many saw as adversity, Bajrang saw as an opportunity. Very soon he emerged as a leader in his own right.

He began to sit on the 'war council' of the agitators, as planner-adviser-expert- participant—all rolled into one. Very few could boast such multifaceted prowess.

Bajrang's biggest opportunity came a few days before the Prime Minister's visit to the state. The agitation had, of late, shown signs of fatigue and shrewd Bajrang had guessed that it was about to dissipate. He acted with remarkable acumen and alacrity. While the other leaders of the agitation debated and hoped, Bajrang made a deal with Chaudhury overnight. He issued a sketchy public statement justifying his volte-face and plunged into the fray—this time on the government's side. Along with his contingent of faithful toughs, he virtually overran the agitation. In a spurt of energetic and unrelenting action, he thoroughly demoralized the agitators and went on to make short shrift of the protest in a few days. It was an incredible feat by any reckoning.

While the Prime Minister addressed the mammoth meeting organized on the occasion, Bajrang moved everywhere like a tornado. He shouted instructions, snubbed possible trouble-makers, glared menacingly at schoolboys and acted as a ubiquitous watchman. Playing this new role efficiently, he succeeded in confounding all the agitators who had infiltrated the crowd to disrupt the meeting. They couldn't do a thing, thanks to Bajrang and his followers. Thus ended the last vestiges of the agitation. The embers soon flickered out.

Naturally, government circles lionized Bajrang and introduced him to Prime Minister Nehru who favoured him with an approving nod. Then followed the party ticket and the election campaign, which further revealed Bajrang's capabilities as a remarkably effective vote-catcher. He needed no public meetings, no canvassing, no visits by ministers to praise him to his constituents. That he, Bajrang Singh, was contesting the election, was itself the most effective manifesto in his constituency. His cadre of toughs went into action and did the rest.

Having taken his seat in the assembly, Bajrang Singh made a speech that became immortal, unforgettable. Members dubbed it the speech to end all speeches. He stood, cleared his throat and uttered exactly six sentences that contained exactly seven swear words—the four-letter variety. Well, why not? After all, he had acquired that vocabulary in the University of Life and employed it to very good effect so far. It was only natural that he should carry it along into the assembly chamber. He was therefore considerably annoyed when fifty members popped up in their seats and chanted, 'Unparliamentary! Unparliamentary! Mr Speaker, sir, please expunge those words from the records! . . .' The Speaker, a dignified man with silvery hair and extra thick glasses, first seemed to enjoy each of those profane gems. Still he ordered them to be expunged—as a concession to the roar of the rabble, Bajrang thought bitterly. He shut his mouth for good, but always remained an MLA to reckon with, speech or no speech. The dynamic go-getter. The genie of the chief minister's wonderful lamp.

Even for Chaudhury, it would have been too much to make Bajrang a minister; but he was too useful and dynamic to be left unutilized. Chaudhury pondered the matter deeply and finally nominated him chief whip of the legislature party. It was a matter of record that the attendance of party members in the assembly improved enormously and quite mysteriously after his nomination!

There were many others whom Chaudhury considered in connection with his ministry. They did not all make it, but even Chaudhury was astonished to find the variety and the multifarious qualities and frailties of his party men. He found the review instructive.

For example, there was Anil Kumar, a man with excessive imagination—always on the wings of romance. He would melt at the mere sight of a pretty female. He had acquired this obsession very long ago, starting with self-abuse and perhaps taking films too seriously. He was otherwise free of vices—a teetotaller, pious, extremely helpful and service-minded, a persuasive orator, an effective campaigner. He had also been elected twice to the assembly . . . In spite of all these plus points, he was known—and known only—as the 'Stud Bull at Large'.

Then there was Shanta Devi, lady member. Good-looking. Conscientious. Learned. Dynamic. However, at the last election, she could not secure the party ticket on these factors of merit.

Instead, she discovered that the only merit that appealed to the then party boss was her luscious body. Well . . . she wanted to refuse the overture, but did not. She thus secured the party ticket and became an MLA. The episode leaked out some time later. That scar persisted ever after that. People called her 'The Bitch'.

Next was Dhanpal. Good background. Efficient. Popular. But money was his blind spot. The trait was altogether unaccountable, since he was fairly rich. He would collect even petty amounts in the name of 'expenses' from anyone who approached him with any request. Collecting money had become an addiction with him. In all other respects he was extremely helpful. He would use his influence to the utmost for the good of the people. He was a much sought-after person. Hundreds thronged to him with all kinds of requests. They paid him, got whatever they wanted done, thanked him profusely, came out of his drawing room and instantly called him 'The Corrupt Bastard'. And that was how he came to be known. The corrupt bastard whom everyone utilized and everyone despised.

Then there was Peter Das, a man no one had ever caught sober. He had picked up the habit of drinking very early in his childhood from his profligate father in one of the city slums. He had come up the hard way and got elected to the assembly. Even in his half-inebriated state—his normal state—he had never done anyone any harm. Wouldn't hurt a fly. Very generous; he would give you the shirt off his back. You could trust him with millions. Or with a lovely virgin on a lonely island. Always cheerful, unmindful of tomorrow's cares. Gloom never came anywhere near him . . . Despite all these humane qualities, they just called him 'The Drunk'. They had almost forgotten his real name . . .

These were a few out of a legion. An incredible mosaic of humanity, each a different mix of hues from all the others. None of them was jet black. Nor was anyone snow-white. Grey was the predominant shade of their characters, their personalities. A kaleidoscope of diversity. The common motivation: power. The common point of unity: self. That was the game, by whatever name you chose to call it.

*Chaudhury was further struck by the fact that each politician came to be identified by his or her main or only vice, which shrouded all the virtues. In the political field, frailty was the banner held aloft over each person's chariot, glaring and prominent, announcing only vulnerable points to the wide world. Which proceeded to see nothing, hear nothing, speak nothing—but evil.*

Then there was the huge, undistinguished, nondescript mass. Not particularly known for anything good or bad. Just plain MLAs. Thrown up by the ballot box, they came, sat in the House for five years and disappeared—unnoticed. All that they earned in their uneventful careers was the prospect of speaking for a few minutes in the House when permitted, and when they died, a condolence resolution and a minute of silence in the assembly. What touching posthumous recognition!

This was the crowd Chaudhury had to choose from, to shape his ministry. In addition to those who had been loyal to him, there were, of course, his former colleagues from Mahendranath's cabinet. They trooped into his drawing room post-haste and pledged their unstinted support and cooperation. Looking at them, he chuckled inwardly at the filthy epithets they had hurled at him barely twenty-four hours ago. They would all 'support' him, he mused, and hurl similar or worse abuse at his prospective rival until he became the chief. Then these stalwarts would switch support to him—and so forth. Well, these worthies were merely the 'chief minister's men', whoever he was. Chaudhury knew he would have to accommodate a few of them in his cabinet, at least for their foul mouths and ability to spew abuse. It needs all kinds to make a cabinet.

But none of the MLAs he had chosen this far would constitute the core. Places in the inner circle would be reserved for the chosen ones, people the new chief minister would have to depend heavily on. Within minutes of his return home after his 'election', Chaudhury sent for Anand. He shook his hand cordially and said, 'Welcome to my residence, Anand. For the first time, I presume?'

'Well . . . er . . . yes sir,' Anand stammered, somewhat guiltily.

'I wish you would come more often. Not to worry, I have thought of a tangible way of bringing you here.'

'What is it?'

'Making you a minister in my cabinet. I see you are in danger of rusting away and need to be put to work.'

Anand could only mumble, 'Thank you.' He had not expected this. His tone, however, sounded even.

'I know what I need to know about you, of course,' Chaudhury went on. 'And you will be in good company, I assure you.' Then he smiled and continued, 'Don't you want to know whose?'

'That's the chief minister's prerogative, I guess,' answered Anand in the same vein.

'That's right,' echoed Chaudhury. 'And I exercise my prerogative to inform you that your good friend Shekhar will be a cabinet colleague of yours!'

Anand was stunned.

# 20

INDIRA GANDHI, PARTY PRESIDENT, GLANCED AT CHAUDHURY'S proposed council of ministers. She did not know any of them well, except Chaudhury himself, whom her father had spoken of as a socialist enthusiast years ago, after the party's meeting at Madras. She had met him and heard about him, since he had kept regularly in touch with the high command as Mahendranath's Number Two minister until he became the chief minister himself. She knew all about their recent feud that had been the talk of New Delhi as much as it had been the talk of Afrozabad. However, she had not found anything to confirm his socialist credentials in anything he said or did. Instead, she found him a pure politician, dealing solely in governmental power and all that it entailed. Both father and daughter were only too familiar with the tribe and did not comment on what had, by then, become the dominant pattern all over the country.

The general secretary's note which accompanied the list pointed out that the size of the council of ministers was rather large. When Indiraji asked him if he had discussed it with the chief minister, he replied, 'Yes, madam, but he says he has to accommodate several castes and also some who are close to his predecessor Mahendranath. So he is constrained by the demand for representation on a group and caste basis.'

The caste factor loomed larger with every passing day, and Indiraji and everyone in the high command had noticed it. This unmistakable trend had appeared in the political process and threatened to overwhelm it eventually. Instances of ministers' interference on the basis of caste in a number of matters that required absolute impartiality from the administration became more and more frequent. Nothing, however, could be done—or so it seemed. A casteless society thus seemed to be impossible, at least in the short run, as matters stood. It was a grotesque irony for a party which proclaimed castelessness as its creed.

Back in the state capital, the atmosphere was very different.

The night before the swearing-in was full of rejoicing for some and of deep introspection for Anand. He remained thoughtful and a bit serious amidst endless hugs and back-slaps and felicitations. His jubiliant supporters filled his living room with talk, laughter and merry-making. There was a momentary lull when Aruna stormed into Anand's drawing room, flushed with excitement. She bustled about like a schoolgirl who had won a prize, greeting everyone; then she started singing a chorus, in which everyone joined heartily. It was real celebration.

After everyone else had left, and he was alone with Aruna, Anand became more serious. She wondered why he seemed so hesitant and diffident. He knit his brows and after a few minutes of ominous silence, said, 'There is still time . . .'

'Time for what?' inquired Aruna, rather puzzled.

'To opt out. To decline Chaudhury's offer.'

'Are you mad?' exploded Aruna. 'Imagine getting depressed just on the eve of the swearing-in! You didn't run after it, did you? What, then, is the point?'

'Look, Aruna, I'm not posing as a martyr. Yet, I am pretty sure I'll have to pay a heavy price for this position.'

'What price? Who's asking you to pay any price? Don't talk in riddles. Give me your wonderful reason!'

Anand said thoughtfully, 'Have you any idea of the real stakes in this proposal, Aruna?'

'What stakes?' enquired Aruna. 'All I can anticipate is that some other fellows may be disappointed. What else?'

'From day one, we'll have to face nothing but embarrassment. Life could become miserable.'

'I don't agree with you at all. Individual embarrassments are too trivial to make you run away from your duty to the country and the state. You shouldn't even think about such things!'

'I'm not thinking about myself at all,' said Anand, rather defensively. 'A man can still survive in a man's world, despite scandals. What about the woman? No, no, Aru, I can't.'

'I don't know what has got into your head!' she exclaimed. 'Tell me, Anand, what's happened? Bothered about your portfolio?'

'Please, Aruna, quit joking! I feel terribly disturbed . . .'

'It's an hour since you started this rambling and you haven't explained one damn thing!' she said sharply.

'Look at the mixed picture and thus the hurdles. I am not afraid of the job, make no mistakes. I feel it in my bones that I shall do very well as minister. But who cares about performance. I have closely watched the predicaments of ministers for some time. In my case, whatever my portfolio, there'll be enough to do, and people working for me will be in for a bit of slave-driving. They will come to hate me like poison. Then there are the politicians. At least half a dozen characters think that *they* should have got the ministerial berth instead of me. They will detest me, and malign me no end. Next, there are some senior leaders in the Opposition who think it's their divine right to ridicule ministers and humiliate them at will. I won't take that sort of insult, and they will not take kindly to me. And lastly, the press. I have some very good friends among them. Personally, I believe that each one is as good as the best in the profession. However, their difficulty is that their job essentially lies in describing the way things go wrong. They look for a minister who could be an easy target. Most reporters subconsciously believe that all ministers are nitwits, or ought to be if they're true to type. Journalists relish the performance of ministers who mess up with wrong answers and cringe for publicity. I'm afraid I shall disappoint them and they'll never forgive me. It isn't their fault at all; some of them are my very good friends. But the fact is, their job can't flourish without something going wrong somewhere. If it is a minister, all the better. Only two days back, one reporter plied me with all kinds of questions, based merely on the speculation of my possible induction into the cabinet. I gave the right answers. He got annoyed, obviously because right answers don't make news. He said irritably, "Coming to you is like milking a he-buffalo!" All in all, looking at it objectively, I shall lose my freedom while finding myself unable to do what I'd like to.'

Aruna's patience snapped. She cut him short and burst out, 'What nonsense is this? Why should you presume that the whole world is against you? As if you are the first minister that ever was and the last that ever will be!'

'I am not thinking about myself at all, Aruna. A man can survive in a man's world, despite being slandered. But what about the woman? Those after my blood will end up spilling yours, in all probability!'

Aruna grew pensive. Exhilarated by the announcement of Anand's inclusion in the cabinet, she had not given enough thought to this aspect. Many people had congratulated her on Anand's elevation, but she had not grasped its significance at the time. The moment Anand uttered the warning, the truth overwhelmed her like a flood. She could see the rest of his argument, logical and clear: you get nothing for nothing! . . . Now, she was all attention.

Anand explained his concern, slowly and methodically. 'So you see the battle-lines. What will they beat me with? They can't ever say I'm corrupt. They can't say I'm inefficient. They can't hope to say I'm unintelligent. They may perhaps say I'm arrogant, that my style of functioning is not what it should be. No one has the remotest idea of what "style of functioning" means, much less what it should be! So, that won't cut much ice and I'll take it in my stride . . .'

'They will say you are a womanizer,' Aruna offered.

'I don't think so,' Anand mused. 'Because that charge wouldn't be serious enough against a male in our society, strange as it may seem! In fact, Aruna, you may not appreciate this, being a woman, but a womanizing man is by no means a contemptible individual, judged by our standards. There is a halo around him. He is a hero of sorts. In a feudal environment, womanizing is almost a status symbol. It is a measure of masculinity. No, Aruna, they won't call me a womanizer, especially when they have a much more serious charge handy.'

'What's that?'

'You . . . and me,' Anand responded with deliberation. 'You see, if it's many women, a whole harem, that's okay. But one woman—no! That is considered the height of immorality. And on top of everything, a minister and a woman together! You see the picture now?'

'I think I do,' murmured Aruna distractedly.

'All this means that a new chapter has to start from tomorrow. I have to part company with you,' she said, as if to herself.

'Can you?'

She looked at him, puzzled and hurt. Then she said, in a determined tone, 'You have to leave me.'

'Can I?'

Suddenly, both said 'No!' together, as if they had found the answers to these vexing questions at the same moment.

They were silent for a long time, ruminating over how to disentangle the convoluted skeins of the problem. They could find no way—or so it seemed.

'The swearing-in, I understand, is in the afternoon,' Anand said at last. 'Meanwhile, I'll manage to get out of it honourably. After all, many others are ready to jump into the berth . . .'

'Don't!' she shouted. 'Please don't! I won't . . .'

'Easy, Aruna, easy,' he consoled her. 'We must sort this out dispassionately and with a clear vision. I'm not enamoured of positions. I don't care for money. I can continue to serve the people as I'm doing now. Then, what's the problem about declining?'

'What about your family, your friends, your followers? How can you disappoint them, especially after the announcement?'

He made no answer, but she could see the troubled expression on his face. It was her turn to counsel calm now. 'Look,' she suggested. 'Let's think about it tonight, independently, okay? I shall leave just one thought with you. I feel that opting out at this point will be extremely awkward. It may land you in avoidable complications. I'm sure there'll be time enough to work out our priorities. Things, after all, will not always be as tough as you imagine.'

'Well, your guess is as good as mine,' said Anand. 'Yet I can't take any chances in this matter. You see, a person in power is a perpetual accused in our society . . .'

'I don't deny that,' she commented. 'Yet, you can't give up in advance. Suppose all of them really go for you. Suppose a choice between power on the one hand, and what you consider more important on the other, presents itself. That has happened to many in history. You can choose your course any day, any moment. Can't you?'

'I am not so sure; it would all depend on how the choice presents itself,' Anand said.

'Don't argue now . . . Just sleep over the problem. Also remember that this is the only thing I shall ever ask of you in my whole life. Decide tomorrow. Wake up with the decision in the morning. Don't tell me, just act. Will you?'

'If you so wish,' mumbled Anand.

There was a long silence once again. The truth was buzzing agitatedly in their heads: you get nothing for nothing . . .

After Aruna left, Anand was about to retire for the night when his friend Dr Sudershan walked in, beaming. It was past midnight, yet they chatted for quite a while, of this and that, without settling on any definite point. At last, tired of evasion, Sudershan said abruptly, 'I know you'll be great as a minister and do fabulously. Power has come to you at the right moment. But . . .' he stuttered a little and forced himself to go on, 'but this Aruna person is going to be your undoing, and no mistake!'

They stared at each other for a few seconds. Then Sudershan added, 'At least, that's what they all say.'

'What about you? What do you say?'

'Dammit!' exploded Sudershan. 'How should I know? And what do I know, anyway?'

'What do you not know?'

Nonplussed for a moment, Sudershan gave a helpless shrug, and then said placatingly, 'Okay, okay . . . Let's say I know what I need to know. Yet the fact remains that you'll get into a lot of trouble because of this woman . . .'

'What kind of trouble? What has she done? Be more specific, will you?'

Sudershan had nothing specific to say, of course. Finding Anand in no mood to receive a general harangue, he changed his strategy and switched again to inconsequential topics. Indeed, he had already said his piece. There was nothing to add.

Yet he had to go on. 'Look, friend,' he began, 'I'm your only comrade, the only one who has stuck to you all these years . . .'

'Like a leech!' cut in Anand.

'Like a leech!' echoed Sudershan with a chuckle. 'And I ask nothing for myself. You and I have been so close, since our student days . . . I feel happy in your happiness, heaven knows why! And you feel happy making everyone unhappy on your account. What is this confounded paradox?'

'Okay, what do you expect me to do, Doctor? Rather, since you refer to "them", whoever "they" happen to be, what do "they" expect me to do?'

'Damned if I know!' bellowed Sudershan. 'There's nothing to blame you for, still maybe you could be more careful. Maybe she could be more careful. I just can't spell out how, so don't ask me!'

'I won't!' responded Anand, so emphatically that Sudershan gaped at him for a while.

'You won't?' he shot back. 'Then what'll you do?'

'Damned if I know!' said Anand. 'Don't ask me!'

Both had a hearty laugh. 'Look,' Sudershan began, 'I don't propose to spoil your joy on the eve of what is undoubtedly a great day in your life—and mine too. I shall leave a thought with you to sleep over. You've always risen above personal predilections . . . Just keep that up as minister!'

Left alone, Anand sighed. He had so many decisions to sleep over . . .

But sleep he could not. A large contingent of MLAs trooped in to felicitate him. Sant Ram, and many others. Their natural leader, of course, happened to be Bajrang Singh. He had somehow developed a special liking for Anand over the years.

Bajrang was particularly happy. He crushed Anand in a hug and slapped his back vigorously, to the delight of everyone present. He lifted Anand off the ground and swung him round and round in total abandon. Then, setting him down gently, he became somewhat serious. 'Be kind to the poor, the *kangals*, Anand *beta*!' he advised. 'If anyone tries to cause trouble to you, just tell me. I'll break his neck the next moment. And don't get a swollen head yourself when you sit in that damned flagged car! If I ever find you going astray, I'll break your neck too! Remember!' Then as an afterthought, he added, 'I know that won't be necessary. I know you'll do very well. I don't know how I know! What does everyone think?'

'You're right!' was the chorus.

The goodwill was overwhelming. Aruna was right, he thought. He was being rather stupid, imagining all those ghastly things. He was perhaps too self-conscious . . . He remembered Aruna's comment: he was neither the first, nor was he going to be the last, to swallow this bitter-sweet political pill.

It was the same story all night. People came and went. Anand received their congratulations, and with immense relief watched their noisy departure. Dawn found him still tense and wide awake. As he stood at a window and watched the sun rise, he suddenly felt with his entire being the mandate of Aruna's determined, compulsive, almost ferocious affection.

# 21

'. . . I will bear true faith and allegiance to the Constitution of India as by law established . . .'

As he uttered the words, Anand's mind visualized the implications of the promise. True faith and allegiance to the Constitution, to fraternity, to equality, to democracy, to freedom—political, economic and social. What immense responsibility, he mused.

. '. . . I will do right by all manner of people without fear or favour, affection or ill-will . . .'

The thought flashed across his mind that the Constitution all but wanted a minister to be a saint. A fleeting comparison with present incumbents, himself included, sent a shudder through him.

'. . . I will not communicate or reveal, to any person or persons, any matter that may be brought to my notice, or become known to me, as minister . . .'

He thought briefly of the plethora of 'top secrets' that appeared in the newspapers. He remembered that someone had defined 'top secret' as a secret that leaks from the top! He felt a little unnerved by what he swore to do, or not to do. Yet, the solemnity of the

217

promise moved him. It sounded like a sacrament.

When he sat down to sign in the register after the oath, his hand was shaking slightly. He felt at once confident and nervous. He had never felt so in the past. It is perhaps symbolic of power, he mused, that nervousness trails confidence like a shadow. You do something that you think is right, but the very next moment you are no longer sure. A host of critics assail you at once. They believe that you can't do anything right anyway, whatever you do. You end up with more doubts. Until you lose your sensitivity and persuade yourself that you're always right, whatever you do!

After the oath-taking, the ministers were profusely congratulated by their friends and well-wishers who had been invited for the ceremony. Aruna formally congratulated Anand and quickly moved aside to address the other ministers. Veena hovered nearby, in a simple but impressive Kancheepuram sari, with the children flanking her. She looked around with pride and satisfaction. Anand remembered his late father and imagined how proud he would have felt to be here on this occasion. He felt sorry that Mother, being too weak after a recent bout of fever, could not come.

From his very first day in office, Anand found that it was not easy to conduct himself as he wished, to resist the temptations of power—maddening, intoxicating, distracting, exciting. He reminded himself of the magic of democracy that had catapulted him into a position of eminence, while many others who had struggled and worked arduously for much longer remained where they had been. He had to intuit and extract the truth from the seemingly trivial events that took place every day. He had to meet crowds of people with a smiling face, without thinking, as some others did, that the riff-raff were wasting his time. The riff-raff—yes, that was what his intellectual friends called the people at large. The unseen foundation of a cherished system. Unseen, ignored, ridiculed, spurned.

Starting at dawn, his compound filled with specimens of 'all manner of people'—so aptly described in the oath he had solemnly taken. They were depressed, sorrowful, cringing, diffident, emaciated, crude, quarrelsome, ignorant, dirty—and remarkably astute beneath their disintegrating rags. They trod upon the lawns at will. Their sticks bored holes everywhere in the damp ground after an overnight drizzle or fall of dew. Their rough homespun blankets appeared in odd places. They sat anywhere, spat where they sat. Some did so out of habit, others were unable to suppress the cough they didn't know was tubercular; no doctor had ever attended to them. They smoked incessantly, noisily drawing long puffs from cheroots made of *palas* leaves stuffed with inferior country tobacco. And coughed and spat all the more. The peons, the sweepers and the civilized gentry—strange coalition—all called them a nuisance.

The 'people' came with all kinds of requests. Ridiculous. Misguided. Silly. Irrelevant. Unnecessary. Mean. Yet they were sincere requests based on genuinely felt grievances, real or imaginary—real for them, imaginary for others . . . And when they mobbed him—which happened at any time of the night or day—Anand read in their supplicant eyes and sunken cheeks the tragedy of their existence—an existence that had once had the potential to achieve sublimity, the birthright of every human being until it was brushed aside by circumstance, destiny, their own unthinking tendency to blunder, and in a number of cases, the rapaciousness of others. From time to time, he would feel awed in their presence, transported by their ignorance and rustic truculence. At such moments his long-standing quest for the other half within, that insubstantial entity that would make him 'complete', would suddenly come to the fore and he would fancy that he saw his 'other half' staring at him like a spirit from the ragged, jostling, coughing, swearing, spitting, pleading crowd. But it was a fleeting illusion; on reflection, he concluded that he would never be able to satisfy the yearning to find his 'other half' in this life.

Amid these crowds of supplicants, he felt transformed from a solitary individual into a very different entity. His own life mattered no more. His joy and sorrow, his family and friends, his likes and dislikes—all were subsumed in a much greater whole. It was the universal and all-inclusive existence of mankind, in the infinite continuum of time, space and human emotions. The phenomenon struck him as the spiritual interpretation of democracy. If as legislator he represented a hundred thousand people, as minister he found himself responsible for the well-being of millions upon millions. That was the big difference—from representation to responsibility. State power, siphoned off from the people and vested in him for the time being, made him a Gulliver; otherwise, he was just another Lilliputian. Oddly, this fiction often appeared more than real. Some politicians believed it to be actual; they paid the price. A few continued to perceive the illusion, yet played their part in the seeming reality with dedication and enthusiasm. Anand wanted to be among those few.

Balancing the moments of transcendence were times of frustration and irritation. He was especially bothered by people calling him 'Honourable Minister'. They welcomed him with addresses that attributed to him countless qualities of head and heart. No one believed the hyperbole, least of all those who presented the addresses. If a minister was expected to possess the virtues attributed to him, it was a misconceived expectation, an impossible demand; if his flatterers proclaimed that he already possessed every virtue, they only betrayed their ignorance. Either way, he felt disappointed, even cheated. He also found, to his consternation, that welcome addresses had a knack of duplicating one another with surprising similitude. Ignorance copied from ignorance, servility emulating servility. He found that some people looked upon him as a new being characterized by arrogance, superciliousness, sensuality, self-centredness and love of sycophancy. Many people took it as a fact of life and proceeded to pander to it the way they knew how . . . He was flabbergasted at this sudden change of attitude of those around him, including a host of so-called friends. As if by becoming a minister, he had degenerated into an inferior and baser individual overnight. What was this due to, he wondered. Was it a reflex or a conditioned response to the general experience? Was it the result of the belief that power always corrupts? Was it the result of an ancient feudal order operating in a highly stratified society? Was it likely, too, that those who danced attendance on him did not really respect him? That they only feigned reverence in a spirit of condescension, in a manner of speaking? In the spirit in which you throw a bone at a dog, to keep it from barking—and perhaps biting? . . . Or, was it a combination of all these and many other unperceived motivations?

He spent long hours meditating on the concept of power. Ennobling. Intoxicating. Corrupting. Which shall it be in my case, he asked himself again and again. He analysed the situation with all the detachment he was capable of, and drew a blank. He found himself neutral to the influence of power.

Ennobling? What is ennobling about power, as one finds it wielded today? Mostly for self, only incidentally, if that, for the people. That is precisely the order of priority of a private individual, isn't that so? . . . Self-interest, either enlightened or unenlightened. In either case, self-interest, nevertheless. With or without the sugar coating . . . Then, what was the difference between a minister and a private individual? If he was unable to reverse this order of priority, what claim could a minister lay to the extra dimension of power? None, Anand concluded. The idea of personal power did not move him.

Intoxicating? Why should power intoxicate? He had seen persons becoming and ceasing to be ministers—all within a week, or even before the ink was dry on their appointment orders. Before official residences and cars were allotted to them. It was a game of snakes and ladders in many respects . . . Anand had never looked upon a minister as anyone extraordinary. Now, having become one himself, he didn't want anyone to see him as different from what he was, beyond what he was really worth. Since all intoxication, including the one induced by power, could only be temporary, it came as no surprise to find it appear and disappear in the case of many others. As for himself, he had not even experienced the intoxication to begin with.

Corrupting? How was it even conceivable in his case? He had no desires or designs that could lead to corruption of any kind. In that respect he was lucky.

As he pondered over these matters, he was struck by the truth about himself, for the umpteenth time: he was unaffected by, and therefore irrelevant to, the context of political power.

As a minister, his style was marked by a fervent idealism that sometimes led to impractical plans; but this was offset by his brilliance, sincerity and an almost maniacal dynamism. He developed his own approach to the question of the deployment of state power.

One day he found himself discussing a variety of concepts with Aruna who, on that rather rare occasion, proved to be a good listener. He said that where motivation was concerned, there was hardly any difference between a caveman and a civilized human being. Also, the desire to live, and live as well as the next man, was common to all. It was the basic human instinct. However, the point at which virtually all of mankind began to develop a sense of discontent was when it discovered the hiatus between desire and capability. Usually, Mother Nature balanced the two. So should human beings, to the best of their abilty. If the hiatus increased, one's equilibrium could be significantly, even suicidally disturbed. At this point, prudent men should cry a halt, step back, reassess their actions.

The same applied to the nation as a democratic entity. This was where man's most potent institution, the state, assumed crucial importance. If the state deployed its power to step up the hiatus further, the organism would break at some point. Sometimes it would break explosively; sometimes it would splinter into a web of hair-thin filaments like the windshield of a car at which a brick has been hurled, breaking into a maze of hair-thin cracks, noiselessly, yet making the shield permanently unstable and unsafe. In either case, there was severe damage. To keep choosing between the one kind of damage and the other was unprofitable. Wisdom lay in preventing or avoiding damage altogether, of both kinds.

The state, then, had to employ its power judiciously to counter the hiatus. To that end, it had to support the disempowered, and protect and assist the weak. It had to neutralize social imbalances, for whatever reason and in whatever manner these were manifest. And some imbalance was created all the time, depending on the nature of political institutions.

Through its manifesto, Anand's party had promised certain

social change. He was now one of those wielding state power, primarily in order to bring about the promised transformation. Only to that extent could he justify state power being in his hands. Beyond that specific function, he could lay claim to no more than could the beggar knocking at his door. From this perspective, the matter was exquisitely simple.

His colleagues had other ideas. They expected him to conform to the familiar pattern. The system was too well entrenched to assimilate any foreign body. It would not absorb or accept original ideas, particularly when the ideas encroached upon the existing order—as Anand's did. To be sure, everything was done in the name of the people. In actual fact, the people figured in the political drama only occasionally—except during elections, of course. They were like the Hindu Deity who never touches the sumptuous food placed in front of Him, in His name. Eventually, the worshipper and the priest share it.

Could someone make the Deity eat the food Himself? And should this come about, would the selfishly motivated priests still come to the temple with lavish offerings not meant for themselves? The comparison wasn't wholly satisfactory, however, for temple deities obviously have no appetite. But the people have all the appetite in the world, unsatisfied since the beginning of human history. They wait for food, real food, but are only fed hollow rhetoric and empty promises . . . Could he, Anand, do something to alter this situation? . . . He had heard of the miraculous power of some Hindu gods. People believed that they did, in fact, partake of the food offered to them. Devotees claimed that the priest placed the food in front of the idol, locked the doors of the shrine and withdrew. Next morning they saw that the Deity had consumed the food overnight. Some deities seemed to prefer liquid offerings. They would consume exactly one-half of the quantity offered—no more, no less. Half a ton out of a ton, half a pint out of a pint. And people worshipped this meticulously impartial divinity with deeper faith because of the miracle—the miracle of the stone idol manifesting human traits . . . What happened to that faith when it came to human beings themselves? Why did it shift, oddly enough, to the being who did not eat any food, to the sadhu who, people believed, ate nothing, to the yogi who could live even without oxygen? Again, a miracle. The stone that ate, the human who didn't—both were sacred, hallowed.

Such, then, was one version of our culture. Worship of the unnatural, calling it supernatural. Why didn't it respect the natural, for heaven's sake, Anand exclaimed. Why must we disdain and ignore the natural?

Could it be that the first makings of the friction between man and man appeared because of the difference in individual capabilities? And then, power? In a plausible sequence, from capabilities to power to domination to subordination? . . . The strongest primitive man freely abducted the most desirable women, seized and devoured the tastiest food, the best of everything that was available . . . and so forth, in all matters. And God, the maker, and the state, the organizer, both contributed to the hiatus, to perpetuate it, to increase it. The family head, the village headman, the parish elder, the king, the emperor—one atop the other. They all added to the hiatus, each in his own way.

Who could have kept the strongest caveman under check? Not another caveman, since he would be the weaker of the two. Many weaker ones together? Perhaps they could . . . Who could bring them together? The strongest, again? Then the result would be the same, or worse. Brute strength would then become organized brute strength. Autocracy would receive a boost through the trappings of democracy. All of which would be inflicted on the weak, eventually.

Could nature restore the balance? A flash of lightning, a cobra gliding out of the bush, a landslide, pestilence . . . But who could say that these would destroy the strongest? Chances were, the stronger the caveman, the safer would be his cave, the more secure his life, the greater his capacity to protect himself from nature's wrath . . . Still, he would be vulnerable to some extent. To the unknown. To God almighty. Like King Parikshit, as described in the *Bhagavata*.

As he spoke to Aruna, Anand realized that the argument looped in an endless circle. The God-man-capacity-power-domination-disparity circle . . . He was himself a part of that circle, rather, a point somewhere on the circumference, maybe somewhere between the centre and the circumference. Certainly not at the centre. Could he change the entire circle—centre, circumference and all; could he exert his will to manipulate objective conditions, to facilitate social change? Glancing around, he often found himself almost alone, opposed and outnumbered. His position in the hierarchy did not permit him to act as a statesman. Even if he wanted to, which he wasn't sure of. Even if he knew how, of which he was even less certain.

What then? Do nothing? Just drift along like many others, take what comes from political power and live happily, think of nothing? After all, when nothing mattered significantly to him, why not be an observer, naturally and logically? . . . However, he found inaction anathema to his way of thinking. He had played with his life as if it did not belong to him, as if it was not precious as human life is. As a 'terrorist' fighting the Khadimaan, he had entered into a dialogue with death many times. He had cherished that life of tempestuous activity—just for the pure excitement, the intoxication and euphoria of danger. As if that was his motivation . . . No, apathetic drifting was out of the question.

A few days after his meandering, rambling conversation with Aruna, he had the opportunity to test his theories and convictions in practical terms, and discovered how different reality and theory were.

While he was in temporary charge of the department of prisons, a file dealing with a prisoner came to him for decision. He was a lifer, convicted for murder. However, he was from a respectable family, the file said. The 'respectability' evidently stemmed from the extent of land he owned. He was used to a comfortable lifestyle, not given to hard work, the note accompanying the file said. Because of his position in society, the secretariat recommended that he be treated as a 'B' class prisoner who would be entitled to a more comfortable time in prison.

Looking closely into the file, Anand read that the prisoner had committed multiple murders in cold blood and in broad daylight. In addition, while on parole for a fortnight, he had had two more murders committed by hired assassins. Anand wondered why he

225

had not received capital punishment. And to think that the secretariat was recommending that he be rewarded with 'B' class. Anand remembered that the Speaker of the legislative assembly as well as some ministers and several influential MLAs had exerted pressure on him in favour of the prisoner. Several deputations had waited on him during the last three days.

It was his first hard decision. The easy course open to him was to okay the file. To follow existing practice and treat the prisoner as a landlord rather than as a convict. After all, the practice had continued for decades. He need have no compunction about going along with it . . . Yet, he hesitated.

'It's the prevailing practice, sir,' the deputy secretary who had come to discuss the file explained. 'No other view has ever been taken in the matter.'

'What is the justification for this practice, may I know?' queried Anand.

'None perhaps; but the practice has continued for a long—'

'That is clear from the file,' said Anand. 'But if it is wrong, can't we change it?'

'Of course we can, sir,' the civil servant replied. 'That is a political decision . . .'

'What exactly is political about it? Was he convicted for what they call political murder?'

'No, sir. It is political merely in the sense that—'

'That politicians are pleading for him . . .' cut in Anand.

'That's true, sir,' admitted the official. 'As you know, these murders are motivated by family vendetta, group rivalry or caste enmity. What we usually call *mens rea* is absent here. That's perhaps the distinction . . .'

'Are there any extenuating circumstances in this case?'

'None,' the other confessed. After a few minutes of uneasy silence, he withdrew.

A very influential murderer, Anand mused. The Speaker of the assembly, ministers, legislators, a long-standing government practice, the favourable treatment that affluent sections of society received, the stability of the status quo, the emphatic recommendation of the secretariat—all these were on one hand.

On the other was ... well, he didn't know what it was, but he just thought the ancient government order merited scrapping. That was not unusual. Governments discard and annul older orders routinely, if they have outlived their utility ... This practice, however, had remained intact for a long time, since British days. It had stood the 'test of time', whatever that meant. It had, however, never been put to the test of justice. He would have to think very carefully before he made his decision, Anand thought. If he was going to act out of conviction, it could signify the beginning of a lone and exhausting struggle against the prevailing order. The chief minister might overrule him yet. He would be exposing himself to criticism for nothing.

But if he was to be true to himself, there could only be one course of action. That could lead, through a variety of twists and turns, to a loss of position—the most dreaded eventuality for a person in power. It was a remote chance, but ... but who could say? Anand's qualms and doubts escalated by the minute, and so did his determination to do what he considered right. He did not know whom to consult. Aruna was not interested. She tried not to interfere with his official duties, even to offer innocuous comment. So he was alone, perhaps in the company of his inner 'other half', which urged him to take the wise, stupid, disastrous but right decision.

He rejected the petition, took the plunge ...

# 22

A REPORTER DECIDED TO WRITE ABOUT THE LANDLORD murderer's case quite casually, perhaps for want of anything more newsworthy that day. The matter seemed to gather momentum at once and Anand's stand on the issue received front page treatment in the *Great India Times*. Almost immediately there was a sharp reaction. It sent shock waves through the landlord class. Anand's phone rang continuously, and he had to stomach bitter tirades from three of his cabinet colleagues. The landlords cursed Chaudhury too, for giving temporary charge of the department of prisons to Anand.

The confrontation began in right earnest. Curiously, every landlord thought Anand had somehow hurt him. True, there was no justification for multiple murders; the landlords offered none. They admitted that the facts of the particular case did warrant the decision Anand had taken. Still, they said, the decision was an affront to an influential section of society. It besmirched their honour. When you convict an offender and sentence him, you vindicate the law, they argued. The state and the offender are quits, as it were, once the former deprives the latter of his liberty and puts him in prison. After that, they said, the state should not refuse the prisoner the treatment commensurate with his status. That would amount to humiliation on top of punishment. And there is no law that permits this. It is clearly extra-legal, if not downright illegal.

This argument figured in some newspaper articles. However, it did not cut any ice because the very idea of treating aristocratic or upper-class murderers with special leniency in prison was blatantly repugnant to public opinion. This made the landlords all the more furious. But they decided to lie low for the time being and await the right opportunity to strike.

The people forgot the issue, more or less. Some landlords approached Chief Minister Chaudhury through his father-in-law, a big landlord. They complained against Anand's intervention in what they considered a matter of class prestige. Chaudhury flatly refused to interfere. He said, with his unerring political instinct, 'What a ridiculous cause to settle scores on! Whoever is behind this is foolish!'

Some of Anand's cabinet colleagues, though, were quick to use this episode as a means to get at him. Their political instincts told them that here was a non-issue with considerable potential to become explosive. They liked Anand, praised him to his face, but resented his regular forays into the affairs of their departments during cabinet meetings. This happened normally in any discussion of a cabinet item. Anand would glance through the cabinet notes briefly and proceed to destroy all the carefully constructed arguments whenever he detected that the note favoured special interest gangs. He had a right to intervene under the joint responsibility of the cabinet. However, in the process, he embarrassed everyone. Even Chaudhury was discomfited by Anand's crusading spirit in some cases. But he did not react; he was giving his idealistic colleague an extra-long rope with which to hang himself.

Other cabinet members, however, did not know how to deal with him. Their frustration was compounded by the fact that he was seemingly invulnerable. He was incorruptible, but that was understandable; many others were equally so. He was competent, but that was also true of several others. What really distinguished him was his neutrality towards state power. Given this trait, he tended to insist on 'doing the right thing' in a rather rigid and uniform way that permitted no exceptions. This approach confounded and irritated everyone, friend and foe alike.

They loved him and they hated him. Why the hell was he, such a fine fellow, so dead set against the established order, they asked angrily. Was it honest to subvert the existing order through its own creature, the government? How would he benefit from such subversion? They found no particular motivation in him, beyond the party mandate. But for heaven's sake, what made him the sole interpreter of the party's policies? How was his stake in the party higher than the next man's? . . . No, it couldn't be that simple, his detractors conjectured, there must be something deeper, something sinister, something extra-political perhaps. Or, was he a 'plant' from some other political persuasion that believed in subversion? That was probably it, they concluded, but said nothing. That hypothesis, they knew, could not be substantiated just then, so they abandoned it temporarily.

Well, how long would he last at this rate, they asked. Every person in authority has a chink in his armour and Anand was no exception. The system has its own staying power, having been tried and tested time and again. One individual could not change it, so one individual should not challenge it, if he was wise. If Anand tried to destroy the system, the system would destroy him, they asserted.

Anand believed that after becoming a minister he had not changed in personality, in habits, in manner, or in the values he upheld. There, perhaps, he was out of step with others. When one is able to change with the changing situation, the relative change is likely to be less marked, less felt. However, an unchanging entity in a changing environment is apt to throw everything out of gear. Anand did just that, unwittingly perhaps. The prevailing order found it inexcusable. Anand was at his brilliant best just then. That was not the time to challenge him. You don't stare at the sun directly at midday, whatever your pique. You wait for the sunset.

Or for a cloud thick enough to obscure the glare.

The wait, as it turned out, was not too long. Within a year and a half, the clouds began to blot out the sun. By this time, people took Anand's success for granted. His brilliant, efficient and upright style of functioning had lost its sheen, its novelty. If he was brilliant, efficient, sincere, that's what he had always been. And a minister must be so anyway. If many others were not like him, that was the variety in God's creation. It was nothing to keep shouting about. But what about the cloud over Anand? Aruna, to wit. A brilliant minister doesn't get a special license to indulge in open adultery, does he?

Aruna was unable to fathom these developments. She was her usual self—frank, self-righteous, obstinate. She basked in Anand's popularity and success. She did not realize that political circles interpreted her pride and delight as arising from personal intimacy. That the allegation had no substance was yet another complication. Anand was indifferent to power and argued with her that it was basically utilitarian and applicational. It had very little to do with emotion or elation. You might feel somewhat euphoric in the first flush of acquiring power; but then you hit a plateau of equanimity. After that power was merely a weapon to use, not to parade about and flourish like a sword. Those who utilized it, did so quietly, effectively. Those who gloated over it only made futile and irrelevant noise. But Aruna, being a natural noise-maker, paid little heed to his advice. She stubbornly became more vocal and extroverted, encouraged by false admirers. She often said 'we', combining herself with Anand. It festered in many ears, rankled in several minds. And gladdened some hearts too.

One could see scores of cars parked in front of Aruna's house throughout the day and late into the night. All kinds of middlemen, transport operators, rice millers, government officials caught in disciplinary proceedings or angling for promotions, contractors, sundry businessmen and a host of other unscrupulous manipulators discovered unheard-of relationships with her—through her husband, her sisters, her sisters' husbands, her sisters' husbands' sisters . . . and so forth, in a never-ending chain. Quite a few classmates and hostel-mates of hers sprang up

231

overnight, though for the life of her she couldn't place many of them. Indeed, it was the height of absurdity when a business magnate claimed to have been her classmate in a college in which she had never studied!

From the status of mere classmates to that of boyfriends and lovers was not a very broad jump. The logic was simple; the gossip had credibility, given the fact that here was a woman in public life who had studied in co-educational institutions. Gradually, the number of ex-lovers grew apace. She was quite a beauty while in college, one of them reminisced. Slim, smart, talkative, sociable—she broke quite a few hearts . . . and . . . well, it fell to his lot, however, to know her a little more closely, as bedmate. Yet another individual who claimed to be a successful lover gave a detailed description of Aruna's erotic skills and added, significantly, 'How I wish to compare notes with Anand!' The immediate purpose of these boasts, however, was to impress on some prosperous associate that he, the former lover, alone could influence Aruna to influence Anand, the current lover, and get the associate's file pushed through the labyrinth of some government department. For a tidy sum as commission to the spurious ex-lover, of course.

Numerous new stars appeared on Anand's firmament too. Classmates galore, playmates and many other associates, real and fake, in various fields of activity. They sprouted from nowhere as if political power had worked as an overnight drizzle on parched land. Said one man who had played hockey with Anand, 'Of course, Anand was on our high school team. He was right-in and I was centre-forward. The fellow was so nimble-footed that none of us could keep pace with him. His stickwork was beautiful, but he would dribble his way to the other goal all alone, so he often failed to score. That was his fault—his penchant for solo performance. I wonder how he operates in politics now! The same way, I fancy . . . solo . . . always solo!'

Then there were those who had played with Anand, or said they had played, all the village games that were popular thirty years earlier—the tree-and-monkey game, hu-tu-tu, *gulli danda*. And lastly, two voluptuous women, of the 'Mata Hari' type, often seen in the corridors of the secretariat, began to describe Anand in intimate detail. They cooed, in meaningful tones, about how in his childhood Anand had roamed with them in the by-lanes of their village. He would go stark naked, his what-do-you-call-it dangling for public exhibition, they added with relish. Their convenient blushing seemed to authenticate their claims. However, the salacious remarks were meant solely to convince an interested businessman that the women could be very effective with Anand.

These degrading episodes galled Anand; yet, he endured them in the larger interest of the people he was determined to serve. One morning, his friend Dr Sudershan who had just returned from a fairly long stint abroad in pursuit of an additional qualification to his existing medical degrees, phoned to say he was back in town. Anand was delighted and suggested a meeting. Then a thought struck him and he said, 'Listen, you have always lambasted the government for its inefficient ways and I agree with much of your criticism. It may be a good idea to see me in action and give me your comments! That would be useful to me in many ways. Why not come to my office tomorrow and spend the whole day with me and observe what it means to be a minister? At the end of the day, you can make use of your fancy degrees to cure yourself of any depression that may hit you!' Sudershan laughed and agreed.

The following day, Anand was in his office, waiting for his friend, when he heard a stormy harangue erupt outside his room.

'Whaaaat . . .? A minister quoting rules? Like the devil quoting scripture! . . . Very well . . . I'll show him! Let me see how long he continues as minister! Just watch what'll happen in the next election! Oh, what ingratitude! What *be-imani*! We toiled night and day to get him elected, spurning very tempting offers from the horse-symbol candidate. We took him round in a procession from village to village in a chariot drawn by fifty pairs of bullocks. We suffered odium from the people of our own caste for not supporting the bicycle-symbol candidate. We lost everything in this confounded election—everything we could have gained by supporting any other candidate, or even two candidates at the same time. Yet we supported this would-be minister, this great Anandji, in the hope that he would help us. And now he reels off rules . . .

Rules indeed! As if we don't know the rules! Ram Ram! What's the world coming to?'

Anand recognized the voice of Bhim Shankar, a powerful landlord who belonged to his constituency. He had wanted Anand to order work to begin on an irrigation tank in his village, against the accepted norms, so that about a hundred hectares of his dry land could turn into fertile wet land overnight. Anand had refused; and here was the bitter Bhim Shankar bemoaning how the world had suddenly changed into an abode of *be-iman* politicians!

The hefty, bespectacled gentleman, wearing a superfine dhoti and a wristwatch with a fat gold strap, harangued the listeners for long moments. His corpulent frame blocked the middle of the most frequented corridor of the secretariat, just in front of Anand's office. Clearly, the man wanted Anand to overhear this peroration.

Within minutes, Anand heard another voice, which he instantly recognized as Dr Sudershan's. Then there was the rumbling of an argument. Sudershan insisted that what could not be done under the rules could not be done. This infuriated the gentleman beyond endurance. 'Mister,' he hissed, 'I know a rule or two myself, I assure you! If something could be done under the rules, the local supervisor would have done it; he is a nice fellow and we often meet in the bar. The district officer would have done it; his wife is the president and my wife the secretary of the local Women's Club. But only when the wretched thing can't be done under the rules does one have to come and cringe before this great personage called a minister . . . See? And he starts quoting rules! Rules indeed!'

Sudershan, somewhat piqued by this logic, tried to counter Bhim Shankar's vitriol. He said, 'So a minister's job, according to you, is to flout rules?'

'To get the damn thing done, rules or no rules—understand? Else, how is he better than a lower division clerk?'

When he entered Anand's room, Sudershan was roaring with laughter. However, the moment he set eyes on Anand, his laughter stopped abruptly. 'Are you okay, Anand?' he enquired with some concern.

'I'm fine, thank you,' Anand answered. 'Maybe a bit exhausted from occasional overwork and tension . . .'

'Goodness! What a change I find in you since I went abroad! You look like you have aged by a decade, my friend!'

'Rubbish! You're exaggerating. I'm in fine fettle, I assure you, Doctor.'

'I'm not surprised you're tired if you have to deal with the likes of that thug I just ran into—'

'He's all right. He's abusive because his interests are threatened, not because he's my enemy,' explained Anand. 'If a small rule, which the minister could twist at will, comes between him and a hundred hectares of wet land, he is bound to rant, and rant like hell. The problem is that a politician has to face something called the next election; that's where he is vulnerable, in most cases . . .'

He motioned Sudershan to a sofa and ordered tea for him. 'Now tell me about the foreign exploits you left out of your letters,' he said. 'Was the training worthwhile, on the whole?'

'Well, yes and no,' responded Sudershan. 'They don't seem to know what we in this country need right now. Strangely, we don't know either. Well, things will change, I'm sure. We're still at the stage when everything foreign looks and sounds valid for all times and all purposes . . .'

At this point, a senior MLA present in the room interrupted vociferously. 'Look, sir,' he asserted, 'if you don't get this fellow transferred at once, our group will be finished. That's for sure, I warn you . . .'

'How can that be done?' protested Anand. 'He has been there hardly three months!'

'That's the point!' was the prompt rejoinder. 'If we kick the scoundrel out regardless of how long he's been there, his successor will be more obliging to our group . . .'

'But I don't order the transfer; the district officer—'

'I know,' cut in the leader. 'Please phone the district collector and ask him to authorize the transfer at once . . .'

Anand began to demur. His voice was feeble; he knew he was swimming against the current. The interest of the 'group' was too strong to ignore. Anything for the group—that was the thumb rule here. No use protesting that he, Anand, had no group. They stamped you with a group identity anyway. In the ruling party, you have to belong to a group, just as anyone born a Hindu in India must belong to a caste.

Another gentleman came up with his problem. Nothing very difficult, he assured Anand. His nephew had passed the BA exam in the third division. He was brilliant, nevertheless. Now he had applied for a senior post in a public sector undertaking. It was true that he had not done too well at the interview; yet he had the minimum qualifications. He was, therefore, qualified. There should be no hitch in his getting the job. The public sector did accommodate such candidates, thank God! However, one always needed a push these days, you see, he said. So, would Anand kindly recommend his nephew to the concerned general manager?

'There are many first class candidates running for this job,' Anand pointed out.

'So what?' countered the gentleman defiantly. 'My nephew has got to get the job, come what may!'

The third visitor wanted a seat for his son in the engineering college. He had no chance on merit, the gentleman admitted. 'You see, this merit stuff is all rubbish,' he pointed out. 'One word from you to the vice-chancellor of the university will ensure the young fellow's future!' He added a broad and almost irresistible smile for effect. 'Just one word,' he repeated.

'That's impossible, my friend!' cried Anand. 'There are many brilliant candidates who must get preference, obviously . . . '

'Had my son been that brilliant, do you think I would be bothering you today?' countered the exasperated father.

The fourth incumbent was more circumlocutory. 'Your speech the other day at Rampur was superb, sir,' he began. 'Believe me, the people were speechless in their admiration. I tell you, they dote on you and never tire of praising you. Which is, of course, so well-deserved!'

'But Sethji, I never delivered any speech that day,' said Anand. 'I had to cancel my visit to Rampur at the last moment!'

Sethji looked foolish, but only for a second. The next moment he plunged into another topic and continued his homily. The object was the same: to praise Anand to the skies. He would neither leave, nor explain the purpose of his visit. His technique evidently was flattery on the first visit. Anand would have to wait for his next to know what he was up to!

Then came visitors with all kinds of requests. To lay this foundation stone. To cut that tape. To open such and such a shop. To preside over the valedictory function of a school. To attend a dinner hosted by someone important. To give away the prizes and address the public at some mela, etc., etc. The reason for most of these invitations was that the other 'group' had booked a minister for *their* function. Minister for minister, they must prove more than a match for their rivals. This was the immutable rule that the group obeyed as if it were a divine decree.

Then a very interesting personage carrying a gigantic garland forced his way into the room, babbling incessantly. The garland must have caused a flower famine in his part of the town. His gait and gestures were too dramatic to describe. At the end of his declamation—rather, during the course of it, since there was no end, really—Anand understood that a certain file was about to reach the ministerial table in a day or two. The gentleman had a personal interest in the matter. Everyone, from the chaprasi upwards, was in his favour. The officials had done a fine job in examining the case thoroughly and conscientiously. There was nothing for Anand to trouble himself about; he just had to affix his signature. That would be it. After all, how could a minister look into all that mass of detail? And what were all those idle fellows in the administration paid for anyway? Would Anand kindly . . . very kindly . . .? The gentleman extracted something like a grunt from Anand, which could have been interpreted in multiple ways. When nothing more definite came, the man took the grunt as a commitment. At last he left, leaving the room frozen in the sort of peculiar stillness that follows a hurricane.

Moments later a red-faced person, who had been sitting rather quietly in a corner of the room, suddenly came to life. He began to speak and expostulate with vigour. Of late, he argued, ministers had become ineffective in the administration. They were too easy-going, too timid and too involved in their political wrangles. They had no time to look closely into the cases coming up for their decision. The bureaucracy was tightening its grip and this didn't augur well for democracy ... Having thus enunciated one laudable principle—contradicting another propounded just a few moments earlier—he came down to his own case. It had been, he said, thoroughly distorted and messed up by corrupt officials. It had landed on Anand's table with a string of comments 'deliberately written against me'. Only the minister now stood between the case and complete failure of justice, 'which would also mean my own complete ruination,' he pleaded. 'I know, sir,' he continued, 'that I'm lucky this case came to you and to no other minister. I know you have the guts and the intelligence to overrule all the officers, including the chief engineer, and ensure that justice is done. I'm positive about it ...' Meanwhile, there was a buzz from the private secretary and Chief Minister Chaudhury came on the line. 'Look,' he said, 'I'm sending that pest to you once again; he's on his way.'

'Which pest?' asked Anand. 'There are so many of them ...'

'You're right, there are so many,' agreed Chaudhury. 'This happens to be the special VIP who thinks that he has made me chief minister. I have no way to put him right and ask him to go to hell!'

'So you've asked him to come to me?' Anand queried, with a glint in his eye.

Chaudhury guffawed. 'That's a good one! Anyway, you do know this character, don't you?'

'Who doesn't? What do you think he wants?'

'Haven't the faintest idea,' replied Chaudhury. 'Talks in riddles all the time. I thought you'd handle him with tact ...'

'That I will,' said Anand. 'Oh, here he comes ...'

And sure enough, the door opened peremptorily and in walked the special VIP, with a supercilious self-assurance all his own. He was neatly dressed and not a hair was out of place—the only disgusting habit he had was his penchant for enormous quantities of snuff that he shoved up his nostrils at short intervals. Then he would blow his nose with a sound resembling muffled thunder and make a nauseating exhibition of his snuff-stained handkerchief. When he wiped his nose with that piece of cloth, it was impossible to say whether the kerchief received the snuff from the nose or vice versa.

'Ah, Minister sahib,' he began in the interval between his first two snuff-stuffing operations. 'Very glad to see you. How are you? Good. Me? Well, getting along, I guess. Feeling exhausted, really. Thought again and again that I could make it to a nice hill station for some well-earned rest. But what can I do? The CM doesn't let me go for a single day. Something or the other keeps turning up all the time. And I can't desert the chief, having once installed him there, you see . . . All in all, this has become a dog's life for me.'

'Must be very strenuous,' ventured Anand tentatively.

'Oh, you have no idea how strenous it is,' said the SVIP (Self-appointed Very Important Person). 'The chief just doesn't realize my plight. He always dumps his worries on my solitary head and goes off on his tours, collecting garlands as usual. I have to run to Delhi and plead his case with the Prime Minister. You know, there are a pack of ferocious MPs thirsting for the chief's blood. Then I run back here and butter up the moneybags for the next election . . . My God! Elections, elections and more elections all the time. Frankly, I don't know why they don't raise an elected government's term to fifteen years. By the time you close your eyes and open them, another election descends upon your head. What kind of democracy is this anyway? I just can't figure out this rank nonsense . . .'

Thus rattled on and on this maker of the chief minister, holding forth on every subject under the sun—politics, philosophy, foreign policy, family planning, inflation and, of course, the socialist programme, which he claimed to have advised the Prime Minister of India to introduce in the·interests of the country . . . All those present in the room were a captive and helpless audience. They sat fidgeting, not knowing how to cope with that torrent of words. At one stage Anand fancied that the man must have run out of snuff and would mercifully stop. But lo and behold! He produced another full packet from his pocket and resumed his disquisition. Only when the private secretary reminded Anand, rather urgently, of a delayed engagement, did the VIP leave the room, still awash on a grotesque tide of bombast.

Then followed a procession of many favour seekers—high and low, male and female, official and non-official, young and old, good and bad. Disposing of all of them quickly, Anand started for the meeting he was to attend. Sudershan wanted to leave—he had seen enough for a day, he said. However, for old times' sake, Anand dragged him along. At the meeting, there were many speeches, in many languages, for many hours. At the end, no one could say who had said what. Everyone, however, said that the meeting was a grand success, and everyone congratulated Anand on his brilliant speech.

They arrived at Anand's residence at last, thoroughly exhausted, almost asleep, and immensely relieved that the day had finally ended. While taking leave of him after dinner, Sudershan asked him just one question, unable to control his exasperation. 'You have been so busy, doing so many things today,' he said. 'If this is your daily routine, when do you find any time to think?'

Anand smiled dryly and said, 'What makes you think, friend, that I think . . .?'

Yes, where was the time to think? It was an unending whirl of action, intrigue—and pleasure for those who desired it. To many it was just another profession, which provided ample opportunities to climb the social ladder, to quench one's material thirst, to satisfy one's egocentric, hedonistic and narcissistic appetites.

Yet politics had another side to it, too, Anand never forgot that. Thousands rejoiced in Anand's rise, with no motive, no particular purpose of any kind. Many of them did not even know him personally; they merely believed that something good in itself had happened when he became a minister—as when an artist paints an exquisite mural on a grimy public wall, or an impoverished street musician suddenly bursts into an enchanting classical *taan*. Those from the rural areas who had known Anand since childhood merely stared at him in awe. They said nothing because they didn't know what to say. They were not adept at ritual declarations of joy and admiration.

On the day he had first visited his village as minister, he had seen an old and blind woman being led up to him, step by laboured step. He had recognized her instantly, leapt forward, hugged her and rested his head on her withered bosom. The large crowd that had gathered to welcome him looked puzzled. One of them asked

Anand if he knew the old woman. He had answered, in a choked voice, 'Do I know her? Do I know my own foster mother who breastfed me, half starving her own son? Do I know her?' The woman was absolutely silent. She didn't even know why she felt so happy. She had merely touched Anand's face, throat, chest and arms with her groping hands. Many eyes went moist for a moment.

When youngsters saw him, their faces broke into spontaneous smiles. Young girls mobbed him for autographs wherever he went. They tore sheets from their notebooks, or seized any paper at hand, and thrust them in front of him. They were overcome by enthusiasm for 'Anand Dada'. Once an audacious girl extended her forearm. Responding to her irresistible demand, Anand tattooed his signature on her fair skin with a ballpoint pen, while her friends collapsed in spasms of uncontrolled giggling.

On a visit to his department's office in his district, he recognized an old schoolmate among the peons who stood in a row to greet him with waist-bending salaams. Anand chatted with everyone else, then went to his schoolmate. He plied him with questions about his family and their old school friends. The peon related this episode for months and months with pride.

Early one morning, Anand saw in his courtyard a wrinkled old man of over seventy, leaning on a stick and looking around distractedly. He rushed out to meet him. The man, astounded at this gesture, said, after some stuttering, 'So you remember me!'

'How could I forget my first guru who gave me the alphabet? Please come in, my teacher, this is a great day for me!' . . . They embraced for a long moment, their eyes brimming with tears.

Such experiences compensated to some extent for the sordid self-seeking that raged all around. However, Anand noted that to do good seemed to take a great deal of effort, like moving a mountain, while to do evil seemed easy. Worse still, many people took evil as the expected norm—until it was publicly detected in the actions of the person in power. Then it was played up relentlessly till it was out of all proportion to reality. Often, the person involved was ruthlessly crushed as a fly under a sledge-hammer.

# 23

ARUNA'S OVERENTHUSIASTIC, OCCASIONALLY EVEN IMPRUDENT support for Anand in public, began to hurt his image. The political fraternity interpreted her aggressiveness and tactless pronouncements as a display of arrogance provoked by Anand's success; they promptly linked it to their relationship. This was not so, in fact; her temperament had always been spirited and confrontational. When Anand was elevated to a position of power, she had rejoiced. Had Anand been trapped in adverse circumstances, she would have lamented his situation with the same sense of identification and earnestness. Either way, she was incapable of assuming a discreet or artificial stance. As with many flamboyant individuals, she was motivated and dominated by her ego, which invariably rubbed people the wrong way. In the high-profile political field, almost every important development could be traced to a clash of egos, sometimes necessary and beneficial, but often leading to catastrophe.

Aruna's personality struck most of her colleagues and others she had dealings with as a baffling web of strong love and hate, compounded by startling inflexibility. Defying all reasonable limits, her hate was as blind and consuming as her love.

She had been this way since childhood. Some of her neurosis could be traced to the fact that she was a typical example of many people who had had access to university level education for the first time in the history of their families, with no specific idea of what they would do with it. They were good, or no good, equally, for every job—from preacher to postmaster. And having achieved academic success, they felt an acute sense of alienation from the feudal, semi-literate, traditional environment they were trapped in. As a result, they were acutely sensitive to real or imagined slights and flared up at the least provocation. In Aruna's case, her naturally fiery temperament only exacerbated the problem.

Aruna's father had died while she was still a child. Being the youngest, she had become the primary object of affection, as well as the focus of all the authoritarianism, in her family. Each brother pampered her, but ordered her about all the time. Her sisters doted on her, but made her life miserable with innumerable taboos and admonitions. No one cared to find out what she herself thought, felt or desired. Added to this, the ghost of supposed ancestral glory haunted her, as though she had been singled out as the one who was charged with restoring the family to a privileged status.

The result was a peculiar amalgam of traits. She was good. She was generous. She was affectionate. She was also extremely stubborn and became more so as a protest against the barrage of do's and don'ts the family imposed on her. Her mother did not matter at all, one way or the other. She was a bit stupid, or was considered so—like so many women in feudal families whom everyone ignores, perhaps because they are not seen as entities distinct from their context. In that ritualistic milieu, a woman either dominates the family, especially her husband, or withdraws into self-imposed oblivion and spends her life in the pooja room or in pilgrimage. There is no other path open to her.

Aruna had understood her predicament well in advance and had revolted, first over her education and then over everything, including marriage. There was a high school in her home town. Her two elder brothers had failed the matriculation examination.

That was nothing unusual; they were feudal lords and did not much care for formal education anyway. But two years later, when Aruna passed the same exam obtaining a first division, all hell broke loose in the family. It was seen as an unpardonable affront that the sister had passed the test that the brothers had failed. Scandalous, wasn't it? It became the talk of the town. The eldest brother Balram, who had by then grown up into an unruly and aggressive individual, ordered Aruna to terminate her 'useless studies' (as he put it), and marry a rich young man from a family that had been close to their own for generations. Aruna was convinced that Balram was forcing the proposal of marriage on her out of spite; and therefore she retaliated by refusing to marry at all. The family home became a virtual Kurukshetra; shouts and arguments became the order of the day—and the night. All members of the family being equally angry and with none of them willing to show restraint, the battle raged for many days. The climax came when Aruna, in a fit of uncontrolled anger and contempt, spat in her second brother's face and burst into loud wailing, as if he had beaten her! She also served an ultimatum, in clear terms, that if she was not allowed to go to college, she would commit suicide, 'before you know what has happened!'

That disturbed the family, which forgave her the spitting episode. After all, she was the adored youngest child. There was a hurried family conference at midnight after Aruna had fallen asleep. They discussed the issue threadbare and finally decided to let Aruna have her way. Peace prevailed once again. Aruna, like the obedient youngest sister they had hoped she would be, fell at the feet of all the elders, showing extra devotion to the second brother, who blessed her with all his heart! It was a bizarre and melodramatic reconciliation.

Two of the older sisters were widows. They had sold the properties that their husbands had left them and settled down with their parents. They were a great help, and brought up the younger brothers and sisters. Both were great devotees of a well-known guru and led a pious life. Several acharyas and sundry sadhus frequented their house almost every day. During navratri, the whole house echoed with bhajans round the clock. Aruna was deeply influenced by this pervading spiritual ethos, which took root in her tempestuous character and somewhat soothed her unpredictable moods. It did not, however, detract from her spirit of revolt. She loved her sisters and respected her brothers, but when it came to taking decisions regarding her own life, she did exactly what she wanted.

Following this practice over a period of time, she had almost become addicted to rebellion. The spirit of revolt provoked her to explore unrelated fields of interest whenever she was attracted to some new idea. At one point, hating the idea of having to spend a whole summer vacation with the family, she settled down in a sanyasin's ashram. She so completely assimilated the lifestyle there that everyone, including her brothers and sisters, gave up all hope of retrieving her into this profane world. However, when July came, she appeared in college one fine morning as if nothing had happened. She baffled everyone, most of all the sanyasins of the ashram, who had patted themselves on the back for having inducted a committed, energetic devotee into their denomination.

Aruna's refusal to marry wasn't unmotivated; after all, it was a means of rejecting her brother's nominee. So when another young man came along, she agreed to marry him. He was an utter stranger. She only talked to him for a few moments. One or two witty answers from him convinced her that he was clever and interesting. After the wedding, however, she found that he did not stimulate her either emotionally or intellectually. She felt cheated and completely deprived . . . However, her strong ego smothered her feeling of disappointment and compelled her to stay within the marriage.

Between ashrams, social service institutions and some prolonged periods of depression, Aruna's domestic life became a shambles. There were occasional extended stretches of wifely devotion, when she accompanied her husband on his long official tours and forced upon him the arbitrary products of her culinary experiments. Some of them turned out to be wonderful, the rest awful. To cap it all, there were 'no food' days too when, all of a sudden, a spiritual fervour would seize her. She would lock herself in a room and go into meditation; this would usually last all day.

And it was the limit when her bouts of *dhyana* coincided with the days her husband had invited guests for lunch or dinner. While he smarted under extreme embarrassment, the guests put aside their inhibitions and enjoyed hours of unrestrained cooperative cooking in an unfamiliar kitchen.

The husband was helpless and hardly ever remonstrated with his wife. How could he protest against the behaviour of a wife so educated, so accomplished? She was more knowledgeable than he could ever hope to be about public affairs. His whole world consisted of obsessions with increments, promotions and keeping on the right side of the bosses. Very soon, he developed an inferiority complex. As for Aruna, she began to feel superior to her husband very soon after they were married. Her launch into the political field brought immense relief to her husband. His tortured nerves celebrated complete freedom after a decade of ceaseless abuse.

Aruna was, withal, a being created primarily to give and receive love. Highly sensuous and unrestrained, her self-inflicted partnership with the wrong man completely fettered her passionate nature. Even so, she was not willing to admit that her marriage was a mistake—indeed, she never accepted her mistakes. She was always right, everyone else was wrong. On occasions, when she could not sustain the illusion or the argument, she used her religious convictions as the central tenet of her logic. When all else failed, and she knew that she had erred, or couldn't win the argument, she would say she simply didn't care.

That wasn't quite true; even as she proclaimed that she didn't care for the opinion of others, she herself realized that she cared very much. The mistakes committed in the past cast longer and longer shadows as she advanced in her public life.

Yet she was too impetuous to be restrained for too long. Her sterile and loveless marriage led her to indiscretions with a few men in the new and relatively free environment she found herself in. But men were only trying to exploit her desperate craving for every aspect of that elusive thing called love. She allowed people to deceive her, believing each episode to be a lasting journey. Naturally, she became disillusioned when the male leeches soon tired of her, or pretended to tire of her. Their interest was wholly and gluttonously carnal. And they feared that their over-possessive wives had begun to get wind of their escapades. A well-known political leader became obsessed with her for some time. When she reciprocated with overwhelming passion, he backed off abruptly, saying, 'My God! I never thought you were so obsessive! At this rate, what'll become of my political career?' That was a typical callous response. Afer a series of similar devastating attachments, Aruna began to develop a loathing for men in general.

From the age-old climate of strict purdah enforced until recently in the state, the sudden change to increased personal freedom began to be seen as indistinguishable from promiscuity. When people saw a man and woman together, any man and any woman, they would make barbed comments that reeked of sexual innuendo. Malicious tongues were desperately and subconsciously trying to violate social barriers by touching on this forbidden subject. It was gossip. It was scandal. It was a sudden release. For some it was also, perhaps unknown to themselves, a manifestation of repressed anger at the transgression of the accepted codes that prevailed from the beginning to the end of people's lives. They resented anyone breaking the shackles of prurience and inhibition.

Placed as she now was in the midst of a politician's life, with myriad opportunities, from the most sublime to the most sinful, Aruna ignored the escalating rumours and tried to assess her situation. Anand's habit of testing everything on the touchstone of the common man, Mahatma Gandhi's *daridranarayan*, appealed to her, but could not satisfy her fiery temperament. A conspicious element of fearlessness characterized all her actions and responses, even to the vilest calumnies. This peobably derived from her implicit faith in God, which went much beyond the prosaic world and became an inseparable part of her being.

In 1957, there were significant changes in the national set-up. The reorganization of states altered the face of the country. The election to the legislative assembly in 1957 presented an opportune moment for Aruna to try her hand. She was too proud to approach the lesser gods whose calibre she already knew, after her tiff with Raghav, the lecherous member of the selection committee. In view of her obvious lack of political acumen, and the fact that she was not willing to barter her self-respect away, well-wishers advised her to return to the kitchen and forget politics for good. Some of her close friends had a vague idea of how disastrous her short stint in public life had been. They told her bluntly that she would never make it. The male-dominated political hell-hole would only turn her into a permanent plaything, and then she'd be dumped in the dustbin on that very count, they warned.

For the first time in her life, Aruna was at a crossroads. Before entering public life, she had hardly considered herself as living. It was the life of a corpse, if you could ever imagine one. How does one merely breathe one's existence away, she had often wondered. She had done everything—revolted at home, acquired an education, married—everything her own way, just to be defiant, to flout anything imposed on her. She now found that this attitude could not persist forever. As she took stock of her own life, it became evident that to begin with, she had wanted freedom simpliciter—in remarkable contrast to her childhood. But once this freedom in general was achieved, what it amounted to was a meaningless spirit of rebellion that drove her to act as she did. On second thoughts, however, she refused to take it as meaningless. In her own confused way she was searching for something. For what? . . . Freedom, of course. Freedom was a quality in itself. But freedom could not be without logic, without responsibility, without an anchor. And in public life, the anchor was extremely important; everything depended on it. This realization hit her like a thunderbolt.

Enough is enough, Aruna decided after the despicable episode with Raghav. Her self-esteem was almost destroyed. However, just when she was preparing to try and sustain a mode of physical and mental detachment, another tempest of revolt began seething within. Why should a woman have to degrade herself at all in order to survive in public life? Surely there were many who did not face this predicament? Then, why must she alone . . . ? It dawned on her, in a flash, that she was responsible at least partly for her own actions and for her fate—at least, a large part of it . . . Her revolt, as such, had not been wrong. Only, at some point she had lost perspective, hurtling down treacherous, addictive, humiliating paths from nowhere to nowhere.

Yet even as she had engaged in erratic behaviour, she had earned a reputation for dedicated social service. While those who failed to lure her into their beds and incurred her unconcealed contempt in the process spread highly exaggerated and specious sexual canards about her 'character' (invariably taken as pertaining to sexual conduct, as far as it concerned a woman), poorer sections of the populace began to worship her. And in 1957, she was inevitably pushed into the electoral whirl. She wanted membership in the legislative assembly. She also decided that if any lecherous male cast an evil eye on her, she would kick his teeth out. 'So help me God!' she said to herself, and set out to secure the ruling party's ticket. The challenge from Raghav steeled her will further.

Just then, Lal Bahadur Shastri visited the state as the high command's representative, to finalize the party's list of candidates. Political researchers hotly debated how to approach Shastriji, making checklists of his friends, friends' friends and friends' friends' friends, until the chain linked with someone they could themselves handle. However, Aruna sought an interview with Lal Bahadurji directly. It turned out to be surprisingly easy. Lal Bahadur scanned her papers and asked her a few questions, curiously enough, about spiritualism. The rest followed quite easily. 'I am highly impressed by her,' said Lal Bahadur. The state leadership readily agreed. Except that they assigned her the toughest constituency, in which the party had lost its deposit in 1952. 'If she doesn't pass through my bedroom, she won't come through the election!' Raghav declared with characteristic malice.

Yet, she came through the election, albeit narrowly. And for over three years, she strode as a powerful presence on the state political scene, fearless, disdainful of her male colleagues, rivals and detractors, extremely compassionate—and hopelessly erratic. She took on all her detractors and was determined to let no one intimidate her or take advantage of her just because she was a

woman. She held her own against all those opposed to her, until
that fateful night when she let Anand embrace her passionately in
the dark cinema balcony. They had entered into the relationship
partly in innocence, partly as an exploratory venture—they were
not committed to anything. That one eloquent embrace caused her
defences to crumble, suddenly and irrevocably. She was
overwhelmed by the sudden sensation of firm ground under her
feet, after treading on quicksand for several wild and anxious
years. Impetuous, ardent, elated, she became part of him without
regret.

As Anand rose in the political firmament, she was exhilarated—
perhaps more than he was himself. She became his most vociferous
champion, his most articulate publicist. This inevitably led to all
sorts of snide talk, because no one accepts that demonstrations of
loyal support in the political field are disinterested. If it is a man,
it is a sell-out; if it is a woman, it is the liaison in bed. In either case,
the person's credibility is lost. 'Why is she singing his praises all
the time? We have never seen her open her mouth except to abuse
someone or something!' commented furious local politicians.

'Everyone knows Anand is good; but when you hear this
woman praising him, you begin to doubt your own judgment of
him . . .'

'What can you do, brother? After all, she wouldn't be hawking
him around if he had not encouraged her . . . With all his
intelligence, he doesn't appear to know where his own interests lie;
rather, where they are in danger.'

'Well, infatuation and sound judgment don't go together, you
see. Where the one takes over, the other retreats . . .'

Some of Anand's well-wishers suggested to her, in the mildest
terms, that she would perhaps do well to be less effusive in her
tributes to him. She resented their intervention and redoubled her
harangues. She became more and more possessive about Anand
and intolerant of others—other women in particular. Her extreme
temper led to many clashes. Other women reacted violently too.
'Since when did this Aruna woman get an exclusive monopoly of
Anand? Why is he letting her dominate him? She has no business
to act as his natural guardian or conscience-keeper!'

'That's a great pity, sister,' cut in another lady. 'She behaves as if she has absolute proprietary rights over him!'

Anand was unaware of all this. Even when some watchful friends warned him, he did not pay attention. He was completely absorbed in the complex duties entrusted to him as minister, particularly in the form in which he envisioned them as part of a huge process of social transformation. He had no time for anything else. Except, of course, Aruna herself. He did find time for her, but she soon felt his attention to be inadequate, although she knew why it had to be so.

# 24

AT A TABLE IN A CORNER OF THE COFFEE SHOP OF THE Intercontinental Hotel in Afrozabad, three men who resembled each other only in girth and the number of chins (three apiece) were seated cosily, talking. The table was strewn with empty glasses, packets of Benson and Hedges cigarettes and plates on which there were well-gnawed bones of tandoori chicken. One of them, Ajit Singh, a Sikh builder, had flown in from Delhi, and the other visitor to town was Sinha, a financier and contractor from Patna with offices there and in Delhi. The third man was Ramprasad; he hailed from a southern state and was also a contractor. He claimed to have important contacts in Afrozabad.

The three contractors were involved in a huge local irrigation project from which they stood to gain a sizeable profit, if only they could get a revised estimate sanctioned by the state government—in other words, by the minister in charge, Anand. However, it so happened that after a careful examination of the claim, he had absolutely refused to entertain any escalation in the cost of the project.

As they called for another round of Black Label Scotch, Sinha said gloomily, 'I haven't come across such a stupid minister in all the thirty-five years I've been a contractor. The fool of a chief minister seems to have got Anand into the irrigation department only to get us all ruined. It's like a hailstorm over a bald head!'

'I don't give up that easily, brothers,' asserted Ramprasad. 'After all, this is Bharat. I am a great believer in God, and I refuse to believe that in this ancient land, He would punish us with such an unmanageable minister.'

'Ramprasad,' Ajit Singh said in a troubled voice, 'you may have local contacts here, but I've done business in this state for over two decades now. And I tell you, *yaar, ki* I have a bad feeling about this bastard. I don't think *ki* you have any idea of how much damage he can do.'

'And I tell you, my dear Sardar,' chimed in Ramprasad with supreme confidence, 'I do know every minister inside out. Every damned minister in the southern states who ever rode in a flagged car since 1952. My friends, you simply have no idea of my experience!'

'Will you quit bragging, Ramprasad?' Sinha cut in angrily. 'Don't you see, we are wasting time while nothing gets done. Let's talk less and get on with the job, as the Prime Minister says.'

'Oh, oh, splendid!' Ramprasad said boisterously. 'When will you stop quoting leaders, Sinha?' He was drunker than the other two.

'When I become a leader myself, that's when!'

'God forbid!' said Ajit Singh, looking up to the ceiling, as if for a possible confirmation of the sentiment from God.

'You fellows have again gone off at a tangent,' complained Sinha. 'We had better . . .'

'All your fault,' cut in Ramprasad. 'If only you'd quit quoting leaders, perhaps we could plan a strategy.'

'Okay, okay, I quit. Now tell me, O oracle of South India, how do we get on with the job? How do we wangle the sanction of an additional fifty crore rupees in the Vijayasagar project from this wretched minister?'

The magnitude of the task, when stated so clearly, was enough to shut them up for a while. They drank and smoked in brooding silence. It was the irrepressible Ramprasad who broke the silence again. 'Listen,' he said, 'I don't think we should panic or throw tantrums. I've managed such situations before, though I must admit this is a really tough one, especially since this pig of a minister thinks that he is an incarnation of Mahatma Gandhi and Satyavadi Harishchandra, all rolled in one. Evidently, he's yet to learn his lesson. A minister doesn't own the whole world, or even the whole country. He is not the highest in the hierarchy, thank God. And he also has a wife, children, friends and political followers, thank God again. Besides, he has elections to fight and win; and any election is at least five times costlier for a minister than for an ordinary candidate. So, my dumb friends, you know the chinks now. Attack, I say to you, that's what we need to do, instead of sitting around and letting him walk all over us.'

The three of them raised their glasses to salute this new-found resolve.

They mounted the attack on all sides. Sardar Ajit Singh singled out Anand's two sons. He made friends with them by bribing the headmaster of their school to allow him to take the boys out to lunch in the city's grandest hotel, the Intercontinental. The boys were only too happy to accompany their new 'Uncle', who claimed to be an old friend of their father, on the jaunt. After they had put away a huge meal, the corpulent Sardar began his pitch.

'Listen, boys,' he said. 'I do admire your father, but I can't appreciate the way he is making his own children suffer. He is brave, intelligent, hard-working and all that. However, he is blind to the aspirations of the younger generation. He thinks there is some great virtue in staying poor, while crooks roll in money and live like princes. I mean, how many times have you eaten in a hotel like this? How many times in a year do you get new clothes? Your father sets extraordinary standards of simplicity and commitment and expects everyone else to be like he was in his student days—one meal a day, wearing a khadi kurta and dhoti . . . He forgets that you boys are the sons of a minister, while he was only the son of a small farmer. Now, tell me, shouldn't he be more liberal? Shouldn't he let his family enjoy themselves a bit more?'

Srikanth and Ramakanth, the lads, were puzzled by the genial Sardar's questions. Although they were old enough to understand the general drift of their new uncle's conversation, they weren't quite sure they'd got the point. They had no complaints about the life they led, and were in fact very proud of their father. They were aware of the high esteem in which he was held by everyone. Besides, contrary to Ajit Singh's claims, they never lacked anything they needed; and while they had never eaten at a five-star hotel before (and it was a meal they had greatly enjoyed), it wasn't something they particularly missed. And, finally, neither of them would dream of taxing their father with a question about his simple style of living; they were too much in awe of him for that.

The younger boy, Ramakanth, spoke for both of them when he said in reply to Ajit Singh, 'In these matters, Father knows best. You'll have to ask him yourself if you want him to do something different.' Sardar Ajit Singh was stumped. Were these children also going to grow up to be as loathsomely monastic and self-righteous as their father? He called for the bill abruptly and drove them back to school with a minimum of conversation.

Sinha concentrated on Veena. First, he sent her a big basket of mangoes bought from the local fruit market, with his compliments. ('From our orchard', the card said). A day later he sent his wife along to pay a courtesy call on the minister's wife. They presented quite a contrast—the sophisticated, city-bred Gayatri Sinha and the homespun, simply-dressed Veena. Initially, Veena felt ill at ease in the presence of the rich, expensively-garbed visitor. But after a few courtesy calls, Mrs Sinha made friends with Veena and several other ladies who were Anand's visiting in-laws. One evening, she suddenly produced a scintillating diamond necklace before them. Everyone gaped and marvelled. Their admiration seemed to be getting the better of them by the minute. Indeed, Veena's starstruck relatives thought by now that the two women were really close and shared a fondness for expensive baubles; it was assumed that Veena could afford them now because of the earnings of her minister-husband. While they were occupied in noisy admiration of the necklace, Mrs Sinha took Veena aside (but within earshot of the other ladies) and said, quite casually, 'There's someone who wishes to present this necklace to you, madam, and . . .'

'Whatever for?' asked Veena, equally casually.

Everyone who saw the necklace and heard Mrs Sinha's statement concluded, despite Veena's disclaimer, that the two had struck a whispered deal. That was Mrs Sinha's plan. She wanted Veena to succumb to the logic that when everyone believed that the necklace had been part of a deal, why not go ahead with the deal anyway? No use getting a bad name for nothing . . .

Veena's attitude floored Mrs Sinha completely. 'Why does someone want me to have this?' Veena asked again. Mrs Sinha had no answer. You don't go about explaining why people present diamond necklaces to ministers' wives, do you? Seems to be a family of idiots, she muttered to herself. But she did not give up.

When Veena realized the reason for the offer of the necklace, she was quick to get rid of Mrs Sinha as courteously as she could, though inwardly she was seething. Mrs Sinha tried to re-establish contact a couple of times, and even sent Veena another fine diamond necklace as a present, but the gift was returned by Anand's secretary with a polite note to say that the minister's wife was out of town.

Ramprasad, who had tried to get to the minister through his followers, fared no better. When they met to compare notes a week later at the Intercontinental bar, he said, 'This fool has infected his entire constituency with the same madness he is suffering from. His followers dote on him like old mothers. They say they like him as he is. In any event, they think he is incorrigible, so why create embarrassment on both sides by trying to get him to do something he has clearly said he will not do!'

'Incredible,' admitted Sinha. 'Do you mean to say that not one of his followers wants to make a quick buck?'

'Oh, yes, there were several. They became disillusioned with his integrity and left him to join a rival group long ago,' replied Ramprasad.

'And there's no one he relies on for support, someone who can create trouble for him if he doesn't oblige him? Isn't there someone we can bribe to twist his tail a bit?'

'No, I don't think so. There were some influential local men who tried to take him on, but they lost heavily in the panchayat elections. After that, no one wags his tail that way. No, my friends, that's a dead end, I'm afraid.'

They tossed back their drinks and addressed the question once more, from a different angle.

'Couldn't we get someone to apply pressure from above?' suggested Ajit Singh. 'Delhi, for instance? Or get a short-notice question tabled in the assembly? I happen to know some leaders, you know . . .'

'Forget it, Sardar,' warned Ramprasad. 'That way lies total disaster. Anand will promptly reject our claims and build our samadhis with concrete. I assure you it will be *pucca* RCC and not like the cement-and-ash mixture you and I build with. Chaudhury, for some reason, will not interfere and Anand has some access to the very top too. We can't do that.'

Irritated, Sinha snapped, 'So are we finished? Is that what you are trying to say?'

Ramprasad didn't reply. They sank into a gloomy silence. Then, in his usual way, Ramprasad brightened. 'You know, if there's anyone who can help us, it's the other important young minister in the cabinet, Shekhar. He hates Anand. And though he isn't strong enough to take him on openly, I'm sure he'll have some idea of what approach we can take.'

They finished their drinks and arranged to meet two days later, after Ramprasad had spoken with Shekhar. As they assembled at Ramprasad's house at the appointed time, he said without preamble, 'We've got him. I don't know why I've been such an idiot, and why we wasted our time with his wife, kids and assorted fools. Everyone in Afrozabad knows there is only one real way to get Anand's attention, and here we've wasted nearly ten days!' He broke off enigmatically.

The other two almost shook him in their impatience. 'So tell us, you rascal, out with it, quick!' Sinha said.

Ajit Singh folded his hands in mock entreaty. 'Please don't kill us any more with suspense, O gem of the south, O Shankaracharya, Ramanujacharya, Rajagopalacharya . . . or whatever charya you fellows call yourselves! I declare *ki* the north surrenders, here and now! Please show us the light!'

Ramprasad said slowly and deliberately, relishing the suspense, 'I visited Shekhar as planned and within minutes he told me something I have known all along, except it hadn't struck me, fool that I am.' He declared solemnly, 'Friends and countrymen, after Shekhar's advice, I remembered that this headache of a minister actually has a heartache. In other words, a . . . shall we say . . . er . . . a girlfriend. I understand that she can influence him fully and completely. This is one hundred per cent correct information, courtesy our good friend, Minister Shekhar, though of course he'll deny it completely should we ever claim that we got it from him.'

The faces of his companions split into broad smiles. And they all began to talk simultaneously. When the excitement subsided a little, Ajit Singh became a bit moody and said, 'My God! This is earth-shaking news, indeed earth-quaking! But Ramprasad, are you absolutely sure *ki* there can be a woman, a flesh-and-blood *aurat* who . . . who can ever become intimate with that . . . that dry-as-dust bundle of virtues, that good-for-nothing Anand?'

Ramprasad flared up. 'Don't be stupid. Go and get a better source, or do as I say! If you dig just a little bit, you'll find that everyone in this city knows about the minister's open secret. If you don't believe me, drive past her house after the assembly adjourns. The long line of cars outside her house should be able to convince you. Count them, and you'll see that most either belong to contractors or to those connected, in some way, with the irrigation department. Or count the number of fellows who hang around her wherever she goes.'

The trio finished their drinks, ordered another round, and got down to planning their next move. Ramprasad told his friends whatever he knew, which wasn't a great deal. He said that in addition to being an MLA, Aruna was also a social worker.

'What do you mean by social worker?' Ajit Singh asked.

'Now, now, Sardarji,' Ramprasad said with a chuckle. 'You're asking questions like a child! Don't pretend you don't know that a social worker is exactly that—namely, a social worker, no further definition needed. But that's not our concern, all that we have to note is that people see her very often in Anand's company. Beyond that I don't know a thing, although lots of stories circulate about them, as usual. But it shouldn't be difficult to get more information.'

After probing for a few days they still hadn't acquired too much concrete information, but they had learned that Aruna Devi was a plain-looking, outspoken, generous and compassionate woman. No one knew how much money she had, or how much more she wanted, nor did they know if she had or coveted jewellery, property, and the other good things of life. This didn't perturb them unduly, for they assumed she was like everyone else when it came to these matters. She was also reportedly very devout and seen frequently in temples and ashrams.

One morning, Sinha called on Aruna, introduced himself as an honest and God-fearing man, a contractor by profession. He said he was a long-time devotee of the Shivanand ashram of Rishikesh, a regular visitor to Sri Aurobindo ashram at Pondicherry, and a generous contributor to the Muktanand ashram near Bombay, as also several other ashrams and religious and philanthropic trusts all over the country. In point of fact, he had never set foot in an ashram, of course. He had simply collected a list of religious centres and institutions from a friend the previous night, in order to make this interview credible. He told Aruna that he was planning a Chandi yagna for which a preparatory committee was to be set up; and as he had heard so much about her interest in religious affairs, he would be honoured if she could serve on the committee and attend its first meeting next Wednesday.

Aruna, impressed, agreed to serve on the preparatory committee, and to attend its inaugural meeting. What was more, she made a handsome donation there and then. Sinha could hardly contain his delight. A tray full of sweets, fruit, and an inviting cup of hot coffee appeared before him. 'Oh, thank you, thank you, Deviji, all this is unnecessary. You are so kind . . . so very kind. I know one shouldn't refuse prasad in a temple.'

'Deviji,' Sinha said, after having partaken of the refreshments.

'There is one snag in our scheme . . .'

'What is it?' she said.

'Deviji, you are like a sister, so I'll be frank with you. I may be a mere contractor, but I've heard saints like you say we're all equal before God. Well, I hate to tell you this, but I have been treated very shabbily, like a dirty dog, I should say . . .'

He feigned deep hurt and Aruna, he was happy to see, looked suitably concerned.

'Who treated you that way?'

'Well, Deviji, perhaps I shouldn't complain. Let me suffer silently.'

'It's all right. Please tell me, don't hesitate.'

'I'm sorry, Deviji, since you insist, I have to say that Anandji, our minister of irrigation, was most unkind to me. I went to him with a request to head the preparatory committee of the Chandi yagna. It's God's work and I wanted him to initiate it. I don't know what was wrong with that, yet I couldn't get an interview. Anyhow, never mind, Deviji, at least you have been so kind.'

'Don't say that, Sinhaji,' said Aruna, 'I'll do what I can to see if Anandji can be persuaded. Give me a call tomorrow morning and I'll let you know.'

After Sinha had left, she went into action at once. She got Anand on the phone and exclaimed, 'What kind of a minister are you? You have no time for a Chandi yagna committee? What do you think is more important than a Chandi yagna?'

'Listen,' protested Anand, 'that contractor Sinha is a scoundrel, I can't . . .'

'You can't what? What if he's a contractor? What makes you think that a contractor is not a human being? And this is, after all, God's work!'

Later, Sinha marvelled at how easily everything had gone this far. After Aruna's intercession, Anand agreed to head the preparatory committee for the Chandi yagna, which Sinha had thought up a few nights earlier after several glasses of whisky.

Sardar Ajit Singh's success was no less spectacular. For at least four generations, his family had lived in Delhi. However, when Ajit Singh called on Aruna, he drew a portrait of himself that would have drawn tears from a block of granite. He said he was one of those who had been traumatized by Partition. His family had been decimated but he had managed to escape and had walked hundreds of miles from his native village near Multan to Delhi. He had had no food or provisions and survived by drinking water from ditches by the roadside. He had slept at night in open fields with snakes and scorpions for company. 'Well, Mataji,' he concluded, in a tone full of pathos, managing to squeeze out some drops from his eyes, 'at last I made it. Did many odd jobs. Didn't have much schooling, but somehow by your grace, went up . . . and up, as a contractor, by sheer hard work, honest work . . . Now I have a problem and you alone can solve it for me.'

'What is your problem?' asked Aruna, almost in tears herself.

'I want to start an institution for vagrant children, such as I once was. Those memories always haunt me. I want *ki* you should be a member of the promoting committee of this institution and would be honoured if our minister for irrigation is its chairman.'

'That's no problem . . .' began Aruna.

'It is, Mataji,' cut in Ajit Singh. 'I know *ki* the minister loves children and children also love him. But unfortunately, when I went to him with this request, he flatly told me *ki* he had no time. I think, Mataji, *ki* he hates contractors like poison.'

'Wait a minute,' said Aruna, picking up the phone and dialling Anand's personal number. When he came on the line, she said with some amusement, 'Minister Sahib, why are you making things difficult for this poor man Ajit Singh who went through such a harrowing time in his youth? In the name of God, I tell you, do something good while you are still in power. God will not forgive you if . . .'

'Very well, madam,' Anand said good-humouredly. 'I surrender to God!' And everything was fixed up, again in no time.

Ramprasad's triumph, however, was the most spectacular of all. To begin with, he had a definite advantage over the others in that he could converse with Aruna in their common mother tongue. He made her his 'Akka', elder sister, thereby immediately establishing a familial relationship that was in the local tradition. He further unearthed some distant relationship with her and claimed that he had mediated in the marriage of Aruna's sister's husband's cousin's daughter. Some two or three visits later he was emboldened enough to invite Akka to visit his modest three-storeyed mansion; there his wife and three children fawned effusively on the visiting dignitary. At the appropriate moment he told her there were to be huge ceremonials—*Kumbhabhishekam* and *Maharudrabhishekam*—in the famous Sangamarudreshwar temple of which he was a trustee. Then he added that he would not hold those religious functions unless Akka and the minister for irrigation both graced the occasion. This, he said, was the Deity's message conveyed to him in a dream. Akka was quick to see the problem and took matters in hand immediately. Anand was inducted as an honoured guest with no further trouble.

Soon after these triumphs, the three gloriously happy contractors met at Ramprasad's house to discuss the next step of the plan. But before they got down to business, they raised their glasses in a toast to Aruna.

'She is an angel born as a human being,' said Sinha.

'I agree. She has a divine quality and I'm positive about it,' commented Ajit Singh. 'I feel furious when I hear fools and rogues speaking ill of her. I feel *ki* they should be shot down on the spot!'

'Yes, I agree with you,' said Ramprasad. 'She is the purest and most virtuous person I have ever met in my life. Even to think that she is Anand's—even to think so is sinful . . .'

'Well, so far so good,' said Ajit Singh. 'Now what about the final assault? Anand is at last involved in all our pious and religious schemes. To proceed any further with them would mean huge expense. Preparatory committees are all right, but how about the real business for which we are enacting all this drama?'

'Sardarji is right,' agreed Sinha. 'We should now quickly get Anand's okay on the irrigation project before we get started, if at all, on the religious ceremonies. Once he approves it, I will not only do a Chandi yagna, I'll make it Shata Chandi (hundredfold ceremony) or even a Sahasra Chandi (thousandfold ceremony) for greater effect . . .'

'You're right,' corroborated Ramprasad. 'Look, I'll tell you what. Let us all three invite Akka to a vegetarian dinner and tell her she will have to pin him down. What about tomorrow night?'

Accordingly, they assembled at Ramprasad's house again. The host smoothed over any surprise Aruna might have felt about the other two guests, by saying they were old friends who were visitors to town and who had told him of their respect for her and her great interest in religion; he thought, therefore, that she would like to see them again. Aruna agreed amiably, and they spent the first half of the evening listening to the devotional songs of Lata Mangeshkar, Vishnupant Pagnis, Vishnu Digambar Paluskar, Chittoor Nagaiah and many others. They sipped fresh black grape juice, a speciality of the region. As they went in to a sumptuous vegetarian dinner, Aruna wondered when they would get to the point, for she was very sure the moment she saw the other two guests that there was more to this dinner than was apparent. Perhaps there were other religious events in the offing for which they needed her support.

As the night advanced, the trio steered the conversation skilfully towards the Vijayasagar Project and the file pending sanction by the minister for irrigation. Gradually, they stepped up the pressure. Aruna naturally said she had no idea what was happening with that project. Finally, the host and his scheming friends were forced to ask her point-blank to influence the minister.

'I don't understand you,' she said at last. 'What has that project got to do with me?'

They couldn't believe their ears. Maybe she was pretending ignorance in order to demand a higher price, they thought at first.

'Akka,' Ramprasad began, 'we will be completely ruined if you don't help us. Please have mercy.'

'It is God alone who can have mercy on man, Prasadji,' she replied calmly. 'I'm sure if you are in the right, Anand will decide in your favour.'

'Mataji,' Ajit Singh chipped in, 'this is a heartless world; even right things need strong recommendations.'

'Not with Anand, I'm sure of that,' she replied confidently.

'Deviji,' explained Sinha, 'in this wretched irrigation department so many matters are right but not straightforward, so to speak. Our case is one such. So unless you persuade the minister, he won't do it. That's the snag.'

'Then that is a real snag, I'm afraid,' Aruna agreed. 'If it is not straightforward, I'm sure he won't do it, persuasion or no persuasion.'

'Akka,' urged Ramprasad, 'you can persuade him, I'm sure.'

'No, I can't . . .'

'Yes, you can,' insisted Sinha. 'We know of your great influence with the minister, Deviji. Please don't put us off. Please pick up the phone and do the trick as you did in my Chandi yagna matter.'

'And my Children's Home proposal,' echoed Ajit Singh.

'And my *Kumbhabhishekam* programme,' added Ramprasad.

She stared at them silently for a long time. Then in a disgusted voice she said, 'What are you talking about? All that was God's work and I did persuade Anand to help. I didn't see anything wrong with that. It's good that in God's work he promised to oblige, but I never interfere in his government work. I'm sorry but I can't help you with your project.'

She rose to leave.

Completely stunned, they mechanically pressed their palms together in feeble namastes as she left the house. None of them had the presence of mind to see her to the gate. They came to life only when her car started up. By the time they rushed out of the house, she was gone.

Enraged beyond description, they abused Aruna with as much ferocity as they could muster.

'The bitch!' muttered Ajit Singh.

'The dirty whore!' spat Sinha.

'The dirty whoring bitch!' exploded Ramprasad.

'We'll put an end to her happiness—and his!' Sinha snarled viciously, and the others readily echoed his sentiment.

# Part III

# 25

WHEN TWO MINISTERS ARE AT LOGGERHEADS, SEVERAL ISSUES could fuel the row. For instance, it could be about a portfolio. About a favour done to someone. About group rivalries in their district. About who is more popular. And quite often, about who is closer to the chief minister. None of these factors, however, applied to the feud between Anand and Shekhar. They were not rivals for the same portfolio; each was happy with what Chaudhury gave him. There was no dispute about any favours; such matters did not concern them too much. Both were popular, each in his own way; that aspect never became a bone of contention. They hailed from different districts and had no local rivalry to hang their quarrels on. Both kept their distance from, or proximity to—whichever way you looked at it—the chief minister; both knew that Chaudhury was nobody's fool. In short, their conflict could not be traced to the usual reasons that divide politicians. Unable to diagnose the phenomenon, 'knowledgeable' political circles often remarked that cause or no cause, Anand and Shekhar couldn't help attacking one another, just for the sake of it. That's the way of politicians—and dogs, someone added contemptuously.

Shekhar and Anand admired and detested each other. Shekhar praised Anand's brilliance, but called him a 'starry-eyed fool'. Anand commended Shekhar's organizing ability but thought him an evil genius; only harm could result from whatever he did. He deserved the nickname Vakra Buddhi (crooked mind) one hundred per cent, Anand opined. Many others agreed with him, but few spoke out. Politicians are discreet while speaking about dangerous individuals.

*

Shekhar had first tasted insufferable injustice when he was a small child. On the day he expected to begin school, he was sent to tend buffaloes. All the other children of the feudal family he lived with entered school with the usual ceremony. Their home was a large rural mansion known as a garhi. It was in the middle of the village, with dismal-looking huts all around. The contrast between the privileged inmates of the big house and the hovels of other villagers made no sense to Shekhar in his years of infancy. He grew up in the garhi, but was never allowed to experience any comfort or enjoy the small pleasures so abundantly available to the other children. He couldn't understand why this should happen until someone older than himself, who suffered from the same discrimination, put him wise one day. 'My dear ignorant fool,' he said, 'you'll understand these things later. Just don't whine; keep your mouth shut. You're not the deshmukh's son; you're a bloody dasi's child. They can kick you out of the garhi whenever they wish. And they will, I assure you, if you don't behave! . . . '

'What's a dasi?' Shekhar shot back, unable to contain his curiosity about the reason for the atrocious treatment he received. Even at five, he knew he was physically and intellectually superior to all the privileged children in the garhi. He had proved this conclusively in the fist fights they had had, and the few singing and recitation sessions at the time of festivals. So he was furious when he was not sent to the private school set up within the garhi for the children of the deshmukh family. Normally, he would have considered freedom from school a blessing, as many others did at his age. Yet, when he was denied entry, he concluded that school must be something desirable. Especially when the other children were forced to attend it, often against their wishes.

'I'm afraid you won't understand what a dasi means,' explained the older boy. 'Didn't you see your mother sweeping the floor and pressing the legs of those other women whom they call ranis?'

'Yes, I did,' answered Shekhar, beginning to see some light.

'Did you ever see a rani pressing your mother's legs?'

'O no,' Shekhar said. 'In fact, I once saw a fat ugly woman kick my mother for no fault of hers. I felt like kicking her back really hard, but my mother looked at me sternly. Then she stopped taking me to that woman's room altogether . . .'

'So, now you understand the difference between a rani and a dasi?' said the older boy triumphantly, glad to have confronted the stubborn brat with a few facts of life.

'I think I do,' answered Shekhar tentatively. 'I don't like it. I don't like it at all.'

'Who bothers about your likes and dislikes, you idiot?' the other boy shouted. 'This is how it is out here. So keep your peace and mind your business!'

Shekhar said nothing, but remained angry. When someone called him 'Shakya'—a derisive version of his name—he would squirm inside at the insult. In a fit of rage, he once called the youngest deshmukh's youngest son 'Seenya' (Srinivas was his full name). Shekhar was soundly thrashed for his audacity by a senior servant of the garhi. More than the physical wounds, he nursed the wound to his self-esteem permanently.

As he grew older, he noticed several strange goings-on. He would often wake up around midnight in their modest quarter, and find that his mother, who had put him to bed earlier, had left the room. He followed her a few times unnoticed and saw her enter the bedroom of one of the deshmukh brothers or of someone who had just arrived as a guest of the family. Quite often some officer came from the town, and his mother carried food for him to the guest house in the garhi's premises. Shekhar often found that his mother stayed in the guest house much longer than she would have needed to place the food there. Sometimes he would peep in and find the door locked in broad daylight, for no reason he could think of. It was all very perplexing; he just couldn't understand what happened behind the closed door.

Sometimes a munim (clerk) or other minor functionary of the estate would walk into their quarter, bringing a toffee or toy for Shekhar. His mother would think up some errand that would keep Shekhar away for more than an hour. Once, when he returned home earlier than expected, he found the room bolted from inside. He felt like pounding on it; but a feeling of embarrassment took hold of him and he fled, not knowing where, until he stood at the other end of the village, panting, wanting to cry. He couldn't explain what he felt, yet the feeling was real, unmistakable.

Gradually and painfully, it dawned on him that his mother was sexually used by all and sundry in the garhi. Fathers as well as sons of the deshmukh clan called her to their beds at will—the former for occasional diversion and the latter for sexual initiation and practice of sorts. She endured the brutality without complaint. She simply considered it her duty, the dasi's mandatory duty in the feudal context. She could not escape it. Generations of serfs had been conditioned in this manner.

By the time Shekhar was eight, he understood enough of the feudal system to seethe with rage and discontent. He was now old enough to tend buffaloes, along with many other urchins. During their day-long chats while the cattle grazed, he gathered a copious repertoire of swear words, a deeper appreciation of the meaning of 'status', a detailed knowledge of sexual matters—and above all, a measure of crude wisdom, the wisdom of the survivor, wisdom that proved extremely useful to him later in life.

His mother was unquestionably the loveliest woman in the garhi, indeed in the village. No one knew who her parents were. They merely believed that the senior landlord, who had since died, had bought her as a child of twelve from her parents in a distant village, when the most devastating famine in living memory stalked the whole district. While the landlord and his wife were struck by the girl's unrivalled beauty, her parents had thought it safest to sell her to the wealthy landlord family. She would at least live a comfortable life, they thought. For the rest, they reasoned, it did not matter what became of her as a woman, so long as she didn't have to go immediately into prostitution to keep body and soul together. In a manner of speaking, the landlords owned her, body, mind and soul—or such was the logic that everyone accepted at the time.

After his mother had had a few forced abortions and was reinstated as the object of everyone's promiscuity and barbaric lusts, Shekhar was born—or rather, allowed to be born. It was not clear if that was a concession to motherhood or just a mistake. His mother never questioned anyone. However, she did feel happy, in a subdued way, when she saw young Shekhar grow up into a healthy and vigorous child.

Shekhar loved his mother, of course. But he had seen so much, he could not decide whether she was an angel or a devil. He tried to avoid that debate within himself. At ten, he developed just one intense, overpowering desire—to perpetrate upon all the women in the deshmukh family exactly what his mother had been subjected to by the clan's swinish males.

His knowledge was very advanced for a boy his age, although the very thought of it, because of the way in which his mother was treated, made him uneasy. However, talk about sex dominated the conversation of the boys he mixed with. Several older boys among them volunteered gossip about the sexual activity in the garhi: some of it was true, but for the most part it was the product of their fertile imagination. While the landlords, they said, ran after maidservants and prostitutes all the time, their fat and ugly wives preyed upon every good-looking young servant in the garhi. Some of the deshmukh wives were reputed to be sexual gluttons; they ordered the poor undernourished boys into bed at any time of the night or day, and milked them dry of all vitality in a matter of months. The husbands looked the other way. One landlord, known to be impotent, always looked at everything except his wife's bedroom! Such were the stories traded among the poor boys in the grazing grounds of the village. They derived immense

271

satisfaction from these anecdotes, toughening their sensibilities into a creed of hate and revenge.

In this, the experience of Shekhar and his friends was no different from any other brutally subjugated class. They chafed and raged and wished all evil upon their employers (who often were also their owners), but eventually served them for the rest of their lives. They had no escape from drudgery, no outlet from slavery. Ironically, the predator landlords often received loyal affection and gratitude from their servants, for the simple reason that the servants, even with their deep hatred, could not hate for ever. At some point, they realized the futility of resisting an oppressive system that had flourished for centuries. At the same time, an instinctive fatalism provided the much-needed philosophical balm, along with a pretext to live.

As he grew older, Shekhar was consumed by an overwhelming restlessness and a constant smouldering anger. Undeniably brilliant, he was not allowed to formally develop his mind. His genius, people said, was due to deshmukh 'seed': after all, the landlord's blood ran in his veins. No one cared to explain why the landlord's own offspring were worthless dimwits, unless they were born of non-deshmukh seed. They called him by various nicknames: *shata-bindu*—outcome of a hundred drops of semen—hybrid, bastard and a host of other derogatory epithets which he found intolerable. He got into countless fights with other boys—even with adults—over this topic. His questionable paternity became his most sensitive point. He could never be respected, whatever his prowess and achievements. He was and would always remain a *dasiputra*, without status. Everything was rooted in this fact.

One morning Shekhar disappeared from the garhi. There was a mild flutter, but everything subsided within a few days. They alerted a few surrounding villages, half-heartedly. His mother, of course, was in no position to search any further. The garhi dismissed Shekhar as dead, lost, abducted, lured away—the deshmukh clan did not care. Those whom his mother served were too callous to commiserate with her. As a dasi, even though she had lost her only son, she evoked no sympathy.

It was a long and tortuous journey for Shekhar. He passed through smugglers' dens, orphanages, jails; he spent time with thieves and pickpockets and children who laboured in the streets, homosexuals, pimps and an endless variety of criminals. He cultivated them, studied them, fraternized with them, loved them, hated them. Above all, he exploited them, made them a ladder for his ascent. Somehow, even in the extreme insecurity and squalor of his wandering life, he managed to teach himself to read and write with a fair degree of proficiency. He also acquired competence in many other areas. He saw this as a means by which he could avenge his mother's brutalization and the insults he had suffered unceasingly as a social outcast.

One day he participated in a raid with an underground resistance group that looted and killed. But they were criminals with a difference, he noticed. They were apparently inspired—in varying degrees—by an ideology. Some had a deep and unalterable conviction that the oppressor class in society needed to be exterminated. Others hypocritically mouthed the group's ideological precepts but remained uncommitted to them. Shekhar was not greatly enamoured of the ideology but he liked the idea of liquidating landlords. He moved with the group for a few months, but found that he couldn't bring himself to spend the rest of his life in perpetual hiding.

His conspiratorial life gave him good connections with the underworld. He became the confidante of a smuggler gang which, it turned out, had close liaison with some important politicians. Shekhar instinctively liked the politicians; more so when he found they responded to his overtures, appreciating his ruthless efficiency. Gradually he began to serve as a trusted carrier of cash and valuables from one side to the other. Both sides were quick to acknowledge how useful he was: being unknown locally, Shekhar could always bluff about the source of the cash, unless the police tortured a confession out of him. But in all likelihood they would take him to be a common thief. He might be thrashed now and then—a small price indeed. The smuggler and the politician were safe. It was a perfect arrangement.

Shekhar was, however, never entirely happy with having to be with smugglers and other criminals. For him, his stint as a smuggler was a temporary halt on his way to better things. Once he got into the politicians' good books, he jettisoned the smugglers. Having equipped himself with some education meanwhile, he began to shine in the political field as a good organizer, campaigner, manager and second-in-command. In the 1952 election his boss got elected to the state legislative assembly, mainly through Shekhar's indefatigable efforts. Or so the boss was made to believe.

The boss had married a second time at a fairly advanced age, creating an extremely piquant situation for himself *vis-à-vis* his young wife. And when a natural liaison emerged between her and Shekhar, there was nothing anyone could do about it. The boss wanted to get rid of Shekhar, whose personal ambitions he found a threat, but the wife became a formidable hurdle in his way. And when the party wanted a younger person as its candidate in the 1957 general election, the choice fell inevitably on Shekhar. His sponsor was none other than his boss, whose wife had him in her clutches and forced him to grovel in support of Shekhar. That was how Shekhar, MLA, shot into the political firmament, superseding many senior party men who had clawed their way up, step by painful step, for decades. This was a notable feat by any standard. It created its own momentum. The rest of the story was well known.

When the battle of the giants in Afrozabad ended in a clear victory for Chaudhury, the scramble for ministerial positions started immediately. Almost everyone, irrespective of which side of the divide he had been on during the conflict, approached Chaudhury, pledged his loyalty and staked his claim for a berth in the ministry. There were a few exceptions, however: people like Anand and Shekhar. Anand knew what was at stake, and so wasn't keen to accept a ministerial position. Shekhar knew that Chaudhury would not trust him anyway. His recent role as Mahendranath's chief henchman was too fresh to evoke any favourable response from the new chief.

So, when Chaudhury offered positions in the new ministry to both men, he seemed to have pulled off the unbelievable. The surprise in political circles bordered on shock. One press hawk who was on very friendly terms with the chief minister grilled him in a private conversation with questions on these selections. They made no sense to any politician, he said. However, Chaudhury had the answers ready. 'Well, when there is a group fight, you have to fight like hell,' he observed. 'No holds barred when you're in the thick of the battle. But when you arrive, you have to find at least a few fellows who possess qualities other than being mere torch-bearers. You know that I have packed the cabinet with as many faithfuls as I needed to. Two efficient fellows added to that crowd from outside shouldn't really hurt. On the contrary, my government will perhaps show results. After all, brother, you have to think of the people at some point!'

'Well, Anand has never been active in any group; he is an unknown quantity to many . . .'

'To many, yes, but not to me. I know him through and through, even if he never indulged in the group game.'

'And the other fellow, Shekhar, indulged rather excessively in the group game, didn't he? So how come he is also in? . . .'

'In his case the logic is different. You see, Shekhar is more dangerous outside the cabinet than he could ever be inside. Besides, his efficiency is available to anyone who befriends him. He doesn't care two hoots for either group, mine or Mahendranath's . . .'

'Then what do you think he is after?'

'I don't know and don't care. All I know is that some persons simply can't be pigeon-holed into groups. They may have their own motivations . . . In fact, they do.'

'They say these two fellows don't see eye to eye. They're sniping at each other all the time.'

'Yes. Suits me fine . . . I can play one against the other, if necessary. Knowing them as I do, however, I don't think I will ever need to do that.'

'How are you so sure?'

'How are you ever sure about any damn thing in this slippery game of politics? You deal in coal, as they say, so you can't hope to keep your hands lily-white all the time.'

275

Well . . . Chaudhury is certainly maturing into a clever statesman, the journalist told himself . . .

# 26

THE STRATEGY TO DEMOLISH ANAND WAS NEAR PERFECT, formulated after deep deliberation. Its main architect was Shekhar, who was careful to orchestrate the action from deep cover. Its executors were a motley crowd of people such as the disgruntled contractors and others who had failed to enlist Anand's support in a variety of their dubious schemes, or had felt aggrieved by his unyielding attitude in taking substantive decisions in his department. Some of his ministerial colleagues who disliked him and had been waiting for an opportunity to strike, decided the time was right; however, like Shekhar, they were careful to operate discreetly as they were not clear where exactly Anand stood in the chief minister's esteem. It would be fatal for their own political futures if they attacked Anand openly and then found themselves at odds with Chaudhury's own position.

The main thrust of the plan to destroy Anand was, naturally, his relationship with Aruna. A whisper campaign was built up, accompanied by selective media leaks, wherein Anand's political success was deliberately attributed to Aruna. Scores of people in whose favour Anand's decision happened to turn out in the usual course, rushed to Aruna to thank her for interceding on their behalf. They said it was she who ensured that 'justice' was done. She didn't know what they were talking about, so didn't know how to react to their effusive gratitude. It was an extremely embarrassing situation. Usually she maintained an uneasy silence, not wanting to offend them by saying they were mistaken or deluded.

Stage two: She was reputed to have unfailing influence over Anand. What do you know? She can literally take hold of his hand and make him write whatever she wants. You don't know anything, your information is hopelessly out of date, friend! The latest is that Anand's files first go to Aruna these days. She writes the orders on a separate sheet of paper and he merely copies the order in the concerned file and affixes his signature. She has now become his most private private secretary. Indeed, she has become his boss. Maybe he is the secretary, if you ask me.

Stage three: Larger crowds at Aruna's residence. Supplicants of all kinds. Those who wanted to buy her influence. Those who tried to pressurize her to use her influence. And lastly, those who wanted to blackmail her into using her influence. None of them succeeded in getting her to oblige, yet inevitably, given the law of averages, some of the supplicants found that Anand had decided in their favour. And, although Aruna had not had a hand in a single decision he made, if he decided in your favour, it was a result of her influence. And if he decided against you, then it was because of the other party having won her over. Either way, the crowds continued to congregate at her residence unabated. There was just no escape from them.

Stage four: Where money, pressure and blackmail failed to work, they tried to appeal to her ego, her sense of her own worth. Madam, this is your duty; you can't refuse. You owe it to the people. You alone can do it. The minister is just and efficient, but he is too busy. If you just recommend my case, the problem will disappear in no time. Please, madam, please, please, please! Alternatively: I'm so grateful to you, madam. God bless you, you saved my family (the family was often present)! The wife and children would fall at Aruna's feet in a dramatic gesture in front of everyone. God bless you—and him! God bless you both . . . both . . . both . . . The concept came to stay. Both. Inseparably both. Minister and lady legislator. The man in authority and his girlfriend.

Stage five: The identification of the two as indivisible deepened, given the public perception that had at first been skilfully orchestrated and had then begun to snowball. At every function, the organizers would invite both of them to be present. He would inaugurate, she would preside, or vice versa. At the very least, she would be asked to make a speech. Meanwhile, a new rumour spread: Anand wouldn't accept any invitation unless Aruna was invited too. Didn't you know that she would harass him day and night if he attended a function without her? Or wouldn't talk to him for God knows how long. And the pity of it is that poor Anand can't breathe without her. Well, well, that is what constitutes a ministerial romance, my dear fellow! . . . No Anand without Aruna, that's the formula, see? . . . Result: more and more invitations, more and more journeys together, more and more dinners together, more and more time together. The comment went round: If you are a minister, you can get away with anything! That's what our democracy has come to, brother!

Stage six: The identification with Aruna threatened to over-shadow Anand completely. Shekhar engineered various meetings wherein it was insinuated to Aruna, very subtly, that she must stick to him all the time . . . closer . . . still closer. You know how political power operates, they suggested. Who knows what will happen, with all those friends, relatives, sycophants (both male and female) hovering around him like flies over a lump of sugar? True, Anand is not amenable to such influences; we know him very well . . . and he is much too devoted to you, Arunaji, to go astray. Still, I'm merely leaving this thought with you, for whatever it is worth . . . You know best, of course. One thing, however, I can't understand, Arunaji. Why do his friends and relatives always talk ill of you? Always, non-stop? Why do they look daggers at you? Why do they keep trying to poison Anand's mind against you? That is what really escapes me. What a pity! After all that you have done for him!

This last was true enough. Anand's friends, relatives, colleagues, were all on one side; Aruna alone on the other. This was the line-up at the personal level. Each side had reasons to dislike the other—all in Anand's interest, as they saw it. They didn't bother to ascertain what Anand himself thought his own interest to be. His friends wanted him to prosper; did it matter that they would prosper too, in the process? How many would sacrifice their own interests for Anand's was another matter. All of them agreed, however, that his association with Aruna would ruin him. On that there was unanimity.

Aruna was equally clear and firm in her line of thinking. The worst enemies of a person in power are his in-laws and self-seeking friends, she asserted. She knew, or thought she knew, about some cases in which Anand's friends reportedly influenced him and made him take wrong decisions. Those who lost out in those cases took great care to brainwash her to this effect, in a variety of subtle ways. These whispers, compounded by those initiated by Shekhar, made her develop an even greater allergy to Anand's friends, relatives, supplicants, colleagues—everyone except herself. And the war between the two sets of well-wishers began to escalate: it would continue, ferocious and implacable, to the finish—to Anand's finish, that is.

This war for possession of Anand proved to be a windfall for Shekhar and the others opposed to Anand. Some of them continued to arrange more and more functions that required the journeys of Anand and Aruna together—on long tours and several halts en route. Others, meanwhile, carried on a campaign of sympathy for Anand. He has fallen, they said, fallen prey to a crafty woman with easy morals. They condemned the woman all the time. It was so much easier—and a more effective strategy in the campaign to destroy Anand.

As the campaign of calumny mounted, there were others who unexpectedly came to Anand's rescue, including legislators who had hitherto been undecided on the issue but now decided that matters had gone far enough. For weeks, the lobbies of the legislative assembly, and other meeting places, were filled with legislators airing one or the other view. One group would say, How shocking! . . . How could anyone be so reckless? What has public life come to, anyway? . . . At this rate, who can survive in politics except scoundrels and adventurers? . . . But, my dear friend, that's what public life is, for heaven's sake—really and truly public. You're always under a searchlight, the most ruthless and probing searchlight. You are accountable for every moment of your life, your movements, public or private. It's an undeniable fact that a person in public life has no such thing as a private life, nor should he expect to have one. That's it, take it or leave it; no point in fretting.

Those opposed to them would reply: What utter nonsense! A person in public life has no private life, eh? Can you show me one public man or woman without a private life? Please talk sense. Whom a man or a woman sleeps with, or how many for that matter, should be nobody else's business. People ought to care two hoots for such nonsense. What a public man does for the public alone is important, or ought to be . . . all else is only meant to divert attention from the main issues. All else is idle scandal-mongering.

My dear free lover, this is India that is Bharat, the India of ancient rishis and munis, the India of Mahatma Gandhi. How can you forget this basic fact? Who will put up with an immoral person here, however efficient or beneficent he or she may be?

Following on these rumblings, Anand's opponents prepared to administer the *coup de grâce*. Some of them wanted to upstage Shekhar—the 'bastard' who had become too important. On their own, they deployed a hugely dirty—and therefore hugely popular—tabloid. The proprietor 'managed' suitably and persuded to instruct the editor to run a major story on the Anand-Aruna affair. True, it was mentioned every so often in the print media, but only in passing; Anand was too popular and efficient a minister for the media to indulge in any exaggerated reporting on this aspect just then. But given the increasingly high visibility of the minister and his 'friend' in public, the press had begun to take a renewed if minor interest in the affair. Now, the tabloid *People's Herald* had a front-page story on the affair, giving dates and times of their assignations, and highly imaginary accounts of their passionate love. At the end of all this description—which was calculated to titillate readers and thereby take good care of the sales of the tabloid—the article suddenly concluded on a self-righteous note, denouncing such behaviour on the part of men and women in public life. Shekhar was unaware of this particular story.

Anand was in Delhi on state business when the story appeared, but Aruna discovered its existence in the most embarrassing circumstances. When she walked into the assembly one morning, a sudden hush descended on the score or so MLAs gathered in the lobby. She wondered what they had been talking about, and what they were trying to hide from her, but then shrugged it off—it was a price you had to pay for being a woman in an almost exclusively male world which had more than its share of crude and vulgar men. She sat down on a sofa and began to examine the day's newspapers arrayed on the table in front of her. Her eye was drawn instantly to the tabloid because of the photograph of Anand and herself on the front page. She picked up the tabloid and began to read aloud. The crowd around her thinned at once as the embarrassed MLAs fled; somehow, even these rough-hewn, often coarse men, many of whom had privately gossiped about the affair, felt this was too much. As Aruna read through the story, she was first enraged, then dismayed, and finally completely crushed. Her eyes filled with tears; then she became conscious of the stares of people around her. Determined not to lose her composure, she blinked back her tears and stood up. Anand . . . she had to speak to Anand without further delay.

She knew he was in Delhi. She looked at her watch; there was an Indian Airlines flight to Delhi at noon. She would take that. She gripped the slanderous paper in her hand and was walking out of the assembly building when Shekhar walked in. He greeted her cordially but his cordiality turned to concern when he saw her distraught face. 'What is it, sister? What is the matter?' he asked, and understood what it was when he saw the tabloid in her hand. Gently, he took it from her and scanned it—for the first time. 'The scoundrel,' he said softly. His first reaction was of anger. The tabloid had overdone the slander—much beyond the worst that the scandal sheet had done in the recent past. The editor at someone's signal, had obviously done what he thought was his best. Shekhar did feel concerned on Aruna's behalf; his war was with Anand and he would destroy him utterly, he had promised himself; but he genuinely liked Aruna and was sorry she was also being destroyed in the process. However, Aruna did not reciprocate his goodwill and looked stern and incredulous.

As Shekhar expressed his concern and surprise, she was sure they were feigned. She was convinced that it was he who had got the story planted in some way. She could hardly believe that he would have the gall to stand there so coolly and pretend innocence and solicitude. She knew just how much he hated Anand and how he would do anything to bring him down. And here he was attempting to assuage her anxiety. She shivered in loathing and her face must have communicated her feelings to him, for his concern was replaced in a flash by annoyance.

'You think I had something to do with this, don't you?' he said in a harsh whisper.

She did not reply but the look on her face was answer enough. He stalked away from her angrily, throwing the paper to the ground. She picked it up and immediately left for the airport.

*

Anand had just finished an afternoon meeting in his room at the state guest house in Delhi with some officials in the Central irrigation ministry when his door was pushed open and Aruna walked in. As he stared at her in surprise, she flew into his arms and began weeping uncontrollably. He held her close, stroked her hair, her face, thoroughly mystified. What on earth was going on? Why had she flown to Delhi when she knew that he was to return to Afrozabad in a day or two? . . . She was so distraught that he didn't know how to calm her down, and decided to let the sobs abate by themselves—which they did, minute by minute. He waited patiently.

Calming down a little, she opened her handbag and pulled out the crumpled tabloid and thrust it at him. As he read the story, he showed no distress or surprise beyond a slight tightening of his lips.

Then between hiccups she told him about her encounter with Shekhar in the lobby of the assembly and voiced her suspicion that he was behind the outrage.

'You're probably right,' Anand said grimly. 'He dislikes me enough, I suppose, for him to want to try and pull me down. Now, contrary to my belief, it is clear that he can go to the extent of destroying you also in the process.'

'You must get him before that,' Aruna said. 'But first I want to destroy the miserable wretch who published this trash. Can't you close the paper down? Surely you can, some infraction of the law, something illegal, I'm sure you'll find something.'

Anand had never seen her like this before. She had always been forthright and never minced words, but this aspect of hers—of revenge through the use of power—was new.

'Tell me, what are we going to do?' she demanded.

He tapped her shoulder and said, 'It's outrageous, and I'm as upset as you are, but there's nothing to be gained by losing control and lashing out. That's what they're waiting for—Shekhar, the editor, whoever. We should take this calmly, plan our next move carefully. And listen, you should calm down, all right? We're both in this together and now that you've told me, I'll work something out. Besides, remember that at the very beginning, when I became a minister, I warned you that we would have to be prepared for something like this.'

He smiled and wiped the tears from her face. When she spoke she was calm. 'All right, I see what you mean. But we can't let them get away with it, can we?'

'No, we can't, Aruna, but this is politics, where everything is fair.'

She looked ready to break down again and he said, earnestly, 'Listen, it will work out, I promise you. It's a dirty game and there is a lot of evil out there but so long as we are together, we'll win, all right?

She nodded and gave him a wan smile.

Even as he comforted her, Anand was fascinated by the paradox she presented—the bold, modern, emancipated woman in public life on the one hand, and a remnant of the traditional Hindu woman on the other—intimidated by taboos, burdened by complexes, and yearning for the complete independence that seemed constantly to be beyond her grasp.

They were silent for a while, then Aruna said, 'Now, tell me, what next?'

'What do you want to do?' asked Anand.

'I want to destroy that fellow!' she said fiercely, pointing to the slanderous periodical that had fallen to the floor.

'Listen, Aruna,' Anand said, 'how do you destroy a nobody? He is a parasite who lives on slander . . . Who doesn't know him? And who doesn't make use of him when needed?'

'But you said you'll take care of him. And Shekhar too,' she said, beginning to whimper.

'Yes, I will, in my own way. But I'm not going to do something foolish impulsively, because they have been very clever, don't you see? They may have got the facts wrong, but who will go into the truth?'

Aruna looked shocked. He quickly placated her. 'Don't misunderstand me, Aruna. All I am saying is there are certain things that we cannot talk about and make a public debate, so we'll have to find a way around them, and solve the problem.'

'What is your way?' she countered, irritated by his lack of obvious anger, his calm air of deliberation.

'I have always dismissed things like this. They can't hurt me, because I am not running after anything. I hardened myself against all kinds of gossip long ago. I can stand the malice and the mockery of others. And when I've arrived at a decision, nothing anyone says makes the slightest difference. The same goes for us. We promised ourselves that we would handle all the problems that cropped up, without getting flustered.'

'But I'd like to destroy those men,' Aruna said again.

'Why? Because they maligned you?'

'No, not at all,' she replied firmly. 'I want to destroy them because they want to destroy you!'

'Why do you think they want to destroy me?'

'Because they're jealous of you, they are your rivals, they want you out of the position you're holding . . .'

'Now, Aruna, listen,' Anand persisted with relentless logic. 'That's only part of the story. They want to destroy me because they think I am out to destroy them. They think I am their enemy. I am one of those in the party about whom they have such apprehensions. But this is not the time for the showdown. I have no desire to fight them on *their* terms, especially because my fight is not with individuals but with what I see is wrong, know is wrong. This is why I'm not interested in wasting my energy trying to destroy X or Y. So I don't care what they say. And this attempt to malign us will just peter out, you'll see.'

'But don't you see that even if they don't succeed this time, he, or they, won't stop until you are utterly destroyed? You might not have any personal animus against them, but they definitely hate you and will not rest until you are finished. You talk like a philosopher but they will continue to attack you. And they have no scruples. They will attack your weaknesses; and this they think is your greatest weakness.'

'They may think they will demolish me on this count, but as I've said, I'll be playing into their hands if I react the way you suggest. My way would be to redouble my efforts to make an undeniable difference to the people. I'll work, work, work—work to distraction or death, so that public support will be overwhelming and trivialities will pale into insignificance. This is what is called drawing a longer line. Frankly, I don't see any other way, for all human beings are imperfect. That's how great achievers have acquitted themselves through the ages; and that's the way I'll fight back.'

Aruna said nothing for a while. Then, slowly but with deliberation, she said, 'Your rationale is correct; but my instinct tells me you won't succeed. My way is different. I shall confront them politically, head-on. I shall not rest until I destroy them or they destroy me, in the process. In that respect, both of us have the same determination. Right now, my impulse is one of unmitigated hate. I don't care what they say about my morals. Yet, the fact remains that they have attacked me on grounds that no woman can or should tolerate being attacked on. I shall break them, break the forces behind them, break the party, if necessary, or be broken trying. And God, I am sure, will be on my side. I adore you, Anand, but right now I can only feel the desire for revenge that is consuming me. You will be scorched if you get in the way. I think you are genuinely above such things, and that is one of the reasons I admire you so much, but I'm sorry I can't be like you. I'm just not made that way . . .'

Anand offered no reply to this, just smiled at her. He stroked her hair affectionately. How beautiful she was, he thought, how strong her will! He could see her point of view clearly, and felt both anger and sorrow at the abuse and degradation being heaped upon her. Yet he was sure that the solution to the problem was not a blind counter-attack on their attackers.

'Aruna,' he said gently, 'I understand your anger, it's not that I don't feel enraged and humiliated myself. But I want you to trust me in this matter despite your instincts and impulses. Promise me you won't do anything rash until I've looked into the matter, all right? I'll take it up as soon as we get back.'

Back in Afrozabad, Anand spent a great deal of time talking to his friends and supporters, trying to get an accurate fix on the situation. Slowly he began to discern the extent of the plot that had been hatched against him. Many of his oldest friends advised him to get out of the cabinet.

Dr Sudershan, his oldest and closest friend, said bluntly, 'I know you won't like my advice, blind as you have become to what is staring you in the face, but I would suggest that you resign your ministerial job. I am more than convinced that from now on, it will only be a non-stop nosedive for you. I know you have no vested interest in political power; maybe if you had, you wouldn't have behaved the way you have. So choose now and be done with the dilemma, in time!'

Anand did not react immediately, but Sudershan's fierce appeal touched him to the core. After all, it was the doctor who had had the last say in convincing Anand to continue in public life. Anand was rather amused to see now that the same brave Sudershan had suddenly developed cold feet—and swift legs to run away—at the very first serious hurdle in political life, a life that is nothing but a hurdle race—and a surprise hurdle race—through and through! Yet, he owed him, at the very least, a genuine response after thinking over the matter dispassionately.

He gave the matter his deepest thought. He did not consult Aruna; he knew that would not help . . . he gave himself just one month's time—to sort out the matter to his own satisfaction.

# 27

CHAUDHURY IMPATIENTLY STUBBED OUT HIS CIGARETTE IN THE ashtray next to him. It was the eleventh cigarette he had smoked since breakfast. For hours he had been pacing up and down his study, trying very hard to order his thoughts and control his exasperation. He read the Prime Minister's letter—the loved-and-dreaded fortnightly letter that all chief ministers received regularly. Couched in the beautiful language characteristic of Jawaharlal Nehru, it was a treat, a beacon light, a timely and educative pointer to the tasks ahead. It contained news, views, fancies, fantasies, literary gems, words of profound wisdom—and much more. It challenged and inspired a few perceptive chief ministers. As for the others who were impervious to everything save their own interests, they probably thought it a waste of time and attention, though no one said so.

Chaudhury alternated between utmost admiration and occasional annoyance when he read Panditji's letters. On international affairs, they were brilliant. Chaudhury was all for non-alignment (whatever that meant, he added in an aside to a few close friends). On internal matters too, he commended much that Panditji had to say—on the subject of a mixed economy, for instance. Chaudhury found mixed economy eminently convenient. 'Pragmatic' was the word, he often reminded himself. He was not so sure about the public sector, yet he saw several virtues in it too. The general managers of the units in the state were eager to oblige him in a variety of ways. Since working for profits was almost a sin in the eyes of the public sector, in those days anyway, there were no stringent criteria of efficiency or any orientation towards achieving results. So you could dump unwanted men by the hundred in any public sector industry. You could satisfy your political friends and supporters, not to speak of your own in-laws.

However, the issue that was nagging Chaudhury that morning was the subject of Panditji's latest letter: land reforms. The letter clearly brought out the urgent need to pass and implement the land ceiling laws. They had been languishing in almost all the states, the letter said. Yet, they brooked no delay, the Prime Minister pointed out. He gave detailed figures of the estimated surplus land available in the country and went on to reiterate the incalculable benefit its distribution would bring to landless people. He stressed that agricultural production would increase dramatically when sharecroppers became proprietors. He argued the case lucidly and definitively. It was clear that Jawaharlal Nehru had made up his mind.

There was a crucial point to consider, however, that pricked Chaudhury like a thorn. He knew that land reform was a controversial and problematic issue that could cause social havoc. How could you implement the land ceiling laws, even if you did manage to get them passed through your party's brute majority in the legislature? How could you make the farmer, big or small, part with his land? And why should he? Land, as seen by the farmer, was not just a means of production; it was much more. It was a status symbol. It was a source of security. The farmer's attachment to it was complete and unseverable. Anyone who sold his land was looked down upon as a failure. He would never be able to live down this absolute stigma . . . Chaudhury thus had serious reservations about the idea of imposing ceilings on land. How is it, he asked no one in particular as he paced the room, that the man in the city could amass money and property to any extent and not be subject to any ceiling whatsoever? Was that fair? Was that just? And above all, would ceilings only on land be practicable?

He felt furious at some other chief ministers and party leaders who had vied with one another in extolling land ceilings at several party forums. They had made the slogan sound holy and inviolable. No free discussion followed—because no one was willing to discuss the issue, once the Prime Minister's opinion on that subject became known. Not that Chaudhury had any intention of speaking out himself. Perhaps he expected someone else to raise the banner of dissent, at the very least present the opposing point of view. And those who held similar views kept looking to each other to speak out. In the end, no one spoke except to lend support to the Prime Minister, which the latter did not need so badly anyway. Chaudhury and his ilk came out of the meeting seething with mute rage and frustration.

When Chaudhury accosted some chief ministers later, he got many interesting replies. 'There's a way to deal with Jawaharlal's ideological flights!' one of them remarked with a glint in the eye. 'Pass the resolutions unanimously and you acquire the right to do nothing in the matter! Very easy! . . . See?'

Another senior leader said sagely, 'You have to understand, Chaudhuryji, that Panditji's vision is not a mere vision; it has great practical utility. It sells everywhere and in the bargain takes the wind out of the sails of the ramshackle Opposition groups. They shout about land reforms all the time, without the faintest idea of what land is. The fellows call themselves parties but have ten leaders for every single follower!!'

A third worldly-wise functionary came straight to the point. 'What is the harm in passing this law anyway? The landholders know that they can enter their lands in the names of cats and dogs and unborn children and grandchildren. They leave nothing except rocks and alkaline tracts to swell the government's surplus acreage figures. Suits both sides perfectly, I should think! . . .'

These interpretations had given Chaudhury some relief. But when the Prime Minister's earnest tone rang in his ears, it was impossible to remain unimpressed. Hypocrisy in the face of such overpowering sincerity felt like a heinous sin. That, in short, was the cause of his annoyance.

He remembered the day, years ago, at the Madras session of his party, when he had made a brilliant speech on the socialistic pattern of society, without meaning a word of it. Jawaharlal Nehru had given him an approving nod, he recalled. Did Jawaharlal still remember? And if he did, what would he expect of him now? . . . He almost regretted having made that clever speech, trapping himself in his own rhetoric. He just could not see how he could take away lands from the landlords and survive as chief minister. And what could be more important than his survival as chief minister? . . . The newspapers had already reported a plot, hatched by Mahendranath and his followers, to instigate the landlord lobby, just in case . . . If Chaudhury pursued land reforms, the lobby would make short shrift of him, they calculated. If, on the other hand, Chaudhury faltered, why, that would also be an ideal stick for Mahendranath to beat him with. He would instantly become *persona non grata* with the party high command.

Chaudhury shuddered at the very thought of a confrontation with the landlord lobby. He was at his wits' end. Smoking and pacing the room did not help a bit. In anticipation of some such directive from the Prime Minister, he had sounded out several loyal followers and colleagues in the past few days. The terror among the legislators was quite unnerving. It was true that some years ago, they had abolished the zamindari system introduced by the British—and not a dog had barked. But that, the MLAs pointed out, was a very different matter. The zamindars had become unpopular with the masses anyway, as a result of their pro-British leanings and anti-people activities during the freedom struggle. To abolish their estates did not present any difficulty. Besides, that was the first flush of the post-Independence enthusiasm for reforms. The exit of the zamindars was therefore an occasion for celebration. The party cited it as proof of its determination to emancipate the people . . . Now, when it came to the landlords—often called peasants or farmers—the situation was entirely different. It was nothing less than suicide for the ruling party to expropriate from the landlords a portion of the land they had held for generations. Several members of the party, especially those who owned extensive landed property themselves, had uttered cries of warning. Chaudhury had heard them all out with the utmost patience.

Then, there were several members—notably those who owned no land and therefore had nothing to lose—who waxed eloquent on the need to immediately apply the land ceiling law. That, they urged, would be an earnest of the ruling party's progressive initiatives, which the masses had endorsed in the last election. There should be no going back, no dilution in the implementation of this measure. The party's credibility depended on what they did now, they asserted. We're all on trial, they warned.

The views held by various people on land ceilings generally corresponded with the size of their own land holdings. Those who owned ten acres, for instance, were all in favour of the land ceiling law, provided the ceiling fixed was above ten acres. And so forth. The arguments at party meetings began to resemble the riotous babel of a lunatic asylum. The grotesque behaviour of the ministers became the subject of much caustic comment and lampooning by the press.

There were a few persons, Shekhar and Anand among them, whom Chaudhury had not consulted in detail . . . He stopped pacing when Shekhar walked in leisurely, greeted him and sat down. 'What's on your mind, chief?' he asked with deliberate nonchalance.

'You know bloody well what it is!' bellowed Chaudhury. 'I'm supposed to kick the landlords out of their lands and distribute the so-called surplus to landless people everywhere. I remember what happened to the lakhs of acres of government land that we distributed to the landless in the past fifteen years. Most of it has found its way back to the landlords. The landless have remained landless. Delhi thinks that the salvation of the country and the party consists in antagonizing the rich peasants, who have stood with us through thick and thin all these years. What the hell do we do now?'

'This was part of the party manifesto, wasn't it?'

'Yes, it was. But the manifesto had umpteen other promises that we could consider to be a higher priority. Why should we pick on this suicidal course alone?'

'Why don't you plead with the Prime Minister and get the priorities changed? If several chief ministers take up the matter, I'm sure Delhi will respond . . .'

'Not that easy, my dear young friend! Do you know that Mahendranath has already become a great champion of land ceilings? His lobby is gunning for me in Delhi, calling me all kinds of names. Do you really believe that the bastard believes in land reforms?'

'The people have voted us in on the programmes we promised, such as land ceilings. How can you back out now when it's time to redeem your pledges? . . .'

'Who's backing out? I don't care what happens to the landlords or the landless millions. My only interest is in keeping the party in power. We're politicians, not pure reformers or do-gooders. Keeping your political power intact, reform any damn thing, I say! The sky is the limit!'

The conversation was leading nowhere. Chaudhury's irritation mounted by the minute, along with his confusion. He believed that political power alone counted; all else was irrelevant. However, the democratic system had made political power completely dependent on what you promised the people, not so much on what you actually did! At least not yet . . . No, not quite so, he made a mental amendment. Power depended on what you made the people believe you would do. And that was where really popular leaders made all the difference. No one, for instance, had much faith in the state leadership, the way they had in Jawaharlal Nehru. At least in the case of national parties (regional parties had not appeared in a big way on the scene at the time) this was so. No one thought even in his wildest dreams that the Mahendranaths or Chaudhurys of the states would take land from the landlords and distribute it among the landless. The people knew them too well to believe this, even in a fit of election-time credulity. They had never taken note of Mahendranath or Chaudhury or, for that matter, the candidate they were voting for. They simply voted for Panditji, the one and only Pandit Jawaharlal Nehru. They considered the state leaders good for gossiping about, grist for the delicious scandals they enjoyed. And that was that . . .

Now, suddenly, Chaudhury found he was to implement some radical and potentially anarchic land ceilings laws, in a sumptuous illusion of distributive justice. He neither believed in them, nor knew how to go about enforcing them. Land ceilings indeed! he muttered scornfully.

Where would his party have been in the election, but for the catchy slogan of land ceilings? Even in his irritation, Chaudhury reflected on this question. His first reaction was that the party would have won anyway, given the state of affairs in the other parties. The fact of the matter was that elections in India were a choice, not of the best, but of the least worthless . . . But the very next moment, new doubts assailed him. How was one sure that his party would have won without the combination of Jawaharlal and land reforms? . . . That's it! he interjected inwardly. The combination of Jawaharlal and land reforms. There was no wishing away the combination, the formidable combination no other party could produce.

So, he was back to square one—to the relationship between political power and land ceilings. If you didn't implement the law, you would violate the party manifesto. And if you did, the powerful landlord class would decimate you. Either way there was disaster—in one case further down the road, at the next election; in the other, just round the corner.

Casting a glance around distractedly, Chaudhury found Shekhar seated comfortably on the sofa. He had stretched his legs out languorously on a small table in front of him and was smoking contentedly, as if everything was just fine with the universe.

'You haven't quite helped me with the problem,' Chaudhury said, annoyance creeping into his tone, when he noticed Shekhar's posture of complete indifference.

'What do you expect me to say?' Shekhar responded, as he stood up and stretched his arms to shake off his lethargy. 'This is strictly between bosses—the Central boss and the state boss. You know what he wants, and more definitely, what you want yourself.

I don't know either. So how can I make constructive suggestions? All I say is, I'm your colleague; rather, you've made me your colleague. So I stand by you.'

'Can't you think of a solution, Shekhar?' asked Chaudhury hopefully. 'Can't something be done to create a chimera of land ceilings and still prevent the landlord lobby from going on the war-path? You're spoken of as a genius . . .'

'Correction!' cut in Shekhar. 'An evil genius!'

'Genius nevertheless,' urged Chaudhury. 'Think up something . . . Think . . . think hard and get us out of this corner!'

There was complete silence for some time, with each absorbed in his own thoughts. 'Shekhar,' Chaudhury said suddenly, as if inspired by an idea. 'Why don't you handle this subject? Suppose I put you in charge of land reforms. . .?'

'A change of portfolio is easy,' Shekhar responded. 'But does it solve your problem? In my opinion, it doesn't . . .'

'Why not?'

'Everyone knows that I don't own a cent of land. They'll say that this is just an eyewash. Alternatively, they'll allege that a fellow who knows nothing about land has been deployed to destroy the land-owning farmer class . . . Worse, Mahendranath's lobby will surely publicize it in the Central Hall of Parliament as a hypocritical gesture . . .'

Chaudhury saw the point at once, especially the last one about Mahendranath's lobby. Lighting another cigarette, he grunted, 'H'mm. Then tell me, who should do this dirty job?'

'Look, chief,' Shekhar began, 'portfolios are your exclusive prerogative and you know who is good at what. I thank you for taking me into confidence. Since you've asked me, my single and unequivocal choice is Anand. In fact, he offers a multiple solution . . .'

Chaudhury burst out laughing. He laughed and laughed for quite a while. 'You are a genius, Shekhar, even if an evil genius, I must admit!' he guffawed. Then he calmed down a bit and asked, 'Now, what is this multiple solution you've discovered?'

'First, he belongs to the landed class, so he has assured credibility. Second, the landlords cannot oppose him openly, although they may not trust him in their heart of hearts. Third, no one in Delhi in Mahendranath's lobby can open his mouth, since you've put one of your most honest and efficient ministers in charge of this very important programme, in deference to the Prime Minister's wishes . . .'

'And fourth,' Chaudhury concluded jokingly but with scathing malice, 'the landlord lobby is sure to destroy him in the process!'

'Which is precisely what I would be delighted to see happen, you may add,' said Shekhar, the sarcasm tinged with seriousness. 'I won't deny this possibility, nor would I drop down dead if what you foresee happens in his case. There is no love lost between Anand and me and that's that. However, let me tell you, there is another angle to the matter. Believe me, there really is . . .'

He paused and stared at Chaudhury, then outside the window at the bounding Alsatian on a rampage through the flowerbeds. He began pacing the room too, perhaps trying to marshal his thoughts.

'Well, go on, Shekhar,' called Chaudhury. 'I'm listening.'

'I know you are,' Shekhar said. 'The matter is so complicated, I don't know how to express it lucidly. You see, Chaudhuryji, this is the moment of truth for us. I don't like Anand, he doesn't like me either. But these are trivial hostilities and don't mean a thing. What in effect the Prime Minister is asking you to do is nothing short of a miracle. He wants you to bring about a revolution through normal legislation, with all its known and unknown built-in loopholes. In the Telengana region not very far from here, there was a fierce armed conflict some years back for a similar cause. It failed and left a trail of blood and misery in its wake. Personally, you are extremely skeptical about the practical implementation of land ceilings. However, unlike many others, you are not a votary of landlordism as a system. You just don't want to lose political power in the process, that's all. I see this as a plus point. I also feel, quite strongly, that all the blood spilt on this soil earlier deserves some divine justice, some retribution if you will. If only we could pull it off somehow, it would be great! The question is, just how? Let's look at the scenario. We have positive inspiration from the Prime Minister. We have a neutral but politically stable and vigilant chief minister. We can also field an honest, efficient and devoted minister-in-charge who knows the subject inside out and is determined to fight his way to success. Given these very favourable factors, I think there is, after all, a chance, an outside chance if you will, to prove the tremendous efficacy of the democratic process . . . That, in my view, is the real stake and we should take the bull by the horns, whatever the risks!!'

'That is a new angle, Shekhar,' commented Chaudhury thoughtfully. 'And a valid one, I admit . . .'

# 28

THE NEWS THAT ANAND WAS TO BE MINISTER OF LAND REFORMS
spread like wildfire, as only political news can. There was as yet
no official announcement, no confirmation. No papers were sent
to the governor to sign, authorizing a change of portfolios. No
reshuffle was in the air. One heard only the normal speculation
that waxes and wanes, depending on more controversial,
significant or sensational news being or not being available from
day to day. In this country, politics is, in a manner of speaking, the
perennial topic of discussion everywhere. Someone said that when
two strangers meet, they talk of the day's weather and the next
day's cabinet reshuffle!

So, the newspapers were full of this single item; some quoted
'authoritative' sources, others referred to 'usually reliable' ones.
Still others simply asserted the news, quoting themselves, as it
were. After all, they argued, if the reported event did not happen,
that would still be news. It would lead to a rich crop of speculation
on the reasons why it hadn't taken place. They could, for instance,
ascribe it to Chaudhury's lack of trust in Anand; after all, the fellow

had never been close as a group man, you see? Then, it could be the chief minister's own lukewarm interest in land reforms. All this fuss, they would say, is because of Jawaharlal's reproving letters; else, who would so much as mention land reforms in this landlord-dominated state? . . . Alternatively, it could be said that Chaudhury had changed his mind for very good political reasons. For instance, how could he be sure that Anand would implement the land ceiling law as he, the chief minister, wanted it? There was no knowing what that uncompromising and ideologically-obsessed fellow could do, including dragging the government into deep trouble! In fact this was precisely why a rift had developed between the two within the last two or three days. This last bit of news was considered a scoop and opened up unlimited vistas for further comment.

Official silence only made the wildfire rage wilder. Most city-bred people began to take note of a programme called land reforms for the first time. If Anand was to handle it from now on, it must be important, they reasoned. First there were seminars and symposia on the subject. Then came 'workshops' that had, of late, assumed respectability through being adopted by the intellectual world. Last came editorials and centre-page articles. They examined the subject from different angles, and came to three different conclusions, though they were all agreed on the end result. First, land reforms were good; but this government would not implement them. Second, land reforms were no good at all in our conditions; but this government was sure to make a mess of implementing them anyway. Third, land reforms were neither good nor bad in themselves; but no matter what, this government would fail to do anything about them. It had flaunted the policy only to seduce voters and catch votes at the coming by-elections. Whether it implemented them or not, eventually this government was sure to plunge the state (and its poor people, of course) into further misery . . . There were several sage comments not so much on land reforms as on Chaudhury, Anand and the whole set of the *dramatis personae* involved. The net outcome was that everything was wrong, everything would be wrong, for the simple reason that nothing had been right with this government, ever . . . In the end, land reforms remained as vague a prospect as ever before.

When the first reports were blazed across the front pages, Anand was in Delhi, the second visit he had paid to the city that month. He had flown to the capital to attend a conference of state irrigation ministers. He had made a name for himself as a minister who knew his subject thoroughly, was articulate, persuasive, effective and earnest. Officials of the Central government respected him, first rather grudgingly, then with growing awe. They cited him as an 'exception', however, confirming their own poor opinion about ministers in general! . . . Such are the subtleties of officialdom.

All of the previous week, after the outcry over the news of their affair in the tabloid, he had pondered the wisdom of quitting politics forever. And then, with his characteristic determination, he had decided to stick it out. He had announced his decision only to his friend Sudershan and to Aruna, telling them that no matter what his detractors tried to do, he was convinced that he should do what he could for the people—and he was best equipped to do that as a politician . . .

On his trip, as usual, Anand was staying at the state guest house. He was looking through some draft resolutions late at night, when the phone rang and Chief Minister Chaudhury came on the line. Anand became alert immediately. After the initial greetings, Chaudhury asked, 'How is the conference going? Anything purposeful, or the usual annual mela?'

'Well,' responded Anand, 'it is a bit of both. Right now I am battling with the important resolutions. If all goes well, I expect them to be different from the run-of-the-mill ones they turn out every year and forget . . .' Then, reminded of something, he continued, 'Anyway, you never showed much interest in these conferences, did you? So, how come you've driven yourself to the telephone in the dead of night? It couldn't be the conference, that's obvious. What's on your mind, really? Anything particular?'

'Don't tell me you haven't been reading the state newspapers!' Chaudhury interjected. 'There is a pretty big storm raging here on land reforms in general and land ceiling laws in particular.'

'Oh, that?' said Anand, chuckling. 'That's the result of your usual enigmatic silence, isn't it? And you enjoy the din and dust meanwhile, of course!'

'I do, I do,' admitted Chaudhury. 'Only this time, it threatens to assume serious dimensions. Our friend Mahendranath is out to exploit it both ways . . . It's becoming a special nuisance.'

'One should expect that too,' said Anand. 'Well, is there anything I can do?'

'Well . . .' and Chaudhury's voice trailed off into a subdued hum. Then, choosing his words carefully, he began, 'Even if there's nothing you can really do as of now, I thought I would consult you anyway. They say you're the cabinet's Brihaspati, after all . . .'

This was Chaudhury's usual dialogue when he was in a good mood. They had given Anand the nickname of Brihaspati, after the god of wisdom in Hindu mythology. Shekhar, however, had a different view. 'I'm not so sure your title is apt,' he would say to anyone who praised Anand's intellect and values. 'I think Anand is good in many ways, but he's no good at politics. You see, Brihaspati was always ready with practical solutions, while Anand does nothing of the kind. He adheres rigidly to what he considers unalterable principles. He could as well belong to another planet; be a sort of extraterrestrial. Such persons are fine museum pieces of humanity, rather than really wise!'

Chaudhury's compliment, which Anand detected was deftly paid in order to allow the chief minister time to compose his next utterance, left him at a loose end. He laughed mildly, mumbling something that sounded like thanks.

'I haven't made this trunk call, spending the people's hard-earned money, merely to praise you,' Chaudhury went on in the bantering tone that had become customary when he talked to Anand. 'If you think so . . .'

'If I think so, it would be a mistake!' interjected Anand. 'And Brihaspatis don't commit such mistakes, let me assure you! That's why I was asking you to tell me frankly. What do I have to do with land reforms?'

'You know,' Chaudhury spoke nonchalantly, something that was characteristic of him when he didn't want to commit himself

302

to a course of action. 'I haven't really decided anything and this is strictly between the two of us at the moment. This wretched land ceiling business could become quite messy down the road. Suppose, just suppose, that you had to handle the portfolio of land reforms. How would you go about it?'

'Too big a question to answer on the phone, I'm afraid,' said Anand thoughtfully. 'Even so, what do you want done in actual fact? What is the end result you foresee?'

'Damned if I know!' blurted Chaudhury. 'I have no fixed ideas, one way or another. I'm not the slave of any ideology, as such—never was in all these decades. Political power is my ideology, if you can call it that, which ideologues like you don't! So whatever you do, I say it should not lead us into the wilderness. Now, is that too much for a chief minister to ask? Or, let's say, for a chief minister like Chaudhury to ask?'

'I don't think any of our party programmes would lead to the wilderness, as such,' commented Anand. 'On the other hand, the accusation is that many of our promises to the people were just for garnering votes. Critics said they were a hoax. Then, why do you apprehend failure in this case?'

'Objective reasoning, I suppose,' Chaudhury replied, rather tentatively. 'Anyway, you're coming back within two or three days, so I thought I should give you a bit of cud to chew meanwhile.'

'Okay, I shall chew it without breaking my jaws!' Anand said with a chuckle.

'Ha ha ha!' Chaudhury burst out laughing. 'That's a good one. Indeed that is the point I was driving at! Chew without breaking your jaws! . . . Brihaspati has put it in perspective, at last, as expected! Good night.'

The conversation ended on this rather intriguing note.

It was past midnight. Anand could not concentrate on the resolutions he had been vetting. Chaudhury's remarks provoked a spell of brooding about a potential imbroglio in which he might soon find himself neck-deep. He sensed intuitively that the idea of giving him the charge of land reforms could have only come from a brain such as Shekhar's. So he was not giving up on his mission to make things difficult for him. Why did Shekhar consider him such a threat? He was not in competition with him. He couldn't care less about political power, Shekhar knew that. So why was he after him? Insecurity? The knowledge that Anand could not be won over to his way of thinking? . . . With a sigh he thought that whatever the tangled mixture of motives that had made Shekhar set out to destroy him, there was very little he could do unless he descended to Shekhar's level. And that he resolutely refused to do. He began to think about the immediate problem facing him. Everyone knew that land reform was pure dynamite in a state where the landholders were so many, so active and so powerful. Some parties had attempted to organize landless labour in the countryside for a fairly long time against the landed gentry—and come to grief. The landholders, big and small, had of late discovered land as the common bond that united them. The attempt to divide the landholders according to the size of their holdings had failed. Combining the small holder with the landless had never been a popular scheme nor a practical success, whatever its theoretical validity. Divisions had indeed appeared among the landless themselves. The landholders had utilized their pervasive influence in the villages to bring this about.

Land was power. Land was the *summum bonum* of the rural context. Land was the omnipotent, omnipresent, omniscient entity in village consciousness. Land was a supreme force that could not be opposed, a fact that could not be denied, a matrix that could not be destroyed. This had been proved over and over again for centuries.

Anand knew of numerous villages where the landlord was literally the Lord. No one dared raise his compound wall higher than the landlord's. No one dared walk the streets with his footwear on while the landlord was anywhere in the vicinity. Smoking in the landlord's presence was, of course, out of the question. All poor women in the village were fair game for the landlord's lust; indeed the women were conditioned to consider his barbarous attention a stroke of luck for themselves. Given this reality in the feudal areas he knew so well, what did land reforms really mean, he asked himself seriously.

The story of land in India is long, tortured, bloody and tear-stained. A number of significant insights Anand had gleaned from authoritative sources, especially books written by experts over the years, suddenly came crowding into his mind. One such pertained to the origin of landlordism as an institution, encouraged by the British in the nineteenth century. It gave a graphic account of how some 'Native leaders, who had risen to power as guerrilla plunderers', levied blackmail, eventually came to terms with the British government and established themselves under the titles of zamindar, polygar, etc., in control of many tracts of the country. For those tracts, they paid a revenue or tribute, uncertain under a weak power, but as regular revenue when a strong power was established. It was remarkable how in these times, the robber, the Raja and the landlord ran into one another.

Anand remained at his desk, contemplating the history of India's land—the mother who had brought sustenance as well as untold misery to millions of her children down the centuries, especially from the beginning of British rule. 'All land belongs to Gopal,' is an old saying. Gopal could mean God or, alternatively, one who owned and tended cows. From the animal to the owner of the animal—that was the sequence. It seemed plausible, since man moved along with the animal in pastoral society. Land thus belonged to everyone who dwelt on it; the tree to every bird that nested there; water to every fish that dived, swam, glided and somersaulted in it with the spontaneous grace of beneficient Creation. Everything belonged to everyone; 'belonging' itself was an all-pervasive phenomenon. There was no record, no registration, no exclusive claim, no individual right.

From that beautiful era to the system of the present day doesn't look like progress at all, Anand commented to himself sadly. However, memories of a romanticized past do not take you anywhere, he told himself sternly. You have to think of the present. You can't bring back the past. The ravages of time don't just disappear; nor do the ravages that man has inflicted on himself and future generations.

He went back to work on the draft resolutions. Most of these documents somehow found their way to him for 'a glance', as they put it. Many thought that the drafts invariably improved when his pencil touched them. There was yet another angle. 'You see,' someone had commented in a tipsy aside at a reception, 'we come to Delhi once in a while and naturally let ourselves go, at times. That goes for officials and non-officials, mind you! Meanwhile, why should this poor devil Anand suffer the agony of idleness? He delights in work and more work, cutting and pruning drafts! So let him enjoy himself too, I say! . . . And in any event, who, either from the steel frame or the khadi frame, bothers about a lousy resolution adopted by a lousier mela called an annual conference of state ministers? . . . Who, barring a bunch of day-dreamers?'

Anand rushed through the draft, perhaps more rapidly than usual. It was at last done with—and on the whole read as it should, he thought after a final rapid reading . . . For once his mind was not on his work but kept straying to his telephonic conversation with Chaudhury . . . He had a fleeting premonition that his life was about to change. And what was all the more mystifying, he could not persuade himself this time that he didn't care, wouldn't care. At that moment, anxiety loomed over his mind like a dark cloud.

He had decided to retire soon after he okayed the resolutions. Now, however, at two in the morning, there wasn't a trace of sleep in his eyes. His thoughts slipped again and again, back to land—Mother Land . . . LAND! . . . The transition from land simpliciter to landed property. From the grazier to the user to the ruler to the registered usurper (yes, the person who fettered land, staked his claim to vast tracts of land, by virtue of his wealth or heredity, was in the most real sense nothing but a usurper!) . . . the integral and inseparable part of *vishala prithvi*, the vast terrestrial expanse; along with sky, water, fire and wind, one of the key elements in the Indian cultural tradition; the repository which carried and nurtured unimaginable wealth of all kinds in its bosom for millions of years with monumental patience. Why is this land, this element (he was not quite sure that the word was an exact rendering of the Sanskrit *bhoota*), this common heritage comprising every atom, animate or inanimate . . . Why is it . . . Why must it be tied to a name someone wrote, or managed to have inscribed, on a piece of paper in a so-called 'Record of Rights' in a dingy room called an office? Why? . . . Why? Suddenly he remembered the Vedic dictum that only small minds think in terms of mine and thine; for noble minds, the whole world is one family, *vasudhaiva kutumbakam* . . . So, he concluded, man's progress has been from the noble to the small-minded . . . That's it; that explained it clearly . . . But again, why?

Precisely at this point, something within him shifted. A part of him began to sneer and chide his sentimental meditation on land . . . Before haranguing everyone else, why not look at yourself? What about the large acreage of land—yes, land, as much a part of *prithvi* as any other bit—entered in your name, the hallowed name of the arch-idealist Anand, none other, in the pages of the *khasra* (land proprietorship register) in the tehsil office? . . . What about that, for heaven's sake?

The harsh reality of this perception abruptly terminated his idealistic flight. True, he had never liked landed property and all that it entailed in his life. That line of defence, however, was neither here nor there. He had to admit that he was a part of the system himself. Any change in the system had to begin with himself, he decided . . . The irony of this perception did not escape him, especially given the way his life and his ambitions and his thinking had evolved this far . . .

When his father died, many years ago, his earlier dreams of becoming a research scholar at Cambridge or any other prestigious university had been abandoned due to the uncertainties of the Second World War, then at its peak. None of the subjects he wanted to study was useful to the family. He could not sacrifice practical utility for sheer personal interest and had therefore joined the law college, as the closest ally to property interests. That way he obeyed his father's injunction to take interest, however marginal, in the family property. And now, ironically, he was being burdened with the task of demolishing his own system. He, a dreamer-insider who observed events from the fringes, who rationalized his momentum, who retained the right perspective and was careful not to be caged within his own rhetoric.

His mind flew into the past once again, to recall that extremely poignant scene of Father's death. Father was perhaps aware that his illness could turn serious, but he knew Anand was to appear at his Law examination and he didn't want him to miss his exam. So he wrote Anand a short letter asking him to come back home *after completing his exam.* Anand realized the risk Father had taken for his sake only when he rushed home after writing the last paper and found that Father's condition was really critical. He was, luckily, fully conscious, though getting feebler by the hour. 'You have come; I am happy,' he had said cryptically. He had suffered from one ailment or another for many years past; but the immediate provocation for the fever that proved fatal had been deeper than physical, Anand gathered later. The facts were ghastly to contemplate. The Second World War was on. The Princely State enforced the 'Defence of Afrozabad Rules'—the state version of the Defence of India Rules. In addition to the harshness associated with the war-time laws, the state government's attitude was also extremely communal. One night, while the whole village was fast asleep, a fez-capped official designated food inspector virtually overran the village. He had a posse of gun-toting police constables with him, threatening the villagers and plundering them right and left. He planted himself in front of Anand's house and woke up his father forcibly, in utter disregard of the latter's ailing condition. He demanded to inspect the grain stocks in his godown, then and there. Meanwhile, a crowd of neighbours gathered, rubbing their sleepy eyes. Seeing the crowd, the inspector's tone became even more insulting. Everyone realized (but no one said, of course) that Father, respected by the whole village and in the immediate neighbourhood, had never been spoken to in *that* language throughout his life. Not even the District Collector had behaved like that when he came to the village, the people recalled, each within himself. When Father pleaded that it was he who had raised the crops and owned the grain, the inspector flaunted the Defence Rules book and threatened to send Father to jail at once. He shouted unspeakable obscenities, deliberately, with an intent to humiliate. As a parting kick, he also made a pointed reference to 'your traitor son studying law outside the state to overthrow *Ala-Hazrat's* benign Government . . .' That, Anand remembered with excruciating remorse, had been the beginning of the end for Father.

Father ignored the *vaid* who was still optimistic, quoting scriptures as a substitute for effective medication. He plunged into a detailed, matter-of-fact discussion with Anand. He called for a full list of the family's land holding. Then he proceeded to describe each plot and its peculiar features. He had observed and mastered them over fifty years of uninterrupted, tender tending. Each plot was a child, as it were. One needed more water, the other less. One was alkaline, the other rich in humus content. One gave a good groundnut crop, but was no good for sesamum. And so forth, down to the last plot.

Once that was over, Father never mentioned land again. He turned to money matters. There was little cash, of course. Yet one could lead a simple and decent life in the village on what the land yielded. 'Starve if you must,' Father enjoined, 'but don't ever go into debt; that's a sin, remember. And most important, don't borrow from a bank or any other outfit that has anything to do with the government. You never know when they will bring a *kurki* (execution proceedings for recovery of debt) or *zabti* (confiscation). Nobody's *izzat* (honour) is safe in their hands.'

He talked fast, with amazing precision, never repeating himself, as if eager to compress whatever he had to say within the very limited time available to him. When Anand broke down, Father suddenly frowned and knit his brows. Then he said, in an enfeebled voice, 'Look, son, we have had no *Lakshmi* (wealth) in the family, ever. We had only one, *Dhairya Lakshmi* (wealth of courage). Don't ever forsake her, or you will have nothing left to sustain you . . .'

Finally, Anand remembered Father, even in his last moments, trying to shout at Mother for crying aloud, while himself shedding tears involuntarily looking at her. Patient like Mother Earth, she had borne his children, his moods and his tempers for over forty years without a word. His tears were perhaps a token of gratitude. He did not wish to express it; they didn't express, only felt. That was the pattern of their life. They lived love, never articulated it.

Then, for the last time, Father began to chant *Ram*

*Naam*—signalling everyone to follow suit. And each successive chant from his lips sounded feebler and feebler, until it became silent lip movement. Presently, that movement stopped too, gently . . . ever so gently. That was the end . . . It was accompanied by a prolonged, loud, heartrending wail from almost the whole adult population of the village. They had gathered there on some uncanny instinct, as if each of them had had a glimpse of Yama's (god of death) messengers come to take Father's life away. For years on end, the village talked of that as a *punyatma's* (pious man's) death, recalling it vividly whenever they saw someone die after long pain or suffering.

*

Wide awake, staring at the ceiling, Anand saw those scenes, one by one, flit across his mind's eye. He lay motionless, just thinking, thinking, thinking about the implications of his new agenda—one that would perhaps persist for a lifetime.

Anand heard someone say, almost aloud, 'So that is the story of Land, do you hear? Which of those plots, those dear children of your father's which he described to you in the last moments of his life, would you choose to surrender to the government? And what right have you to do so, any more than to gift a younger brother away? . . . Granted that in your own case, land perhaps became a shackle to your genius (which you think you have, but who knows?); it came to you in a package of gain and loss, as almost everything in life comes. Granted that your life has not been happy the way you would have wanted it. Yet who but a few freaks like you would spurn that very package? So, you are the misfit, really; and that is the system, you idiot! Why cavil at the system? Replace it if you can, with a better one. Fight the enemies, exploiters and predators who foul up any system under the sun. Yes, fight them if you have the guts. Quit mouthing empty slogans. Stop conjuring up atavistic golden dreams, for heaven's sake!'

Somewhere in a jhuggi cluster within earshot of the guest house, a rooster crowed, seemingly in full-throated confirmation . . .

There was no going back to sleep now, Anand decided as he

got out of bed. He felt a bit exhausted, not so much by lack of
sleep, as by the rigour of sustained introspection. Standing in front
of the mirror to shave, he found a pair of bloodshot, swollen eyes
squinting back at him through barely-visible slits. God! What are
land reforms going to do to me at this rate! he exclaimed to himself.

There was a buzz from the guest house PBX and the operator
said, 'Good morning, sir. Trunk call from Afrozabad. Someone
from UNI wants to speak to you urgently . . .'

UNI . . .? So early? Anand hesitated a little, then said, 'Okay,
put the call through.'

Incredible! he thought, while the UNI gave him the news about
the governor's announcement, late the previous night, of a change
in portfolios. So, he reflected, the die is cast. Apparently,
Chaudhury didn't want to give him any time for second
thoughts—indeed for any thought! Great tactician, our chief, he
thought. He must now brace himself for the confrontation of a
lifetime. The UNI reporter had also gathered a few 'first reactions'
to the change-over, ranging from utmost gratification to
unconcealed anger.

Thanking him for the tip-off, Anand was about to hang up
when the correspondent suddenly shot the question at him, too
quick for him to duck it. 'What is your reaction, Mr Minister?
How do you see your new job? Exciting? Risky? Messy?
Dangerous? Easy?'

He's using all the adjectives he knows, Anand thought irritably.
Then came the thunderbolt, 'Or, shall I say you said you don't
know yet?'

'Please don't say that!' Anand snapped, while a headline
reading 'Anand does not know his job!' flashed across his mind.
Then, collecting his thoughts, he said, 'Look, my first reaction is
that I see my job as partly everything you described, but only partly
. . . As to the relative magnitude of each part, I shall tell you on my
return, after consulting the chief minister . . . Okay?'

'Okay,' said the correspondent unenthusiastically.

'Thanks for being the earliest harbinger of the news anyway,'
Anand said soothingly, trying to make up for his earlier evasive
reply. He was sure the UNI man would consider it flat, indifferent

and a waste of UNI money. 'I have always been impressed with UNI's promptness.'

He had a hurried breakfast, after which the rapporteur of the conference came to collect the texts of the resolutions he had vetted the previous night. However, Anand's mind had already strayed from irrigation and begun to wade through a maze of jumbled ideas and thorny new problems. Some were precise, others hopelessly imprecise. Don't cavil at the system, change it if you can; replace it with a better one if you know how! he reminded himself fiercely . . . Was he prepared for it, he kept asking himself.

The morning conference concluded at last, with a valedictory address by a Central minister other than the one who had inaugurated it. That was the main difference between the two addresses. Everyone complimented everyone else. Last came the vote of thanks, covering every person and organization under the sun. Since the urge to make a speech is irresistible to Indians, the proposer of the vote of thanks threw in some of his own ideas on the substantive issues of the conference. He took his own time, virtually wreaking vengeance on the organizers who had not included his name among the main speakers earlier. When he concluded at last, Anand thought that another vote of thanks was due to him for ending the speech! . . . He felt intolerably restless, remembering the UNI reporter's inquisition and his own arbitrary replies.

The news of the change in Anand's portfolio had spread to the conference room already. Members began congratulating him, adding that they expected 'solid results' in his new assignment. He acknowledged their good wishes, convinced in his own mind that he would need every ounce of sympathy, support and cooperation from the highest to the lowliest in the hierarchy. All that and much more would be required, to bring about radical changes in the entrenched system. First, he had to understand the system itself, where it had gone wrong, why, how and because of whom . . .

He arranged to pay a courtesy call on the Central minister in charge of land reforms. He also wanted to know what the Central government in general, and that minister in particular, thought about the subject and the programme. He wanted to find out if the government's views were in fact identical to the Prime Minister's. This aspect, he thought, was important and would affect the programme very substantially . . .

The minister received him with all courtesy, and served him a cup of tea which, in colour and taste and smell, was as indifferent as that served in all departments of all government ministries. Then the minister gave him a fat file, duly stamped and adorned by a compliments slip, evidently untouched at the ministerial level. To several questions that Anand ventured to ask, the minister's forefinger pointed to the file, thus saving much time and trouble. On further enquiry, Anand was told that the minister was city-born and city-bred and his link with rural India didn't ever go beyond mandatory attendance at government functions.

When, at the instance of the minister, the two officials from the ministry called on Anand later at the guest house to discuss land reforms in greater detail, he found them alternately indifferent and over-enthusiastic. In both cases, they were far removed from grassroots realities. They had worked in their respective states twenty years ago and drifted leisurely from one ministry to another in the Central government—from defence to health to forests to irrigation—with occasional postings in Western countries, where they had similarly handled widely differing jobs. Like other career bureaucrats, they had probably been efficient, knowledgeable and agreeable throughout their careers. But when they had been forced to take on land reforms, just as they were on the verge of retirement, they had obviously begun to sulk, if their present attitude was anything to go by. They gave you the feeling that they considered this last posting as a punishment visited on them for no fault of theirs, other than lack of 'pull'. . . . There is no person more pathetic than a retired bureaucrat who has wielded uninterrupted authority while in service, has really enjoyed it and suddenly finds himself reduced to a nobody upon retirement. Some officals in the department of land reforms were bracing themselves for that distasteful eventuality . . . Overall, Anand was unable to visualize a fruitful future for land reforms. Somewhat depressed, he reflected that it was a weak start for him.

Back in the state capital, he found himself flooded with a variety of reactions, advice, warnings, good wishes and, of course, taunts. Sudershan came to see him, fuming with indignation. 'This chief minister definitely wants to destroy you!' he roared. 'You could perhaps get out of the cabinet now and live safely ever after, since there is no happiness in your horoscope anyway!'

'Is that the advice of a brave friend to another brave activist?' Anand asked ironically.

'Of course not!' Sudershan said promptly, stiffening. 'But don't you see behind this a conspiracy to decimate you? Can't they leave you alone? What have you done to harm them?'

'You know, Doctor sahib, that this idea has emanated from Jawaharlal Nehru. Chaudhury doesn't like it, but can't oppose it, obviously. Never mind who planted my name in Chaudhury's head; he has his own head, which is not all that empty. But tell me, forgetting for a moment that I am your friend and you don't want my head on the chopping block, who do you think could implement Panditji's mandate effectively, out of the present cabinet?'

'For God's sake, Anand. Why ask me such things? I know I can't think beyond you, really. Even so, why you, I ask? Is every other minister being chosen on merit alone? You want me to believe that there is no ulterior motive in this? You talk as if you wanted this portfolio yourself!'

'You know that the landlords don't like me,' Anand explained, without reacting to Sudershan's outburst. 'But so far, that was only a general attitude, which did not matter too much. But now Chaudhury has created an oppositional relationship between them and me. I may possibly destroy them as landlords. I don't know if this is part of a scheme to destroy me. Either way, it suits Chaudhury fine. Either he gets rid of a fellow who is not his 'own' man but whom he can't dump unceremoniously, or he becomes a hero himself by implementing Panditji's favoured programme. Success would be his, failure would naturally be mine, along with the risk involved. Many of the landlords are my personal friends and know that I won't hurt them out of ill-will. I am also one of them and stand to lose a sizeable portion of land myself. What I

314

am about to do is what the party manifesto enjoins. However, there are many others in the party whose interpretation of what the party enjoins is very different from mine. So, if they can destroy me before I destroy them, they will stand to gain, without violating the party mandate . . . Rather complicated, isn't it?'

'I am amazed,' Sudershan commented. 'Are you saying that the party doesn't want its government to implement its own firm promises?'

'In essence, there are some party members who think so,' answered Anand. 'However, they couch their argument in different terms, for obvious reasons. They take the party programme more as something to flaunt, rather than implement. They lay more store by gimmicks to be employed at election time. I am talking only about some, not all the activists in the party. The question is really of comparative pull. My approach is not election-oriented at all. I want social transformation for its own sake, which is what I believe the party stands for, votes or no votes. And in the ultimate analysis, the party programme is not inimical to its electoral prospects. What will indeed affect our electoral prospects, if that should ever happen, is our vacillation and the gaping chasm between precept and practice . . .'

'I'm afraid much of this theory goes over my head,' commented Sudershan. 'Some landlords who spoke to me wonder why you're so fanatical about this social transformation ideology when you belong to the same class and background as they. They would normally expect you to be the champion of their cause! How did you come to believe what others in your class don't, inside the party or outside? People find this so mystifying in a person whom they otherwise adore so much . . . '

Anand fell silent. Then, as if speaking to himself, he began, 'Yes . . . How, indeed, did I come to believe in social transformation? . . . I'm not sure that I have the complete answer. Like many others, I believed in the need for change of the existing order. But as I looked around, I understood that nothing short of a radical change would do now. My experience convinces me that the institution of property—the concept of mine or thine—has caused much misery to mankind in a variety of ways. It does not

315

matter whether the property is big or small. The most dismal shack ignites the same passions as the tallest mansion; a few cents of land could prove as explosive as a whole estate. So I came to care not so much for wealth, as such; I came to believe that the basic need is happiness. And I shall fight a system that equates happiness with wealth and proceeds to build social relations on the basis of that preposterous proposition . . . I don't know if my talk makes any sense to you; but the way I am made, I think the most sacred right of man is the right to be happy. And whatever detracts from that right—be it property, custom, power, prestige—deserves to be stamped out. This, then, is my fight. In turn, I am willing to court destruction myself, which may turn out to be more likely. Still, there shall be no compromise on this. And why should I compromise? What do I get from such compromises? Nothing that I want, surely! Then why? What's the point? You know I have no animus against anyone, again because nothing matters to me.'

'You may be right, Anand,' Sudershan declared. 'But I predict failure, if you'll pardon my saying so!'

'You sent me into this life in the name of the dreamers, remember?' Anand said, looking straight into his friend's agitated eyes.

'I remember,' replied Sudershan. 'Even as someone who knows almost everything about you, this aspect of your job is beyond my comprehension. All I can say, therefore, is that I wish you the best in your endeavours!'

# 29

SOON AFTER THE CHANGE IN PORTFOLIOS, ANAND HAD HIS FIRST
problematic encounter with Chaudhury. The chief minister was
harsh, almost vitriolic in his criticism of Anand's approach.
However, the clash brought about an understanding of
sorts—between untempered idealism on the one hand and
unabashed opportunism (euphemistically called pragmatism) on
the other. Chaudhury had been talked into giving the land reforms
portfolio to Anand. Later, however, the more he thought about it,
the less convinced he was of its correctness. He wanted to help the
landless poor, certainly; but not by arbitrarily seizing the ancestral
property of the landed sections. And that was precisely what he
was now afraid Anand would do.

Chaudhury had numerous reasons for his reservations about
land reforms. He felt uneasy about socialism in general, especially
about its willing, almost effusive acceptance by his party. After all,
did he not know the score? Whom are we trying to fool, he asked
himself. He had no illusions as far as this issue was concerned.
Socialism in the party was Jawaharlal's brain-child all the way.

317

Several younger members of the party (who were nicknamed Young Turks) were indeed attracted to socialism. But they did not wield much influence in the party, which was dominated by established leaders. Some of their critics sarcastically remarked, 'Our brilliant socialist friends are absolutely unique in terms of popularity; you can't accuse them of having contested or won a single direct election so far!' This was true in those days. Yet the socialists had in their ranks several brilliant and devoted leaders such as Acharya Narendra Deva, Jaya Prakash Narayan, Achyut Patwardhan, Dr Ram Manohar Lohia, Asoka Mehta and many others, each of whom was highly regarded in his own right. However, they were unable to build a party at the national level and function as a united Opposition. Fractured by internal differences, the group broke up into the Socialist Party, Praja Socialist Party, Samyukta Socialist Party and other small groupings. Their immediate impact began to dwindle soon, and they only came into prominence much later, during Indira Gandhi's regime.

Then there were the converted socialists—a special brand who supported the party for strictly personal reasons. Chaudhury represented this group. He used his supposed allegiance to socialism solely to steer himself close to Jawaharlal—nothing more. Yet a person of his experience and intelligence could not have remained neutral forever. He was a thinking animal in his own way. And he did have his beliefs. These beliefs, though, could change at will—to suit his political interests. That was the virtue of pragmatism. Chaudhury had mastered it over the decades, by patient observation and careful scheming and plotting.

He had also indulged in what was called 'here and now' rhetoric. Socialism here and now. Nationalization (of everything) here and now. Land reforms here and now. Many party men, infuriated by his grandiose sloganeering, which they knew did not mean a thing, had begun to call him 'Here-and-Now Chaudhury'. The nickname had stuck. All that, however, was part of the game.

So Chaudhury continued to mouth socialist propaganda, injecting vigour into his tired rhetoric by quoting Nehru shamelessly and extensively. This had diminished over the years, as he steadily climbed the ladder of political power. He had not believed in it at any time anyway. But he could not disclaim socialism openly, since it had become the party's creed and also because of Jawaharlal Nehru's reported confidence in him as a socialist-minded party man. Circles 'closest' to the Prime Minister had told him so. To identify those 'circles' wasn't possible; everyone had to go by his own belief—or superstition. Reports also had it that Chaudhury's ascendancy had been due to the Prime Minister's confidence in him. In his rare moments of introspection, Chaudhury repented having created a false impression about himself in the great leader's mind. It also meant that it was easy to deceive Panditji! At this rate, how many more impostors were prowling about in Delhi, Chaudhury wondered, masquerading as God knows what, and basking in Jawaharlal's misplaced patronage? . . . He never expressed these thoughts, of course; but he knew that a number of party men shared them. Many tried to exploit Nehru's innate generosity and credulous liberalism. Side by side, systematic but subtle efforts were on to create almost a glorious and resplendent image of the 'Nehru Family'. The effort was restrained mainly for fear that Panditji himself might not like it.

Anand and Chaudhury were meeting that day at the latter's official residence. They had had a light lunch and had been discussing Anand's new responsibilities, with Chaudhury doing most of the talking. Chaudhury first turned to one of his pet themes: socialism. As long as it was applied to industries in urban areas, labour unions, nationalization and the like, inculcate socialism by all means, said Chaudhury. Coming to land and land relations, however, he found socialism a thorn in the flesh. It simply wouldn't work, he declared. Agricultural labourers received their wages in kind in most rural areas. Each year there was some bargaining between the landlord and his workers. When there was a bumper crop, everyone got a generous deal; it was Mother Earth's bounty. When there was drought or flood or pest, everyone received less. Yet, barring acute famines when both men and cattle had to migrate from the village, what they got even in lean years could prevent starvation. The collective conscience of the village always ensured that. Each artisan served several farmers and got a little, albeit less than normal, from each. Each farmer reaped a poor harvest, yet managed to keep body and soul together. He postponed extra projects like the construction of a house or a cattle-shed, digging a new well, improvements to land, even a daughter's marriage if necessary—to better years. That was a compromise with the inevitable. Ideally, the impact of the good as well as of the not-so-good affected all, more or less. Rural society had subsisted thus for centuries. Wasn't that the essence of socialism?

Granted, Chaudhury commented, that feudal relations had distorted the agrarian context to a large extent in recent times. The process had become worse through the big farmer's exploitative methods of functioning. Granted that the landlord had become a tyrant and a grabber. Granted that capitalist tendencies polarized rural society into the rich and the poor, and exacerbated tension between them. Granted that injustice and discrimination had eaten into the system like cancer for several decades . . . Granted that all this has happened, but what was the remedy today, Chaudhury asked. Did the remedy lie in imposing an alien, artificial graft—which was what, in essence, the contemplated land reform proposals were? Would this not be a disaster? Was this the sum total of the party's wisdom?

Look at recent history, Chaudhury explained. For example, the man-made famine of Bengal in 1943, when millions died of starvation. Men and dogs had battled in the streets of Calcutta over the crumbs and leftovers from sumptuous dinners in expensive hotels. No wonder the British had agreed to leave India. They must have considered post-war reconstruction an impossibility, given a fiercely hostile population and a near-bankrupt economy. Since the time of Independence, however, a gradual change had become evident in the country's fortunes—gradual but unmistakable. The credit truly belonged to the Indian farmer. Yet politicians had appropriated it, election after election. If there was drought, it was an act of God. If there was a bumper harvest, it was solely due to the party's policies and their implementation by the government! . . . But, if one was being honest, the farmer was the unsung and unhonoured food-giver and life-saver. And the farmer in India came in different sizes—big, medium, small, marginal . . . And, through their own efforts, the country's farmers continued to improve their own and thereby the country's position. For over a decade now, pump sets had appeared on thousands of wells in the countryside. Canals now flowed from gigantic reservoirs through arid lands, where the only water one could see in earlier decades was the tears of living human skeletons. We still went round the globe with our begging bowl held out, still squirming under the humiliation of PL 480. Yet, we might, hopefully, in a few years' time, manage to achieve self-sufficiency in foodgrains. While the country was thus in sight of a real breakthrough, would it be wise to disturb established land relations and to disrupt rural life from its roots? If that happened now, who would pick up the pieces later? What would happen to our tall claims of achieving self-reliance? What would happen to national self-respect?

And lastly, continued Chaudhury, there was the political aspect. Election after election, it was the farmer who had stood by their party consistently, at least in this state and a few around it. The landless had been against them, by and large. The voting figures made this crystal clear. The urban areas had almost invariably gone against the party. They were anti-establishment, whatever the establishment. They grabbed every conceivable concession from the government and still kicked it in the teeth with unerring regularity. The rural areas groaned helplessly or suffered the repercussions of the party's policy in silence. The party didn't have the guts to touch the urban rich, reportedly in deference to their fund-giving potential. It was unable to penalize the middleman, the trader, the industrialist, the trade union leader, the intellectuals, the professionals, journalists—and almost all of them detested the party. Some journals had made a fine art of extolling Jawaharlal personally twenty-four hours a day, and denigrating each and every other person in his party, possibly for twenty-five hours! It would appear that Jawaharlal Nehru was an angel leading a party of a million devils! Amazingly, they got away with such descriptions! And this being the political scenario, must their party insist on alienating the only force that had saved it every time? If other parties were shouting in favour of land reforms, it suited them eminently because those who would lose lands were their enemies anyway. Must they also, in this savage competition of slogans, destroy their friends, their only friends? What kind of political sagacity was this, for heaven's sake?

And suppose they made this suicidal move, in order to appear progressive. If they were defeated in the next election, due only a year from now, which other party was going to implement all this futile socialism? Where would political stability be in this country? And once instability set in, particularly at the national level, where would the country be? . . . Where were they headed, for the sake of a doubtful ideology about which no one was clear, including Jawaharlal Nehru? What was the point of all this?

Chaudhury's presentation, elaborately argued and impeccably logical, apparently left no chinks for detractors to penetrate. As chief minister, he had done what Jawaharlal Nehru expected him to do. His own inclinations were clearly in the opposite direction. Yet in the end, he had reasoned, Jawaharlal was the vote-catcher anyway. He, Chaudhury, had no beliefs, as such. He only had to ensure that he retained his position. From his point of view, he knew that nothing succeeds like success. And by the same token, nothing fails like failure.

Anand sat motionless, keenly attentive throughout the presentation. Then, as if coming out of a trance, he said, 'Thank you, chief. You haven't yet told me what I'm to do! That was what I thought we were to figure out at this meeting.'

'I know, I know,' Chaudhury said. 'I assumed you would think hard and find a way out. There is no instant or complete solution. We shall have to muddle through somehow, I suppose.'

'Is that what you want done? I mean, do you want me to muddle through?' Anand queried pointedly.

'I don't know what else is possible, with the general elections round the corner . . .' Chaudhury murmured.

'We shall come to the election issue later. The main question is in which direction are we to proceed, with such a sharp division of views in the party itself?'

'This has always been the case perhaps,' Chaudhury mused. 'Our party carries as many contradictions as our society does.

That's why it has something for each section, some hope for each group.'

'And some patch of hunting ground for each anti-social gang!' cut in Anand with a chuckle.

Chaudhury laughed to disguise his annoyance. 'You speak as if you don't have faith in your own party!' he remarked edgily.

'Do you?' countered Anand.

'All right, I get your point,' Chaudhury said sardonically. 'We do and we don't! That's what you wish to say. In that respect too it's a mixed crowd with mixed beliefs and mixed motivations . . . Well, where does this discovery lead us?'

'If it is a mere discovery, there is another scenario.'

'What do you mean, another scenario ?'

'True, ours is not a cadre-based, closed-circuit party. It is more a platform, a forum, an organization. Yet, whatever its structure, or lack of it, it has never been aimless, rudderless. The party was always aware of where it was going. From stage to stage in its history, it knew its own mind. Different leaders expressed the goal differently from time to time. Still, what they said resonated with the people every time. It entered their collective consciousness. The question today is, what is our goal now? Where do we go from here? After Independence, we seemed to be groping for a while. That was the moment when Mahatma Gandhi wanted the party dissolved, and replaced by another with more distinct objectives, maybe. The party did not accept that advice, again because it thought it had still to accomplish the task of integration. Jawaharlal Nehru is spearheading that process today. Sardar Patel completed the political integration of the country. However, the emotional and economic aspects of integration remain far from complete. We are indeed only beginning to probe them. What the country has always had, despite varying vicissitudes, is cultural integration. The British tried to destroy it, but luckily, great Indians like Vivekananda, Sri Aurobindo and Gandhi saved it. We have to build on this mixed foundation left over from a series of historical and colonial ravages . . .'

Chaudhury was restless. He had made umpteen speeches himself on national unity, as the main stock-in-trade of political campaigning. He gestured to Anand to pause, then he said, 'My dear scholar, will you come to the point? What has all this integration stuff got to do with land reforms?'

'Sorry, chief,' Anand hastened to say. 'I didn't mean to pontificate, nor to advise one of Jawaharlal's favourites! I know that is entirely unnecessary . . .'

'You mean irrelevant, really!' exclaimed Chaudhury with a burst of good-natured laughter.

'I prefer the word "unnecessary",' Anand clarified. 'When I said the British tried to destroy our cultural integrity, I was referring to culture as the sum total of our rural life, including land relations. The British tampered with them for more than a century. That is how the need for land reforms has arisen today. What we understand by reforms is largely a return to our traditional non-exploitative pattern. There will, of course, be changes warranted by the changed circumstances. New factors will have to figure in the pattern. For instance, we have a much larger and rapidly growing population to look after today. There is much greater pressure on land, with none of the rural industries that flourished in the last century to relieve the strain; the British destroyed them. The feudal set-up they encouraged led to exploitation and social degradation. Unemployment and under-employment are plaguing rural India. Millions of young people from villages migrate to the cities and lose their soul and identity for ever. Doesn't this very familiar scene and its clear nexus with land reforms make any sense to you? Or do you think that I am merely trying to argue for argument's sake?'

This question stung Chaudhury. For a brief moment, he almost felt sorry for himself and those like him who had come into the political field with an entirely self-centred approach. They lacked the fundamental commitment to egalitarianism and justice that formed the root of Gandhian socialism. They had spent all their lives chasing transient glory, worshipping the false god of political power for its own sake. They had rejected the significant indigenous models of statecraft, such as those of Rama, Chanakya, Asoka, Akbar. An entirely new system of professional politics had emerged in India, based on the Western model, but without the training, preparation and methodology built into that model over centuries. The Indian model was cumbersome, straitjacketed, convoluted—neither fish nor fowl. Chaudhury responded defensively, 'You are right, Anand. Go on . . . Let me hear you out. We don't have all day. Can't delay decisions any longer.'

'There is nothing much to add, really,' Anand said, making it sound inconsequential, as an atonement for the slight aspersion he had cast on Chaudhury by his previous question. He shouldn't have done that, he told himself. 'We have to grapple with the familiar context I have tried to describe. In my considered view, the only effective beginning of any reform now would be with land relations. Land still is by far the sheet anchor of our economy and all else stems from it. Still, I don't want to be dogmatic; I am subject to reason and correction. Could you, Chaudhuryji, think of any other starting point?'

Chaudhury paused for several moments, possibly searching for an answer, then said, non-committally, 'Please go on, will you?'

'As you wish,' Anand continued. 'Land reforms, which evoke such mixed and intense reaction at the moment, would mean a reorganization of agrarian relations as a whole—nothing less. Reform is nothing if it is not a full package; piecemeal, it would be disastrous. We have already achieved the abolition of zamindari, more or less. When you end a system, what do you replace it with? There should be another self-contained system, obviously; else everything will be scattered in total confusion. In our well-intentioned campaign to distribute government land to the landless, we have created hundreds of thousands of marginal and tiny land owners. They were otherwise indigent, living as labourers. They were in no position to take on the responsibility of land ownership. There was no concomitant programme of making each of these recipients viable in his new occupation. Besides, there were so many delays in giving them even the documents of ownership that they could not raise bank loans in time. They did not know the intricate system of financial assistance anyway. Meanwhile, the revenue officials at the lower rungs found the programme of land distribution a gold mine for themselves. They went on a rampage, with the ready connivance of the village officers . . . The overall frustration created by these endless hurdles was simply unbearable. So, the poor beneficiaries sold most of the land assigned to them, at unbelievably cheap rates, to big landlords or to medium farmers. Whatever our rules on paper prohibiting such transactions, you cannot, indeed dare not, resume that land from the ultimate transferees. We should not repeat these mistakes. We should, as I said, bring in a self-contained flexible structure. In effect, we should, within a short time, conceive and create an effective alternative to the existing system that took shape and has become more and more complex over the last two centuries. This is the task that history has assigned to our generation . . .'

Anand spoke in a low, steady voice. His eyes were half-closed. For a split second Chaudhury envied the young visionary. His life, he thought, would perhaps come to nothing; but whose life, including his own, would ever come to anything anyway? The thought flitted across his mind for the first time, igniting a brief spark of discomfort.

'Chaudhuryji,' Anand continued, 'you just said that the landless are against our party. Why did that happen? After all, the abolition of zamindari was the party's crowning achievement, wasn't it? With that background, why would the landless labourer go against us, unless he felt that we did not care for him? Unless he believed that we were wooing the landed gentry? As a party worker, I had occasion to talk to hundreds of landless labourers in the rural areas. I personally cultivated some persons from my own village who had been my childhood friends. They are now floating around, rootless, as weavers or barbers in Bombay or Sholapur. They serve some rich boss as wage-earners in their own profession. Many are plying rickshaws in towns. They earn money and squander it in the liquor shops; some of them manage to send a little to their families in the village . . . Now, what is their stake in life? And whatever their individual differences in attitude and behaviour, I find that many of them still want to go back to their village and settle down on a piece of land of their own . . . if possible; that is the big if.'

'And that is why you want land to be redistributed ?' queried Chaudhury.

'I am not confining myself to land specifically. The point I am making is that the village is getting drained of its multifaceted talent. The artisans are leaving, the landless able-bodied young men are leaving, all hard-working individuals are leaving. At this rate, where will the Indian village find itself? . . . The agrarian society in the past was a hub of activity, with land as the main focus. When feudalism disturbed that, everything woven round it was similarly disrupted. It spilled over to the towns in the process. We have not devised any village-town-city-village cyclic system based on mutual strengthening. Several interests, badly fragmented, are working at cross-purposes. The hunger for land has increased so tremendously because village industries have perished . . . So I think we should begin with land reforms and weave a new self-contained system around it. Had we made a beginning some ten years ago, I am reasonably certain that in our own state and some others like it, we would not have lost the support of the rural landless. It is not too late even now. Meanwhile, we have to keep an eye on what you have referred to as farmers' support. Are you sure you have it today as much as you did during the days of the zamindari abolition? We are all farmers; but I am no longer sure that we enjoy that unqualified support, although it is still considerable . . . What do you think?'

'I agree; but why is the support dwindling?' Chaudhury shot back. 'Is it not because we have started putting our foot right in our mouth by talking about land reforms, redistribution of land and so on? Is that not enough to scare the farmers and cost us their support eventually?'

'You do have a point there, I admit,' said Anand. 'But who is a farmer, may I know? As against a non-farmer, such as a landless person, farmers may unite. But how about their own internal differences? What about caste? What about class? What about the big and the small? What about their conflicts? Those conflicts become all-pervasive during elections. Caste rivalries appear from nowhere and will not let the farmers' vote remain undivided for long. Casteism is already cutting across political party lines, as we have noticed in elections and by-elections. We never tire of talking about a casteless society, but always try to derive an electoral advantage from every caste situation . . . In the face of these undeniable facts, how can we expect to sustain the party's strength on the basis of a single section that is itself fragmenting? You seem to be lukewarm to the idea of land distribution under a ceiling law. In point of fact, how many land-holders will actually lose their land? In my own village that consists of about a thousand peasant proprietors, I can count only three or four surplus land-holders, including myself. And their surplus land would go to a much larger number of landless persons, obviously . . . So, I should think that if we go about this programme methodically, our party should be a net gainer of electoral support and not a loser . . .

'You talked about political instability and I agree that there lurks a real danger. Yet, how long do you think Jawaharlal Nehru's personality and persuasion can see the party through, election after election? We have seen that while he has championed socialism forcefully, he has also agreed to make compromises. For instance, the moment the Ganatantra Parishad merged with our party, was it not evident that our party had lost its élan? The thrust of socialism inevitably was eroded from within, in spite of Jawaharlal. In fact, his own faith in socialism became suspect to some extent in this process. When he finds that his party men have reservations about the ideology he envisions, he faces an unenviable choice—between immediate instability and ultimate decline. And his sense of history drives him, perhaps rightly, to make compromises to keep the country together. History will always remember his regime for political stability—plus some amount of ideological dilution as the price for that stability. Now, between ourselves, Chaudhuryji, just imagine. When Jawaharlal is no longer on the scene, don't you see the country left with neither political stability nor ideological thrust? I clearly see regionalism, language politics, ethnic divides, Centre-state tensions and a host of other maladies waiting to come into play, once there is a personality vacuum at the top. So, even from the narrow angle of political advantage, is it not urgent to enlist the solid support of the base of the popular pyramid?'

'You seem to be turning my own arguments against me,' Chaudhury remarked. 'When are you going to present your remedy for all the problems we have both listed?'

'Forgive my saying so, chief,' Anand continued, 'but you and I are thinking of different time-frames. Your sights are on the immediate future, maybe five years. I am at least ten years younger and naturally think long term, say fifteen to twenty years. You think of how the party could sail through smoothly with Jawaharlal as the political salesman. I take this period as secured already and try to look beyond Jawaharlal. I don't mean his life span—we all wish him a long, long life—but more notably, his effectiveness in the fast-changing situations at home and abroad. He has done, and is doing, a great job. We are all proud of him, naturally. Yet every leader's relevance and influence fluctuate, for reasons beyond everyone's control. The change may also be totally unrelated to his intrinsic merit. It has happened many times before. We shouldn't rule it out now, even if it does not actually happen. With the emergence of post-Independence generations, I am afraid the criteria of judging political parties will change. The nostalgia of the freedom struggle will abate more quickly than we tend to believe. The aspirations of the young will soar as never before. They will notice the progress that other countries have achieved. From a distance, that achievement will look even more spectacular . . . So we cannot, in my view, avoid focusing on the base, which, in India's context, is the village—and land, undeniably . . . If we ignore this base, we'll be building on sand. Nothing will remain firm, nothing will materialize . . .'

'Why can't we wait a few years, until we achieve a breakthrough in the farm sector and are no longer deficient in food at least?' asked Chaudhury.

'I have often thought of that, Chaudhuryji,' answered Anand. 'Why not have enough before you embark on distributive justice? What can you distribute right now except poverty? . . . The argument sounds plausible. However, can you show me one example where a country waited to produce enough before beginning to distribute? And succeeded by taking that route? Is such a sequence at all practicable, given the nature and propensities of an acquisitive society? Which producer will ever agree that we have produced enough and may now proceed to distribute?

Poverty and riches are relative terms; where exactly do you draw
the line? You find the rich and the poor in all countries, although
the rich in one country may be below the middle class in another
. . . In addition, Chaudhuryji, I stumbled onto yet another reason
when I scrutinized the wait-some-more argument. What is the
outcome of the breakthrough we are heading for, really? You
create massive irrigation facilities. You supply all the inputs: good
seed, effective farming practices, fertilizer, pesticides. You bring
about soil conservation, produce green manure, arrange for soil
testing. Last but not the least, you give sufficient bank loan support
to finance all these operations. Millions of acres of arid land get
irrigation water overnight. All the big landlords with thousands of
acres of dry land become the lucky owners of thousands of acres
of fertile wet land overnight. Yes, the small farmers also will get
some benefit; but I am talking about the overall impact. Imagine
the massive disparity this process will create in rural society. How
much wealth it will dump in the lap of the landlords! What have
they done to deserve that windfall? Nothing! Have we made any
socio-economic assessment of that extraordinary situation? I have
a genuine apprehension that our present rural society will find this
sudden spurt in disparity unendurable. It will become disrupted
and destabilized. It will bring in a new norm, an alien fashion—of
vulgar consumerism, of the so-called good things of life. The rich
will flaunt them, the poor will feel even more deprived. This will
create further tension. In the feudal context, it was power and
prestige that constituted distinction. In terms of wealth, even the
feudal lord was not too high above the middle class. Remember
how many nawabs of the old princely states were heavily in debt
to moneylenders. The moneylender gave the nawab exaggerated
reverence; the nawab's ego was satisfied. Now, with the advent of
money power, it is going to be a much more sickening game.
Villages will lose their soul, I am afraid. Urbanization will grow
beyond our wildest dreams, since the new god of money will
possess everyone. And the city is where the money is. On the
political front, party loyalty will become the casualty; money will
loom large everywhere—in giving party tickets, in securing votes,

in arranging campaigns . . . in everything. Where will the poor party worker or candidate find himself in that set-up? . . . What can possibly result from this scramble, except political instability?'

'You are talking like an astrologer, Anand,' Chaudhury commented with a mixture of humour and sarcasm. 'You seem to have become a modern version of Nostradamus!'

'I am nothing of the kind and you know it!' said Anand. 'You are only pulling my leg, but I have faced worse situations due to my unorthodox views. Still, no one has told me why I am wrong and whether I am only being paranoid and imagining things. My simple formulation is that in every agrarian society already burdened with age-old disparities, socio-economic reform should logically begin with land reform. The correct order should be: distribute the means of production first; enable all to produce more; avoid increase of disparities. We did not achieve our freedom through a bloody revolution. Nevertheless, the revolutionary zeal attending our freedom was no less intense. That momentum, as I see it, was enough to usher in any change, however fundamental or however radical in its impact. However, presumably for very valid reasons, Jawaharlal Nehru and his colleagues at the top decided not to take advantage of it; they let it pass. They settled for stability; they got it. Now, will it remain after Panditji? This is the question of questions. And we do not seem to have ensured it through our programmes. All that we can do is to hope and pray for the reappearance of charismatic leadership each time. Frankly, I am worried . . .'

His voice trailed away and his reflective eyes met Chaudhury's. The chief minister shifted uncomfortably under that gaze. He rose abruptly, hugged Anand, slapped him on the back and said, with a touch of extra fervour, 'Thank you, young man. You have won the case; you got the decree. As for the mode of execution, I shall give you the procedure in a few days' time, after I make a brief trip to Delhi . . .'

The next moment, Anand remembered an adage which he had heard at the law college, that the troubles of a litigant in India begin *after* he obtains a decree and wants to get it executed! He said nothing, and tried not to visualize the new schemes being hatched in Chaudhury's frenziedly churning brain.

# 30

FOR SEVERAL DAYS, AS HE PLOTTED AND PLANNED, SHEKHAR TRIED
to suppress his furtive joy. How many birds he was about to kill
with one stone, maybe even with no stone! he exulted. He owned
no land, belonged to no caste. The nicknames he had had to put
up with were legion. 'Bastard' was, of course, the most common.
He could not blame anyone in particular for these epithets. He had
become quickly conditioned to receiving the derogatory references
to illegitimacy that were so ingrained in people's minds and
tongues. He seethed within, while externally he kept moving from
success to success. The revulsion and hostility still continued
unabated, but now, for the most part, they took place behind his
back. His public achievements concealed the stigma to some
extent, but it was always there, festering and rankling, like a
wound no salve could heal in all the cycles of birth and rebirth. He
surrendered to pervasive and intoxicating fantasies of revenge, in
which he systematically destroyed representatives of the class that
had brutalized his mother and the thousands of women like her
who suffered continuous physical and emotional abuse. For hours

he fantasized about the annihilation of a society that would never grant him status or respect, or allow him to live within it with honour.

God! How he detested the world, the whole stinking world! Here he was, just Shekhar, Shekhar Nothing. Not Shekhar Rao, not Shekhar Reddy, not Shekhar Chaudhury, not Shekhar Naidu, not Shekhar Iyer, not Shekhar Gupta, not Shekhar Yadav, not Shekhar Tyagi, not Shekhar Shastri, not Shekhar Jatav, not Thakur Shekhar Singh, not Shekhar Mishra, not Shekhar Patil, not Shekhar Menon, not Shekhar Bannerji, not Shekhar Patnaik, not Shekhar Chaliha, not Shekhar Paswan, not Shekhar Gujjar, not Shekhar Padayachi . . . Well, the list was endless and would remain so, he mused, as long as each caste, sub-caste and sub-sub-caste advanced its claim for separate recognition in the sharing of political spoils. He alone had no nook in this ever-widening field of demands based on the accident of birth . . . Yet how, he asked himself angrily, was a brahmin or a Reddy or a Yadav or a Jatav or any other caste-labeled fellow sure that his mother had not slept with a stud-bull of another caste and begotten him, complete with caste seal and label? How could anyone assert that this nation, or any nation, did not consist of a vast number of unidentified bastards? Unidentified because the mothers were married? Why should that piece of thread called a mangalsutra, or a wedding ring, or any other external mark of marriage, make such a difference in all those cases? Why? . . . Why? . . .

And here he was, Shekhar Nothing, yet a blazing success story if ever there was one. Brahmin pandits and chandalas alike prostrated themselves at his feet in his office or drawing room for this or that favour. They sang his praises in his presence, but referred to him as 'that illegitimate son of a prostitute' as soon as they were out of earshot. There was no way out, no way he could convert himself to a proper caste, be it scheduled or unscheduled. The brahmin had dominated Hindu society for centuries, keeping his learning a closed preserve, unavailable to others. And now, the scheduled caste had become a closed preserve too, out of bounds to outsiders. If only the founding fathers of India's Constitution had had the imagination—and perhaps the honesty—to provide adequate reservation to those of illegitimate origin, millions would be procuring, selling and otherwise dealing in false and fake certificates of bona fide illegitimacy to get jobs and concessions from the government. Each of them would, Shekhar speculated with delight, cite the Indian Evidence Act to prove his illegitimacy conclusively. He would produce clinching evidence that at the probable time of his conception, his lawful father was so far away from his mother that he could never have begotten him! Legitimacy would then have become a sin everyone tried to run away from . . . And as a desirable consequence, caste would go out of fashion, ushering in a truly casteless society. Instead of merely stating it in the Preamble of the Constitution, why didn't the great champions of a casteless society pass legislation banning marriages within the same caste, for heaven's sake, if they had really meant what they shouted from the housetops? If there could be prohibited degrees of relationship for marriage—as there are in several scripture-bound personal laws—why not prohibit intra-caste marriages on the same grounds? . . . They never did that, nor will they do it now, the hypocrites, Shekhar reflected bitterly. They just keep talking of a casteless society, talking ad nauseam without believing a word. Everything they do, in fact, only emphasizes racial purity, caste superiority, family history, aristocratic blood. They encourage each of these in its most virulent form and still expatiate on the equality of men. Why, they think in terms of pedigrees in horses and dogs—that is a highbrow science. How futile, then, to expect any attitude of equality among human beings anywhere in the world!

Rage consumed him night and day. He was thus condemned to remain Shekhar Nothing, until the disposal of his dead body. They might even break one another's heads on the method of disposal. There would, in all probability, be a riot between a group favouring cremation and a gang urging burial!

And so, that morning, the embittered Shekhar Nothing raised again and again within himself, with excruciating irony, the forlorn voice of a casteless citizen crying out for a caste, in a self-proclaimed casteless society. But he was committed to his life's mission—to succeed so handsomely that the world would have to kneel to him, at which point he would avenge himself by spitting on it. There would be no backing out.

He remembered his mother. She had been dead about fifteen years. She had died under circumstances that submerged him in a torrent of agony and hate. What caste had she belonged to? No one knew; she had told no one. So who would marry her? She was useful only for sexual slavery, not for marriage. Had she had a caste, he, Shekhar, could have called himself Shekhar Something. Had she been ugly like most other women, she would perhaps have ended up being one person's mistress and would have perhaps been treated more humanely, by that one person. As it was, she was too beautiful to be allowed to remain the chattel of one particular landlord. She had to service many, having been bought for hard cash. The landlords' fornicating sprees were interspersed with assaults by honoured guests, petty officials and whosoever happened to wield power locally. She had undergone umpteen abortions, ordered by the landlords and carried out by an old hag in the village whom everyone hated but many utilized regularly. Her last abortion had apparently led to some ailment that caused intolerable pain in the abdominal region. Meanwhile, a police official was on a visit to the village in connection with an investigation in which the landlords had to please him. The dasi was detailed to service him. The encounter resulted in profuse internal bleeding and finally a collapse. A childhood friend of Shekhar's who happened to know his address in the city had managed to scribble a letter to him. Shekhar was at that time living with pickpockets in a slum. By the time he had rushed to the village along with a compounder acquaintance, his mother, who had died (of septicaemia, the compounder said) three days earlier, had already been cremated. He had gone to the pyre. By then it was cool, allowing him to grope for the remains of his mother in the ashes. He broke down and wept—for the first and last time in his life. He had vowed, there and then, that he would drown all of the perpetrators of that crime in a sea of their own tears. His own eyes, he had told himself, would never be moist again, ever.

He had done his bit over the years, making full use of his

scheming brain. Crooked according to others, absolutely clear and logical according to himself. He had changed parties, enunciating a new principle for each change. He not only got away with it, but added to his own importance at every step. And someone always wanted him; an efficient conspirator is never unutilized in the political field. With every operation, he left a debris of broken friendships behind. With every step he took, he sowed a fresh crop of deep-rooted suspicions that could never be resolved—and he saw to it that they remained unresolved.

Thanks to him, Mahendranath and Chaudhury were implacable enemies. Their cohorts at all levels were in confrontation, eyeball to eyeball. And in the bargain, Chaudhury had made Shekhar a minister, to take advantage of his inside knowledge of Mahendranath's camp. Mahendranath fumed at him, but Shekhar couldn't care less. He had stepped off the uppermost rung of the ladder and then kicked it away from under him, as almost everyone does in political life. He had even managed to use his illegitimacy to his advantage. Given the umpteen sub-groups within groups in the party, based on caste, region, sub-region, religion, language, ethnicity, Shekhar's skill at manipulating the various permutations and combinations ensured that the politicians were fighting amongst themselves all the time. And he succeeded fabulously, being the only casteless, classless, mobile politician around, without affiliation to group or creed. This increased his value enormously. It was an exquisite paradox that for once his illegitimacy gave him a rare advantage over all the other leaders shackled to their castes.

His strategy was mainly to demolish, one by one, every person in his own party who mattered, or would matter at some future time. Set them against one another and let them do the rest; just watch the fun, stoking the fires now and then. The last on his hit list for the time being was Anand. 'He is so easy to destroy, such a sitting duck! How I pity him!' he had often told himself. However, it had been easy to banish any compunctions he might have felt once he had targeted Anand. Step one: get him embroiled in controversy. That was easy enough, especially at the surface level, given his association with Aruna. Anand was a committed

337

devotee of logical thinking. He had overwhelming compassion for the afflicted. He suffered from a total absence of personal ambition. He possessed a storehouse of knowledge accumulated over a long period of diligent study and reflection. His ideological bent and visionary nature would be his undoing. Shekhar knew this inclination was the antithesis of practical politics, such as was in vogue: Jawaharlal did the thinking—and got away with it, because he was Jawaharlal; the 'Panditji' in him did the explaining and then, everyone else did the violating! Neat division of labour, Shekhar mused sardonically.

After he had failed to dislodge Anand through the exposé he had inspired in the tabloid, Shekhar looked around for some other way in which to get rid of his foe. Fortunately for Shekhar, he had persuaded Chief Minister Chaudhury, rather too easily he thought, to give Anand the new portfolio of land reforms. Now, he set out to protect his flanks and direct the assault.

Right then, as he ruminated in his drawing room, he was expecting a very promising visitor who could play a key role in the unfolding drama. He was Balram, Aruna's elder brother. A big landlord in his area, Balram was impetuous, breezy, ruthless. He had dropped out of school very early when he found Aruna had been promoted to his own class, while he had failed to make the grade. The humiliation was intolerable. He had therefore insisted, as the eldest member of the family, that Aruna terminate her studies too and get married. She flatly refused to do so and went off to the city to enter college, assisted by a distant cousin; the family had to acquiesce. But Balram's male ego was badly bruised. He had become a good farmer and the local sarpanch, an effective leader in dealing with the toughs of the locality, at once a despot and a shrewd tactician. He had finally managed to live down his inferiority in education. Yet, with all the brotherly love he showered on Aruna, he had not quite forgiven her for having outstripped him at school, years ago. There were violent arguments as well as displays of extremely tender affection between them whenever they met. They baffled people by their volatile shifts in mood.

All in all, Shekhar reflected, Balram was going to be a tricky customer. In some respects, brother and sister were alike—erratic in temperament, daredevils in action and inexhaustible reservoirs of love. Balram was also the master litigant of his area. Unpredictable and mercurial, he would sometimes espouse seemingly lost causes: a helpless widow harassed by her late husband's in-laws; an indigent scheduled-caste tenant arrested by the police at the instance of a rich landlord; a poor girl in love with a young man but forced to marry a stinking old fellow with property . . . In cases such as the last, Balram had got the couple married in his own house at his own expense and got the unjust police officer transferred overnight. People were intimidated by the prospect of opposing him in any way. However, all that influence was the direct outcome of his extensive landed property and the fat income he derived from it. Without that property, he was, or would have been, a nobody—neither clerk nor coolie. Not even equal to an ordinary wage-earner or to any of his own numerous farm servants. That fact was undeniable. So, Shekhar guessed shrewdly, Balram wouldn't exactly relish the prospect of having to surrender almost half of his land to the government.

Shekhar had done his homework extremely well. Like many big landowners, Balram also gloated over some family history, he noted. Some boot-licking ancestor of his in the last century was 'honoured' with a *laqab* (title), presumably for 'distinguished services' rendered to one of the past Nasir Jahs. The *laqab* had instantly turned the family's blood into blue. It became bluer and bluer with every succeeding generation, until Balram began to claim that there was no trace of any other colour in it. That was a significant obsession, Shekhar noted again.

Shekhar was musing on these traits with grim contempt when the peon announced Balram's arrival. Instantly, he slipped on a practiced mask of geniality. He advanced towards the door to welcome Balram, who strutted in pompously. What a striking contrast in this respect between sister and brother—between Aruna, simple and completely unselfconscious, and this arrogant, conceited blighter!—Shekhar thought as he shook hands with Balram.

'Welcome, Raja sahib, welcome!' Shekhar exclaimed, inflating

Balram's ego no end. A minister calling him Raja Sahib! Balram's self-esteem was in spate. And why not? Who was this minister yesterday? How was he different from any of Balram's own illegitimate progeny scattered in many villages and in many families, under different paternities? After all, a bastard is a bastard, whatever else he may or may not be!

'How are you, Minister sahib?' said Balram. 'I wanted to come and felicitate you earlier, but just couldn't make it, you see . . . I am so glad you have become a minister . . .'

'Thank you, thank you very much indeed!' smiled Shekhar. 'It is all due to the goodwill of respected citizens like your good self, Raja sahib . . .'

'I hear that there has been some change in portfolios lately?' queried Balram casually. 'To tell you the truth, I don't care about the change, since it doesn't affect me one way or another. I don't know why the newspapers are all overflowing with this news alone!'

'You know how the newspapers are these days, Raja sahib,' Shekhar commented with seeming ingenuousness. 'This time they have collected a big bundle of opinions across the board, as you must have noticed. By the way, did any of the journalists contact you? I thought they couldn't possibly miss a personage like you, any more than they could miss the Qutub Minar in Delhi!'

'Oh yes, some fellow from some . . . what do they call it, some agent, he said . . .'

'Yes, yes, you mean news agency . . . the same thing, you know? Was it UNI by any chance?'

'Yes, yes, I remember now . . . Some name like that. He wanted to come over. I invited him to dinner tonight. I don't know what the fellow is going to ask me . . .' This, of course, Shekhar already knew because it was he who had tipped off the UNI correspondent about Balram earlier in the day. The newsman had not been very enthusiastic but he had been galvanized into activity when he was told that Balram was Aruna's own elder brother. What a stroke of luck, he had told himself, realizing at once the news potential of Aruna's brother battling it out with Aruna's boyfriend!

'They're all like that, you see,' Shekhar said. 'They never tell you what they'll ask. Just shoot the questions directly. Of course, you have all the answers ready with all your rich experience and knowledge. He might ask you anything under the sun, yet I'm sure you wouldn't bat an eye. So, how does it matter whether or not you know what he wants in advance?'

Balram couldn't agree more. He thought, this minister is quite intelligent after all and is able to assess people correctly. While he was thus complimenting Shekhar mentally, completely taken in by the latter's adulation, Shekhar added, rather casually, 'Maybe, Raja sahib, one of the topics this newsman would like to ask you about is land reforms. You know, a new portfolio of land reforms has come into being and my good friend Anand is the minister in charge of it . . . ?'

'Oh yes, I know. I know everything,' echoed Balram, eager to show that what he knew was nothing short of everything. 'I have known Anand well for quite some time now. He has been in the city, yet he knows so much about land, agriculture work, cattle etc. Nice fellow . . .'

Hmm, thought Shekhar, that way lies a road block. The goodwill between Anand and Balram was a sudden and unforeseen barrier. A thought occurred to him. It had occurred dozens of times before, but he had suppressed it ruthlessly, uncompromisingly. At that moment, however, when he was face to face with Balram, it seemed particularly tempting. Should he, in his own subtle way, hint at the Anand-Aruna relationship? Should he impress on Balram how the name of his illustrious family was about to suffer through this scandalous connection? That the *laqab* earned by a forebear of his generations ago would change into a *laqab* of notorious adultery? For a man, it was not shameful; indeed, it was a badge of virility. Balram was a shining example of a compulsive womanizer himself. But a daughter of the family . . . What could be more disastrous?

It was easy. It was at the tip of his tongue . . . Yet Shekhar suppressed it again with a supreme effort of will. He remembered the moment he had first observed Aruna in Anand's company on the day of their swearing-in, her dusky face and large lustrous eyes aglow with pride and delight . . . It was then that he had called her 'sister'—and had continued to do so ever since. He had always longed for a younger sister, from his days as a lonely child in the garhi where he was born, and where he continually received the unforgivable taunts about his 'corrupt' bloodline. He could have had a sister, if only his mother had been spared one, just one of those umpteen abortions the landlords had forced on her with sickening regularity. That was not to be . . . So though he hated Anand like poison, he had tried his best not to harm Aruna. Sometimes he despised himself for this vulnerability, which was in total contradiction to the ruthlessness he took pride in. But he could not bring himself to plot Aruna's destruction. He could not help this lacuna in his conversion from man to fiend. It remained, a marshy spot of persistent emotion.

'What do you think Anand will do as minister in charge of land reforms?' he asked Balram, reverting to the one subject he knew he should concentrate on.

'How do I know?' Balram countered, shrugging his shoulders. 'I believe they will pass some law; let us see. For the rest, you should know, being a minister . . .?'

'The law is yet to come,' said Shekhar. 'The party policies are well-known. Didn't Aruna give you a rough idea at least?'

'Aruna?' guffawed Balram. 'What does she know of land anyway, poor thing? She was born in the village, but that's about all. After that, it was city life for her all through. I don't think she knows whether paddy grows above the ground or underground! I wouldn't pay much attention to what she says about land or land reforms.' His ego demanded that he emphasize how his sister, with all her education and status as MLA, was ignorant in at least one area.

'Maybe you could ask Anand himself,' Shekhar suggested as a new inspiration struck him with all its possibilities. 'Straight from the horse's mouth, you know . . .'

'Yes, that's a very good idea. I'll ask Anand. Maybe early tomorrow. I'll ask for an appointment.'

Again, Shekhar wanted to say, 'Why not ask Aruna to get the appointment fixed immediately?' But he restrained himself. He noticed again and again that even in his plan of total annihilation, he wanted one person saved. He knew that a holocaust does not make any exception. Yet, that was his puzzling, arbitrary and absurd wish, if you will. It was as clear and unambiguous as the other wish—the wish to destroy.

'I have some idea of party policy,' continued Shekhar, unwilling to let Balram meet Anand without being 'properly' prepared. 'In the first place, the party thinks that concentration of too much land in a few hands is bad for the people, bad for the landowners themselves and bad for efficient agriculture. So there should be some kind of cooperative farming. Next, there should be a law giving fixity of tenure to tenants and share-croppers. Rack-renting and frequent substitution of tenants must end. And lastly, no family should own more than a given extent of land, called a ceiling. All surplus land over and above the ceiling should go to the government, to be distributed among the landless in the village . . . Well, this is only a bare outline, as you can see.'

Balram heard him out carefully, then burst out laughing. After his amusement had subsided a little, he said, with a broad smile, 'And the officers of the revenue department will implement these laws, I presume?'

'Well, I think so,' answered Shekhar rather lamely. 'Who else can do it?'

'Thank you very much for this information!' cut in Balram. 'I welcome the laws, indeed any number of laws, more the merrier! Please get them passed and implemented at the earliest, I say!'

This was the opening Shekhar was looking for. He seized the chance. He put on a serious look and said, 'Raja sahib, please don't be too complacent about this matter. The party will carry out its mandate, come what may; no question about it. And don't forget, we now have a minister who knows his job as no one knew it before. Besides, he is a fanatic land reformer, let me tell you. You don't seem to realize whom you will be dealing with from now on. As for myself, I may have all sympathy for the landowners, personally. I may not agree with this over-zealous programme of forcibly seizing land from owners who have lived on it for centuries. Yet, I am a disciplined soldier of the party and I can't see how you or I or anyone can stop Anand from doing what he is sure to do . . .! He knows all the tricks of the trade. He is fully aware of the possible loopholes in implementation that you seem to be relying on. Don't ever think that Anand will not plug each of those holes and curtail your options forever! No one can challenge this mighty government and get away with it, don't you understand?'

Raja sahib panicked a little, but he was not completely shaken by Shekhar's poorly-disguised venom. No minister can go to every village to administer any law—any damn law, he told himself. What is this bastard raving about with such new-found zeal? At the moment, it looked like a riddle. After a few more sallies that brought no answers, Balram rose to go. 'Thanks for the information anyway,' he said. 'I shall follow your advice and get the real facts from Anand himself . . . From the horse's mouth, as you said.' They shook hands.

'Yes, that's right,' echoed Shekhar as he escorted Balram to the car. 'Only, I shall wager anything on my forecast that this horse will not open its mouth wide enough to tell you what he is actually proposing to do! . . . Sorry I have to leave you with this disquieting thought, but being your well-wisher, I must be blunt in telling you the whole truth . . .'

Balram got into his car rather absent-mindedly. The end of his dhoti got trapped in the door as he slammed it. Watching the flap of starched white protruding from the door as the car pulled away, Shekhar found himself brooding somewhat irritably at the deeply ironic twist his scheme was taking. Why—why on earth—was he trying now to help the landlords, a class which had tormented him from his earliest years, against a person who was engaged heart and soul in a struggle to end landlord privileges once and for all?

# 31

AFTER HIS MEETING AT CHAUDHURY'S HOUSE TO DISCUSS HIS NEW responsibilities, Anand did not go to his office for a day; he decided to stay home to think through, as best he could, the way to proceed with his new job. After spending a morning in quiet reflection he thought he could now see both sides of the picture more clearly. It was good this way, he concluded, particularly if one was going to tackle the root of an issue and not just superficial problems.

Four days later, Aruna suddenly materialized one afternoon, fuming in her usual style—a style Anand had come to understand and humour. It was an amalgam of several factors, but chiefly she was fretting at her inability to meet him as often as she wanted to. She often taunted him, saying, 'I see you are more devoted to your work than anything else. How do I become your favourite book or file for a change?' To which Anand replied, 'You are already my favourite book, indeed an epic, written by a great poet gone berserk!'

At this time, while Anand's career seemed to have taken off, Aruna was going nowhere. She spent her time in pointless activity ranging from meetings without agenda to grossly exaggerated gossip about male politicians. She was disgusted at the swarm of self-servers who mobbed her, seeking favours from the state government in general and from Anand in particular. Even when he was no longer minister of irrigation, some contractors approached Aruna, urging her to get things done by chief engineers through Anand. They came with wide-ranging offers in exchange, which incensed her. She flew into uncontrollable rage when someone referred to Anand in derogatory terms in her presence. This last had almost become a regular ruse to provoke her and add to the fast-expanding scandal about her and Anand. Her antics on such occasions only made matters worse; but she never cared to control her temper. Anand remained characteristically neutral, giving her no advice or suggestion in this regard, for fear that she might do just the opposite!

'What's the trouble, Aruna?' Anand asked, planting a light kiss on her forehead.

'You, of course!' she snapped. 'Who else? What else?'

'That's well-known now. You don't react so explosively to such commonplace things, do you? . . . There must be something special this time!'

'You are special always!' she said. Then, cooling down a little, added, 'For me, of course . . .' and clung to him.

'All right,' Anand began. He seated her on a sofa and girdled her waist with his arm. 'Let's see what the problem is. Too many recommendations? Too many snide remarks? Too much activity that takes you away from someone?' When she shook her head at each of these guesses, he added, 'Well, I have exhausted my powers of speculation. I give up. Now tell me.'

'This new portfolio of yours worries me. The comments I hear scare me out of my wits. It seems extremely dangerous.'

'You must have heard a lot, of course. Can you list a few gems that you consider particularly dangerous? And dangerous for whom or for what?'

'I don't know where to begin, but I'll try. In the first place, they say you brought tremendous pressure to bear on Chaudhury to put you in charge of land reforms. You lobbied intensively in Delhi.

You even persuaded the Prime Minister to advise the chief ministers on the urgency of this programme. Then you got someone very close to the Prime Minister to ask Chaudhury to give you this portfolio at once. At once, because you wanted everyone to believe that it was forced on you, even while you were away from the state headquarters. And when a prominent journalist contacted you for immediate comment, you were very evasive. That was your game of fooling everyone . . .'

'Perfect!' commented Anand. 'And why am I doing all this? Any idea about my motivation? Or, do they think I have become a fit case for the lunatic asylum?'

'I was coming to that,' Aruna added. 'Your alleged motivation seemed to vary from group to group. The landlords are certain that you are out to destroy them.'

'Do they care to explain why?' asked Anand.

'There's no unanimity on that. One imaginative rumour has it that you demanded that a landlord sell you one hundred acres of his dry land. It will become wet land shortly, when a huge irrigation project gets commissioned. You offered him the price of dry land and he refused, naturally. Justice was obviously on his side. So, you took a vow to strip all landlords of their lands and make them paupers.'

'And what are the comments of other groups?'

'They're varied too, as you can expect,' responded Aruna. 'One comment is that when you found land reforms unavoidable, you schemed to have the portfolio assigned to you, so that you could help the landlords to the maximum. After all, they add, you are from the same class yourself. You would not like them decimated by any unsympathetic minister such as, say, Shekhar. In fact they believe that there was a tussle between the two of you for this prize portfolio . . .'

'What do the common people say, if I may ask?'

'I went to my constituency for a few days. In fact I was in a far-off village only yesterday. The mass of the people do think that you will give them land; but they're not sure they will be able to keep it. They say it'll revert to the landed gentry somehow. They are oscillating between hope and despair at the same time . . .'

'Your constituency is full of Left activists, isn't it? Did you get any reaction from those quarters?'

'Well, yes . . . Their general reaction is that all this is just another gimmick of the ruling party. However, this time I could see they were angrier than usual. They don't dismiss the matter lightly now.'

'What does that signify?'

'I don't know. Maybe they are either afraid or unhappy or both.'

'H'mm,' mused Anand. 'Did you discover why they're unhappy?'

'Not quite,' said Aruna. 'One of their party men who is a bit too talkative said that they may lose one of their stock issues against the ruling party. He still asserted that nothing is going to emerge in concrete terms; yet, with you in charge, he is no longer that certain. He says his party men are also vague about land reforms, but since they're not forming a government to carry out the programme, they only have to make political capital out of the issue and keep the landless on their own side.'

Here she stopped abruptly and, looking straight into his eyes, said, 'But what am I babbling about? I started with the complaint that you're too busy with land reforms and you end up by making me talk of nothing else! I must stop this!' She embraced him, and pretended she wouldn't talk at all.

After a while, their patience exhausted, they began talking again about Anand's new job. That was the one topic on the agenda, whether they liked it or not.

'What have you got into, for heaven's sake?' Aruna resumed worriedly. 'They say even my brother Balram is unhappy with you. Did you two have an altercation by any chance? He was so fond of you always . . .'

'We haven't even met to discuss this subject,' Anand said. 'In any event, he is entitled to his views, as also his unhappiness.'

'Even without talking to you?'

'Why not, if many others have talked to him about me and told him all that you reported a few minutes back?'

'Now, tell me, what is all this trouble about? Why have you

become a common target suddenly? What does everyone think you are going to do? Why did you get into this messy job in the first place?'

'I really don't know, Aruna,' Anand replied. 'Circumstantially, what you heard had an element of truth. For instance, Chaudhury created the new portfolio and allotted it to me when I was away in Delhi, as you know. What prompted Chaudhury to do so is not at all clear to me, even after my detailed talk with him. There is a maze of devious motivations operating behind my back. I seem to be merely at the receiving end. It is also well known that I own land myself and would stand to lose a good portion of it under the proposed land ceiling law. So, they had to invent different interpretations, one to explain my ostensible support to the land owners, the other to account for my alleged antagonism to my own brotherhood. The fact is that no one has worked out a way to convert a slogan into a programme. Implementation always comes much later, you see . . . For my part, I shall await further instructions from the chief minister—which would really be those from the party high command. I see nothing else I can do at the moment.'

'You hold strong views on land reform, don't you?'

'Yes, it so happens that I do.'

'And so do others. Their views are diametrically opposed to yours, aren't they?'

'Yes, they are.'

'What happens if there is a showdown?'

'I don't know. Let us see.'

At this point the phone rang. While he said 'Hello!' to the caller, Anand cupped the mouthpiece with his hand and whispered to Aruna, 'Your brother!' Then he continued, 'How are you, Balramji? Why, what is the difficulty? You know I don't stand on formality. You can walk in any time. Would you like to come now?'

'In fact I am on my way,' came the reply. 'I left home an hour back; I am speaking to you from some other place.'

'Then you would be hardly a couple of minutes from here. Please come over . . .'

There was a short, uneasy, suspicious silence. Then Balram said, 'Good heavens! How did you know I am so close by?'

'Just a hunch, you know,' replied Anand. 'Anyway how does it matter how near or far you are? I am waiting.'

'Where is he?' Aruna asked when Anand put down the receiver.

'A stone's throw away, literally,' Anand said with a grin. 'The exact spot from where stones are thrown at me all the time—Shekhar's residence!'

Aruna made a face and became serious.

'Cheer up, Aruna,' Anand said with a chuckle. 'Your big brother's on his way. You don't want him to think that you and I have just had a quarrel, do you? After all, a sister needs a brother to quarrel with! And what a brother!' He gave her another quick hug before Balram's Impala glided into the portico. Then they sat at a respectable distance from each other on the sofa.

'Anandji, glad to see you!' shouted Balram as he entered the room with his usual royal swagger. Anand met him halfway, shook his hand and showed him to a sofa. It was then that Balram saw Aruna. She looked at him smilingly and said, 'Hello, bhaiya! How are you? How are bhabhi and the children?'

'They're all well, thank you,' Balram replied. 'When did you arrive here? What are you doing?'

'She has been making all kinds of complaints against you!' Anand said, bursting into laughter.

'I don't believe you on this at all!' snapped Balram. 'I know my sister better than I know myself. She doesn't complain; she explodes. And she would abuse me to my face rather than complain to a third person. We fight and make up all the time. It is a family trait, you know . . .'

'A wonderful trait, no doubt!' commented Anand. 'However, innocent third persons such as myself get the benefit of the family trait sometimes!'

All three laughed heartily. After they had had coffee, Balram lit a cigar and in a casual and leisurely manner, broached the topic of the day. 'You see, Anandji, I don't understand all this tumult and confusion about land reforms. Not that it worries me, but there is an element of anxiety in the countryside. Tensions are also mounting visibly. Can nothing be done about this situation?'

Balram looked genuinely apprehensive, which Anand seemed to appreciate entirely. His sympathy at once established a friendly equation between them. If Balram had come prepared for a fight, he now found none in the offing. 'You see, Anandji,' he began in a conciliatory tone. 'I respect your deep knowledge of the countryside and insight into the minds of the rural folk. That's why I like to talk to you on equal and cordial terms, which is something I am unable to do with many other ministers. Tell me, what should we do now? What do the projected land reforms hold in store for us?'

Anand was surprised too, and a bit baffled. He had also braced himself for a fight, at least for some plain-speaking. Balram's sudden mellowness disarmed him. 'We do know the problems of the rural areas, Balramji,' he began matter-of-factly. 'Don't you think we need to go into the reasons for the present situation? Take your area, for instance. What is the average number of murders per year in your district? Any idea?'

'Quite high,' replied Balram.

'And out of them, what percentage are about land?'

'Again quite high, I must say.'

'And this has been the case for decades, I presume?'

'Yes, that's right. There has hardly been any respite from crime and tension about land ever since I remember.'

'So, you see that tensions in the countryside are not traceable to land reforms or to anything of recent origin. Isn't that so?'

'Yes, but the talk of land reforms is adding to the tension now,' observed Balram rather feebly, when he found his main allegation virtually demolished.

'Let us assume that this is so. Now supposing there had been no talk of land reform, did we have any plan to resolve the existing tensions?'

Balram felt annoyed. He had come to elicit information from Anand and to virtually demolish the whole scheme of land reforms. He had not bargained for a cross-examination of this kind. He was not the type who would sort out complex subjects through discussion. According to him, he was invariably right, and his logic always trustworthy.

'Why do you ask me?' he said testily. 'I am not running the government. I could have lived with the old tensions because I knew where I stood then. I had the necessary clout to deal with them, both legally and in other ways. All that was familiar ground.'

Anand's patience was running out. Still, he did not want to be the first to lose his temper. 'Look, Balramji,' he said, 'we are not talking of power here. Can't we talk of what is right, for a change?'

'You don't mean to suggest that I am being unjust?'

'I suggest nothing of the kind,' Anand retorted. 'I am only trying to understand your viewpoint . . .'

'Look, we have done no injustice to anyone,' Balram went on. 'We protect the people in the village, provide them with leadership, give them employment, keep them from devouring one another, and in general, maintain public order. We try to help them survive famine and pestilence. We do everything to keep them happy. Heaven knows that you can't do all this without being a bit harsh sometimes. That is part of the game. I don't see why anyone should complain about this . . .'

'No one is complaining, as far as I can see,' Anand said. 'The system of kingship had several good characteristics. For one thing, the king made it unnecessary for the people to think for themselves. Yet we have done away with kingship in about five hundred native states, haven't we? In a feudal set-up, no great responsibility rests on the people. They merely have to exist and obey. However, when aspirations change, there is friction between the old and the new systems. This is what we have to contend with, the good and the not-so-good . . .'

Balram's temper rose abruptly. He was not willing to concede that he belonged to a community threatened with potential obsolescence. 'I have heard such lectures hundreds of times. I don't agree that any far-reaching change in the system is necessary. I speak for my entire class when I say that we will resist any such ruinous change. And by God, we will succeed!'

'Let's not jump to questions of success and failure, Balramji,' Anand pleaded. 'We are not at that stage now and there is no need for conflict. We have recent experience of the effects of a confrontation on agrarian issues. Fortunately, your area has been peaceful; but it's only a question of time before all areas are engulfed in uncontrollable turmoil. Let's face it, there is too much land in too few hands. However benevolent you are, you will never be able to make a landless person feel like a land owner, even a marginal land owner.'

'What do they need land for?' Balram cut in with controlled fury. 'They will only sell it for liquor and become landless again.'

'I know that this has happened,' agreed Anand. 'But this is besides the point. You and I are also aware of a number of landlords who are debauched and who have frittered away their entire property as a result. On the other hand, I can also point out thousands of landless persons who have started a new life for themselves with the small plots of government land assigned to them. So we cannot advance such instances in support of or against the concept of land reforms . . .'

'Whatever you say, Anandji,' Balram said with finality. 'You are not being realistic in this matter. I do not see how the land owners can cooperate with you and sign their own death warrant.'

'They're not signing their death warrant, I assure you,' Anand said earnestly. 'Land reforms will really free big landlords from the shackles of unwieldy and unproductive farming. Reforms will enable them to diversify their economic activity. They can fan out into industries and a host of other fields and utilize their financial resources for more profitable investment. In the feudal areas, there is a social stigma attached to any landlord selling his land. Selling is interpreted as evidence of going bankrupt. Land reforms will remove that and set a new trend to treat land strictly as a means of production. It will no longer be a status symbol or a dead asset. The whole agrarian scene will become dynamic. Rural areas will be buzzing with diversified economic activity. Just imagine what the new scenario will be like, Balramji . . .'

'All I can imagine is my becoming a non-entity in all respects,' Balram retorted. 'No . . . I won't abide by or succumb to your reforms, come what may.'

Aruna had been agitated by the conversation between her

brother and Anand. She had restrained herself with a great effort. She had tried to intervene each time Balram's hostility threatened to obstruct the dialogue. Finally, Balram brushed her aside brusquely and said, 'Will you keep out of this? You know nothing about the subject!'

'I know enough to see that you are unreasonable!'

Anand cut in, just in time to avert a major confrontation.

'Aruna,' he said, 'we are trying to sort this thing out. I would welcome suggestions from you, since you are in close touch with your constituency. In fact you and I could have another long chat on the subject. Okay?'

That was the closest he could come to asking her to keep quiet. Then, he turned to Balram and said, 'You said you could resist change and still succeed. How will you resist? How will you succeed? Could you elucidate a little?'

'That is our precious secret, Minister sahib!' Balram replied with a burst of laughter. 'When it comes to the crunch, you are just an individual swimming against the current. The truth is, the entire administrative machinery of the government is behind the landlord class. I assure you of this fact!'

'Well, we have our precious secrets too,' Anand retorted. 'And as for the government, all I can say is, let us see!'

'So, the die is cast!' said Balram.

'You say so . . .' countered Anand.

They sat for a while in simmering tension. The silence was broken by the shrill ring of the unlisted telephone. Anand answered it and heard Chaudhury on the line—from Delhi. 'I have been talking to our leaders here,' the chief minister said. 'The situation on our northern borders is none too happy. There seems to be considerable tension and confusion. However, despite the distraction of the Chinese threat, preparations for the third general elections are on. The party manifesto is on the anvil, with land reforms as an important issue. They have put you on the drafting panel. So get ready, dreamer; fill it up with as much hope for the people as your imagination can manage. Soar to your heart's content on the wings of your words. I'll discuss the rest after my return. Good luck!'

# 32

THE STATE GOVERNMENT GUEST HOUSE IN DELHI WAS JAM-PACKED
with ticket-seekers, their supporters, sycophants and opponents.
So were the guest houses of all state governments, as well as many
hotels with various 'star' ratings. All of them overflowed with the
torch-bearers of democracy. The crowds swelled and swelled.
From several states, particularly those not far from the capital,
Indian Railways carried ticketless travellers by the thousand. The
urgency of the need to obtain a party ticket dispensed with the
need to buy a rail ticket. Indian Airlines, on the other hand, wiped
out its chronic losses and made a clean profit during each election.

Anand observed the mêlée with keen interest and a
bewilderment verging on wonder. Large contingents of politicians
of all sorts and grades were everywhere. They made the rounds of
the central ministers. They made a beeline for the members of the
Central parliamentary board of the ruling party. They also
thronged around astrologers who mushroomed suddenly at
election time. Lastly, they ran after hundreds of opportunists who
claimed to be close, very close, to this or that leader. They could

make him sign on the dotted line, they asserted. The near-deserted, sleepy roads and footpaths of New Delhi suddenly came alive. As if by magic, human beings sprang up like unseasonal weeds and wild plants everywhere. Peons and jamadars at ministers' offices and residences collected tidy sums by way of *bakshish* from the thousands who lined up in their courtyards as mendicants of political power. Many ticket-seekers who were otherwise tough and arrogant in their own areas, assumed imploring masks and made placating gestures devised and practiced specially for the occasion. The lust for power softened their attitudes overnight.

Party men—and women—moved in batches of varied size and composition. Each candidate rejected at the state level arrived in Delhi to appeal to the party high command. About one-fourth (often less) of each representation consisted of the appellant's record of service that, according to him, entitled him to the party ticket. The remaining three-fourth (often much more) contained a diatribe against each of the other ticket-seekers from the constituency and reasons why each of them merited rejection out of hand. The negative part was much more elaborate and consisted of horrendous stories of the wickedness of all applicants other than the appellant. If you went by this and believed it in all cases, you would conclude that the party did not have a single good candidate to field! If it was a male applicant, he was corrupt to the core and a womanizer of the worst kind, according to his opponents. If the applicant was female, she was of easy morals, a blot on Indian womanhood. How could you tolerate her in a party blessed by Mahatma Gandhi? Applicants dug up one another's criminal records. They produced certified copies of court judgments in support of their allegations. These instances created pathological irritation and suspicion all round. After all that the applicants alleged against one another, it was impossible to find one among them whom the others could support with a clear conscience in the campaign. The selected candidate thus stood alone, to fend for himself. He had to face the candidates of the other parties, as well as many saboteurs from his own.

Then, there was the political branding. Candidates charged one another with being opposed to Nehru's ideals—which ideals, they did not spell out. None of them seemed to know these ideals. It had become a mechanical process, a slogan, a shibboleth. One claimed to be a progressive, dubbing the others as reactionaries. One claimed to be extremely popular in the constituency, while others said everyone detested him. There was no way to verify the truth in Delhi. And the most important factor, loyalty to the Nehru family, gradually assumed crucial importance. Candidates began to be labelled accordingly. The phenomenon had no recognizable origin. Yet it became a palpable truth, particularly in the northern states.

Anand had to make frequent trips to Delhi at short notice during this period. He was baffled by the way 'loyalty to the Nehru family' became a criterion and a talking point. Soon it was perhaps the main talking point. He had seen Jawaharlal Nehru's career for at least twenty years now, from the last five years of the freedom movement through Independence and the first decade-and-a-half of his Prime Ministership.

Panditji's personality fascinated Anand. He mused over Nehru's exemplary traits. His indomitable courage. His attempt to introduce modernity in a tradition-bound ambience, to blend both in viable harmony. His buoyant idealism that countered the depressing forces of social injustice. His possible shortcomings in judging men and so on . . . All of Anand's admiration, however, could not reconcile him to the new slogan of 'loyalty'. Loyalty to the party, even to one individual of Nehru's stature, was understandable. But when the slogan extended to the family . . . Anand remembered the king's regime. He recalled his early revulsion towards the concept of loyalty to the king, even in the context of hereditary rule. Now, in the new context of democracy, the slogan saddened him. There was no question in his mind that attitudes needed to change radically in free India.

In recent years, Nehru's speeches had tended to become a bit halting. The change was noticed by penetrating observers. As the country prepared to go to the polls in 1962, the thinking Indian was no longer as sure-footed in his onward march as he had been in the previous decade.

What had gone wrong, or was about to go wrong? Anand

mulled over the complex question. It was perhaps disillusionment, because performance had fallen short of expectation. Maybe the expectation itself had been pitched too high to begin with. The people had perhaps taken Independence, at least subconsciously, as an all-powerful panacea for the country's ills. No one said so, certainly not Panditji. But it was true that the local satraps of the party did not choose to dispel that impression. In the short term, they had won two general elections without having to make the people aware that India's complex socio-economic and ethnic problems could not be solved by the application of any single formula or methodology, or the energy of any one historical or political phenomenon.

Parties vied with one another in making fantastic promises to wrest electoral advantages, in utter disregard of any government's capacity to fulfil them. Nehru was again the exception to this. He not only did not make promises, but went one step further and desisted from making a direct appeal to the people to vote for his party. Nevertheless, his charismatic personality made the people presume, with ample justification, that what his party men said, he would certainly do. 'Panditji is too dignified and too principled a person to ask for votes in so many words,' they concluded. His halo served the party well, but the law of diminishing returns began to operate gradually. Yet it was unquestionable that Jawaharlal was still a greater asset to the party than anyone its rivals could muster. No other party had a Jawaharlal to head it.

There was an air of unease that no one could quite understood. Anand analysed it more closely, to get a feel of it, if possible. It was a fact that while Nehru grappled with the nation's problems almost single-handedly, those who were expected to share his burden seemed to be foisting more and more problems of their own making upon his shoulders. Many of his irresponsible party men became a liability to him. They had nothing effective to contribute. Besides, many of them had no understanding of Nehru's vision anyway. And when Nehru's public appearances decreased and he showed signs of slowing down, it became obvious how difficult it would be to find an effective replacement. The tone he had set was high and unique. As a result, the void that would result after him looked all the more difficult to fill. No one thought his departure was imminent, yet everyone seemed to be expecting it. Everyone took that event subconsciously as the next watershed, as it were, in the country's unfolding history. Dozens of speculative books appeared on the subject of Nehru's possible successor. They signalled just one problem staring the nation in the face. All other issues paled into insignificance for the time being. In fact this was *the* problem—to find Nehru's successor. And there were no credible options. It threatened to be a long and futile quest.

The problems were indeed many; they could be categorized as mainly regional, linguistic and communal. Lal Bahadur Shastri, as the home minister from a little before mid-1961, battled with these problems, paying visits to several troubled areas on behalf of the Prime Minister. Some clashes had erupted even before 1961; for instance, in 1959 the Assam Sahitya Sabha made a demand that Assamese be made the official language of the state of Assam. There was an area and some tribal pockets in the state as it then was where the people spoke Bengali. Obviously, a formula to satisfy both linguistic groups was needed. Unfortunately the matter went beyond the politics of language alone and spilled into the streets. Violence broke out in 1960, and in May 1961 there was extensive violence, especially in Cachar district, a Bengali majority area. Lal Bahadur visited Assam and a formula was thrashed out, which was accepted by both sides. It attempted to do justice to both the linguistic groups and allayed their fears and suspicions. In the process, ironically, it benefited English most.

Even worse was the anti-Hindi agitation which roused tremendous passions in Tamil Nadu and in some other pockets. It had other features including class conflict and some north-south ramifications as well. The unrest raged for quite some time and had far-reaching political implications.

Chief Minister Chaudhury and some of his ministerial colleagues, including Anand, had a very grim but instructive experience during that agitation. One of the senior ministers of Tamil Nadu was to celebrate his daughter's marriage in Madras; unfortunately the auspicious day fell during the week when the anti-Hindu agitation hit a climax. There was no question of

Chaudhury and his ministers avoiding the wedding. All of them would go, they decided. And they went with some misgivings; for all they knew, not being from a confirmed anti-Hindi state, they might provoke the agitators further. Worse, Chief Minister Chaudhury's public criticism of the anti-Hindi agitation was only a few days old. No one could be sure that it had been forgotten.

They were lodged in a nice hotel, but some distance from the wedding mandap. After the muhurat, they were told that at around 6 p.m. there would be a cultural programme at the mandap site, where a temporary stage had been erected, very tastefully decorated for the occasion. When Anand, out of curiosity, asked the person in charge what the main feature of the programme was to be, the man's face became a bit pale while he answered, Kathak dance recital by Birju Maharaj. Everyone within hearing collapsed with shock. No one, of course, said anything to betray nervousness, but the implication was clear. The Tamil Nadu minister had evidently wanted his counterparts from North India to enjoy the cultural programme; so in addition to a musical recital by a famous South Indian Bhagavatar, he had, some months ago when things were calm, finalized Birju Maharaj's inclusion in the programme.

Birju Maharaj thus faced some kind of 'direct action' that evening as a penalty for his mastery over a school of dance which was admittedly non-Dravidian. At around 5 p.m. people started gathering around the compound in which the wedding mandap was situated. The police presence was reinforced, but in that emotionally charged atmosphere everybody knew that anything might happen. Just that morning, the newspaper headlines had announced two self-immolations for 'Tamil Mother' in different parts of the state. This created ripples of unrest around the site of the wedding mandap. By six o'clock the gathering crowd seemed ominously tense and alert.

The invited members of the audience took their seats at last, looking furtively around on all sides, perhaps to familiarize themselves with emergency escape routes. Cold drinks were served and on the stroke of six, the recital began. Loudspeakers had been arranged for the singing and music; but for the dance recital, the loudspeakers only served to whet the urge to watch. Within ten minutes thousands of people outside the compound had jumped the wall and rushed towards the stage. In another minute or so there would have been either a lathi charge or firing, or some other violence; the recital would disintegrate, that was certain. The faces of the invited guests were fraught with anxiety.

Then the crowd, surging like flood water on all sides, suddenly stopped, and everyone sat down. Birju Maharaj was just warming up to his first rapid beat. The strange quiet that descended over the unruly gathering seemed to inspire him a hundredfold. He gave the performance of his life. As the tempo increased towards the end, the people—in particular those who had jumped the compound wall—themselves began to respond, dancing to the same beat as Birju Maharaj. They seemed to bless and consecrate the great guru's life-long sadhana, completely forgetting where it came from; they found the exquisite sounds and rhythms which pervade the whole world . . . and maybe the universe. There seemed to be some energy present that was much more powerful than that of hatred and anger; it was the sublime rapture of aesthetic perfection that prevailed as a unifying force.

However, this was an isolated instance of harmony. The anti-Hindi agitation had by now spread to several other areas. The emotional issue of language seemed to defy rational solutions. Hindi enthusiasts, most of them with Hindi as their mother tongue, went to the extent of labelling as traitors the anti-Hindi agitators, and all those who did not like the imposition of Hindi. Hundreds of provocative and hostile incidents, small and big, exacerbated the turbulence.

According to the original provisions of the Constitution, Hindi was to become the sole official language of India from 26 January 1965. This deadline intensified the urgency and heat of the anti-Hindi agitation. Lal Bahadur as home minister presented the Official Language Bill in the Lok Sabha in April 1962, according to which English would continue to be used in government and parliamentary proceedings even after 26 January 1965. Nehru also assured the people and parliament that Hindi would not be imposed. Even if one state wanted it, English would continue to be the associate official language. But none of these measures stemmed the rising discontent.

Anand and many others saw at first hand the anger that rose out of the anti-Hindi agitation whenever they happened to visit Tamil Nadu and other areas affected by the agitation. A medical college in the state had invited Anand to preside over its centenary celebration. Midway through the well-attended function, a large crowd of agitators, aided by some students of the college, raised slogans and obstructed the meeting. They demanded that the minister declare, on the spot, that he would change his pro-Hindi attitude immediately, and pledge that he would work against Hindi from now on. Anand declared that he was only following the policy of his party and its government and there was no question of his changing it. Immediately, the meeting was terminated forcibly and Anand was gheraoed. The agitators surrounding him said they would not leave the college until he committed himself to supporting them. There was a stalemate and some of the organizers of the function also joined the gherao. Anand sat in the principal's room quietly and the slogan-shouting went on for some time. The gherao continued into the small hours of the night; Anand seemed in no great hurry to leave or to argue with the agitators. At last the district collector negotiated with the demonstrators and brought them round to giving a memorandum to the minister conveying their views. After that, the students suddenly mellowed and expressed regrets for their disruptive behaviour.

An interesting tailpiece to this agitation was provided by a Tamil MP from the party carrying on the anti-Hindi movement. Anand knew him very well, having met him several times in Delhi. One day, the MP arrived at Palam airport from Madras at the same time as Anand was about to leave Delhi for Afrozabad. They happened to meet in the VIP lounge. The MP was accompanied by his teenage son, whom he introduced to Anand. Then, with some amount of paternal pride, he said, 'You know, he is studying in Delhi and always comes first in his class in Hindi!'

Surprised, Anand said, 'And you don't know a word of Hindi and agitate against it all the time!'

'This is politics, you see?'

'Yes, I see. I see better now!' replied Anand.

The separatist agitation by some parties continued despite the legal protection provided by the new legislation on language. A clear secessionist trend began to develop. As a consequence, a bill to amend the Constitution was presented in May 1963, with the proviso that any expression of secession from the Union of India would be treated as treason. These were some new complications the nation faced, as Nehru's health and authority declined.

But by far the biggest setback the country faced in the early 1960s was its war with China. For over a decade India and China had maintained excellent relations but it was clear that this amity had deteriorated. The frequent friendly visits between the countries, when highly evocative slogans of *Hindi-Chini, Bhai-Bhai* had rent the air, turned into sullen silence. Tension mounted on the borders. Hostilities had not started yet. Still, it was obvious that Jawaharlal's dream of the two great Asian giants clasped in close friendship for ever had begun to dissolve—perhaps forever. Some giants do not believe in equality. Others who do are seen as weak, on the grounds that only the weak aspire for equality.

Things had not got out of hand—they would not, as long as Jawaharlal Nehru was around. He was the idol of the masses. He continued to be the country's chief inspiration. He alone could enthuse and mobilize the people, although one found doubts cropping up more often than before with regard to his capacity to deliver. And of course, for how long would he be around? And what then?

Some of his old colleagues had deserted him, to form or lead other parties. In terms of their capacities, they were perhaps adequate; but they simply were not effective. Their reputation continued to derive from their services in the freedom struggle, up to the moment they parted company with the 'mother' organization. The common man tended to look upon them as traitors, rather than as blazers of a new trail more glorious than the undivided party's. Their genuine motivation to float a new and vibrant Opposition in the interests of democracy got no real recognition. Many saw them only as disgruntled individuals. The reasoning, at the grassroots at any rate, was surprisingly simple.

The people vote you to power, so you initiate legislation and implement the policy that will benefit the people. What is this new thing called the Opposition? The people just did not know. They had never heard of this concept either when kings ruled or when feudals held sway. The idea never really registered. It was alien. It looked strange. It sounded odd. It failed to carry conviction and gather support. Instead, the people tended to vote for or against the 'mother party'. They did not choose *between* parties.

However, all this was never spelt out clearly. Quite often the people reacted to local situations such as the mother party granting candidature to an unpopular person; replacement of the party's sitting member for 'unjust' reasons; or another very popular and powerful candidate being in the field, either set up by another party, or standing on his own. In this latter case, it was essentially a vote for the person and not for the party . . . and so forth. The offshoot of all this was that party democracy, in the real sense, did not get established. In addition, several leaders who had left the mother party found that their position in their native areas had become unstable. They switched constituencies at every election and by-election—now from Bihar, now from Karnataka, the third time from Madhya Pradesh. They searched for 'safe' constituencies each time there was an election. Sometimes, they became 'guest' candidates, wherever a temporary combination of parties and individuals needed a big name. The idea was to defeat the mother party somehow, on any pretext. The party system stayed wreathed in its own dense convolutions. As a result democracy suffered.

Leaders who had left the mother party found themselves marginalized, isolated and completely frustrated. Jawaharlal Nehru had a monopoly on all the attractive slogans—socialism, land to the tiller, planning for development, science and technology, building modern India, cooperative commonwealth, democratic decentralization called Panchayati Raj . . . well, everything. When Nehru's rivals raised the same slogans, they were unconvincing.

When the critics saw no ideological chinks in Nehru's armour, they turned their attention to corruption. The idealistic matrix of the freedom struggle had practically disintegrated. Politicians and administrators tended to become 'realistic', with more flexible consciences that adapted like chameleons to each context. Several 'scandals' surfaced. Almost all of them involved a minister or some other senior person in the government or bureaucracy. In the relatively uneventful political climate that had emerged because of Nehru's unassailable authority, the issue of corruption tended to become the main talking point. Slowly but surely, the scandals gave rise to the belief that everyone in the ruling party was immersed in the pervasive climate of corruption—barring Nehru and a few others.

This had some definite consequences. A strange cynicism developed among the people. They began to perceive corruption in the entire public life of the country. Since they believed that this had happened in Mahatma Gandhi's party, they concluded that no positive values did or could survive. Concepts of honesty, simplicity and truthfulness steadily lost ground. Everything was relative; nothing mattered. There was a near-absolute general demoralization. The new atmosphere of nauseating opportunism only encouraged more corruption. And none of those whose nefarious dealings were exposed ever repented. It turned out to be a self-fulfilling indictment.

What is the use of Panditji talking in the air about principles, people remarked. He cannot control his own party men. He looks on helplessly while rampant corruption, nepotism, favouritism, casteism and communalism sweep across the country like hurricanes. Indeed, corrupt politicians in the ruling party get full cover and protection under Jawaharlal Nehru's leadership. If this had not been so, public life would be much cleaner indeed, as in the past . . . This view was too sweeping and simplistic to be true, and the critics knew it. Yet it was partly true, and that was enough to make it a talking point in the absence of anything more compelling.

Then there was the question of elections. Increasingly, the electoral process had become riddled with corruption, in addition to being tainted by the worst aspects of feudalism. Indeed, elections gradually lost their original purpose—a means to ascertain the wishes of the people for the governance of the country. Instead, elections became an occasion to wage war, an opportunity for both groups and individuals to settle scores. Anyone could change his party at will. Anyone could desert any party at any time and re-enter it later, at his convenience. Caste and community determined the voting pattern to a large extent. Political scruples became less and less significant, resulting in unrepentant cross-voting.

While elections to parliament remained largely political, it was tragic to see elections and by-elections to the state legislative assemblies becoming devoid of political content. Candidates captured polling booths like enemy military posts in war. They used firearms freely, to influence voters or to scare them away—as the situation required. This became the norm in some northern states. Political parties became litigants, political workers behaved like touts. It was a continuation of the feudal past. The true spirit of democracy became a tattered illusion and a pathetic shadow of the autocratic ambience that had existed in the country for centuries.

Cracks began to appear in the country's internal unity. Jammu and Kashmir presented a Constitutional problem. The concept of granting 'special status' to any one state, as distinct from all the others, made many eyebrows rise. Yet, given the heterogeneity of geographical areas and their complex ethnic and socio-cultural backgrounds, mechanical uniformity would simply not work. Jawaharlal Nehru tried hard to find a solution to this dilemma. It worked for a time, but fissured the wavering sentiment of national unity. All in all, it was a period of creeping disenchantment, with nothing much to enthuse the masses. It was a mere holding operation. The fact of the matter was that only one person was holding India together with the fragile power of his somewhat fading charisma, while corruption and apathy spread through the country like a demonic cancer. One person made the difference between unity and disunity, between stability and turmoil. No one else mattered.

Against this depressing background, Anand was commissioned to take part in the drafting of the party manifesto. He did his best, yet remained unsatisfied. And in this process, he discovered the rot at the core of New Delhi's political labyrinth. It was something he would have to battle with in the future, as his political fortunes rose.

# Part IV

# 33

FROM 1959 ONWARDS THE SITUATION ON THE BORDER WITH CHINA became increasingly tense. As the general elections approached, it became a cause for national concern. Perhaps for the first time in independent India, an international issue assumed significance on the national scene, belying the common assumption that Jawaharlal Nehru would somehow 'manage' the international aspects of the country's policy. The belief that India would continue to hold a place of prestige and honour in the world no longer held firm as before.

The third general elections in 1962 brought another victory to the ruling party. The sense of anxiety, however, thickened further. No credible rival emerged to Nehru and his party; yet both became visibly weaker.

Chaudhury became chief minister again in Afrozabad and things were as before at the state level. The Chinese question, however, worried him as much as it did any other chief minister, despite the fact that his state was a long distance from the northern border. He had been carefully studying the Prime Minister's fortnightly letters to the chief ministers which dealt with the China issue. In fact, he had compiled a file of all such letters from 1949 onwards, and thumbed through it occasionally. Since he could accurately intuit personality clashes, he had had a hunch—indeed more than a hunch—about the divergence of views between Nehru and Sardar Patel, and wondered what would have happened if the titans had openly fallen out. In a way, he could see how something unthinkable had been averted when the great Sardar passed away in 1950.

One morning in October, Chaudhury was gripped by a peculiar restlessness. The northern border seemed particularly menacing. There was a creeping feeling of something imminent—a feeling that an old political hand, well-versed in dealing with political disasters, gets unerringly . . . And it happened—the full-scale Chinese invasion. And as India reeled under the shock of betrayal, the Chinese invaded and occupied Indian territory.

On 20 October 1962, massed Chinese artillery opened heavy fire on the Indian garrison in a narrow sector of the Nanka Chu valley of Kameng Frontier Division, in the North East Frontier Agency (NEFA). Chinese infantry advanced 160 miles into Indian territory, reaching the Brahmaputra valley by 20 November. The Indian forces were ill-equipped, unacclimatized and ill-trained for mountain warfare. The NEFA Reverse, as this short battle was named, rocked India's political and military foundations and gave rise to a defeatist mentality. India had accepted the possibility of conflict with China over the undemarcated Indo-Tibet border, but had not considered the probability of a major military conflict. The government had not prepared the nation for war. India's reaction was one of shock, disbelief and indignation. 'We have been negligent and credulous,' exclaimed President S. Radhakrishnan. In a courageous but sad admission of failure, Prime Minister Nehru said over the radio, 'I am grieved at the setbacks to our troops that have occurred on the frontier, and the reverses we have had. They were overwhelmed by vast numbers and big artillery, mountain guns and heavy mortars which the Chinese have brought with them.' V.K. Krishna Menon, the defence minister, admitted, 'The

Chinese have very considerable superiority in numbers and fire power. We have been heavily outnumbered and out-weaponed.'

India's foreign policy was in disarray. The nation reacted with anger to the absoluteness of the NEFA Reverse. The army was virulently criticized and ridiculed. National indignation was accompanied by national despondency as the border state of Assam was increasingly threatened by the Chinese advance. India's humiliation intensified when after thirty days the Chinese announced their intention to withdraw from the areas they had occupied. In the words of Brigadier John Dalvi: ' . . . 1962 was a national failure of which every Indian is guilty. It was a failure in the Higher Direction of War, a failure of the Opposition, a failure of the General Staff (myself included); it was a failure of responsible public opinion and the Press. For the government of India, it was a Himalayan Blunder at all levels.' [*]

Anand was on tour in a distant village when the shattering news of the Chinese invasion was announced. Within hours, there was an astonishing metamorphosis in the prevailing atmosphere. There was a community radio set in the village which, in normal times, people were not particularly keen to listen to. However, that fateful morning the whole village gathered in front of it, listening to each bulletin with extraordinary attention. It was a roadside village and the radio set was housed in the *panchayat ghar*. As the radio blared the news of the invasion, all traffic on the road came to a grinding halt. Truck drivers left their vehicles, joined the crowd and gritted their teeth as the details of the invasion reverberated in the air. On any other occasion, the keeper of the small tea stall at the bus stand would have been bustling about, handing out hot tea and snacks to the unexpected crowd of customers. It would have been a virtual godsend for him. But the keeper was stunned that morning; he did

---

[*] The events described here are reconstructed from Brigadier John Dalvi's book *Himalayan Blunder*. To fully explore the ramifications of a very complex issue, I would also refer the reader to *The Chinese Betrayal* and *My Years With Nehru, 1948-64* by B.N. Malik, *Nehru: A Political Biography* by Michael Brecher, and *Guilty Men of 1962* by D. R. Mankekar, which have helped me to arrive at an understanding of the events of 1962.

not even place the tea kettle on the stove. Even his regular customers went without tea. Except for the lone troubled voice that came from the radio, there was a numbed silence all around. Scores of children who either did not go to school at all or had dropped out after a year or two, and normally scampered about all day playing games, today just stood like statues with glum faces. It was difficult to say if they had ever heard of China or realized what it meant for one country to invade another. The only uniformed person they had ever seen was the local police constable. They could not imagine anything like the army, navy or air force, leave alone a war. Yet, the news had dazed them, as though they had just come back from the battle front. Reports of the invasion had travelled fast—faster than sound, since those who had not listened to the radio also knew it simultaneously. It was the speed of the mind, called *manoveg* in Indian parlance. Every citizen was in the grip of an indescribable mixture of anger, anguish, a sense of disappointment and, above all, a feeling of unity with every other Indian, wherever he might be living within the vast expanse of the country.

Anand fidgeted in the open veranda of the small dak bungalow, listening to his transistor. He scrutinized the road map of India that he always carried in his briefcase. It gave no details about anything connected with military operations on the border. However, it did show clearly the long distances between available road heads and the border. The enormity of the logistic disadvantage was unnerving. Anand had learned that for each army jawan fighting on the front, about a hundred and fifty persons had to work in fields and factories, night and day, funneling their energies into the most unproductive human activity yet devised: war. Yet, it had to be done . . .

He wanted to return at once to the state capital, but the local sarpanch and others had arranged a big function just at that time. He thought it would be good to give the youngsters an idea of the trial they were all in for. He went to the meeting and explained to the children, with the help of the school map, the implications of the Chinese invasion and the uphill task that India faced. They all heard him with rapt attention, with grim faces and knit brows. They said very little; young and old, they were all lost in deep thought and deeper emotion.

Just when Anand was about to leave, a lad of about ten came forward. He approached Anand gingerly and greeted him, obviously eager to say something. Anand returned the greeting and asked, 'What is it, son? What's on your mind?'

The lad put his hand in his shirt pocket and produced a twenty-five naye paise coin. He held it out tentatively and stammered, 'This is my contribution to defeat China . . . '

Anand accepted the coin and hugged the boy. He controlled his emotion with some difficulty. 'Thank you, son,' he said. 'I shall send this invaluable donation to Panditji on your behalf. You'll get an official receipt!'

The gesture electrified the atmosphere. For the first time faces brightened somewhat. 'Why not raise a fund in the village?' said the sarpanch.

'Yes, why not?' echoed everyone present.

'In this village and all the villages of the country . . .' added the sarpanch.

'Yes!' interjected another villager. 'We must give and give and give until it hurts! Each a little more than he can afford to . . .'

Anand couldn't believe his ears. Barely twenty-four hours earlier, he had despaired of that very village. Everyone opposed everyone else. No one was willing to part with a single rupee for the common benefit. They wanted the government to do everything. It was the same with the country. A house hopelessly divided against itself, if ever there was one . . .

God! Does this country need the threat of external aggression to unite it internally? he wondered as his car turned into the highway.

*

Two trends were discernible in the country during the dark days after the Kameng fiasco. First, to the people smarting under the knowledge that India had never, in its long history, won a single war, it was even more agonizing to witness continuing failure in this regard, especially since India had achieved independence and was being piloted by an illustrious Prime Minister. Secondly, there was a surge of fierce anger at the unexpected—and apparently purposeless—betrayal. It was impossible to believe that two huge and ancient countries with deep-rooted and stable civilizations, with no history of antagonism for as far back as one could remember, could suddenly engage in a war which no one could explain or justify—on any grounds. (It is highly doubtful if, even after so many years, the Chinese invasion has found even a modicum of justification, leave alone complete validation.) The combined effect of these two trends shook the country to its roots.

The debate in parliament was long, bitter and recriminatory. All the parties upbraided the government. Nehru tried his best to pacify the Houses and to give the people a detailed briefing on the historical and political aspects of the issue. And once again, wheels within wheels turned freely as arguments were marshalled and accusations of incompetence were levelled at the government. The Kameng defeat was put down squarely to the failure of Nehru's foreign policy. There was much circumlocution, but the core of the argument was not far to seek—to wit, the futility of non-alignment and the desirability (suggested very subtly) of aligning with one of the superpowers. 'One' was only a way of expression; the answer to the question, 'Which one?' emerged loud and clear from those quarters that had first raised it.

At the end of the historic debate, the Houses, with all members standing, unanimously adopted the following Resolution:

*This House approves the Proclamation of Emergency issued by the President on the 26th October, 1962, under clause (1) of Article 352 of the Constitution.*
*This House notes with deep regret that, in spite of the uniform gestures of goodwill and friendship by India towards the People's Government of China on the basis of recognition of each other's independence, non-aggression and non-interference, and peaceful co-existence, China has betrayed this goodwill and friendship and*

376

*the principles of Panchsheel which had been agreed to between the
two countries and has committed aggression and initiated a
massive invasion of India by her armed forces.*

*This House places on record its high appreciation of the valiant
struggle of men and officers of our armed forces while defending
our frontiers and pays its respectful homage to the martyrs who
have laid down their lives in defending the honour and integrity
of our Motherland.*

*This House also records its profound appreciation of the
wonderful and spontaneous response of the people of India to the
emergency and the crisis that has resulted from China's invasion
of India. It notes with deep gratitude this mighty upsurge amongst
all sections of our people for harnessing all our resources towards
the organization of an all-out effort to meet this grave national
emergency. The flame of liberty and sacrifice has been kindled
anew and a fresh dedication has taken place to the cause of India's
freedom and integrity.*

*This House gratefully acknowledges the sympathy and the moral
and material support received from a large number of friendly
countries in this grim hour of our struggle against aggression and
invasion.*

*With hope and faith, this House affirms the firm resolve of the
Indian people to drive out the aggressor from the sacred soil of
India, however long and hard the struggle may be.*

*

Obviously, the story did not begin in 1962 with the Chinese
invasion. One has to go back several years to see what led to the
invasion and why. One view that gained currency was that India's
basic policy on China was against her national interests. It was
only a question of time before a major conflict overtook India, as
a direct consequence of a complacent policy based on the belief
that there would be *no war* between the two countries. The other
view was that the basic policy was sound, predicated as it was on
the vision of Sino-Indian friendship on a lasting basis, in
accordance with historical facts. This view held that the present
invasion was an act of perfidy and treachery on China's part, an

event that could not have been normally anticipated.

For a long time in history, there had been no common border between India and China. Our northern neighbour was Tibet, which was practically an independent country. India and Tibet had enjoyed friendly relations for centuries without any history of hostilities. With China, Tibet had an undefined relationship called 'suzerainty' whose content varied from time to time depending on the relative capacities of the countries either to enforce it or to resist such enforcement. The Chinese had, however, been talking of the 'liberation of Tibet', and even the regimes preceding the communist government had claimed Tibet to be part of China. The Chinese Liberation Army entered Tibet for the first time in 1950 and this posed a very difficult problem for India, with ominous and long-term repercussions. Any intervention from the Indian side would not have been justified, because the Indian government only stood in the shoes of the previous British Indian government which had continued to recognize China's 'suzerainty' over Tibet, for its own reasons. Whatever that relationship meant, it was not congruous with total Tibetan independence. India was merely Tibet's neighbour and despite cultural and religious links extending over centuries, they had no defined political relations, except for what the British imperial power had extracted from Tibet under the treaty of 1914.

The only snag with this line of reasoning was that the content of 'suzerainty' would, according to the Chinese, be bound to increase whenever they chose to step it up with the use of force; that was the very purpose of keeping it vague. India's recognition would likewise have to vary according to what China chose to foist on Tibet, China being the stronger of the two. This would militate against India's friendly intentions towards Tibet, in the ultimate analysis. How could India resolve this paradox?

The counter-argument was equally ticklish. Being the successor to the British Indian government, it was difficult for Nehru's government to exceed its predecessor's position. The only way to do so was by force of arms, by entering into a war with China. Such a war would have been utterly untenable. Besides, anyone who understood the preoccupations of Nehru's government—the country's Constitution was still in the making, and the multifarious problems in the wake of Partition required immediate solutions—would think ten times before recommending a war at that time. So what was the way out?

All these alternatives were, it appears, discussed even in 1950; they were not ignored, nor did they go unnoticed. No less a person than Sardar Patel, the strong man of the Indian government to whom goes the great credit of integrating India politically, drew Nehru's attention to the threat posed by China. In a detailed letter containing some truly prophetic formulations about China's intentions and plans, he warned Jawaharlal Nehru of the dangers of complacency and strongly urged a serious reconsideration of the entire China policy and the various steps that needed to be taken to meet the new situation.

After giving a lucid account of the changed situation in Tibet after the consolidation of Communist China and her army's march into Tibet, the Sardar said, in his letter:

Thus, for the first time, after centuries, India's defence has to concentrate itself on two fronts simultaneously. Our defence measures have so far been based on the calculation of a superiority over Pakistan. In our calculation, we shall now have to reckon with Communist China in the north and north-east—a Communist China which has definite ambitions and aims and which does not, in any way, seem friendly disposed towards us.

In my judgement, therefore, the situation is one in which we cannot afford either to be complacent or to be vacillating. We must have a clear idea of what we wish to achieve and also of the methods by which we achieve it. Any faltering or lack of decisiveness in formulating our objectives or in pursuing our policy to attain those objectives is bound to weaken us and increase the threats which are so evident.

Then the Sardar, in his clear-cut style, went on to list 'some problems, which, in my opinion, require early solution and round which we have to build our administrative or military policies and measures to implement them.

a) A military and intelligence appreciation of the Chinese threat to India both on the frontier and to internal security.

b) An examination of our military position and such redisposition of our forces as might be necessary, particularly with the idea of guarding important routes or areas which are likely to be the subject of dispute.

c) An appraisement of the strength of our forces and, if necessary, reconsideration of our retrenchment plans for the Army in the light of these new threats.

d) A long-term consideration of our defence needs. My own feeling is that unless we assure our supplies of arms, ammunition and armour, we would be making our defence position perpetually weak and we would not be able to stand up to the double threat of difficulties both from the west and north-west and north and north-east.

e) The question of Chinese entry into the UNO. In view of the rebuff which China has given us and the method which it has followed in dealing with Tibet, I am doubtful whether we can advocate its claims any longer. There would probably be a threat in the UNO virtually to outlaw China, in view of its active participation in the Korean war. We must determine our attitude on this question also.

f) The political and administrative steps which we should take to strengthen our northern and north-eastern frontiers. This would include the whole of the border i.e. Nepal, Bhutan, Cecum, Darjeeling and the tribal territory in Assam.

g) Measures of internal security in the border areas as well as the states flanking those areas such as Uttar Pradesh, Bihar, Bengal and Assam.

h) Improvement of our communications, road, rail, air and wireless, in these areas, and with the frontier outposts.

i) Policing and intelligence of frontier posts.

j) The future of our mission at Lhasa and the trade posts at Gyangtse and Yatung and the forces which we have in operation in Tibet to guard the trade routes.

k) The policy in regard to McMahon Line.'

*

It is not easy to enunciate a historically and legally clear-cut account of the political positions taken by China, India, Tibet, Russia and other important countries in the nineteenth century, and how they stood at the time of India's independence. Further, India's foreign policy in the early years was, strictly speaking, not India's, but that of the imperial British power inherited at Independence. British protection of India's interests was contemplated, naturally, as part of the empire's wider interests in the area. Thus, Britain's Tibet policy was, at that time, conditioned by its perception of its interests in the Central Asian region—the most dominant factor in that perception being the fear of Russian domination in the region.

It is here that Indian opinion on several imperial policies and actions in Tibet and other weaker countries was uniformly critical. Long before India's independence, the Indian National Congress had made many formulations about what independent India's policies should ideally be. As a result, after Independence, the Nehru government's policies could not, in the very nature of things, be mere carbon copies of those of the previous British governments of India. Even as the rightful successor, Nehru could not pursue the old policies *in toto*, disregarding his own orientation and that of his party. In effect, it had to be, and therefore was, the policy of the government of independent India—nothing less. This very vital distinction needs to be borne in mind while examining the policies and actions of Nehru's government.

All the chief ministers received the following letter in July 1950 from Prime Minister Nehru:

> India has, within the inevitable limitations imposed by events, tried to follow her own independent policy in foreign, as in other affairs. No country can be hundred per cent independent in such matters because every act or policy flows from other acts done before and other things happening in the world. But within those limitations, one can be more or less independent. We have preferred to be more independent. That was not only an idealistic approach but, I think, an eminently practical way of dealing with current problems. Also it flowed naturally from our past. Any other policy would have come in the way of our natural development and stunted us, apart from creating a great deal of internal friction . . . We have been following a certain policy in

foreign affairs and that policy has undoubtedly brought credit to
India and made us in a small way an influence for peace. If we and
some other countries did not do so, undoubtedly war would have
been much nearer, apart from the internal difficulties that we
might have had to face. We have, in any event, to carry our people
with us, and no policy, that has not got large-scale public
approval, can be carried on for long. To have changed our old
policy at the first touch of harsh fact may have brought approval
from some quarters, but it would have been to the great discredit
of India and she would have counted for little in the great drama
that is taking place. So we tried to adhere to that basic policy,
though there was a variation of it under stress of circumstances.

Unlike China and many other countries, India's main weapon
for gaining freedom was not armed rebellion or war with the
imperial power. India was unique in this respect. Gandhiji's
strategy had taken firm root in the minds of the people; the
shocking violence of his assassination only served to strengthen his
influence. Gandhian non-violence did not instantly receive any
measure of acceptance as a practical—or practicable methodology;
yet, as every other methodology, every method of diplomacy, every
act or threat of force and blackmail administered to weaker
countries by the powerful ones failed to bring results, the yet
untried Gandhian way has come to seem more and more inviting
over the decades. The world continues to be nudged one step closer
to Gandhi by this peculiar dialectic.

Gandhi's idea of a non-violent Indian state was based on his
conviction that such a state could be built—as was once done by
Ashoka. He did not, however, insist that it was immediately
implementable. Gandhi's non-violence, so integral to the national
movement, was not just a matter of intellectual theory here; it was
actually applied, and generated the belief that the Gandhian
prescriptions of non-violent mass action were feasible, irrespective
of the context. Only recently, questions have been raised whether
Gandhian methods would have succeeded against Hitler or, within
the country, against the particularly despotic rulers of some
princely states. (In point of fact the anti-ruler agitations in some

princely states contained an element of armed struggle also, apart from non-violent agitation.) These questions are valid, but one has also to realize that a methodology evolved primarily in a given context cannot immediately be applied to all conditions. At the same time, it should not be ruled out completely elsewhere, without a genuine effort at application with appropriate alterations.

Jawaharlal Nehru held a somewhat different view on the issue of non-violence. While Gandhi was committed to non-violence as a basic creed and principle, Nehru was more flexible and ready to resort to the use of force for purposes of defence, *till the methodology of non-violent defence was perfected so as to be effective.* Nehru felt that until then, it would not be possible to adhere to non-violence as an unalterable creed. Looked at a bit carefully, both approaches were two sides of the same coin; there was no real contradiction between them. His use of force in Junagadh, Kashmir, Hyderabad and Goa would highlight this. On 23 February 1950, he warned Pakistan that India would have to use other methods if its peaceful offers were not agreed to. On 11 August 1951, replying to the debate on the President's address in parliament, Nehru declared, 'Whatever happens, India is not going to be invaded. Even if there is war, do you imagine that we will wait idly to be invaded? Certainly not.' In the same speech he said, 'I have ruled out war as a measure for the easing of Indo-Pakistan relations, but I cannot rule it out independently or unilaterally. Since the other party brings it in and talks and shouts so much about it, I have to be perfectly ready for it.' In fact, at that stage, when Pakistan's Prime Minister Liaquat Ali Khan, in the course of a belligerent speech, shook his fist publicly at India, the Indian army was moved to the border. This action sobered Pakistan. It was an example of coercive diplomacy and had the desired effect.

Non-violence, Nehru said, could only be a policy and a method promising certain results and by those results it would have to be finally judged. In the forties, while the national struggle was drawing to a successful close, these basic questions had intensely engaged the attention of the Indian National Congress. The lively debate proved to be a mine of new ideas for the young men and women engaged in the struggle at the lower rungs of the party. It was, at that stage, no longer just a matter of theoretical debate, since hard decisions would have to be taken soon about its role in the formulation of national policy once the country attained freedom.

Nehru expressed his intense dislike for militarism on several occasions, including in his writings. Combined with this attitude was the high priority he gave to development and industrialization. In fact he made it a point to emphasize that without industrialization, neither could the country's defence needs be met, nor the growing needs of a growing population languishing in abject poverty as a result of continued foreign exploitation. This led, for the first time, to a clear-cut connection being established between development and defence. Speaking in the Rajya Sabha on 3 September 1962, Nehru traced the events that had led to the reduction of expenditure on defence, including the cutting down on defence personnel, before the worsening situation, first with Pakistan and then with China, reinforced the importance of military preparedness. He recalled that in the early fifties, the Congress and 'every public man' in India, including himself, had strongly criticized the heavy expenditure on defence and the army. After all, the real strength of the country, even from the defence point of view, was the industrial apparatus supporting it, for one could not always depend on getting arms from abroad in an emergency. A country that was not industrialized could not be militarily strong.

Because of the shortage of foreign exchange and a desire to divert maximum funds towards development projects, it was decided that less would be spent on defence requirements. This, as Nehru admitted, 'was because we did not expect any attack from China at that time . . . We thought that the more we built up the industrial background of our country, the better it would be, for defence also ultimately. That was the most important consideration. You cannot just have a factory to produce aircraft. The whole process is correlated—a powerful defence apparatus with scientific infrastructure.'

Nehru concluded his speech with a forceful plea for all-round economic development: 'I do not wish to apologise for what the Government has done or not done. There was a certain compulsion of events and no Government, however much it may have differed from our way of thinking, could have functioned very differently from what we did, keeping in mind the fact that the real thing before us was to strengthen India industrially and not superficially, by getting an odd gun or an odd aircraft. Raising the economic potential of the country is very important because no country can fight unless the economic potential is very good.' The persistent demand that the government should suspend all development projects and divert the resources meant for them to defence alone, was effectively countered by Panditji's formulation.

Nehru had actually seen much violence in the wars then raging. He had visited several countries engaged in war to appraise the conditions there. He abhorred war, but having seen the realities on the ground, he had developed a certain immunity to fear. In *The Discovery of India* he wrote:

> Much as I hated war, the prospect of a Japanese invasion of India had in no way frightened me. At the back of my mind I was in a sense attracted to this coming of war, horrible as it was, to India. For I wanted a tremendous shake-up, a personal experience for millions of people, which would drag them out of that peace of the grave that Britain had imposed upon us, something that would force them to face the reality of today and to outgrow the past which clung to them so tenaciously, to get beyond the petty political squabbles and exaggeration of temporary problems which filled their minds . . . That war was not of our seeking but since it had come, it could be made to harden the fibre of the nation and provide those vital experiences out of which a new life might blossom forth. Vast numbers would die, that was inevitable, but it is better to die than to live a miserable, hopeless life. Out of death, life is born afresh and individuals and nations who do not know how to die, do not know also how to live. Only where there are graves, are there resurrections.

Closer studies reveal that the debacle of 1962 did not occur for want of men and equipment. As Nehru pointed out in his speech in the Rajya Sabha on 3 September 1963, there was enough equipment, but it was rather spread out all over India. It may not have been available at a particular place, because we had to face the situation rather suddenly and we did not have time. He also admitted in the same speech: 'There has been a slant in our minds that China would not attack us. It is perfectly true. There had been a slant in our minds in the past, not completely but partly.' Apart from a detailed analysis of this slant, it would be pertinent to note that such slants are by no means uncommon in history. A brief look at the genesis of the Second World War would clearly bring out a similar slant on the part of the British government. The Munich Pact was concluded with no less bonhomie, and the confidence that Hitler would not attack Britain. Exactly at that time, Nehru was loudly proclaiming his anti-Fascist views. Like human beings, nation-states also take decisions on the basis of a certain mutual trust which, when violated treacherously, leads to crisis and calamities.

India's slant was of two kinds. According to the Intelligence Bureau, since the Chinese had not used force when they came up against an Indian post, they were not likely to use force against a line of Indian posts set up to prevent their further encroachment. There was sufficiently plausible logic underlying this assessment and hence, perhaps, it commanded significant credibility. No one, however, raised the question, 'What if the Chinese now decide to change the pattern of their behaviour?' For not anticipating that eventuality, several people—generals, senior civil servants in the Foreign Office and the Ministry of Defence, cabinet members and above all, Jawaharlal Nehru—must be held responsible.

The second slant originated in the minds of senior military men and probably influenced the thinking of Jawaharlal Nehru. General Thimayya, then Chief of Army Staff, wrote in an article in July 1962 that as a soldier, he could not envisage India taking on China in an open conflict on its own because China's military strength, with the full support of the USSR, exceeded India's military resources a hundredfold. The only way to counter Chinese aggression on the border, according to him, was to attack the enemy in the Himalayan passes, which were practically impossible to cross for six months of the year. Here, the Indian army could make full use of its manpower and light equipment against a Chinese force deprived of the use of its heavy equipment including tanks and heavy-calibre artillery. In case the Chinese got through to the plains and foothills, guerrilla tactics would have to be used to harass their lines of communication. The Indian army's superior firepower and manoeuvrability would then have to be brought into play to defeat the enemy forces.

Jawaharlal Nehru also, in his pronouncements, talked in terms of alternative possibilities of either patrol clashes with the Chinese at high altitudes, or a full-scale invasion in the Indian plains.

In all these arguments, the possibility of the Chinese launching a carefully controlled limited operation, with limited political objectives, appears to have been overlooked altogether, both in the Services and political circles, and by the Prime Minister. In the end, troops had to be moved from the plains to the high altitude regions in the Kameng division in a hurry, at the eleventh hour. They should have been there earlier. As Air Chief Marshal Arjan Singh later pointed out, there was insufficient appreciation of the problems of operating aircraft from high altitude airfields. If those problems had been thought through, there would not have been as much reluctance to use Indian air power in support of our operations in 1962 as there actually was.

From these factors, it appears that the debacle of 1962 happened not because of Gandhiji's advocacy of non-violence or Jawaharlal Nehru's plea for non-alignment and rational solutions to international tensions, but because of our failure to anticipate the Chinese strategy in time. While the Indian political and military leadership was thinking of engaging in either patrol clashes or a full-scale war, the Chinese thought in terms of a quick thrust, a military humiliation followed by rapid disengagement and territorial control.

It might be argued that whatever the total strength of the Chinese army, only a part of it would be deployable—and therefore it would not be quite one hundred times that of the Indian army, in actual terms. But then, the deployable part on the Indian side would also have been similarly less and it would still have been a grossly unequal confrontation. Besides, the Chinese army had been continuously fighting for the last twenty-five years, if not longer, thus remaining fighting fit from every point of view. The Indian army, on the other hand, was an 'inherited' army. As Nehru put it in his speech in the Rajya Sabha on 3 September 1962, 'Immediately after independence, we succeeded to an army. It was a competent army, a good army. Nevertheless, it had always been a small part of the British army . . . All our policy was laid down in Whitehall . . . We got all the material for our armed forces from England.' In the face of these obvious facts, no Prime Minister could have had any illusions about how heavily the dice were loaded against India in any confrontation with China at that point of time.

It is obvious that neither Prime Minister Nehru nor Defence Minister Krishna Menon anticipated the timing of the Chinese action. They would not otherwise have gone out of the country in September. Not only that, the Chief of the General Staff, Lt. Gen. Kaul was on leave and the Director of Military Operations was away on a Vikrant cruise. It appears, therefore, that the Chinese decision to take military action was kept a well-guarded secret and further, India's intelligence agencies completely failed to get wind of it.

India, on its part, was determined not to become embroiled in a dangerous conflict with its neighbour, unless its vital interests, such as control over the Himalayan border states of Nepal, Bhutan and Sikkim, were openly threatened. Nehru was disturbed by the evidence of Chinese penetration into the Himalayan border states and had made it abundantly clear that he considered them to be in India's 'sphere of influence'. Nor was he oblivious to the rivalry between Democratic India and Communist China for the leadership of Asia. He was also aware that the contest between Delhi and Peking, particularly in the economic realm, was being watched closely by the rest of the world to see which system could 'deliver the goods'.

Tibet was another major bone of contention. Nehru's reply to parliamentary debates in 1950 made it clear that India had no territorial or political ambitions in regard to Tibet, and desired only to preserve cultural and commercial relations with that country. Tibet had no arms and was no threat to China; yet China insisted it was going to 'liberate' Tibet—from whom, it was unclear. Critics of India's stand on Tibet ignored the fact that the Simla convention of 1914 had practically recognized the *de facto* independence of Tibet but under conditions of Chinese suzerainty. The Republican government of China had refused to sign the Simla convention. The Nationalist government that succeeded it had not only ignored the convention but tried to secure its dominance over Tibet whenever and howsoever it could. This government considered itself to be superior to the new government of India and assumed a patronising stance. In such a context, had India urged a treaty revision, the whole issue would have opened up again and perhaps even questioned the validity of the McMahon line on which the Indo-China frontier was based. Any unilateral recognition of Tibetan independence would have been simply unthinkable, whatever may be said today with the benefit of hindsight.

The Chinese army at the time was the most powerful in the world. It threatened India's Himalayan frontier as well as the remote tribal areas which the British had not troubled to administer. The McMahon line existed only on the map—it did not function as an administrative boundary because there were no Indian personnel posted within a hundred miles of that divide. Had India tried to engage China in war at that time, the Chinese might have been in a position to extend their frontiers to the foothills of NEFA and detach Bhutan, Sikkim and Nepal from India's sphere of influence. China could also have threatened the hill areas of Himachal Pradesh and Utter Pradesh; large parts of Ladakh in Kashmir would have been vulnerable.

In order to salvage Tibetan autonomy as much as possible, Pandit Nehru adopted a policy of non-interference, which succeeded in eroding Chinese suspicions and consolidating India's hold in NEFA and the frontier regions, while maintaining some of the Dalai Lama's authority in Tibet upto 1959.

When Premier Chou En-lai visited India he claimed that he had never heard of the McMahon line, but now that such a crucial issue was at stake, and the line was an established fact, friendly relations should be preserved between China, India and Burma. The Chinese government had not included the Tibetan mandate with regard to the official recognition of the McMahon line, but proposed to do so.

As conditions became congenial from 1952 to 1958, India supported China's admission to the UN year after year, and did not initiate diplomatic relations with Taiwan. But there were several cases of border violations by the Chinese in Uttar Pradesh, Himachal Pradesh, Ladakh, and parts of NEFA. The Chinese also utilized this interval to build roads, consolidating their hold on Tibet.

It was a time when natural calamities—droughts and floods—ravaged the nation, resulting in chronic food shortages. Western countries predicted that India would never be self-sufficient in foodgrains, and was doomed to inevitable balkanization as ethnic fissures grew deeper. Suddenly India's defence preparedness became the first priority. In such a situation, it was clearly not feasible for India to take on China militarily. The responsibility for India's security rested squarely on the shoulders of senior diplomats and politicians.

As if in anticipation of that demand, in his first broadcast as vice-chairman of the Executive Council in charge of the external affairs portfolio on 7 September 1946, Jawaharlal Nehru had declared:

We propose as far as possible, to keep away from the power politics of groups aligned against one another, which have led in the past to world wars and which may again lead to disasters even on a vaster scale. We believe that peace and freedom are indivisible and the denial of freedom anywhere must deny freedom elsewhere and lead to conflict and war. We are particularly interested in the emancipation of colonial and dependent countries and peoples, and in the recognition in theory and practice of equal opportunities for all races. We repudiate utterly the Nazi doctrine of racialism, whensoever and in whatever form it may be practised. We seek no dominion over others and we claim no privileged position over other peoples. But we do claim equal and honourable treatment for our people wherever they may go, and we cannot accept any discrimination against them.

We send our greetings to the people of the United States of America to whom destiny has given a major role in international affairs. We trust that this tremendous responsibility will be utilized for the furtherance of peace and freedom everywhere.

To that other great nation of the modern world, the Soviet Union, which also carries a vast responsibility for shaping world events, we send greetings. They are our neighbours in Asia and inevitably we shall have to undertake many common tasks and have much to do with each other.

This radical comment put forward the doctrine of non-alignment. It was the first such formulation by any nation in the immediate post-World War II era. It was remarkable that Nehru was expounding the basic security and foreign policy doctrine of India eleven months before India became free. It was also fifteen years before the formation of the non-aligned movement, as such. Yet another noteworthy aspect of the speech is Nehru's reference to the Soviet Union as 'our neighbours in Asia', and the inevitability of having to undertake many common tasks with them. This was at a time when the Soviet and other Communist parties were denouncing Nehru as a stooge of the imperialists. It was obvious that he was looking far beyond the immediate future and was taking into account the geo-strategic compulsions that would bear on India and the Soviet Union.

The policy of non-alignment was not easily appreciated even by very senior politicians. It was questioned in parliament by stalwarts such as N.G. Ranga, H.V. Kamath, Maulana Hasrat Mohani and M.R. Masani. For some it meant being neutral; for some others it meant creation of a third force.

Non-alignment was an assertion of autonomy in an international system which was dominated by the bipolar concept. In the initial stages of the rivalry, the leaders of the two camps insisted that every country must perforce join one side or the other, and denounced non-alignment as immoral neutrality or as a cover for supporting and pandering to imperialists. The two camps had a shared perception of the entire international system as ideologically bipolar. The concept of non-alignment rejected this view, and the non-aligned countries refused to be drawn into the Cold War.

India had already come under considerable pressure from the West in regard to the Kashmir issue and the question of military assistance to Pakistan from the United States. Meanwhile, the Soviet leaders advised the Indian communist leadership to desist from the path of insurgency. It was under these circumstances that India concluded the Panchsheel treaty with China.

By 1955, the Soviets had extended their support to India on the Kashmir issue, as well as on the issue of the decolonization of Goa. As the relationship between the Soviet Union and China began to sour, the Soviets sought an alliance with India, going so far as to hold China responsible for the war of 1962. Then followed a period of friendship between the two countries as the Soviet Union supplied arms and advanced technology to India.

At the time of his visit to Peking in 1952, Pandit Nehru is reported to have said, 'Some day or other, these two Asian giants are bound to tread on each other's corns and come into conflict, and that would be a calamity for Asia. That is an eventuality which we should all strive hard to avert.' On 27 November 1950, Nehru declared in parliament that India had to take note of what the new China, after the revolution, was likely to be. Subsequently, on 9 December 1959, he referred to the Border Committee, which was appointed in 1951, and said that since 1950 the picture of the two powerful states coming face to face with each other on a tremendous border conflict had been before the government, though they might have 'differed as to . . . when that would happen: Whether in five years, ten years, fifteen years or thirty years'. These facts confirm Mullick's assertion that, from the beginning, Nehru had his reservations about China.

There is today ample evidence to show Nehru's perception of the Chinese threat from the early 1950s. Some leaders claimed that they warned him about the Chinese threat and that he did not take timely action. In this context, what 'timely action' meant at given specific moments needs to be examined. Defence preparedness does not become a reality overnight by a mere warning. The timeframe to build up military preparedness—of the scale required in this case—is extremely relevant. Taking all these factors into account, as also the equally crucial priorities in other areas of national development, it would not be reasonable to charge Nehru's government with any negligence in the field of building up the country's defences, as such. The point to be noted in this connection is that in those years (and even today), there were 'cold warriors' in India who were keen on pushing India into the Western camp. They included not only politicians, but several senior bureaucrats, both civil and military. Further, as mentioned earlier, from 1959 onwards, Nehru talked openly about Chinese hostility in parliament and to the press. It is, therefore, very difficult to understand how the 'Hindi-Chini, bhai-bhai-ism' of the 1954-58 period alone explains the unpreparedness of 1962.

In 1945, replying to Gandhi who insisted on the 'Hind Swaraj' model for the future of India, Nehru said, 'The question of independence and protection from foreign aggression, both political and economic, has also to be considered in this context. I do not think it is possible for India to be really independent unless she is a technically advanced country. I am not thinking for the moment in terms of just armies, but rather of scientific growth.' He thus decided to adopt a policy which would contribute to India's national security by bringing about a mutually countervailing balance of forces in this part of the world. Given the geo-strategic location of the United States, the Soviet Union and India, and given the American predilection in favour of Pakistan and colonialist and neo-colonialist forces, Nehru seems to have deliberately decided to cultivate the Soviet Union as a countervailing factor.

*

In retrospect, one would say that those who fought in Ladakh and laid down their lives did not do so in vain. Nor could it be said that the battles of Nanka Chu and Walong were fought to no purpose. But for those battles, Arunachal Pradesh would not have continued to be Indian territory. When we come to the sequence of events of that fateful November in the Kameng Division, we encounter myths that have been deliberately created to confuse the whole issue. The available evidence shows that in Kameng, the Fourth Indian Army Division was not given a chance to fight by its own commander, and the failure was entirely a local one. The Division, contrary to popular belief, was not out-weaponed. It had tanks and field guns which the Chinese did not have. It had enough supplies to hold back the Chinese for at least seven days. If it had done so, it is doubtful whether the Chinese would have been able to sustain their campaign. In fact, if it had held them back for those few days, the history of the 1962 war would have been very different.

It is difficult to analyse what the Chinese were aiming to gain by their operations. However, the thesis that they acted in self-defence is absurd. In retrospect, the Chinese, by their deep penetration into Indian territory, and a subsequent withdrawal from Arunachal Pradesh, validated the Indian title to the state. The long slice of land about twenty kilometres in width where they overran and occupied our checkposts in Ladakh was not worth the price of completely alienating India and triggering off a major Indian rearmament programme. Consequently, one should look for their motivation in political spheres. They may have aimed at toppling the Nehru government or at pushing India into the Western camp in the hope of scoring a point *vis-à-vis* the Soviet Union in their ideological debate. In either case, the Chinese have not achieved their objectives. The Indian military humiliation was not a policy failure. The military commander who failed had an excellent combat record and had been decorated earlier. In the absence of more specific evidence it can only be characterized as one of those unforeseeable random events of history.

During the period 1947-64, India's stature in the world rose high and then plummeted badly following the 1962 military debacle. Indian security was safeguarded at this time through the Kashmir operation, the integration of princely states and the decolonization of the colonial enclaves. Insurgency was successfully countered and the impact of Pakistan, which had become part of the Western military alliance, was contained. Even in respect of China, buying time through the Panchsheel treaty and consolidating our own position in Arunachal Pradesh were no mean achievements. If, in fact, our achievements outweighed our failures by an enormous margin, the credit for this should largely go to Prime Minister Jawaharlal Nehru. At the same time, to be fair to him, a wholly uncritical attitude towards his achievements should be avoided, and an impartial analysis is necessary to understand the reasons for his enormous successes as well as what has to be termed as his one costly failure.

His successes are particularly astounding if we are to consider the extreme paucity of assets and resources with which he had to build India's place in the international system and safeguard Indian security during its perilous adolescence. India was no small country—it had a large population, was situated in an area of vital global communications, had a centuries-old history, had attained its independence through prolonged, non-violent struggle under the banner of democratic values and goals, had a rising middle class with relatively developed skills by world standards, and had a reasonable administrative and economic infrastructure. At the same time, the population was largely poor, there was as yet no adequate industrial base, freedom had been achieved at the cost of enormous bloodshed, violence, communal hatred and forced migrations of incomparable magnitude. Hundreds of princely states at different levels of development had to be merged, and some of the larger ones, which had threatened to secede, with encouragement from outside, had to be integrated, with the use of force in one case.

The two communist giants, the Soviet Union and China, were not friendly (at that time) and communist insurgency had to be faced within the country as well. The British and, under their influence, the Americans, were partisan on the Kashmir issue and had converted it into a contest between Indian secularism and the Pakistani two-nation thesis. Within the country, most of the politicians looked at the international situation through the distorting prism of the Cold War; many civil servants, senior personnel of the armed forces, and the media in general were oriented towards a Western perspective. In these circumstances, it required extraordinary vision and far-sightedness on the part of Prime Minister Nehru to formulate the policy of non-alignment and to sustain it through a very difficult period. No doubt, the prolonged freedom struggle and the civilizational concept associated with India over millennia made it logical for an Indian Prime Minister to look at the world from an Indo-centric point of view, refusing to concede that the US-Soviet relationship was the axis of global politics.[*]

---

[*] The subject of India-China relations in the half-century following India's independence has been examined in several studies by scholars and researchers. There also exists a great deal of literature about the earlier periods that take into consideration the changing conditions of this region from time to time. In most cases, what has been extensively and intensively commented upon is the Indian policy—to be more exact, Nehru's policy—which is defined as right or wrong (more often wrong than right), depending on the researcher concerned.

Incidentally, these studies revealed that Nehru, and Gandhiji too in his own distinctive style, had openly and unequivocally declared, even before India became free, that non-alignment with the power blocs would be the bedrock of independent India's foreign policy. This factor, at a time when non-alignment (meaning *not* being with the West, in this context) was considered and branded as immoral, must have come as a disappointment to those of a Western persuasion, and must have coloured the views of Western scholars to some extent at least, especially while they were formulating their positions on India-China and India-Pakistan relations—indeed, on any issue in which India was a concerned party. These scholars knew all about India, from official records to grapevine gossip to South Block rhetoric and counter-rhetoric, while about China they had only one—the official, inflexible and final—version. That one version, in the absence of any other, tended to become the gospel—at least the solitary—truth. On the Indian side, however, differences abounded as various versions and perceptions circulated, as is natural in an open system. The erstwhile Imperial government might well have deliberately retained contradictions and ambiguities in some cases, presumably for valid reasons. Alternatively, the British government may have been alert to a particular issue but, overwhelmed by the event of Indian independence, it may have been unable to thrash it through. In all such cases, the outstanding differences afforded researchers the widest imaginable scope to cut, prune, interpret and distort. They would come up with findings inspired at least partly by their understandable annoyance with a leader who not only differed from

Understandably, Prime Minister Nehru decried the role of force in international relations. In a world threatened by burgeoning nuclear arsenals, it was necessary to urge strategic rationality in the interests of human survival. This style also befitted him as an ardent champion of peace and international development. Such pronouncements at the highest levels of leadership should not have inhibited intensive debates at other appropriate levels on the country's security problems, and detailed professional consideration of measures to safeguard the country's security. Unfortunately, Nehru's pronouncements were often converted into a convenient alibi for inaction and lack of cerebration. They

---

the Western viewpoint in every way, but was in fact proceeding to build up, along with other eminent world leaders, a distinct personality and identity for the Third World, gradually but unmistakably.

I have carefully gone through some treatises written in the late eighties viz. twenty years after the Sino-Indian conflict. I have found them interesting, also useful in some respects. But I am sorry to say that the post-factum analysis they offer is based largely on hindsight. For instance, it is true that the government's style of functioning would not have been the same if someone other than Nehru had been the Prime Minister. But whether at the level of consultation or decision-making, the Prime Minister was bound to be a dominant figure. Howsoever standardized and impersonal the machinery of government may be, the person at the helm—particularly given the situation in the country then—was bound to assert his personality and opinions on the decisions taken. Given the inscrutable nature of Chinese functioning, it is not surprising that Nehru's government was not quite able to divine the hidden intentions of the Chinese accurately. Again, to certify that Nehru behaved during the 1962 crisis just as any other leader would have, is not a particularly illuminating discovery. For the rest, there were deficiencies galore on the Indian side, as there were in the internal working of the Allies in the Second World War, regardless of their eventual victory. It may also be added that the deficiencies that came to light in the 1962 debacle were promptly set right and India's defence preparedness has been methodically built up to conform to the required level, despite the competing claims of many development programmes. Indeed, figures show that there has been a steady build-up of India's defence capabilities from 1950 onwards, and Nehru cannot be blamed for being remiss in this regard. In fact, his great contribution to the overall thinking on national planning has been to make development and defence two sides of the same coin.

Nothing, however, remains static in international relations in a dynamic world. In the post-Cold War situation, both India and China are having to redefine their bilateral relations, as also their roles in the world in general. There have been considerable changes in regard to the border as well, though the matter has not been finally resolved. As demanded by wisdom and statesmanship, a treaty has been concluded to keep the border free from tension, pending the final settlement of the border question—Author.

were also repeated down the line as mere slogans.

Today, in view of the rising political consciousness and the high cost of forcible occupation, we are no longer in an age when war can be used as an extension of policy. This is the age of coercive diplomacy, when the projection of forces in intimidatory, deterrent and defensive roles has become an inextricable aspect of international relations. *

---

\* These comments are partly based on the views of K. Subramanyam, former defence secretary, Government of India, and a well-known commentator on defence issues—Author.

# 34

JAWAHARLAL NEHRU NEVER REALLY RECOVERED FROM THE SHOCK of the Chinese invasion. He saw in the event a complete undoing of all that he had tried to achieve for several decades. The idea of Asian solidarity became a shambles overnight. The conflict shattered the dream of the two ancient civilizations jointly assuming their rightful role, to find a new path for mankind's survival in a world that seemed bent on annihilating itself. That role had inspired Panditji and swayed the Indian people for a decade and a half. In a pathetic summing up after the invasion, Nehru admitted that he had been living in an unreal world.

The country took several months to absorb the shock. But it did recover, slowly but surely. And it stood solidly behind Nehru in the hour of his failure. There was no one, no single leader who could turn Jawaharlal's discomfiture to his own advantage. No single man could convince the people that he could be a viable alternative to Jawaharlal. Besides, the people loved Jawaharlal to a degree where temporary eclipses did not really count, not decisively, at any rate. Panditji was Panditji: what did success or failure on an isolated issue mean, really?

Yet the damage had been done. India's image plummeted considerably after the 1962 debacle. The focus on economic development became diluted. The obsession with victory and defeat in war revived atavistic notions. It reminded the people that India had never won a major war throughout her long history. She had been a perpetual loser in all encounters. Many began to interpret the country's philosophy and heritage as the foundation of its weakness.

Then followed a period of fitful and incoherent activity. The people listened to Nehru's words with the usual regard, but came to take them less seriously in practice. He was in no position to enforce compliance of his precepts. His failing health added to the problem. Rumour went round that ill-health had impaired his powers of concentration. He was unable to provide real guidance. It was reported that during a meeting of Indian heads of missions convened to take instructions from Panditji, he kept dozing off, leading to embarrassment and disappointment. The government was drifting, it had lost direction.

In the wake of these developments came the Kamraj plan. It was the brainchild of a few of Nehru's close associates at the Centre. It raised, perhaps for the first time, a controversy that persisted ever after. Over the years, almost all the talented leaders had been inducted into either the Central or state governments. Those who did not win elections, or were not accommodated in government for some reason, were made party functionaries. There were of course several exceptions to this, but the trend was unmistakable. The Kamraj plan essentially suggested the removal of some important leaders of the party from government—including chief ministers of states and ministers in the Central cabinet—to be drafted for party work. The need and rationale for this shift was evident. However, it so happened that some of those removed from government were not qualified to do party work with any success. They were just dead wood. In any event, most of them were not in fact drafted for party work. The Kamraj plan thus operated for a purpose other than its avowed one. The plan lost much of its credibility. And once this chink appeared, wild speculation and comment aggravated the damage. Many began to believe that its authors wanted to steer the post-Nehru line of succession in a given direction. Which, in turn, meant that the succession was indeed imminent.

When the Kamraj plan first came out, it mentioned no names. Nor the number of those who would come under the axe. It authorized the Prime Minister to choose them. Speculation raged all over the country. Political commentators and media people had their hands full for several days. If according to a newspaper Chief Minister X deserved removal, a learned editorial soon appeared in it, recounting his service to the party in the past. In case he did not possess such a past record, the learned editor still concluded that Chief Minister X was excellent for party work. He should be shifted under the Kamraj plan, the editorial added. For a few days, work in all government offices in the country came to a standstill. Secretariats hummed with frenzied discussion.

Chaudhury was no exception. Mahendranath's camp lost no time in spreading the word that Chaudhury would be the first to go. The Prime Minister trusted no one else as implicitly as he did Chaudhury in party matters, they asserted. In fact, they added, the Kamraj plan came into being primarily to draft Chaudhury for party work. It would include some others as well, first because they had become dead wood anyway, and second, because the Prime Minister did not wish to make a high-sounding plan for a single individual. No, sir, that would invest this Chaudhury fellow with disproportionate importance. Alternatively, the true intention of the Kamraj plan being the elimination of unwanted persons from government, it was obvious that the plan simply could not exclude Chaudhury. To the Mahendranath lobby, it did not matter how Chaudhury was to go and on what grounds, so long as he did go.

Concomitant with this speculation was the question—who was the next chief minister to be? The choice was wide open. Which meant that the personal fortunes of many reporters took a positive turn. Dinners (wet, of course), lunches, mysterious little envelopes of varying thickness passing from hand to hand . . . in a word, it was just wonderful for them. The services expected of them were innocuous and inconsequential. All they needed to say was that if A could succeed Chaudhury, so could B or C; it was that simple. The columnist cared very little about who actually succeeded the incumbent. He could write about different clients on different days. Some high and mighty journalists catered to so many clients that they ended up with oblique references to all their negative characteristics and concluded that their uniform worthlessness made the choice doubly difficult! . . . This was the only media support received by those hopefuls who did not dig liberally into their pockets. Soon, the likely candidates stopped campaigning by proxy and began attacking each other directly. Each of the probables recounted stories of the horrendous vices of all the others. It was again a field day for the newspapers. When political power appears on the horizon, no one takes chances. Both Mahendranath and Chaudhury marshalled their lieutenants with equal gusto. It was a free-for-all.

After several days of tension, the names of those being axed under the Kamraj plan were announced. The omission of Chaudhury's name from the list was an anticlimax. It started another round of speculation and comment. Chaudhury's group saw it as proof that he was indispensable to the running of the state. Mahendranath's men countered this assertion, saying that Panditji could never trust a scoundrel like Chaudhury for party work anyway. Besides, they said, quoting 'very reliable sources', he had bought his retention as chief minister by paying 'crores' in Delhi—to whom, no one cared to elaborate.

The final result of the Kamraj plan was dismal. Kamraj himself became the party president, but no one else undertook any party work. In effect, the plan amounted to the dismissal of some. No one shed tears about the removals, but the way in which it was done was criticized. Panditji's credibility was affected, giving rise to the feeling that the country had been misled. It was so unlike Jawaharlal, said many.

The people had in fact shown extreme indulgence to Nehru in absolving him of the responsibility for the Chinese debacle. They saw him mainly as a victim of betrayal. Nevertheless, Jawaharlal clearly saw the ground slipping under his feet. His party's image sagged as never before. No one had believed this could happen in Panditji's lifetime, least of all Panditji himself. In the plenary session which Kamraj presided over, the party adopted the new objective of 'socialism' to replace 'socialistic pattern', its previous goal (which hadn't been too popular). Not many could grasp the difference between the old label and the new. Members acquiesced to the change-over. There was not much evidence of any cogitation in the party ranks on the change.

Midway through the session, Jawaharlal suffered a stroke—mild according to some, severe according to others. A stroke, all the same. This sad event largely overshadowed the euphoria anticipated from the upgraded objective of socialism. The political effort of the session did not seem to bear fruit.

So callous was the indifference to basic principles, particularly at the state level, that within a few weeks of the advent of socialism as the party's creed, no one seemed to remember it . . . These developments stunned Anand. Where he himself was concerned, the party's adoption of a far-reaching ideology in its entirety was something which humbled him and made him think deeply about each decision he made. When a file came to him for disposal, he felt something within him stir and ask, 'Is your decision going to be in conformity with the spirit of socialism? Aren't you going to make every administrative measure fit into the new creed? How will you implement the party's objectives unless its ideology permeates all actions by the government and the party?' While many party men were similarly conscious of the new direction, some of his colleagues did not grasp its critical significance. They did not believe that a shift in ideology should lead to a corresponding change in the government's programme and methodology . . . For many of them it was once again business as usual. Mahendranath and Chaudhury resumed their collision course. Not that they had ever stopped; only, they now went ahead with redoubled vigour. It was impossible to believe that both belonged to the same political party. They used every political event as an occasion to attack each other.

The earliest of such events after the adoption of the new ideology took place during the biennial election to the state legislative council.

Afrozabad, like other large Indian states, had a bicameral legislature. The legislative council, called the upper house or the second chamber, is an important component of the legislature in the Indian parliamentary system at the state level. It is a compact institution, comprising representatives of different important interest groups in society and a fixed number of intellectuals and professionals from the community at large such as medical experts, economists, scientists, jurists, engineers, academics, litterateurs and so on, nominated by the governor of the state. Special interest groups in the state, such as teachers, registered graduates, representatives of local bodies etc. are listed as voters in specially delimited constituencies and elect their respective quota of members to the council.

The legislative assembly (the lower house) is also one such constituency, and its members (MLAs) elect a fixed number of members (other than themselves) to the legislative council. These are generally the different components of the upper house. The legislative powers of the council are the same as those of the assembly, and each piece of legislation needs to be passed by both houses in order to become law, after receiving the governor's assent. The only subjects the council is not entitled to vote on are money bills, such as the budget, taxation proposals and so on. However, the most important feature to be noted is that a member of the upper house has the same status as one from the lower house. Barring nominated members, any member of the legislative council could be included in the council of ministers. Which is what makes the membership of the upper house well worth the effort ambitious people put in. Needless to say, the effort is multi-faceted and extremely absorbing.

The election by this last category, namely the MLAs, is held according to the system of proportional representation with the single transferable vote. Since it is so different from the simple majority system we all know about, it is crucial to understand at least the essentials, to know why it was introduced into the electoral process originally, and how it came to be misused to a large extent later.

This system is useful where a single constituency has to elect more than one candidate at the same time. For instance, where three candidates are contesting and two are to be elected, if one of them gets fifty-one per cent of the votes he is declared elected at once, while there is a tie for the second seat between the other two. But if no one gets fifty-one per cent by himself, any two combined could defeat the third, obviously. Which two of them are to combine and how? Herein lies a second choice or preference available to the voters in the system of proportional representation. This principle helps political parties, minority groups or interests to get their respective numerical strengths reflected in the result of the election more accurately than through a simple majority poll.

The method works roughly in the following way:

Suppose the total strength of the MLAs in the given assembly is 122, of whom three are absent on the day of polling and 119 are present and voting; out of these 119, suppose two votes have been rejected as invalid for some reason. The remaining 117 are the valid votes polled. Suppose they are to elect five members to the legislative council, and the total number of candidates standing for the election is nine, A, B, C, D, E, F, G, H and I . . . So, now, each voter (MLA) is given a ballot paper containing the names of the contestants, A, B, C, etc. in alphabetical order. As per the rules, the voter is asked to mark, according to his preference, the numbers 1, 2, 3, 4, 5 etc. opposite the names. He could mark only 1 (only one candidate, the first preference) or 1 and 2 (the first and second preference, and so on) leaving the others out, if he so wishes. Obviously, different candidates will get different numbers of first, second, third etc. preference votes in such voting.

Next, there is a formula which determines the minimum number of first preference votes (called the quotient or quota) which a candidate should get in order to be declared elected. For the convenience of calculation, to avoid small fractions, each ballot is given a value of 100. Then the quota is arrived at by dividing the aggregate value of the total valid votes polled, by a number which is one more than the number of candidates to be elected, plus one, ignoring the remainder if any. In the present example, we multiply 117 (being the valid votes) by 100, viz. 117 x 100 = 11700; we then divide this by 5 + 1 = 6, which gives the figure of 1950. Adding one to this quotient, the quota for this election would be declared as 1951.

Now it is clear that all the nine candidates standing for election cannot be elected, since there are only five vacancies. Let us assume that out of the nine candidates contesting—A, B, C, D, E, F, G, H and I—the values of votes polled by candidates C and F exceed the quota of 1951; suppose C gets votes whose value is 2100, while that of F's votes is 2462. They need only votes of the value of 1951 each, this being the quota. So C has votes of the value 149 and F has of 511 over and above the quota of 1951 respectively. What happens to these extra votes? In a simple majority election, they would be wasted and would not give any advantage to the party or group or interest that got these extra votes. However, in the system of proportional representation with single transferable vote, these extra votes would be transferred to the other candidates of the party, for whom preferences such as 2, 3, 4 etc. have been marked by the voters. Thus the party candidates will get the extra votes of other candidates of their party proportionately. Now, taking the surpluses in the descending order of their values, the highest surplus, namely F's 511, has to be transferred first. Suppose that three voters out of those who gave their first preference vote to F have marked preference 2 for candidate D. Suppose further that D has already got first preference votes of the value of 1600 by himself. D would only require 351 of F's 511 extra votes to reach the quota of 1951. The extra votes of the remaining value of (511-351=)160 would then be transferred to A, for whom preference 3 has been marked and who is, say, trailing with first preference votes of the value of 1400 of his own. Now A will reach votes of value (1400+160=)1560, in his effort to reach the quota of 1951.

In this manner the surplus votes obtained by the candidates are transferred to the other candidates as marked by the voters. This marking is done normally for the candidates of the same or a like-minded party, under the directions of the chief whip of the party.

After the surplus votes are thus transferred, we come to the list of candidates and their votes, inclusive of the transferred surplus votes. Let us assume that after three candidates—F, C and D—have been declared elected on crossing the quota as shown above, the remaining six candidates are still below the quota in the total value of their original and transferred votes. Then the elimination process begins, starting with the candidate with the least number of votes, say G in this example. Suppose G has got votes of the value of 840 by himself, plus transfer, if any, as described above. These are again transferred to the other candidates as marked on his ballot paper. Suppose three out of these eight are marked 2 (second preference) to F; but since F has already been declared elected, he no longer requires these votes. In that case, they are transferred to the candidate for whom 3 (third preference) is marked in G's ballot paper. If this candidate needs these votes to move up to the quota, they are transferred to him. And so on, until five candidates reach the quota. Those five, who are necessarily from different parties according to their respective strengths, are declared elected, while the other four lose the election.

It will thus be seen that a party's or group's votes in the system of proportional representation are fully utilized for the party's or group's benefit. The votes are also from all parts of the constituency, from wherever votes were polled. The main virtue and benefit of this system is that the end result is much closer to the actual wishes of the electorate than in the simple majority system generally in vogue.

This is only a brief outline, taking a simple example. In reality, the process is much more intricate, especially when it comes to resolving situations such as two candidates polling votes of equal value, or working out how the votes of eliminated candidates are to be transferred and so on.

When elections to the upper house are to take place, the usual practice of any party setting up candidates is to divide the votes of its own MLAs plus those of any independents supporting them, among the candidates set up by that party. All parties participating in the election do the same with the votes available to them. The party allots a pre-calculated number of first, second, third, fourth (and so on) preference votes to each of its candidates, so that all the candidates of the party get the requisite number of preferential votes each, and win the election as per the seats due to that party on the basis of its total strength. To ensure this, the party managers give a slip containing the preferential order of voting to each party voter, which he is supposed to copy accurately on his ballot paper while voting. For instance, if you are a party MLA and are placed, say, in candidate B's list for first preference, candidate A's list for second preference, and so on, party discipline requires you to mark your ballot paper in that order, namely, mark 1 against B and 2 against A and so on, as directed in the slip.

This, then, is the system followed at elections to the legislative council, as prescribed by law. So far, so good. But here comes the rub. The party may ask you to mark your first preference for a candidate whom you detest with all your heart, for whatever reason. Indeed, you might want to give your first preference vote to another candidate to whom the party has not allotted your vote. What then? It is this intriguing question that baffles the voter in an indirect secret election. You may, for instance, surrender to party discipline and vote as directed, against your own wish. That would be normal voting; no excitement, no romance, no likelihood of any quid pro quo. The alternative is that you could protest against the party decision and leave the party. Well, nobody does that any more. It is not easy to leave your party, especially if it happens to be the ruling party. By a logical process of elimination, you arrive at the third option, the best yet. If this is the course you have chosen, you now follow the following procedure—you continue in the 'camp' of the candidate to whom the party has allotted you; you keep running about and actively canvassing for him, you make him believe that you are his chief lieutenant. Then you get into the polling booth, mark your first preference vote in favour of the other candidate to whom you were *not* allotted, yet whom you always intended to vote for. Finally, you come out of the polling booth with an expansive smile, go straight back to the candidate to whom you were allotted but did not vote for, and make him thank you for having cast your vote for him—and live happily ever after. A classic piece of political adultery.

Then, of course, there are the uncommitted independent MLAs, for whom the sky is the limit. You can hardly imagine any occasion that independents find more enjoyable or profitable.

Thus the current election to the upper house by the members of the lower house inevitably became a welter of party and group politics. It fully reflected the Mahendranath-Chaudhury conflict, as did everything else. Indeed, it became the dominant factor in the drama. First, each group wanted its own yes-men to get the ruling party's ticket to the council. Eight members were to be elected from the assembly and the ruling party's strength was enough to get five of its candidates elected outright, plus around sixteen extra votes which by themselves could not get a candidate elected, but were invaluable for any candidate who could, by hook or crook—in practice often by crook—manage the remaining votes. Mahendranath and Chaudhury did everything they could to influence the selection of the candidates through their contacts in Delhi. However, the result of their efforts was far from clear this time, since some of the candidates themselves had considerable pull in Delhi. Party tickets fell into their laps straight from there—or so they claimed. As if to confirm these claims, the list of the ruling party's 'official' candidates came straight from Delhi, sending the legislators in the state capital into a frenzy.

The list caught everyone unawares. Yet no one said he was surprised. That is another characteristic of politicians—never to show surprise. Surprise is a sign of ignorance, vulnerability, stupidity, perhaps worse. No politician can ever afford to appear less than all-knowing. 'Well, the list is no surprise to me,' everyone said. 'I had got wind of it at least a couple of days in advance. You see, my sources of information in Delhi are very accurate. They haven't let me down so far.' Both the Mahendranath and Chaudhury camps made the same claim with equal vehemence. Then each began to claim a majority among the candidates in the list as 'our men'.

One of the ruling party's candidates named Ramgopal was said to be the weakest among those fielded by the party high command. This assessment was repeated many times over—and was accepted. One person accepted it because the other person accepted it—and so on, all along the line. A consensus was built up by itself due to this repetition and for no other reason anyone could cite. Eventually it was discovered that he had been dubbed the weakest candidate because he was the poorest; he just couldn't afford an indirect election. Besides, he was a somewhat strong-willed fellow, and not very friendly with the dubious characters who tried to manipulate him. He refused to be pigeon-holed as anyone's camp follower. So, as a matter of strategy, neither Mahendranath's camp nor Chaudhury's claimed him or did anything to cultivate him. He was a senior party man, but group-wise he was just an orphan. So everyone predicted that Ramgopal would lose. No one thought that as many as thirty-six MLAs would cast their first preference votes for him, that being the minimum number required for any candidate to get elected in the first count, in a secret ballot—even under the direction of the party whip. The other four candidates of the ruling party either had their group backings or blessings from Delhi. Their MLAs could be persuaded to defect, too, for suitable inducements, but their cases were not as hopeless as Ramgopal's.

By contrast, the 'Fat Four', namely Someshwar, Bihari, Ratanlal and Babu Mian, were in a different class. These four, again by consensus, were a perfect fit for an indirect election. They were wealthy, and widely known to be rank opportunists. They now seized the opportunity to participate in the kind of election that was in line with their genius. Corrupt candidates of their type had become a regular feature of all indirect elections for some time now. Their largesse was of great help in the election, it was claimed. They belonged to no party. No one could tell which of them was close to Mahendranath or to Chaudhury in the ruling party. For their part, they were too clever to be aligned with any group, because they had been, and would always be, milking both groups for their own umpteen interests.

How the Fat Four became candidates at this election was also a remarkable story. If the ruling party had sixteen extra votes after allotting thirty-six to each of its official candidates, the other parties put together had seventeen extra. Where would these sixteen plus seventeen go? And which sixteen and which seventeen, in a secret ballot? The aspirations of the Fat Four were rooted in this conundrum. Their mutual rivalries contributed not a little to their candidatures; in other words, each man compulsively and inexorably jumped into the fray because the others did so. All as independents, hoping for defecting votes from all parties!

As far as political parties went, none had 'openly' pledged support to any of the Fat Four. The ruling party had sixteen extra votes, but the extras in the other parties were rather scattered. One party had four, which was neither here nor there; still the four could prove a great boon for that party, if only its leaders knew how to cash in on them—which they did, of course. Then there was a party cobbled out of seven independent MLAs who had otherwise nothing to do with one another; they called themselves a party merely in order to bargain better—a party was always stronger than an individual. However, their marriage of convenience was based on a very insecure foundation; each of the seven was capable of deserting the party the moment he found it more profitable to do so. Then there was a two-member party, one of them being its leader, and the other the deputy leader-cum-secretary-cum-treasurer-cum-chief-whip-cum-executive member. And the most remarkable was a one-member party, with one person as everything and everybody in it. Yet it was well-known that that member was the most vociferous thunderer in the entire assembly, if ever there was one. When he rose to speak, the weatherman could almost forecast an unseasonal storm.

With this line-up, it was clear that the impending indirect election could turn into a free-for-all. Both Mahendranath and Chaudhury, the main gladiators of the ruling party, let loose their followers after the Fat Four, while the Fat Four thought, in turn, that they had let themselves loose on the MLAs in general, regardless of their party affiliations and whips. Seeing all this, someone quipped that partyless democracy was already in action in that election!

The four millionaire candidates lost no time in setting up their organizations—'shops', in common parlance. Their agents swarmed all over the state capital. They also visited the home towns and villages of the MLAs in a bid to 'book' them in advance.

Someshwar and Bihari each hired fifty air-conditioned rooms in two luxury hotels to begin their assault in grand style. However, their arrangements to entertain prospective voters became public news instantaneously. People began to refer to the two hotels with a wink and a nod. Not that the candidates cared; yet public opinion had it that it was outrageous if one indulged 'openly' in such things; a bit of discretion would perhaps be tolerated. No one believes that you are drinking lemonade sitting in a liquor shop, even if you do so in fact. To any observer, the drink goes with the shop. Indeed, true discretion would lie in drinking liquor in a lemonade shop—if you could manage it. Which was precisely what the other two millionaire candidates, Ratanlal and Babu Mian, did. Ratanlal booked all the guest houses within five miles of the capital. He made catering arrangements and had the bedrooms redecorated. Fresh stocks of foreign liquor were made available. He arranged for interesting companions to be at hand at very short notice. He did everything possible to treat the MLAs like princes—until the poll, of course. However, even Ratanlal's 'show' was not quite secret. He had to involve government officials in the elaborate process of booking and refurbishing the guest houses. As a result, many officials, while happily partaking of the fare at the guest houses, still talked about Ratanlal with certain bureaucratic disapproval. That was the special privilege of government officials—to enjoy themselves while at the same time sitting in judgement on the source of their pleasures.

The most discreet arrangement was Babu Mian's. Almost no one knew what he did. He secured individual well-furnished rooms exclusively for the entertainment of the voters—one room per head. The rooms were in different localities—all posh, of course. Babu's intimate friends supervised the arrangements personally. There was a detailed master plan listing where each voter was to stay, who would look after him, how and when. It earmarked the 'company' for each. Everything worked perfectly. Babu Mian left nothing to chance or to human error.

The battle lines of the election were drawn with absolute precision by the millionaires, as Ramgopal and the other poor candidates watched in anger and frustration. Many of the voters allotted to them were lured into the hotels, guest houses and private apartments of the Fat Four. Whenever Ramgopal approached one of his voters, he had a nasty feeling that the latter looked at him uncomprehendingly, as if unaware that a candidate called Ramgopal existed. Just three days before the poll, everyone knew that at least twenty voters out of the thirty-six allotted to Ramgopal and an unknown but fair number from all the other candidates had succumbed to the Fat Four; maybe all the thirty-six allotted to Ramgopal would desert him on election day, someone said ominously. So, his defeat was inevitable, while the chances of several others were also feeble. No one knew this better than Ramgopal himself. The irony was that as of that day, he got sympathy and promises in plenty, but no prospect of votes; while the Fat Four got no sympathy from any quarter but they were sure to net all the votes.

As the hours ticked by, the election process slowly took on a different complexion. Hitherto, it was the diversion of votes from the poor candidates to the Fat Four. By now, almost everyone believed that the poor candidates were virtually out of the reckoning and the millionaires began to fight among themselves for votes. This operation was both more ruthless and more subtle. It was a fight to the finish—it had to be, for obvious reasons. The tussle was no longer for the membership of the legislative council; that was over for all practical purposes. The real stake now was of ministership, for which all four were serious contenders. Each of them began trying to get the other three defeated in the election. Intrigue and vilification crossed all limits of decency—assuming, that is, that there are any such limits in electoral politics. No holds barred, no resources spared. You didn't have to make an inquiry to know the nefarious side of any of the four. You just had to note what each said about the other three. That made you an authority on all four. You could write a book on each one and get it published with the generous help of the other three!

The funniest part of the drama was that the Fat Four were all independent candidates, but each of them, through some private source, had received the assurance that he would be admitted into the ruling party after being elected as MLC and made a minister.

Some MLAs were too shrewd for the Fat Four. Take, for instance, the case of Jagmohan Sharma, an MLA allotted to Ramgopal. Soon after the allotment, he had started complaining about all the voters allotted to Ramgopal. 'What's the use?' he said. 'Even if a few honest voters like me do vote for Ramgopal, everyone knows he isn't going to make it. The Fat Four have managed too many defections already. There is no discipline in this party. I am certain there will be massive cross-voting. And in the end, they will blame only the honest voters, I'm afraid. I just don't see how Ramgopal can win, with all that's going on . . .' With this preface, Jagmohan built the foundation of his own defection. He visited the camps of the Fat Four, lecturing everyone on honesty, and deploring the epidemic of defections. Meanwhile, he made a careful assessment of what could be gained from each of the contenders, taking in every strength and every weakness.

When he visited the hotel rooms hired by Someshwar, he ran into many MLAs allotted to Ramgopal and other party candidates. The congregation looked like a social gathering, if you confined your observation to the spacious lounge. However, inside the closed rooms you could see—rather, could have seen if you had the chance to—a variety of transactions in progress. Jagmohan's perceptive eye observed everything, inside and outside. He made another little speech on the evils of defection, had a sumptuous breakfast and departed. As he sank into the back seat of his car, a big head with a thick moustache and dirty protruding teeth thrust itself into his face and whispered, 'Twenty thousand?' Surprised but undaunted, Jagmohan hissed back, 'You scoundrel! How dare you try to corrupt an honest legislator! Now get out!' He slammed the door shut and instructed the driver to speed away. As the car whirred off, a hand rested on the shoulder of the man with the big head and someone said, 'Serve you right! That's no way to tackle honourable MLAs! You've no class, my friend!'

Meanwhile, Jagmohan reached the hotel where Bihari's supporters had gathered. Again he found several fellow-voters from Ramgopal's list and other MLAs from all parties. They sat or stood listlessly in the lounge and the corridors. They threw furtive glances all round, feeling out of place, fidgeting. When Jagmohan entered the corridor, their faces went pale but lit up with knowing smiles the very next moment. They felt the burden of their sin weigh less on their conscience, with one more—and an 'honest' one at that—joining them to share it. They suddenly began to laugh and joke boisterously and succeeded, temporarily at least, in drowning the nagging inner voice of their scruples.

Jagmohan's next stop was one of the guest houses engaged by Ratanlal. He saw the same unabated revelry there among the MLAs belonging to his party and others, and snubbed those who tried to tempt him to participate. By then he had created an impression of himself as absolutely incorruptible. They all said that Ramgopal was indeed lucky to have a voter of Jagmohan Sharma's rectitude. He became a leader among voters!

The following morning Babu Mian invited him to one of his private homes. By then, each of the Fat Four had decided to secure Sharma's support. The attention showered on him at Babu Mian's haunt would have corrupted any lesser mortal. But not Jagmohan Sharma; he came out of the den unscathed. Then he disappeared mysteriously. Each of the Fat Four suspected that one of the other three had abducted Sharma. It was amazing how they considered winning him over a special achievement! They felt the way a seducer feels about his 'conquest' of a virtuous housewife. Within a day of his disappearance, each of the Fat Four was willing to pay any price just to keep Sharma away from the other three. And Sharma managed to keep free and clear of all four, making all of them beholden to him in the process.

It was not for nothing that Sharma had become such a powerful magnet. Apart from being seen as honest, word had got round that there were at least fifteen MLAs, from all parties, in his grip and he controlled them fully and completely. No one knew how this piece of fiction was conveyed to the Fat Four, but each believed that he alone knew it and he alone would eventually bag Jagmohan and fifteen others for himself. Never was the combination of wealth and stupidity so transparently obvious as in this electoral wizardry!

Long after the elections, Jagmohan Sharma found himself in Ootacamund, the beautiful hill station in the far south. 'Accidentally', he ran into Ratanlal's niece and gave her his gentlemanly protection in a hotel room . . . His financial problems disappeared one by one, as Bihari quietly attended to them. His son got a comfortable job in an undertaking in which the managing director was a close friend of Babu Mian's. And finally a nice house began to take shape, brick by brick, in the name of his widowed sister-in-law. She neither needed the house, nor could she afford it; it had materialized with Someshwar's manager acting on her behalf. No one knew about these developments, apart from those concerned; and Jagmohan continued to be held up as a shining example of the honest voter.

To return to the election. The Fat Four continued to believe that Jagmohan could sway those fifteen votes allotted to the poor candidates. So they kept up their efforts to win him over. The poor candidates, meanwhile, kept saluting and supplicating him with folded hands and imploring faces. That was all they could do. Ramgopal, of course, would have lambasted him; but Jagmohan didn't give him that chance.

Hafeezullah, MLA, was in a terrible dilemma. The party had allotted his first vote to Ramgopal, and for that very reason, each of the Fat Four assumed they could buy him off cheap. They knew that Hafeezullah had no chance whatever of retaining his seat at the next election; indeed, it had been a great surprise that he had retained his seat in the 1962 election. He had been the beneficiary of yet another wave. But there would be no next time, they were sure, especially as Panditji's health had begun to deteriorate; no one, however, said so.

Three nights before polling day, Hafeezullah was returning from a friend's house when four hefty men pounced upon him at a dark street corner. They tied, gagged and blindfolded him in a flash. He was then stuffed like a sack of rice into the rear seat of a waiting taxi. By the time Hafeez regained control of his senses, the taxi had travelled several miles and come to a stop in the middle of a deserted country road. The man seated next to him thrust a wad of blue currency notes, securely stapled, into Hafeez's pocket, and barked, 'Here's ten thousand in crisp new notes. Your first preference vote goes to Bihari, candidate number one on the list printed on the ballot paper. And listen, no nonsense. If you don't comply, remember that you won't live to complete your term! Is that clear?'

Stupefied and helpless, Hafeezullah mumbled something incoherent. He was terrified but at the same time he felt hurt and insulted. To think that this was happening in Nehru's India!

The interview in the taxi was just about to end, when a big van roared past and came to a dead stop. Immediately, seven or eight men in khaki jumped out of the vehicle, rifles at the ready. Shouts rent the air. Hafeezullah was pushed out of the taxi, and the taxi drove off at amazing speed. Covered with mud, nursing a sprained ankle and clutching a wad of ten thousand rupees, Hafeezullah watched in terror as his new assailants approached him. His fear abated when he saw the khaki uniforms. The police, he thought, with immense relief. He would remember to pay a handsome tribute to them while speaking on the demands of the Home department in the budget session of the assembly.

His relief, however, proved short-lived. He discovered to his consternation that his khaki-clad rescuers were Ratanlal's men. They had donned fake police uniforms to scare Bihari's hoodlums away. Hafeez began cowering in redoubled fear. However, Ratanlal's men preferred a different method of attack. They did not resort to any show of force. On the contrary, they were friendly, and claimed that in rescuing him they were acting in the best traditions of democracy. All they wanted to do was to restore to him the right to vote as he pleased. Sounds too good, thought Hafeez, as he thanked them and waited to hear what came next.

The veil began to lift, slowly. 'You know, Hafeezullah Sahib, that Ratanlal is from your district. You know that he is a millionaire and wields tremendous influence. You know that he has a definite say in your constituency and has been the deciding factor in all the elections so far. You know that even you, popular as you are, have no chance of winning without Ratanlal's active support. That support will be very much enhanced if Ratanlal becomes an MLC in this election. And if he doesn't win, he will contest the assembly election and be your rival in your seat, see? . . . Now, you are supposed to cast your first-preference vote for that good-for-nothing Ramgopal; but you know that he isn't going to win anyway. If you feel it's all right, my dear Hafeezullah Sahib, why not switch your vote to Ratanlal . . .?'

Why not? How convincing they have made defection sound, and in his own interest! thought Hafeezullah. He mumbled something as he frantically tried to compose his answer. It was fascinating to see Bihari and Ratanlal employ opposite techniques for the same purpose. All roads seemed to lead to defection during those days!

Bansidhar, the scheduled caste MLA, was also allotted to Ramgopal in this election. He was known to be impeccably honest, so none of the other candidates approached him with any inducements. Instead, they started a subtle rumour against him. How long, they asked, could good old Bansi keep his large family of three sons and four daughters at near-starvation level? He had already missed the bus many times on the way to the council of ministers. Now he simply could not afford to spurn the generous amounts offered by the Fat Four. And you know what? He had already collected his reward, though, of course, no one would believe that about him. Rubbish, absolute rubbish, this talk of honesty . . .

No one believed this rumour, but precisely for this reason it spread fast—the sad truth of an honest man's first ever act of dishonesty. Even if no one believed it, no one could deny it either. After all, who knew the truth? As journalists say, rule out nothing, but nothing, ever. The more fantastic the rumour, the better; in any event, it excites greater curiosity. And when something is repeated over time, people will begin to believe the unbelievable. So the rumour about Bansidhar's defection (from honesty, that is) gave sadistic pleasure to many. They gloated, as it were, over Bansi's entry into their own fold. It was an acquisition. A long-awaited triumph. A hypocritical thorn removed from their flesh.

When rumour became belief, as only a political rumour can, more and more people sympathized with Ramgopal, the abandoned candidate. And concluded more deals to bring about more defections. If Bansidhar could defect, who wouldn't?

The drama played out in the matter of the votes of Bansidhar and Hafeezullah was repeated with other MLAs right up to the eve of the elections. The legislators' hostel hummed with activity. As the night wore on, the participants shed all pretences in this political striptease. Kidnapping, intimidation, money, liquor, carnal pleasure, cajoling and every other form of inducement was used; but the players knew with certainty that finally no matter what they tried, the voters would vote just as they pleased. 'Damn this secret ballot!' exploded Bihari to his chief organizer. 'The devil himself must have devised it! Here I am, in a tight hole, lavishing everything on these dirty pigs for over a fortnight now. I've almost no money left, everything has gone into this bottomless pit. I could as well have built a temple or a hospital, as my father has been telling me to! But no! Not Bihari, the politician and patriot! And where am I now, on this accursed night? Nowhere, that's where! They're all enjoying themselves as though this night is to be their very last—and they know it, the bastards! I've bribed seventy voters in all, in one way or another—in fact, many in more ways than one. Still, I'm not sure about even one single rascal. What each will do is his own precious secret—the secret of the ballot!'

As the Fat Four fretted and fumed, the poor candidates spent a sleepless night. Ministers kept an all-night vigil in the legislators' hostel, along with their staff. They were detailed to keep an eye on the party MLAs from their respective districts—mainly by keeping the intruders, and their inducements, out of the way.

The activity of non-voting politicians who were not candidates was the most intense. Mahendranath's henchmen did their best to make it known that Chief Minister Chaudhury's lieutenants were causing defections. They wanted to put the blame on Mahendranath, they claimed, in order to get him expelled from the party. Chaudhury, they said, was exploiting his proximity to the high command to wreak vengeance on Mahendranath. Chaudhury's henchmen, on the other hand, began to shout from the housetops that Mahendranath's men were busy causing defections, to get some 'official' candidates defeated. They were determined to dirty Chief Minister Chaudhury's name. All these charges and counter-charges confused everyone further. Ultimately, they said, you couldn't rule out anything. The safest thing was to disbelieve nothing. In effect, you were free to believe what you wished to believe.

Rumours of defection, re-defection and re-re-defection hung in the air like smog. Everyone suspected everyone else. Everyone chased and spied on everyone else. Central Intelligence personnel scurried all over the place, sniffing their way about in an attempt to forecast how many ruling party candidates were in danger of defeat. They took 'guesstimates' and opinions from everyone who was anyone. Then they completed their own deductions and sent their reports to Delhi. 'They will rehash our guesses and present them as their own deep research!' commented one cynical MLA. 'That is Central Intelligence for you!'

Behind all this hubbub and hustle, somewhere, unseen, unsuspected, a subtle manipulation of the voting MLAs, the key players in the drama, went on. When the process of massaging their egos and wills was complete, their minds would have been irrevocably made up. After all the action of the past weeks, this was the end game. Incredible, but true. Imperceptibly, the chief minister's levers of power went into action. The handiwork of the past fortnight—the obscene and excessive use of money, liquor and sex which had reached a point of oversaturation—began to slowly crack. A mysterious alchemy began in the minds of those who would vote in the morning. An unaccountable sense of anxiety gripped them from within.

Simultaneously, the corrupt practices of the Fat Four cancelled each other out, leaving none of them with any solid advantage. As the hours passed, ministers who hailed from the districts of the Fat Four suddenly became active. They did nothing overt, yet their activity which was primarily one of omission and exceedingly subtle commission, meshed to bring about the eventual result: the defeat of the Fat Four. While the Fat Four believed their positions impregnable, internal operators now began to gnaw into their foundations. Every person in power, whose rivals the Fat Four could have become, served as a stick of dynamite in the sabotage. They employed power to block others from coming to power. Nothing was visible on the surface, however. The revelry went on, bcoming more and more bohemian and reckless as the campaign entered its last stage.

Another unforeseen reaction surfaced at the penultimate hour and caused great commotion in the camps of the Fat Four. In their anxiety to please and win over the defectors, the camp managers of the Fat Four had unwittingly ignored some voters and activists who had been sincerely working for them. This was a grievous lapse, a tactical blunder; but it was not surprising. It was the same as the husband's preference for the concubine over his wife; of the wife's preference for the paramour over the husband. It was the difference between what one takes for granted and what one has to get through further effort; between the assured that seems ordinary, and the uncertain that seems alluring. However, in political life the dividing line between the wife and the concubine, the husband and the paramour, the reliable and the dubious, is extraordinarily thin. One can merge with the other with no great effort. The neglected voters who had toiled honestly for the Fat Four boiled over with resentment. If defection was so respectable and profitable, to hell with loyalty, they thought bitterly. Who in his right mind wants to be a poor relation?

A new philosophy began to emerge as the night advanced into the small hours. When the sun shines, you bask in it, gratis; you don't owe a thing to the sun. So with money; it is common wealth, you take it as and when it comes—which isn't very often anyway. So with drink; it's the soma of the gods, it belongs to all, as much as the gods belong to all who worship them. So with sex, since everything is fair where the fair ones are concerned. Hail to the revised slogans. Land to the tiller. Money to the taker. Liquor to the drinker. Woman to the womanizer and so forth, *mutatis mutandis*. Thus, by the time dawn washed away the night, a brand new philosophy of maya predominated. By and large, the voters felt obliged to no one. After all, this was a free country and they were free men and women, they mused tipsily. Who did the Fat Four think they were anyway? Can they buy us, honourable legislators that we are?

The poll passed off peacefully the next day. Admirers of the Fat Four, armed with huge garlands, took over the premises where the counting was taking place. Each camp expected its hero to be sworn in as minister very soon. Ramgopal and the other presumed losers were huddled together in an obscure corner, perhaps waiting for the humiliation to end even before it had begun. No one noticed them. The first count was about to end and the results were expected shortly. The smiles on the faces of the Fat Four and their supporters were expansive and relaxed.

A harried, balding, middle-aged man dressed in a dhoti and kurta rushed out of the counting room and whispered in the ear of a Bihari supporter. The other repeated the whisper. Soon it became a hiss, a murmur, a prolonged groan. They stared at one another, speechless. 'The crazy fools! The double-crossing scoundrels!' exclaimed one of them angrily under his breath.

Then it gushed forth in a torrent: Ramgopal alone declared elected in the first count with—astonishingly, unbelievably—forty-nine first preference votes! Forty-nine! 'Forty-nine!' the crowd roared.

Ramgopal was leaning back in a corner, his eyes shut. Someone pounced on him and shouted, 'Forty-nine!' Ramgopal repeated the figure mechanically, uncomprehendingly, 'Forty-nine . . .?' Then, registering the full impact of what he had just heard, he gave a loud cry and slumped to the ground, unconscious. The tension that had accumulated within him finally overwhelmed him.

There was a lot of pandemonium and the last that one heard was the Returning Officer's frantic calls for the ambulance . . .

# 35

ON 27 MAY 1964, PANDIT JAWAHARLAL NEHRU DIED. HIS PASSING was not unexpected. Almost everyone in the country and many abroad had been talking about it for quite some time, with genuine concern, especially after the debacle of the China war. They believed it was just a question of time. Still, it came as an enormous shock. A defeated nation whimpered at this second deadly blow.

God! Not at this time! everyone said in utter disbelief when the news first came. Not at this time, when the country is still reeling under the depression of defeat at the hands of China. Not at this time when Jawaharlal Nehru is indispensable, being the one person who can hold the country together . . . Not at this time when the void after him would be too ghastly to contemplate . . . Not at this time when no other leader worth his salt can hope to redeem the party's pledges to the people, even remotely. Not at this time when cantankerous and mischievous men at home and abroad are waiting for his end to come; they could do nothing while he lived.

Anand was in the midst of a heated discussion at the meeting of a joint select committee that afternoon. On what basis should the government levy house tax in the municipalities? This was the question at issue. There was near unanimity in the view that the rental value of the house should be the basis. Several members themselves, or their near and dear ones, owned houses within municipal limits. They put their foot down against any change in the 'time-tested' principle of rental value. Anand was on the committee, to help his colleague, the minister for municipal administration, about whose competence Chief Minister Chaudhury happened to have rather a dim view. 'Then why did you make him a minister at all?' someone had once asked him. 'It takes all kinds to make a cabinet, my dear friend,' Chaudhury had replied. 'Those who are dumb also serve. In fact they serve better, if only they are born in the right caste!' Anand was thus a guest participant at the meeting. Yet he joined issue with the majority and argued, to everyone's exasperation, that the basis for house tax should be the market value of the property. The concerned minister, who chaired the meeting, did not agree; he was infuriated, yet he dared not take a public stand other than Anand's. He thought him a meddler, tagged on to the committee merely on Chaudhury's whim. However, it wouldn't do to annoy the chief minister, although he was not too sure that Chaudhury himself would concur with Anand's fantastic suggestion.

The argument went on desultorily. How can you abandon a long-standing principle? How do you know that the other basis will really work and bring in more revenue to the municipalities? Has it worked in any other municipality in the country? One member commented, with biting sarcasm, 'Minister Anandji seems to be an expert on every subject under the sun. However, I would like to remind him that we are considering the question of raising resources, not purveying ethereal views on socialism! How can we run the risk of changing the system of taxation all of a sudden? We know that under-valuation of properties for purposes of sale and purchase is rampant already. If we accept Anandji's new-fangled idea, I have no doubt that all sale documents will record ridiculously low prices to dodge taxes. In the end, the municipalities will stand to lose even the revenue they are getting now. Will Anandji hold himself responsible for those enormous losses? Would he recommend, by this legislation, the closure of all municipal councils?'

Anand realized that he was under attack from all sides. When the chairman invited him to reply, he began, in a deliberate tone, 'Mr Chairman, I would like to point out that we are considering a new comprehensive law for the administration of municipalities in the state and not merely the issue of house tax. Taken in isolation, every single proposal for change looks uncertain and risky. In the new context, however, we have to raise resources primarily from those who can pay, should pay and have to be made to pay. My simple idea of taxing housing property on its market value is not only sound but inescapable. Honourable members from other parties may choose to scoff at socialism, but that happens to be the ruling party's chosen policy. What I suggest is exactly what the member derisively mentioned now. I am converting a utopian view into a new hard-headed municipal law. My authority for doing so is none other than our revered Prime Minister, Jawaharlal Nehru . . .'

Precisely at that moment someone brought in a slip and handed it to the chairman, who glanced at it, then looked again and yet again. The room became silent; a terrible suspense gripped everyone. Slowly, in a deeply troubled voice, the chairman announced, 'Friends, this is shocking news. Our beloved Prime Minister Jawaharlal Nehru is no more.'

A groan of anguish rose from those attending the meeting. Within seconds everyone left the room, except Anand. He sat there for a long time, with his elbows resting on the table and his bent head supported between his palms. He felt more afflicted than when he had lost his father years ago. Jawaharlal had woven a new world of ideas and created a sense of optimism, euphoria and possibility among the masses. He had helped India define her place in the world. Never before had a starving nation been able to hold its head high and look rich countries in the eye. Never before had the arrogance of power and wealth been shown its place, as when Jawaharlal stood up to speak in world councils . . . National honour got priority over dead GDP (Gross Domestic Product) figures. The rich did snigger in their sleeves, but only in their sleeves. However, when it came to internal policies and their implementation, many of his own party men had flouted Jawaharlal—flouted him with great reverence! And now, Anand thought, what'll happen now that he is no more? Will it be possible to retain even a semblance of ideology? He felt orphaned, empty, despairing.

He felt a gentle touch on his shoulder and turned to find Aruna, her eyes red-rimmed. They left the hall and headed for the park. They sat on a bench in a distant corner, absorbed in their grief.

Anand was lost in memories, distant and recent. His school authorities had once penalized him for reading Nehru's autobiography. He had not seen Panditji in person until he had left the state secretly, with the money saved over several months from out of his merit scholarship, to attend the plenary session of the party at Haripura in the Gujarat area of what was then Bombay Presidency. He had never seen such a huge crowd. On entering the wide maidan, he became immediately trapped in a solid human phalanx. He could neither press forward nor get out. He thought he would die of sheer suffocation. However, the thrust of the crowd itself pushed him, inch by inch, into the enclosure of the open session. Once in, he forgot the discomfort immediately and, like the Kathiawari villagers around him, became engrossed in identifying the leaders of the nation individually—Jawaharlal Nehru, Subhas Chandra Bose, Sardar Vallabhbhai Patel, Maulana Azad, Pattabhi Seetharamayya, Khan Abdul Ghaffar Khan (towering over everyone) and many others. He heard Jawaharlal for the first time, with his earnest voice, now halting with emotion, now surging like a river in flood. Anand would remember that occasion and that voice to the end of his days. Nehru's head, so handsomely topped by the Gandhi cap, became indelibly etched in his memory. He had been fascinated by Nehru's qualities—of patriotism, of idealism, of liberalism, of an indefinable, almost transparent calibre of sophistication rarely found in others. What impressed Anand the most was the rare combination of all these qualities in one individual. After that session, he rummaged through several more libraries for Jawaharlal's writings.

426

Undoubtedly, Nehru was the first and most important political influence on him.

The next encounter that had left its mark was the plenary session of the party at Tripuri, a small village near Jubbalpore, on the banks of the Narmada in what was then Central Provinces. Anand had perfected the technique of going out of the princely state unnoticed, to attend political meetings in British India. He had a glimpse of Jawaharlal's short temper at Tripuri. While Nehru spoke at a public meeting, a stray aeroplane circled around making a loud noise and diverted the attention of the audience. Jawaharlal shouted in unconcealed anger that no aircraft should come anywhere near the meeting. Anand wondered who was to carry out that vehement order! However, the aircraft in fact did not approach the area again. Anand was struck by Nehru's peremptoriness, apart from his other qualities. He almost came to fancy that a bit of short temper (genuine or assumed) was perhaps a necessary ingredient of a leader's personality. There are many who have little patience with patience, he told himself with an inward chuckle. He became especially conscious of it because he knew he lacked this trait himself, almost completely. Having trained himself to control anger and annoyance and not to let the world know if these emotions were corroding him from within, he came to admire Jawaharlal all the more.

He remembered another occasion in his youth when he had witnessed a show of temper by Nehru. Anand was visiting Pune for a party meeting that was being addressed by Nehru. Before the meeting the Prime Minister addressed the students of Fergusson College. Anand recalled an interesting episode of that meeting. Anand, on a visit to Pune (then Poona) to see a friend at that college, was in the enthusiastic crowd gathered to listen to Panditji. The gathering was definitely larger than the college amphitheatre could accommodate, and consequently, there was utter confusion even after Panditji's arrival. Some students wanted to drown the noise in cheering and slogan-shouting (*Panditji zindabad* etc.), perhaps to mollify him to some extent! This became counter-productive and Panditji was even more furious. He had just returned from some war-torn country, having seen extensive suffering there at first hand, which was fresh in his memory. Eventually, when a modicum of order was restored, he lashed out at the irresponsible behaviour of the students, at how they did not realize that there were tragedies happening just then in some other countries. He was so angry that he said that the students would realize this if a few bombs were deliberately dropped at some places in India! (Mercifully he did not mention Pune!) After that outburst, pin-drop silence prevailed and Panditji went on to deliver his impassioned and inspiring speech.

Anand recalled, one after another, the various facets of Nehru's versatile personality. He had given the country a lead in more fields of thought and action than one cared to count. He had lent lustre to whatever he touched—and he had hardly left any field untouched. Whenever he was in jail, he produced writings of permanent value, each remarkably solid and lucid. Many said that when Jawaharlal was in jail, literature gained, and when he was out of jail, politics. He had high refinement, reinforced with utter sincerity. He could carry conviction to the Western mind, even in its most cynical moments. There was not a trace of crudeness in him. On occasion this made him look odd, almost a misfit in the company of his colleagues, their own fine qualities notwithstanding. Anand had sometimes wondered if Panditji wasn't an 'alien' of some kind on the Indian political scene. He had laughed within himself at this outlandish thought.

One particular event stood out in Anand's memory. Jawaharlal had visited the state to lay the foundation of an irrigation project on a mighty river. The audience of a hundred thousand villagers, most of them illiterate, had gathered for his 'darshan'. Panditji simply lost himself in the breathtaking scene of the river and the green hills around. He delivered a classic speech on the River Valley Civilization, about which he had written extensively. His rhetoric was brilliant, yet informative and simple. When conveyed to the unlettered crowd through the interpreter, it kept all the men and women spellbound for about an hour and a half. Anand had no doubt that every villager had understood every word of Panditji's exposition and felt the glow of national pride as much as he

(Anand) did himself. It was an unforgettable performance. It had come straight from Nehru's heart.

Non-alignment, the scientific temper, mixed economy, socialism, the concept of a commonwealth of independent republics, the public sector, the advent of national laboratories, the birth of the Planning Commission and the Five Year plans, disarmament and economic cooperation among nations, the abhorrence of war, the role of the United Nations Organization, the establishment of the Akademis of literature, music and dance and art, the institution of national awards—a never-ending sequence of thoughts and images crowded Anand's mind.

Seated next to Aruna on that fateful afternoon, Anand spoke incessantly, now in a choked voice, now in an agitated monologue. He would become pensive in the middle of an idea and whisper, 'What now . . . !' He saw the past dissolve, as it were, and the future loom menacingly close, while the present moved relentlessly and inexorably forward . . . Aruna listened silently, running her fingers through his tangled hair again and again, trying to console him. Gradually Anand's mood changed, as doubts about the nation's future possessed him completely. He trembled under the combined impact of fury and anguish.

'Now, what has this great man done to insure us against future shocks?' he almost shouted. Aruna was taken aback, wincing at Anand's irreverence. 'He gave us lofty ideas, great personal example, remarkable deeds, unmatched respect in world councils, elaborate physical infrastructure, firm ideological anchorage, something to look forward to . . . yes . . . yes . . . YES! But where is the human inheritor of all this? He has made a glorious place for himself, but where will his successors take the country? If he was Mahatma Gandhi's heir, who is *his* heir, for heaven's sake? Collective leadership? For what? For whom? Why did he not realize that his personality alone was sustaining the fabric he had woven for the nation's future? How would it carry on when he was no more? Where is the faith? Where is the vision? Where is the lamp lit by this lamp before it went out? Who can give us the assurance that the party will remain wedded to Nehru's concept—Nehruism, as it has been labelled? What is a mixed economy worth, if the mix is deliberately tailored to maintain the status quo? What will national planning achieve if it leaves out the human element in its anxiety to create physical infrastructure? What is the actual blueprint of socialism going to be? Will it be deliberately fashioned to eliminate inequity? . . . I know I am too small a fellow to ask these big questions. Yet it's a fact that we're going to be ruled by smaller men now, like it or not. No other Jawaharlal is waiting in the wings. If only he had lived for five more years, his picture of socialism would possibly have emerged in concrete shape, after its final and unequivocal acceptance by the party at Bhubaneshwar just a few months back. What is the guarantee now that in the name and style of socialism, something unintended will not follow? . . .'

Anand ranted on and on. He did not realize that he, a non-entity in the overall scheme of things, a mere speck in the country's vast political expanse, was raving against a giant who had earned a permanent place in world history. Aruna tapped his shoulder lightly and said, 'What has happened to you? Why are you so pessimistic?'

'I am not pessimistic, Aruna, don't get me wrong,' Anand said fiercely. 'I mean no disrespect to any leader in Delhi or anywhere in India. They are patriots, great freedom fighters, good administrators, good organizers, untiring workers. Yet I don't find a visionary in our party now. Which, to my mind, means the danger of losing ourselves in trivial clashes, inevitably pulling the people down to those levels too. Which, again, spells the ascendancy of caste, community, group, region and so on to an extent quite disastrous to the country . . . Nehru's foremost concern was the unity of India. How is unity achieved? What does it consist of? Should it not essentially relate to national objectives? Should it not be, in essence, ideological? How can one expect unity to exist when people and groups are working at cross purposes, each claiming to be serving the country? I am referring to basic approaches, not personal feuds and conflicts. One would have expected that the unanimous acceptance of socialism would have made it the essence of government, the basic goal of the nation. Not the socialism borrowed from other countries, but India's own indigenous socialism, as Panditji so clearly and repeatedly emphasized. Our wise men call it Yuga Dharma (ethos of the age). It would become the touchstone to judge every action of the government. Frankly, I don't see this happening from now on. I feel the first casualty of Panditji's death is going to be socialism. '

It was a long day, at the end of May; the nation's loss made it seem longer, more dreary. The poplar and cypress trees in the public park began to cast long shadows. Subdued and emotionally exhausted, the two got up to leave. On reaching his residence, Anand learned about the hundreds of condolence messages from all parts of the world pouring into the country in a torrent. It gave him an idea of the huge aching void created by the event—a void at home, a void abroad, a void everywhere.

Even while arrangements for Nehru's last journey were being made, the issue of political succession erupted. The President of India appointed Gulzarilal Nanda 'interim' Prime Minister, but the question 'Who next?' exercised millions of minds during those few eventful days. While there was intense lobbying among members of parliament from the ruling party, thinking men and women all over the country perceived a watershed in the political landscape. It was not just a question of power. It was certainly not a mere question of personality. It was not even a question of popularity. It was partly all these, but much more. It was a question of leadership, posed as 'leadership for what?' It was a question of the nation's future, really. The media, however, largely missed this question of questions. Many among them saw it as a choice between candidates who were neither competent nor stable. Their portrayal of the current situation was a gross oversimplification. An impression was effectively planted for all time in the minds of the people that the political process was nothing but a cut-throat scramble for power and aggrandizement.

Within a day, all the chief ministers converged on Delhi. Chaudhury was among the earliest to arrive. He asked Anand to accompany him, 'to test your contacts in the country and pick your brains,' he said good-humouredly. Seated side by side on the Indian Airlines flight, they cautiously began to talk about the internal bickering in the party. 'He died at the wrong moment,' said

P. V. NARASIMHA RAO

Chaudhury. 'There will be a lot of confusion in the party.'

'Why do you think so?' Anand asked deftly, to draw the chief minister out.

'I don't know and I can't quite figure it out,' admitted Chaudhury. 'This is one of those cases where everyone knows the event in advance and still no one dare say or do anything about it in advance. We just hope that the event will not occur. It is all so strange, so illogical.'

'Could it be,' suggested Anand, 'that the end of this great man is itself a great event whose dimensions are difficult to evaluate? Could this be the reason why those around him have always been so worried and so deeply divided? So worried indeed that they chose to ignore the writing on the wall, until the event was in fact upon them?'

'Could be . . .' mused Chaudhury. 'I know, to some extent, that they are still divided . . .'

'Divided on what? . . . Succession?'

'Yes . . . I think so . . . Succession.'

'Because there is no obvious successor?'

'Because there is no acceptable successor,' responded Chaudhury. 'But this diagnosis also seems to be an over-simplification. I think the matter is much more complicated. Only, it's all so unclear.'

'Does it have anything to do with the party's ideology?'

'Well, yes and no. The ideological and personal angles are very much mixed up.'

'Which do you think is dominant?'

'You know I'm not much of an ideologue. I don't think that ideology is dominant here, but I am not very clear one way or the other . . . Now tell me, my dear Brihaspati, what do you think we are in for?'

The dialogue was interrupted when they arrived at Palam airport. They were pulled into different groups and were on the move the whole day. In the evening they met in the chief minister's suite in the state guest house, after separately participating in individual and group meetings, including some in the Central Hall of Parliament. Passions seemed to run high and charges and countercharges filled the air. There was even mention of monetary inducement. Anand felt the onset of slow despair.

Despite the confused situation, he discerned an alignment. 'Panditji's men' were on one side, a so-called 'anti-Nehru' coterie on the other. It was a fuzzy pattern, with several confusing factors; yet one could glean it from the utterances, backgrounds and known attitudes of individuals. Lobbying and whispering campaigns took care of the rest.

The press, Anand noted, depicted it as a succession struggle, pure and simple. They had all been Panditji's colleagues till yesterday; then what was the sense, some editorials asked, in branding one section as anti-Nehru? It was a canard, they concluded. A propaganda stunt. A nefarious design to misuse Nehru's name for personal ends. There was no ideological substance in this polarization. It was dubious. It was fraudulent. It was a naked scramble for power, nothing more, nothing less.

Having closely observed the wheels within wheels, Anand had fancied that it was more than a mere personal bout between two claimants for power. He had wandered for some time in the Connaught Place area during the day and visited Old Delhi to meet a friend. There was unmistakable tension in the air. He felt that every citizen was taking part in a notional poll and expressing himself candidly and with vehemence. The people were keen—and anxious—to save something, to uphold something, of Nehru. No one could have spelt out what, of Nehru, was under threat and how. They simply wanted it saved—whatever it was.

These scenes flitted across Anand's mind while he collected his thoughts and prepared to report on the prevailing situation to Chaudhury.

'Who are the persons you met during the day, if I may ask?' Anand queried.

'I met all the leaders, other chief ministers, party functionaries. Several MPs from our state called on me.'

'Well, I moved in a different circle,' Anand said. 'I took to the streets, virtually . . . I heard people talk among themselves animatedly. I talked to several myself to gauge the depth of their feeling. I went to Chandni Chowk to move among different sections of the people. I visited the Delhi University campus to meet a few academics about a seminar next month.'

Chaudhury was a bit impatient. He wanted a straight answer, yes or no.

'I don't want the details of your diary,' he cut in. 'What is the relevance of these noble and not so noble citizens of Delhi that you have met in this political wrangle? This is an intra-party affair . . . It is vital for us in the states, in the sense that we cannot afford to back a losing horse in this tussle; else we'll be finished. If we have a vindictive Prime Minister next, unlike Jawaharlal Nehru, and he thinks we have opposed him in this election, we could go to the dogs and the state would go down the drain . . . That is the real measure of the Prime Minister's power, if you want to know! So don't give me any socialistic nonsense about your street encounters!'

'That's one angle, Chaudhuryji, and a valid one,' said Anand. 'Still, what I was trying to know was how the common man looks at this succession. It is extremely important to see how far our parliamentary party is in step with the people's thinking. This may be irrelevant for this succession, as you say, but more than relevant for the future of the party. After all, the people voted for Jawaharlal's leadership for the full five-year term. They have no say in choosing the party's leader for the rest of the term now, but they will draw their own conclusions on how much the party is in line with the leader they had voted for the last time. Isn't that so?'

'Yes, that is so,' admitted Chaudhury. 'But how does this question arise at all? The people elected the party, didn't they?'

'Did they? Are you sure? Could you say Jawaharlal's personality had nothing to do with it? Don't you agree that the people voted for the party under Jawaharlal Nehru?'

'Yes . . . yes, I suppose I do. From that standpoint you're right,' said Chaudhury. 'I agree that he was the main vote-catcher. And since this is the first intra-party election after Nehru, the people have a right to expect the party to continue his line. It has no mandate to do otherwise. Yet, isn't all this a distinction without any essential difference, Anand? After all, whosoever the party elects as its leader would implement Nehru's policies, wouldn't he?'

'Would he?' countered Anand.

'Well . . . I believe he would.'

'The people in general don't believe so . . .'

'Why do you say so? How are you so sure ?'

'That's where my street encounters come in,' answered Anand. 'This is a trying time and the man in the street has reacted spontaneously to it. A clear polarization of popular views has already emerged, believe it or not. The view that the Nehru philosophy should continue has overwhelming support. It was quite obvious to me . . . When they talk of the possible successors, they clearly identify one of them with Nehru and the other, equally clearly, with the anti-Nehru line. No one could tell me why, but in fact they do. It seems to be a fairly widespread opinion. Our party can ignore this phenomenon only at its peril . . .'

'What you say may be right,' Chaudhury began tentatively. 'Tell me, how do they distinguish between the pro-Nehru and anti-Nehru line?

'I'm sure they can't articulate it clearly, neither can I,' Anand answered. 'However, let me tell you what happened in this guest house about an hour back. Returning from my visits, I felt hungry. Instead of ringing for the bearer, I strolled into the kitchen to see what they could prepare for me quickly. When I was just about to enter, I saw the bearers, with their backs to the door, engaged in a loud conversation. It turned out to be on the impending succession. One of them said, "*Arre bhai, yeh to paisewalon aur garibon ke beech ka muqabala hai*! (Brother, this is a contest between the rich and the poor!)" . . . They see the pro-Nehru persuasion as pro-poor. And they see Lal Bahadur Shastri as the pro-Nehru candidate. The other claimant is Morarji Desai. This may be an oversimplification, but this, in essence, is their view of the matter. No amount of rationalizing can change it . . .'

'And which side do the people see me working for?' asked Chaudhury jokingly, but not without some seriousness.

'My taxi driver, whose stand is close to our guest house, put you squarely in Morarji's camp!'

Instead of laughing aloud, as Anand expected him to, Chaudhury was silent for a while. Then he said, 'There's a point in what you say, Anand. I shall speak to the other chief ministers and leaders. I'm sure they're taking all aspects into account, yet a little emphasis on known public perceptions would be useful . . .'

He called his private secretary and asked him to fix appointments, some at once, others early the next morning. He remembered the scene in the hotel bedroom at the hill-station years ago, when a prostitute had unwittingly given him his first insight into 'make-up'. Now, he argued to himself, the party's make-up would need to be refurbished, given that its sole mask had slipped. Even in that sombre moment, his native cynicism surfaced for a while. Till yesterday, Jawaharlal in person had been in constant demand. From now, it would be his name and memory.

The following day, Anand accompanied a member of parliament to the Central Hall and spent a couple of hours there. That is the cauldron in which they first cook the nation's fortunes—before delivering them to the legislatures. Mingling with members, non-members, journalists and others, he witnessed an intense non-stop debate. He paid attention to everything they said on the impending election in the party. In particular, he tried to relate the Central Hall activity with the conversation he had overheard among the guest house bearers the previous afternoon.

As the hours ticked by, the lobbying intensified. Everyone met everyone, spoke to everyone, convinced everyone—it was all so confusing. Towards nightfall, when Chaudhury and Anand met again to compare notes, Anand found his chief beaming with happiness. Chaudhury exulted while announcing that they could avert a contest for leadership in the party.

It was the result of hours and hours of effort and conciliation by chief ministers, senior leaders and a host of wise men from everywhere in the country—whether they held positions for the time being or not. It was a nationwide family responding to a nationwide peril. After earnest deliberations, they had arrived at a consensus to choose Lal Bahadur as the Prime Minister. Morarji Desai had, of course, been persuaded to agree.

Anand listened to Chaudhury attentively and said, tentatively, 'I see . . .'

Chaudhury was furious. 'What has come over you?' he exploded. 'Nothing we do seems to please you. Here we have deflected a grave crisis in the party and you, the so-called wise one, put on a long face. Don't you see that there will be practically no change from the past, since the Union cabinet will look more or less like Jawaharlal's?'

'Yes, except that Jawaharlal will not be there . . .'

'Of course he won't be there. Do you think he can be brought back? Yet, barring that, the country will contine to move along the tracks he laid.'

'That's precisely what remains to be seen,' Anand commented cryptically.

# 36

WAS HE AT A CROSSROADS? WAS INDIA AT A CROSSROADS? WAS HIS
party at a crossroads? Indeed, did Jawaharlal's exit signify a
crossroads?

Was the nation in transition? Was society in transition? What
did Jawaharlal's death have to do with the transition? Or vice
versa? What was the nexus, overt or subtle?

Like the proverbial drop of water on a lotus leaf, Anand had
exercised power and yet remained untouched by it—at once a
participant and observer. Like millions of his compatriots, he had
subconsciously come to take Jawaharlal Nehru as
immortal—almost. He had seen no inclination or urge in his party
for . . . succession? No, he corrected himself . . . for ideological
succession. In other words, the urge to maintain continuity. Also
to reorient and reinterpret the basic tenets of this ideology to apply
it to changing times and situations. Simply put, there was no one
to serve Nehru or his ideals, in the manner Nehru had served
Mahatma Gandhi and his ideals.

The Central government was more like a coalition within the
same party, an unequal coalition. It was altogether a strange

phenomenon. 'Panditji's men' were present in numbers, but they continued to be only Panditji's men. They merely chanted his name and swore by his ideas all the time. One could safely call them Panditji's parrots. They were the preservers of his image. Yet they fulfilled a useful function, keeping his memory alive, albeit without the ability to keep it fresh. The memory, incidentally, provided them with their own survival . . .

Then there was the 'anti-Nehru' group, labelled thus for want of a more accurate description. They had been with Jawaharlal; most of them were as loyal to him as anyone else. Only, they could never reconcile themselves with what they called his flighty dream-world, his impractical approach to problems, his illogical vision. The group called him names behind his back but agreed with him to his face. They even praised him to the extent necessary to keep up appearances and keep detractors at bay . . .

When the Nehru sycophants branded them anti-Nehru, they resented it intensely. They were not 'anti' anyone. They just did not like rapid change. They did not expect a new and perfect era to dawn overnight. And the lesser among them also had an entrenched interest in the status quo; their bread was buttered on that side. In their view, any change was likely to be a change for the worse—for them, to be sure. And most extraordinarily, they cited Gandhi in support of the no-change approach . . . Gandhi and Nehru had been part of a common ethos of change but their followers now conveniently ranged them on opposite sides.

No less dramatic was the change in the political ambience of the state. Leaders now tended to lay greater emphasis on 'realism'. Commendations of 'pragmatism' became more frequent. While Nehru was alive, he constantly shed light on his policies and the revisions he made of them. That era ended abruptly. The most that anyone said was that Nehru's policies would continue. No one took the trouble to elucidate them any longer. Legislative proceedings degenerated into a ritual of remembrance.

All this happened gradually, yet it didn't take too long. Also, nothing happened visibly, though it was politically palpable. Within twelve months the change was clear. The rhetoric did not change drastically, yet its impact—or lack of it—was no longer a matter of speculation. India became cautious, inward-looking. Language, religion, region, caste: all these volatile factors began to throw longer shadows.

New centres of gravity appeared in the states. Chief ministers gained in power and influence. The Prime Minister, by contrast, appeared pliable; however, no one said so openly. Lal Bahadur was a stalwart in his own right, Jawaharlal's right-hand man. The whole country respected him as a humble, sincere and gentle soul. He had given proof of his moral fibre years before, when he resigned as minister of railways in Nehru's cabinet, consequent on a railway accident somewhere in the far south. Many tended to look upon the resignation as bordering on the absurd. It stretched the area of a minister's ethical or moral responsibility to ridiculous lengths. Some critics ridiculed the idea, saying, 'At this rate, brother, the Union cabinet will become a railway platform where ministers keep coming and going like trains!' 'That's an understatement!' chipped in another. 'In fact, the only activity in the Union cabinet will be resignations and swearings-in every day! And home ministers, in particular, would have to change every hour, considering what's happening on the law and order front in the country all the time . . .!'

'That's not correct,' commented a Constitutional expert. 'You forget that law and order is a state subject under the Constitution. And normally it is under the chief minister . . .'

'That's capital!' responded the first man. 'Then Chief Minister Chaudhury should quit with every murder committed anywhere in the state!'

Despite such snide remarks, Lal Bahadur had effectively, through personal example, established the principle of moral responsibility, based on the Gandhian approach. That reputation, however, proved inadequate to give him effective authority as Prime Minister. The contrast between Jawaharlal and Lal Bahadur was so striking, it overshadowed their similarities. Their kinship in thought was itself far from clear anyway. The cosmopolitan, the visionary, the mass leader, the writer, the aesthete, the scholar, the historian, the scientist, the 'Chacha' figure—Lal Bahadur reflected none of these. The people saw him as a trusted lieutenant of the former Prime Minister; therefore, only a shadow. His own substance remained largely unproved. Undoubtedly, he was a Gandhian; but when the anti-Nehru group appropriated the Gandhian seal and stamp, he became nondescript. He was a good follower, but an indifferent interpreter of policy. And one who is a mere follower, howsoever good and faithful, cannot lead the country as Prime Minister for long . . . Things appeared to be slipping, drifting, under him. Side by side, the internecine struggle raged relentlessly—now in the open, now under the surface.

There was a new Prime Minister, a new government under him. Yet, to any careful observer, it was obvious that the issue of Nehru's successor still remained undecided. Many believed that Nehru had wanted Lal Bahadur as his successor; but that was by no means unambiguous or accepted. The temporary truce between factions did not improve matters. It merely postponed the inevitable showdown.

Besides the two major factions, the Nehru coterie and the anti-Nehru camp, a new grouping formed around his daughter, Indira Gandhi, who was included in Lal Bahadur's cabinet as minister of information and broadcasting. No tremors were felt for a few months; yet the younger generation in the party and the country—and of course, the women—gravitated towards her naturally and inevitably. Besides, being Nehru's daughter, she received the affection the people retained for her father and naturally and inevitably transferred to her.

Lal Bahadur Shastri took some time coming into his own. He built bridges with all the state chief ministers and tried to establish himself as the standard-bearer of the Nehru line. The people responded to him. They tried hard to find Nehru's reflection in Lal Bahadur. They wanted to believe that the latter was an effective substitute for the former. They just didn't relish the prospect of being leaderless. Yet the make-believe did not seem to work as they wanted it to. The fault was neither theirs nor Lal Bahadur's. The harsh fact of the matter was that no one could improvise a complete replacement for Nehru.

As the months passed, the country witnessed an unprecedented scenario of centrifugal tendencies. There was a vertical division in the ruling party in every state. Where the configuration was not a direct Nehru–anti-Nehru dichotomy, it was an incumbent–dissident cleavage—in other words, the struggle between the haves and the have-nots of power. Those opposed to each other within the party were more inimical to each other than either of them was against the Opposition. The reason was simple: the ruling party believed that no Opposition party would capture political power in the coming elections. This was a complete miscalculation of the people's mind and mood. Scrambling for power within the ruling party became the order of the day—twenty-four hours a day. Sant Fateh Singh in Punjab threatened self-immolation unless a Punjabi Suba (state) came into being. The north-eastern region presented a picture of near anarchy, with Reverend Michael Scott and his ilk fanning the flames of rebellion and secession. Several strong chief ministers disappeared from the scene. Pratap Singh of Punjab fell to assassins. Bakshi of Kashmir and Patnaik of Orissa had to go. Their successors found it very difficult to cope with the complicated political situation in those states.

In foreign policy, the turmoil and instability after the Nehru era was most striking. The architect of non-alignment as a positive national option in international affairs was no more. He had interpreted non-alignment in terms of India's hallowed tradition of the 'Middle Path' as in the ancient texts, besides its modern ramifications. To India, it came easily as an article of faith, not as a mere construct of expediency. But the country's leaders did not elucidate this at the popular level. First, they did not consider foreign policy relevant to the common people. Next, there was no way its nuances could be understood by the masses. Only Nehru spoke on foreign affairs on every possible occasion, while many of his colleagues privately called it one of Panditji's 'fads'. You have to put up with it somehow, they whispered in one another's ear. The party's leaders generally failed to spell out the connection between the country's crushing domestic problems and its relations with the rest of the world. Foreign policy largely remained a 'South Block' activity, or Nehru's favoured project, having nothing to do with the psyche of the people. And now, only two years after the non-aligned movement had formally come into being, death had

442

snatched away its principal Indian exponent. He did not live long enough to elaborate on the theme and carry it to the people in his inimitable style. What remained with Nehru's successors was a collection of his speeches, made on different occasions, on different aspects of foreign policy. They were unquestionably lucid, but fragmented. The new set-up under Lal Bahadur—including the Foreign Office—found itself groping to understand the core principles, while adhering faithfully to the rhetoric. In the absence of any real focus, diplomats in the Indian Foreign Service came in for labelling—some as pro-Soviet and others as pro-American. Only a few chose to bear the mantle of non-alignment . . .

Lack of conceptual authority led to criticism, which did not encourage debate, but made light of the policy. When Prime Minister Lal Bahadur Shastri went to attend the non-aligned summit at Cairo, the media largely focused on where and how he made his chapatis and cooked his vegetarian food. The 'copy' for the press was that he had never been abroad before—this 'homespun' Prime Minister. The bewildered heads of other governments did not know how to approach the new incumbent and continue the close rapport they had struck with Jawaharlal Nehru.

Detractors saw India as friendless, trudging along what they called the lone and senseless path called non-alignment. If Yugoslavia's Tito followed non-alignment, it was the only policy open to him in the context of his country's peculiar position, they said. In contrast, they asserted, India's non-alignment was clearly impracticable, unnecessary and suicidal. You have to join one bloc or the other; you simply cannot remain neutral or non-aligned. (They considered the two words as synonymous and interchangeable.) Some influential politician had already called India 'neutral on the other side'—obviously annoyed at her not being on his side. Someone else had, in his wisdom, branded non-alignment as immoral . . . Many detractors within the country quoted these gems with relish. However, when it came to recommending the bloc that India should join, there was a sharp division. Some prescribed the Soviet bloc, since India had adopted socialism. Others recommended the Western bloc led by America, since India was a democracy—the largest in the world. When India adopted democratic socialism, it seemed to baffle both blocs. They could not pigeon-hole India as this or that!

On top of all this came the news of Lal Bahadur's ill-health, giving rise to a host of uncertainties. The Prime Minister of India needs nerves of steel and a body of cast iron. Nothing less will do. Nehru had fortunately possessed these till a few months before his death. His immediate successor could not afford poor health, especially not a heart condition. And Lal Bahadur suffered from just that.

Meanwhile, competing with other chief ministers, Chaudhury arranged a three-day official visit of the Prime Minister to the state. The people of Afrozabad showed keen interest in the visit, if only to savour the contrast between Nehru, the leader and Shastri, the loyal follower. They had grown fond of Shastri within the few months he had been Prime Minister; they were only too willing to shower their affection on Nehru's successor, without mentioning his calibre. Even his short physical build, his rather raucous voice, so very different from Nehru's vibrant tone, appealed to them in its own way . . . However, all that was indulgence, and did not necessarily amount to confidence. It seemed as though in their view Shastri was on a probation of sorts. They supported him and wished him well, certainly. However, they had not decided to uncross their fingers, yet . . .

When the Prime Minister arrived at the airport, there was a big crowd to welcome him. People lined the streets in large numbers and gave him an ovation worthy of his position. Yet Anand, like many others, found—or thought he found—that there was a subtle difference. Nehru's appearance electrified the atmosphere and moved the crowds profoundly. The sedate presence of Shastri, with his slight build and deferential manner, had a very different effect; the masses tended to shower a kind of parental affection on him. And there lay the strong—as well as weak—point of Lal Bahadur Shastri. Anand was at once fascinated and perplexed.

Chaudhury introduced his ministers. When Anand shook hands with the Prime Minister, he thought he found the latter's face a bit pale. Fatigue shadowed his features. Anand dismissed the thought as a figment of his own imagination. He stepped up, alert, as Chaudhury said to Shastri, 'This is Anand, minister for land reforms, your official interpreter on this tour . . . and all tours from now on to this state!' Before Anand could recover from his astonishment, he pinched his shoulder and whispered, 'Buck up and go ahead; you have a job to do!' When Anand looked down the line, he saw a rather grotesque scowl appear on Shekhar's face even as he shook Shastri's hand.

The tour programme was absolutely jam-packed. If Chaudhury's group had five public meetings in one day, Mahendranath's outfit would insist on an equal number for his own areas of influence. Neither group cared to realize that in their eagerness to score points over each other, they were forcing the ailing Prime Minister to attend ten public meetings, and thereby possibly cutting short his life. Shastriji was too obliging to put his foot down on this thoroughly exhausting tape-cutting spree, despite the protests of his physician. And it was the absolute limit when a very influential trustee of a temple managed to get a visit to this temple slipped into the programme through the chief minister's henchmen.

When the programme was being finalized, Aruna happened to learn of the scheme. She rushed to Chaudhury in uncontrolled rage and shouted, 'What are you doing? Have you forgotten that you have to climb one hundred steps to reach that temple gate? Do you want to kill the Prime Minister and send his dead body to Delhi?' The chief secretary who happened to be present there reported, with bureaucratic pride, that the administration had 'duly' taken note of the steps and had made efficient arrangements to carry the Prime Minister to the temple in a comfortable chair. That made Aruna even more furious. She said, 'So you want to proclaim to the world, with photographic evidence, that the Prime Minister of India needs a chair to climb the steps of a temple? What a spectacle you would be making of him! Shame on you!' She raved on until they quietly deleted the temple visit from the programme. The trustee of the temple and some legislators lashed out at her viciously, in the filthiest possible language. 'Since when did this bitch become Lal Bahadur Shastri's keeper?' they asked. The trustee had planned to attract the Prime Minister's attention on this visit, in a bid for a seat in the Rajya Sabha at the next biennial election. Now all his plans were dashed to the ground. He had wanted to exploit God—and the Prime Minister—but Aruna's officious meddling and loud mouth frustrated him.

Inevitably, this controversy appeared in the next day's newspapers, almost overshadowing everything else, even the Prime Minister's speeches and inaugural functions. Box items appeared everywhere, the size of the boxes and their content varying with the newspaper proprietor's disposition towards the ruling party. While interpreting the Prime Minister's speeches on the second day, Anand found Shastri's ideas become less coherent, his emphasis rather halting. Anand surmised that the box items had been brought to his attention.

The box items—and everything they implied—were certainly scrutinized by another personage—President (Field Marshal) Ayub Khan of Pakistan. To him, unlike any Indian newspaper reader, it was not a mere news item. It was the opportunity of a lifetime—his country's lifetime. God had been unduly harsh to Pakistan in the twin events of Jinnah's demise within a month of the country's birth, and Jawaharlal Nehru's perfect health and long life across the new border. Now, after almost eighteen years, Allah presumably was about to reverse His dispensation. Near-chaos within and an ailing Prime Minister, still not established as the nation's leader—this decline in fortunes on the Indian side was too good for Ayub Khan to let pass. It was now or never for him.

Soon the rumbling started, on a front of the least consequence—the Rann of Kutch. The venue made no sense except as one for rehearsal, to camouflage the real target—which was, and could be none other than, Kashmir. No one seemed to take the Rann episodes seriously, including the bulk of the Indian press. Neither could anyone say that something more menacing was brewing. The press dismissed the border skirmishes as a diversionary tactic of the government to create a bogey of Pakistan's evil intentions and distract the attention of the people from the real issue facing the nation. No one knew what to do, while Pakistan virtually won the first round by fomenting a controversy where none existed.

In a few weeks' time things seemed to settle down. Ayub, for his part, had carried out the first probe. He had wanted to ascertain the vulnerability of the Indian defence forces in the event of a short, swift, determined thrust in a theatre of his choosing. On the Indian side, nothing was proved or disproved. The generals did not want a confrontation in the Rann; they knew it was not worth the effort. They could not take any other initiative either, since India had no aggressive intentions anyway. Everything remained at a loose end . . . which, the media claimed, was a confirmation of their view that the alarmist postures on the Indian side were all unsubstantiated. Yet, in point of fact, when reports of stray incidents came in day after day, no one described them as inconsequential. The atmosphere of mistrust and unease intensified till people's nerves were on edge. War was the sole topic everywhere—at public meetings, in parliament, in coffee house conversations. It was especially loud in the secretariats, where officials made it a valid pretext to suspend normal work.

Anand found himself largely unemployed as minister. Who would bother about land reforms when the nation was under threat of war? Colleagues seized the chance to mock his obsession. Don't you see you're becoming a laughing stock? Is this the time to alienate the landlord lobby? How can you press for such a controversial and divisive measure, when the need of the hour is total unity? What are the dictates of patriotism at this crucial moment? Have you thought of that? . . . Fuming in utter exasperation, Anand made no reply. He had least expected Field Marshal Ayub Khan of Pakistan to become the ally of India's landlords overnight.

He was reading the daily newspapers one morning when the attendant brought in a slip bearing the name 'Afzal Khan' in Urdu. Under the name was written, *zindagi aur maut ka sawal hai* (it is a matter of life and death). The name was familiar, but he could not quite place it. He reflected for a moment and asked the attendant to usher the visitor in. Within minutes, an old man, supporting himself with a walking stick, entered the room with unsteady steps. He salaamed to Anand several times and was about

447

to fall on his face in the process, when Anand steadied him, quickly getting out of his chair. He then had a good look at the old man and cried, 'Chacha! Is it you . . .?'

'Yes, *sarkar* . . . I am the same unfortunate Chacha whom you and your friends in the village knew so well . . .'

In a split second, the scene flashed vividly in Anand's memory. The Janmashtami festival in the village . . . the final day . . . children enacting Krishna Leela . . . Anand's friend Karim missing for some reason . . . some of them going to his house to find him . . . Chacha berating them with a distasteful scowl on his face and some supercilious remark about Hindu festivals . . . Karim . . . yes, Karim, his closest friend . . . The last Anand had heard of Karim was that he had migrated to Pakistan . . . And here was the same Chacha come to meet him after thirty-five years! Anand felt grateful for having remembered the visitor, while the old man felt unspeakably grateful to Anand for receiving him.

Anand seated him on a sofa. Indeed, he had to force him to sit, so reluctant was the old man to sit next to 'sarkar'. Serving the old man a cup of tea, he waited for an explanation for the sudden visit.

'Bade Bhai Saheb is critically ill . . .' Afzal began. Anand understood at once that Bade Bhai Saheb was Karim's father. He tried to recall him. A jovial fellow who always preferred to stay in the village, engaged in farming his five-acre holding and doing odd jobs in his spare time . . . No one knew his name; the whole village called him 'Bade Sahib'. He knew many verses from the *Bhagavata*, as well as several Ayats from the Koran, and would readily join the people in all festivals, Hindu or Muslim. Above all, Bade Sahib was like the Supreme Court. All local disputes found their final adjudication in front of his humble house. The villagers looked upon him as justice personified.

'This time we have lost all hope,' Chacha went on. 'The doctor says it's a matter of days. Bhai Sahib had not bothered much about his sons and daughters earlier. He felt happy that they were all happily settled. But this time, he insists that all of them be at his bedside. All of them are in fact there . . . except . . . as you perhaps know . . . Karim. Bhai Saheb repeats Karim's name all the time. He seems to be holding on to life just to set eyes on Karim for the last time . . . And . . .' here the old man folded both hands and said, in a choked voice, '*sarkar* alone can help us. We just don't know what to do . . .'

'Chacha,' queried Anand, 'I am sorry I could not keep track of Karim all these years, I only know he is in Pakistan. I'm sure he must have come to India several times; the rogue never informed me, let alone met me. What is the difficulty in his coming here to see his father now? What's he doing in Pakistan anyway?'

'He's some officer in the Pakistan Army—Karnal or something. I don't know what that means . . .' Chacha's reply came haltingly.

Anand was stunned. For a fleeting moment he imagined himself as a colonel in the Indian army, repulsing an attack from Pakistani troops under Colonel Karim.

'H'mm,' he began cautiously, 'I shall do what I can, Chacha, though I can't promise, you know . . .'

'Yes, I know . . . It's all *taqdeer* (destiny),' responded the old man in the midst of a coughing bout. 'God bless you . . .' And after making another back-bending salaam, he ambled out painfully.

When Anand studied the papers left by Chacha, he found that the Central government had already turned down Karim's request for a visa to visit India. To get that decision reversed was obviously an uphill task. When he spoke to the minister of state for home in the Central government, the latter sounded unenthusiastic. However, the following afternoon a police official called on Anand to inquire about the antecedents of Colonel Abdul Karim of Pakistan. Anand realized with a slight shock that he knew next to nothing about Karim, besides his childhood association and his family background. He gave a very short, almost cryptic account. Still, after the explanation the official seemed sympathetic, to Anand's immense relief.

However, the following day, news of the imminent Indo-Pak conflict erupted all over the country. Leave granted to all defence personnel was promptly cancelled. The Indian government could perhaps have been convinced to permit Colonel Karim to see his dying father; General Ayub Khan willed otherwise. Bade Saheb died within a few days. And Anand heard nothing further about Karim. All that remained was the report, carefully noted by

449

Shekhar, that Anand had a very close friend in the Pakistan army.

The information was of no use to Shekhar at the moment. Yet this valuable innuendo, that Anand could be a security risk for the country, had explosive potential and could not be ignored. All that Shekhar would need, he calculated, was a crucial occasion and a reliable press reporter to publicize this extraordinarily interesting news about Anand's intimate friend in the Pakistan Army. And through an efficient and determined whispering campaign, Shekhar could ensure that this nugget reached the ears of those in the highest echelons of power.

# 37

CHACHA AFZAL KHAN'S SHORT VISIT SET ANAND THINKING. Chacha had apparently changed in the past thirty odd years. Or had he? He had torn Anand and Karim apart, in a manner of speaking. This sudden realization made Anand shudder. Why was that so? He compared the brothers, Afzal Chacha and Bade Sahib. The former was essentially a city-bred parasitic functionary. He was an outsider, though born in the village. He had imbibed the notion of *An-al-Malik* (I am the king) which was the badge of a Muslim citizen in the kingdom of a Muslim monarch . . . So when the monarchy came to an end, Chacha and those of his persuasion found themselves at a loose end. Chacha's obsequious salaam seemed to signify the recognition of the new truth—'I am *not* the king; you are, no matter how much I detest it!' This perception made Anand extremely embarrassed—and filled him with a vague sense of sorrow.

In sharp contrast, Bade Sahib was of the soil. He worked, played, celebrated, fought, fornicated, shouted choice rural obscenities like a mobile thesaurus, suffered droughts and floods, participated in umpteen riots arising out of land disputes, made peace, dispensed impeccable justice when quarrels of all kinds came to him for adjudication—in one word, he *was* the village. He had begotten fourteen children by four wives, one of whom was a non-Muslim before he married her. He could also boast a considerable number of progeny on the side, with different labels of paternity. In his youth, which apparently extended well beyond sixty, many village women had enjoyed his amorous attentions. The village abounded with convenient nooks for liaisons, and he had made full use of them. A standing corn crop; the secluded platform of a machaan erected to scare birds away when grain began to ripen on the cobs; a grassy dip between mounds of earth rimming an irrigation well; an inviting clearing in the midst of a thick cluster of plants taller than shrubs but shorter than trees. To be fair to him, he was not the only stud in the village. He was just one of several incorrigible characters known for their lead roles in an ongoing sexual carnival. And in all this feverish activity, no discrimination on the basis of religion had ever entered anyone's mind.

Decades later, even after the flesh had refused to respond, Bade Sahib's good-natured jokes and anecdotes continued to proliferate. They titillated the young boys and girls of the village, particularly the latter whose bashful giggles made his life worth living.

In this placid existence, unchanged for generations, Chacha Afzal had ignited a communal fuse. Who slept with whom also became crucial from the religious angle. Sex was permissible only when the male partner belonged to a particular community. That flowed from the logic of *An-al-Malik*. The logic gradually extended to every aspect of village life. One community was granted primacy. It was now almost above the law, a law unto itself, evoking entirely predictable reactions.

Under the British, communalism had been mainly a political weapon, to divide and rule. Under a Muslim king, it was transformed into absolute Muslim hegemony, in all respects. The theoretical basis for this dispensation was that in a Muslim kingdom every Muslim citizen was supposed to reflect, or contain, a part of that kingship; hence he or she had a special position.

Came the Partition and there was a change. It was, however, superficial. Communalism continued to flourish, albeit insidiously, side by side with the rhetoric of secularism. Communal tension erupted into violence in some pockets, and gradually became endemic in these areas. The two-nation theory, which had resulted in the creation of Pakistan, had been rendered irrelevant in India. Yet, the ethnic and psychological cohesion characteristic of a single nation did not quite become all-pervading. It became the slogan of institutions, subsisted in the vast rural area as a tradition, but did not come to dwell in hearts and minds in urban areas. Grievance on the one hand, suspicion on the other, began to permeate the life of the nation. The estrangement between the communities deepened year after year. The new virus mutated stealthily within the body of India. Whenever there was a riot anywhere, the first spark of discord came generally from outside that area. Communal violence managed to remain faceless by an ingenious device. Hindus and Muslims killed one another, but in a vast majority of cases the murderer and the victim were strangers. Normally, no one participated in any communal killings in his own village or *mohalla*. So the murderers would go to another locality to vent their fury. The carnage was impersonal. There was no hatred for the subjects of this mindless rage. Neither was there any compassion. It was mechanical, killing for killing's sake, arbitrary slaughter.

Military conflicts with Pakistan made matters worse in India. Nehru's supreme effort to weld the nation into a secular entity did succeed to a considerable extent. Yet that success was almost solely due to his personal charisma. Hindu suspicion of the Muslim minority increased to such an extent that Nehru's constant struggle to establish the secular ideal had often drawn derisive comments. One such remark, attributed to a senior leader, was that the only nationalist Muslim in India was Jawaharlal Nehru! . . . Thus, Nehru became the sole crusader for secularism, while many other leaders, both Hindu and Muslim, only mouthed secular slogans with little conviction. The secular ideal appeared to be solid and pristine, but was not fully effective. The reason was obvious: the

453

presence of a separate country across the border, as a living monument to the two-nation theory and the outright negation of secularism. Thus while secularism became India's creed under Jawaharlal's tutelage, it did not have a stable axis or a dependable foundation. The nauseating anti-India tirade from across the border increasingly complicated the situation. It was clear that the leaders of Pakistan were more interested in India-baiting than getting on with their own urgent task of nation-building.

It was not easy to bring about a completely secular atmosphere on the Indian side. During the worst days of the communal riots, Nehru had gone into the affected areas and accosted rioters personally—confronting aggressive bullies, catching hold of stabbing hands. Stories of such personal courage were widely circulated, but did not succeed in curbing the violence or inspiring other people to follow Nehru's example. One such anecdote described how Jawaharlal, moving in a riot-torn area of Delhi one day along with his daughter Indira, saw someone suddenly grab Indira's arm and pull her towards himself. Furious beyond words, Nehru slapped the fellow. The man calmly rubbed his cheek, smiled a tragic smile and said, 'Panditji, if you could fly into such fury over what I just did, what would you expect me to do after what was done to my wife and sister in Lahore?' Panditji allegedly burst into tears and apologized to the youth.

Nearly two decades after Partition, however, life as a whole in the subcontinent was peaceful. Peaceful co-existence was evident on both sides of the Indo-Pak border. The common people in the border areas were not particularly prone to violence. And where they were, they came from the same stock, and sporadic skirmishes had been a habitual feature among these people from long before Partition. They were—and are—mostly nomadic breeders of cattle. In the Rann of Kutch there was no farming for the Rann was under sea water for six to seven out of twelve months, year after year. Smuggling and other kinds of illicit trade flourished—after the Partition these continued across the new border. This indeed was a natural fallout of the geopolitical context. Local families had kin on both sides of the border, and were thus ideally positioned for any activity that required cooperation and secrecy.

Partition was an altogether peculiar development. Simply put, leaders mainly from Bombay, the United Provinces (later named Uttar Pradesh) and from other parts of undivided India, had decided with the British, to split the country into two, drawing an entirely artificial frontier. The people in the border areas themselves had little or no role in that decision. The decision, by itself, could not therefore transform the people along the border into strangers overnight. Brothers could not snap their bonds. Friends and relatives could not break ancient ties of blood, custom and marriage. Mutual economic symbiosis could not immediately vanish. Whatever the leaders of the two new countries willed, they could not establish a real border. In any event no one precisely knew where the border lay.

And what a border! There were no landmarks, no watersheds, no features or barriers that normally keep inhabitants within their territories. There were no attributes of an international border. A village, for instance, fell on one side, its agricultural lands and various extensions on the other. Both became meaningless. How can boundaries be drawn among fluctuating sand dunes? Fences could be erected, but who could guarantee that interested persons or groups did not alter their location? And who administered these sites, anyway? To those whose entire world consisted of the revenue limits of the village, what happened outside those limits had never mattered—Partition or no Partition. They were content to let life go on as it had, for centuries.

There is a peculiar feature of the sand dunes in the border areas of Rajasthan: where they run parallel to the border, their slope on the Pakistan side is gentler. This gives a tactical advantage to Pakistani troops. Where the dunes run perpendicular to the border, advantages and disadvantages are common to both sides. No one had noticed these features before, but after the Partition, they became important—sometimes crucial—overnight.

To the north of this area lies a large territory fissured by rivers and canals, right up to the northern tip of the Punjab, on both sides of the border. Beyond this lies the the real object of Pakistani ambition—the state of Jammu and Kashmir, partly in India and partly in Pakistan. Rugged and mountainous, it is fractured by rivulets, ravines and other barriers. This is the real battleground in the continuing Indo-Pak conflict.

It is not necessary to catalogue individual sectors and segments, each of which could be a potential theatre of military conflict. Major engagements could take place at some points, hit-and-run guerrilla activities in others.

The first conflict of 1947 over Kashmir fomented unbridgeable antagonism. The second minor engagement in the Rann of Kutch in 1964 whetted General Ayub Khan's appetite for vengeance. It gave him the notion of Pakistani superiority over India, both in the fighting capacity of its armed forces and in its armour and weaponry. There could be no relenting after the foretaste of victory in the Rann. Ayub planned to inflict a crushing defeat on India within a short time-frame.

Kutch had experienced the first rumblings as early as in 1956. It subsided quickly, with the Indian Central Reserve Police patrolling the area for the following eight years, until May 1964—in other words, until a change in India's leadership became visibly imminent. Some thrusts from Pakistan followed, taking advantage of India's possible complacency during the preceding years. The notion on the Indian side had been that this area would never see any serious fighting.

The scene of action was the area around Kanjarkot, about three miles within India. Pakistan had constructed a road, intruding into Indian territory about one-and-a-half miles deep at several points. Indian authorities discovered it only after they heard the rumblings in late 1964. After a few diplomatic exchanges, Pakistan claimed that Kanjarkot had always been part of Pakistan. When India insisted that Pakistan vacate Kanjarkot, the latter responded with gunfire. Pakistani troops, overwhelming in number, succeeded in making the small Indian Central Reserve Police withdraw after a fierce battle of fourteen hours. Pakistan then proposed negotiations. India rejected the proposal and insisted on Pakistan vacating Kanjarkot. Meanwhile, Pakistan planned a heavier thrust. The Rann area came under the danger of inundation by the sea in May. Pakistan refused to vacate areas occupied during the exchange. Prime Minister Lal Bahadur Shastri hinted at suitable measures elsewhere to neutralize the Pakistani occupation. That sent an unequivocal message to Pakistan, and the British Prime Minister promptly intervened and suggested a cease-fire. Another month or so of sporadic thrusts brought about the cease-fire. Pakistan agreed to vacate the areas it had occupied recently, including Kanjarkot. In return it received the right to patrol a nearby road. And while this theatre was cooling down gradually, the real action began in Jammu and Kashmir.

The recent experience with the Chinese *bhai* (brother) was still fresh in the Indian mind. The Chinese brand of enlarging 'national liberation', coupled with the new Sino-Pak friendship, posed a clear threat to India. Its base was anti-India, pure and simple. The more military backing Pakistan got from Peking, the stiffer became the attitude of the Indian people. Military officers, in particular, were naturally alert against subversion in Kashmir. This was more likely than an overt Chinese attack. Far from intimidating New Delhi, Pakistan's new-found closeness with China heightened Indo-Pak tensions and steeled India's will.

Whatever Pakistani propaganda claimed, it was undeniable that India was neither motivated nor prepared for an aggressive attack on Pakistan. As analyst and author Russell Brines puts it:

The disposition of these forces in mid-1965 was another essential consideration in measuring intent and the balance of strength. India maintained an estimated garrison of 150,000 men, at least three divisions, in Kashmir. They were required to guard the Ladakh front against Communist China and the 470-mile cease-fire line with Pakistan. Part of this force may also have been used to cover the northern edge of the 800-mile border between India and West Pakistan. Another six Indian divisions were positioned in the Himalayas and near East Pakistan. A portion of this garrison was expected to contain the one Pakistani division stationed in East Pakistan; New Delhi sources said a maximum of two or three divisions would be sufficient. The balance of this Indian force was required to protect the 1800-mile border with China, less the Ladakh section. This means the Indians had eight divisions left from their known standing strength for use on the

Indian-West Pakistan border, for strategic reserve and other purposes. Of the seven divisions stationed in West Pakistan, four or five were believed to be in the Kashmir-Lahore section, with three in reserve.

If these figures are correct, or close enough to be indicative, they suggest that India was not in a condition or in a position to launch an aggressive attack that could be expected to precipitate major fighting. Half of the regular army was pinned down to defensive commitments and could not be feasibly used for action elsewhere, as long as there was a valid threat of a two-front war, with Red China and Pakistan. Some of the best units were located in Kashmir where, theoretically at least, they could be occupied and immobilised by the efficient use of Pakistani irregulars. The half of the army available for action in the critical Punjab, the most feasible area for opening offensive action, was not large enough to launch an offensive attack and still maintain the necessary reserve. In general a three-to-one advantage in manpower is considered necessary for attack, particularly over the fortified terrain in the crucial Punjab areas. When the possibility of a two-front war subsided, the Indians used one or two mountain divisions in the Punjab, but even so their manpower superiority was minimal for offensive purposes. Thus the Indian army was not logically positioned to initiate major hostilities, although it was capable of responding vigorously to single-front attack with limited offensive action. Pakistan was in a more favorable position for a quick, limited offensive. The bulk of her regular forces was concentrated in the Kashmir-Lahore section of the Punjab, the main battle area. Her supply lines were shorter and more effective. She had no worries about a second front and no long border with a third power to guard by herself; her aid pact gave her assurances of support against communist assault. In terms of over-all manpower and, particularly, in industrial capacity, the Pakistanis could not match India's potential staying power in a long war. But it was far more feasible for them to initiate a quick attack.

The contrast between the political policies of the two countries was noteworthy. India steadfastly followed the non-aligned line. Pakistan joined regional combines like the CENTO (Central Treaty Organisation) presumably to neutralize political influence with military might. The 1962 debacle had stepped up the criticism of Nehru's policy of non-alignment. Non-aligned India seemed indeed friendless, with little hope of external military assistance, compared to what was so readily available to Pakistan. In Brines' words:

> India had emerged from the crisis of 1962 with a profound sense of international isolation. She had been rebuffed, says an Indian writer, in a global search for adequate arms. 'Indian diplomacy met with scant respect abroad. We slumped in the esteem of Afro-Asian opinion. It looked as though we had not a friend in the world.' The 'efforts for a break-through resembled those of a caged animal desperately trying to break out'. It is evident that this sense of isolation also contributed substantially to a hardened Indian response to Pakistani initiatives.

The practical facets of non-alignment became evident again and again. In practice, there were temporary set-backs to the principle, while immediate advantage accrued to those who aligned with power blocs. To quote Brines:

> This isolation was a concomitant of Nehru's philosophy that a non-aligned nation would determine its position, and therefore its compatriots, on the merits of each international episode. As with individuals, the nation practising this independence has considerable freedom but few friends. Thus, both of the belligerents devoted considerable attention to the attempt to establish power positions which quickly fell apart, without exercising the same diplomatic initiative towards preserving peace.

Policies inevitably impinged on relative preparedness, at least in the short run. There is in fact every reason why a non-aligned country, precisely because of its expected 'isolation', should remain vigilant and prepared. This was well-recognized in India, as her policy of long-term self-reliance in defence clearly spelt out. It is the short-term needs that a non-aligned country has to assess and try to fulfil. This is a test of her vigilance as well as diplomacy.

Brines says:

> Nevertheless, the evidence is convincing that Pakistan prepared and launched the guerrilla attack and carefully deployed her mechanized Army to give it maximum support. Indian authorities were alert to the guerrilla threat, if incompletely prepared to meet it, but generally they were oblivious of the potentialities for conventional attack. In July, officials of the New Delhi Home Ministry met with state authorities in Srinagar and decided that guerrilla sabotage was possible but that Pakistan was unprepared for a major conventional war against India. On August 2, a senior Indian Army commander told officers in Srinagar that the next phase of the Kashmir struggle would not be overt organized power but murder and terrorism. On the other hand, a variety of intelligence agencies received solid information during this period about a build-up of Pakistani conventional power. In July, a European official of a specialized U N agency returned from the Punjab with the information: 'The Pakistanis are assembling a massive Tank force in the Punjab. The Indians are asleep, and they won't know what hit them.' Some foreign observers with access to unpublished information had concluded at this same time that Pakistan had decided to attack in a desperate attempt to change the course of history.

The Pakistani plan was elaborate and meticulous. It was to begin in Jammu and Kashmir and culminate, incredible as it may now seem, in a victory parade in Delhi. General Ayub Khan was convinced that this dream could be realized. The Rann of Kutch probe somehow confirmed the myth in Pakistan that one Pakistani soldier was equal to four of the Indian army. The events in fact had demonstrated nothing of the kind; yet the relentless propaganda grafted onto a fanatical psyche in Pakistan did the trick. To General Ayub, the day of supreme glory promised to dawn very soon.

The Pakistani commanders planned to execute the attack along two fronts: the Jammu and Kashmir sector from Chhamb to Kargil in the north; and from Chhamb to Fazilka in the Punjab sector in the south. In the Kashmir sector, they deployed forces from

Pakistan-occupied Kashmir and a large number of irregular 'volunteers', fully supported by Pakistani artillery. Regular Pakistani troops were in readiness to go into action at short notice. The regular Pakistan army, along with the air force, was to operate in the Punjab sector. Pakistan expected that with a short and sharp thrust along these two fronts, Jammu and Kashmir would fall in a few days and the victorious Pakistani force in the Punjab sector would overrun the Indian territory between the border and Delhi. The campaign would culminate in a victory parade in Delhi. In General Ayub Khan's exquisitely-tailored fantasies, he would accept the Indian Army's surrender and dictate his terms to the Indian government.

In April-May 1965, Pakistan made five raids on Indian installations. The purpose was to browbeat India and to obtain sensitive information about the installations. The Indian soldiers retaliated by occupying a Pakistani post. They returned it, however, after UN mediation. This was near Kargil in Ladakh, and the move proclaimed the strength and determination of the Indian army. Significantly, India returned the post on the same day on which the two countries signed the Kutch Agreement. However, within three weeks, violent skirmishes broke out again in the area. A large number of Pakistani infiltrators had entered Indian territory. Heavy fighting took place in several areas, although there was no unusual disruption of normal civilian life. It was evident that the Kutch Agreement meant nothing to Pakistan, since its leaders had finalized the plan to attack Jammu and Kashmir much earlier.

The war soon spread over a front described as 1,200 miles long and even longer, if the extreme flank areas of periodic confrontation were included. The main fighting, however, remained in the Punjab. On September 8, India began to advance westward in the desert along the border between Pakistani Sindh and Rajasthan, some 400 miles south-west of the central combat area. It was later explained as a diversionary thrust. Indian commentators concluded the purpose was to keep Pakistani forces pinned down in the principal city of Karachi, west of the area of the desert advance . . . to quote Brines again:

On the Lahore front, Indian forces achieved initial tactical surprise when they moved forward at 5.30 a.m., September 6. The Pakistanis had deployed their Tenth Division in defensive positions forward of the city only a few hours before the attack, and there was no Pakistani armour east of the BRB canal. At this point, say competent sources, the Pakistanis still doubted that India would dare to cross an international border. They were also startled by the vigour of the Indian attack, for the vision of Indian ineptness remained strong, nurtured by the relatively feeble response in the Rann of Kutch crisis. The Indian offensive involved three armour-supported divisions, by Indian accounts, but it is known that eventually five divisions were involved. Initially, the assault proceeded with relative speed. By nightfall, the centre column had captured two key villages. Infantry units of the northern column, proceeding along the Grand Trunk Road, reached the outskirts of Lahore and were driven back by heavy opposition. This particular advance created a belief that the Indians intended to capture the city and were prevented from doing so by stout defences. The Indian version is that the infantry outraced its armour in an unplanned over-extension and was recalled. Thereafter, the campaign in this sector settled down to hard and continuous fighting for strategic waterways, bridges and fortified villages. Combat was continual from D-day until the cease-fire on September 23, swirling from the border to the canal and involving all types of heavy weapons. Eventually, the Pakistanis blew up some seventy bridges across the BRB canal, and it served as a defensive moat for both sides against further armoured assault in this salient.

In one of the key battles, Indian forces captured the village of Burki on September 10, after a full day's battle. The objective of the central advancing column, Burki was situated in a dominating position on the east bank of the canal and had been made into a major fortified position, guarded, the Indians say, by eleven concrete pill-boxes, camouflaged to resemble rural mud huts, with three-foot walls, steel-shuttered gun openings and ample supplies for a three-man garrison. The battle, which began at night, involved tanks on both sides and unusually heavy fire from Pakistani artillery, ranging up to 150-millimetre guns. Control of the village and supporting operations by other units gave the

Indians command of a considerable stretch of the Ichhogil Canal in the central area, although they remained under Pakistani artillery fire. This position was some twelve miles from the centre of Lahore but only about five miles from its airport; so the Indians reported, with some pride, that American authorities asked for their co-operation in suspending fire while American residents of the Pakistani city were evacuated by air.

Farther north, a second major battle was waged continually for Dograi village, another fortified position on the east bank of the canal. The village, seven miles inside Pakistan due west of Amritsar along the Grand Trunk Road, was part of the outer defences of Lahore, eight miles distant. Dograi changed hands at least three times, in some of the fiercest fighting of this campaign, before the Indians captured it a few hours in advance of the cease-fire. In one of the first eye-witness stories of the war from the Indian side by a foreign newsman, Thomas F. Brady of the *New York Times* reported that the Grand Trunk Road had been fought over yard by yard, from the border to the canal. Near Dograi he saw extensive debris of war and at least a dozen immobilised tanks, many destroyed by fire or explosives. Dograi itself was badly damaged after the final battle, but Pakistani troops were positioned near it in deep trenches, supported by Sherman tanks and a line of recoilless rifles. Brady's dispatch, filed September 23, was never published, because of the New York newspaper strike at that time.

Pakistani military sources confirm this account of the Dograi campaign but contend that the Indians succeeded only in capturing the western outskirts of the village just before the armistice. They failed, however, to capture the Batapur bridge across the canal in this region, an objective the Pakistanis claim was the primary Indian objective. Control of the bridge conceivably could have allowed the Indians to send an armoured thrust deeper toward Lahore along the Grand Trunk Road. Farther northward along the canal, the Indians launched a flanking movement toward another key objective, the Bhiani bridge, but failed to capture it, the Pakistanis say, after making fifteen attacks to clear a path for tanks. The ferocity of the fighting around Burki is reflected in Pakistani accounts which, however, claim this campaign was a major Indian mistake because of its intensity.

The fighting in this area was waged almost continuously and involved weapons from tanks and heavy artillery to bayonet charges. Competent foreign sources report that the Pakistani counter-offensive at one point drove the Indians back almost to their line of departure, seven miles from Dograi, before some of the territory could be regained. The Pakistanis, contending they were outnumbered four-to-one, regard this campaign as a heroic defence of Lahore during which the Indians were unable to penetrate their main defences.

By the end of the campaign, the Indians claimed control over more than thirty miles of the east bank of the canal. The implication is that they held positions on the canal itself, but Pakistani sources say the actual line of control ran irregularly to the eastward of the waterway. In any case, the canal in this sector had become a barrier against the movement of armour either eastward or westward, because all the principal bridges were destroyed. Indian forces held a wedge of land of the Pakistani side of the border totalling around 140 square miles, a figure generally confirmed by independent sources. If the purpose was an offensive-defensive attack to destroy the enemy's striking power without attempting to penetrate deeper into Pakistan, as the Indians say, the major objective seems to have been accomplished. But the Pakistanis insist that the occupation or encirclement of Lahore was the primary objective and that the Indians launched thirteen major attacks of brigade strength or greater without breaking Pakistani defences. The 'victory' continues to be extolled in Pakistan and a monument to the battle is being erected in Lahore.

Pakistan launched its major counter-thrust on the Indian left flank to the south. The Indian column advancing from Ferozpore through Khem Karan towards Pakistani Kasur, took its initial objectives easily. But the opposition was so slight that the commanding officer, fearing a trap, halted the advance and withdrew to the west bank of the Sutlej river. The Pakistani armoured attack beginning on September 7 forced the Indians back to their starting point. Indian intelligence had reported that the main Pakistani tank force, the First Armoured division, was in the Sialkot sector. But the Pakistanis had concentrated it around Kasur to prevent a feared encirclement movement towards Lahore. The division, created and trained by Americans, was equipped with heavy American Patton tanks, light American Shermans and medium French Chaffees. This column of clanking land warcraft, with its artillery and infantry, constituted the principal threat to New Delhi if such a threat existed, for a second American-organised armoured division was incomplete. India's pre-war concern over the American equipment was perhaps reflected by the fact that an official citation commending a non-commissioned officer for his heroism noted his action against 'several of the supposedly invulnerable Patton tanks . . .'

The Pakistan First Armoured and a supporting infantry division opened a major offensive on the night of September 8, choosing darkness because Pattons are equipped with infra-red 'eyes' for night-fighting, whereas the heavy Centurion tanks, India's best, were blind after sunset. Indian accounts say that more than 225 Pakistani tanks were involved, but the active strength for such a division is between 125 and 150 tanks; further, the Pakistani commander is said to have held substantial forces in reserve. In any case, Pakistan threw a heavy concentration of armour into the battle, outnumbering the Indian Centurions and Shermans by a substantial ratio, if somewhat less than the Indian figure of four-to-one. In this most decisive engagement of the war, Pakistan launched five separate attacks at Indian positions during the next day and a half, seeking a breakthrough which was never achieved. At one point, the attackers penetrated fifteen miles into Indian territory, but were beaten back. Originally, the assault exceeded expectations; then it was stopped. The attackers were able to send such an extensive force across the BRB canal, the Indians say, because they secretly built a tunnel beneath the waterway. New Delhi had incomplete prior knowledge of this installation.

The Pakistanis sought unsuccessfully to implement an operational plan to trap Indian forces—the plan which the Indians later obtained. It called for the armoured conquest of a substantial segment of territory between the border and the Beas River, extending north-west from Khem Karan to the Grand Trunk Road. At the road, the Beas and its vital bridge lie twenty-seven miles east of Amritsar. One armoured column was to take this position after a thrust roughly parallel with the river. The western attacking column was to capture Amritsar, or at least to put it out of action. A third column, in the centre, was ordered also to reach the Grand Trunk Road. If successful, this operation would have cut off Indian forces between the Beas and the border, exposing them to piecemeal destruction. 'If it had succeeded,' says Mankekar, 'east of that point, upto Delhi, the Grand Trunk Road lay open, practically undefended, with all our forces on the other side of the Beas—thus bringing within an ace of realization Ayub's dream of "strolling up" to Delhi.'

The battle plan was a logical manoeuvre, designed to circumvent major terrain liabilities. In that area, numerous canals and drains run roughly north-eastward from the area of the border. The Pakistani columns were ordered to advance along the waterways, instead of attempting to cross them, until they reached the more manoeuvrable Grand Trunk Road. The Indian defence also was logical; it blocked the approaches to the road by utilizing the terrain as fully as possible. These defensive plans were formulated by field commanders before the Pakistani battle order was captured. The evidence as confirmed by post-battle investigation is that the Indians won the engagement by superior use of territory and equipment against a potentially stronger attacking force.

Indian armour and infantry, by Indian accounts, fell back from Khem Karan in order to draw the Pakistanis into a huge horseshoe-shaped trap near the village of Asal Uttar, a short distance away. Entrenched infantry and concentrated artillery beat off preliminary attacks piecemeal. On the morning of September 10, the Pakistanis threw the main force of their armoured division, with supporting infantry, into vigorous outflanking efforts to get behind Indian positions. The manoeuvrability of the armour was hampered by irrigation ditches and by flooded areas created when the Indians cut key dykes. The principal tank attacks were then diverted into fields of sugar-cane, left standing some nine feet high, behind which a force of Indian Centurions crouched in ambush. The narrow terrain and the newly created marshlands cut down the superior speed and mobility of the Pattons. The high cane-fields reduced the attackers' visibility and thereby helped to curtail the superior gunnery range of the Pattons, which the Indians say is 1,800 yards to around 1,000 yards, for the Centurions. Moreover, the Indian tanks were hidden while the waving sugar-cane exposed the position of the Pakistani Pattons.

When the Pakistani armour rounded a corner of the fields and exposed itself, dug-in Indian tanks, mostly old American-designed Shermans, opened fire. The Indians profitably used Canadian-designed 76 mm high velocity tanks guns. The tanks were supported by jeep-mounted 106 mm recoilless rifles, which were American-designed but were being manufactured in Indian factories. Two Pakistani outflanking attempts were blocked on this general pattern by Indian tanks, artillery, aircraft and infantry. The offensive was halted. Pakistani forces fell back to Khem Karan, where they dug in and, at the cease-fire, held a strip of Indian territory three miles deep and ten miles long. Indian officers in the battle area said they had destroyed sixty Pakistani tanks and captured another ten intact; later Indian estimates were a total of ninety-seven destroyed or captured. Independent sources say Pakistan lost perhaps forty tanks in this engagement. There is no doubt that the Indians won a significant victory in what was probably the most important single battle of the conflict, as Indian military sources say. These sources, however, do not claim that the Pakistani offensive was aimed at New Delhi, nor do they reveal any indication that the Defence Ministry believed Pakistan had the military capability of threatening the capital.

August 1965 saw heavy fighting on several fronts in the Jammu and Kashmir area. Pakistan took the plunge to capture at least a part of the Kashmir Valley. It also cut the line of control of the Indian army at several places. The infiltrators were to keep the Indian army divided into small detachments in the forward areas, so that it could not cope with the massive attack of the Pakistani army when they unleashed it, at the moment of their choosing.

Prominent places involved in the fighting were Kishenganga Valley, the Rajouri sector, Uri, Kargil, Tithwal, Bedore, Poonch, Kahuta, Rajachand, Mendhar, Naushera, Chhamb—and of course, the Haji Pir Pass and the Haji Pir 'Bulge' where Indian troops fought an epic battle for about three weeks in August 1965.

When the Pakistani infiltrators started tasting defeat, the Pakistan Army initiated regular action. The famous American Patton tanks and Sabre Jets came into operation but were crushed by the Indian forces. Eventually these became objects of such ridicule in India that the country that manufactured them was significantly embarrassed, to the point that it later requested India not to exhibit captured Patton tanks.

Pakistan launched its attack in the Chhamb sector on 1 September 1965, deploying a force far superior in number and armour to the defending Indian troops. The Indian Air Force provided sterling support to ground troops until the cease-fire on 23 September.

The crucial step in the operations was India's decision to open a second front in the Punjab sector, to relieve the pressure exerted by Pakistanis in the Chhamb area. It was a decision involving considerable courage and determination. In substance, it was a defensive step in every sense of the term. The Indian army crossed the Ichhogil canal and reached the outskirts of Lahore. As expected, Britain and the USA promptly objected to this, totally disregarding the fact that Pakistan had been treacherously invading and infiltrating Indian territory by stealth for many months.

The Indian people rose as one man, with tremendous patriotic fervour. Another war imposed within three years of the 1962 Chinese invasion—it was too ghastly an option to contemplate. Yes, as Anand noted, the nation faced this trial heroically—the first after Nehru's death. India was fighting under a leader whose gentle image seemed incongruous with the brutality of war. Would he prove equal to the task? This single unarticulated question perplexed everyone. The conflict would take its toll, regardless of whether it was sustained and gradual, or short and absolute. Worst of all, India had no choice except aggression, because Pakistan was entirely responsible for initiating and exacerbating hostilities.

Eventually, however, the conflict came to an end within twenty-two days. Lal Bahadur's position as the nation's leader was instantly enhanced. His firm statements, coupled with decisions without the slightest trace of vacillation, brought him unprecedented glory in a matter of days.

Then came the Tashkent Agreement.

# 38

IT WAS TWO A.M. THE SHRILL RING OF THE DIRECT TELEPHONE IN Anand's bedroom sounded shriller by its suddenness. It jolted him out of a doze that was just turning into deep sleep.

Until after midnight, he had been travelling long distances, addressing public meetings to explain the country's stand in the Indo-Pak crisis. There was a feeling of general relief that active hostilities had ceased, and the Tashkent dialogue had begun. Yet, persistent reports of a breakdown in the talks poured in. The possibility of further hostilities fuelled uneasy speculation.

'Sleeping . . .?' boomed the voice at the other end of the line.

'Not quite, Hariram,' answered Anand, at once recognizing the UNI correspondent's voice. 'You know I can't invoke the White Horse that puts you and some other lucky pen-pushers to instant sleep!'

'Quit joking,' cut in Hariram ominously. 'There is bad news. Lal Bahadur is dead. Heart attack at Tashkent . . .'

Anand sat bolt upright in bed, wide awake.

Since the Tashkent parleys began after the cease-fire, Anand had found a peculiar mixture of hope and increasing anger among the people. It was palpable even in areas far from Delhi. There was an unending debate on whether Prime Minister Lal Bahadur Shastri was right in agreeing to the Tashkent mediation. There was a feeling that once the Indian army crossed the Indo-Pak border, the advance should have continued, to put India in a commanding position. Lahore should have been taken and a Pakistani surrender forced. The Haji Pir 'Bulge' was specially mentioned in critical newspaper comments. Critics insisted that Lal Bahadur had succumbed to the pressures of outside powers, by agreeing to the cease-fire; this, they asserted, was contrary to the country's security interests.

According to rumour, there had been a sharp exchange between the Prime Minister and the chief of the army staff, General Chaudhuri, on the return of some pockets of Pakistani territory occupied by India during the hostilities. Some newspapers speculated that the army chief had threatened to resign, or had in fact resigned, as a protest against the government's weak-kneed attitude. There was another equally strong rumour, exactly the reverse of this speculation; it said that it was the army chief who recommended acceptance of the cease-fire. Lal Bahadur in fact wanted to know if any military advantage was expected (such as whether the Pakistani side had exhausted most of its ammunition, while India still had large stocks in reserve, or so the rumour went) by continuing the action for some more days. (This latter version has now been confirmed authoritatively by L.P. Singh, the then Union home secretary, in his book on Shastriji published in 1996.)

The stirring concept of national prestige naturally occupied a central place in the countrywide debate, both in and outside parliament. There was jubilation at the Indian Army's achievement in the war. However, many saw the government as vacillating. It was willing, they charged, to forego the gains achieved by the fighting forces, for the dubious advantage of placating international opinion ... And finally, the Soviet government's offer to hold the Tashkent parleys also became the subject of tireless comment. Various quarters attributed various motives to the Russians. It was believed, for example, that the Soviets wanted to 'increase their influence' in India to prevent China and Washington from profiting from the conflict. Likewise, they wanted Pakistan to appreciate their efforts, so that they could steer that country away from China's grasp. Finally, both Moscow and Washington wanted India and Pakistan to sink their differences so that they could provide a united front against Chinese designs of increasing its strategic hold on the area. Yet none of this was altogether clear when the Tashkent Conference opened on 4 January 1966. Almost everyone believed that it was foredoomed to failure. In the prevailing atmosphere, no one hoped for any accord between India and Pakistan on any item. The cease-fire held but the fire had not exactly ceased. Both sides maintained inflexible positions. The bone of contention, again, was Kashmir. India wanted it out of the agenda, Pakistan insisted on its inclusion as the main item, if not the only one. All other issues, howsoever important and urgent, paled into insignificance.

Anand and his colleagues in state cabinets everywhere in India faced an extremely complex situation. Some among them, perceptive enough to look into the future, could see that the country was in for a long economic crunch. The mood of the war would subside in due course, but the ravages on the country's economy would be inescapable. Their task was to see that what was inescapable became acceptable to the people. That would mean continued deprivation to those who had suffered for ages and were just looking for the beginning of social justice for the first time . . . These deprived millions should not look at the country's defence as a curse that would destroy their future. How did one prevent that contingency? How did one tailor austerity programmes so that they did not interfere with accepted socio-economic goals? These were the trickiest questions the country's policy-makers faced. And at the end of the day, everything depended on educating and convincing the people.

Both countries faced each other with smoking guns. Neither could immediately remove the tension of war. Yet the imperatives of lasting peace were irresistible. There was a very severe drought in India, countrywide. The foremost duty of preventing starvation deaths forced the Central government to turn to the rest of the world, to buy food wherever available. Along with food, and sometimes even without it, India received transparent disdain and long lectures on self-reliance, in the firm belief that she would never attain it. The prospect was at once depressing and extremely difficult.

Yet, despite the hostility between the two sides at the Tashkent Conference, it was clear to both of them that they would have to make some sort of a beginning towards a settlement as neither could afford an endless arms race. However, the leaders of both nations were virtually under a mandate not to agree to anything, come what may. No one had actually given that mandate, but when there is a give and take—as there must be in any accord—both leaders negotiating on behalf of their countries find themselves under the threat of being accused of betrayal. People of both countries saw agreement—any agreement whatever—as capitulation.

The gruelling negotiations proceeded on expected lines, neither side giving anything away. However, just as both sides were about to terminate the dialogue and part company, the Soviet Prime Minister brought about a miraculous breakthrough, after long and arduous rounds of shuttle diplomacy. The mention of Kashmir in the text of the pact, which had become the subject of total disagreement, was at last managed through using phrases which temporarily satisfied both sides. Yet, there appeared to be no hope of an accord. 'Unless a miracle happens,' reported an Indian correspondent, 'the Tashkent Conference should end . . . on an unmistakable note of disagreement . . . a *détente* on any basic issue is considered impossible.'

All this was a great ordeal for the peace-loving Lal Bahadur Shastri. Added to this was the history of his previous heart attack. Before anyone knew how to react, he was dead, felled by a massive heart attack.

Chief Minister Chaudhury took the first morning flight to Delhi to attend Shastri's funeral and to be available for consultations on the next step. The nation was devastated by the death of the Prime Minister. Nehru's death had stunned the country a year and a half earlier, but it was not quite unexpected, although his colleagues and other leaders had done nothing to prepare the nation for that eventuality. Lal Bahadur had emerged as the interim Prime Minister manifesting all the inhibitions inherent in the compromise. He had not begun to establish himself in the eyes of the nation until the Pakistan hostilities when he began to emerge as a leader in his own right. The lingering doubts about the Prime Minister's competence had been laid to rest, at last . . . This made his abrupt end even more ironic and tragic. It was like the last bright flicker of a lamp.

Chaudhury brought four of his ministers with him to Delhi, including Anand. They frequented the Central Hall of Parliament, restaurants and other well-known spots where meetings went on, including condolence meetings. There was a good deal of interaction among chief ministers belonging to the ruling party. Kamraj, the president of the party, and several other stalwarts worked overtime to sort things out. It was the most trying moment in the country's history. If Nehru's death had left a void a year and half earlier, Lal Bahadur's sudden exit from the centre of the political stage now led to another vacuum, coupled with confusion. After Nehru, the choice had at least been between two senior leaders of the party. However, after Shastri, no acceptable senior leader was visible. Some persons fancied Kamraj himself for prime ministership, but the fancy turned out to be a fleeting one, no one knew why. Instead, everyone assumed that his 'nominee' was to be the Prime Minister. His image as a wise kingmaker, probably in line with his own wish, became established. He thus became the pivotal person in the succession drama. No other president of the ruling party since Independence had become so important all of a sudden, commented many perceptive political pundits.

As for Kamraj, his enigmatic comment in Tamil, 'Parkalam' ('We'll see'), reverberated throughout Delhi. Yet, who was not his choice was more or less clear—to wit, Morarji Desai. The reasons and arguments were the same as those cited after Nehru in 1964. Memories were still fresh. The feeling still was that Morarji was not a supporter of Nehru's policies . . . To that was added the belief that Kamraj just did not like him.

Meanwhile, a younger band of legislators was working ceaselessly to project its candidate, Indira Gandhi, as a candidate for the top job. Yet this alternative was not taken too seriously at first. She was, of course, well-known in the country, but largely as her father's daughter. Her elevation to the position of party president a few years earlier was largely seen as a concession, or homage, to her illustrious father. Her own initiatives, which were quite important in themselves, often went unnoticed since they were subconsciously interpreted as Nehru's, or of both. People and politicians began to take serious notice of her for the first time after Lal Bahadur's death. She was the minister of information and broadcasting in his cabinet, not an outsider. Anand and many like him could not understand whether there had been a move to groom her for succession while Lal Bahadur was still alive. Reports to this effect, however, did circulate now and then. Indeed, some people hinted, and others asserted, that Lal Bahadur's succession to the prime ministership was itself meant to pave Indira Gandhi's way. To some it looked far-fetched, but many believed it. In any event, it was interesting enough to persist in some minds, and controversial enough to keep media speculation going.

The general election of 1967 was hardly a year away. It would be the first without Nehru. This consideration loomed larger than ever before, more than anything else. Far-sighted leaders in the party realized the crucial importance of charismatic leadership. Was Indira Gandhi the answer? A report, considered authentic, had it that the moment Kamraj received the news of Lal Bahadur's death, he had muttered to himself, 'Indira . . .' No one knew the truth, but it sounded like a typical monosyllabic Kamraj reaction.

The going, however, was very rough. The party's senior chief ministers tried to pull off a compromise, as they had done in 1964. Their effort failed this time. A showdown became inevitable. For the first time in the ruling party's history, its members in parliament were to elect their leader by a divided vote. It was the moment of truth.

They drew the battle-lines again, but according to a different set of criteria. While Morarji remained Morarji, Indira Gandhi appeared as Nehru's torch-bearer and descendant. She had no rival as the party's vote-catcher for the 1967 elections. Hereditary privilege, charm, youth and promise—the combination was too formidable for anyone else to match.

Chaudhury, like some other chief ministers, had a very difficult time trying to ride two horses. At one point, he almost faced the prospect of antagonizing both. That meant that he was himself sure to be out of the saddle, whichever horse won. However, his clever deployment of colleagues helped him to stumble into the winning side. He kept both channels open, one through Anand and the other through Shekhar and another minister who was one of the old guard in the party. Chaudhury himself marked attendance in both camps, leaving his wife Nalini Devi to concentrate on Indira Gandhi's camp.

Thus Anand, whom younger party circles knew well for some time past, received his first exposure to the avowed socialists. They were bubbling with enthusiasm, some to bring Indira in, others to keep Morarji out. Although these were the two main reasons why people supported Indira Gandhi, there were other considerations as well: personal ambition as also various rivalries. The web was extremely complex; Anand, who was not personally involved in the race, found it fascinating.

He had no personal rapport with Indira Gandhi, but many of her close co-workers knew him. He had himself met her once in the state capital which she had visited some months earlier to inaugurate a function connected with the ministry of information. Again, at that function Anand had been asked to stand in for the regular information minister, who had just fallen ill.

As the final countdown to the election began, both candidates began to acquire a fairly distinctive image in the eyes of the people. Morarji's image was pro-rich; in contrast, Indira Gandhi's was, or became, pro-poor. Like shade and light, they tended to highlight each other. Closer scrutiny would perhaps have exposed the fissures in this simplistic categorization. However, not many were in a mood for closer scrutiny. The people, and a majority in the party, simply wanted a person to shower their affection on. For that purpose, they found Indira Gandhi more to their liking. The rest of the rationalization followed later.

The night before the showdown, Chaudhury summoned his

ministerial cohorts (spies, if you like) for a pre-final confabulation. Support was distinctly veering towards Indira Gandhi, although party members were far from absolute in their public utterances. Many stories about the surreptitious activities behind the scenes came into circulation. The outcome seemed anybody's guess.

Shekhar and the other minister, Chandra Mohan, detailed to reconnoitre the Morarji camp, had made their rounds separately and gave rather contradictory reports. While Minister Chandra Mohan, elderly and rather credulous in nature, asserted that Morarji had a solid majority, Shekhar merely said, 'I don't believe a word of what our senior colleague has gathered. My assessment is that the chances are even. Only the actual count will bring out the truth . . .'

'Why do you think so?' queried Chaudhury.

'It's quite simple; but let me put a counter-question. Why are you, the chief minister of a large state, firing a double-barrel gun? Why have you kept one foot in each camp?'

'Because I know that it is suicidal not to be on the right side of the Prime Minister, whoever he is going to be. I know, without any illusions, that we have only one power centre in the country—the Prime Minister. If a chief minister is out of step, he is out of the saddle, as I have said again and again . . .'

'Agreed,' and Shekhar. 'Now, why not apply the same yardstick to the hapless members of parliament as well? Nehru had selected them; he is no more. Shastri might have known many of them; but Shastri is no more. And now between Morarji and Indiraji, how do they know on which side their political bread is buttered?'

'Agreed,' echoed Chaudhury. 'Why do you think the MPs are feigning support only to Morarji? Their support to Indiraji could also be equally fake, for all I know . . . How do you explain this?'

'Easy,' responded Shekhar. 'There is a psychological dichotomy here. They feel that Morarji, having once stood down in favour of Shastri, has a stronger claim to the prime ministership this time. Moreover, they know it is now or never for him, in terms of age . . . On the other hand, they don't like him and don't feel secure with him. He is rigid, unbending, and vindictive—this is the Central

Hall opinion, whatever the truth. By comparison, they see Indiraji as gracious, soft and . . . perhaps what they really mean is, pliable.'

'In that case they should, logically, have lined up behind Indiraji solidly . . .' argued Chaudhury.

'Yes, but there are two hurdles. One, some state bosses fully support Morarji. They are breathing down their MPs' necks. Second, and what is really crucial, MPs in general don't like to oppose a vindictive candidate openly . . . Secret ballot is a different matter.'

'On the whole, your feedback is plausible,' commented Chaudhury. Even as he said it, he saw Minister Chandra Mohan's face turn a bit pale. Chaudhury turned to him and remarked, in a mollifying tone, 'You see, my friend, seniors like us don't go into these intricacies. I am pretty sure that even if Shekhar's theory sounds plausible, things may not quite work out that way. Events may prove you right, after all.'

Shekhar and Anand exchanged faint smiles.

Chaudhury then turned to Anand and bantered, 'And what is our Brihaspati's report? How do Indiraji's prospects seem to you? Great? Bleak? Middling? . . .'

'Great, of course,' responded Anand, 'if the party MPs have at least their eyes and ears open, whatever their private opinions.'

'That's a big if, isn't it? Do you think they have in fact kept their eyes and ears open?'

'I believe so. This is an unprecedented moment for the party. No member can afford to ignore it. Indiraji will win, if there is a contest, as seems imminent . . .'

'The contest will gladden your heart, no doubt,' Chaudhury remarked somewhat caustically. 'I remember your long face when we patched up the differences between Lal Bahadur and Morarji. Now your prayers seem about to be answered . . .'

'They are not *my* prayers alone. Anything to polarize the party and launch it single-mindedly on the course of its own promises is welcome . . .'

'In other words,' Shekhar said, with a snort of derisive laughter, 'Anand is dead certain that Indiraji's regime will see the instant

477

implementation of land reforms!'

'I am quite certain under whom that will not happen. We will attempt it under Indiraji, despite all the Shekhars of India,' Anand retorted grimly.

# 39

INDIRA GANDHI WAS ELECTED LEADER OF THE PARTY IN
parliament and became Prime Minister. She included Morarji
Desai as deputy Prime Minister in her cabinet. Anand was among
those who were, on the whole, gratified at the result, but he
remained discreetly in the background. He tried to analyse the
implications of the fact of a Prime Minister installed on a divided
vote of the ruling party and working with a deputy Prime Minister
who was—and was known to be—at variance with her in his views.
Was it a danger signal? Or an unprecedented opportunity? In either
case, the event presented a formidable challenge which few people
were willing to perceive or acknowledge at the time. Many were
busy celebrating or jockeying for positions. Being at the state level,
Anand had no such preoccupation, nor did he have the inclination.
As far as the state was concerned, he credited Indira Gandhi's
victory to Chief Minister Chaudhury. Not to please Chaudhury,
he told himself, but to prepare him for the trials ahead . . . Indira
Gandhi, he discovered, had her own opinions. When he chanced
to meet her briefly and described how sincerely Chief Minister

Chaudhury had toiled for her, she simply said, 'I know . . .' and smiled, suggesting, in no uncertain terms, that she knew the truth!

By the same token, Shekhar advised Chaudhury to slow down his blatant attempts to align himself with the new Prime Minister. 'You see,' he said. 'We wish her well; she is a fine person and all that. Still, no chief minister can afford to forget that the shadows of instability have appeared at the centre. Circumspection is called for at this delicate juncture.'

They returned to Afrozabad, having played their respective roles. Chaudhury's star rose in the political firmament. He was *the* state leader, people said of him, one of the Prime Minister's closest advisers. Everyone talked about him with awe and called him a very successful chief minister with the state securely in his grasp, or *mutthi*, to quote his Hindi-speaking followers. People of lesser consequence, such as Anand, went unrecognized. There was no particular need to recognize them. The chief minister's footprint, like an elephant's, was wide enough to contain those of all others. Many gloating opportunists in Delhi lionized Chaudhury, just as they had praised Mahendranath to the skies a few years earlier, albeit for different reasons.

Mahendranath's group was furious. They couldn't bear to see Chaudhury being praised and fawned over. At this rate, they predicted, Indiraji is sure to get into trouble. Chaudhury is a *badmaash* (rascal) and a most unreliable fellow masquerading as a loyalist. He will surely abandon her, mark my words, said many a disgruntled leader. Chaudhury will only make use of her for the 1967 elections. Then he will be secure for the next five years, while he knows Indiraji may not last that long. The blackguard!

What made Mahendranath's followers frantic was not so much Indira Gandhi's future as their own. With Chaudhury firmly in the saddle less than a year before the general elections, what seemed to be in store for them was political wilderness. Sure as hell, they would not get the ruling party's tickets, even in proportion to their strength in the present assembly. Chaudhury would fight like a wild boar to destroy them. It was too late to resort to flattery; Chaudhury would not be taken in, would not let them come anywhere near himself. They found themselves condemned to bear Mahendranath's label, like a widow still compelled to bear her late husband's name, no matter how long he had been dead.

Still hoping against hope, several among them moved heaven and earth to curry favour with Chaudhury. As the elections approached, their frenzy became more and more ludicrous and pathetic. In public they castigated Mahendranath, their hero until yesterday, with epithets that no one, even in Chaudhury's group, had ever employed. They tried to propitiate everyone who was anyone in Chaudhury's camp. Not excluding—indeed, in particular—his personal staff, notably his *jamadaar* (head-peon). It was freely rumoured that this man came to own three large buildings and two taxis in the state capital, plus fifteen acres of double-crop wet land in his native village. Just a *jamadaar*, mind you!

All this nefarious activity by Mahendranath's erstwhile faithfuls stemmed from the assumption that they were now widowed for good, politically. In other words, they believed that Mahendranath, once their lord and master, was now absolutely dead. And here lay their worst blunder, as it turned out. Just as some of them poured their most scathing vitriol over Mahendranath, the news of his elevation to an important post at the Centre smote them like lightning. It nearly electrocuted all of them.

Chaudhury had, of course, learnt of the Centre's intention a few days earlier. He was too familiar with Delhi either not to expect this to happen or to remain indifferent when he saw even a hazy signal. He promptly rang up the Prime Minister and recommended to her, quite categorically, that since Mahendranath had been cooling his heels too long, the PM must accommodate him in Delhi in whatever slot she thought fit. He gushed with love and admiration for Mahendranath. This, he told a journalist confidante, was a double master-stroke. In the first place, Delhi could come to the conclusion that he (Chaudhury) and Mahendranath had somehow made up and would combine forces if Mahendranath was accommodated in Delhi. In which case, he added gleefully, Mahendranath would get nothing and end up holding bullocks' tails for the rest of his life in the village. The other alternative, of course, was that Delhi would think of befriending Mahendranath as a weapon against Chaudhury, in case such a need ever arose. In either case, he (Chaudhury) could take some credit—either for Mahendranath's rehabilitation or for his downfall and destruction, as the case may be. And in any event, it was good riddance for him and the state.

Fully aware of how genuine Chaudhury's love for Mahendranath was, the Prime Minister merely said, 'You want him *here*?' Chaudhury understood the inflection in her voice at once. Tempering his earlier effort at cleverness, he replied, honestly this time, 'Madam, I just want him out of *here*!' He imagined her smile, her iron self-control intact even when she was immensely amused.

Equally promptly, Chaudhury personally contacted Mahendranath via a midnight trunk call to the latter's village in his district. Considering the honey that flowed along the wires both ways, no one in his wildest dreams could have believed that they had not been on talking terms until that moment . . . A car was specially rushed to Mahendranath's village, carrying the district collector. Until the previous day, the collector had been rather confused about how to conduct himself in relation to the former chief minister because he feared that the current chief minister scrutinized him with a thousand eyes. 'You can't imagine the hazards of poor civil servants these days,' he had groaned to a friend just the other day. 'Believe me, it's hell!' Now, while driving to Mahendranath's village, the collector's face beamed with relief, as if he had just been promoted as chief secretary in one single jump. Mahendranath's impending departure filled him with joy. Not that Mahendranath ever interfered in the collector's work; the official had no such complaint. It was just the natural attitude of a civil servant who feels weighed down by the mere presence of any VIP anywhere within his jurisdiction.

When Mahendranath stepped into the VIP lounge at the airport in the state capital, he found Chaudhury waiting to welcome him with a huge garland. There was an assortment of followers from both sides. The recent turncoats were not there at all, except some of the less blatant ones. These hovered uncomfortably on the periphery, eager to mark attendance but afraid to engage in conversation with Mahendranath. They knew his tongue too well to go anywhere near him.

Mahendranath had no doubt that his migration to Delhi was the Prime Minister's way of obliging Chaudhury. 'I'll teach her a lesson. I'll show Delhi how hot I can make matters for them in their own dens. They'll repent for the rest of their lives!' he fumed. His outward behavior, however, changed perceptibly. From being a 'poor lady' a few weeks back, Indira Gandhi became a 'great lady' in his estimation—in his public utterances, that is.

The sniping between the pro- and anti-Indira Gandhi camps continued for months. While both maintained an uneasy truce within the parliamentary party and let the government run its term, both prepared for a real fight to the finish. The fight would continue through the process of selection of candidates and go on into the election itself, with each group determined to prevent the other from winning seats. While other political parties, and notably independents, stood to get a windfall, the ruling party was in for self-destruction.

Mahendranath and Chaudhury braced themselves for a grand showdown in the state. Now that Mahendranath occupied a position at the Centre, the fight was no longer unequal. If Chaudhury found himself outfoxed by Mahendranath's presence in Delhi, he said nothing about it—indeed could say nothing, since he had recommended it himself. It was Delhi's normal balancing act; he had been its beneficiary himself not so long ago when Mahendranath was the chief minister. There was only one way open to him now. *Fight.*

Plans for mutual destruction began long before the party as a whole took stock of the electoral scene. Both groups were ready with lists of their candidates in pairs, one pair for each constituency. Of the pair, the group would urge that one should get the party's 'official' candidature. In case he failed to secure the ticket, the group would set up the other as an independent, with its full support. The support was to come through different categories of party workers. Some were to campaign openly against the 'official' candidate (belonging to the other group, mostly). Some others were to become inactive on some pretext or the other, contributing to the defeat of the official party candidate, by any means fair or foul, mostly foul. The most intelligent of the lot were to remain throughout with the party's official candidate and act as Trojan horses to sabotage his chances from within. This last technique had been developed over the decades. Both Mahendranath and Chaudhury were experts at it. However, while they had practised the art together against common opponents in the past, they now invoked it against each other, with unprecedented ruthlessness. The same technique was followed in almost all the four-thousand-odd assembly constituencies in all the states at this election—proving, once again, that the country was one both in principle and in practice!

Anand had been nursing his constituency regularly with as much personal attention as he could bestow upon it, consistent with his duties as minister. The people in general seemed satisfied with his performance. Yet he did not realize till very late in the day that there was trouble in his constituency. Superficially everything seemed fine, but beneath the surface there was something brewing. Initially, he didn't see this, for his constituency was rather backward and the people, in general, were simple and straightforward. They would not abandon him—or so he believed. Then one day, when he was poring over some files in his office, Aruna suddenly appeared from nowhere. They had not been meeting frequently these days, busy as they were with political activity in different localities. She came straight to the point.

'Is anything wrong in your constituency?'

'Nothing that I know of,' answered Anand, a bit surprised, considering that she hadn't taken much interest in his constituency in the past.

'You are too busy with your dreams of land reform,' she said testily. 'You have failed to take note of the landslide that's about to hit you in your constituency!'

'What's the matter? What's happening?' Anand asked, his curiosity aroused.

'Do you know a landlord named Shyam Sunder? Does he

belong to your constituency?'

'Oh yes, he is a close friend of mine. He has a good hold on two or three villages in my constituency.'

'Well, all I can say is that you will do well to beware of this close friend of yours. He and I happened to be with the health minister's private secretary in his room in the secretariat. He doesn't know me personally, of course. He bragged to the secretary all the while about his great influence all over your constituency and how he was going to get you defeated in the coming election. Later, while returning from the minister's office, I saw him entering Shekhar's office. All this may not mean anything, but I think you had better watch out . . .'

Aruna caught her breath and waited as Anand sat lost in grim concentration for a while.

'That's good solid advice, Aruna. I'll look into it . . .'

'What? You'll look into it? Like any routine matter coming to your notice every minute? Your best friend in the constituency turns against you and you say you'll look into it, in typical ministerese? Wake up, Anand, before it is too late! Don't forget you're facing this election as the most controversial minister in the cabinet . . . And look at your complacency! My God! You'll look into it, eh?'

'Well, that may not be the appropriate phrase,' Anand said, with mock seriousness. 'I shall give it my most earnest and urgent consideration!'

'Ministerese again!' shouted Aruna, and laughed almost hysterically. After a few more stray remarks, she left. Anand remained in deep thought. He had, of late, noticed some change in Aruna's manner and attitude. Or was it only his own imagination?

She was more impatient, more jumpy, more tactless than ever before. She picked quarrels right and left. And finally vented all her temper on Anand. This last, of course, he could understand. She had no way out. And her angry outbursts invariably ended in repentance. He had to comfort her all the time, after enduring her fury and turbulence. He wondered what was coming over her.

His private secretary told him on the intercom that Shri Shyam Sunder had just dropped in. He had an urgent request, and could he come in for a minute . . .?

'Of course, send him in,' responded Anand, Aruna's outburst still echoing in his ears.

Shyam Sunder was hefty and haughty, every inch a feudal lord. He had been a schoolmate of Anand's. Somehow, he had taken a special fancy for Anand, next only to shikar and good food. His village, situated on the periphery of the Reserve Forest, was completely at his beck and call—to the last man, woman and child. The one accursed thing he could not control was diabetes, and he was furious about it. Of late his blood sugar, his intake of his favourite sweets and his dosage of insulin injections had meshed in an escalating spiral, with which his natural irritability kept pace.

Shyam Sunder had virtually adopted Anand—his old school friend, he announced proudly—as his own ministerial exhibit (not many feudals could boast of a minister as a close friend). When Anand visited Shyam Sunder's village—and he insisted that the visits be as frequent as possible—Shyam Sunder was the sole master of ceremonies throughout. Lunch at Shyam Sunder's residence, public meetings in front of Shyam Sunder's *kothi*, presided over by Shyam Sunder—well, it was Shyam Sunder all the way. Not a single person in the village could come anywhere near Anand. Shyam Sunder's servants collected petitions from the people, tied them in a bundle and handed them over to Anand's personal assistant. Many villagers, however, came to the state capital or the district headquarters to meet Anand separately. They described how they suffered under the feudal tyrant's atrocities in the village.

In the last two general elections, Shyam Sunder's village had supported Anand overwhelmingly. Very few votes had gone against him. It was difficult to divide the credit for this victory between the powerful Shyam Sunder on the one hand and the downtrodden, afflicted villagers on the other. Shyam Sunder, of course, had claimed all the credit for himself, with hardly anyone else in the village daring to contradict him openly. And Anand had quietly managed to keep everyone pleased, to the extent he could.

For about a year, however, Anand had received several disquieting reports about Shyam Sunder's deep involvement in the illicit felling of high-quality teak trees in the Reserve Forest. The timber was sold secretly in the city. Shyam Sunder was using about a hundred bullock carts regularly for the purpose, with the help of as many poor labourers from his village. Petty local officials of the forest department, of course, cooperated willingly in return for a share in the profits. What angered Anand most was a recent report (yet unconfirmed) that when an uncommonly honest forest range officer, just posted in the area, confiscated a large load of timber, he was promptly told by Shyam Sunder's agent that the stuff was meant for Minister Anand. 'Don't you know the minister is constructing a house in Afrozabad?' the agent asked the officer in a menacing tone.

These thoughts came to Anand's mind while Shyam Sunder shook his hand, slapped his shoulder and said, 'Namaskar, Anandbhai, mighty glad to meet you . . . How do you manage to keep so trim in spite of so much work?'

'I'm glad to know I look trim,' Anand replied with a smile. 'When did you come and what brings you here? Is everything all right in the village?'

'Yes, by the grace of God. Look, I know you have a cabinet meeting in the next half-hour, so I'll come straight to the point. All right?'

'Of course, if you so wish . . . Go ahead.'

'You know in all these years, I have not asked you, my closest school friend and minister, for one single favour. Isn't that so?'

'That is so, and I am grateful for all that you did in my last two elections. You've been a real friend in need.'

'Now, Anandbhai, I have come to beg of you a personal favour—my first and last, I assure you . . .'

'Oh, why do you say all that, Shyamji? Please go right ahead and tell me what you want me to do. You know I will not hesitate.'

'I know, I know. The matter is quite simple, really. A close cousin of mine is an executive engineer. I am personally beholden to him. He has been suddenly transferred from the irrigation project where he is working. Somehow, his retention there for a year more has become a question of prestige—his prestige and mine. In fact it is now my prestige more than his. I want the transfer cancelled at any cost . . .'

'Hmm . . .' Anand began. 'The chief minister himself holds the irrigation portfolio at the moment.'

'That's why I came to you,' said Shyam Sunder, 'since I don't know him personally. The chief engineer is scared to oblige me without the chief minister's consent . . .'

'I shall certainly speak to the chief, Shyamji,' Anand assured him. 'I think it shouldn't be too difficult.'

'Nothing is difficult if only you take it up seriously,' Shyam Sunder asserted. The comment sounded like a compliment, but also contained a note of warning. Subtle, but noticeable all the same. Then Shyam Sunder wound up his entreaty with yet another loaded statement. 'You know, Anandbhai, that I never bother about these things,' he said. 'I lead my life the way I want to. However, when it comes to my prestige, I stop at nothing. Call it my arrogance, but that's the way it is in my family. I hope you will do me this favour without fail . . .'

Again, Anand thought, a veiled threat. Or, was he imagining things? he wondered briefly. Was he judging Shyam Sunder in the light of Aruna's revelations?

*

After the cabinet meeting a little later, Anand followed Chaudhury into the latter's ante-room and told him about the executive engineer's transfer. Since this was perhaps the first ever request of a personal nature he was making to Chaudhury, he took pains to explain how important Shyam Sunder was in his constituency and how his continued support would be needed in view of the impending general elections. Chaudhury took careful note of the particulars and promised to speak to the chief engineer.

Soon after this, there were a series of public holidays, following which the chief engineer left on a longish inspection tour. Meanwhile, Anand kept making inquiries about the fate of the executive engineer and learned, to his utter amazement, that he had received further orders to hand over charge 'at once', and to report at his new place of posting and intimate compliance, 'within twenty-four hours'. His intervention, Anand saw, had made matters worse for Shyam Sunder's cousin. He had to approach the chief minister again, urgently.

Chaudhury was chatting leisurely with a journalist friend of his when Anand telephoned. He seemed to relish every word of Anand's anxious account. At the end of the conversation, he remarked coldly, 'I'll look into it, Anand,' and put the receiver down.

Chaudhury pressed the buzzer on his intercom with unusual force and barked at his secretary. 'Get me that nincompoop chief engineer from the irrigation department. Now!' The astute secretary not only got the chief engineer on the phone, he also gave him a timely tip. 'Sir,' he warned. 'I don't know why, the boss is furious. He is in a rotten mood . . . Now speak on . . .'

'So that corrupt bastard is still in his old post and bringing political pressure to bear right and left, is he?' shouted Chaudhury when the chief engineer greeted him reverently. The boss's outburst, with no name specified, confused the chief engineer completely. Either the chief minister was too angry to talk coherently or, in his view, you could call any engineer in the irrigation department a 'corrupt bastard' with equal validity. All that the chief engineer could do in response was to stammer incoherently.

Chaudhury resumed, in a softer tone, 'You can't place the fellow? The executive engineer from Minister Anand's district who is throwing money all round to be retained on that big irrigation project . . . Hasn't he left?'

'Sir, we gave him orders by telegram yesterday!'

'Blast your telegram!' exploded Chaudhury. 'Place him under suspension for not complying with government orders. Today. Now!' He slammed the receiver down with such force that it fell outside the cradle.

'Amazing!' spluttered the journalist. 'I've never seen you in such a rage!'

'Sometimes anger is necessary, with a few abuses,' Chaudhury replied calmly, his equilibrium already restored.

'Why can't you oblige Anand, your own colleague?' asked the journalist, somewhat perplexed.

'Why should I?' Chaudhury shot back. 'In the first place, he is not in my group, so I don't have to bother about his future. I am sure Shekhar, my other colleague, will take care of that . . .'

'And why do you want that good fellow defeated?'

'Who says I want him defeated?' snapped Chaudhury. 'I want him to stew in his own juice, as everyone is made to in politics. And I have no doubt he will win; I have ascertained that to my satisfaction. What I want you to appreciate is that I don't owe him a damn thing. I don't belong to the do-gooder fraternity . . . Besides, if he is not pegged to his constituency, he will move all over the state for many other candidates and they will begin to worship him. I would be a fool to let that happen!'

'Is that executive engineer really honest, as Anand says?'

'I don't know and don't care; nor does Anand. In any event, I don't waste my time looking for ridiculous needles in haystacks,' Chaudhury remarked sarcastically. 'You miss my point, Sharma. What kind of man is this dreamer? When it comes to his own election, he is out to please one influential landlord—good, bad or indifferent—in his constituency. At that rate, how many similar landlords do *I* have to placate in the whole state in order to win the damned general elections? Particularly with the present uncertainties due to Nehru's absence . . . And between you and me, Sharma, there are many other considerations here.'

'Such as . . . ?'

'Such as my own uncertainty. How do I know where I'll stand with the new Prime Minister, once she gets a thumping majority in the Lok Sabha poll? How am I sure that her future whim will not select some ideological animal for a change?'

'Like Anand . . .?'

'Or any other cousin brother of his—I don't care, so long as it is not good old Chaudhury who gets dumped.'

'I told you again and again,' asserted Shekhar, 'that my dear colleague Anand hates the landlord class, like poison. Whether you were his schoolmate or classmate, his attitude is exactly the same . . .'

'So I see, so I see,' responded Shyam Sunder.

'What was the great favour you asked of him?' continued Shekhar. 'One small, simple cancellation of an unjust transfer . . . You request a retention, and your altruistic schoolmate minister grants you a suspension in return for your services in two consecutive general elections!'

'The ungrateful bastard!' Shyam Sunder said, grinding his teeth. 'I swear I'll teach him a lesson. I'll show him! But what can we do about my cousin? The poor fellow depended solely on me . . .'

'And you, in turn, like a perfect simpleton, depended solely on your brilliant schoolmate and friend!' Shekhar sneered. 'Still, no matter, Shyamji, your worry is over. I arranged everything even while you were hovering round Anand. Just an hour back I got word from a barrister friend that the high court has stayed the government's order suspending your cousin and all other action, until the writ petition he filed yesterday is disposed of. Which means two years at least. And you wanted his retention only for one year, isn't that so?' Shekhar's face beamed triumphantly as he repeated, 'So, relax now . . .'

'Relax?' shouted Shyam Sunder. 'No, thank you! I shall relax only after I see my beloved and trusted schoolmate defeated at the damned polls!'

Shekhar smiled maliciously.

# 40

'PERFECT!' SAID SHYAM SUNDER WITH GENUINE APPRECIATION WHEN Shekhar finally unfolded his plan. He christened it Operation Anandocide. They had had several long sessions before the plan emerged. First, they drafted the bare outline. Then, bit by bit, they completed it in detail, with all the appropriate hues and colours.

First, the candidate to contest against Anand. They agreed that no hopeful worth the name was immediately available. No one good enough *against* Anand anyway. They considered several names, but when approached, the persons refused. Some were interested at first, particularly when they knew how much money Shyam Sunder and Shekhar were ready to spend. However, somewhere down the line, these worthies developed cold feet and backed out. One or two of them even reported the proceedings to Anand, as if to clear their conscience. They knew Anand had rendered yeoman service to their villages . . .

Then, there were several who were unwilling to contest, but willing to support and work for the rival candidate. Their enthusiasm was impressive. When someone asked why, they gave a particularly interesting reason. 'You see,' they said. 'Money,

492

liquor and so on have never figured in this constituency since Anand came to contest here. It's time to end that drought. Some benefits must come to the voters during the election, apart from the MLA's services after it . . . And in any event, men like us prefer only to serve. We don't get into trouble. We are like the midwife who is always safe, while the danger is to the mother, or the child, or both!'

When the search for a candidate made no real progress, Shyam Sunder became impatient and offered himself. There was a detailed analysis of the pros and cons; eventually, Shekhar's advice went against the proposal. He explained the matter lucidly and persuaded Shyam Sunder to let the search continue. 'You have supported Anand in two elections,' he said. 'You have been one of his closest friends; even now not many people know that you have fallen out. They will not take your sudden emergence as a rival candidate seriously. They will attribute it to some isolated conflict over something in which he, as minister, may not have obliged you. In either case, your candidature will be without cause or substance, which is what it really is, if you'll pardon my saying so. No, Shyamji, you have to think of another person, I am afraid . . .'

Next they discussed the political party, if any, to which Anand's rival must belong. With Shyam Sunder's support coupled with the influence of his other friends, several parties were in fact willing to field candidates against Anand. They calculated that even if their chances of success were slim, they would be making a debut in the constituency through this election. On their own they began to send feelers to Shyam Sunder—through emissaries, relatives and party workers. Yet, here too, Shekhar put his foot down. 'Look,' he warned Shyam Sunder. 'Take it from me, Anand has made the constituency a virtual fort for the ruling party. No other party can hope to prosper here. And against Anand, well . . . just forget it. He will make mincemeat of every other candidate. In fact, any other political party contesting here would enhance Anand's chances of success. He can always appeal to party loyalty and swing the people to his side . . . No, Shyamji, no other party will do.'

'What do you suggest then, for heaven's sake?' demanded

Shyam Sunder in a vexed tone. 'We seem to be coming back to square one each time . . .'

'Easy, easy, Shyamji,' Shekhar began. 'To defeat a ruling party candidate like Anand is not a simple task, I assure you. Please don't get impatient. While we have been searching, I have done some homework on the side. I have finalized everything, in a manner of speaking.'

'Finalized everything?' Shyam Sunder asked in surprise. 'Why didn't you tell me earlier? Why should we have gone on this blind chase?'

'Please, Shyamji, let's understand the issue,' Shekhar pleaded. 'You and I look at the matter differently, with just one common objective, namely Anand's defeat. Your approach is personal, mine is personal and political. In a way we are making use of each other for the common end. Now, there are many implications of our different approaches. We need to sort them out before we take the next step . . .'

'You're damned right,' observed Shyam Sunder. 'But how long are we to ruminate over these implications? And what are they anyway?'

'To give you one example,' Shekhar pointed out. 'Anand's defeat should not weaken the ruling party in the constituency . . .'

'What do you mean?'

'Exactly what I said. You see, Shyamji, I oppose Anand, but in the process of getting him defeated, I don't want to ruin my party. My own political future is involved here . . . Besides, we have to mobilize the whole landlord lobby against Anand. This is possible only if we convince the landlords that despite their attempt to defeat a prominent ruling party candidate, the party is favourable to them. And finally, I don't want another political party to get a foothold in Anand's constituency. It is not good for the people, including, of course, yourself . . .'

'How does it make any difference to me?' Shyam Sunder asked with a shrug. 'I don't understand all this political nonsense anyway.'

'It does make a difference to everyone, Shyamji,' Shekhar explained. 'Still, I shall not go into any more details. As I said, I am now ready with my blueprint. I have some idea of the candidate who could fit the bill.'

'Who is he? Why don't you tell me immediately?'

'Before I disclose the name, Shyamji, I have to explain the specifications I had in view. In case you don't agree with any of them, you may tell me, so we can review them . . .'

'My God, Shekharji,' cut in Shyam Sunder tartly. 'I'm getting really frustrated with all this stalling. Please, let's just have the name!'

'Please bear with me for a minute,' pleaded Shekhar. 'As I was saying, we don't want a candidate from another party; he has to be an independent. He has to be from a powerful caste, such as yours. He has to be a young person with nothing against him, at least nothing for or against. An unknown entity has a special appeal to voters. They often presume that he is good—bless them. And of course, he has to be a middle-class person, not seen as rich. Lastly, he must have a presentable personality, so an average voter tells himself: why not give this innocent youngster a chance? There are many voters who want a change just for change's sake. And now . . .' At this point Shekhar paused theatrically and finally declared, 'without further delay, let me name him, Shyamji. He is your brother-in-law's brother-in-law, Ravi Kumar!'

The plotting and underhand methods that were being used against Anand were repeated thus in most of the four thousand legislative assembly constituencies all over the country, before the 1967 elections. It was at this time that the rot really set into the electoral process.

*

The 'ticket season' started and thousands of ticket-seekers from all over the country, along with ten times as many hangers-on, invaded Delhi as usual. There was absolute confusion about the real focus of power. Was it the Prime Minister? Was it the president of the party? Was it the chief minister of the state concerned? To what extent was the chief minister crucial in selecting candidates for the Lok Sabha? Was that choice to be left to Indira Gandhi? . . .

The ruling party's post-election set-up at the Centre depended on this last question.

Chief ministers converged on Delhi as usual, but for the first time they were unsure about the political permutations and combinations that had arisen with the advent of Indira Gandhi. Suspicions about one another dogged them all the time. Eventually, they fell back, by and large, on their own sources in Delhi but the sources were themselves dubious and unreliable.

A new conclave around Indira Gandhi, nicknamed the 'kitchen cabinet', had come into being at the Centre. It was still a little-known entity, at least for those belonging to far-flung areas. The aged levers of power and influence creaked and groaned, while still claiming to turn effectively. The new levers had not appeared clearly; perhaps they were still in the making. Delhi had become a conundrum even to seasoned politicians.

Indira Gandhi was another question mark. To the established leaders she was mainly a vote-catching device, intended to be used to bring the party back to power. They did acknowledge that she could do that job better than anyone else. However, at that point, as they saw it, her utility ended. Once the party was in, she would take, or they would make her take, a back seat—where they thought she really belonged. A more experienced leader—whom they did not, rather could not, name—would have to take over and run the country. Her turn may come too, some of them said ... or may not, some others pointed out. In any event, her continuance as Prime Minister after the election was unlikely.

'And very undesirable, if you ask me,' said a senior chief minister from a northern state to a leader from a neighbouring state.

'Well, my friend, you seem to be living in a fool's paradise! Rather a damn fool's!! You think the Nehru family is ever going to relinquish power, having got hold of the top position once? You don't know anything about Indira Gandhi—how obstinate, how wilful, how tough she is. Don't you remember that she married Feroze Gandhi against Mahatma Gandhi's wish? You think Jawaharlal approved of it ? Ask me, I am from Allahabad proper ... I know everything about the Nehrus ... No, I tell you no one can dislodge Indira Gandhi from the gaddi now!'

'You may be right in assessing her, but she can never deliver the goods. There will be endless trouble. It is one thing to be her father's daughter and attract the masses for a moment of transient glory. But to run this country . . . My God! How can you ever believe that a woman, Westernized, far from grassroot realities . . . How can you think of such a Prime Minister for a regular term?'

So ran the reactions of many politicians of the ruling party. Their main preoccupation was with the immediate future—their own, rather than the country's. Everyone believed that in the face of all the question marks on the horizon, one could take no risks. One *had* to be in a position of vantage politically, at this juncture, come what may. Chief ministers, ministers, legislators, members of parliament—both current and aspiring—each had to gain or retain a place of security for himself or herself in the impending election. That place of security would serve as a weapon, both defensive and offensive, to steer through the uncertain times ahead.

In their present mood nothing but the ends mattered.

Opportunism had indeed been rampant in all the previous elections. However, there were two distinguishing features about the expediency that had existed in the earlier polls. First, there was a touch of ideology about the various parties that helped the masses make up their minds. The Communist party in the south, the Jan Sangh-Ram Rajya Parishad combine in the north. Each had its separate identity. When the Ram Rajya Parishad put up a candidate against Jawaharlal Nehru, it had to project its orthodox Hindu, anti-reformist identity. The party thought it would work, at least in one election—and it nearly did. Panditji won with a margin that was not as massive as his eminence would merit. Yet, once he won, it was the verdict of the Hindu masses, loud and clear. The people wanted reform in Hindu law, as Nehru and his party envisaged . . . And the reform came accordingly, through legislation by the nation's parliament.

Second, Nehru had continously sharpened his party's radical image. What he achieved in point of fact was not relevant, since the masses believed implicitly that he would do what he promised he would . . . And he did what he could, almost single-handedly.

At any rate, the people believed that he tried to do what he promised.

These two factors had disappeared long before the 1967 election. The war with Pakistan had a far-reaching psychological effect. It inducted a new and overriding element of concern: the country's defence against hostile neighbours. The threat from China had receded somewhat from the people's mind, but Pakistan was a serious concern. The talking point for the election was: Who would build the country's defences efficiently? Whatever they said in party manifestos, this was an important consideration . . . With a woman running for Prime Minister and a coterie of senior leaders trying to elbow her out, this consideration began to obsess the people. Afraid and confused, and without the familiar figure of Nehru to reassure them, they could not be expected to vote according to traditional patterns.

Two main questions emerged. Would Indira Gandhi, if she became Prime Minister again, deliver the goods in the extremely difficult situation the country found itself in? And if the answer was no, who would . . .? To both the questions, no reliable answers were forthcoming . . . The election, in effect, promised to be a leap in the dark. If the people were confused, all the politicians were concerned about was their own survival. Ideology and commitment were given short shrift and opportunism took their place.

Ideology taking a second place, electoral choices were made for different reasons. Casteism, for instance. Not that it did not figure in earlier elections; it did indeed. However, caste became a powerful electoral plank now. A tacit understanding developed among the voters, to vote according to caste, cutting across political parties. Local leaders of all parties who belonged to a given caste held secret meetings. It was not quite clear which party or caste benefited from this political promiscuity. More or less all the parties appeared to profit from their exploitation of the caste factor. A deep rot started in the political process, from which the country never recovered.

They devised caste combinations to ensure a majority, depending on the caste composition of each constituency. They drew up caste-wise lists of voters, down to the last polling booth. Each candidate wore, as it were, an invisible but self-evident badge of the caste he belonged to. In some cases it was a distinct disqualification. In others it was a qualification. University scholars undertook research on matters concerning caste. In the process, casteism almost became a respectable activity.

With casteist overtones everywhere, caste conflicts became the order of the day. Several caste groups organized their own private armies. Rioting and pitched battles disrupted the peace and tranquillity of the rural areas. The common purpose of the armies was to prevent voters (particularly certain sections among them whose electoral preferences were well-known) from going to the polling booths. These battalions of thugs armed themselves with long lathis that rained on human heads and broke them like coconuts. Frequently the lathis were replaced by swords and daggers, and then by firearms and country-made bombs . . . These coercive measures, however, were often tempered with liberal rewards. If a voter agreed not to go anywhere near a polling booth, he would get enough money to drown himself in drink throughout the day of the poll. Middlemen sprang up in the countryside, earning tidy amounts for their ability to organize voters of a caste or a locality—either to vote for a candidate or not to vote at all, as the candidate wished. A new brand of electoral zamindari appeared, particularly in the northern states, and spread all over the country in a few years.

The extraordinary phenomenon called booth-capturing rapidly developed into a fine art. A hundred hefty men, armed either with lathis or firearms, would surround a polling booth. They would overpower the polling staff and the one or two police constables posted at the booth. Finally, they would stamp all the ballot papers in favour of their candidate and stuff them in the ballot boxes. Any genuine voter who went to the booth after that would find that someone had cast his vote already, leaving him with nothing to do. If the polling staff cooperated, they received generous rewards—money, liquor, women . . . if they resisted, they were just pushed aside, while the marauders went ahead with their mass stamping and stuffing of ballot papers. No one complained, since each party resorted to the same tactics wherever it could. It was part of the game. If one party failed to capture more polling booths than the other, well, it was a pity; that was all. Once everything was deemed 'fair' during elections, the country had nothing but fair elections!

Shocked by these developments, Anand knew he had to nevertheless find a way to cope with the new situation.

It was the penultimate day for filing nominations. Anand paced up and down his lawn restlessly, waiting for Sridhar, a sarpanch in his constituency. Sridhar had been his proposer in the previous elections. He was a mild and hard-working person, a close follower of Anand's. He had managed to get facilities such as a primary health centre, a veterinary hospital, an approach road and a high school sanctioned for his village through Anand's help. He was grateful to Anand and admired him for his dynamism and erudition. Each time Anand toured the constituency, Sridhar made it a point to take him to his village and hold a public meeting.

When he finally appeared at the gate Sridhar came straight to Anand, looking slightly pale in the face. He was a little out of breath, and said, 'Sorry, sir, to keep you waiting . . .' he did not elaborate. Anand did not even ask him to sit, and simply said, 'It's all right, Sridhar.'

'Did you get your nomination papers filed, sir?' Sridhar began. 'There is very little time left now. Tomorrow is the last day and the returning officer is a hundred and fifty miles away.'

'I have been waiting for you for the past three days,' Anand said. 'You know I don't want to break the tradition of the past elections. You will be the proposer on the first nomination paper I file. So, let's reach there this evening . . .'

When they arrived at the district headquarters, several of Anand's followers virtually mobbed him and recounted instances to prove that Shyam Sunder's men had bribed Sridhar to desert Anand. They opposed the idea of Sridhar being Anand's proposer—'on any nomination paper, first or last, we don't care,' they concluded emphatically.

'But this is incorrect!' protested Anand. 'Sridhar has accompanied me here, to file my nomination paper tomorrow.'

'Something is wrong, we are warning you,' they told him bluntly and repeated their misgivings again and again. They realized, however, that Anand could not change the proposer at that stage. The topic was abandoned, but his followers continued to shake their heads sceptically.

Sridhar filed Anand's first nomination paper with the usual fanfare, followed by three others. (Each candidate can file four nomination papers, according to the election law.) A large crowd had gathered in front of the office to pledge their support. When the people saw Sridhar accompanying Anand out of their office, their cheers suddenly turned into sustained angry jeers. They all seem to know what *I* don't, Anand told himself, surprised. There was something remarkable in the wisdom of the crowd; it is unfailing.

'Why is that fellow still with you?' someone shouted.

'He is a traitor!' yelled another.

'He is going to desert you, sure thing!' proclaimed a third, viciously.

Anand tried to pacify them. They lapsed into a sullen silence at his pleading. Meanwhile, Sridhar disappeared unnoticed from the scene. No one knew when and where he had slipped out. A paanwala at some distance from the crowd volunteered the information that he saw Sridhar get into a jeep covered with posters of Ravi Kumar, the rival candidate. The informant added that while buying a packet of cigarettes from his shop, Sridhar had sneered, 'All right, I'll show those bastards what a traitor can do!'

Anand had no way to verify the paanwala's version, but Sridhar's behaviour certainly lent credence to it. Yet, he paused to think, could it be that his followers had given Sridhar grave and sudden provocation to do what he did? In any event, nothing could be done now. The arrow, as they say, had left the bow.

Within an hour, a pamphlet was brought to Anand. It was signed by Sridhar and was vituperative in the extreme, and listed a long series of alleged corrupt activities either sanctioned or deliberately overlooked by Anand.

Anand had done nothing worthwhile for the constituency, it declared. People had entertained high hopes when he became a minister. However, Minister Sahib had apparently no time for the constituency. He had become inaccessible even to important sarpanches of the constituency, being always busy with his private activity ... At this point the pamphlet's language became salacious, describing how instead of serving the whole constituency, Anand had chosen to serve one woman! Finally, Sridhar went on to allege that Anand had forced him to sign the nomination paper, but God had opened his eyes when a bunch of Anand's hired sycophants had openly called him a traitor. They had also tried to assassinate him in broad daylight in front of the office of the returning officer. He repented, he said, for every minute of the past several years when he had been so completely taken in by Anand. Finally, he exhorted the people to 'throw this arrogant, immoral, corrupt and anti-people minister out for good and to save the state from such highly undesirable upstarts'.

After that, there were daily tirades against Anand. Ravi Kumar's posters were plastered on every wall in every village in the constituency long before the ruling party could put its electoral machine together. It was an object lesson in electioneering. Like Sridhar's first salvo, the opposition had obviously planned everything in advance and executed it efficiently, leaving Anand's followers standing and gaping. The first round of the campaign had clearly gone to Ravi Kumar . . . or Shyam Sunder . . . or Shekhar. To Shekhar, really . . . There was visible discomfiture among Anand's followers, bordering on demoralization.

There was, in effect, just one point of attack: Anand's 'affair'. It rose as a wave all of a sudden and became the talk of the town and the village. Since the people in the far-flung villages had not heard of it in the past years, they looked at the posters and at one another, as if to say, 'Is that so?' Then they seemed to pause, questioning the information, wavering in their assessment of the many lascivious details provided by the poster ... They waited for further developments.

The ruling party's lumbering election machine began to move at last, slowly, very slowly. It took quite some time to reach out and make an impact in the villages. Mahatma Gandhi came to its rescue. Jawaharlal stood sentinel to safeguard its interests. Indira Gandhi, still described as 'Nehru's daughter' in the countryside, appeared on the election scene in a big way . . . There was keen competition among the party candidates to have Indira Gandhi visit his or her constituency to campaign. They all believed, with ample justification at the time, that her mere appearance would enhance their chances of success in the election.

Chief Minister Chaudhury appointed a committee consisting of Shekhar and two others to draw up Indira Gandhi's election tour programme. Shekhar worked very hard and produced an itinerary that seemed to please almost all the party candidates. He allotted a whole evening to Anand's constituency, making it the last item of the day. Everyone praised Shekhar's fairness, considering his known hostility towards Anand. When someone mentioned this to Chaudhury, the latter responded with a broad smile . . . Anand said nothing. He had asked for a slot for his constituency, but had not made any special effort to get it, since Shekhar was in charge of the programme. He had also felt it rather indelicate to deprive many other party candidates clamouring for a visit.

When they finalized the visit, he began to make arrangements in the constituency. Indira Gandhi was to reach a centrally located village in his constituency around 9 p.m. People began gathering at the venue in large numbers about five hours before she was due to arrive. The crowd swelled and swelled, reaching a size never seen before anywhere in the area. However, several unfamiliar individuals had positioned themselves at all points of entry into the village. They persuaded the arriving crowds to go back. 'Indira Gandhi's tour programme does not include this village,' they said emphatically . . . They also added that Anand had played a dirty trick on them for the purpose of gathering a huge crowd so he could address it himself. 'And since no one would think of coming all the way to hear him, that immoral, wily son-of-a-bitch told you a damned lie. You will see for yourselves; Indira Gandhi will never come to plead for this bloody sinner. He is a characterless wretch and a blot on the government and the party!'

Despite these efforts to turn them back, the crowds gathered and stayed. By the same token, Anand's anxiety mounted as the appointed hour came and went, with no sign of the Prime Minister. Some well-wishers advised Anand to abandon the meeting. They claimed that the inconvenience caused to the people would prejudice them against him. Anand had never met these well-wishers before; they were from outside the area. From their accents, Anand guessed that they must be from the city—probably the state capital. The inference was obvious: Shekhar had laid a trap to convince the people that Anand was a liar.

It was past midnight. A tentative message arrived that the Prime Minister would arrive in an hour's time. However, it was futile to announce anything in view of the prevailing uncertainty. When there was yet another message to say Indira Gandhi would be further delayed, Anand decided not to make any announcement at all. He merely hinted that it was for the people to wait or leave, as they wished. As for himself, he would wait as long as necessary.

Almost everyone waited, to the disappointment of the dissuaders. When Indira Gandhi did arrive, towards the crack of dawn, the crowd was overjoyed to have her darshan. No one heard, nor cared to hear, what she said. No one could hear anything clearly anyway. What they understood was only the party symbol. For the rest, they forgot the fatigue of the all-night vigil.

After some investigation, Anand came to know the cause of the delay. While delays were normal during an election campaign, Shekhar had taken special care to cram that evening with a large number of unscheduled stops and meetings. His intention was that Indira Gandhi should not reach Anand's constituency that night. He managed this, but the people foiled his scheme by waiting loyally till she came.

Again, Anand said nothing. More than anything, the new phenomenon of darshan in election campaigns struck him as odd. People had clamoured for Nehru's darshan in earlier elections, he recalled. Yet Nehru would insist on explaining the issues at stake to the people. The people would listen in complete silence as he spoke to them. Now, all that the people came for was a glimpse of the Prime Minister. Watching the exhausted crowd disperse, he wondered if this phenomenon, this dependence on presence and charisma, just darshan and nothing else, was a sign of things to come.

# 41

AS FEARED, THE RESULTS OF THE 1967 GENERAL ELECTIONS threatened to engulf the country in confusion and near instability. A plethora of political parties and groups sprang up from the electoral free-for-all. Opportunistic alliances mushroomed overnight in several states. Strange combinations formed coalition governments. Democracy appeared disoriented for the first time in India. Again, this was the result of Nehru's absence.

Anand's victory in the election had remained uncertain till the counting of votes. It was touch and go throughout the campaign. He confined himself to his constituency, unable to help many others who had depended on him earlier. Ravi Kumar's aggressive election campaign had demoralized Anand's followers, and he had to give them back their confidence as also convince the villagers to vote for him. A river of liquor flowed in the constituency two nights before the poll, thanks to Ravi Kumar. Practically no one in any village was sober. Self-respecting people virtually went into hiding behind bolted doors. Anand and his workers made several nocturnal rounds of the area, but the villagers avoided them. The situation became grimmer when gangs of young men on motorcycles went from village to village openly threatening the voters with dire consequences, including murder, in case they did not vote for Ravi Kumar. The show of firearms was massive and truly intimidating.

All this activity, however, did not seem to brighten Ravi Kumar's chances. The night before the poll, for instance, Anand's followers caught hold of a sarpanch who was particularly close to Anand. The man was hideously drunk. He almost fell down at every step, and was completely out of control. When he saw Anand arrive at his house, he jerked himself back into some kind of sobriety. He greeted Anand and began to fuss about, ordering tea and food for the guests. Anand spoke to him as usual, as if the man was completely sober, and asked him about the election prospects in his village. The sarpanch's face showed some annoyance and he said, rather sharply, 'Why do you ask me, sir? Do you suspect this village?'

It was a difficult question to answer, so Anand said nothing beyond a tentative 'Oh, no!' Then one of his followers began a harangue on corrupt electoral practices and how the people would stand to suffer if the voters fell prey to any kind of bribe. The sarpanch listened to the tirade for what seemed an unusually long time, considering his condition. Then he retorted, 'Don't spoil my mood, my dear friend. Minister sahib knows me very well, so stop your sermon, will you?'

The other man fell silent; but he was about to say something again when the sarpanch cut him short.

'To hell with your preaching!' he shouted. 'Here is a candidate offering us a little drink for the first time in the constituency's history. Must you interfere just at this time with your wretched homily? Hungry people have watched the zamindars revelling in good food and drink for decades. If the poor are being given pulao to eat for the first time in their lives today, why is your stomach getting upset? Forgive me, sahib,' he said, turning to Anand. 'Ask this follower of yours to pack up and go. You don't need the support of such men to get you votes in this village. Understand?'

'I understand perfectly,' echoed Anand, trying to look cheerful.

P. V. NARASIMHA RAO

This was neither here not there, as the person who had given the sermon could see. The sarpanch, as he understood it, was justifying what the law clearly defined as a 'corrupt practice'. This was not right, he told himself, and began a fresh sermon, this time even more passionately. 'It is a shame that votes in this constituency are being sold for money and liquor . . . ' He was about to proceed further, but the drunk raised his hand and all but slapped him in the face. 'I'll break your bones here and now if you utter one word more!' he shouted. 'How dare you insinuate such a thing about my village? You idiot, what have this free drink and food got to do with voting? Who are you to make me vote or prevent me from voting? Who do you think you are, anyway? My master, eh? And which master can ever know which way his servant is voting?' And he whipped up such a furore that Anand preferred to abandon the meeting. The sarpanch had, in his own drunken way, given him, Anand, a sermon on the sanctity of the secret ballot . . . As it turned out, the overwhelming majority in that village voted for Anand. So did many other villages, but not before shaking his equilibrium considerably.

\*

Indira Gandhi formed the Central cabinet. It was difficult to say that the government inspired confidence.

Chaudhury became the state chief minister again and Anand continued in the cabinet. However, nothing was the same to him any more. Including Aruna. She had changed. She became increasingly irritable and critical of everything, including of her party. The uncertainties of the political situation in the country completely confused her and plucked at her taut nerves. She suggested nothing positive, condemned everything. By her persistent dabbling in personal politics, she managed to make enemies everywhere. Not merely for herself but for Anand.

Many were of the view that her irritation was the result of stagnation—as a mere legislator. This was natural, some of them said, since no one can do without a promotion forever—be he a politician, civil servant or businessman. That was the truth. It assumed a special significance in Aruna's context. 'She has a case, brother, a cast iron case,' said one of the critics posing as a sympathizer. 'The trouble is, both she and Anand can't be ministers.'

'Why not?' interjected another, grinning. 'Where does the Constitution say that intimate friends can't be cabinet colleagues?'

'Nowhere, I am happy to say,' replied the other with an obscene wink.

'What a nice prospect for Chaudhury and his other ministers!' put in a third, savouring every word. 'There'll be some action in the cabinet . . .'

'Yes, why not?' chipped in a ubiquitous press reporter. 'At least that will make news, at least for a few days, at least for a day . . .'

It is a truism that there comes a time when even a politician finds politics futile. It holds no promise, brings no rewards, affords no satisfaction. On the other hand, it leaves one increasingly vulnerable to relentless maligning from all sides. There is no way one can get out of it, since one does not know whom to fight and ends up throwing punches at shadows. Thus, Aruna bustled around, for or against nothing in particular, against no one in particular, yet getting on everyone's nerves. She left everyone wondering. Political circles thought she was smarting under extreme frustration. And total isolation, added some. 'Even Anand seems to be running away from her,' said others in mock sympathy. Aruna is in a state of political menopause, remarked some particularly vicious party men. Despicable as the gossipmongers were, the sad truth remained that Aruna did betray frustration.

It was the grand plaza, the point where the road one has taken so far terminates. After that, however, there are other routes to choose from. You could, in anticipation of retirement or an electoral defeat, amass wealth, using your influence and contacts. You could prepare for a full-blown return to your old profession, if you had one. You could cultivate an altogether new interest and decide to pursue it from then on. Or you might decide to stay on and on as legislator, for want of a viable alternative, with waning interest and mounting boredom, although it must be said that in some cases the legislator continues to be as active on the last day of his life as he had been on the day he entered politics. There are a few such perennial spirits.

Unfortunately for Aruna, she had no options to choose from. And politics bored her; she felt there was a huge vacuum in her life. She had once admired Anand's concentration on his work. However, his commitment to unending politics began to gall her, though she would never have admitted it. And the sense of purposelessness grew within her. From simply being the subject of snide casual gossip, her behaviour became an intimidating reality she could neither deny nor wish away.

Her isolation from relatives and friends was almost total. They could say nothing to her face, but condemned her on a double count behind her back. Their logic, perhaps callous, was nevertheless clear. She had disgraced her kin, they said, by going too close to Anand. Having done so, why didn't she at least atone for it? Couldn't she dissuade Anand from his pigheaded resolve to destroy the landlords? Why should he concentrate his mania for ceilings on land alone? What about urban properties—the high-rise mansions, the glittering heaps of jewellery and gold, the stocks and shares? What about the thriving black markets, the ever-spiralling salaries, allowances and myriad perquisites extorted from the government under the constant threat of strike and dislocation? What about the kickbacks, the various shady deals behind closed doors and under the tables? What about the free sale of jobs and positions, concluded around card tables and in the beds of five-star hotels? How about the contractor kings who could make the Nizam of Hyderabad (at one time the richest person in the world) seem a pauper? Why did no policy of reform ever seem to touch these classes? Why couldn't Anand divert a bit of his attention to these areas of horrendous parasitism and exploitation? Why must he insist on exterminating the source of his own roots?

They argued and argued with her, as if *she* was the accused. And she was, in their eyes. This only added to her irritation and isolation: irritation at Anand and isolation from the world around her. She did not care to argue with him. She had neither the patience nor the conviction to argue, one way or the other. She only knew that she was caught in the cross-fire of this political battle and could not see a way out.

Elsewhere on the national political scene, the ruling party became a house divided against itself as never before. Colleague against colleague, member against member. Indira Gandhi came in for much criticism. One senior party member complained loudly to a colleague in a state guest house in the capital: 'Why is she scared of her own shadow? Now that she has become Prime Minister by hook or by crook—Aha! You object to by hook or by crook, do you? Then what was it, really, if not by hook or by crook? . . . But never mind . . . Now that she has become Prime Minister, why doesn't she put together a team and begin serving the people? Why must she try to prove, day in and day out, that she deserved to be Prime Minister, that she and no one else was *always* the natural, destined Prime Minister? Why does she let her kitchen cabinet hounds loose on her senior respected colleagues? What have they done to deserve this shabby treatment?'

His friend replied: 'Well, my dear friend, you overlook some simple facts of human psychology, if you will pardon my saying so. Take it from me, Indira Gandhi will never, repeat never, get over her complex—a very complex complex indeed. It consists of a sense of inferiority, a feeling of insecurity, and an admission of inadequacy. There is a persistent insistence on her own tremendous potential—coupled, above all, with the consuming ambition to attain immortality, to eclipse her great father . . . And much more, of course. And because she is a woman, the enigma deepens infinitely. Mark my words, brother, Indira Gandhi has come to stay. Make no mistake, she will be the country's main national topic for a long time to come. The country has to learn to live with her, rather under her, for better or for worse.' These sentiments were echoed with varying degrees of intensity in some quarters in the country.

Aruna rejoiced that Indira Gandhi had become Prime Minister. There was no ideological basis for this feeling, nor was it the outcome of any strong feminist streak. It was simply an extension of her dislike for men in general. She felt gratified to see Indira

Gandhi give a bloody nose to those 'male pigs' who had tried to humiliate her.

All this elation was only temporary, however. Aruna's problem, whatever it was, seethed on as before. Until one evening, she suddenly rushed to Anand in a state of high excitement.

'You seem to be under some divine inspiration, Aruna,' Anand teased. 'Anything to be shared with ordinary mortals?' He spoke to her with his usual tenderness, making her sit comfortably.

'I've been debating precisely the same question for several days,' she began. 'So much has happened and so much has changed. They drove me to a point of rebellion, as you know. I have burnt my boats with the party. It seems to have no more use for me and many others like me.'

Anand said nothing. He remembered numerous instances when Aruna had reacted unpredictably in the past; it was best to let her wriggle back. He preferred to let her negotiate her own balance. He worried about her, but did not know what to do. Yet, strangely, everyone expected him to do something about her unpredictable frenzies. Some thought he should control her, others had no doubt it was time he jettisoned her. Still others believed he was helpless.

'I don't expect Indira Gandhi to be different from any other Prime Minister,' Aruna commented, rather tentatively. Then she added, almost as a quick afterthought, 'Of course, we all had good reasons to support her; I don't regret that part at all. Yet, I feel disillusioned to some extent. I can't spell out why. I don't know what I had expected of her. It all looks so silly on my part . . .'

'I don't think it is silly. It is probably quite significant, but you haven't been able to reason it out,' Anand said. 'That doesn't mean you're wrong.'

'Nor right,' shot back Aruna.

'Yes,' Anand agreed. 'Sometimes, one simply can't figure things out.'

'I am not looking for philosophical generalizations,' Aruna retorted good-naturedly. 'What I'm really bothered about has to do with my own feeling of restlessness, I think . . . I've been feeling for some time that I must do something really remarkable to prove myself.'

'Such as . . . ?' Anand queried, making it sound casual. He was sure she had not thought anything through and he did not wish to set her off on the irrational and emotional storms he knew she was capable of producing. But he asked the question anyway.

'I don't know really . . .' Her voice trailed off. However, within seconds, her whole body seemed to quiver vigorously like a creeper in a strong breeze. Then she said fiercely, 'Yes . . . That's it! I rebel against the party . . . I repudiate it . . . I defy it . . . I oppose it . . .'

Anand was stunned. He regretted having goaded her a minute earlier. He ought not to have done that. He said nothing further.

'Don't you want to know what I am going to do? You don't care what I do, do you? Couldn't care less?'

She had cornered him again. How could he say he didn't care? 'Whatever you want to do, Aruna,' he said gently, 'I want to know why you **want** to do it.' That way, he could divert her line of thought **for a while**, he reflected.

'Why?' **she** echoed. 'Didn't I say I wanted to prove myself? In this wonderful party of ours, I am merely your friend and sycophant. I have no other identity. Heaven knows I have done nothing earth-shaking for the country, but no lousy leader can say that I've done nothing beyond clinging to Minister Anand. Don't wince at my bluntness for a moment. Reflect a little, for heaven's sake, and tell me if what I just said is not the naked truth in our party circles. I don't know if I shocked them when I came into your life, but I am definitely going to shock them now.'

Still Anand did not ask her what she wanted to do. He hoped she had not devised some concrete plan. He kept stroking her head tenderly, as if to lull her into forgetfulness. Several minutes passed in uneasy silence.

'Know what?' Aruna jerked and blurted out. 'I'll sabotage the party in the Presidential election. I'll support Subba Rao!'

'What?' shouted Anand, unable to believe his ears.

'Yes, Subba Rao,' repeated Aruna, stressing the name with utmost deliberation. 'Koka Subba Rao! I don't know him at all; I only know he is the one candidate who has the guts to stand against our party. I must say that's a great virtue in my estimation right now!'

513

And she began to sing, 'Koka Subba Rao . . . Subba Rao . . . Subba Subba Rao . . . Rao Rao Rao . . .!'

'Will you stop this nonsense?' Anand said furiously. 'You are out of your mind! I tell you, this is the limit!'

'What is the limit, Minister sahib?' Aruna sneered. 'You will see the limit expand now, in a few days. You will see the party functionaries at my door, on their knees. I am sure to get a sweet letter from Indira Gandhi, maybe a call from some member of her kitchen cabinet . . . But why am I blurting out all this? I shouldn't tell you anything, Anand! You are the loyalist, I am the rebel. Why should I disclose my hand to one in the opposite camp? The enemy camp, to be more precise?'

Anand needed all his power of restraint to not lash out under such provocation. He could feel her uncontrolled anger and bitterness, suppressed for years. He knew she had nothing to lose. She wanted nothing, at any rate nothing from those whom she had come to look upon as a gang of perpetually conspiring foes. And that's where most leaders miscalculate the motives of their followers. At least some followers. There is a presumption that every politician is a careerist. That he or she is out to get something. And that he or she would do anything for that something. That is his or her price—the be-all and end-all. Put up with defeat, disappointment and above all, humiliation . . . While the presumption is true enough in most cases, there are exceptions. Aruna was one.

*

The President of India is a Constitutional authority. He is comparable to the King or Queen of England, with one important difference. The succession to the British throne is hereditary, while in the case of the President of India, it is by election. A limited electoral college consisting of members of parliament and the state legislative assemblies elects him. The President has no real political power, yet his position has the highest prestige and honour the nation can give any individual. The government's decisions are all issued in the President's name. He is the commander-in-chief of the country's armed forces. He 'appoints' the Prime Minister, ministers, judges of the Supreme Court and the High Courts, governors of states and a host of other very high functionaries in government. He accepts the credentials of ambassadors of foreign governments. He addresses the houses of parliament, to expound on what 'my government' proposes to do—even if that actually amounts to reading the 'address' prepared for him by the government. And most important of all, he is looked upon as the eldest in the family, the father figure whom the government headed by the Prime Minister looks to for advice and guidance.

Both the previous Presidential elections had been foregone conclusions. The candidate fielded by the ruling party won hands down—Dr Rajendra Prasad and Dr Radhakrishnan, the former for a second term also. There had been some reservations each time—first about Dr Rajendra Prasad's second term, and then about Dr Radhakrishnan's candidature, since he was not from the nation's political leadership. However, once Jawaharlal Nehru had made up his mind, that had been the end of it. The party had put its imprimatur on its candidate, and its nominee had walked into the Rashtrapati Bhavan in style.

There had been some controversy for a while on the President's powers while Dr Rajendra Prasad was in office. There was protracted correspondence on this subject between Rajendra Prasad and Jawaharlal Nehru. There had been no discernible rancour of any kind. No one had believed the rumours set afloat by Delhi's political busybodies, trying to foment the illusion of a clash of personalities . . . In any event, the controversy had tapered off long ago.

Now, in 1967, fissures were increasingly evident in the political world. For the first time, Indira Gandhi decided to field a candidate from a minority community—Dr Zakir Hussain. No one was against Zakir Sahib. His credentials were immaculate. Erudite, dignified, secular, a great freedom fighter, an educationist par excellence. All thinking sections of the people acclaimed his candidature. Many said that Mahatma Gandhi's soul would feel supremely happy at the decision. Indira Gandhi received genuine accolades. All seemed well.

Then started the internal smouldering. No one knew if Indira Gandhi had consulted her 'senior' colleagues on Zakir Sahib's nomination. No one was sure that she, or any Prime Minister, ought to, as a rule or convention. According to some, it was a party issue; the decision lay with the party parliamentary board. But then, the board largely consisted of the same 'senior' colleagues. So it was a self-defeating enterprise. However, word promptly went round that it was Indira Gandhi's individual decision. The collective wisdom of senior party men with decades of experience was not taken into account. And that reason alone, the argument said, vitiated the decision—however good it was.

It was a question of principle, they asserted. And so it was, on the basis of the facts alleged. No one, however, wondered if principle would have figured at all if Jawaharlal had been the Prime Minister. So, once again, the personality of the Prime Minister made the difference. How could they let Indira Gandhi dominate over this crucial issue by taking a subjective and individual decision? It should not be allowed, those opposed to her asserted.

However, it was not easy to find a candidate comparable to Zakir Sahib. Several hopefuls shied away. First, because no Presidential candidate stood a chance if he was contesting against the candidate of the ruling party. And second, in this case, the secular credentials of the nation were being tested, as it were. So, not many eminent persons wanted to stand against a minority candidate of Zakir Sahib's eminence. It seemed sacrilegious to oppose him—or so they thought, at least subconsciously. No one said so, but it boiled down to a question of conscience. 'Look what a thorny dilemma this Indira Gandhi has thrust on us!' senior politicians remonstrated angrily. 'She has put us right on trial! . . . If we support Zakir Sahib, we become her meek and unquestioning flock while she garners all the glory for herself. And if we oppose his candidacy, the people will call us Hindu communalists!'

While he was Chief Justice of India, Koka Subba Rao had made history with his judgment in what became a classic of sorts—the Golaknath case. A controversy over the judgement had raged for a long time. So, for better or for worse, he fulfilled one important criterion of a candidate in a presidential election: he was well known. Well known and equipped with an ideological armour of no mean significance. By then, the Golaknath judgment had generated Constitutional thunder that soon became a political dust storm. Its subject matter was of grave public concern. Briefly put, the full bench of the Supreme Court under Subba Rao had declared that the fundamental rights enumerated in chapter III of the Constitution of India are inviolable. In particular, they override the directive principles of state policy set out in chapter IV. In other words, if any measure contemplated by the government in pursuance of the directive principles of state policy was construed by a court to interfere with a 'fundamental' right—of expression, association, profession, etc.—that measure would be null and void under the Constitution and could not be carried out. Clearly, Subba Rao had stirred up a hornet's nest. Millions of ordinary people would be affected . . . or so it seemed at the time. Public opinion in this regard rose to a crescendo. Its repercussions are still being felt.

There was more to Subba Rao's candidacy than a mere Constitutional conundrum. He appeared as a champion of every conceivable right of the Indian citizen. A great man. A great candidate. It is a pity that the great political party which brought freedom to the country should seek to defeat the great upholder of rights and freedoms. How absurd! How sad! Is there no one in the ruling party who has the courage to cry a halt to this madness? Why must the party fly in the face of fundamental rights guaranteed by the Constitution . . .?

Several other political parties joined forces behind Subba Rao. Although there was no question that his supporters could put up a good fight, his eventual defeat was certain. Even with its reduced numbers in the parliament and the state assemblies after the 1967 elections, the ruling party was a sure winner. Only a sizeable defection from the ruling party could upset the result—and teach Indira Gandhi a lesson, as her detractors within the party fervently wished.

At the other end of the spectrum were Subba Rao's detractors who had been active ever since the Golaknath judgment hit the courts, long before Subba Rao figured as a Presidential candidate.

They called him the champion of unlimited freedom, total license and, in economic terms, unbridled private enterprise. It was the antithesis of socialism and everything Jawaharlal Nehru had espoused. The Golaknath judgment, they asserted, was sure to bring the government's welfare and development measures to a grinding halt. Any cantankerous individual could hold society to ransom. Chapter IV of the Constitution would ever remain a dead letter. The only state policy to survive after Golaknath would be complete capitalism. Was that what the people of India wanted their Rashtrapati to epitomize?

Two views co-existed within the ruling party. One was the overt, 'official' pro-Zakir Sahib view. The other covert, equally fervent view favoured Subba Rao. No one pleaded openly in support of Subba Rao, but preparations for defection were well underway. It wasn't a choice between Zakir Sahib and Subba Rao, really; coming to the crunch, it was between Indira Gandhi's ascendancy and undoing. And going to the state level, it became a choice between one group and another within the ruling party. Plus the choice dictated by individual vendetta. To some, Zakir Sahib was a demi-god; to others, Subba Rao was a prophet.

One morning, Aruna sat in the Central Hall of Parliament in New Delhi, in the midst of an all-party MPs' group that extolled Subba Rao's great qualities. The group became larger and larger as the desultory business in the houses went on. A free-wheeling debate took place within the group; yet no one committed himself or herself, one way or the other. The discussion only added to the prevailing tension. It was whispered that some in the group sat there only to spy on the other participants. Indira Gandhi, it was asserted, got a verbatim minute-to-minute report of the proceedings. She was busy making her own calculations. It's a matter of her prestige, they reminded one another.

The arithmetic became more and more confusing. Many from the states projected unbelievable numbers of those intending to defect from the ruling party. Out of members of parliament alone, they counted about a hundred—and named them—as having committed their support to Subba Rao. None of them were, however, present at the time of counting. Some vociferous members argued that it was absurdly myopic of Indira Gandhi to foist a Muslim candidate on the nation, so soon after the 1965 war with Pakistan. It wasn't fair, especially for Zakir Sahib, they added with great fervour. Suppose—just suppose, they said—that he loses, how extremely embarrassing it would be for the country! Is this risk worth taking, they asked, at this juncture? Aruna was carried away by the logic of defection. There were scores of MLAs in her state who admired Subba Rao, she asserted. There would be massive defections, she predicted. She became a well-known person in the Central Hall overnight. The newspapers lionized her.

When journalists approached senior leaders for comment, their replies were largely evasive. 'The party will of course vote for Zakir Sahib, as per the whip,' one of them said, in a grudging tone. 'I don't think we should comment, at this stage, on the selection of the candidate or the timing of the election. You see, what is done is done, there's no use going into that. You want to know, what if he doesn't win? I have no comment on that; I am sure Zakir Sahib will win . . . But after all, victory and defeat are part of the game, aren't they? You want to know who made the selection? My friend, how does that make a difference? Suppose Indiraji alone made the choice, so what? Do you want me to say the Prime Minister did not consult me? That, as you know, matters very little. We all endure the consequences, don't we? The party has to stand or fall by the leader's decisions. So it has been; so it will be . . .'

Paraphrasing this circumlocution, the press correspondent reported, 'Senior party leader repudiates leadership. Says Presidential candidacy was Indiraji's individual decision. There was no consultation with party top brass. Zakir Sahib's position is at grave risk. Responsibility for defeat will be entirely on Prime Minister . . .'

To a colleague who was present at the interview, the correspondent said, 'Well . . . he didn't say that exactly . . . But he can't say he meant anything but that!'

Indira Gandhi did not pause in her tracks. The die was cast once again. Apparently, no one contacted or cajoled the intending defectors. And amidst persistent speculation forecasting the ruling party's defeat and the Prime Minister's complete loss of face, Dr

Zakir Hussain won the Presidential election against Koka Subba Rao.

'I know what happened,' said another senior leader of the party. 'And I knew that was going to happen. You see, Indiraji had already enlisted the full support of the leftist parties. What a shame that she should lean on communists in order to score points over her own party colleagues!'

'Well . . . I am not surprised at all,' commented another leader who was rumoured to have been in touch with Subba Rao's close relatives in his home state. 'Mark my words, Indira Gandhi is sure to push the country into the communist fold. She is determined to do so . . . She is not very different from a communist herself, if you want to know my frank opinion!'

Her opponents never forgave Indiraji her audacious victory.

# 42

INDIRA GANDHI TRIUMPHED—OVER WHOM, IT WAS NOT EASY TO spell out. Her victory inevitably began to add to the bitterness amongst colleagues in the ruling party. It became increasingly clear that the party, once again in its long history, faced a split due to internal conflicts. The split took its time coming, but there was no doubt that it *was* coming.

The political landscape in the country at the time held no promise of a committed path to progress. The various factions that bickered with each other endlessly ensured that nothing constructive was done. All the parties voiced their concern about the issues that faced the country, but they had neither the time nor the inclination to do anything about them; they were too busy fighting among themselves. The ruling party began to deplore the growth of separatist and parochial tendencies. Its leaders started to blame one another for these developments. They did not realize that the emerging trend of regionalism was largely due to the absence of a dominant national personality. There had been no change in the people, as such. It was the nation's political

521

leadership which was projecting its own inadequacy on the masses.

Since the 1967 general election, one verdict had sounded loud and clear: Indira Gandhi was *not* Jawaharlal. Neither collective leadership (which was non-existent anyway) within the ruling party, nor a collection of heterogeneous leaders outside it, could provide the answer to the tough new situation. The party needed to produce a strong leader or face a political situation bordering on anarchy—that was the writing on the wall.

Once the need for a leader was established, the search could hardly go beyond Indira Gandhi. She was *not* the leader—yet. However, she was a better answer than anyone else to the question, 'Who could be the leader?' . . . This summed up the situation accurately at the time. Incidentally, the country's requirement coincided with her own ambition, which could no longer be doubted or denied. Her detractors blindly opposed her. They did not realize the fact that the nation needed her tough will and determination to be in control of the situation. It was difficult to see how any of them could fancy himself as better entitled to the leader's position. Apparently, no one made any such crucial comparison. Many simply harped, in various devious ways, on what they considered Indira Gandhi's lack of legitimacy as leader. Above all, no one knew where he or she stood *vis-à-vis* Indira Gandhi any more than Indira Gandhi herself knew where she stood *vis-à-vis* the old guard. The sense of insecurity was thus mutual—and complete. Under the circumstances, even a modicum of understanding and goodwill—as distinguished from clichés of courtesy—seemed out of the question.

Had the objective conditions continued as before, the country could have taken the political splits and splinters in its stride. However, it was passing through an unprecedented crisis—indeed, a series of crises. It urgently needed political stability as never before. Some crises were internal, others external. For instance, famine and pestilence were purely internal, whereas the Chinese invasion and the war with Pakistan were external. It would not have been too difficult to deal with these sets of problems separately. However, the new phenomenon that appeared on the north-western frontier of West Bengal in 1967 was an extremely complex combination of external and internal factors, which threatened to shake the Indian socio-political system to its roots. The new challenge to the country's polity was Naxalism.

The movement began in Naxalbari, a pocket of sixty to seventy villages, mostly tribal, tucked away in the foothills of the Himalayas in the district of Darjeeling in West Bengal. It was located within easy trekking distance (forty to seventy miles) from the country's borders with Nepal, Sikkim, Bhutan, Tibet (i.e. China) and East Pakistan (later Bangladesh). The new force followed the Communist party (Marxist-Leninist) line, and its objective was the total destruction of the existing socio-political system, presumably to be replaced by a new one. It intended to wrest power via 'the barrel of a gun' as suggested by Mao Tse Tung, and it intended to create a network of Naxalbaris in the country, to organize the rural population and to capture state power. Its constituency comprised poor and downtrodden tribals, sharecroppers, students and other sections oppressed by landlords and the police, and it found that the chaos that prevailed in the country after the 1967 elections provided ideal conditions in which to grow.

The new entity came as a complete surprise to the establishment. Soon after the party came into being, it held complete sway over the villages. Many individuals were branded enemies of the Revolution by 'People's Courts', and physically liquidated. All these events in quick succession compelled many politicians to sit up and take notice. The new phenomenon sent shock waves throughout the country, far beyond the confines of the rural pocket in which it had first erupted.

Anand was disturbed by the development and, ironically, so were the landlords ranged against him. The legislative battle that raged between them became almost irrelevant. The new scenario engulfed all aspects of society—ideological, political, social, economic and administrative.

Yet for some time there was an element of complacency in the state. Naxalbari was more than a thousand miles away. It was somewhere in an obscure border area beset with special problems. So, legislators reasoned, one need not take an unduly alarmist view 'just now'. Nevertheless, many perceptive individuals clearly noted the portents of Naxalbari and the long shadows it could be expected to cast.

One morning, Anand found a police report on his desk, sent to him by Chief Minister Chaudhury. The report said there had been a small uprising in a few villages in a tribal district of the state, deep in the Reserve Forest. The normal administrative machinery did not operate in that area effectively. The area was 'ruled' by forest guards, the landlords or their agents, and moneylenders. They completely controlled the lives of the tribals—and had done so for several decades past.

Since the British rule, Agency laws did not permit any plainsman to buy land in the tribal areas. Yet for several decades, landlords and big farmers from the plains had done precisely this, through a variety of illegal but legal-looking subterfuges. The petty officials of the revenue department connived at the fraud. Consequently, the tribals had become landless and were reduced to complete penury. The report also said that for some years past, the tribals had been demanding their lands back from the landlords. In return, the landlords had begun to oppress them with utmost barbarity.

A week earlier, the report went on, a stranger (later identified as Charu Majumdar) from a distant part of the country had arrived in the area and held meetings with local tribal leaders. A local school teacher served as interpreter. The same night, about a hundred tribals got together from various villages and attacked a landlord who was visiting the area to collect his dues. They had killed the two bodyguards who accompanied him, dragged him out of the jeep he was driving and hacked him to pieces with axes and knives. By the following morning the news had spread throughout the area. Within three days, all the resident landlords had fled for refuge to the district headquarters. Equally promptly, a deputation of landlords had waited on Chief Minister Chaudhury and urged him to order effective measures to check lawlessness in the area forthwith. Several legislators had expressed public concern through press statements. Some leaders of the Opposition parties had squarely condemned the state government for its complete failure to maintain law and order in a 'sensitive' area of the state. After some days, they issued another public statement. They followed up with yet another. All from Afrozabad.

While Anand ruminated over the police report, wondering why Chaudhury had sent it to him, there was a phone call from the chief. 'Seems to be pretty grim, Anand,' he said. 'There is a heavy exodus from the area and no one knows what to do. People are arriving in the towns with stories of atrocious brutality. They are adding to the tension no end. It's a bit mystifying how such an utterly peaceful area could go up in flames overnight . . .'

'Maybe it hasn't happened overnight, Chief,' Anand commented. 'Obviously the situation has simmered for many decades. It only needed someone to fan the flames.'

'Why do you think so?'

'Because I have been studying the regulations made for the Agency tribals—made by the British government long before Independence. Our land-grabbing gentry from the plains have violated even the old British laws. From the decennial census figures, there is clearly a steep rise in the non-tribal population in the tribal areas. How can we explain this away? Did our friends from the plains go there to serve the tribals? The exploitation of the tribals by outsiders has been brutal.'

'Well, all that is water under the bridge today,' observed Chaudhury. 'We have to take up the threads now, such as they are. Why don't you come over in the evening? Let's rack our brains, if we have any . . . I shall call some others also.'

'Shekhar and his landlord cronies,' said Anand to himself, even as he promised to be present.

*

Chaudhury had assembled an impressive group at his residence. Shekhar was there, as Anand had expected. Balram represented the landlord fraternity. A senior police officer had come with the latest information from the field. The fourth was a young man of about twenty-four, whom Anand had never met. He was introduced as a research student at Calcutta University. He had all the relevant information about the theory and practice of Naxalism and its origin in the Naxalbari area. He had now come to study its influence in the distant pockets of this state. That's how he had come in contact with the local police, through whom Chaudhury had invited him to talk things over at this meeting.

The young man's account was lucid and sincere. It was not quite clear whether he was purely a researcher or also a party activist. Anand was about to ask him his name, but suppressed the question at the tip of his tongue. He remembered his own underground days, when he had never used the same name on consecutive days. Anand was struck by the young man's earnestness, and fancied that the vision of a golden era prompted the words he spoke . . . Activist or not, he was no doubt an enthusiast. Anand's own dream world of the late forties flooded his memory.

The young man traced the history of the communist movement in India. 'The communist view of the Indian polity, as it has evolved, is that India's independence was illusory and that the parliamentary system will not provide the real answer to the country's ills. The communists did not accept adherence to Constitutional means only in solving problems. I am sure there is, at the core, a consensus on this among all hues of communists. The differences consist of how to utilize, in the party's interests, the Constitutional and legal opportunities that have opened up after Independence—partial as it was, even fake, according to some of them.'

'That position has changed now in some groups of communists, hasn't it?' asked Chaudhury.

'Yes and no,' the young man said. 'I am not at all sure they have accepted parliamentary democracy without reservation, whatever their party resolutions may say from time to time.' Then, as an afterthought, he asserted, 'My own view is that even outside the communist fold, acceptance of the system is neither unanimous nor final. In fact, it cannot be final . . . and it should not be, if you don't mind my candidness.'

Surprisingly, Chaudhury said nothing very sharp to counter this view. However, Anand joined issue with the young man. 'Since you have come from Calcutta, let's call you Comrade Bannerjee for the duration of this meeting,' he began. 'Will you elaborate this last point a little more? Why are you so categorical in your reservations about democracy?'

'I'm not talking about democracy per se. And in any case, they do have that word in the communist vocabulary also. The real issue is the parliamentary system, the British model this country follows. Being only twenty-four, I haven't seen too many elections closely. The two I have observed convince me that the system is fast approaching complete breakdown. It'll be a new feudalism with the trappings of parliamentary democracy. Nothing good will come and benefit the masses, beyond crumbs from the table.'

'I can't see why you think that the substantial benefits our people received after Independence are mere crumbs from the table,' cut in Shekhar. 'If you compare today's India with the India of 1947, the difference is enormous, too glaring to shut your eyes to, by any reckoning . . .'

'That may be so,' commented Comrade Bannerjee. 'But you have to look at a given situation from the people's standpoint and not as a mere statistician or historian. You cannot possibly argue that the British did not give us anything good. They did give us some infrastructure and a sense of nationhood, perhaps forged under common adversity. And in any case, there are still many who praise the British rule. That did not make the people of India wish for British rule to continue. For a poor man in the village, the local landlord or a tyrant among the petty officials was the embodiment of the British government. That was how he judged Independence, not by the Imperial proclamations . . . And that is why, judging by the experience of people after Independence, the CPI (M-L) has concluded that the result is the same, whether it is because of the policies of the legislature of this state, or of West Bengal where one brand of communists are in power . . .'

He then proceeded to explain a lot of Marxist theory, including the allegiance of the CPI (M-L) to the Chinese brand of revolution and the shades of difference between the different revolutionary groups. Much of it was not relevant to the immediate problems of the state, but it was clear that the theoretical fermentation that had gone into the emergence of Naxalism was deep and intense. What seemed to be final, however, was the Naxalite rejection of the parliamentary system in India. They did not believe even in exploiting the system for party ends. They just wanted a total break. They had decided to work for a new system, starting from scratch.

'And the new system is the one that began in Naxalbari and whose foretaste we have just had in this state a few days back?' asked Shekhar, with a tinge of sarcasm in his voice.

Bannerjee at once noticed the dig. But he neither faltered, nor lost his temper. He said, matter-of-factly, 'Acts committed during war cannot be judged by the standards of normalcy. However, I am not aware of what you are referring to, so I can't offer any meaningful comment. I don't belong to any political party; I am only a researcher. I am not competent yet to make a political forecast. Indeed, it would be wrong for me or anyone to be dogmatic right now about the ultimate fallout of the Naxalite movement. All systems seem to be in a fluid state at the moment, notwithstanding the elections you have had since 1947. I am not sure the people are themselves committed to a system finally and irrevocably . . . I may be wrong in this judgment, so again I don't want to be dogmatic. Everything perhaps boils down to the ability to deliver the goods.'

For the first time, Balram took the cue. 'He is right,' he asserted. 'Everything boils down to delivering the goods, whatever the rhetoric.'

Chaudhury, Shekhar and Anand comprehended the significance of the utterance at once—they noticed the convergence of two extremes: the landlord and the Naxalite who was out to decimate him. It appeared quite confusing at first. Yet, one could not dismiss it. Could it be, Anand wondered, that basically these were the only two forces relevant to the Indian village? Could it also mean that eventually Mahendranath, Chaudhury, Shekhar, Anand—and, consequently, Indira Gandhi—would become irrelevant to Mahatma Gandhi's Indian village? Similar disquieting thoughts seemed to be nagging the other two, while Balram seemed quite relaxed in the immediate presence of his own most significant enemy, as it were.

'The Naxalite movement is so tiny and isolated, how do you expect it to succeed and deliver the goods, Comrade Bannerjee?' queried Anand.

'Well, I am not sure that the Indian National Congress was exactly massive when it began in 1885. The point is that Naxalism has the potential to take root and its leaders believe that conditions are ripe for its success in India. They believe that India today is even more inclined to armed struggle than China originally was. The struggle can first develop in a few impregnable pockets and then easily spread all over the country in due course.'

'Who are the party's main allies in the countryside?' asked Anand. It sounded like a question whose answer the questioner already knew. Yet, he put the question anyway.

'That part is well known,' responded Bannerjee, as expected. 'The landless segment and the small peasant are the bulwarks of the movement, while the intention is to involve the whole peasantry. With these sections securely involved in the struggle, the countryside will become extremely inhospitable to the few landlords and agents of the government in the villages. They will promptly quit the scene, as is already happening. This process can be suitably intensified or speeded up at will, by a few killings intelligently timed and spaced out. In due course, every village will become a citadel of the Revolution, where the government's writ will just not run. The fall of the cities will then only be a question of time . . .'

'Where is the need for the landlords to leave the village?' queried Anand. 'How will the landlord fit in the urban environment? He has neither the training nor the attitude to thrive in the city right now. Don't you agree?'

'I agree,' responded Bannerjee. 'In the first place, the Naxal leadership need not bother about this. The landlords will no doubt fend for themselves. Some will migrate to cities, but many, I am sure, will adjust to the new rural dispensation and get absorbed in it. They know how to cross that bridge, once they come to it . . .'

Anand looked at Balram for confirmation. Balram stared back and said vaguely, 'All this is only speculation. Your guess is as good as mine.'

'Right,' said Shekhar. 'We were only wondering about your guess, Raja sahib.' He wanted to draw Balram out, hoping for a sharp altercation between him and Anand. It was important to provoke the landlord and the Naxalite against the socialist dreamer, if possible.

'My guess, if you want to know,' said Balram, rather sharply, 'is that the landlord will survive in some form or the other. He has enormous staying power. You can't destroy him, either by force of law or force of arms . . .'

Chaudhury intervened to put the discussion back on the rails. 'Look, we want some information from Comrade Bannerjee. Anything more to ask him?'

'It is not fair to ply him with too many questions,' Anand commented, almost bringing the dialogue to an end. 'I was just wondering, Comrade Bannerjee, why you think you can bank upon the rural population supporting the Naxalites under all circumstances? There was an armed struggle in Telangana; what we heard about that experience doesn't justify your confidence. We were told that when the underground movement lost its punch, the people deserted it. Many of them became informers. And the movement itself petered out when several activists misused the resources they were given, for their own personal benefit.'

'You may be right,' admitted Bannerjee. 'The combined effect of money and secrecy can sometimes destroy the positive aspects of a movement. Yet, there are many points of difference between the Telangana struggle and the present Naxal movement. For one thing, the Telangana struggle had no model such as the Chinese revolution to follow. Besides, the Telangana struggle had not quite established, over any area, the kind of complete control that the Naxal leadership has, at least as of now. In any case, I am not making a final prognosis, as no one can or should. The unmistakable fact is that the system your party leaders decided upon for India seems to be about to crack at the base as never before.'

The issue was clearly spelt out. The conference was over. Comrade Bannerjee rose to leave. Just then, Anand shot the last and most crucial question at him. 'Suppose, Comrade,' he said, 'just suppose that the main causes of discontent at the grassroots level are removed. Then what?'

'Then nothing,' Bannerjee beamed. 'You are only begging the question. The basic postulate of Naxalism is the firm belief that this system of yours cannot do what you want me to suppose it will do. So, where does this speculation lead us? All I can say is, I shall continue crystal-gazing meanwhile.'

Bannerjee shook hands with Chaudhury and the others and withdrew, accompanied by the police officer. There was a longish silence, with each of the four remaining men trying to take in the situation. Chaudhury was the first to speak. 'Well, well,' he said, in a disproportionately loud voice. 'What do you think of the picture?'

'Pretty grim down the road,' commented Shekhar. 'However, I am not so sure that Naxalism will succeed eventually. They are too idealistic and naive to be taken seriously. They might as well be from another planet.'

'What about now, for heaven's sake?' shouted Chaudhury. 'What do you see now? Bloodshed; total failure of law and order; the state chief minister put on the mat; statements, counter-statements; exaggerated reports, lurid interviews, a feast for newshounds; Mahendranath bragging day in and day out in Delhi that such things never happened during his regime and that all this is the result of my incompetence . . . God! What a prospect!'

It was rather a shocking reaction. Chaudhury worried about *now*, about what would happen to his position. And obsessed about how Mahendranath would malign him in Delhi . . . It was a most extraordinary situation. Momentous socio-political issues threatened to cast ever-lengthening shadows far into the future. Yet, Chaudhury only saw them within the limited present. The system was being decimated from the core. Yet, state leaders thought only about their own individual future . . . There was no Jawaharlal, Anand lamented within himself, to transcend the present and to dream ahead of his time. Expediency tended to be the sole dictum.

'You haven't said anything, Balramji,' Chaudhury said, calm again, after the first spontaneous outburst. Perhaps he regretted it inwardly. 'After all, politicians will come and go; but this new phenomenon threatens your class specifically, doesn't it? How does the scenario appear to you?'

'It is ghastly, but not quite unfamiliar,' responded Balram, in a troubled yet controlled voice. 'You may take me as mad, but for once I'll be blunt, since you asked for it. It is your ruling party, I think, that is out of step with grassroots realities. You thought that the moment Independence came in 1947, the Indian people, to the last man, woman and child, had imbibed the spirit of democracy. You believed that India had become a democratic republic overnight. After that, it was just elections . . . elections . . . more elections. Promises . . . promises . . . more promises. And, of course, breaches . . . breaches . . . more breaches of those promises. Indeed, often the people could see, or you made them see, only the breaches, not positive results. In the system you devised, each political party loudly propagated the failures of the others. Not many other political parties have had the opportunity of doing anything so far, since they have not gained power. So everyone has only one song to repeat, the song of your party's failures. The people have quite naturally became failure-oriented and believe that there have been nothing but failures all round . . .'

'What has all this got to do with Naxalism, Balramji?' queried Chaudhury, rather impatient at Raja Sahib's rambling.

'I am not highly educated, unlike all of you,' Balram said with a sneer. 'But I know the rural people inside out, having lived with them all my life. Your party exploited the failures of the feudal system; the Naxalites, in turn, are now exploiting the failures of *your* system. These are even more glaring. This is only divine justice, if you ask me. This time, power is not going to come from counting votes. The Naxalites are asking the people to reject the system in which the fluctuations in politics degenerate into a perpetual game of enthroning and dethroning one's enemies and even one's closest friends. This system lets no party that comes to power think of anything but power, retaining power. When you were on top, you thought the people had accepted your system. That was wishful thinking. The feudal order also thought so, I imagine, when it reigned supreme. Now it's the Naxalites' turn to think so. With whatever consequences.'

'Your comments are not fair,' Chaudhury cut in. 'Anyway, I shall not argue for the moment. What, according to you, is the system the people want?'

Balram thought for a moment, as if weighing the pros and cons of speaking frankly. For a long time he had been fuming about the impending threat of the land ceiling law. Apart from his honest view that this was a ruinous measure for the country, he abhorred the prospect of having to surrender a major portion of his own land if the law was implemented. If it was implemented . . . In that 'if' lay his survival. And the law would not come about if he could prevent it. Presently, he broke the brief silence slowly, deliberately. 'Since we are all friends,' he began, 'we can be honest with one another. You asked me what system the people want. In my honest view, the people are in no position to make a value judgment about any system. You may wax eloquent in your public speeches about their good sense and wisdom; but I think they are still dumb, by and large. They act under inducement or threat, never of their own free will, yet. I kept them under my thumb; they came to no harm, in the ultimate analysis. I believe they were content in their own way. You and your party kept them under the spell of palliatives and bribes. That spell is being ruptured. The Naxalites will coerce them into doing whatever they want, in the name of the Revolution . . . until a superior force shatters them once again, sooner or later. Where is the people's free will in this endless tamasha? . . . I don't know what they want; all I know is that a firm hand is what they understand and comply with. That is where the Naxalites and I are of the same mind and kind, whatever the difference in rhetoric . . . I know, Chaudhuryji, you don't like what I said. Just forget it as the babble of an uneducated person. I have had my say; I don't care about anything else!'

Balram's tongue-lashing left a peculiar stillness in its wake. After a few uneasy moments, he rose to take his leave. As he shook hands with them and headed for the door, he turned abruptly and said, 'I must add that the Naxalites are no friends of the landlord. Nor are they his foes. They simply have to kill the landlord to become heroes in the eyes of the people. And then they will be much more despotic than the feudals. Your democracy did away with feudalism, only to deliver the people to the Naxalites. You are only a passing phase, a conduit, really.' And he swaggered out in his usual style.

The three men left behind stared vacantly at one another. Something new weighed on their minds—the imminence of a systemic crisis. Well, we are all insignificant; it is for the national leadership to sort these things out . . . That seemed a good alibi. Yet, who or what was national leadership? Indira Gandhi? Morarji Desai? The splinter groups fattening on Indira's political largesse and basking in her glory? The Opposition splinters (none of them were even 'parties', technically)? . . . Suddenly, it occurred to them: what would Jawaharlal have done when faced with a situation of this kind? Despite their differences, a thought crossed all their minds—if only Jawaharlal were here now!

Chaudhury looked at Anand and said, 'You have been very quiet all afternoon. What is cooking in your mind? Is it anything positive? Are we any wiser for Brihaspati's dialogue with Comrade Bannerjee?'

'I don't know,' Anand replied. 'Once again since Independence, there is a serious challenge to the system we have chosen. I am coming back to the same question . . . Can we make it deliver the goods and save India?'

# Part V

# 43

THE SIGNAL OF THREAT TO THE SYSTEM WENT UNNOTICED. THE power game became more and more relentless. There was no way the ruling party could avert a split. The only course was to unite on the programme already committed to the people and implement it without further delay. That, however, was now out of the question. The programme no longer enjoyed unanimous support within the party, whatever the public postures. Differences surfaced in respect of the content, and even more glaringly, the pace and time-frame of implementation.

The picture of instability was complete when governments in several states fell. They had sprung up in 1967, mainly through opportunistic alliances to gain power. Their fall, ironically enough, came about due to the same opportunism. It couldn't be otherwise, and they fell midway through their five-year term. This took the country unawares. It was like a downpour in midsummer for which neither the land is ready nor the farmer: it is good for neither, bad for both.

The hunger for power, however, grew apace—the inevitable

result of ideological promiscuity. What the government did or wanted to do, was now no longer news. The only news that interested any reader was who became a minister or was kicked out of the ministry. Power became a game, a source of entertainment, like the fights between gladiators in the Roman Empire or cockfights and bullfights in medieval Indian principalities . . . The people figured nowhere. Anand and those of his bent of mind looked on, helpless. He had met several ministers and legislators of coalition governments in the northern states, besides those of his own party all over the country. When their acquaintance deepened, they invariably began to confide in each other. And the same anguish poured forth from almost everyone.

In August there were torrential downpours in some states while drought conditions continued in others. Nature was so erratic and cruel sometimes that just when a state government was about to implement a drought scheme prepared after much effort, overnight cloudbursts upset everything and the government had to switch to flood relief measures. The unpredictability of the monsoon and of the twists and turns in the political drama had become equally noteworthy in the Indian scene.

\*

Anand was on one of the usual visits to Delhi on conference work. An MP friend got him a pass to the Distinguished Gallery of the Lok Sabha and to the Central Hall. He sat in the Gallery for some time and then strayed into the Central Hall.

There was tension in the Central Hall. If you had the eyes to see or the sensitivity to perceive, you couldn't miss it, couldn't mistake it. The moment you entered, you felt in your bones that the nation was in for something terribly important.

Honourable members of parliament were locked in whispered confabulations—in twos, threes and fours. There were also a couple of larger huddles with eight to ten participants in distant corners of the Hall. Bearers from the canteens moved slowly up and down the aisles and between tables. They carried trays full of the food meant for the nation's law-givers. Presumably, the stuff determined the course of the law—and, consequently, the fortunes of the nation—in no small measure. The bearers, by their bearing and pace, symbolized the country's onward march. Their progress was leisurely, laconical, unhurried, yet with a dignity all its own.

On that day, however, all the familiar scenes of Central Hall were wrapped in an unfamiliar sense of foreboding. Members talked in hushed, agitated tones. Anand found the attendance in the Central Hall unusually heavy, in sharp contrast to the House where he had just heard the quorum bell ring time and again.

The first group of legislators, sitting nearest the main entrance that day, consisted of Shri Pandey from Uttar Pradesh, Shri Menon from Kerala and Shri Bandopadhyaya from West Bengal. All were from the ruling party, middling in seniority, bantam weight in influence. They were exceedingly voluble and were often fielded to speak on crucial issues. Aggressive supporters of the Prime Minister, they were in their element when she was present in the House.

'I tell you, it's going to be massive this time . . .,' said Menon, glancing furtively around.

'I don't know,' mused Pandey. 'We've heard this so often . . .'

'It's not like other times,' confirmed Bandopadhyaya. 'From all indications, I agree it's going to be massive, really . . .'

At this point entered Doctor Chintadripetapadu Veera Venkata Lakshmi Prasanna Rama Somayajulu from Andhra Pradesh. Unable to handle this speech-long name from the south-central region, MPs had abbreviated it suitably. Joining the first and last syllables, they simply called him Dr Chilu. The moment he heard the word 'massive', Dr Chilu stopped, as if he were braking suddenly. Being a good physician he couldn't imagine anything massive to be other than a heart attack. He asked, with some concern, 'Massive? Who is it? Who has had the massive heart attack?' And before anyone could reply, the doctor-MP continued, with transparent anxiety, 'Too bad, too bad. I'm coming from the Willingdon Nursing Home. Looks like half the parliament is permanently there. You could hold a session in the nursing home with an assured quorum. Too bad . . .'

'Relax, doctor. Relax,' cut in Bandopadhyaya. 'Take it easy; no heart attack—yet. We're talking about the cabinet reshuffle.'

The doctor's compassion at once turned into the politician's crafty animation. He sat down heavily. 'Oh yes, yes,' he crooned. 'I heard something too. The air is full of cabinet reshuffle. Like pollen, or pollution—I don't know which!' And he joined the others as they plunged into a detailed review of the possibilities, timing, etc. of the approaching changes.

About six benches to the right sat another group consisting of Somanna of Karnataka, Chaudhri Ramnarayan Singh of Haryana, Papeshwar Jha from Bihar, Stephenson from Meghalaya and a heavyweight lady member with a clearly visible moustache that looked like a neat strip of unmown lawn on her upper lip. The moustache almost proved the equality of the sexes guaranteed under our Constitution. Her waist was of equatorial girth and appearance; it made her look like a moving globe. She belonged to a state where a visible moustache, such as hers, adorns the upper lip of most women—or so they said.

The median age of this group was within the septuagenarian range. Having weathered five stormy elections—now sinking, now sailing—they had successfully made it to parliament in the recent election. Naturally, they were speculating how many senior ministers would get the axe in the coming reshuffle. They were irritated at the extraordinary durability of some septuagenarian ministers. These toughies lived on and on; what was worse, they also stayed on and on in power. This was obviously unfair to other septuagenarians, who now stood in the dreadful danger of not coming to power at all. They also fumed at the recent new-fangled nonsense about the need for young blood in the cabinet—and fresh flesh, they added sarcastically.

'This time, there is going to be a clean sweep of the old guard,' said the Chaudhri, relishing every word. 'I just can't imagine why the PM has kept so many of them on for so long. It's preposterous. No wonder nothing happens in their ministries and the country goes to the dogs, meanwhile . . .'

'And no experienced women legislators either,' added the hirsute lady member. 'I don't see how you can expect these tired and eccentric men to understand the woes of the housewife. What an irony that this should happen when a lady is Prime Minister!'

Stephenson joined in the tirade heartily, adding some bitter parenthetical remarks about the neglect of minorities from the very sensitive and difficult north-east region . . . Their discussion trailed off suddenly when they saw Shri Nag, a minister with a major portfolio, approaching them, squeezing his way through the rows of benches. Shri Nag was one of the redoubtable septuagenarians who refused to leave the ministerial ranks under anything short of a divine decree. His rotund figure appeared to be composed of three spheres. The first and the largest, of course, was the torso. On that rested the second, the melon-shaped head. Upon this bloomed his gigantic nose, a mass of warts and bumps. Indeed, his face was all nose and little else. It had earned him the nick-name of Shri Naak (Mr Nose). He naturally gravitated to the group of fellow-septuagenarians and stood near them for a while. They requested him to sit down but he refused politely because once he sat down, it would be a tremendous task to stand up again. The group thought that he looked rather crestfallen. His face, they thought further, confirmed that some of the oldsters were in for the axe. Shri Nag exchanged a few pleasantries with them. He knew that they knew that he knew the end was at hand.

Then there was a sudden stir. The Prime Minister appeared and walked briskly across the Central Hall, evidently on her way from one House to the other. Suddenly everyone stood up, and the simultaneous movement created an optical illusion as though the domed ceiling of the Central Hall had risen higher too. She proceeded at a steady pace, acknowledging greetings, sprinkling smiles, tempering authority with grace and shrouding both authority and grace in a palpable aura of suspense and mystery. Every member felt his pulse throb a bit faster. They had, of course, seen her a thousand times; yet, during the 'reshuffle season', each member tended to fancy that she had thrown at him a special glance. The glance meant a favour and an indication. The indication conjured up an image in his mind: his swearing-in as minister. And since the Prime Minister did things unexpectedly, even those who normally did not expect to be ministers expected to be ministers. Such was the fascinating logic of ministry-making.

Further down, southwest of the septuagenarian group, sat a few young MPs, mostly first-termers. It was difficult even to consider them for ministerial positions. They simply had no chance—yet. They were sprightly and cheerful. They were enjoying themselves irreverently at the expense of the elephants in the rat race. In this group was Mirza, the poet-cum-satirist from Uttar Pradesh, with a beautiful doll-like face, delicate lips and hippie hair. Urdu couplets appropriate to the occasion flowed spontaneously from his shapely mouth, along with a constant spray of paan spittle. Then, there was Chowbe of Madhya Pradesh, whose spittle-spray was no less copious. So were his smutty jokes which made him very popular, particularly among women members who made it a point to protest what they called 'such woman-baiting ribaldry'—*after* they had heard it with relish, of course. The next was Bedi from Punjab, whose jet black beard furnished a perfect frame for his classic, fair-complexioned face. He was also a master of ribaldry and claimed with pride—with no one from anywhere else to contradict him—that in this respect too, as in many others, Punjab topped the list in the whole country. Besides these members from the ruling party, there were a few from the Opposition. Their position would remain unchanged. They were not suffering from any tension. So, they drew intense vicarious pleasure from watching the agonized deliberations of members of the ruling party. They brought to mind some of the impotent nawabs of medieval times, who derived satisfaction from watching orgies from close quarters, as the nearest substitute for participating in them.

'Take it from me,' Mirza assured the group, 'the minister over there, whispering to that male lady member will get admitted to the Jaslok Hospital in Bombay in a day or two . . .'

'From Lok Sabha to Jaslok Sabha, you mean?' quipped Chowbe.

'Surely better than the Parlok Sabha, isn't it?' punned Bedi.

They cracked jokes and made fun of the ministerial aspirants. Just the same, you could find in their talk an undercurrent of what you could call derision for the unattainable. All in all, even this group felt the tension, though for no particular reason. They were not concerned, yet still concerned very much—why and how, they could not explain. The tension was all-pervasive; no one was immune.

Anand remembered that it had all started with a two-column dispatch sent from Delhi by the special correspondent of a southern daily newspaper. Shorn of its circumlocutory verbiage, it said that the Prime Minister was looking for fresh talent within her party. She wanted to give her cabinet a new look and make it more efficient and dynamic. Going a step further, the correspondent had predicted the possible removal of a lot of 'dead wood' that was cluttering up the cabinet. For one thing, the whole tribe of deputy ministers, the journalist pointed out, was redundant. Some of them would get promoted, while other heads would simply roll. And so on up the line, including some septuagenarians who had outlived their utility.

Many readers believed this special correspondent to be well-informed. His forecasts only rarely came true, but his readers believed every such forecast. Some who found it favourable to themselves believed it the more. Others whose prospects the report discounted, hoped that it was just another figment of the correspondent's imagination . . . The result of this fascinating bit of journalism was that within twenty-four hours, all the ministers who were touring all over the country converged on Delhi. They left their inspections, conferences, seminars, symposia, constituency visits, rest camps and pleasure jaunts—everything— halfway. Those who had gone abroad, leading delegations or on assignments to explain India's stand on this or that issue, returned to Delhi as soon as Air India could find them a seat. They left the rest of their tasks to their seconds-in-command, deputies, Indian ambassadors—and to God. And all the hopefuls, too, scurried back to Delhi in record time from wherever they were, by whichever mode of travel was available. No one had sent them notices. The fugitive aroma of power needed no notice and waited for none. And the Central Hall of parliament came alive.

Every cabinet reshuffle has its own rationale. In this particular instance, since it was to be massive, it had to be a plus-and-minus, add-and-drop affair. Taking the drop part first, many ministers could be dropped, of course. There were some who definitely had to be dropped—their identity depending on whose opinion you solicited. Shri Sundaram, for instance, had proved a failure as a minister. In case he got the sack, Shri Armugam, MP, stood, or thought he stood, a fair chance of entering the council of ministers. So Shri Armugam waxed eloquent on what an unmitigated disaster Shri Sundaram had been, on how he had brought a bad name to his (their) state, on how he could be of no use in the impending elections, and so on. Only a month earlier, Shri Armugam had praised Sundaram to the skies. However, that was a full month ago—too long a period for politicians to keep their opinions unchanged. Besides, there was no cabinet reshuffle in the air then. The situation had now changed qualitatively. And in any event, hadn't someone said that consistency is the virtue of a donkey?

Everyone said that Shri Pyarelal, Shri Kutty and Dr (Mrs) Sharma were useless as ministers. Yet, each of them had his or her own plus points. If X got the axe, he would go back to his state and make the chief minister's life miserable there. If the Prime Minister dropped Y, the landlords in his state would start an agitation for or against something or the other—no matter what. If Z was dropped, he would just drop down dead; he was a chronic heart patient and political power alone sustained his heart, contrary to all diagnostic criteria known to medical science . . . And there was another minister whose powerful caste lobby, which he took great care to nurse, would be furious if he were to get the sack. Yet another minister was so worthless that the Prime Minister would not find it worthwhile even to remove him . . . All of which meant that dropping ministers was not as easy as some people believed.

Nor was it easy to induct new ministers on sheer merit. And speaking of merit, you had to admit that for purposes of ministry-making, merit was, or had come to be, of many kinds—such as merit of birth, merit of money, merit of potential mischief, merit of unquestioning personal loyalty, and so on. It was not just a question of picking the best man—no sir, it was not that simple. Not like the Union Public Service Commission. For instance, if there were already two ministers from a state, a third from the same state, even if he had excellent credentials, could not get in through the normal channels. His chances would therefore depend on the stars of the other two—in addition, of course, to his own. Then, there was the complicated question of the Russian and the American lobbies. No one seriously believed that the Prime Minister listened to any lobby. Still, those lobbies, whatever they were, came in handy in political circles, as an alibi for those who had hoped to become ministers but did not. After all, it was more respectable to be called the victim of the capitalist or the communist lobby, rather than be branded as just not good enough for a minister's post. Reports had it that some ministers were to step down umpteen times in the past, but this or that lobby had saved them—how, no one cared to explain . . .

Many incidents had conspired to make a major reshuffle appear imminent this time. To several ministers, it was a real question of 'to be or not to be'—in Delhi. One persistent rumour had it that the Prime Minister was demanding letters of resignation from ministers. This meant that a convenient absence from Delhi for some days could perhaps stave off the danger temporarily. There was always the hope that meanwhile the PM might have second thoughts on the resignations, or something unforeseen would make the proposed reshuffle less urgent. And once you were able to stall something, it would, hopefully, get stalled indefinitely. That was the common experience of those long entrenched in the government. This resulted in a sudden spurt of extended tours of ministers all over the country, and wherever possible, abroad. There was thus a two-way traffic of ministers returning to Delhi in a hurry and leaving Delhi in a panic.

Too many senior ministers had entered the Willingdon Nursing Home, Delhi. From there, they had graduated, as it were, to the Jaslok Hospital, Bombay. Some had even managed to get their ailments internationalized, by proceeding to New York, Boston, Houston, London or Vienna. Yet, according to their own statements, these ministers never suffered from any ailment. They needed nothing more than a 'check-up'. This time too there were many check-up admissions, but the check-ups became unusually long. Soon, their detractors triumphantly crowed that some ministers were 'unadmittedly' sick.

A couple of weeks before the current session of parliament, feverish activity and mad speculation gripped New Delhi. This was just the time for the reshuffle. Another week, and you could forget about it, because there was usually no reshuffle during a session or immediately before it. So, it was either now, or not for quite some time. Speculation on the fortunes of the hopefuls fluctuated from day to day, hour to hour. Shri Nag was going, they said one Saturday. But a photograph appeared in the Sunday newspapers, showing the Prime Minister and Shri Nag laughing, possibly over something funny. Promptly Shri Nag's followers used that photograph as a flag to wave, as a club to beat their opponents with and as a magic wand to hypnotize everyone. Who says Shri Nag is going, they asked, brandishing the photograph. Don't you know, you ignorant fools, that Shri Nag is very close to the Prime Minister these days? . . . The anti-Nag faction would not give in that easily. Let's see who has the last laugh, they countered quizzically. Look at the very picture you're waving about. While the Prime Minister's smile is natural and absolutely charming, Shri Nag's grin looks grotesque. It clearly betrays nervousness and panic. Even a blind man can see the difference. No question about it, Shri Nag is on his way out . . . Besides, what do you know about the Prime Minister? My dear misguided and over-optimistic friends, don't you know that when she appears more cordial than usual and showers more smiles than necessary, it means a pleasant farewell? That's history, my dear sinking comrades, history for you. She reserves her broadest smiles for the outgoing. So what are you bragging about, hoisting that photograph? You ought to be organizing a farewell meeting instead!

Thus raged the controversies, interpretations, claims and counter-claims, provoking a nerve-shattering guessing game. It was said that Friday and Saturday were crucial for reshuffles. Statistics indicated that most reshuffles took shape during Saturday night and took place on the following morning. Whatever the fact, this was the superstition. And as Sunday approached, tension grew by the minute.

On Friday afternoon, the Prime Minister inaugurated an

international meet on science and technology in Vigyan Bhavan. To the utter amazement of the foreign scientists attending the seminar, Indian MPs occupied the entire front half of the hall. There was virtually a nodding competition among them while the Prime Minister spoke. However, after she left, the front half of the hall became practically empty . . . One eminent foreign scientist, fascinated by the keen interest of Indian parliamentarians in science and technology, asked one of them about it. The MP did not know English, so a journalist served as interpreter. To the foreigner's question, the MP gave a forthright answer—in his mother-tongue, of course. Said he, 'Science and technology?No, brother! We came because the PM came!' 'Sir,' the journalist interpreted, smiling ingratiatingly,'under the inspiring leadership of our Prime Minister, all members of parliament have developed a remarkable interest in science and technology!'

No less interesting were the goings-on in the Central Secretariat, Anand learned later. While the normal movement of normal files practically came to a standstill, some files started moving with abnormal speed. They were disposed of with unusual thoroughness and efficiency. No one could say which of the ministers would go. Everyone made a forecast according to his wish. And why not? Until the event actually happened, one forecast was as good as another. It provided the sadistic satisfaction that human beings constantly seek in one another's downfall. Consequently, the presumption was that almost every minister was on his way out. The secretary of Shri Nag's ministry was busy obstructing every file from going to Shri Nag. He interrupted circulation by raising silly queries. He passed interim orders to send the files back. Wherever that was not possible, he just stuffed some crucial files in his 'confidential' locker, from where no one else could retrieve them. He had been at loggerheads with Shri Nag for quite some time. About two years ago they had come into fierce conflict over the grant of a license. The battle had developed into a 'scandal' and attracted many inconvenient mentions in parliament . . . Now was the time for the secretary to settle scores. Eagerly awaiting Shri Nag's ignominious dismissal from the cabinet, he did everything to retain on record every trace of the minister's guilt and misuse of power. He was already making out a case for the appointment of a commission of inquiry that would damage Shri Nag's public reputation for good. He had also chosen, with great care, members of the Opposition to whom he would pass on the relevant information, along with photostat copies of all important documents.

Saturday night. The tension became simply intolerable. Each minister's private secretary tried to elicit the latest information from every other minister's private secretary. Ministers' wives invariably turned to God that night with non-stop prayers, trying to exert last-minute pressure on the Almighty. All long-distance telephone lines in the country were blocked. The operators, already harassed for almost a month, found it impossible to cope with the unprecedented number of lightning calls. The calls would eventually be certified as 'official' and debited to the government, Central or state . . .

Has the axe fallen? Have the outgoing ministers submitted their resignations? Who are they? Has the Prime Minister finalized the new list and sent it to Rashtrapati Bhavan? . . . Are you absolutely sure? Is there any unusual activity in Rashtrapati Bhavan at this time of the night? What about the Prime Minister's house? Are press correspondents bustling about, missing their customary booze at the Press Club? . . . And when the telephone lines went dead in the middle of a conversation, exasperated politicians shouted louder and louder. They insisted on shouting across the country, even without the phones . . .

One thing was, however, universal. No one's sympathies lay with the ministers who were about to get the chop. Those who had presented them with long-winded welcome addresses in silver caskets, had praised them to the skies and pampered them twenty-four hours a day, were now busy finding clinching reasons for their removal. They asserted it was already long overdue. The message was clear: barring a few exceptions, every person in power stood alone, at the moment of his fall, as at the moment of his death. And death appeared to be the better of the two, since it evoked sympathy at least.

The fateful night wore on and on.


On Sunday morning, newspapers reported a communiqué issued from Rashtrapati Bhavan. It said that the President of India, on the advice of the Prime Minister, was pleased to order an interchange of the portfolios held by two deputy ministers . . .!

Such anticlimaxes became frequent. Time and again, a reported cabinet reshuffle raised hopes and created excitement. It featured prominently in the news, but nothing came of these reports. The speculation about the reshuffle—which did not eventually happen—had thrown up many names and sullied many reputations. This led to all-round suspicion and anger. These fomented bitter personal animosity. Added to this frustrating atmosphere was the endless bickering and the overriding compulsion to come into power or retain it at any cost. This led to a situation where legislators became permanent antagonists, behaving like permanent enemy groups. The activity was political, but the minds behind it were feudalistic and implacable all the way. They simply could not co-exist in the same party. All these factors led to the disastrous split, by far the most decisive in the party's recent history.

MOMENTOUS EVENTS LIKE THE VERTICAL SPLIT IN A RULING PARTY
are triggered by complex motivations. Yet the actors in the drama
are often blinkered by their own obsessions. It was the same in the
split of 1969. No other event had such a decisive impact on
subsequent developments in the political life of the nation. Every
politician had contributed in some way to it, yet when it eventually
took place, determined efforts were made to blame it on one
person: Indira Gandhi.

Everyone could see it coming; indeed before it happened, the
country itself had split into two schools of thought. There were
regional variations of course, and local differences that resulted in
clashes, but as time wore on, the people on either side of the divide
had come to be perceived as either pro-rich or pro-poor.

Anand was busy with some complicated files one day when
Chief Minister Chaudhury rang up to introduce a respected Delhi
journalist. He was the former editor of a national newspaper, and
was a trusted figure in Central cabinet circles. He had come down
to the state capital to explore a lead. Would Anand see him and

550

discuss the national scene?

'As you say,' Anand responded. Immediately, some instinct was aroused within him. He asked, 'Since you know him well, could you give me a tip? Has he come here with a message from one of the groups poised for the coming intra-party Kurukshetra?'

'How do I know? You will have to probe that yourself, I'm afraid,' replied Chaudhury.

'Given the eminence of the person, his intimate connections at the highest levels, the current intense political activity in Delhi which no responsible Delhi-based journalist would normally miss by visiting a state . . . Don't you think there is something more to this visit?' Anand persisted.

'Could be,' said Chaudhury. 'But why are you shooting these questions at me?'

'Just in case he has given you some inkling of why he is here. If so, you could perhaps tell me what you want me to ferret out . . . and more to the point, what to tell him!'

Chaudhury was silent for a few minutes. Then he said, 'Look, I wouldn't want to influence your own judgment one way or another. I prefer you chart out your course yourself . . . No clues from me at the moment . . . And report to me as soon as possible.'

The cunning fox! Keeping his options open, even while creating confusion! Anand was positive that Chaudhury *did* want to influence his (Anand's) judgment, albeit in a devious way. Or alternatively, to set up a debate and watch its progress, sitting comfortably on the fence. He wanted Anand to advocate Indira Gandhi's cause openly, and perhaps wanted some other minister to take the opposite side, while he kept quiet himself until the result became a foregone conclusion. In any event, this journalist could not have come here without Chief Minister Chaudhury having a hand in it.

Anand made a mental note of all these factors and said, 'Okay, please send him at once. I'll keep my files aside and order a cup of coffee for him, meanwhile . . .'

In about twenty minutes, Anand's private secretary ushered in the neat, stocky and self-assured Shanker Das. There was something very correct in the poise and demeanour of the man.

His clipped and short sentences and pointed sallies revealed a sharp mind. He must have written many forthright editorials in his heyday and created ripples in all circles. On the whole, he struck Anand as a well-meaning, extremely well-informed, suave, clear-headed, no-nonsense old-world journalist and political commentator. His approach was essentially patriotic and bore the stamp of the freedom struggle. He was the product of a dedicated era in the country's recent history. At seventy-four, he was hale and hearty—and proud of it, like many others of his generation.

Das at once struck up a personal rapport with Anand. He compared him with his own son and introduced his wife and other members of his family, in absentia, wrapping up this sidelight with a standing invitation to Anand to visit the family, have a 'meal and a chat' as often as he could manage, when he was in New Delhi. He established a 'no formality' relationship—or tried to. This remarkably relaxed attitude of the old-timer, at once earnest and consummate, impressed Anand.

Then followed a wide-ranging discussion on the current political situation in the country and abroad. Das waxed eloquent on the country's economic chaos. He said he could clearly see the after-effects of the recent war with Pakistan. Catastrophic droughts and floods had worsened the situation. He regretted the lack of coordinated and effective measures to stem the rot. His presentation was lucid, realistic, unexceptionable.

Finally, he came to the thrust of his argument. Is *this* the time to split the ruling party, he demanded. Can't she (meaning Indira Gandhi, of course) consolidate the party during the rest of her term? Shouldn't she face the next election—her second—with greater unity?

The questions sounded like a chargesheet. Though politely phrased, they were partisan in the extreme. And worse still, Anand found them simplistic and rhetorical.

Anand was surprised—and a little saddened. When urbanity serves as a mere mask, bluntness is perhaps the answer. However, Anand did not resort to that weapon. He knew it would be effective, but he also feared that it could impair the rapport that the elderly visitor had built up within a few minutes. He didn't want the link full of future possibilities to erode.

'Dasji,' he said. 'You have seen many vicissitudes in the country's history. Please tell me, is there a specified time when the ruling party is allowed to split? Are any such a priori conditions conceivable?'

'Well, normally no,' Das conceded.

'Exactly,' Anand responded. 'Next, I must say I don't know much about Delhi politics and I depend entirely on you to enlighten me. Now, who is forcing the split? Is it Indira Gandhi?'

'Undoubtedly,' Das asserted. 'She has no confidence in her senior colleagues, but can't jettison them. So, she wants her own empire and hopes to make it acceptable to the people all by herself, even at the risk of ruining the party in the process . . .'

'Dasji, two years back there was a general election in which all the old stalwarts in the party had their full say, as far as I know. The only new person on the scene was Indira Gandhi. Why did the party get such a drubbing in a major part of the country then?'

Das jumped at the opening offered by this query. 'That's precisely what the elderly leaders argue,' he declared. 'This is the time to close ranks, not to split . . . See?'

'I quite see their point, but tell me, Dasji, what do we mean by closing ranks? Doesn't it mean, in simple terms, that Indira Gandhi, the leader, should follow her senior colleagues? Isn't that the essence of their opinion?'

'Well, that is not how *I* would put it, really. The cabinet, after all, is a team and must function as a team. That's how it has been since Panditji . . .'

'Many don't share that observation, I'm afraid,' Anand commented. 'Panditji's cabinet, they say, was just Panditji; others only toed the line, at any rate after Sardar Patel's death. And the suggestion now seems to be that they simply reverse these roles, since Indira Gandhi is not Panditji. She should confine herself to the vote-catcher's role, while all else comes from the senior colleagues . . . As a party worker, I'm not concerned with these roles; I merely want results. And the fact remains that the programmes dictated by the senior leaders fell short of the people's expectations in the 1967 election. They need change, overhaul, reorientation, reinvigoration, a face-lift, partial reversal—call it what you will . . . And they need it urgently . . .'

'You seem to have made up your mind, more or less,' Das commented, showing some impatience for the first time. 'How do you react to the general belief that the party's debacle in 1967 was mainly due to disunity?'

'I don't think there was any single reason for the party's bad showing,' observed Anand. 'Unity is always essential in a political party, but unity for what? And to what effect? In my district, for example, we were all united in 1952, with Jawaharlal Nehru as our supreme leader. Still, we lost almost all the seats, because there was a more compelling political force operating to influence the voters. So why don't the leaders sit together now and thrash out a new programme to attract the voter? This would be a direct attack on the problem, wouldn't it? And if the leadership does this together, that would be excellent, of course. Please tell me, Dasji, will that happen? What have you concluded from your observations of these Delhi intrigues?'

Shanker Das was silent for few moments. Then, with a helpless sigh, he began, 'Alas! If only that could happen! I'm afraid, Anandji, that as long as Indiraji flouts tested policies and programmes, there is very little scope for united action in the party. That, I think, is the real hitch . . .'

'Wait a minute, Dasji,' Anand interjected. 'Why do you club policies and programmes together? I thought that the basic policies of the party were never in question; they are right and time-tested. No other political party has improved upon them. However, programmes are a different matter. They can, and must, vary with the needs of the time. Their thrust can change, priorities could differ, their presentation should be altered to suit the mood of the people . . . The 1967 elections have proved beyond doubt that it is imperative to institute change. And as far as I understand, the difference, in essence, is in the areas of programmes . . .'

Again Shanker Das reflected a little before he spoke. 'I am not quite certain that the distinction you have made is valid,' he commented. 'Even granting it is, I know that Indira Gandhi does not support the idea of forging an agreed programme. She is leaning more on communist ideologues than her own colleagues in the party. She is, in effect, shattering the party's unified ethos and culture . . .'

'I am not competent to pronounce judgement on the ethos and culture of a a political party,' Anand countered. 'Nevertheless, I believe that even the ethos and culture of this party have changed from time to time. At every decisive turn in the party's history, there came a change. When the masses of India came into the party's fold in a big way under Mahatma Gandhi, there was a great change in its base and culture. When Gandhiji gave the call to "do or die", there was a similar extraordinary change. When he linked political agitation with economic self-reliance, there was a definite change. Earlier, when the party switched its objective from Dominion Status to Poorna Swaraj, its ethos was completely transformed . . . Even granting that Indira Gandhi is trying to change the ethos of the party now, the change is neither the first nor the last . . . So why can't the leaders see what is coming and let it happen painlessly?'

Shanker Das found the argument getting out of hand. Listening to Anand, he realized how subjective his own arguments were. He shrugged his shoulders a little and said, 'Your reasoning is plausible but many people see it only as an unseemly scramble for power—nothing more.'

'In that case, I have no reason to participate in that treacherous game, do I?' retorted Anand. 'Here, we are grappling with numerous intractable problems at the grassroots level. Why should we look at the situation except with the eyes of the common villager? I don't mean to say that there is no scheming thirst for power here at the state level; of course there is, and it's even more unscrupulous. And when the chips are down, our divisions here eventually get aligned, somehow, at some point, with those at the Centre. But what stares us in the face now, Dasji, is the next election . . . and the one after that . . . and so on. We need to do something for the masses on a continuing basis, in the party's own interest, if nothing else. If a village got a drinking water well before one election, we cannot harp on the well in the next election. That is where the party's programme becomes important and relevant.

While I find myself too small to compare the personalities of national leaders, I can certainly compare their programmes and come to a judgment . . . Don't you agree, Dasji?'

'I do, but where do you find a difference in the programmes? It is the party's programme, not that of an individual—any individual's, however highly placed . . .'

'I have no problem with that,' observed Anand. 'However, as a party worker, and a potential candidate in the next election, I would like to make sure that I can sell the party's programme and get myself elected. Tell me, Dasji, are you sure that such a programme is on the anvil in the party high command?'

'I am not quite sure,' replied Shanker Das. 'Anyway, I don't know the whole story—yet. What I am positive about is that there are serious differences in the high command on items like the nationalization of banks . . . The move may look popular and attractive, but in the new set-up banks will have to advance loans to too many poor people, without security. Their losses will be too heavy and the country's economy will be in a shambles before you know what is happening . . .'

'What makes you think so, Dasji?' cut in Anand. 'On what basis was that conclusion about poor loanees arrived at? Were any studies conducted at the field level?'

'I don't know,' observed Shanker Das. 'Indeed, I don't see why a study is at all necessary. Is it not natural that a person who is too poor to repay a loan will just not pay?'

'Do you know the experience of thousands upon thousands of private moneylenders operating for centuries in the rural areas? Do they find it impossible to recover the loans they advance to the poor people? If that were so, how do you think they have stayed in this profession and, in fact, become richer and richer over time? And about prompt payments, Dasji, don't you know that the heaviest land revenue arrears are due from the biggest landlords? Indeed, getting away with heavy arrears to the government is a status symbol in our rural society!'

From where they sat in the drawing room, they could clearly see, through the window, the wide street and the movement of traffic. They could hear persistent human cries, and the cacophony of vehicles: purring, humming, hissing, grating, chattering, clattering, rumbling, thundering . . . the whole orchestra typical of the Indian city. A never-ending procession of buses, cars, trucks, taxicabs, three-wheelers, motor-cycles, bicycle-rickshaws, bicycles and a great many carts and push-trolleys laden with vegetables passed before their eyes. Shops and beggars occupied all the footpaths. Pedestrians overflowed onto the main road, causing frequent traffic jams. Here and there on the pavement, astrologers sat with their holy books. Some of them had cages of *mainas*—small birds believed to be the medium through which God conveyed His messages regarding the future of humans. The astrologer, in turn, re-conveyed them, with his own gloss and advice, to anxious clients—for an immediate payment, of course. Even with all these presences, this footpath was rather less heavily encroached upon, since it was right in front of a minister's residence. Which, of course, the citizenry cited as government's undue partiality to its own ministers. 'They don't give a damn about what happens to others!' they commented bitterly.

Shanker Das and Anand both watched the street scene for several minutes, perhaps mesmerized by its frenetic activity, perhaps to gain time to recover from their bout. Suddenly Anand turned to Das and said, 'Shall we collect some live data here and now, Dasji?'

Shanker Das looked at him mystified, but Anand added, 'Live and instant data, I assure you!' He picked up the phone and gave some crisp instructions to his private secretary in the local language. While Shanker Das watched with growing interest, a security guard escorted a woman inside the compound, along with her pushcart laden with vegetables. Her face betrayed a mixture of fear, hope and confusion—fear because she couldn't figure out why a policeman had herded her here, even after she had paid the daily *mamool* of two rupees to a constable just a half hour earlier; hope because she thought her fresh vegetables had at last caught someone's eye in the important bungalow; and confusion because she had never experienced anything like this before.

Anand escorted Shanker Das out of the drawing room and began to talk to the vendor—gently, kindly and encouragingly. He drew out, slowly, and with utmost tenderness, a poignant narrative that no one had ever cared to write down. He asked his puzzled private secretary to buy vegetables from her, and permitted her to go, after making her feel that he was pleased with her and her wares. Then he ushered Shanker Das back into the drawing room. The man did not know what to do; he merely followed Anand, tongue-tied.

'Thank you, Dasji,' Anand began. 'Your questions inspired me to make a quick and random probe into this poor woman's mind. Her story is both fascinating and heart-rending. She hails from a village thirty miles south of the city. Along with her husband, she came here about ten years ago. The husband plied a bicycle-rickshaw, which he had got on hire-purchase from a businessman. He had to pay the daily hire amount to the owner, which left him with very little to live on. They could hardly make both ends meet. In a bid to buy off the rickshaw, the man worked harder and harder, day and night—and suddenly died of some disease no one cared to diagnose or treat. The widow had nothing to fall back upon, so she borrowed five hundred rupees from a moneylender, bought the push trolley and began to sell vegetables in the streets and lanes of the city. You will see hundreds of such trolleys all over the town; who knows what tragic story the owner of each of those trolleys has to tell. For working capital, this woman borrows about fifty rupees from another moneylender every day and pays him two rupees towards interest every evening, along with the fifty rupees. Every day, mind you, she repeats the transaction; you can calculate the interest she is paying. And the shocking part of the story is that she is immensely grateful to the moneylender and blesses him from the bottom of her heart. After four years of excruciating labour, she still has to clear the amount she had originally borrowed to buy the trolley. She is just able to pay the interest; it is clear that she will never be able to repay the principal amount.'

Shanker Das did not need further elaboration. 'I understand your case for the nationalization of banks now,' he said, trying to sound genuine. 'How I wish the matter were as simple as it looks from the vegetable vendor's standpoint! At any rate, I realize why

558

no one can avert a split in the party any more. God bless you and save the party!'

The following morning, the news of President Zakir Hussain's sudden death stunned the country . . .

# 45

THE DEATH OF A CONSTITUTIONAL HEAD SHOULD NOT, IN THE normal course, cause a big political storm. Yet Dr Zakir Hussain's passing became another ordeal for the ruling party. His election two years earlier had brought about internal fragmentation. It had tested Indira Gandhi's authority and skill to the fullest. The developments after his death hastened the split in the party and made it irreversible.

The new struggle for succession took a distinctly different form. This time no candidate outside the ruling party came forward. It was clear that whatever the internal divisions, an outside candidate could never hope to win a Presidential election, even with the combined support of the Opposition. Koka Subba Rao had come closest to winning the election, and that was that. And the country did not have many Koka Subba Raos. In any event, circumstances had changed vastly since that fateful election two years earlier. Again, the election had nothing to do personally with the candidates. The split in the ruling party and the Presidential election merely coincided, to compound the situation. Two parties were born after the split, as a result of deliberate decision, *not* because of chance events.

The selection of the ruling party's official candidate for the election became a bone of contention. Who selects the candidate for the Presidential election? The parliamentary board of the party? The highest executive of the party? Party members in parliament? . . . There was an animated discussion—in the media, in the Central Hall of Parliament, among intellectuals . . . everywhere. As often, it remained inconclusive because each view tended to change with the changing situation. In this confusing context, two candidates emerged from the ruling party itself, heralding the split. The party's parliamentary board selected Sanjeeva Reddi as the party candidate, by a majority for the first time in its history. Indira Gandhi signed his nomination paper as proposer. Within a few days, she shifted her support to Giri, the incumbent vice-president. Everyone believed that Giri came into the field only at Indira's instance. The volte-face proved expensive in the long run, and exposed her as one who could sacrifice principles for group purposes. Not even for group purposes; to be more correct, for her own survival.

Yes, that was it. For her own survival, as she perceived it. As the others perceived it too. To begin with, the manner of the candidate's selection created the distinct impression that the future President was either to act as a check on the Prime Minister or, alternatively, be a mere rubber stamp. The 'powers' of the President under the constitution had been discussed during Subba Rao's election campaign earlier. A vague opinion had emerged, by no means widely held, yet articulated in influential circles, that the President of India, even while functioning as a mere Constitutional head, could sometimes overrule, or at least pressurize the Prime Minister and influence his or her decisions on vital issues. That notion became the centre of the debate in the current election.

The conflict saw the party president and the Prime Minister ranged on opposite sides. The top body of the party, the working committee, split into two. The party president removed two members of the working committee from it. Everyone could see that this action was a step to convert his own faction in the working committee from a minority into a majority.

Party members all over India became more and more disturbed by the Delhi intrigues. Chaudhury in particular was extremely upset. There came a stage when all state leaders and chief ministers had to stand up and be counted. The choice was extremely silly, Chaudhury thought. It was, he said, an absurd and bizarre choice between the left eye and the right eye. He fumed as he foresaw his own future being jeopardized by this enforced choice.

Left to himself, Chaudhury would have opted for the status quo. He found Indira Gandhi's behaviour arbitrary and autocratic. He was in daily touch with several other chief ministers who thought the same way he did. Yet he was equally certain that they were trying hard to curry the Prime Minister's favour too, all the time, just as he was. In addition, he had to ward off the abuse Mahendranath's outfit hurled at him in the state. This was not easy, since Mahendranath himself was in Delhi, vigilant and ever busy with his machinations against Chaudhury.

Neither faction, however, had shown its hand yet. It was the twilight period when everyone tried to cultivate everyone else, in a bid to conceal duplicity and fraud. Several self-appointed leaders who moved in high-command circles in Delhi—often for lack of their own base or support in any state—became active overnight as 'observers' and 'envoys'. They moved to state capitals to study the political situation. They would report to the Prime Minister or the party president: there were two separate focuses now. These busybodies were a nuisance to everyone in the state, but no one could say so.

One such 'envoy', Ranjan Babu, was due to visit the state capital the following day. Chaudhury detested him, Mahendranath hated him with all his heart. For once both factions were unanimous in their opinion. Yet both factions vied with each other in spreading the red carpet for him. They knew that whatever his political clout, he was a master manipulator. Everyone also said he was an inveterate bribe-taker.

Anand and Shekhar both burst out laughing when Chaudhury,

in all seriousness, gave them instructions on how they should give Ranjan Babu a princely welcome. 'What amuses you fellows so much?' asked Chaudhury irritably.

'The wonderful wart of democracy about to storm the state tomorrow,' Shekhar commented, laughing again.

'Why don't you ask him to go straight to hell?' interjected Anand.

'Are you both plotting to get me thrown out?' said Chaudhury, sardonically. 'This fellow will promptly become Mahendranath's accomplice if we don't treat him well!'

'Let's treat him well, by all means,' said Shekhar. 'But why is this character so important? You think the Prime Minister listens to him? What exactly is his influence?'

'You don't go into these details and waste your energies, my young friends,' Chaudhury counselled. 'The golden rule is, give him what he is looking for, and get rid of him quick. You don't keep a dead body at home for long, do you?'

'We don't,' agreed Anand. 'But dead bodies are much less trouble, I'm sure. What precious training you are giving us!'

'Look,' asserted Chaudhury, 'I know what I am doing, I assure you. I care nothing for this Ranjan fellow. Yet when leaders fight among themselves, filth like this predator floats to the surface. Till this moment, I do not know for sure if any leader really deputed him to visit this state. I suppose he must have bragged to some minor functionary in the high command that he knows this state like the back of his hand. He must have promised to assess the position here for the coming Presidential election. Take it from me, many more such self-appointed fact-finders are floating around the states. And no one knows on which side their loyalties lie.'

The legislators again found themselves caught in the group crossfire. Both the candidates in this election were from the same party background, so the group-fight syndrome loomed even larger. No one could grasp the rationale of the contest. It was unprecedented. How could the high command maintain discipline in the party ranks if it was riven by naked factionalism at its very top? It was a depressing and demoralizing scenario. Scruples seemed to have taken leave of the party more than ever before.

It was an equally bizarre situation for the other political parties. They had no candidate of their own; yet they had to conjure a 'Subba Rao II' in the image of one of the candidates. It was a political necessity for them. And they were drawn, willy nilly, into the ruling party's faction fight. Soon they plunged in with gusto, some for Sanjeeva Reddi and others for Giri. They advanced arguments vehemently on behalf of both candidates. The political parties of India thus seemed to fade away. What remained were two huge factions. Will the future political historian record these events while laughing in his sleeve? Worse, will the future generations dispense even with the sleeve and burst out in open derisive laughter? . . . Why was all this happening? Was it not, Anand reflected, due to Jawaharlal Nehru's absence?

The mushrooming of Ranjan Babu and his ilk was not surprising, given the general atmosphere of influence-peddling and middlemanship. It was an altogether obnoxious activity. Many impostors appeared overnight and masqueraded as the conscience-keepers of the opposing groups. Some identified themselves with Indira Gandhi's kitchen cabinet and others declared themselves the authentic mouthpieces of the Morarji camp. They virtually tyrannized all state leaders, including chief ministers.

Anand kept largely aloof from the rough and tumble of Ranjan Babu's visit. Shekhar, on the other hand, was the master of ceremonies. 'I don't want this great event to be messed up by an inexperienced person like you,' Chaudhury had told Anand jokingly yet truthfully in his inimitable style. Anand noted that no one remembered the Presidential election of two years ago. A new alignment of forces began to take shape. Many members of the ruling party promptly changed sides. Both Indira Gandhi and Morarji had to ignore the past election in their bid to forge new links of support for the present one. The voters were the same, but sandwiched this time between two huge grinding stones, as it were. The factions encouraged them to resort to defection as a respectable activity; there was no odium attached to it any longer. Defection naturally led to re-defection and re-re-defection. Anyone could now get away with anything, if only he or she had a vote.

Aruna, as usual, was in the thick of the fray. There was hardly any discussion anywhere in which her loud voice did not reverberate. She only added to the confusion by associating with both lobbies and urging arguments from both sides.

The fact of the matter was that she could never get back to mainstream politics, having once strayed from it on the Subba Rao trail two years ago. Paradoxically, however, she and many who had climbed onto Subba Rao's bandwagon had found their importance enhanced in the past two years. They had proved their potential for mischief. Both groups now went all out to cultivate or retain them. The consistent faithfuls paled into insignificance.

One morning, Aruna made her way into Anand's drawing room while he was looking through some papers. She entered stealthily from a side door and put her hands over his eyes from behind. 'It can't be a sane person!' Anand remarked, identifying her instantly.

'You rogue!' she chided him mockingly. 'You aren't scared to see a dissident enter your house? What will Indira Gandhi say if her spies tell her? Is your job going to be safe?'

This had become routine banter between them since her Subba Rao phase, when she had been marked out as a 'prominent dissident'. Prominent because, unlike many others, she had made no secret of her defection. She had clearly developed a psychological complex, compounded by her innate honesty on the one hand and obstinacy on the other. Anand had tried to remove it, in his own unobtrusive way, but his effort came to naught, as he knew it would. And her bitterness—against whom, she was unable to spell out—increased even as she pretended to bask in her new-found 'prominence'. She knew she was out of step with the party. Indira Gandhi's leadership was firm now, strengthened in no small measure after the result of the previous Presidential election . . . Worse still for Aruna, she was equally out of step with the opposite camp, not being essentially group-oriented. As a result, while others were assimilated into one or the other group, she remained the odd woman out. Anand knew there was nothing to be done about Aruna's predicament. Only a new situation could perhaps rescue her—from herself.

Her behaviour often embarrassed him. Even Chaudhury had

hinted at the odium he was earning. Yet, he resolutely avoided interfering with her. He merely responded to her self-conscious jibes in a carefully nonchalant way, taking care not to evoke any sharp reaction from her. He was pretty sure that she had, in fact, realized, without the slightest intention to publicly acknowledge the fact, that she had not acted ethically in the last Presidential election. And what would she do now, given her stubborn temperament? Strangely, Anand's detached approach increased her irritation. She interpreted it as indifference to what she did and therefore indifference to herself. Yet, she also knew that had he indeed tried to influence her actions, she would have resented it all the more. Frankly, she did not know what she wanted him to do.

'You have given up on me completely,' she complained now. 'You seem to have concluded I am incorrigible, troublesome, and a pain in the neck!'

'I don't know what you mean,' Anand answered calmly. 'And I don't know what you are driving at . . .' And he patted her on her cheek.

'For two years you have let me roam on an uncharted sea,' she continued in the same strain. 'Shouldn't you have advised and controlled me? Wasn't it for you to steer me out of the morass I got into?'

'I don't agree with you on that point at all,' Anand countered. 'Don't you remember what you told me two years back? You asserted that defection would enhance your importance. You said you were only proving yourself. You said Indira Gandhi would seek you out, send for you, cajole you . . . Strange as it may seem, you may not have meant all you said then, but I believed you were right in your own way, that those who supported Subba Rao would eventually gain in respectability. So what was the point in steering you or stopping you, even if I had wanted to, even if I had been able to?'

'Have you been following my movements at all?' she asked.

'What do you think?' he put a counter-question.

'Never mind what I think,' she ducked his query. 'Aren't you eager to know what happened on my recent Delhi visit?'

'I'm not sure you are eager to tell me,' Anand commented, rather slyly.

566

'You're absolutely right,' she responded, snuggling on the sofa. 'I've decided to tell you not because of my eagerness, but because I know you are dying to know!'

'All right, you win,' he agreed. 'Now tell me.'

She snuggled closer and began, 'Guess who I met in Delhi, among others . . .'

'Your question suggests the answer—Indira Gandhi . . .'

She beamed with joy. 'I am so happy,' she said. 'She was all smiles and she received me with such kindness. I thought I was a fool not to have met her before. I have been making all kinds of vituperative statements about her. She must have got all the reports. Still, she treated me with deep affection . . . I think she is one of the most gracious persons I have ever met. I am so excited about this trip to Delhi . . .'

Anand guessed that the tide had turned, at last. From now on, he thought, it will be Indira Gandhi all through Aruna's rhetoric. He commented, modestly, 'I'm glad to hear this, Aruna; I am sure Indira Gandhi has a good opinion of your abilities.'

'That sounds a pretty left-handed compliment!' she retorted. 'However, I won't blame you for it any more. I forgive you, as of this moment!'

'To what do I owe this great and gracious reprieve?' Anand teased.

'To Indira Gandhi, of course!' she answered unhesitatingly. 'As of today, I'm going to work for Giri day and night, until he wins and gets installed in Rashtrapati Bhavan!'

'Oh, so you have decided?' said Anand, feigning surprise. 'Now what do you advise me to do? . . . And why?'

'Simple,' she asserted. 'You do the same . . . As for reasons, don't ask me! I don't believe in reasons, as you know!'

'I know,' he replied. 'You act on inspiration; but I don't get these bouts of inspiration, unfortunately! I have to think and act.'

'Don't think!' Aruna exclaimed. 'Act first, then search for reasons and arguments! That's the only way to be effective in politics!'

'Thanks for the advice,' Anand said teasingly. 'I shall think about it!'

'Think, you said again?' she demanded. 'Didn't I say don't think?'

'You did, and I shall think about not thinking!' Anand said, patting on her shoulder.

'You are incorrigible!' she responded to his tap.

'All the way . . . I plead guilty!' he confessed.

It was a good enough truce for the time being. It helped that they were now on the same side of the fence, but this did not completely resolve their differences. The gulf between them widened further because of the snide remarks that continued to be aimed at them by friends and foes alike.

Aruna's latest decision to support Giri came in for its share of adverse comments. Indira Gandhi seems to have tamed her, as only one woman can tame another, said some. And in turn, some others added, Aruna has tamed Anand, who was all the while thinking . . . thinking . . . thinking endlessly, as if the world's survival depended on his thinking!

The backlash was logical. Those who had banked on her to play her noisy part from their side were angry to find her making the same noise, even louder, from the other. To be sure, she had made no commitment to either side earlier; she had been blowing hot and cold, overpowering the hot with the cold. That pleased both camps for some time. However, the moment she made up her mind—very close to the poll—it upset the balance violently. Very few were as articulate or as determined as Aruna. Few could match her in crusading spirit. So her jump into Indira Gandhi's camp sent many minor leaders tumbling. Of course, this was not unexpected, one of them said. I had a hunch even when she began her tirades in the Central Hall this time, said another . . . No one but Indira Gandhi could condone the Anand-Aruna partnership; so the two have chosen the right quarters, averred some others. In the bargain, they dragged Indira Gandhi's name into the mud and maligned her too.

All this only added to the inhibitions that plagued Aruna. Somewhere deep down in her psyche, her vilified (or was it stained in her own subconscious estimation?) public image began to bother her. It was vague at first, then swiftly assumed more palpable dimensions. 'Who bothers about what that bitch says?' she heard her detractors say viciously when they couldn't contradict her. It was an easy way out. A good alibi for their own stupidity. And again and again she found Anand not matching her intensity of indignation. She found him too reflective, too hesitant, too uncommitted. From that she promptly concluded that he didn't care. And why should he, she reflected. The male can do no wrong. So he is cool and patient, while she, Aruna, became the target of relentless slander . . . She found the situation intolerable.

The worst of her doubts, however, surfaced suddenly when she found, or thought she found, that Anand's coolness towards her had something to do with his position as minister. Once this thought crossed her mind, she believed it fully and completely. Anand had no inkling of this suspicion, naturally; neither did she mention the topic to him. This act of conscious suppression, by a person who never suppressed anything, started a drip of poison, as it were, which eventually began to drive them apart. For his part, Anand strictly observed the decorum of the office he was holding, and maintained his distance. It was entirely proper. Aruna had also considered it proper a few months earlier, but she found it humiliating now . . . And since she did not express her feelings this time, she swiftly became their victim.

Once she began spinning around in this circle of unreason—and feeling—there was no stopping her, as usual. She became hugely aggrieved by his ostensible indifference. She almost lost her sense of balance but checked herself just in time to save the situation; however, she could not rectify it completely. She had to reconcile herself to a creeping coolness towards him. Almost a retaliatory coolness. Yet she knew she could not have jettisoned her feelings for him, nor could he do likewise.

Fortunately, their relationship received a temporary reprieve in the much more urgent context of the Presidential election, and concomitant with that, when Ranjan Babu's visit was announced; all hostilities would have to be put aside in order to make the important visitor feel welcome.

# 46

'YOUR ATTENTION, PLEASE, LADIES AND GENTLEMEN, YOUR attention. Indian Airlines announces the arrival of its Boeing Flight 987 from Delhi. I repeat . . .' In the terminal building of the Afrozabad airport, there was a peculiar hum, a murmur, a movement. It was the unmistakable sign of the presence of a large crowd with a common focus of expectancy and excitement. A solid phalanx of khadi garments and Gandhi caps moved, by its own momentum, onto the tarmac. The ground signalman had a piece of equipment in his hand that looked like a yellow table-tennis racquet; he used this to wave the giant aircraft into position. He looked like the ringmaster of a circus who makes an elephant veer round and sit on a stool. The huge jumbo finally sat, as instructed, emitting an angry, monotonous hiss all the time. Meanwhile, the khadi phalanx positioned itself in front of the door. Grudgingly, it allowed the stepladder to inch with considerable difficulty towards the aircraft.

When the door opened, the VIP was, of course, the first passenger to emerge. He folded his hands neatly, in the

570

characteristic namaste posture. The diamond rings on his fingers glittered in the bright morning sun. Thousands of eyes peered at this man—with his snub nose, protruding teeth and bald pate. He could have been described as a classic example of ugliness. Yet he was sought after for his 'political beauty'. He was the current idol of the political mendicants of India. They believed he was 'very close' to the high command . . . In one moment, hundreds of garlands, of all sizes and kinds, virtually crushed him under their weight. Shouts of *Ranjan Babu zindabad!* rent the air, competing with one another in full-throated pitch. All in all, it was an inspired spectacle of fawning adulation.

'Welcome, Ranjan Babu, a most hearty welcome!' exclaimed Chief Minister Chaudhury. 'How wonderful to have you in our state after a long time! We are extremely grateful . . .'

'Oh, don't mention it, please. It was my duty to come, *hanji!* And thank you indeed for this very affectionate welcome!' Ranjan Babu sounded appropriately modest.

'How about your baggage, sir?' asked the more practical Pramod Rai, MLA. As everyone knew, he represented the Mahendranath faction. 'Could I have the tags? Where is your briefcase? Is your personal assistant accompanying you?'

'I'm a simple man, my friend,' said Ranjan. 'I've no PA, no briefcase. Only one suitcase. Here is the tag.' He fumbled in his pockets and fished it out. Pramod Rai took it promptly. Anything to please this personage—the mouthpiece, if not the mouth, of the high command.

The phalanx, this time swirling round Ranjan Babu, moved back into the terminal building. It left a few chinks, which some redoubtable gentlemen of the press managed to penetrate. They got within shouting distance of the honoured guest. Their questions had to be yelled over the heads of the local leaders as these worthies would not, come what may, allow any outsider—be he pressman or postman—to gain further entry into their own compact throng.

'What is your mission, sir?' asked PTI.

'Oh, it's simple enough,' crooned Ranjan. 'I'm a simple man with a simple mission, you know . . .'

'We know that, sir,' retorted UNI. 'Your simplicity is common knowledge throughout the country. We were wondering if you would care to enlighten us on your simple mission . . .'

'Well,' began Ranjan. 'It's not so simple to disclose, you see.'

'I see,' said *Samachar Bharati*. 'Suppose we help you to spell out something, sir . . . er . . . er . . . Is it true that the high command has sent you here to look into the serious complaints against the chief minister?'

Not to be outdone, PTI shot a no less ticklish question. 'Maybe you have come to assess the strengths of the groups here in the context of the Presidential election?'

'What are the prospects of the high command's official candidate?' queried the reporter of a local magazine. The magazine, as a matter of policy, never ascertained facts, always fabricated news as required.

'Is it a fact that Chief Minister Chaudhury has been sitting on the fence? Have you come to persuade him to favour Giri?' asked another correspondent. His paper was carrying on a vicious tirade against Sanjeeva Reddi.

'Don't you agree that Sanjeeva Reddi is the party's official candidate?' shouted a special correspondent. His paper always expected him to report on something going wrong, or at the very least something controversial. He had come to believe that any report he sent, of anything positive happening anywhere, would cost him his job.

The questions threatened to multiply and get more awkward. Since the crowd was in motion, the reporters were eager to unload their questions in a row, expecting the answers to roll out in a row likewise. However, Ranjan Babu had other ideas. There were too many questions flying around, none of which he wanted to answer anyway. Now he discovered a neat way out.

He drawled, with a forced smile, 'My friends, you are going too far, too quick, shooting too many questions, I must say, *hanji* . . . Some other time, maybe . . . For now, good day!' And he stalked out like an unbending stick, leaving the infuriated journalists fuming.

The impromptu mobile press conference having been

concluded, the hosts conducted the simple Ranjan Babu to a simple air-conditioned special suite in the simple Hotel Chandragupta Intercontinental.

Then started the welcoming race. Local newsmen had no other item to report, at any rate nothing as newsy as Ranjan's visit. The local sycophants had sent them an unending torrent of statements eulogizing Ranjan Babu's long record of devoted service to the country, which were now reproduced, for lack of anything else, in the newspapers. From the volume of the statements, it was difficult to see how Bharat Mata could ever repay the debt of Ranjan Babu's patriotic service. The statements depicted his visit as a great boon to the people of the state—why and how, no one bothered to explain. They said people welcomed him with gratitude, from the bottom of their hearts, etc. etc. No one believed a word of all this—neither the writers nor the readers.

As the race to welcome the dignitary peaked, the flood of invitations for lunches and dinners, teas and breakfasts, became unmanageable. The *seths* of Chaudhury's group vied with the *sahukars* of Mahendranath's outfit. There were open clashes between the toughs of the rival groups, including a stabbing incident. The young hooligans on both sides came to blows in the streets several times during that day and night. Rival processions of Mahila Mandals unleashed hysterical tirades describing each other's morals. All these vituperative biographies were complete and unabridged.

Next came the invitations to Ranjan Babu to 'grace' public functions. Chaudhury's admirers had already arranged a wrestling match between two teams of female film stars. Ranjan Babu was to inaugurate it—and, the younger wits started to speculate with relish exactly how he would do this. On the other side, Mahendranath's protégé Pramod Rai arranged a choice programme of qawwalis by a bevy of young women, average age under thirty, selected strictly on the basis of visual merit. Two parallel bar associations placed Ranjan in an invitation tie. One styled itself 'Progressive'; the other called itself 'Democratic'. Their membership was mutually exclusive. Ranjan had to make up his mind between progress and democracy. The legal luminaries saw the two as mutually irreconcilable . . . A number of new associations came into being overnight, solely to invite Ranjan Babu to their ceremonial events. Many printing presses got a lot of work, printing unheard-of letterheads with unthought-of names of office-bearers. So much creation within so short a time—it was a marvel, rather a double marvel, since both groups accomplished it simultaneously.

Ranjan Babu's visit to the state capital was crucial, coming as it did at a crucial time. There was uneasy speculation in the Central Hall of Parliament—the 'third chamber' that serves as the political barometer of the country. The Hall echoed with acrimonious discussions on the imminent split in the ruling party. All chief ministers were embroiled in the internecine war of nerves and political horse-trading.

This was not unusual because the Centre constantly kept the chief ministers guessing about their standing with the party high command. Initially, each chief was a hero, but after a while he became a villain.

It had happened to Mahendranath some years ago; it was Chaudhury's turn now. So MPs of Mahendranath's faction began a virulent Chaudhury-is-going campaign. They asserted that Chaudhury had tried to ride two horses at the same time. Result: both threw him. Morarji Desai hated him anyway, they said, while Prime Minister Indira Gandhi had at last realized his treacherous nature and blessed the idea of kicking him out. So, they concluded, Chaudhury, the scoundrel, is out, sure as anything.

Things were set in motion as usual when a delegation of these MPs waited on the Prime Minister and appraised her of Chaudhury's 'very serious' lapses. They told her categorically that Chaudhury: a) could not carry out the party's programme; b) would not be able to secure success for the party in any forthcoming election; c) could not maintain the stability of the state government, since he always acted with a group bias; d) did not enjoy the confidence of most legislators; e) was corrupt, and known to be so; f) was not of a 'progressive' outlook; and g) most important, he was not loyal to the PM. In his very private circles, he had spoken disapprovingly, at any rate not as approvingly as he ought to have, about her actions in connection with the impending Presidential election. They had unimpeachable proof, they said, that Chaudhury had pledged his support secretly to Morarji Desai at a private meeting recently arranged between the two at Bombay. They repeated that Chaudhury was thoroughly unreliable and unworthy of trust in the bitter struggle against 'vested interests'. The only way to save the party and strengthen Indira Gandhi's hands was to throw him out of the state chief ministership, 'at the earliest'.

The Prime Minister had heard them out and smiled, without saying anything one way or the other, which she never did anyway. Even so, most MPs had become expert interpreters of the Prime Minister's smile—or so they claimed. Soon after their interview with Indira Gandhi, the group of anti-Chaudhury MPs asserted, on the basis of the Prime Minister's smile, that Chaudhury would get short shrift any day. Just a question of time, they said.

However, another delegation of MPs from the state, who belonged to the Chaudhury faction, also waited on the Prime Minister, close on the heels of the first. This delegation impressed on her that: a) Chief Minister Chaudhury was doing wonderful work; b) he was a man of quick decisions and quicker action; c) he was most loyal to the Prime Minister—nay, to the Nehru family; if his chest, like Hanuman's, was ripped open by a thoracic surgeon, one would see the PM's portrait engraved on his heart; and d) the only way to ensure stability in the state and success to the party in the coming elections was to continue to support Chaudhury as chief minister and to strengthen him in every way ... The Prime Minister favoured this delegation also with a smile. Being equally unfailing smile-watchers, they concluded that the high command was backing Chaudhury one hundred per cent, for the simple reason that the percentage of support could not be increased further!

The same groups called on Morarji, and urged their cases for or against Chaudhury, with equal vigour. Version one: Chaudhury is an evil person, as you know, sir. (How do I know? retorted Morarji; the delegation interpreted that curt query to mean that Morarji did know. After all, they reasoned, how could Morarji say that he knew? And further, how could he not know such a self-evident truth?) He has become Indira Gandhi's *chamcha*, and is all out to malign you, sir . . . We have been your admirers for decades, sir. (Morarji noticed that some of them were too young to claim that.) We thought we should bring these facts to your notice, sir. He is bringing tremendous pressure on the MPs and MLAs of our state to vote for Giri *en bloc*. He is openly criticizing Sanjeeva Reddi, our official candidate, sir. Perhaps you are not aware of these dirty tricks he is resorting to . . . (Why do you think so? You just said that I do know, didn't you? Morarji shot back.) Version two: Thank you for receiving us, sir. Some persons are spreading a lot of misinformation against Chief Minister Chaudhury, sir. Fact is, he is working day and night for Sanjeeva Reddi, our official candidate, sir. (What is so extraordinary about a party chief minister working for the party candidate? Morarji countered. That poured ice-cold water on the delegation immediately.) As you know, sir, Chaudhury is your great admirer. (If I know, why do you have to tell me? snapped Morarji.) He opposes Indira Gandhi tooth and nail. (Is that a special qualification? cut in Morarji.) Sir, you must support him strongly . . . (Is he standing for election? queried Morarji.) And so on. After these question-and-counter-question interviews, neither group knew where it stood. And precisely for the same reason, each believed and claimed that Morarji concurred with its version.

When word got round that Ranjan Babu was to visit the state for an on-the-spot appraisal, both groups noisily and passionately claimed that they were responsible for that excellent choice. Both claimed Ranjan Babu's close personal friendship—in addition, of course, to the blessings of the high command.

*

In Afrozabad, Ranjan was in high spirits but he was guarded in his remarks about Chaudhury. It was past midnight and he was unwinding in his hotel room with a doctor, a bosom friend who was in town 'accidentally'—having been specially flown in from Trivandrum by the practical-minded Pramod Rai, just to 'keep

Ranjanji company'. Ranjan responded with what sounded like encouraging grunts when the doctor mounted a vicious attack on Chaudhury.

'He's corrupt to the core,' he said.

'H'mm . . . tons of money, eh?' responded Ranjan.

'Yes, and a hopeless womanizer . . .' added the medical man.

'Aha!' exclaimed Ranjan. 'Maintains a private harem, eh?'

Ranjan's responses were quick, but not quite as hostile as the doctor had hoped. He pulled out his next weapon. 'And everyone knows he drinks like a fish.'

'That completes it,' commented Ranjan. 'His cellar must contain a reservoir of foreign liquor, the size of Bhakra! . . .'

The doctor couldn't quite interpret these comments. 'Too damn devious!' he thought to himself. He tried his the next gambit. 'This chief minister is downright disloyal to the Prime Minister. That's common knowledge in the state. He is working against Giri in the Presidential election. Going all out. Leaving no stone unturned. His recent utterances leave no doubt about this aspect . . .'

'Right, doctor,' Ranjan replied. 'I know how to deal with the man, leave it to me. And now for old times' sake, let's . . .' He reached for something that looked like a bottle, in the darkened room.

*

'No, my friend, I'm terribly sorry,' began Ranjan. 'You are the chief minister's close confidante, so I must give it to you straight. I'm afraid I have heard too much against him from too many people.'

Shekhar was enjoying the interview with a mixture of contempt, exasperation and amusement. For over an hour, he had tried in vain to convince Ranjan Babu (without necessarily believing in what he said) that Chaudhury was absolutely innocent, that there was a conspiracy against him, that what all his detractors said was a tissue of lies, and so on and so forth. This was the concluding interview, after two long days—and nights—of marathon consultations with individuals and small groups. The chief minister's detractors unfolded fantastic stories of corruption and maladministration. The stories sounded too fantastic to be true, yet their purveyors claimed they were the gospel truth. During these interviews, Ranjan had indicated his annoyance with Chief Minister Chaudhury, although his comments were apparently non-committal—as was appropriate for a representative of the high command.

Shekhar had done his own investigation and had put Ranjan Babu down as a political windbag and parasite of the worst type. But now, within that cosy room, facing that flamboyant character, he could not speak his mind. He had come to 'humour' him, as Chaudhury had asked him to. 'And so, Mr Shekhar,' Ranjan concluded in a bantering but ominous tone, 'good luck to you; I have to report what I have to report. Goodbye.' Shekhar felt like punching Ranjan's flat nose there and then—but he suppressed the impulse and showed excessive courtesy to Ranjan.

Aruna struck the only discordant note in this smooth exercise in hypocrisy. She knew nothing about Ranjan Babu. However, the moment she saw him on his arrival at the airport, she felt an immediate loathing for the man. She began to fulminate against him in public. In the process, she fell foul of both the rival groups. Each tried to identify her with the other, which annoyed her even more. 'Chaudhury and Mahendranath are two big humbugs,' she shouted everywhere. 'And this genius descending from Delhi is a bigger fraud than both.' Some legislators tried to argue with her, in a last-minute bid to save the situation. They wanted to get Ranjan's visit over with somehow, with least damage to their respective groups. Maulana sahib, for whom Aruna had some respect, tried to calm her down. 'There may be a point in what you say, Aruna,' he reasoned. 'Yet, what good will your tirade do to the party? Don't you see it is passing through a critical phase?'

'What good do such opportunistic adventurers do to the party, Maulana?' she shot back. 'What do you expect to achieve by hovering round him like dogs?'

'I can't argue with you,' Maulana said in a tired voice. 'I am certain that the fellow will complain against Chaudhury to the Prime Minister.'

'I don't care about his complaints, but I'll expose him in Delhi. I shall report to Indiraji myself!'

I don't care . . . I don't care . . . I don't care . . . That was her refrain. Yet, there was no one who didn't care. No one believed she didn't care either. It was all an exercise in self-deception. Everyone did care about what Ranjan Babu would report.

Consequently, Aruna became the lone crusader who spoke openly against Ranjan. No one thought she was wrong, but no one said she was right either. Many said she was wrong, many more said nothing. They simply treated her as an outcast.

*

A lake of white-capped heads filled the airport again. Mahendranath's followers virtually danced. Their feet almost floated in mid-air. Their heads were high in the clouds. And why not? They had scored a magnificent victory over Chief Minister Chaudhury. Ranjan Babu's smile, while talking to Pramod Rai and his other colleagues the previous night, had been celestial. A heavenly smile lighting up an exquisitely ugly face—it was incongruous, but true. Word got round, about midnight, that Ranjan Babu's report would most certainly cook Chaudhury's goose—within a week, a month, you name the time according to your optimism. How hard they had worked for this day! What a tough nut Chaudhury had proved! He had manipulated all the available legislators and made his position almost impregnable. But now Mahendranath's coterie had proved they were no less adept in every department of the game.

Young and ambitious Pramod Rai's entry into the legislative assembly in a recent by-election, coupled with his meteoric rise, had proved a godsend to the group. Pramod knew the ropes at least as thoroughly as Shekhar did . . .

'*Ranjan Babu zindabad!*' shouted Pramod Rai's crowd. Not to be out-shouted, Chaudhury's gang also raised similar slogans. Ranjan said his goodbyes and cracked many stale jokes, while the captive political audience forced themselves to laugh their heads off.

'Thanks, Chief,' Ranjan said to Chaudhury. 'I had a lovely time in your lovely town; *hanji*, it was extremely useful too . . .'

'Not at all, Ranjanji,' cooed Chaudhury. 'The pleasure is entirely ours . . .'

'I can't understand where you keep this incredible reservoir of energy,' Pramod Rai chimed in. 'Did you realize, sir, that you've been working almost round the clock since you arrived here? You have put all of us youngsters to shame. When do you ever get any time to relax?'

'Well, my work is my relaxation,' said Ranjan modestly.

'Ladies and gentlemen, your attention, please. Indian Airlines announces the departure of . . .' As the departure announcement began, the Gandhi-capped phalanx moved on to the tarmac. Just then there came a sudden ripple, the peculiar movement you see when a single fast-moving vehicle penetrates a solid mass of slow-moving traffic. A police officer from Chief Minister Chaudhury's personal security staff rushed up, as all last-minute arrivals do. But there was a design in his rush, a sense of timing in his haste. He squeezed himself easily and smoothly through the crowd; but not without knocking against many knees and thighs with a biggish briefcase, nearly the size of a suitcase. With a visible flush on his face, panting audibly, he caught up with Ranjan Babu at last and said, breathlessly, 'Sorry, sir, you forgot your briefcase in the hotel. I got it back just in time, thank God . . .'

For just a moment Ranjan Babu looked blankly at the briefcase—then recognized it instantly. How couldn't he? It was his, of course.

'Oh! *Hanji*, thank you, thank you indeed!' he said, his voice unnecessarily loud. Thousands of eyes were riveted on the forgotten briefcase, while Ranjan painstakingly and elaborately explained his forgetfulness. The officer carried the briefcase with utmost care, like a time-bomb, to Ranjan's seat in the aircraft. In a few minutes Ranjan was on the top step of the ladder, waving to his admirers, presenting his neat namaste posture, beaming like a satisfied angel while the diamonds on the rings on his fingers glittered in the morning sun once again.

# 47

TWO PARTIES BEARING THE SAME NAME EXPLODED ON THE political scene together. Neither would give up the 'goodwill' accumulated over eight decades of struggle, sacrifice and public support. However, when it came to the crunch, it was obvious that the party that received the stamp of the original party would be the one with the leader whom the nation accepted. And sure enough, that was where Indira Gandhi's distinct advantage lay. The other party had no such trump card.

Precisely for the same reason, Indira Gandhi's entourage gradually tended to become a motley crowd. A baffling variety of followers gathered around her for different and often conflicting purposes.

The nature of her following remained largely obscure in the first flush of her party's victory. That was not the time to analyse the ideological hues reflected in the party. Stability was the crying need instead. She must command a majority in the Lok Sabha to rule the country. All else was secondary . . . This need proved a virtual 'open sesame' for unrestricted entry into her party. Mahendranath,

Chaudhury, Anand, Shekhar, Aruna, Rehman Khan, Sant Ram and a host of others, both within and outside the legislatures, claimed to be in her charge. Not one of them went over to the other party, their internal irreconcilable conflicts notwithstanding. People from all walks of life—landlords, tenants, capitalists, labourers, princes, paupers, beggars, women, weaker sections *and* their exploiters—all of them followed, or said they followed, Indira Gandhi. No one could explain how a party that claimed a sharper ideological thrust than the others could allow this influx. Partial explanations abounded; but they were vague and unconvincing. The palpable fact was that Indira became the confluence of multifarious interests.

'Why don't you decide one way or the other?' Anand had asked Chaudhury a few days after Ranjan Babu's visit to the state capital. 'The Presidential election is just a few days ahead and you're still sitting on the fence. At least that's what many newspapers say . . .'

'If I don't sit on the fence, it's likely that I'd find myself in a tight hole,' Chaudhury snapped, gritting his teeth. 'This Ranjan fellow must have reported against me, sure as hell.'

'Despite the big briefcase that went with him?' Anand asked, in amazement.

'Who knows how many more briefcases have reached him? They only cancel each other out, you see . . . He'll still report against me, I think. So, Indira Gandhi isn't going to trust me, even if I support her candidate. Morarji's camp somehow doesn't think I support them either; they fancy that Mahendranath is more reliable. I don't know what the hell to do. . .'

'How is your inaction going to help?' Anand asked agitatedly. His anxiety to push Chaudhury into Indira Gandhi's camp was obvious. Still, Chaudhury just dug his heels in and said, 'I know what you're up to. I won't budge until I know what Mahendranath is going to do.'

'In other words, if you know he is on one side, you'll be on the other . . .'

'Exactly. I don't want to be in the same camp with him. He will be the senior leader there, having been my boss once. I'll be a second-class citizen. Am I being unreasonable?'

'Certainly not,' conceded Anand. 'But how are you going to ferret out Mahendranath's designs? He is covering his tracks too, equally cleverly . . .'

'That's where the Brihaspathi of my cabinet has to do his bit,' cut in Chaudhury. 'Look, wise man, I didn't bother you with Ranjan Babu. I put him in Shekhar's lap. Our MLAs are already busy on the election front, creating all the confusion I want them to . . . Now is the time for hard information, leading to a definite decision. Understand?'

'Yes, I understand,' Anand responded tentatively.

'And don't ask me how to do your job . . . Understand?' Chaudhury snapped ferociously.

'I understand,' Anand said with assumed meekness. 'Anything else to understand?'

'Yes, yes,' resumed Chaudhury. 'The most important thing is the time constraint. I give you forty-eight hours from now. If you don't do your job, you forfeit your right to advise me to get off the fence.'

'I understand,' Anand said simply.

Yet mere understanding meant nothing. This was a fight in which Mahendranath and Chaudhury were trying to exploit both Morarji Desai and Indira Gandhi in order to save their own skins. Naturally, they made their plans and moves with the utmost secrecy. So, how was one to know the hand either of them played against the other at any given moment? Anand returned home, lost in deep thought.

In a few moments his private secretary announced on the intercom, 'Pramod Rai, MLA, wants to speak to you, sir.'

Anand was a bit intrigued, but agreed to take the call.

'Could I come to see you for a few minutes, Anandji?' Pramod asked him, in a neutral tone of voice.

'You're welcome, Pramod,' responded Anand. 'By the way, what about?'

'I have an important public function in my constituency tomorrow. The Central minister who had agreed to inaugurate it has suddenly taken ill and cannot come. I thought you could come to my rescue . . .'

'Okay,' Anand said, after a short pause. 'Come immediately, let me see what I can do.'

What Pramod Rai told Anand was, however, not the whole truth. For a whole day after getting the Central minister's refusal, he had tried to persuade as many as three other ministers, including Shekhar, but all of them had refused. They gave several reasons, but the real reason was that no one wanted to hobnob with Mahendranath's first lieutenant just then. However, Shekhar, while excusing himself, had hinted that the only minister who would 'perhaps' oblige him (Pramod) was Anand; the caveat 'perhaps' was appropriately emphasized to import credibility into the suggestion and to make it appear casual.

Pramod Rai was not a regular visitor to ministers' residences. He was a fire-eating dissident, serving Mahendranath's group interests in the state. Mahendranath had pulled numberless strings in Delhi to get Pramod the party ticket in a recent by-election, in the teeth of Chaudhury's most determined opposition. Then, Mahendranath had marshalled all his forces, financial and political, to get Pramod elected. Pramod won by the skin of his teeth, against an independent candidate who boasted Chief Minister Chaudhury's 'full blessings' . . . That candidate received a lot of covert support from the district bureaucracy, which reflected the chief minister's 'blessings'. Mahendranath made a strong complaint on this to the high command; Chaudhury stoutly denied it. As usual, nothing more happened.

It is universally believed in the ruling party that every one of its candidates faces two kinds of opponents. One is from the other political parties, which is normal. The other, from the dissidents within the party itself, is invisible but much more damaging. If the candidate wins against both, he is a great asset; otherwise, he is worthless . . . Pramod Rai was elected and Chaudhury promptly presided over the public function to felicitate him. Pramod thanked the chief minister profusely for his 'invaluable' support in the election. The audience gaped in utter astonishment at this hypocritical exchange.

Pramod lost no time in organizing Mahendranath's scattered cohorts in the state to confront Chaudhury every inch of the way.

He lambasted the ministers and ridiculed them on every possible occasion. He indulged in umpteen innuendos to suggest that ever since Mahendranath had stepped down from the chief ministership, the state had gone to the dogs. And there it would most certainly stay, he added with the authority of an infallible astrologer.

Chaudhury fretted and fumed at this unscrupulous upstart who threatened to undermine the party's foundations. With his scathing criticism and biting sarcasm, he put the government to shame, always taking care to assert that he did so 'in the best interests of the ruling party'. Very soon he outstripped several leaders of the Opposition groups in effectiveness. He discovered more and more secret deals within the administration. He gave all the relevant details to the media or tabled them in the legislature, complete with references and photostat copies of documents ferreted out from the bureaucracy. Even on the rare occasions he failed to get concrete evidence of malfeasance, he still raised a terrific din, until he succeeded in casting suspicion on his victims. However, the two ministers who did not present a single chink to Pramod were Shekhar and Anand. Their departments were under efficient stewardship, and functioned like well-oiled machines impervious to external attack.

Between the two, Pramod was quick to find the difference. He thought that Shekhar was more villainous than necessary, even for the norms of political activity. His destructive genius seemed to emanate from something deeper than the normal political motivation of self; indeed, it was selfless in its own way, but the antithesis of public good. Pramod put him down as a special, perhaps pathological, specimen of an evil designer, efficient and dangerous. He maintained neutral relations with Shekhar, keeping a well-defined distance.

Anand, in Pramod's eyes, was at once an enigma and an open book. He had tried attacking him a few times on the floor of the assembly, but Anand was ready with his answers, tempering them with a humour that blunted the edge of Pramod's sallies instantly. Pramod found Anand easy to communicate with but difficult to convince. He could not figure out which group to pigeon-hole

Anand into; he seemed a misfit in the group pattern. He stood solidly by Indira Gandhi, but the nature of his loyalty was complex. Indira Gandhi is *of* the party, Pramod had often heard Anand say—which was very different from what many others had to say. Anand looked upon Indira Gandhi as the symbol of the party, not as an individual. Pramod thought this was just hair splitting. In his opinion, Anand was attempting to save her from the queenly and dynastic image that was being fostered by her sycophants. The attempt to paint Indira Gandhi as the new regent was understandable in a country where kingship had been the main building block of the socio-political structure for centuries. While Pramod appreciated the struggle that Anand waged against the short-sighted idolatry which opportunistic time-servers foolishly thrust upon her, he was unable to convince himself that Indira Gandhi had acted honestly in this Presidential election. He had to agree, however, as Anand asserted, that the country would benefit much more by projecting Indira Gandhi as herself, even with her faults, than in a mere role as her father's daughter or as a usurper-politician or someone superhuman and extraordinary.

Pramod had sized up Chaudhury quite realistically as a politician first, and a politician last. He wanted to remain chief minister as long as he pleased and destroy his opponents inside and outside the party. On the surface, however, Chaudhury dripped honey. Entirely understandable, Pramod thought. He could even see himself being Chaudhury's confidante one day . . . some day. He knew roles could change.

Well, whatever the future held, Pramod was Mahendranath's hatchet man in the state for the time being. He never asked himself if he liked that role. As an insignificant junior legislator who had made his debut in a by-election entirely due to Mahendranath's support and patronage, he knew it was not for him to question why. He only had to do his best—or worst—to keep Mahendranath's banner aloft . . . He rarely met Chaudhury because he knew the latter would never oblige him. Besides, he knew that even a casual association would set many tongues wagging. They would say that Chaudhury, the spider with an infinite capacity to seduce legislator-flies, was out to draw Pramod into his web. On the other side, Mahendranath's propensity for suspicion and fury was equally unlimited and terrifying . . . So Pramod decided to adopt the attitude of the virtuous Hindu wife—forbidden, according to some, even to look at any male other than her husband. He would behave as a bona fide *pativrata*.

However, Pramod had a job to do. He could not afford to sit in purdah, just to prove his single-minded loyalty to Mahendranath. His loyalty demanded that he gather solid political support for Mahendranath's candidate in the Presidential election. And who was that candidate? Frankly, he did not know, beyond the description that he was the one other than Chaudhury's. And who was Chaudhury's candidate? Obviously the one other than Mahendranath's. Which left everyone guessing as to who was whose candidate. An example of consummate political sparring.

Pramod had his own suspicions about where Mahendranath's and Chaudhury's loyalities lay, but he couldn't say anything openly—was not supposed to, while the speculation was on. Yet he had his hunches and he kept trying to confirm them in every way possible so he could communicate his findings to his leader. He found Anand useful in this process.

So, when a hostile-looking private secretary ushered him into Anand's drawing room, Pramod reminded himself that the invitation he had extended to Anand on the telephone earlier had a dual purpose; the public function as well as his intention to probe Anand's mind, if possible. He would have to be sharp to pick up any clues Anand let fall. Anand received him cordially. He also realized that in his own mission, he had stumbled on a person who could be useful. This mutual convenience lifted the veil between them rapidly. 'How do you substitute a Central minister with a state minister, Pramod? Aren't you encroaching on Centre-state relations?' Anand asked jestingly, while Pramod sipped coffee.

'Maybe I am,' Pramod replied. 'However, I couldn't look for another Central minister who had not fallen ill and was willing to drive two hundred kilometres to my constituency from the state capital. And, of course, you know this road so well . . .'

That tail-piece was a mild jibe at the state government, which Anand noticed at once. The road was bad; but then, all roads were bad and Pramod Rai knew why, as well as anyone else.

Anand ignored the comment. He wanted to edge towards the subject of his probe. He was sure, more or less, that Pramod would also talk about it. 'Ill or well, Pramod,' he said, 'how can any Central minister find time to visit the states when everyone is busy with the Presidential poll?'

'You are right,' observed Pramod. 'And that's another reason why I didn't bother any other Central minister. I thought of you instead . . .'

'Thanks for that, Pramod,' said Anand. 'But why not postpone your function by a couple of days? You could meanwhile tell the people who is coming and who isn't . . . Else, they could find me a poor substitute for a Central minister . . .'

'I'm not at all afraid of that,' responded Pramod, meaning to pay a compliment to Anand. 'Unfortunately, no postponement is possible since I have to leave for Bombay the day after the function . . .'

'Then why not put off your Bombay visit by a couple of days?'

'Oh no, that's impossible,' Pramod said quickly. 'Many others are to come . . .'

The replies came naturally, yet Anand knew they were playing out an elaborate charade.

'All right, I shall attend your function,' Anand said and asked his private secretary if he would be free on the following day.

The private secretary hesitated to answer, not because Anand was not free, but because he didn't like the idea of his boss visiting a known dissident's constituency. 'You are free tomorrow, sir,' he said reluctantly on the intercom. 'However, you may have to check back with the chief minister. He has asked all ministers to stay at headquarters for some days.'

'That's okay; I shall tell him. Please issue the tour programme. Inform the district collector by phone, there is no time to send the programme by post.'

The secretary said, 'Yes, sir,' with ill-concealed hostility.

And he was right, of course. Chaudhury was furious when Anand phoned to tell him about his impending visit.

'I don't know why you're wasting your time,' he grumbled. 'I gave you a job to do and—'

'You also told me,' Anand cut in, 'that I shouldn't ask you how to do it, right?'

'Yes, but—'

'Doesn't that also imply that no one should ask me, in the meantime, how I do the job?'

'Well, I suppose it does. Go ahead, it's your funeral.' Chaudhury hung up abruptly.

No one knew how the news spread, but Chaudhury had already received a few phone calls about Anand's foolhardy decision to visit Pramod Rai's constituency. Scandalous, said many; madness, added some. At this rate, our group will definitely go down the drain, asserted others ... And when Shekhar made a particularly ominous comment, Chaudhury was really shaken, in spite of the scepticism with which he normally took Shekhar's remarks about Anand.

At last, unable to contain himself, Chaudhury telephoned Anand once again and asked, without any of his customary preamble, 'Are you sure you're doing the right thing by hobnobbing with this fellow Pramod? Can't you call it off even now? Suppose I fix an urgent meeting of the cabinet to pre-empt your visit?'

Anand was not very sure himself why he had suddenly agreed to make a nearly day-long trip in the company of a potential enemy. At the very best, all he was operating on was a vague hunch sparked off by something Pramod had let slip during their conversation—'Bombay . . . Impossible to postpone . . . Many others are to come . . .' All that could well turn out to be a figment of his fertile imagination. But if he let go of this intuition, what was he left with, in order to carry out the probe Chaudhury had entrusted to him? To Chaudhury's question, he said, 'Haven't I been absent from cabinet meetings in the past?'

'Yes, I suppose so . . . You're impossible,' fumed Chaudhury. 'Look, I just wanted to point out the risk in—'

'Chief,' cut in Anand. 'I'm sure I know what I am doing. Let me try to explain, even if I don't have to, as per our understanding.

You give me forty-eight hours to find out what Mahendranath is going to do in the election. Promptly, indeed luckily, I attach myself to the person who is right now Mahendranath's conscience-keeper here. Does my action make no sense at all to you?'

'Well, it does, but how far—'

'I know there are all kinds of risks in this,' Anand interrupted him again. 'But you don't get results from inaction. Probably Shekhar doesn't like what I am doing. That somehow convinces me that I am on the right track.'

'This has nothing to do with Shekhar,' asserted Chaudhury, without much conviction. 'I thought I should warn you, that's all.'

'So what do you want me to do? You said I shouldn't ask you this question, didn't you? You want to go back and sit on the fence?'

'We both know that's no longer possible,' admitted Chaudhury. 'So go ahead with your crazy plan, whatever it is. And get me results . . .'

'I'll do my best . . .' said Anand.

'Remember, I want results,' repeated Chaudhury, sounding as grim as he could.

Early the next morning, Anand and Pramod began the long drive to Pramod's constituency. For about an hour they talked in monosyllables, each trying to work out his opening gambit. Characteristically, Anand was feeling a bit guilty. Was he not deceiving and exploiting the unsuspecting Pramod Rai? Was it fair to take advantage of the latter's need for a minister? Then, his thoughts took a different turn. What sin was he about to commit? he asked himself in exasperation. Why was he being so squeamish about something that everyone does in an election? And how was he sure he was going to succeed in tapping Pramod, who was no simpleton by any stretch of imagination? How was he, Anand, so sure that the other fellow was not up to the same game and would not turn the tables against him? Relax, my dear dreamer, he told himself.

Pramod also found himself prey to confused thoughts. He had sized Anand up as honest and decent. And here he was trying to probe Anand's mind. About what? Well, there were several things he could think of. For a start, he could see if he could bring Anand close to Mahendranath. After all, if Chaudhury opted for the candidate other than Indira Gandhi's, Mahendranath and Anand would find themselves, willy nilly, in the same camp—to wit, Indira Gandhi's. That would perhaps be an ideal situation. Pramod had done his homework earlier. He had had long chats with Aruna who had told him everything about Anand's (and now her own) commitment to Indira Gandhi. So Pramod conjured up a Pramod-Aruna-Anand-Mahendranath-Indira Gandhi combination—with Chaudhury thrown out of the window into some endless wilderness . . . He soon realized, however, that this was nothing short of a utopian scenario. He was not at all sure that his boss, Mahendranath, liked the prospect of being a follower of Indira Gandhi. He also knew, very definitely, that Indira Gandhi would never prefer Mahendranath to Chaudhury. She would at best balance both—as she was doing already. But jettison Chaudhury for Mahendranath—no way. And 'jettison Chaudhury' was Mahendranath's only demand. He could no longer remain in the same camp as Chaudhury, whether it was Indira Gandhi's or someone else's . . . He would gladly go to hell rather than share his heaven with 'that scoundrel'. Pramod slowly resigned himself to doing whatever Mahendranath had asked him to do, in this election at any rate.

That was the catch—in this election. And what about after this election? Pramod was unable to figure that out. He was the creature of a by-election, and had an uncharted (perhaps unchartable) political future. As of now he was the appendage of Mahendranath, who was himself in no particular camp (despite paying lip service to Indira Gandhi) at the national level. Mahendranath was a national leader of sorts himself. Yet, if there was one leader who could underwrite any follower's future, Pramod knew it was Indira Gandhi. He could thus see his own predicament—the conflict between future interest and present loyalty . . . Switch to Chaudhury, he would not; join Indira Gandhi, he could not . . . However, he could open a channel to Indira

Gandhi, just in case—yes, why not? he reasoned. And this is where he could use Anand.

Lost in these ruminations, he did not realize that he had begun talking to Anand animatedly, excitedly and earnestly—on the subject of his own future. 'I don't know what to do. I don't want to end up in the company of the out-going. I am young and don't want to be a straggler in the onward march of historical forces.'

He looked into Anand's eyes intently—and expectantly, Anand thought. And Anand responded at that crucial moment. 'You don't have to,' he said simply.

Pramod was suddenly jolted into silence. He had not intended to say so much about himself. He wanted to probe Anand on a number of things and though his own future was one of them, it wasn't of any great importance at this time. Yet, when he had opened up, the incidental had happened to be uppermost in his mind and he had expressed it involuntarily. There was nothing he could do about what had been said but it was time to stop; he began to talk about the impending Presidential election.

Before either could warm up to the subject, the car passed through several roadside villages one after the other. They had to stop at each village—now for a simple greeting from the people, now for a cup of tea, and everywhere to collect a pile of petitions. People customarily presented these to visiting or passing ministers—with no high hopes of any redress on them. Caught in this routine, Pramod and Anand temporarily suspended their discussion.

Meanwhile, people in every village made a special note of this unusual duo. So much had been written about the group combinations in the ruling party that it was disconcerting to see two politicians who were ostensibly in rival camps travelling together. Eyebrows went up many times over during the long drive that morning. When they arrived at their destination, everyone stared at them in utter disbelief. There was an extraordinary outpouring of astonished comment before, at and after the function.

'Good times are in store for the state now; Anandji and

Pramodji coming together is indeed a happy augury,' said some. 'Perhaps this means that Mahendranath and Chaudhury are drawing closer together, like the good old days.'

'Please, please, for heaven's sake, don't let your imagination get the better of you. These two gentlemen coming together means nothing, just nothing more than nothing, nothing other than nothing . . . Mahendranath and Chaudhury can never, repeat never, come together again . . . No return to that golden period, thank God, when both of them together had held the ruling party in the state to ransom . . . When political activists were mere serfs . . . When the two of them ruined the careers of scores of promising and upcoming young men, cutting everyone to size, indeed to nothing.'

'Whatever that may be, Pramod has pulled off a miracle, I must say! He is the bridge between Mahendranath and Anand now, as everyone can see. They will now work together in the Presidential election, leaving Chaudhury, the scoundrel, high and dry. After all, it's good that decent people are at last coming closer . . .'

'I am not sure of your prognosis. My hunch is that this is a trap laid by Chaudhury and Anand; our by-election MLA Pramod is just walking into it, even as we look on. Your hypothesis to the contrary is absurd, if you don't mind my saying so. It is like the tail wagging the dog.'

'I don't agree with you at all; you don't know young Pramod's capabilities. He is more than a match for people like Anand and Shekhar. He will make short shrift of this scourge called Chaudhury, mark my words.'

And so forth. It was a feast for gossips. And in the surrounding uncertainty about who-supports-whom in the impending Presidential election, the Anand-Pramod combine allowed political groupies and pundits to give full vent to their imagination.

The public function carried on amid loud cheers, spirited whistles and persistent whispers. Anand had drawn a blank so far on the subject of the Presidential election. He began to regret the leap in the dark he had taken in accepting Pramod's invitation for this visit. However, things began to brighten suddenly at the crowded lunch after the function. Anand's easy and friendly demeanour seemed to loosen many tongues and he heard a variety of comments against Chaudhury and Indira Gandhi. Obviously those who spoke so candidly to Anand took him as a new convert to the Mahendranath-Pramod fold, to which they also belonged. With each repetition, the version became more outspoken—in other words, more critical of Chaudhury and Indira Gandhi. Evidently, every comment was based on the assumption of Chaudhury *and* Indira Gandhi being together. The truth gleamed through the desultory talk, slowly but surely.

Pramod had not bargained for this. He had hoped to parade his own association with Anand, with a view to confusing Chaudhury's camp. What in fact happened was very different; his own constituents overshot their mouths and lumped Chaudhury with Indira Gandhi. They announced, by necessary implication, that Mahendranath was with the anti-Indira camp, working for Sanjeeva Reddi. They had uncovered the mystery—without meaning to, of course.

Pramod was embarrassed. He made some feeble attempts to dilute the enthusiasm of his supporters to some extent. 'You see, Sunderji,' he drawled to one of his most vociferous colleagues. 'You are exaggerating and jumping to conclusions too soon. After all, neither Mahendranath nor Chaudhury has clearly indicated his stand in the Presidential election . . .'

Sunderji was bubbling with enthusiasm. His irresistible desire to show off his political insights got the better of him. He failed to take Pramod's hint and continued with his perceptions of the political scene. 'Whatever you might say, Pramod, I'm pretty sure that I have read the situation correctly. Mahendranath's decision may be a secret to the world; but not to you and me. Besides, Anandji is wise and friendly. He has come to Mahendranath's side at the right time, like a godsend. We may as well share our hunches with him. Indira Gandhi may be Prime Minister, but she has antagonized almost all her senior colleagues. Look at the formidable line-up: Mórarji Desai, Kamraj, Atulya Ghosh, Nijalingappa, Ram Subhag Singh, S.K. Patil, Sanjeeva Reddi . . . What a galaxy of patriots! And who is Indira Gandhi left with? All light-weights. She can't command a majority in her parliamentary party any more. So, her days as Prime Minister are numbered. Imagine proposing one candidate's nomination and setting up another to contest him! It's the height of political immorality!'

Anand found it extremely difficult to stand this relentless onslaught. He had to call up every ounce of his forebearance to keep listening silently. Sunderji was in his element now: 'I was absolutely sure, Anandji, that you would take the right decision at the right time. We have great respect for you, but since you are in Chaudhury's cabinet, we couldn't talk to you freely. Of course, being in his cabinet doesn't mean toeing his treacherous line all the way. After all, you are a minister because you deserve to be one. Now, you will naturally distance yourself from Indira Gandhi, the earlier the better. You have a long way to go and you should be in the right camp at the national level.'

Pramod tried his best to divert Sunderji's attention to some other topic, but the latter would not, come what may, let go of Anand, his captive audience and target. The longer he spoke, the more he felt he impressed his listener. He thought Anand would remember him as a man who could be useful in future political contingencies. After all, this upstart Pramod Rai had suddenly become an MLA from nowhere, thanks to that brute Mahendranath's crazy fancy for the fellow. In reality, wasn't he, Sunderji, himself the genuine claimant for the party ticket in the by-election that had elevated Pramod? Sunderji had not forgiven either Mahendranath or Pramod for this, yet he had had to swallow the bitter pill. What else could he do? The whole district was firmly in Mahendranath's control; not even Chief Minister Chaudhury could penetrate it, with all his money and guile. Besides, the district was known for rough and ready justice, by simply cutting throats whenever there was non-compliance. So there wasn't much political opposition to the 'acknowledged' leader, Mahendranath, anywhere in the district. Sunderji thus had to play second fiddle to Pramod. Yet, this was an occasion to parade his own brilliance and prowess—indeed, his better claim to be MLA from the constituency, compared to Pramod . . . He had bragged about himself to many visitors since the by-election.

Today it was Anand's turn to listen. All this had nothing to do with Sanjeeva Reddi and Giri, the candidates in the Presidential election, or with Mahendranath or Chaudhury, the state-level gladiators out to destroy each other. Yet it had its own significance in the political arena, where nothing could be ignored.

Sunderji's thwarted ambition thus frustrated Pramod's plan of secrecy through his enthusiasm and misplaced confidence in Anand as a convert to their group. Anand had stumbled onto the precise information that Chaudhury had charged him to ferret out. Meanwhile, Pramod was regretting his utter folly in inviting Anand to his constituency.

Anand guessed Pramod's predicament. He appeared not to evince any interest in Sunderji's information, even as he noted every word of it carefully. He knew that Pramod knew what had actually happened in this battle of wits. Pramod had over-reached himself and would perhaps pay for it dearly when the truth came out, as it was going to within a few hours.

On their way back to the capital, Pramod was mostly sullen, as if castigating himself. After about an hour of this ordeal, he broke down completely and blurted out the truth—which had come out at the function just an hour back, anyway—that Mahendranath had decided long ago to throw in his lot with Sanjeeva Reddi. While he volunteered this information, his attitude was still ambiguous.

'You're certain, of course, that Sanjeeva Reddi will win the Presidential election, aren't you?' Anand asked him non-committally.

'How does it matter to me, or to anybody for that matter?' Pramod shot back. 'We're only operators; we operate, that's all.'

'Why do you say so?' Anand queried. 'Doesn't that signify your group's victory, and a bright future at least for the main operators?'

'Now that you know everything, Anandji, let me tell you the only fact you don't know yet. I don't see the future as particularly bright. I am working for Sanjeeva Reddi, but there is no candidate-voter relationship between him and me. I don't know him, except perhaps as a former chief minister of another state and a former president of the party ten years ago when I was a student. The fact of the matter is that I am gathering votes for Mahendranath. I am his captive voter, his bonded labourer. I don't believe in groups, yet I am a slave of the group and can't get out of it. Returned in a by-election for the first time, I have a long way to go, maybe five more elections, and I can't figure out what future I shall have with Morarji Desai and Sanjeeva Reddi. I respect them, certainly, but hitching myself to them is quite another matter, isn't it?'

'I suppose so,' answered Anand tentatively, trying somewhat sympathetically to deflect the spate of remorse in Pramod's rambling. 'You know, Pramod, political situations are always dynamic. There is always the next crossing and always a way to zigzag your way around, if you feel impelled to do so by conviction and circumstances.'

'I know that,' Pramod said. 'Yet, why should it be so? I ask myself, why should I choose between two candidates from my own party? Am I choosing between Indiraji and Morarji Desai in this Presidential election?'

'Well, yes . . . you are, in a manner of speaking,' responded Anand.

'I am not,' snarled Pramod. 'I don't find that choice open to me at all.'

'Look, Pramod, you do have the choice, but you are unable to exercise it. The group game prevents your free choice as of now. When more and more young men and women with an ideological bent come into the political field, independent choices will become easier. I don't know if that will actually happen, but I hope and pray it does. The Gandhi-Nehru hegemony cannot last forever; so there is bound to be a sudden dip in the ruling party's confidence. Groupism, casteism, communalism and a host of other such tendencies have grown fast. Weeds grow in the absence of good farming practices, don't they? We all have to work hard to sharpen the party's image. There is no other way.'

'What can I do with Mahendranath as my mentor? Make no mistake, I owe my position to him, so I have to obey him. Yet, how do Mahendranath and ideology go together? The same goes for Chaudhury, of course.'

'Don't jump the gun, Pramod,' Anand said. 'You don't get ideal conditions to work in; else you wouldn't have any work to do.

597

Keep to your group, but don't become its slave. Keep your eyes and ears open. I am sure things will work out.'

While he quietly offered this excellent advice to Pramod, Anand was unaware of what had happened during his absence from the state capital that morning. Only Chaudhury, and Shekhar, were aware of Anand's visit; everyone else got to know about it in bits and pieces. Some had witnessed Anand and Pramod driving away together. Some got phone calls from the villages where the two had halted to receive greetings from the local people. Finally, many got detailed information on the goings-on at and after the function in Pramod's constituency. Every comment there reached newspapers and political busybodies word for word, even while Anand and Pramod were on their way back. As a result, when they reached Anand's residence, a crowd of press correspondents and ubiquitous hangers-on greeted them with knowing smiles and damning questions.

They saw the day's events as a watershed in the state's political history. Had Anand defected to Mahendranath's side? Or had he succeeded in seducing Pramod Rai to Chaudhury's side? Some imaginative commentators offered an altogether new explanation: that both Mahendranath and Chaudhury had realized the folly of their endless personal conflict. Anand had convinced them that they should come together, somehow, for which, supporting the same candidate in the Presidential election offered as good an occasion as any.

The questions thrown at Anand and Pramod reflected all these speculations. They were mutually contradictory and all that Anand had to do was to consider each question in the light of the others and to laugh them all away. Yet, at the end of the interview he had to tell them cryptically, 'Wait for an hour or two; no more questions meanwhile.' That wasn't exactly a headline, yet it was something, a promise of a headline . . .

The following day, the papers screamed, 'CHAUDHURY BACKS GIRI!' . . .

# 48

V. V. GIRI WON THE PRESIDENTIAL ELECTION, BUT IT WAS DIFFICULT to say that Sanjeeva Reddi lost it. What about Indira Gandhi? Some said this was a pyrrhic victory for her. Enthusiasts said she had finally vanquished the reactionary forces, that she had smashed the vested interests. Sycophants chanted: She is great, great, great . . . Careful observers, however, said she had just managed to avert a disastrous defeat.

Considering the odds against Indira Gandhi and her stake in the election, it was a signal victory. It showed she had the potential to be 'great', as her admirers claimed. Yet, the very narrow margin showed that she had just scraped through. Besides, she had secured a sizeable number of votes from other parties—notably of the Left. If the votes of the ruling party alone were counted, those who thought she had lost also seemed justified in their opinion. The fallout of the Presidential election was that Indira Gandhi's position, and by extension that of her government, became precarious.

To run the government effectively became increasingly difficult.

The bureaucracy dodged decisions, prevaricated and generally behaved as though Indira Gandhi's 'minority' government was on its last legs. And all this when her term was just over half-way through. A slow drift began. No one was sure where the government was going. No one understood Indira Gandhi's policies; they had possibly not crystallized, as of then.

The nationalization of banks was indeed the first real item of her policy, meant as the first frontal attack on poverty. She started it, but the bureaucracy took its own time to implement it countrywide. It wasn't its fault either. The very idea of giving loans to rickshaw-pullers and vegetable vendors was shocking to the banking establishment . . . Besides, nationalization entailed bureaucratization. It gave rise to some unavoidable absurdities. How does an ordinary public servant don the mantle of a money-lender overnight? And worse, how does a bank, which works for profit, suddenly become altruistic and throw its money around for purposes such as making a non-viable poor man viable? It might have suited Indira Gandhi's populist image to promote such measures, but how could the country's economy run on a bankrupt banking structure? On top of everything, no one could make the new scheme yield results overnight, even with the utmost sincerity—which wasn't there anyway. The infrastructure was nowhere near ready in 1970. Meanwhile, a propaganda barrage erupted against the scheme, throughout the country. Although some quarters protested openly, the adverse reaction to her initiatives was mainly disseminated through an extensive and intensive whispering campaign.

'In Indira Gandhi's new dispensation, banks have become charity centres. This is the truth, whatever the verbal camouflage. Now, where do the banks get their money from? From deposits made by millions and millions of middle-class people from their hard-earned incomes. It is from you that it is taken, my brothers and sisters, from the five rupees and ten rupees that millions of wise housewives in the country put away for a rainy day. They cut down their immediate needs—maybe better clothes, better food, sometimes the few ornaments every woman naturally desires to wear. They make savings for future needs—a daughter's marriage, a son's college education, money to build a small house after struggling and saving for ten years, maybe twenty . . . That is how the banks get *your* money and invest them for *your* benefit . . .

'But now, now, my sisters and brothers, you had better forget all these dreams and schemes. Your money is going down the drain. Your sons will beg in the streets, your daughters will become old maids or prostitutes; no decent marriages for them . . . And all this for no fault of yours, my friends—that's the most tragic part of this drama Indira Gandhi is enacting. No fault of yours, I repeat. You deposited your money in banks, not in charities. Yet, the banks have to throw your money away now, thanks to our great Prime Minister Indira Gandhi . . . I am not sure you can even withdraw your money. In any event, please remember, no one ever returns charity, so it'll never come back to you, ever . . .' Yet, the middle class, on the whole, did not panic. The run on the banks, which some reputed economists and politicians predicted, proved to be mere wishful thinking.

Meanwhile, Indira Gandhi gradually assumed the halo of a martyr. Look at how. these old blackguards are harassing that beleaguered woman, the people told one another. After all, she is Jawaharlal's daughter, isn't she? The same fellows who licked his boots yesterday are dragging his daughter over the coals today—the ungrateful swine!

Thus, Indira Gandhi's political support came to depend largely upon public compassion. In one speech, she emitted a little, momentary sob, while describing the way she was tormented by her senior colleagues. Many called the sob artificial; but it left an imprint on the minds of the masses, particularly women. The 'Syndicate'—the nickname for the group of Indira Gandhi's main detractors—had no answer to this.

Chaudhury felt uncomfortable. He did not like the concept of bank nationalization, but had to second the resolution favouring it in the crucial meeting of the party. He realized the immense political potential of the measure, of course; but he was somehow uneasy about it. He sincerely felt it was something just not done.

Other politicians and legislators, while understanding nothing about bank nationalization, began to count its benefits in terms of votes. They had no time to debate on how the party should orient the new scheme to the realities of the rural areas. All they could see were votes . . . votes . . . votes . . .

Likewise, those who opposed Indira Gandhi—both outside her party and within it—intensified the whispering campaign against bank nationalization . . . Some saw it as largesse coming gratis from Indira Gandhi. Others labelled it as Indira Gandhi's grand scheme of national bankruptcy. Very few tried to project it as a bold attempt to mount a frontal attack on the vicious cycle of poverty-indebtedness-poverty. Very few understood it as a breakthrough that would improve the lives of the millions who had been a perpetual burden on the country's economy. Very few, again, looked at it as an effort to stabilize the national economy by shoring up its vast but extremely fragile base.

Anand felt depressed. Chaudhury praised bank nationalization to the skies in public. Then he denigrated it in private conversations with his close friends. All over the country began a scramble to grab the largesse by hook or by crook. Influence-peddlers and middlemen sprouted overnight to 'help' the loanees get loans. The real plan, however, was to siphon off part of the money into their own pockets.

In the months after it was announced, there were innumerable problems with the scheme. There was a long gestation period before a loan could be processed and even with the middlemen's help, not every poor man or woman could get loans from the banks. There was no marked impact on the ruling party's immediate electoral prospects. Besides, the banks could earmark only a meagre amount to be loaned to the poor. The all-round sniping that the scheme received in advance from its detractors made it a doubtful starter at best. The opponents of the scheme fully realized the electoral advantage of the measure to the ruling party. It was a grave menace to their own prospects. It spurred them to do everything to vilify and defeat it. Bank managers found 'incentives' to delay the processing of loans. The process of obtaining a loan became extremely frustrating and tardy. The more the delay, the larger the cuts they could impose for their own illegal gratification. The popular joke was that any manager of a small village bank who did not make a lakh of rupees a year was an idiot. You see, they said, the whole scheme is a grand charity show. Charity begins—and in this case also ends—at home! Given the big cutbacks, repayment became ruinous and back-breaking for the loanee.

At the same time, the loanees got some kind of assurance, in subtle and unsubtle ways, that the loan was only a loan in name, that it would not need to be repaid at all, eventually. 'Ever heard of any fool repaying government loans? You have to be a bit smart, my dear friend! Catch hold of a dozen MLAs or a couple of MPs and make a hell of a noise for postponement of repayment—and later for a total write-off. That's how you measure the legislator's influence, see? In any case, the middlemen are ready and willing to take care of all these delicate aspects. Nothing to worry about. If the ruling party gets you a loan, my poor dear friend, *my* party will see to it that you don't have to repay, I promise you . . .'

As the controversy continued unabated, the government found the going rough. With a precarious majority in the Lok Sabha, Indira Gandhi found herself stymied at every step. Frequent divisions in the houses on flimsy issues made a mockery of the proceedings of these august institutions. After all, voting is an inalienable right of members; but when taken to ridiculous lengths, the voting process becomes at best a repeated joke, at worst an irritating pastime. It loses its democratic depth and sanctity. Unruly scenes within the houses of parliament became a regular feature. Lung power almost completely replaced the power of argument.

Critics now started focusing on personal aspects of Indira Gandhi's life. A story connected with a very expensive mink coat was unearthed or invented—no one was sure which. They said that some rich foreign tycoon had presented the coat to Indira Gandhi and that she had retained it against government rules. The innuendo was that Indira was open to the temptation of money and fabulous possessions. Said one prominent Opposition leader with biting sarcasm, 'Jawaharlal Nehru made a will that bequeathed his ashes to the nation and the family jewellery to his daughter!' The reference was to the highly evocative words Panditji had used in his last wish. He wrote that he belonged to the whole country, body and soul, and wished that the ashes of his mortal remains, after cremation, be mingled with the motherland's earth and rivers . . . While the average Indian wept at these sentiments, this leader from the Opposition chose to denigrate it. It was shocking.

Despite Indira Gandhi's vulnerable position, it was not possible for her critics to find anything blameworthy about her from the people's point of view. Yet the lack of a clear majority in parliament hamstrung her policies, and largely eroded her effectiveness. She could rule, but only just. She could bring about no radical change in any sphere, since each critical issue needed a majority. And each time she sought the cooperation of the communists, her critics severely criticized her as a fellow-traveller, as a Russian stooge, as the antithesis of the democratic national ethos, as authoritarian and so on.

It was 1970. Still two years, two long and barren years to go before Indira Gandhi could turn to the people for a fresh mandate. Two weary years before the electorate—the illiterate, poor, ignorant but wise electorate of India—could resolve the stalemate in ideas and ideals, one way or the other. The wait was impossible to endure. Besides, the general stagnation meanwhile would lead to destructive unrest. Marking time for too long in a rapidly changing political environment would produce nothing but further confusion and anarchy.

The fact that Indira Gandhi was constrained by her lack of clear majority was not lost on the people. They had not wanted this to happen when they had voted her into power in 1967. Obviously, in the next elections they would opt for a stable majority—for one of the leaders, one of the parties who towered above the rest. Which was that party to be? Who was that leader to be? . . . You can decide after two years, the people were being told. However, they were not in a mood to defer their mandate, any more than Indira Gandhi was.

There was another side to the issue which had is own impeccable logic. This was that not even one per cent of the legislators were willing to face a fresh poll two years before it was due. Such a prospect was too frightening for them to contemplate. You're insulting the people by forcing them to vote again in the middle of the term, they argued. What right have you to do that? They voted you to power for five years, but your party split and splintered. You created all kinds of ideological conundrums in a naked scramble for power. You introduced personality clashes within the party and indulged in open name-calling at the highest levels. You divided yourselves into groups and sought to divide the people too on the basis of fraudulent slogans. You let your intolerance cross all limits of decency. And now you want the people to decide, before the due time, which of you they prefer. What audacity!

You didn't ask yourselves the question—why should they have to choose just between the two of you? Why should they choose between two gangs of the same party, which is what your so-called two parties really are? . . . And in any event, the MLAs and MPs have committed no sin. They are innocent. They have only played the leaders' game, following them like sheep—faithfully, unquestioningly. Now, instead of rewarding them for their loyalties, on both sides, you want to throw them to the electoral wolves! Shame on you! . . .

Chaudhury was furious. He had, of course, echoed Indira Gandhi's line—just the previous day. But this morning he was furious having just heard a disturbing new rumour. 'This is preposterous!' he roared to a group of loyalists. 'At this rate, we'll face an election every bloody month of the year. And the chief ministers will be doing the donkey's work all the time! God! What are we coming to!'

'Why didn't you tell the PM so yesterday when you called on her in Delhi?' asked someone present at the conclave. 'After all, she would like senior chief ministers like you to give her proper and timely advice . . .'

'Easy for you to say that in a cosy drawing room,' sneered Chaudhury. 'You don't understand my predicament. No other chief minister opens his mouth. Everyone endorses Indira Gandhi's decisions in advance. And gangs of MPs from the states keep telling her day in and day out that the chief ministers are all against her and on Morarji Desai's side. My good friend Mahendranath is working overtime on the same theme . . . I am not willing to tender unsolicited advice to the Prime Minister and get his prayers answered. She knows what to do.'

'Then why are you fretting?' asked the other.

'God! Can't a fellow fret in his own drawing room?' shouted Chaudhury, sending everyone present into peals of laughter. 'If I don't fret here, I'll go mad. You fellows will see me tearing my hair and stripping my clothes off in the street for public entertainment!'

That was the predicament of most chief ministers. Not only of those who disagreed with the idea of the mid-term poll; also of those who supported it. For this latter category, the approach was different, naturally. Suppose a chief minister strongly advocated mid-term polls and the election did not eventually take place, for some wretched reason or the other, where would he be then? This was already happening to one chief minister whom the dissidents in his legislature party were harassing mercilessly. They promptly spread the rumour—through the active support of a section of the press, of course—that the chief minister was desperately working for a mid-term poll in the state, along with a mid-term poll for the Lok Sabha. His motivation, it was said quite plausibly, was to curry favour with Indira Gandhi; to teach MLAs a lesson by driving them to the electorate far ahead of schedule; and most importantly, to call the shots as chief minister and deny the party ticket to all those sitting MLAs who did not toe his line . . . While the main question of the mid-term parliamentary poll still hung in mid-air, one important and reasonably stable chief minister thus fell into deep trouble . . . If Chaudhury didn't want to become the second in this train, you couldn't blame him, could you?

Shekhar was very active—on both sides, as one could expect of him. It was obviously a difficult game, involving risky acrobatics, but he managed it with finesse. He had extensive contacts in many constituencies and was quick to learn which MLAs were vulnerable. He concentrated on the shaky MLAs and convinced them that 'someone' was pressuring Chief Minister Chaudhury to push for a mid-term poll for the Lok Sabha and the state assembly . . . Shekhar also subtly insinuated that if there was a mid-term poll to the Lok Sabha, Chaudhury would secure the party tickets for his *chamchas* and plant them firmly in the Lok Sabha. They would, of course, be with Indira Gandhi, but their real loyalty would be with Chaudhury. His bargaining power *vis-à-vis* Indira Gandhi would endure for all time, to the complete exclusion of Mahendranath. Shekhar took care not to attribute any motives to Chaudhury directly. He always hinted at 'someone' or 'some force'. Those who listened drew their inferences. The needle of suspicion often pointed towards Anand.

Anand frequently confirmed the suspicion by his straight talk. What is the use, he said, of Indira Gandhi's regime if she has no parliamentary support to do anything meaningful for the poor? Since her colleagues deserted her, she has no one else but the people to turn to. They are sure to give her an unequivocal mandate if she approaches them, he asserted.

Shekhar was not so sure. In this, he was in an impressive majority among 'knowledgeable' persons. In the first place, he said, no one could gauge the will of the people; indeed, no one should. Since Indira Gandhi still had more than a year and a half before the due date of the poll, she could certainly utilize this time to establish her bona fides, even if she could not do much, given her obvious limitations. It was possible that if she then went to the people, they would give her another term. On the other hand, if she went to them now, she would only irritate them. In the process, she might irritate and alienate a large number of her loyal followers. After all, why had they supported her against heavy odds? Not to unseat themselves in mid-term, surely?

When Shekhar talked to party men who had lost in the last election, as also many 'hopefuls' who pined for a mid-term poll to the assembly, he struck a different note. Chaudhury, he said, was in favour of a mid-term poll. He wants younger and better talent to enter the Lok Sabha and the state assembly. However—he would add after a suspenseful ten seconds—someone is stopping him and he, in turn, is stopping Indira Gandhi. And my young friends, who could this someone be except one who is not sure to succeed at the polls again? Maybe someone whose image is so tarnished that he knows people will dump him this time . . . Maybe someone who is a minister and wants to continue as minister till the last day of the term, in other words the last day as minister in his life! Again, the target of his attack could be none other than Anand. Everyone understood.

Confusion mounted by the day; no one talked of anything else. One morning, Anand's drawing room was full of agitated MLAs who wanted to know what was happening. Anand wanted to put across his point of view as clearly as he could but he wasn't making much headway. The MLAs were determined to have their say and from their remarks it was clear that they had been well tutored by someone before they arrived at his house. He changed his stance and sat back patiently, while his private secretary organized tea and snacks.

Maulana, the oldest MLA in the assembly, said without preamble, 'This is my last term in the assembly, Anand,' he said. 'You have decided to cut it short halfway . . .'

Good old Maulana was beside himself with fear at the prospect of defeat. Understandable, Anand conceded; but the old man's diatribe upset him. It was unfair in the extreme.

'You know, Maulana,' Anand began patiently, 'My respect for you puts a seal on my lips. I don't intend to join issue with you. Now, tell me, why do you think anyone would want a mid-term poll in the state?'

'That's what everyone says,' declared Maulana.

'Who is this "everyone" you are talking about?' Anand shot back.

'Everyone is everyone,' Maulana said, unwilling to be more forthcoming. In fact, in that fleeting moment, he realized that the 'everyone' he had referred to was in fact just one: Shekhar.

'Okay, let's analyse this a bit,' said Anand. 'You think Chief Minister Chaudhury has lost his majority in the assembly?'

'Of course not,' asserted Maulana, with all the others supporting him in a chorus.

'Does he find himself unable to run the government for any other reason?' queried Anand.

'Not at all,' echoed the others.

'Then, why should there be a mid-term poll in the state? What justification did "everyone" mention to you, Maulana?' Anand persisted.

Maulana had no answer. Someone else hazarded a guess. 'It is rumoured that you, Anand, strongly favour a mid-term poll to the Lok Sabha and simultaneously to the state assembly,' he declared.

'Now don't confuse the two,' said Anand. 'I am certainly in favour of a mid-term poll to the Lok Sabha. The reasons are obvious: Indira Gandhi's mandate is not unambiguous. It is not as strong as she needs it to be, to carry out her programme. She needs to get that programme endorsed or rejected again by the people, as they choose. She can't be marking time, in my view, for another two years . . . And that's my view, as I said. I am neither a member of parliament nor a Central minister. I have no say in the matter. At the state level, however, we don't have any of these factors to contend with. I don't see how we could justify a mid-term poll here . . .'

'Well, someone told us—' began one MLA tentatively.

'Never mind what someone told you,' cut in Anand. 'Consider the issue yourselves and draw your own conclusions.'

While the discussion went on inconclusively, Anand's private secretary quietly slipped a piece of paper into his hands and withdrew. Anand glanced at it and announced, 'Here's news, ladies and gentlemen. The Central government has just lost a snap vote in the Rajya Sabha over the bill to abolish privy purses . . .'

There was stony silence all round for a few minutes. Then someone found his voice and said, 'That's shocking; but they could still re-introduce the bill, couldn't they?'

'A snap vote is no indication of the government's strength,' asserted another. 'I am sure they can retrieve the bill and pass it eventually.'

Opinions were exchanged noisily for a few minutes, while Anand sat in silence, looking out of the window. That attracted immediate attention and everyone started to gaze at him intently, in ominous silence . . .

'What a splendid springboard for mid-term elections to the Lok Sabha!' Anand said slowly, almost inaudibly.

The others had some misgivings but there was nothing they

could do about it; in any event the general feeling among them was of relief because Anand hadn't been talking about elections at the state level; they were now certain that *their* term wouldn't be cut short. Shekhar had raised a false alarm. They sat for a few minutes and trooped out, relieved and pleased.

Anand sat still for some time. Doubts assailed him again. He did not know if Indira Gandhi would opt for a mid-term poll. If she did, would that be the right decision? He thought so, but the battle between the pros and the cons raged violently in his mind. What it really amounted to was a clash between audacity and circumspection. A tussle between being a visionary and playing it safe. These choices were dangerous, like the choice between the right eye and the left. How do you choose between two equally essential things? Indira Gandhi herself somehow constituted a dangerous choice, albeit a compelling one. Anand believed that she was the right choice to lead the country; but how many in the party really thought the way he did? The way they sang Indiraji's praises—even the absurd words they used, the epithets they employed—did no justice to Indira Gandhi's essential nature, her will, her strength, her determination and motivation.

On the other hand, the split had had its impact. Anand and some of his friends had exulted over it; they still stood by it. Yet, he could not help noticing that the split did not work out the way its authors had intended. It brought about a polarization between enthusiasm and caution; from another standpoint, between rash inexperience and complacent passivity. And on both sides of the divide, unhealthy factors tended to dominate—impulse and inaction, political idolatry and barren superciliousness. The favourable characteristics were submerged, at least overshadowed, on both sides.

But it was clear to him that Indira Gandhi must free herself from her shackles, find her wings to fly. He was convinced that the only way this could take place was through a mid-term poll. There were other things that she needed to do urgently. She would need to pick a team that could help her in the task. Everyone who criticized Morarji Desai or the 'Syndicate' could not arbitarily or automatically became her ally. Conversely, all her sycophants and hangers-on were not necessarily the right people to help her implement her programme.

Within a few days of the snap vote and its aftermath, Anand could see what should have been even more obvious to Indira Gandhi—that the choice of her human tools was now more crucial than ever before. He found too many little-known men and women strutting around as Indira Gandhi's 'loyal' followers. He noticed that too many persons who had neither talent nor conviction got accelerated promotions in the party. Many who had not proved their mettle even in local elections now became fancied candidates for the Lok Sabha, in case of a mid-term poll. Several vacancies had arisen as a result of the split; many more would become available when the time for selections came. It was whispered that many who were still with her and were not quite 'loyal' would be replaced.

Where the opportunists and cynics were concerned, the emphasis was already on the party ticket, almost to the exclusion of the party programme. If there was to be an 'Indira Gandhi wave' this time, why not climb on to her bandwagon immediately? What difference did ideology make anyway? After all, what was needed now was loyalty . . . And this was measured by how loud one shouted '*jai!*', how many times one mentioned Indira's name in public speeches. Fantastic hyperbole became an important criterion of loyalty. If you said that the sun rose in the east and the rains came on time because of Indira Gandhi, you were a loyal follower—'soldier' was the word in fashion.

Anand found, to his horror, that Indira Gandhi's camp almost overflowed with men and women who could only be a dead weight on her, who merely wanted to bask in her glory, who were out to benefit from her position. They couldn't give her an ounce of strength in return; they didn't possess any themselves. This was the depressing side of an otherwise exhilarating prospect, a noble dream. The dream promised a break from the past, the dawn of a new era in Indian politics—the politics of committed action.

Then came the announcement of the mid-term poll to the Lok Sabha, as expected, as dreaded.

# 49

THE COUNTRY PLUNGED INTO INTENSE ACTIVITY. THIS WAS THE very first election to the Lok Sabha before its due time—a full year ahead. This fact was widely discussed, criticized and variously interpreted. The initial reaction in most quarters was: Would Jawaharlal have allowed such an event to come about? Of course not, everyone agreed. From this point on, people's opinions diverged. Had the sober Morarji Desai become the Prime Minister instead of Indira Gandhi the ruthless power-seeker, there would have been no split, some asserted. No sir, you are completely wrong there, others retorted. Under Morarji Desai the party would never have come to power in 1967. Never. Indira Gandhi has saved the party, make no mistake about that. She has trimmed the party and energized it after the split. And now her party is trying to ensure a more homogeneous programme for the country by ordering a mid-term poll . . . and let's face it, there is no Jawaharlal now. To claim that Morarji would have continued to provide the stability that Jawaharlal did is idle speculation . . . In any case, it hasn't happened that way. So why propagate a useless hypothesis?

What needs to be done now has to be done, so let the people decide . . . In short, in every corner of the country, the impending poll was the subject of animated, even frenzied, discussion.

Anand was touring an outlying district of the state when he heard the news of the mid-term poll on the radio. The broadcast specified that the election was only to the Lok Sabha. There would be no elections to the legislative assemblies simultaneously, as had been the practice till then.

'When will you go to polls for the assembly?' the village sarpanch, who was also listening to the broadcast, asked Anand. 'Next year,' Anand replied.

'Thank God,' said the sarpanch. 'How is this election to parliament different for us from the assembly election next year?'

The question was rather complex. The issues in a Lok Sabha poll were different. The people should understand this in terms of their own benefit; Anand realized, with regret, that the party had neglected to explain this. It was merely telling them that Indira Gandhi was taking on Morarji Desai in the mid-term poll.

Several villagers gathered around him—some to see him, others to be seen by or near him. The mid-term poll was the sole topic of conversation. The people shot questions at Anand from all sides. Above all, they wanted to know what was in it for them. Not in vague generalizations, but in concrete, measurable terms.

Anand began by telling them about the stature and image of Indira Gandhi. That was the best opening gambit available. It worked instantly and there was all-round approbation. Then one octogenarian said, in a feeble voice, 'What is Indira Gandhi going to do for the country?'

Anand had been expecting the question, and he began telling them about how the abolition of privy purses was one of the many things that Indira Gandhi was planning to do to redistribute wealth and help the country at large.

'What's a privy purse?' the old man asked.

Anand was not surprised by the question. He hadn't really expected the villagers to know about privy purses. He explained what privy purses were and told them just why Indira Gandhi wanted to abolish them. He told them why the princes had no right to privy purses, how these payments to the elite class of a bygone era deprived the people of funds that the government could spend on their development instead . . .

Yet he found a wall of blank faces in front of him. At last the octogenarian, after a few moments of hesitation, said, 'You mean the kings who ruled over us until some years back are going to lose their money?'

'Yes, exactly,' Anand answered, somewhat relieved that the man at last understood the point.

'How is it fair to deprive them of what they were getting?' asked the old man. 'After all, they owned everything in their states before. How will they live now, if you take away their purses—or whatever you call them? Do you want them to beg in the streets? Is it right for Indira Gandhi to treat them like this?' Then he embarked upon a convoluted description of how generous the kings had been, how they showered benefits on some individuals unexpectedly, on a whim, and how his generation had always been loyal to the king. 'If he is king and I am a poor subject, it is karma,' he concluded. 'Why should he suffer for it? And how much money will you save by driving them to penury? How much of that money is each of us going to get?'

The old man's stance stunned Anand—the insistence on personal loyalty even now, even after the advent of democracy, perplexed him all the more. The question of whether kings had ever lost power in the eyes of the people mocked him. No, Anand concluded, the privy purses issue was irrelevant in the rural context. He found it astonishing that the people had forgotten the tyrannies of the princes. Perhaps it was due to the varied misdeeds of the succeeding regimes. Yes, everyone loved and respected Jawaharlal Nehru, but wasn't he, Anand asked himself, some kind of substitute for a great king in the villager's mind? . . . The people despised a corrupt sarpanch or legislator more than a corrupt businessman or feudal lord: curious, but true. The businessman was naturally corrupt in the public eye; the feudal had to be despotic and corrupt anyway. But what about this sarpanch fellow? He was begging for a small loan just a year back. Now, having become sarpanch, look at the double-storied house he has built! Why, it is as big as the deshmukh's garhi, which took generations to build. So, has the country changed for the better? Or are things much worse?

Anand had no answer to the villager's unforeseen reaction. A change in the person of the exploiter is no change at all; no, he corrected himself, it is a change for the worse. 'Give me back my king, who ruled from the distant capital,' the villager seemed to say. 'Get this upstart sarpanch-cousin of mine off my back, for God's sake! He humiliates me with his authority twenty-four hours a day, here, in the same village! I hate his face! To hell with his new-found power!'

So, what has Indira Gandhi to offer these men and women, Anand wondered. It should be something they understand completely. It should be something they believe they will benefit from. They should be convinced that it will bring about a real change in their lives . . . What, in heaven's name, could that be? He began to think—and fervently hoped that millions would begin to think like him. Including, of course, Indira Gandhi.

Take the rural poor, for instance. The government had promised them land for more than a decade. He, Anand, was in the game right now. How much land had he given them so far? Not much, he admitted to himself. The landholders had violated the land ceiling law in a vast number of cases. He knew he could do nothing about it. He passed more and more stringent orders day after day, but nothing happened. The district officials pretended to comply with the orders, mainly to send reports. Almost no action was taken . . . Why was it so?

In the first place, Anand noted, the ceilings in force so far were too high to yield any sizeable surplus for distribution to the landless. He had surveyed many villages at random, including his own. Under the existing law, they could find very few owners with surplus land, even if the government enforced the law honestly. So, he asked himself, does Indira Gandhi intend to make land ceilings effective? Until now, the answer was no; several senior leaders in her party did not allow the measure to go through. They wanted rhetoric without change, claims without results. That's how it had been, despite the efforts of a determined few like Anand.

As such, a rehash of the ongoing—more correctly, non-going—programme would not enthuse the people. Besides, the other party would claim it too, since it had been common to both in the undivided ruling party. So this time the programme had to be distinctive, Indira Gandhi's own, which the other party could not—dare not—claim nor duplicate . . . These were the crucial parameters.

Then there was the twin of rural land: urban land. Over the years, the government had enacted laws of sorts on ceilings for rural agricultural land. However, the expensive land belonging to the rich in the cities had no ceiling imposed on it. Whatever the niceties of the argument, the undivided ruling party could not justify this discrimination. The farmers had accused the government of a pro-urban bias. There was no way to counter the accusation by argument.

Here, then, was another distinctive programme available to Indira Gandhi, if only she would quickly seize the chance to implement it. Anand's hunch was that the other party—the Syndicate—would not take to this programme with fervour. They would, at best, mention it in passing. Was it possible, then, for Indira Gandhi to project this programme forcefully? Would she make so bold as to incur the displeasure of the urban rich? Would she or wouldn't she? . . . He thought she would, but wasn't sure. He wasn't sure of anything in this game where election promises had lost much of their credibility and party manifestos were reduced to mere scraps of paper . . . Would Indira Gandhi change that? Would she invest the manifesto with the sanctity of the Magna Carta? Would she, in effect, decide to stand or fall by that document? So much was at stake for democracy in the answer to that question, Anand reflected.

Why not go into the basics first? The two-year-old split, in the people's perception, was not a routine political event. Mahatma Gandhi's legacy was being divided into two. Jawaharlal Nehru's vision was being snapped in the middle. The whole ethos of a party that represented the aspirations of millions was being bifurcated. But surely that was incorrect, Anand mused. How could you split

Mahatma Gandhi's legacy? How could you fracture Nehru's vision? Each was a unique and indivisible phenomenon. No one could dismember the aspirations of millions; that was absurd.

So what did this split in the ruling party really signify? Go to the basics, Anand repeated to himself. There are two camps in the ruling party today, he noted, each calling itself *the* party. Since no one could bifurcate the common legacy, each called itself the original and whole party and dubbed the other a group of expelled persons. There is only *one* party, each claimed, and ours is that. That is how there was one party seen as two, or two parties giving the illusion of one . . . Which was the truth? The question could be debated times without number without necessarily arriving at a satisfactory answer, Anand concluded.

Meanwhile, the practical implications of the split surfaced. Everything relating to the undivided party became an issue between the two new parties. This created total confusion everywhere—among the people, in the party ranks. Litigation was initiated by both groups for the name, flag, election symbol, offices, records—everything. Where the election symbol was concerned, a ridiculous situation arose. Both parties claimed the same symbol. To be sure, the symbol meant a lot. People were familiar with it. It projected the party as the original one; the other party became a newcomer by implication. So the fight over the symbol was the most bitter. And the Election Commission adopted the only course possible under the circumstances. It 'froze' the old symbol and allotted new symbols to the two parties.

The names of the parties presented yet another difficulty. The Election Commission at last settled it by permitting both parties to have the same name, adding the first letter of each party president's name in brackets. Thus the party headed by Indira Gandhi had the suffix (I) . . . and so forth. It became a joke for some time. What would they do if the names of both the presidents began with the same letter—or worse still, if both had identical names? Would they bring in the father's or husband's name to distinguish their parties? someone quipped.

The undivided party had hundreds of office buildings throughout the country. The possession of these buildings presented a major problem. Litigation apart, musclemen had a field day. They captured, recaptured and re-recaptured premises. The process went on for months—in some cases, years. It tarnished the image of both parties. Newspapers at home and abroad described the skirmishing in lurid terms. Intellectuals saw the disintegration of the ruling party—'even as we watch helplessly', they added for emphasis. Many ambassadors in Delhi sent long dispatches to their governments predicting the eventual—some said imminent—break-up of the country, since there was no other political party that could keep it together. Several political mouths began watering—in regions around India and in far-off former colonial capitals. And, of course, media commentators decided unanimously that Indira Gandhi was the 'splitter'—the sole agent of disintegration.

In the geopolitical context the split in the ruling party was a dangerous development that the nation could not afford to ignore. Wasn't it a similar situation of seeming instability that had tempted General Ayub Khan of Pakistan into an adventure after Nehru's death? Now it was General Yahya Khan who was a threat. There was little difference otherwise.

Indira Gandhi could not risk being labelled the splitter of the party and wrecker of the country. Indeed, it had to be the reverse. She had to turn the split into a factor of strength and stability for the country. In other words, her party had to win handsomely in the 1971 Lok Sabha elections. There was just no other way. It was apparent that the other breakaway party—the Syndicate—could not give the country a stable and strong government. Its leaders claimed they could, but their claim did not carry conviction . . . All they seemed to be able to do was reduce Indira Gandhi's chances at the hustings. This meant the weakening of the country, in addition to weakening Indira Gandhi.

It was again Indira Gandhi on whom all eyes were centred.

This brought Anand back to the blunt question the old villager had asked. What does Indira Gandhi offer to the poor, the downtrodden, the helpless, the powerless? The question was not limited to the impending mid-term election alone. It was a question addressed to all Prime Ministers of India, present and future. It wasn't a mere selfish question, Anand noted. It was in many ways a patriotic question, a question of the nation's strength and stability. It concerned the wide base of the social pyramid.

When Anand returned to the dak bungalow after chatting with the villagers, he was exhausted. He realized that although he had been acting as Indira Gandhi's surrogate for so long and so persistently, it was true that he had no close acquaintance with her, certainly no insight into her mind or opinions on vital matters of policy. Was he justified in almost being her mouthpiece? Hadn't he constructed an image of Indira Gandhi in the mould of his own thinking? How was he sure he was right? Wasn't it just another brand of personal loyalty, the problematic concept that he had been debating in his mind ever since his school days? Wasn't it hypocritical?

These nagging doubts stung him like bees. He was committing himself to an extent that made no sense. At such moments, he found Shekhar's logic more plausible. He and Shekhar had both been in favour of the split. Both had supported Indira Gandhi. However, their reasons for doing so were poles apart.

Shekhar saw the split simply as a fact of life. Where there is no Opposition worth the name, the ruling party splits naturally, providing the Opposition with the fuel it needs to run the vehicle of democracy. All that one has to do is to manoeuvre oneself on the right side of political developments. The right side need not always be the ruling side. Sometimes being on the other side for a short while might bring better dividends. It may catapult you into a longer spell of power—particularly if the split occurs not long before an election.

Why had he thrown in his lot with Indira Gandhi? 'Simple, my friend,' Shekhar was reported to have said. 'She is winning this election. What she will do then, I can't say. That is in the future. I believe in first things first, see? So I have to be with the winning side. Also, I hope that with its massive resources and power of intrigue, the other side will be returned in viable numbers too. You see, this country simply can't afford total unity in the ruling party, ever!'

This and similar comments from other party members incensed

Anand. Yet on reflection he had to admit that one could not expect identical motivations for the variegated actions of political beings. He did know that many in Indira Gandhi's party had differing motivations, quite unconnected with ideology. And ruminating thus, he suddenly stumbled onto the question, the question of questions: what about *her* motivation? He dismissed the question instantly, biting his lip and feeling guilty of something akin to blasphemy.

He returned to the state capital and met Chaudhury who was, as usual, in high spirits. The reason, believe it or not, was that at last—at long last—Mahendranath had just declared his allegiance to Morarji's party. Chaudhury was virtually dancing like a happy peacock in his drawing room when Anand stepped in. 'Laugh aloud, man! This calls for celebration . . . the scoundrel has left us . . . left us in peace at last! Now . . . now . . . You'll see good old Chaudhury in his element. I'll get him defeated if he stands for election. I'll rub his nose in the mud. You'll hear no more of Mahendranath after this . . . Look, why don't you draft a nice epitaph for him? Your drafting talent couldn't be put to better use!'

'He may not stand for election,' Anand pointed out.

'Oh yes, he will, I assure you!' Chaudhury ejaculated. 'You don't know him as I do, for heaven's sake! He will stand, will stand, will . . .'

With each repetition, his emphasis grew less and his assertion more uncertain. Then in a flash he shouted, 'If he doesn't stand, he stands exposed! That itself will be his epitaph! See?'

Anand didn't quite see the matter the way Chaudhury did. This was a peripheral issue for him. He didn't quite consider victory or defeat as anything to be excited about. In a storm of this intensity, individuals were bound to rise or fall. That wasn't important for the country. The really crucial issue was the total tally of seats the party won and how the millions of voters responded to Indira Gandhi's promise to change their lives.

The most disquieting aspect of the election, as he saw it, was that there would be confusion unless the voters were able to think seriously before voting. They had not been put to hard thinking in any of the previous elections, because of their implicit faith in

Jawaharlal Nehru. Some went into the details and hard facts, many didn't, and the party came back to power. Even while Jawaharlal was alive, some disenchantment had set in—not about his leadership and other qualities, but about his ability to actualize his dreams. He is great, said many. But there were some who commented that because his head was in the clouds, he was not aware of the landslides under his feet. People had begun to feel that merely having a great visionary as Prime Minister was not enough. You cannot fill your stomach with visions, they pointed out.

And, of course, you kept coming back to the basic fact that Indira Gandhi was not Jawaharlal. In her case, visions wouldn't work at all. She had to deal with realities. And the reality was there for everyone to see: the rich were becoming richer, the poor were becoming relatively poorer. Even if the poor gained something from the government's programmes, this went almost unnoticed because the rich were growing much more in wealth by the day. Their growth—coupled with the near-stagnation of the poor—became a permanent festering abscess. As it was, the benefits of government schemes, such as there were, did not reach those they were intended for. With these increasing inequities, social tensions mounted. The Naxalite movement in some parts of the country—not extensive yet, but significant enough—stood testimony to the proven limitations of the democratic process itself as practised in the country. Logically, the new creed of socialism needed to include a measure of levelling down which would make the much smaller 'levelling up' seem tolerable. The two sides of the coin were vitally interlinked, whether some leaders liked it or not. How did Indira Gandhi propose to meet this situation head-on—which was the only way to meet it?

Out of this challenge was born the most evocative symbol of total response. The basic root—as well as the totality—of the malady being poverty, the slogan *Garibi Hatao* (Remove Poverty) took shape. In no time, it caught the people's imagination. It spread to every nook of the country—without language versions, translations, annotations, explanations. It was *Garibi Hatao* in Tamil, it was *Garibi Hatao* in Manipuri. It was a thunderbolt. It

621

was a revelation. It was a revolution. No one perhaps knew the originator, or the coiner of the slogan; nor the source of his or her inspiration. But he or she must have been a person inspired to the depths of the soul. The slogan was sheer poetry, celestial music, a Vedic hymn. It was everything to everyone . . . It was fantastic in its impact. It almost matched the Quit India call of 1942 in its impact, its brevity, its exquisite simplicity.

There was nothing to beat it—just nothing. It generated a wave—a wave which no one could resist. Many straws who happened to coast upon it reached the shore in grand style. Many solid mountains who resisted it crumbled and were submerged.

The words had sculpted a political miracle.

Nothing else mattered—candidates, castes, creeds, speeches, campaigns, alliances, stratagems, money, muscle . . . nothing.

The people just awaited the counting of votes; they knew the result even before the campaign had begun.

*Indira Gandhi ki jai!* echoed everywhere.

Her leadership came of age overnight—and for good.

# 50

THE COUNTRY CELEBRATED INDIRA GANDHI'S VICTORY. THE POOR man in the village began to walk with a bit of a swagger—because of a combination of naïveté and a genuine awakening of consciousness. He assumed that his *garibi* would soon be *hatao*-ed (removed). And, in the euphoric early days of her victory, a genuine scene of jubilation pervaded all sections of society.

This was amply clear, for instance, from the enthusiastic support Indira Gandhi got from no less a person than Balram, the embodiment of the feudal order. He had improvised his own logic as to why the landlord class, as a whole, must support Indira Gandhi. He was active in the Lok Sabha elections and made some speeches too. He argued well, often better than some of the ruling party's star performers. Speech-making had never been instinctive with him. Indeed, his feudal mentality had looked down upon all electioneering as unmitigated fraud. At this election, however, he convinced everyone—as only a feudal aristocrat can—of the need for land reforms. 'Look at these Naxalites,' he would point out. 'They're playing havoc with the lives of the people in the villages.

P. V. NARASIMHA RAO

The landlord looked after the village so far; but somehow he doesn't fit into the landscape any more. So, what does one do? Indira Gandhi says, give land to the landless and rescue them from the Naxalites' clutches. I agree, one hundred per cent. So, friends, vote for Indira Gandhi's party. Save the villages from bloodshed and save yourselves from murder and extortion!'

Aruna would often burst out laughing at these speeches during the campaign. Anand was also present at some meetings and marvelled at the flexibility of the feudal class. There was no situation they could not cope with—from fascism to Naxalism. Anand's task at the campaign meetings became much easier. When the landlord pleads for land reforms, what more can the minister of land reforms add? So he merely endorsed what Balram said. Yet, he could not help suspecting the other man's motives. He wouldn't concede that all that new-found rhetoric was just the result of a change of heart.

Aruna wasn't convinced by her brother's sudden desire for land reform. 'There is something mysterious in your transformation, bhaiya,' she teased. 'You must be finding some benefit in Indira Gandhi's camp!'

'I find benefits in every camp,' snapped Balram.

'Including the Naxalite camp . . . ' sneered Aruna.

'Yes, of course. I find some special benefit in that camp,' replied Balram nonchalantly.

Thus, all social forces began to find their equation with the Indira Gandhi dispensation. It was a different Indira Gandhi now. She was supreme leader in her own right, no longer just Jawaharlal's daughter. Gone were the comparisons between father and daughter that had taken Jawaharlal as the standard and measured Indira Gandhi against it. People had found her wanting in some things, deficient in some others, almost equal elsewhere. The outcome had been invariably unfavourable to Indira. Now, after her grand victory of 1971, Indira, though she didn't quite become the standard, didn't have to stand comparison with anyone any more.

She could not, however, confine herself to governing the country and solving internal problems. India has an international

624

role that no Prime Minister can disown. Nehru excelled in it and made a name for himself and for the country. He was, in his time, among the world's great statesmen. Obviously his role, as also the country's, had not ended with his death. In fact, it had become more complicated with the worsening world situation and the tension in India's neighbourhood. Pakistan was not a stable entity and its internal contradictions and divisions gave rise to a situation that eventually culminated in the greatest event of the decade: the birth of Bangladesh. Indira Gandhi's role in that historic event came soon after her electoral triumph of 1971. It was her finest hour. It made her a permanent object of fear and hatred in the ruling circles of Pakistan. Also, it gave them a standing alibi for their own failure to keep the west and the east wings of their country together.

\*

Bangladesh was an epic narrative indeed—of drama and heroism, of revolts and betrayals, of struggles and fulfilment, of suppression and, finally, freedom.

For more than two decades after its formation, military dictators ruled Pakistan, with short spells of civilian government. It was a geographically and ethnically diverse country, and it did not possess an inherently democratic environment. For this reason, among others, military governments found it easy to take control.

In particular, there was very little in common between the peoples of the west and east wings of Pakistan. Religion alone bound them as a nation-state. The physical distance separating them added to the problems of integration—apart, of course, from the lack of the basic will to integrate. From the very inception of Pakistan, the two wings had been unequal in many respects—in their numbers in the armed and civilian services, in economic prosperity, and so on. For instance, among the 133 officers of the Indian Civil Service who opted for Pakistan at the time of Partition, only one was a Bengali.

The East Pakistanis did consider themselves superior in two respects: language and cultural heritage. So, when the leaders of

West Pakistan sought to make Urdu the official language of the whole country, there was an immediate demand in East Pakistan to recognize Bengali as one of the state languages. Besides ethnic sentiment, language was directly related to job prospects and social standing. Both the Urdu and Bengali-speaking sections of Pakistan were keenly aware of this.

Differences on this score had indeed appeared in 1946, even as Pakistan was being conceived as an entity. But the euphoria of a new identity was too strong to allow conflict over what seemed a minor issue then. However, once Pakistan was born, the realities of the language question came into bold relief. The backlash started as early as 1948, when the government posted a large number of non-Bengalis in the Dacca Secretariat, and at lower levels. An East Pakistani litterateur, Abdul Mansoor Ahmed, wrote:

> If Urdu is made the state language (of Pakistan), the educated section of the people of East Pakistan would be rendered 'illiterate' and thus unfit for Government jobs instantaneously, (just) as the Muslim educated class were made 'illiterate' and 'unfit' for Government jobs in a day by the British imperialists when they declared English as the state language in place of Persian in the middle of the nineteenth century.

The proposal to make Urdu the sole official language of Pakistan drew its authority from Jinnah himself. He refused to accept a bilingual dispensation. The Qaid-e-Azam's verdict was final. Jinnah stuck to the theory that a single national language, Urdu, was the hallmark of the Pakistani nation. It did not matter to him that the people of the eastern wing, who constituted a numerical majority in the new country, did not know or speak Urdu. He dubbed those who demanded that Bengali be recognized as one of the official languages as 'enemies of Pakistan' and 'fifth columnists . . . who are financed by outsiders'. He also threatened to come down heavily on them. His strategy was to forge unity in Pakistan by doing away with East Pakistan's distinctive linguistic and cultural features. Other leaders also pursued this strategy persistently after Jinnah. Another categorical announcement on Urdu being the 'sole' official language of Pakistan came from the then Prime Minister, while he was on a visit to Dacca.

There was a spontaneous pro-Bengali insurgency in 1953 in East Pakistan, in which many brave young men faced bullets. Language, however, was just the thin end of the wedge. It only indicated the unrest that gripped East Pakistan on a variety of issues. It soon developed into a struggle for the liberation of East Pakistan from what the people perceived as the 'colonialism' of West Pakistan. The link of religion became weak. The vision of a secular nation, instead, caught the imagination of the people of East Pakistan—at least the thinking sections of the people.

When language politics ignited the first spark, other issues— equally vital, perhaps more—surfaced too. Being an area with a majority population, East Pakistan asked for a proportionately bigger share in the nation's legislature and its governance. Coupled with this was the demand for autonomy for East Pakistan—with a few specified subjects under the Central government. This was totally unacceptable to the western wing. Consequently, the process of Constitution-making dragged on for several years and ended abruptly in 1954.

Then came the 'Parity Formula', which sought to implement equal representation for the western and eastern wings, with two state languages and cultural autonomy. Both wings accepted it at first, but almost immediately, the western wing violated the understanding, with Ayub Khan's military regime finally hijacking the political process.

Ayub attempted several fiats. He wanted to change the Bengali script to Roman. He tried to 'reform' the language by weeding out Sanskrit words and replacing them with Persian and Arabic equivalents. Finally, he banned the inclusion of Hindu poets who wrote in Bengali in the school syllabi. The official media and newspapers under government tutelage sought to banish Rabindranath Tagore from East Bengal. These steps only added enormous fuel to the raging fire. The leading poets of East Bengal promptly composed and sang soul-stirring patriotic songs, heralding and welcoming an independent nation.

From the economic point of view, East Bengal was at a disadvantage from the beginning. In 1947, Bengal was partitioned into east and west, on the basis of its Muslim population being predominantly in the east, which then became East Pakistan. While West Bengal soon became integrated with the rest of India economically and industrially, the other segment remained geographically and culturally isolated from West Pakistan. Indeed, whatever development took place was at the expense of East Pakistan. A kind of colonial relationship developed between the two wings. The eastern wing was an exporter of jute and tea; but its foreign exchange potential only helped West Pakistan's industrialists to accumulate capital. East Pakistan became a captive market for the manufactured products of West Pakistan.

This was just one instance of how the western wing exploited East Pakistan economically. The state invested larger amounts of capital for West Pakistan's development than they did for the eastern wing. Between 1963 and 1966, private investment in East Pakistan was just over one-fifth of the country's total. The government employed several administrative devices to camouflage this disparity. The devices only made it more transparent and painful. The net transfer of resources from the eastern wing to the western was estimated at $200 million a year. It was too glaring an injustice to escape attention. Clearly, East Pakistan's poverty contributed to West Pakistan's prosperity.

There was also gross neglect of the eastern wing in respect of education, health and social services. Starting from a better position at the time of the Partition where literacy was concerned, East Pakistan slipped to a far lower position in education by 1970. The western wing had thirteen out of sixteen research centres. It received the lion's share of scholarships and training facilities.

In Talukdar Muniruzzaman's words:

All this led to the Ayub Government losing its raison d'être for most people in the East. This resulted not only in a loss of legitimacy. The loss was much greater than that. As economic development was raised from the instrumental sphere to the transcendental level, and as no compensatory ideological and political values were developed to cushion economic frustrations, continuous talk about economic disparity between East and West Pakistan created a severe sense of deprivation among the educated classes of East Pakistan. It prepared them mentally to accept the argument—advanced forcefully by some East Pakistan leaders—that the economic advancement of East Pakistan could not take place until the colonial yoke of West Pakistan was totally broken . . .

No principles of political justice were applied to make up for the 'deprivation' on the economic front. On the other hand, the hopes of the East Pakistani people for genuine parliamentary democracy (with a fair share of power to the eastern wing) came to nothing in the Presidential elections of January 1965. Ayub had so tailored the rules of the election that the people could not remove him even if they did not want him. Such was the genius of the new system he had devised.

Even in the context of the Indo-Pak war of 1965, the western wing alone featured prominently. The people of East Pakistan were not consulted or involved in decisions by the rulers in West Pakistan. This distrust struck deep into the psyche of the East Pakistani people. They also realized that West Pakistani leaders did not see the defence of the western and eastern wings of Pakistan as an integrated whole. India, for instance, could have cut off East Pakistan completely during the hostilities and there was nothing the western wing could have done, or perhaps even wanted to do. So, the people of the eastern wing reasoned, each had to fend for itself separately.

Somewhere through these vicissitudes, a new consciousness also surfaced, that East Pakistan itself was self-sufficient in every way. It had a beautiful and rich language, an ancient culture, ample natural resources, and a highly intelligent and emotionally united people with a shared aversion to the subservient regional position foisted on them through the decades. Their fertile imagination visualized a resplendent future.

This situation saw the emergence of a charismatic leader in Sheikh Mujib-ur-Rehman. He presented a blueprint of

near-independence for East Pakistan, which he couched as a
formula for 'autonomy'. Ayub Khan stuck to his 'language of
weapons'. This only deepened the crisis of confidence between the
two wings, now intensifying at the popular level. Ayub promptly
charged Sheikh Mujib with fostering conspiracy 'to bring about
the secession of East Pakistan with Indian help'. His trial by a
special tribunal, with the proceedings reported in the newspapers
every day, added to the simmering tension. The people grew
increasingly hostile. When Sheikh Mujib came out of prison, the
inevitable happened: he became a hero and the foremost fighter
for national independence.

In the 1970 general election, Sheikh Mujib's party, the Awami
League, swept the polls in East Pakistan, capturing 160 out of 162
seats. Its main plank was the friendly relations with India. A mixed
result was seen in the western wing, with the majority going to
Zulfiqar Ali Bhutto's Pakistan People's Party, wedded to the slogan
of 'a thousand years' war with India' and a strong Central
government in Pakistan. The verdicts in the two wings were thus
predictably contradictory. The people on both sides chose to go in
widely differing directions.

Even so, the result of the election required that Sheikh Mujib
head the Central government of Pakistan. This would have placed
the responsibility of preserving the country's unity squarely on his
shoulders. It would have forced him to modify his 'confederation'
demand and find a *modus vivendi* for the whole nation.

At this point, however, personal factors supervened. The
political leaders of West Pakistan opposed Sheikh Mujib's
becoming leader of the whole of Pakistan. 'We don't want to be
ruled by Bengalis,' was the unequivocal slogan in the West. It
reverberated throughout the region and accentuated the inherent
regional, ethnic and cultural differences between the two wings.
The West Pakistanis considered the East Pakistanis inferior in all
respects. This psychological complex had been present throughout
the conflict. It erupted when the stewardship of the country was
about to slip into Bengali hands after the 1970 general elections.

The ambivalent West Pakistani attitude toward the East drove
Bhutto from one absurd position to the next. He declared that

there were 'two majority parties' and 'two Pakistans'.

This latter declaration was about to become prophetic.

*

Across the border, Indian Prime Minister Indira Gandhi was about to face a crucial election to the Lok Sabha. The Pakistani leaders saw her, as well as India, as vulnerable. They had always been on the lookout for such a situation. Or perhaps they assessed Indira Gandhi's real potential accurately and wanted to prevent her ascent in time. Consequently, they made her the sole target of their political assaults. They mounted an extremely vicious anti-India campaign, in a desperate bid to divert domestic public attention from the internal crisis. They tried to distort and cover up the origins of the East Pakistan imbroglio.

On 30 January 1971, an Indian Airlines Fokker Friendship aircraft, with a crew of four and twenty-eight passengers aboard, was hijacked to Lahore. The hijackers let the passengers leave Pakistan after a gruelling forty-eight hours in captivity. The Pakistan government readily gave asylum to the hijackers and its media described them as heroes engaged in the mission to liberate Kashmir from India. The hijackers demanded the release of some 'Al Fatah' saboteurs arrested in Kashmir earlier. Indira Gandhi promptly rejected the demand. She strongly criticized the authorities in Pakistan for abetment, incitement and encouragement of the crime of hijacking. She pointed out how the hijackers blew up the Indian plane in Lahore in full view of the Pakistan army authorities. It also became clear that the two hijackers had received intensive training in guerrilla warfare in Pakistan.

In March 1971 Indira was returned to power with a massive margin in the Lok Sabha elections. The Syndicate and all others who had sniped at her for months on end were convincingly thrashed. She reigned supreme; yet, her detractors were down but not out.

She had to wage an extended struggle to survive, fighting with her back to the wall. Given the circumstances, it was unthinkable that she could have conceived or plotted the dismemberment of Pakistan. However, the exodus of refugees from East Bengal into West Bengal had begun in the meantime. It demanded immediate attention. That meant Indira Gandhi's deep involvement in the crisis that had triggered the migration.

Everyone in India, government and people alike, had watched the developments in Pakistan with more than ordinary interest and concern, for months and months—in fact, years. They had no choice, really. The Partition had made both countries focus obsessively on each other.

Even so, the Indira government was reluctant to make any public statement on the issue. On 15 March, Sheikh Mujib made a unilateral declaration of East Pakistan's autonomy. Yahya Khan came to Dacca for talks to find a solution, and Bhutto joined him a few days later. The Pakistan army, meanwhile, continued its slaughter in the eastern region. On 25 March, Yahya left for Karachi, leaving the army to deal with the situation. Soldiers arrested Mujib, raped a large number of women and murdered hundreds of workers, intellectuals, students and anyone who came within range. Immediately, through a clandestine radio station calling itself Swadhin Bangla Betar Kendra, the Sheikh declared the seventy-five million people of East Pakistan as citizens of independent Bangladesh. (The deep emotions of the suffering people can be gleaned from excerpts from the diary of Jahanara Imam, a housewife and mother of a young freedom fighter, included at the end of this chapter.)

*

At the cabinet meeting one day, Anand found Chief Minister Chaudhury beaming. He was happy about something that he alone knew as of that moment. 'Events seem to be happening fast,' he said enigmatically, and then went on to the items listed on the agenda.

The hint he had let slip preyed on all their minds. No one was in a mood to concentrate on the cabinet issues at hand. They deferred some, approved others without the customary discussion and debate. For once there were no sharp exchanges between Anand and Shekhar, which the other ministers normally anticipated and relished. Chaudhury, in particular, enjoyed their mutual sallies and had once told a friendly journalist, 'I am afraid too many *pahelwans* like these have come into Indira Gandhi's camp after the recent elections. Each of them swears by her; but each swears at the others . . . Well . . . I have deep admiration for her, but my sympathy is deeper . . .' He never made such observations openly, of course, and those journalists who were close confidantes never quoted them in their columns. Yet, they largely reflected the unspoken opinion that many of Indira Gandhi's 'seasoned' colleagues held about her.

As the cabinet meeting carried on desultorily, an attendant quietly brought in a piece of paper. It looked like part of a longer document and contained English text in capital letters. With all the respect he had learned to show, the attendant made a platter of his upturned palms together, with the piece of paper resting on it, text up, and presented it to the chief minister. He waited until the latter picked it up and then withdrew, walking backwards. All eyes converged on the document. The cabinet forgot the meeting for a while.

'Must be PTI or UNI news all right,' observed Anand, glancing at the capital letters from where he sat. 'Well, we are all dying to know . . .'

Chaudhury glanced at the paper, then looked back into the cabinet papers and murmured, with a faint smile, 'There are a few more items to dispose of, I see.'

The suspense of the telex message gripped everyone. There was a chorus around the table, urging Chaudhury to share it with them at once. For several weeks now, the events in East Pakistan had become an obsession in India. Something big was in the air—no one knew what. The newspapers were full of descriptions of the atrocities perpetrated by the Pakistani soldiers in East Bengal. Sheikh Mujib was already a well-known and well-admired leader in India. The Indian mind responds to suffering and sacrifice spontaneously. It is an unbroken legacy, stretching down the ages from the Buddha to Gandhi. So, the people had adopted the Sheikh as a hero—'our own' hero.

'This is great news,' Chaudhury began, scanning the telex. 'Bangladesh is born!'

'Bangladesh?' repeated a senior minister, a bit puzzled.

'Yes, Bangladesh now; East Pakistan until yesterday,' explained Chaudhury. 'A new country, a new nation . . . They couldn't call it by the old name, could they?'

'Bangladesh!' chorused the whole cabinet, savouring the beautiful name.

'The provisional government of Bangladesh has asked for recognition by other governments. Our Prime Minister has been informed,' said Chaudhury, not quite indicating his own view.

'We must accord recognition at once,' declared several ministers.

'India must be the first!' shouted Anand.

'Yes, absolutely!' echoed Shekhar.

'Not so simple, my friends,' began Chaudhury. 'I have a full account of the situation in the letter the Prime Minister sent yesterday to all chief ministers. The Pakistanis have always been accusing her of fomenting trouble in their eastern wing. They are screaming murder all over the world, with the instant backing of those who don't like Indira Gandhi.'

'Why don't they like her?' mused one of the ministers. 'After all, she has done nothing beyond winning a Lok Sabha election. She hasn't hurt any other country in any way.'

'That is a long story,' Chaudhury said. He turned to Anand and asked, 'Why do you think they don't like Indira Gandhi right now?'

'It appears to me that for historical reasons some powers cannot and will not treat India and Pakistan equally. There has to be a tilt towards Pakistan. It is inherent in the very creation of that country. That, I think, is the wider question. Well, I don't claim to know much . . .'

'He doesn't know much beyond land reforms anyway,' someone tried to pull his leg.

Anand ignored that remark. He knew that land reform wasn't exactly popular with many of his colleagues. He resumed speaking calmly, 'None of us knows much about international relations. We don't deal with that subject here. Right now, I think some Western countries dislike Indira Gandhi. It's not what she has done that bothers them, in my view, but they are afraid of the action she will take on many issues, including that of Bangladesh . . .'

'What do you suppose they think she'll do on the subject of Bangladesh, if I may ask?' queried another minister, in a tone tinged with sarcasm.

'Look, Saeed sahib,' shot back Anand, 'we don't know—at least I don't. Yet, each of us has a hunch; we are too deep in this game to pretend innocence or ignorance. Right now, what it really amounts to is a sort of second partition of undivided India. Those who helped the first partition obviously don't like this second one. It spells a chronic failure of their designs, almost a slap in the face. With Indira Gandhi supporting Bangladesh, the sting in that slap will be unendurable . . . I think the Prime Minister is taking her time, weighing the pros and cons.'

'You're right there,' endorsed Chaudhury. 'From all accounts, she is being extremely circumspect on this issue . . . But why should we be so diffident? The Pakistanis and their mentors the world over are already crowing like nobody's business.'

The cabinet meeting tapered off unnoticed. Speculation on Indira Gandhi's next step continued endlessly—everywhere in the country. Will she or won't she? Should she or shouldn't she? Can she or can't she? To this last question, the invariable answer was in the affirmative. She *can*, they said, if she *wants* to . . .

To declare one's country independent was one thing; to make that independence a reality quite another. The announcement on the provisional government of Bangladesh came on 28 March 1971. On 10 April, the Sovereign Democratic Republic of Bangladesh was born at a secret spot in that country. A ceremonial proclamation came on 17 April. The village of Muadanga in the liberated area, renamed Mujibnagar, became the capital of the new republic.

The new government could now secure the services of several Bengali diplomats and officers then serving in Pakistan. Hossain Ali, Pakistan's deputy high commissioner in Calcutta, declared his loyalty to the new government. He converted his office into the

Bangladesh diplomatic mission. Bangladesh got a foothold on Indian soil.

The uphill task of liberating the country still remained. The new government was in no position to accomplish it in a short time. Pitted against the mighty Pakistan army, the newly-improvised Liberation Army of Bangladesh, later renamed Mukti Bahini, initially had little chance.

Throughout the length and breadth of India, pressure was building up in favour of recognizing Bangladesh. Indira Gandhi's government was under constant attack for its vacillation and its weak-kneed approach. The Prime Minister gave several indications of her thinking and tried to pacify the parliament and the people. Yet, the torrent of public opinion and the wave of sympathy for the suffering people of Bangladesh left her largely on the defensive.

'This is just dilly-dallying,' shouted many young members of the ruling party. 'Listen to what the other parties are saying. We will be out of step with the people, whatever we may do eventually.' Indira Gandhi tried her best to argue, in parliament, that in view of the delicate nature of the issue, the government should say as little as possible. She also hinted that the government would take the right decision at the right time—'not just expressing a theoretical view,' she added significantly. She insisted on following 'proper international norms'. The government mounted a campaign all over the world to explain India's position. Indira Gandhi pointed out India's massive responsibility of looking after the very large influx of refugees from Bangladesh. The numbers increased with each passing day.

'All this is futile,' said many critics bitterly. 'No one is going to sympathize with India on this issue. They will readily buy the Pakistani propaganda that India is at the root of the trouble in the eastern wing of Pakistan. I don't know what Indiraji is waiting for and whom she wishes to convince. Meanwhile the atrocities by the Pak army in Bangladesh escalate by the day. They will destroy the whole country before she decides to act . . .'

And sure enough, the Pakistani propaganda machine worked overtime to paint India as the villain of the piece. The Central leadership had perhaps already lost hope of retaining the eastern wing, judging from the irrational manner in which it acted and reacted. The number of charges the Pakistanis levelled against India were legion—notably the allegation that the Awami League and Indira Gandhi were conspiring to dismember Pakistan.

A sovereign independent country had come into being on the strong base of a common religion less than twenty-five years ago. Here was one half of that country struggling to break loose from the other half—absolutely determined in its resolve. There had to be solid reasons behind this urgent drive to secede. Slowly but surely, the truth behind the creation of Bangladesh began to trickle through the barriers erected by the Pakistani government. More and more newspapers around the world penetrated the veil of secrecy. They unearthed the truth about the type and extent of the slaughter that the Pakistani army unleashed upon the people of East Pakistan. Soon, it was clear to everyone everywhere that an independent Bangladesh was inevitable. No power on earth could avert it . . . And eventually, the powers that counted decided that they should not avert it.

Indira Gandhi's government still refused to recognize the government of Bangladesh. However, both the government and people of India were committed to assisting the freedom fighters in that country. They spared nothing, no effort, no resources.

On the humanitarian front, the problem of Bangladeshi refugees became extremely difficult to tackle. Unlike the earlier refugee influxes of single communities across the Indo-Pak border, this influx from East Pakistan had no communal base. It was political, pure and simple. The people wanted independence. The government of Pakistan persecuted them, waged war against them, forced them out of their hearths and homes. They were victims of war, as Indira Gandhi described them. By October 1971, about thirteen per cent of East Pakistan's population had already arrived in India, seeking refuge. 'So massive a migration in so brief a period is unprecedented in recorded history,' Indira Gandhi pointed out. Her policy was not to accept the refugees permanently. India would look after them for the time being and enable them to return to their homes when conditions had been created for their safe return. Which meant that independent Bangladesh should come to stay. There was no alternative.

A Bangladesh Aid Committee came into being in Afrozabad, with—astonishingly—Balram as chairman. Who formed it and how, was a long story; in any event it became a fait accompli before anyone realized what had happened. And to be fair to him, Balram put his heart and soul into its activities. He earned quite a name for himself and for the committee. For the first time in his life, he tasted the flavour of patriotism. He found it quite intoxicating. Some of his friends and well-wishers started the rumour that he was preparing to stand for the next election and inevitably, to become a minister. The landlord lobby greeted the rumour with enthusiasm.

'I didn't instigate Pakistan to get into this mess,' protested Balram when Aruna commented on his activity. 'I didn't get India and Indira Gandhi embroiled in the Bangladesh crisis. No one has control over these matters. And when the country is so tangled in a problem, even the hated landlord has to lend a helping hand. Put a politician at the head of this Aid Committee, and I can bet ninety-nine to one that the fellow will misappropriate half the funds.'

'I didn't criticize your activity, bhaiya,' said Aruna, rather surprised at this sudden outburst. 'I just wondered . . .'

'I know, I know, you just wondered why I am so active in this Bangladesh Aid. My dear sister, I know you mould your views on that minister-ideologue Anand's advice. That's why I think it's time for you to realize that the country's life doesn't begin and end with land reforms, nor with making paupers of all landlords. Just because our forefathers—yours and mine—have left us some land so we can live a comfortable life, doesn't mean that we are the worst sinners imaginable. I will prove the worth of the landlord class now. You just watch!'

Aruna found her brother's aggressive posture rather mystifying.

'You have humiliated the landlord enough,' Balram continued. 'Your election promises and rhetoric have singled him out for decimation. You had to find a victim to set the hounds on! That was the only way to generate a wave and garner votes . . . But watch out now! Let us see if Indira Gandhi cares more for the landless or for her own glorious place in history . . . You know what, sister? Didn't you hear about our great-grandmother Bimla Devi who fed the whole village from out of her grain stocks when there was a terrible famine in the area some eighty years ago? Haven't you seen how she has become immortal in the village? Every drought year brings in Bimla Devi's memories, embellished by new stories . . . If there had been a relief committee of politicians then, not one of them would have helped with a single grain from his own stock. In fact, they would have divided government funds and grain in aid of themselves, leaving nothing for the hungry.'

It was indeed a revelation to Aruna to find her near-illiterate brother produce such strong logic to defend the landlord class. She had seen his transformation at the last Lok Sabha election, but had no idea how deeply he hated politicians.

'Why do you compare Bimla Devi with some corrupt politicians to score a point?' she demanded.

'I'm not scoring points,' Balram shot back. 'I am telling my very educated sister a few facts of life she doesn't know a thing about so far . . .'

'A few months back you waxed eloquent on land reforms and socialism in the election campaign, didn't you?'

'Of course I did,' said Balram. 'I still do . . . Land reforms are good; socialism is good. However, no one wants to implement them, barring a few visionary fools and ideologues like Anand. As for Indira Gandhi, I have no doubt she too wants land reforms; but her desire for land reforms is part of a wider strategy for capturing and retaining political power. She now has the spectacular issue of Bangaldesh that will bring her power and glory. So, my dear sister, she will utilize everyone who can help her to achieve greatness. And in my own way, I am one of those.'

Balram's logic was not far off the mark. When Aruna reported this conversation to Anand, he became thoughtful for a moment and said, 'I don't know what Indira Gandhi will do, but the nation has been obsessed with Bangladesh for eight months now. The party's manifesto has receded into the background . . . It's a pity. The party is about to lose a grand opportunity to come into its own. Only the leader's greatness will have to sustain it now, as before.'

Months dragged on, but a Bangladesh born of the people's will remained unformed. Genocide by the Pakistani troops continued and the political picture continued to be indeterminate. Yahya Khan refused to talk to Sheikh Mujib, the undisputed leader of the eastern wing. Instead, he wanted to negotiate with India. Indira Gandhi refused to oblige. She reiterated that the Pakistani leaders must settle it amongst themselves. India would not interfere.

To the leaders of Pakistan, however, India was clearly the root cause of the Bangladesh problem. When Indira Gandhi refused to be dragged into the conflict, they concluded that the solution lay in attacking India. Unable to cope with the guerrilla activities of the Mukti Bahini, they shelled areas within the Indian border. The Indian side retaliated, and slowly the border skirmishes escalated into a full-scale war. India's defence minister Jagjivan Ram declared on 28 November, 'If the military rulers of Pakistan want to inflict war on India, it will be fought on Pakistani soil and not Indian.'

On 3 December, it was announced that the two countries were at war. Naturally, the versions of the two governments were diametrically opposite. Pakistan raided Indian airfields in the west as a pre-emptive bid, as also to relieve Indian pressure on the eastern front. However, nothing worked in favour of Pakistan.

Two days after the war broke out, India recognized Bangladesh as an independent nation. The two countries concluded an agreement and announced a plan for joint military operations, return of refugees, and other crucial issues.

The war ended in fourteen days. The Pakistani army surrendered in Dacca on 16 December. Bangladesh was liberated. Indira Gandhi's fame exploded all over the world. She was loved in some countries, hated in others, feared in a few, but respected everywhere. Atal Bihari Vajpayee, a prominent leader of the Opposition in the Indian parliament, referred to her as Durga and Kali.

When the Bangladesh war had broken out in December 1971, government had postponed the state assembly elections, scheduled for January 1972. With the conclusion of the war—and Indira Gandhi's renewed glory—the country promptly went to the polls in March of that year.

'This time, it will be an incredibly easy win for the ruling party,' everyone predicted.

And it was.

*

Jahanara Imam's Diary: Extracts

Wednesday, 10th March 1971

The young people cannot come to a consensus on the autonomy-independence debate. Meanwhile the octogenarian Bhashani yesterday demanded outright Independence at a public meeting at Paltan. Yesterday at 3 p.m. the Bengal Independence Movement Co-ordination Committee held a meeting where Maulana Bhashani presided. He said, 'If the Government does not grant Independence to East Pakistan by 25th March, then I will launch a movement with Mujib as I did in 1952.'

One statement of Bhashani made a deep impression on me. He said, 'It is more honourable to be a leader of Bengal than to be the Prime Minister of Pakistan.' It reminded me of a quotation from Milton's *Paradise Lost*: 'It is better to reign in hell than serve in heaven.'

Sunday, 14th March 1971

Expressing their solidarity with the autonomy movement, the poets and authors have formed a committee by the name of Authors Movement Centre. Hasan Hafizur Rahman is the convenor. Members include Sikander Abu Jaafar, Ahmed Sharif, Shaukat Osman, Shamsur Rahman, Badruddin Omar, Ronesh Das Gupta, Syed Aatiqulla, Burhanuddin Khan Jahangir, Ruknuzzaman Khan, Abdul Gaffar Chowdhury, Sufia Kamal, Zillur Rahman, Abdul Ghani Hazari and many others. Today at 5 p.m. there was a meeting of the committee at the Bangla Academy. Ahmed Sharif presided.

Ronesh Das Gupta, Alauddin Al Azad, Burhanuddin Khan

Jahangir, Hasan Hafizur Rahman, Rabeya Khatoon, Ahmed Safa and many others gave eloquent speeches on the role of poets and authors in the autonomy movement.

I am neither an author nor an orator. I sat on a chair at the rear of the hall but couldn't help being touched by the fiery speeches. After the meeting a procession left for the Shaheed Minar which is close to the Bangla Academy. My knee trouble has reappeared. I did not dare to join the procession.

The artistes have also come forward. From the 1st of March, all the artistes of radio, television and cinema joined the non-cooperation movement. Now they have formed an organization by the name of Artistes Movement Committee. Ali Mansoor is the President and Syed Abdul Hadi the Secretary. Laila Arzoomand Banu has been appointed Treasurer. Members include Mustafa Zaman Abbasi, Aahedur Rahim, Firdausi Rahman, Bashir Ahmed, Khan Ataur Rahman, Altaf Mahmood, Golam Mostafa, Qamrul Hasan, Ajit Roy, Hasan Imam, Kamal Lohani, G.A. Mannan, Abdul Ahad, Samar Das, Gahar Jamil, Razzak and many others.

The Artistes Movement Committee has very strongly opposed deployment of troops at the radio and television stations.

Thursday, 18th March 1971

Dhaka Television has taken the autonomy movement to its peak through its superb music programmes. We have never seen such programmes before. All the top artistes of Dacca, Firdausi Rahman, Sabina Yasmeen, Shahnaz Begum, Anjuman Ara Begum, Khandakar Farooq Ahmed, Ratindra Nath Ray and others have been rendering highly emotional songs singing of the glory of the movement. Through some camera trick these turn into thousands of faces and cover the entire television screen, creating storms in the hearts of viewers all over the country.

I asked Masuma, 'How do they do it?'

Masuma replied, 'These are the doings of Uncle Montu.'

Montu—Mustafa Manwar—is the Director General of Dacca Television. I caught hold of him at an opportune moment and asked him how the few faces on the television could turn into thousands of faces. With a bashful smile he replied, 'We don't have modern equipment. We are somehow managing with mirrors and other simple instruments.'

It is Montu's nature not to claim credit for anything. He's always modest when talking about himself.

A few patriotic songs became quite popular through these novel programmes of Montu—'My house has been set on fire, my peace has been snatched away', 'Blessed is my birth in this country', 'O my single-stringed instrument, sing the glory of this land'. The more the songs are televised, the more the comfort-loving, normally peaceful Bengalees are inspired to join the patriotic struggle on the streets, in the meadows, at the ports, at the crossroads.

Wednesday, 4th August 1971

The days and nights are now crowded with events. There is an unending stream of visitors and we are getting used to frequent sounds of explosions. We don't sleep well unless we hear one or two loud bangs. Dada Bhai, Murtaza, Banka, and Fakir all feel the same way. Some of my friends jokingly say that the sale of Valium has gone down because the sound of explosions works as an excellent sleeping medicine. Some nights if I don't hear the sounds I feel alarmed. Have the Pakistanis caught the boys?

No, that is not true. Even if there is no explosion in the early part of the night there is invariably a blast later on to soothe our nerves.

The boys are getting more and more daring everyday. The people have nicknamed them 'The Scorpions'. Yesterday, just before sunset, some of the Scorpions threw a grenade at the Army checkpost near the State Bank. The soldiers could not get any of them. The Swadhin Bangla Betar reports that those of the Scorpions facing the Pakistanis in a frontal warfare at the borders are also showing tremendous courage and valour, disregarding all hazards to their lives. They are fighting for a cause and they believe that death for the motherland is a death of honour. They would rather embrace martyrdom than dishonour.

Someone was singing on the Swadhin Bangla Betar—

We the young sailors must cross this turbulent ocean;
We the young soldiers fight for our freedom,
We the young ones have no anchor and no sense of time.
We only know to hold the rudder firm and row forward.

As I listened, tears rolled down my cheeks.

Thursday, 12th August 1971

I have hardly seen Rumi during the last three days. He comes home for a couple of hours and then disappears again. The day before yesterday he brought home two of his guerrilla friends, Bodi and Jewel, for lunch. Bodi was doing his Masters in Economics and Jewel is a renowed cricketer. After lunch the three of them left and didn't return at night. Yesterday we had called Dholu and Chisty for lunch. They will go back to Islamabad on the 15th of August. At the dining table Dholu asked, 'Where's Rumi? Isn't he going to join us?'

I said, 'He's gone out. He will be back any time now.'

But by the time Rumi returned it was evening and Dholu and Chisty had already left. I told Rumi that he should go and visit his Uncle and Aunty before they leave for Islamabad. Yesterday also, Rumi left in the morning and didn't return at night.

There is nothing I can do but I do have sleepless nights. I am worried and nervous. I wish Rumi was more frank with me.

Today I kept Rumi's lunch on the dining table and waited for him. He came in the afternoon and said, 'Mother, I am famished. Give me something to eat.' As he looked at the table he said, 'You are great, Mother! The food is already laid.'

As I was serving him his food I said, 'You know what happened at the Hotel Intercontinental last evening? Some of the Scorpions exploded a grenade in one of the rooms.'

'Yes, I know. It was not in one of the rooms; it was in a bathroom on the ground floor beside the lounge.'

'Were you there? Do you know who did it?'

'Mother!' Rumi sounded annoyed. I also lost my temper. I said, 'Okay, you don't have to tell me anything, but remember I have my own sources. In this city news travels faster than jet planes.'

Rumi smiled and I angrily left for my room upstairs.

After a little while, Rumi entered my bedroom and sat beside me. He said, 'It was not a grenade, it was a plastic explosive commonly known as PK.'

I didn't say anything. Rumi continued, 'You don't know the boys who did it. I also didn't know them but I got to know them in Melaghar.'

I remained silent. Rumi also kept quiet for a while and then said, 'PK looks exactly like putty that is used by the furniture manufacturers. It is yellow in colour and looks harmless.'

Still there was no word from me. I had learnt my lesson. I knew that Rumi would tell me exactly as much as he wanted to. I cannot get anything more by pressing him. Rumi whistled for a while and then recited a poem:

What do you look like?
What is your attire?
Do you have a loose robe on or tight trousers?
Is your hair long or short?
Do you stay on the branches of the trees
Or do you hang around the teashops?

They are looking for you,
The troops, the Secret Service and their stooges,
They look for you house to house.

I sat up and said, 'Who wrote it?'

'A famous poet of Dhaka. I don't recall his name. Shahadat and Alam took this poem to Melaghar. We kept a copy and sent the original to a journal in Calcutta.'

'This poem is about you people.'

'Yes. It is titled "Guerrilla". Listen to the rest of it:

They would have rent the blue vastness of the sky
Or entered the depth of the ocean
To find you out
You and the future are moving forward

645

hand in hand
I can hear your footsteps all around.

I sat quietly for a while and then asked, 'Why don't Shahadat and Alam come any more to Dacca these days?'

'They do, but they don't stay long.'

'Didn't they come with you?'

Rumi smiled and said, 'Mother, you are simply incorrigible!'

Defensively I muttered, 'I only wanted to know the name of the poet from them.'

Rumi said, 'I knew the name but I have forgotten it. He lives in Dacca. I think it is better that we all forget his name. That is safe for us as well as for the poet.'

The two of us play this cat and mouse game. Rumi said, 'The less you know the better it is because you might give out vital information under torture.'

I listen to him but then I forget and keep asking him all sorts of questions again. I smiled and said, 'As I am getting old, I am getting more forgetful. It seems we have switched places. You are the big daddy now and I am your little daughter!'

# 51

THE 1972 ELECTION TO THE STATE ASSEMBLIES BROUGHT ANOTHER grand victory to Indira Gandhi. It was as though the people had at last found their destiny in 'Amma'. They genuinely believed that they could now sit back and watch her solve their problems one by one—or even all at once.

They were in for disillusionment, regrettably. And, as always happens, the more intense the euphoria, the deeper—and quicker—was the disillusionment. Since Indira had reached the pinnacle of her glory, she couldn't go any higher, some said. To be precise, others clarified, she was doomed to fall. It was sad, as some saw it; it was an outcome that was inescapable, according to others. Both groups appraised her future entirely out of self-interest—to them the fate of the country was irrelevant.

Comments varied. How does one keep oneself at the pinnacle? Is it at all possible? How soon will the inevitable slide begin? A few months perhaps, some suggested. What is the ruling party supposed to do meanwhile? . . . Party, did you say? What party? Where is the party? My dear friend, don't you know that Indira Gandhi is herself both the party and the leader? Who else do you think can function while she rules?

Politicians of the ruling party—many of them, not all, of course—saw a whole range of vistas opening up before them. They thought they only had to manoeuvre themselves into vantage positions politically. How did one do that? Well, the process was a bit involved. It consisted of making Indira Gandhi hear about you, then see you, take note of your qualities—and above all assess your unquestioning loyalty to her, sometimes to the Nehru family. This last, however, was not obligatory just then. The reason was simple. She was not at ease with those who had protested their loyalty to Jawaharlal Nehru round the clock. Their numbers were legion and multiplied by the day. They wanted her to realize how close they had been to her father—and to acknowledge and reward them accordingly. Else—they tried to say but didn't—she was ungrateful. It was blackmail, subtle and suggestive, which she must have resented. Besides, didn't she have to fight many of those Jawaharlal loyalists for her own survival? So what she preferred was loyalty to herself, for the time being. And by and by, to her younger son Sanjay . . . gradually, ever so gradually.

Given her unquestioned supremacy, Indira began to alter the contours of the political situation in the country. She was able to do this because she did not owe her position to the Bangladesh triumph alone. She had done something quite extraordinary before Bangladesh—her audacious 1971 Lok Sabha triumph—by giving *Garibi Hatao* the pride of place in the party's manifesto. However, when it came to the crunch, most of the programmes she initiated were within the jurisdiction of the state governments. The Centre had little to do with them directly, except in granting funds to the states. But now, because of her absolute dominance, what Indira Gandhi ordained necessarily had to happen. This was easiest in the states where her party ruled; here the chief ministers gave her unquestioning obedience and thereby became her instruments of national power.

In one imperious but mysterious sweep—swift and bafflingly decisive—Indira Gandhi ended the careers of some of her party chief ministers. She did not dismiss them, of course; but without doubt, she eased them out. Just when they were basking in the glory of her Bangladesh triumph. Just when they had begun to plan for the imminent assembly elections which would give them another term in office.

The sweep had a stunning effect. For the first time, it devalued the chief minister—a creature of the Constitution almost equal with the Prime Minister, within the confines of the state. The post now appeared to be one to which the Prime Minister—rather the leader of the party—'nominated' individuals. Moreover, Indira replaced the old and powerful chiefs with those of a different kind: these were 'her' chief ministers. Weighed on conventional political scales, they were 'lightweights'. Yet, she hand-picked them, presumably as special agents to implement the revolutionary changes she had conceived. This was one interpretation which her staunch supporters advanced. Not that they knew her mind, but they argued the case for her anyway.

This development sent shock waves throughout the political hierarchy. It shook the old 'bosses'; Indira could name anyone boss now. There was commotion and confusion in the ruling party. The only tangible outcome from this was Indira Gandhi's absolute control, bordering on ownership, of the party. 'She has had the last word so far,' commented many party men. 'Hers is the only word now, first to last . . .'

That was the way many in the country perceived the situation. That Indira Gandhi was absolute . . . That the party somehow 'belonged' to her. She had come to appropriate it for herself.

Anand strongly disagreed. He admitted that she had absolute power now. 'Yet, absolute power is not an end in itself—nor intended to be so,' he argued.

'All right, then what is the end?' demanded Shekhar, articulating the suspicion that nagged millions of minds across the country and abroad. They were discussing Indira Gandhi's latest move in the entrance hall of the assembly, as they waited for the day's proceedings to begin.

'Shekhar, there is no single answer to your question,' Anand said, measuring every word carefully. 'I hold no brief for Indira Gandhi; she hardly knows me. I only try to know her mind from a distance, the way political activists try to know their leader. If you believe she wants absolute power, I believe she wants it for something. It simply can't be power for power's sake. Why don't you speculate on this latter question as well? Why does she want absolute power, granting that she does? I believe that her purpose primarily concerns the people. She may be right, or she may go completely wrong. At the end of the day, the people might say that she did nothing for them. It's we who are talking about her now; we, her colleagues and followers, if you will. We, who have no business to be with her unless we understand her . . .'

'We have covered that ground times without number,' Shekhar said, a bit tartly. He did not like to answer the question as to why he was with Indira Gandhi. 'She is the leader of the party; she is the Prime Minister. She needs followers to run this anarchic entity called India. And run it according to the rules borrowed from a different people six thousand miles away, because they happened to be our masters for a hundred and fifty years.'

'That's a good reason,' commented Anand, 'but that's not the whole story. There is something that doesn't quite explain our being Indira Gandhi's followers, while so many senior leaders have deserted her. I believe that I am trying to help her achieve something—exactly what, I can't explain. The people can't explain either. I believe it has to do with the country's future—something not merely concerned with our own political interests. I believe I speak for all of us, Shekhar, not merely for myself.'

'I don't know,' argued Shekhar. 'Sometimes your dreaminess becomes infectious. I am no dreamer. I feel that all this is just realpolitik, nothing more, nothing less.'

'Then why don't you join those who are out to denigrate her?' asked Anand bluntly. 'You agree with them all the way . . .'

'Not all the way,' Shekhar hastened to add. 'That's the trouble. The others only denigrate; beyond that, they have nothing to do. That's a dead end for them. They don't know where they propose to take the country and don't seem to care . . . My position is quite different. I believe that whatever Indira Gandhi wants to do with her absolute power, the people do not primarily figure in it. They are there, of course, always; but more as a means to an end than an end in themselves . . .'

'Then what is the end she has in view?' queried Anand.

'How do I know?' retorted Shekhar. 'These motivations are so complex anyway. I just told you what I feel the end isn't; I am in no position to spell out what it is. It could be ego. It could be the consuming desire for glory, for a place in history, for immortality, for. . . anything, just anything . . . You and I can't figure it out just now. It may also be nothing, nothing in particular that she has reasoned out herself.'

These, then, were the lines of speculation. Fierce arguments from both sides cancelled each other out. The negative opinions had an edge in private conversations within the party; in public, it was all positive. In the media, those who were critical of her were in the majority. Abroad, they saw a dictator in the making.

The people were positive all the way. Some among the few literates who read the newspapers raised their eyebrows now and then. They could not, however, go about with permanently raised eyebrows, so they also joined the chorus—*Indira Gandhi ki jai*!

The regular reshuffling, dismissal and appointment of sundry chief ministers didn't create much of a ripple among the people. Among people who followed politics it was noted with interest. The masses remained largely unmoved. In general, their response was to acquiesce in—and sometimes welcome—whatever Indira Gandhi did. If she wanted a chief minister out, something must be wrong with him, they assumed. When Indira Gandhi installed a new person (rather unknown) as chief minister, the public opinion was that he must be someone brilliant, congenial and sensitive to the people's needs. The political sharks must have muffled and masked him all these years, that's why he has remained unknown. After all, it is dog-eat-dog in politics anyway . . . So let's see what the new man does. We have nothing to lose; nothing worse could possibly happen to us.

To Anand, it was a disconcerting but challenging spectacle. He did not quite realize that he had been romanticizing Indira Gandhi's leadership. Why was that? Just because he was entirely with her and had lost a realistic perspective? Had he taken Indira Gandhi as a messianic figure unquestioningly, in a fit of idealism and hero-worship? Had he lost all sense of logic and objectivity?

Sometimes he felt he was a laughing stock among his friends and colleagues. He almost began to believe Shekhar right and himself wrong. But even as the thought came to him, he squirmed in revulsion.

What nonsense! How could such unabashed cynicism be right? He conceded that Indira Gandhi was an enigma to him. So was she to Shekhar and to many others. To him at least, Indira Gandhi was a medium, a means to an end. (He didn't like the cliché, but found no better way to describe the way he saw things.) He was serving the people and the country, not Indira Gandhi. His mind was clear on that, even if few understood the nuances. To her denigrators, curiously, she was the end—end-target, that is. As Shekhar had admitted, they saw nothing beyond . . . So, he, Anand, had to live with the enigma, but serve the people in the process. That was the real catch—*in the process.*

The process baffled him—all the more because he had to interpret it in terms of the enigma. The latest in the process was the removal of chief ministers who had served the party well for years and kept its power base intact in their states. Chaudhury, for instance. He had played dirty tricks by the dozen and exploited every known weakness of those he had to deal with—and tamed them. He was no ideologue, no fancy 'socialist', but his main motive was to benefit the people to the extent feasible, without endangering his position. He was not against Indira Gandhi, although no one could wager that he would commit political *sati* with her. In any event, she could not complain about his political acumen or his skills as a strategist . . . Yet, Chaudhury's future was in the doldrums now. Would he go? When? How? And why?

Why should he go? He had complete hold over the members of his party in the state legislature. Whenever he wanted, they would pass a near-unanimous resolution affirming their confidence in him. The state administration understood and obeyed him without demur. He had proved to be a contrast to the abrasive and arrogant Mahendranath. Chaudhury was both kind and exacting without being insulting—this was the attitude that the bureaucracy liked and respected. No one thought he was a shining example of rectitude, but he had not gathered a web of money-related scandals around himself either. He had a way with the people who tolerated him. 'He's no angel,' they said, 'but the angels fled our planet long ago anyway. You live among damned human beings and this Chaudhury fellow isn't the worst of them . . .' So why should Chaudhury go? . . . The question echoed and re-echoed all over the state.

Yet, there was another point of view, even among the unbiased. How long do you want Chaudhury to stay on, doing more of the same? Which amounts to more and more of nothing for the people, really. They say change is the spice of life, so why not try a new masala? After all, a chief minister is not a king. You change everything—your clothes, your shoes, your fashions, your lifestyles . . . So, why not change your chief minister—for a change?

The flippancy was galling. It was the streak of cynicism that kept the people going. It was the bridge between the known and the unknown. Between what you have and what you think you must have. Between the one-half that you are and the other half you keep desiring to be through life.

Meanwhile, Chaudhury laughed and joked aloud, but fretted and fumed inside, to the utter delight of Mahendranath and his cronies. Mahendranath needed two hundred hands instead of two to pull countless strings—in Delhi and in the state. Incidentally, since he was not in the ruling party any more, he had to take recourse to a more complicated strategy than before to maintain his clout and his stature. It is interesting how no one who was once in the ruling party ever really leaves it. He fiddles with the party in many ways even from outside, never losing his stake in it. He does not wish to rule out his own return to the party some day, in some way. Indeed in many cases, the very act of leaving the party is part of a grander strategy to return to it with greater power after decimating the splinter factions and potential traitors now entrenched within it. And every party in the country is busier manipulating the ruling party than improving its own performance!

Strangely enough, the flippant view expressed by some sections of the people and political circles on Indira Gandhi's regime gave Anand the clue to develop his argument. It is just not enough to go on and on with more of the same. That becomes counter-productive; indeed, it has already. The system, as anyone can see, is generating more and more disparities. The Naxalites have served notice that social tensions can lead to unmitigated disaster. There has to be change. Indira Gandhi represents that change, like it or not. She simply doesn't represent more of the same. However, she has to engineer the change in full. It can't be peripheral or partial. Her changing of chief ministers is complementary to the change at the top—the advent of a newly empowered Prime Minister. In a very real sense, it is the other half.

While he argued his case forcefully, he was painfully conscious of his own ignorance. He had no verifiable basis for the thesis he presented with such gusto. The very structure of his ideas could collapse like a house of cards. What if facts proved him completely wrong? What if Indira Gandhi was pursuing a path different from what he imagined? What if the schemes he was imagining exploded in his face? Where, then, would he be? What would become of Anand the dreamer, of Anand the confirmed socialist, of Anand the unselfish altruist and servant of the people?

He had heated arguments with all his friends. Not one of them lent full support to him. They were not against Indira Gandhi; everyone made that clear. Indeed they made a virtue of not being against her. Very few tried to spell out what they supported. Most of them praised Indira Gandhi sincerely. But they confused personal adulation with political support. Anand found the empty praise exasperating, but could not say so. At last he could stand it no longer, and one afternoon when Aruna made one of her infrequent appearances at his residence he exploded in anger.

'This is preposterous!' he shouted. 'These fellows are out to destroy Indira Gandhi, out to destroy the party!'

'Easy, day-dreamer,' Aruna responded. 'Don't hit all round the wicket. Indira Gandhi may or may not be a dictator, but you certainly aren't one, are you? So why do you throw a fit at what ordinary mortals can't help saying or doing?'

'Aruna, can't you see the stakes?' Anand protested vehemently. 'Don't you see the price we're paying in terms of values? Can we afford this? Can the country afford this?'

'What are you talking about? Be specific, will you?'

'Too many things are weighing upon my mind now,' he began, conrolling his rage. 'Let me try and explain it to you. It's true that we have just won a glorious electoral victory in most of the states, and that Indira Gandhi is at the peak of her power and popularity. But how long can she remain at that peak? How long can she ride on the crest of the wave?'

'You're right,' said Aruna. 'The wave may recede soon and many party men worry about it, as you do. So why are *you* asking questions? *You* are Indira Gandhi's interpreter and conscience-keeper—self-appointed, of course. So, why don't *you* find the answers? At the moment, few seem to understand Indira Gandhi. No one knows why she is doing what she is doing. Imagine the Prime Minister toppling her party chief ministers! Was anything like this ever done before? If her followers find this autocratic and arbitrary, why do you blame them? They don't speak their minds because she is all-powerful. They know they can't take up cudgels against her. They can't criticize her, so they praise her—simple, isn't it, if you realize that politicians cannot be silent on any issue for long? Why don't you understand why they praise her? You don't believe their praise is genuine, do you? If it is, it means they all support her. If it isn't, as you know it isn't, you have to understand its real meaning. Either way, you've no business finding fault with them . . . The fact is that you, Anand, are the one who is confused. You don't know Indira Gandhi's mind, yet you try to interpret her. You justify her actions, but you know you don't have a strong case. So, you end up criticizing everyone. What in blazes is all this nonsense!'

Anand did not respond. He tried to absorb the impact of her hard-hitting comments. They were not hers, he knew. They echoed the thoughts of many who were uneasy and angry. He also knew that Aruna alone could express them to him fearlessly—while others kept their mouths shut, or gushed hollow praise.

Aruna realized that she had been harsh—harsh because she had presented the alternate view. There was no other way to make Anand see anything other than his own version of the political scenario, based on observation and interpretation. Some of its components were imaginative, and often drastic, far-reaching, audacious. They tried to match the complexity of the existing situation, but with no guarantee of success, because everything depended on one person—Indira Gandhi. Everything hinged on how she would build the party and the party's response to what she proposed to do . . .

Given her mercurial nature, Aruna suddenly turned pleasant. 'Don't be angry,' she cooed, in a sweet and soft voice. 'I know you always want to try and do the right thing, but as things stand, to be efficient, you need to invoke Indira Gandhi's might. How on earth will you do that? She's in Delhi—*Dilli dur ast* (Delhi is far away), as they say . . . So far away from one of the few who try to understand our Prime Minister critically—which is the only way to understand . . .'

Anand looked into her eyes that brimmed with understanding. They had both passed through an emotional crisis in which political compulsions had overwhelmed personal relations—much against their will. Aruna found Anand's involvement in his work too intense to do anything about. For his part, Anand found Aruna given to excessive irrational action; moreover, he realized she was less and less synchronized with his being. They had not anticipated these developments, and now they could not escape them. Besides, the pall of advancing age had descended on their lives—making them ponderous, hesitant and aloof. Ten years ago, they had believed they could, and would, change the world. They were no longer as confident now. Yet, life had not disappointed them. And they had not given up.

'You are so kind, Aruna,' Anand began. 'You just want to find me right and I'm grateful. Yet, I want you to test my thoughts rigorously and tell me if I am wasting my time. As a free nation, we chose parliamentary democracy on the Westminster model. Many people said it wouldn't work, but Panditji and his colleagues asserted it would. Nehru argued this elaborately in his speeches and writings. He talked the people into accepting the model. As long as he lived, he nurtured the model and tried to weave grassroots democracy, economic self-reliance and planned development into it, based on secular nationhood and the concept

656

of unity in diversity. He reasoned out every complex detail and harmonized it with every other complex detail. He made the resultant amalgam look remarkably simple and natural. Looking back, we know what happened after him. We have seen the gradual crumbling of what he tried to build and sustain with his persuasive personality . . . I sometimes believe that when Nehru died, his legacy was split into two. Both Indira Gandhi and the so-called Syndicate were part of him, albeit harmonized parts. The two parts separated and are struggling for supremacy. Keeping personalities aside, this is the state of affairs today . . . The two parts cannot come together any more; they cannot coexist mechanically, they can be together only in harmony. And after Nehru, the harmony vanished, for want of the cohesive factor. Again, I am not talking about personalities; politicians are a mobile lot anyway. It wouldn't surprise me if Indira Gandhi's denigrators were to team up with her overnight. Even then, that would not amount to Nehru's resurrection. The two parts he consisted of would still remain apart. The new combination would, in effect, adopt one of the parts as its creed, jettisoning the other. The choice is thus clear. Indira Gandhi has to chart out her own path, for better or for worse . . . I am sure she knew this the moment she decided to enter active politics. Some of her bold and independent actions as the party chief, while her father was alive, corroborate this view. She has had the benefit of sizing up many leaders of the party for what they were at that time and what they are today . . . She is the Prime Minister now, she is supreme. That's the end of Chapter One . . .'

'Now tell me about Chapter Two,' urged Aruna. She knew that when Anand warmed to his theme, he was a fascinating speaker even though she often disagreed with his interpretations and opinions. These days she also found him more obstinate in his views, especially when it came to his various crusades against injustices in the social and political order. She often missed the clear-headed Anand she had known for years. He has changed, she told herself. You can't pinion a crusader for long, can you? He slips away from you each time! But, God, let Anand's crusade succeed for his own sake!

'Chapter Two is right before us,' Anand continued. 'It is Indira

Gandhi all the way—unchallenged and unchallengeable. Just after her spectacular triumphs, some of her actions are somehow beginning to hurt the country's image. The removal of chief ministers is eroding the democratic values we cherish. It is not unconstitutional, the way it is done. Yet, it is extra-constitutional, which is no better, if not worse . . . If this is not the entire story, if there is an uplifting motive behind it, as I believe there is, then the real purpose should be explained to the people. I try to say what I can to explain her actions, to the extent that I understood and am able to interpret them, but I am too insignificant to carry conviction. Meanwhile, the press goes to town and adds disaffection—which is unavoidable in any one-sided campaign. You know I don't talk in this strain to others. In public I'm Indira Gandhi's out-and-out supporter. My support often draws ridicule from friends who say I'll commit *sati* with her. They don't know my agony, which mainly emanates from my support for her, of course. So, Aruna, I have to open up before you. Lately this has become unbearable.'

'Why this agony? You're a politician and politicians don't agonize. They face situations, and either master them or go under. I don't see why you should—'

'You're right, this is not agony in a personal sense,' Anand explained. 'It concerns the country and the people. Indira Gandhi happens to be the centre of their universe today. What she does, and how, is very important to them. To them and to the system . . . And most important to every one is that she should succeed.'

'I agree,' responded Aruna. 'The government is the chief actor in the drama of people's lives in developing countries. Right now, Indira Gandhi is the focus of the people's hopes and aspirations in this country . . . You say she hardly knows you, although there is no reason to suppose that the Prime Minister doesn't know about you. You're not as unknown as you think. But never mind . . . Now, what is your agony about? What causes it? Tell me just one thing that bothers you immensely.'

'Right now, Aruna, I'm afraid the people have receded into the background. The change of chief ministers is the sole talking point at the moment. The arguments against that action sound plausible;

even Indira Gandhi's admirers can't defend her on this point. I feel, however, that there is logic in her viewpoint. There is nothing personal in her move. These chief ministers are solid, they have done well, they stood by her when she needed their support. If she wants to replace them now, it must be for something they *can't* do.'

'How are you so sure they can't?' Aruna countered. 'After all, you admit they're reasonably efficient, don't you? They will certainly do what she wants. Besides, you can't condemn them without putting them to the test, can you? So her jettison-chief-ministers scheme is pretty indefensible. The only explanation is that she is unsure of their loyalty and wants them out, just in case . . . Isn't that so?'

'That's what I hear all the time. Yet, I refuse to buy the argument that Indira Gandhi has a paranoid fear of the chief ministers and wants them to go just for her own sense of security. I reject that charge outright. *My* question is, is there nothing at all our chief ministers can't do? I don't agree with the assertion that they can do everything. I believe that we have a set of good status quo chief ministers. They will do, as they have no doubt done, a fine maintenance job. I am not at all sure, however, that they can bring about basic change. They can't discard the modus they have lived with for decades. They can't question their own genesis, cut their own umbilical cords . . . It is not their fault, of course; I have no doubt on that point.'

'Wait a minute,' Aruna interrupted him. 'Aren't you levelling a serious charge against the chief ministers, Anand? Whatever you think, I am sure no one will accept this idea, which sounds more like a pretext than an assessment. What's the evidence for your allegation—or whatever else you may prefer to call it?'

'This is no allegation, I assure you,' Anand said earnestly. 'I have every respect for our chief ministers . . . Look, you have to consider the situation as a whole, I repeat, as a whole. The Indira Gandhi phenomenon is itself a turn in our history. It had to be so. She had to give a new message, send a new signal, bring in a new era, promise a new future—for the people. She couldn't possibly have gone on doing and talking about more of the same, meaning, more of 1967. At that point, the country had reached a crossroads. The choice was clear and final—between change and disaster. If it had to be change, someone had to herald it, head it. It happened to be Indira Gandhi. Yet, Indira Gandhi is only an agent of change, not a substitute for it. The distinction is clear to me—crystal clear. This is where I differ from the Indira Gandhi idolaters. And this is what worries me.'

'Why should it worry you? Indira Gandhi is changing everything, isn't she? She is operating as an agent of change, isn't she?'

'Well, upto a point,' Anand replied after an extended pause, feeling trapped by Aruna's blunt question. 'There are two snags that I see. One, critics and friends alike look at every aspect of change in isolation, without seeing it as a part of a larger whole. So they criticize each action of Indira Gandhi individually and separately. She is autocratic, she is selfish, she is only building up personal power, she is a dictator. Second, even if she takes all this flak in her stride, will she deliver? And deliver what? Will that come up to the people's expectations? The idolaters emphatically say, Yes! I am not so sure, though I wouldn't say No—yet . . .'

'You almost sound blasphemous when you say that!' remarked Aruna, laughing. 'Her fanatic camp-followers will lynch you if they ever come to know your secret thoughts. Now, tell me, what do you expect of her in specific terms?'

'It is difficult to spell out,' Anand elaborated. 'Absurd as it may seem, I think her position is both strong and not so strong. She is supreme, she is great, she is the architect of Bangladesh, she is now a world figure. She has a great mass following, but lacks complete ideological support at top levels. She wants to bring about radical changes, but her unenthusiastic colleagues and a wooden-headed bureaucracy inhibit her. She is brave, but has to contend with extremely crafty vested interests who sabotage her from within and attack her from outside. She has many critics. That is understandable. But she has many more serious enemies who hate her, who pass off as genuine critics. These opponents are remnants of the feudal past. Critics are a democratic innovation—or ought to be so. The tribe is still evolving, I think. And more harmful in their own way than the critics and the hostile opponents are the host of sycophantic fools who worship her. These fellows simply don't know why she is great, what she wants to do and how they could themselves lend real support to her—which they don't. They trumpet her praises for the wrong reasons, thus inflicting the worst possible damage upon her. With these assets and liabilities, she has to make the system of parliamentary democracy work and yield results. It may be premature to say so, but I believe that Naxalism, of whatever brand, will be her main adversary. In the ultimate analysis, she has to show that a revolution is possible without the gun. Mahatma Gandhi preached non-violence. I believe it has fallen to Indira Gandhi's lot to prove it in practice, in the context of the modern state . . .'

'You think she is throwing out chief ministers just to prove Mahatma Gandhi right?' queried Aruna with a touch of sarcasm, laughing aloud.

'I see your scepticism, Aruna,' Anand responded calmly. 'That means I didn't argue the case cogently. Believe me, you cannot save this country by maintaining the same stagnant position. And certainly, no chief minister is a holy cow—including my chief minister, for whom I have affection and respect, as you know. The fact is, Aruna, it is so difficult to separate the personal and the impersonal now. Yet, I think we must do so; else we are in trouble. Right or wrong, Indira Gandhi wants to try new chiefs in place of the old. Criticism won't change that now. The question is: what kind of men are the new ones and what kind of agendas will they follow? Alternatively, what agendas were they given to implement, when they were "nominated"?'

Anand knew that he was in a minority. The removal of chief ministers, especially the way it was being done, had no visible justification. It became a fait accompli, but without acceptance. It would be accepted by the country at large only if it yielded dazzling results that drive doubts away.

Chaudhury was cool. Dangerously cool, Anand thought, and many who knew Chaudhury agreed. He did not appear sullen; he was willing to discuss the question of his impending departure with anyone at any time. He had a foolproof way to manipulate the reports about himself that reached Indira Gandhi. Through these he convinced her that he was ready to lay down office, like yesterday's shirt, if only she, in her wisdom, wanted it. It was a perfect act by any standard. Everyone, including Indira Gandhi, knew that it was an act. And it was perfect, everyone agreed—unlike some other chiefs who made transparently pathetic efforts to cling to office.

As time went by, the attitude of the chief ministers who were about to be axed became the central point of discussion. Each of them was assessed in terms of how grabbing or detached he was about the position he held. The ethics of arbitrary and summary dismissal were—most amazingly—gradually forgotten. At any rate, they receded into obscurity. So, Indira Gandhi was proved right by default. Not a dog—well, not many at any rate—barked when she eased a chief minister out. The political rabble would immediately begin to discuss the deficiencies of the victim and dissect the prospects of all the leading contenders for the position. No one thought of the outgoing individual.

Chaudhury suddenly became philosophical, surprising everybody. 'After all, how does it matter who the chief minister is?' Chaudhury asked a small group of legislators one evening in his house. He feigned a nonchalance that he knew would fool no one. 'I have had my innings. It is only fair that someone younger and more competent gets a chance to run the state . . . ' His blasé description of the chief minister's job made it sound like a shift in a factory. Some of those present (as well as most perceptive observers) saw in his attitude a desperate attempt to conceal the extreme frustration that corroded him from within. Worst of all was the feeling that his enemy Mahendranath, even if out of the party, was supplying the opposition with powerful weapons to destroy him. Chaudhury believed this, on evidence that was at best scanty. Yet his paranoia forced him to believe it; no one found it worth their while to contradict him. For all the others, it only added to the drama.

No one knew if Chaudhury would go, much less when. So as good politicians should, they promptly bypassed these questions and concentrated their attention on his successor. Of course,

Chaudhury is going, most asserted. The more ignorant the person, the stronger his assertion. Some said, trying to sound convincing, that Chaudhury would stay; but their voices were feeble and lacked conviction. And in any case Chaudhury's going was more sensational news than Chaudhury's staying—for the press, as also for many readers with no stake one way or another—and so it received greater attention.

Chaudhury had done nothing to merit an unceremonious removal. That was more or less the opinion. Change was in the air, nevertheless. And change was now being seen as inextricably linked with Indira Gandhi's absolute power. Power must be capricious; it is nothing if it doesn't defy logic and reason. It must stun, it must shock . . . Therefore, Chaudhury is going, concluded the politicians and, of course, hordes of ravenous journalists.

Anand was on a visit to another state capital to attend a conference of state ministers of land revenue and land reforms. There, a new chief minister, known to have been hand-picked by the Prime Minister, had just taken over. He had never been prominent in the party. He had spoken at party meets now and then, but had never attracted enough attention to make any member at the meeting on his way to the coffee enclosure pause and listen to him. With his elevation, all that his colleagues could see was the mask of Indira Gandhi covering his face from ear to ear, as it were.

Anand knew his counterpart in the host state well, having met him at several similar meetings in the past two years. In all that time, the minister had sulked for being landed with the land reforms portfolio. He detested the subject with all his heart. He wailed that he was stuck with it for want of enough pull with the previous chief minister. He now hoped for a better deal at the hands of the new chief—at least a transfer to the excise department, if not to finance and commercial taxes.

The participants at the meeting discussed several issues, took several decisions—all for the record. Anand found it an exhausting exercise. Consequently, he paid little attention to the proceedings. Instead, he cornered the disgruntled minister who was hosting the conference and plied him with questions about the new chief minister's antecedents and attitudes. 'He has turned out to be the darkest horse you can imagine,' his colleague told him. 'Some called him a nobody, others nicknamed him minister-for-nothing, still others said he didn't even deserve a nickname.'

'What is his attitude on programmes like land reforms, land ceilings and others mentioned in the party manifesto?' asked Anand pointedly.

'Very strong,' the other replied emphatically.

Anand suddenly felt elated; but his exhilaration plunged sickeningly when his colleague explained, 'I mean very strong against any measures that disturb the status quo.' Then he hastened to add, 'But of course, he is all for Indira Gandhi and her programme!'

Anand took some time to absorb this comment. He could see that in this state at least there was no ideological basis for the change of guard . . . Depression crept over him.

'What will your previous chief do now?' asked Anand, as an afterthought.

'What he will not do is leave the party,' began the other. 'He knows that the alternative is political wilderness. Mahendranath, the once undisputed leader of your state, is a pale shadow of his former self today, as a standing deterrent to others. No, our ex-chief will stay put in the party all right. And he will give all of us hell until Indira Gandhi makes amends—amends that he considers adequate. He will not revolt, of course. He will not ask for any other post. He will accept what she offers him, and still continue to cause trouble in the state. He will pretend to be a very good boy . . . yet, he will, sure as anything, lay highly explosive mines every inch of the new chief's way and finally blow him to bits!'

'Why is he so bitter? Don't they get on well together?'

'Oh yes, they do. They are good friends, as friends go. Still, you see, this is a matter of prestige. How could anyone, even the Prime Minister, remove a chief minister? Is he her personal servant? Don't you see the real issue?'

'Yes, I do,' agreed Anand, his heart sinking.

On his way back home, Anand had to pass through Delhi. He

stayed there overnight and gathered all the gossip he could about Chaudhury's impending fate. Late in the night, an elderly gentleman with a graying moustache, stately build and penetrating eyes, clad in spotless khadi, came to see him at the state guest house. Anand knew about him, but had never met him. He did not hold any post at the time, but politicians widely believed him to be one of the powers behind the throne. He talked very little in public, which only enhanced his importance. The gentleman's sudden desire to see Anand at that unusual hour was intriguing. Strange indeed are the ways of Indira Gandhi, he had heard people say time and again. This time he too joined the chorus inwardly.

They talked of nothing in particular for about a half hour. Anand imagined that the man was probing and assessing him with uncanny shrewdness. However, he did express his emphatic view that Chaudhury had provided stability to the state and should continue as chief minister. The gentleman grunted agreement—or so Anand thought. The visitor left as quietly and as abruptly as he had arrived. He left a bemused Anand on the guest house steps, puzzling over his arrival and departure.

# 52

'WHERE WAS THE NEED FOR HIM TO GO TO DELHI? WASN'T IT FOR overnight consultations? In other words, conspiracies? You may not know, but your Brihaspati has been cutting the ground from under your feet in Delhi for quite some time. You won't believe me because I am at loggerheads with him. But I just can't help telling you whatever I know . . .'

Shekhar had been talking for almost half an hour in an attempt to convince the unusually sullen Chaudhury that Anand was the man behind the move to replace him. As there was little he could find to falsely implicate Anand, Shekhar seized upon his rival's overnight halt in Delhi as proof of his malicious intentions. However, in actuality, the only route back to the state capial was via Delhi and an overnight halt was necessary as there was no direct connecting flight to Afrozabad. So, Shekhar concentrated on Anand's meetings and calls in Delhi—especially the visit by the elderly party leader. That looked ominous to Chaudhury and made him thoughtful.

Something was wrong with his Delhi arrangements. He had

overlooked something somewhere. He had tripped, he told himself with annoyance.

'You are imagining things,' he told Shekhar sardonically.

'Don't believe me if you don't want to,' Shekhar exclaimed in a hurt tone. 'But don't accuse me of what I am incapable of doing. I am a down-to-earth fellow and you know it. Imagination is Anand's special quality, not mine. So please yourself with wishful thinking by all means; it's your problem . . .'

After Shekhar left, in a feigned huff, Chaudhury began to pace his drawing room like an animal in a cage. He thought furiously, examined his political strategy in minute detail. He wondered what could have transpired; where and how in his foolproof plans had this hairline chink appeared. He regarded both Anand and Shekhar as inconsequential. The former had no idea of the Delhi developments; he was just a spectator. The latter, however he phrased his protests, was trying to find a stick to beat Anand with. So where had he gone wrong? And why hadn't he got a scent of all this until now? Clearly, Chaudhury ruminated, his own sources in Delhi had double-crossed him. They had let him down badly. Should he go to Delhi and intervene personally? He decided against the idea at once. No chief minister should hobnob in Delhi at that moment. It was too dangerous. You would only find masks there, no faces. He felt like a paratrooper who jumps with supreme confidence, only to find that his chute has failed to open. Too late to do anything.

Chaudhury was angry. He knew Mahendranth and his ilk, both in and out of the party, were gunning for him. He hadn't been unduly perturbed; he expected nothing different from them anyway. They didn't deserve even a thought, he mused in passing . . . However, he was furious, absolutely furious, with Indira Gandhi. He had considered himself one of her few pillars of strength in the country. If you recalled every event since Lal Bahadur Shastri's death, bit by tiny bit, detail by minute detail, he had consistently passed the twin tests of loyalty and effectiveness. He would even have relinquished chief ministership honourably, in a natural course of events. (This thought occurred to him for the first time.) But to be eased out . . . out . . . out like this! He just could not stomach the prospect. He still had no hard information about his fate, but began to consider the worst case scenario immediately. What if he was no longer chief minister? Then who? Anand? Shekhar? Bipin Chandra, Number Two in his cabinet? The safe Number Two, the oldest of them all, so good and harmless no one even took note of his presence? Or were some MPs quietly pushing one amongst themselves to be sent down to the state? . . . If so, who?

His reverie was broken by a light knock on the door and Anand entered. He greeted Chaudhury and exclaimed 'My God!' looking at the ashtray that overflowed with cigarette stubs. Chaudhury noticed it too, for the first time, with some surprise. He laughed and said, 'Good to think of God! Someone has to save us all! When did you return, wise man?'

'Morning flight,' answered Anand, and almost added, 'as Intelligence must have reported to you!' Instead, he added, 'After a sleepless night in Delhi, for no fault of mine!' Intelligence must have reported this to Chaudhury—and to Shekhar, who had his own set of spies.

An awkward silence fell. There was none of the customary jest and banter today.

Suddenly, Chaudhury said, 'Cut out all the details. Tell me, does she want me out?'

Anand replied without thinking, 'Yes, but I have no proof, no clue . . .'

'I didn't ask for proof,' Chaudhury cut in.

This cryptic exchange disturbed Anand. No reason, no clue, no background; yet, both agreed on the answer. Anand tried to backtrack on his impetuous reply. Chaudhury dismissed it with a peremptory wave of his hand and said, 'We are talking of Indira Gandhi; nothing to do with you. Now, look into the future and tell me what you see . . .'

'I'm afraid I can't see anything clearly, if the change of chief minister in the state I visited two days back is any indication.'

'One state is no indication of another,' Chaudhury declared. 'Answer my question on the merits of this state, without any indication from elsewhere.'

'I think it is wrong to think of changing the chief in this state; and I am not saying this to please you . . .'

'I know you are not a sycophant; no need to convince me about that. Yet, you just said, didn't you, that you see a change coming? So—'

'You didn't let me complete my sentence,' interrupted Anand. 'A change here needs to be averted, at least for some time.'

'How?'

'That's your job,' said Anand decisively.

'Sorry, that is impossible,' Chaudhury responded, equally decisively. 'I haven't exactly been gazing at the stars these past weeks. I have done my best—without hawking my self-respect around, that is. Ended up with nothing. A change will come—or it won't. No one knows.'

'Seems a dead end,' commented Anand thoughtfully.

'Dead as dead can be,' snapped Chaudhury, keeping a forcible grip on his growing anxiety and his long-suppressed rage.

He was absolutely right, thought Anand. Each state stood on its own merit. The change in one gave no indication of the change, or no-change, in the other. It was futile to search for a pattern—or so it seemed, on the whole.

A thought, which Anand at once dismissed as fantastic, crossed his mind. Was what was happening simply change for the sake of change? If there was no discernible pattern, was change an end in itself? Just a violent shake-up, so no one could feel secure, no one could strike roots in one place? Did Indira Gandhi want chief ministers who owed her not only their exalted positions, but even their political existence? Did she want political dwarfs, or better still, dwarfs of all persuasions, in all areas and disciplines and ministries, who could be politically painted and scrubbed at will—her will? The thought was uncharitable in the extreme, Anand admitted to himself. Yet, he found 'enlightened' opinion in the country fast veering to that position. It meant, in effect, that the people saw the Prime Minister destabilizing the country herself, sowing the seeds of disaster, just in order to make her personal authority unshakable for all time . . .

Anand rejected the allegation as rank nonsense. He fervently hoped that some dramatic development would expose the absurdity of the charge and enable Indira Gandhi to emerge unscathed. Could some new chief ministers disprove this grave charge and demonstrate that changing chief ministers had really been in the best interests of the people? Strangely, it occurred to him that her vindication within the country, in the eyes of her own people, was much more important than her triumph in Bangladesh ... As he saw it, she had only one armour against the many attacks being mounted against her: the Indian masses.

Chaudhury was lost in his own thoughts and Anand's mind took another track. How, he wondered, could Indira Gandhi suddenly conjure up ideal chief ministers to avoid the charge that she was replacing the existing lot for selfish reasons? And even if the new chief ministers were committed to the party programmes, would they be loyal? Anand reasoned that if the person had both these characteristics, the former could bring benefits to the people and justify the latter; After all, one could argue that it was not a sin to be loyal to Indira Gandhi—at least, not in the eyes of the masses.

Indeed, why should he suppose that Indira Gandhi was not aware of these criteria for choosing the new chiefs? True, in one state he visited recently, the new incumbent perhaps did not measure up. That assessment was itself based on scanty information. Anand could not take it as wholly reliable. So, even if he was right in that one case, why should he beat his breast in advance about other states? And which other states? Why was he fussing over nothing in particular?

As he took his leave of Chaudhury, he was thinking about the relationship between Indira Gandhi and the teeming millions of India. If that nexus was intact, Indira's position would be secure. And he was confident that Indira Gandhi would do her utmost to ensure that the masses continued to love her; this was how she would ultimately prevail!

*

The tension in the state capital grew. Aruna, the political

unpredictable, now adopted a new stance. She raised the slogan that Chaudhury should go. As usual, not many took her seriously. Why should he go? they asked. She had no answer, but shouted that there was not a single reason for him to stay. Indiraji wants a change in the states. Why should this state be an exception, Aruna demanded. What is so extraordinary about Chaudhury? Is he honest? Is he pro-poor? Has he done even one miserable thing for the state, beyond feathering his cronies' nests? What can the people expect of him in the new context? When other states are to go ahead with revolutionary programmes, why should one individual hold this state to ransom?

Aruna's extraordinary force of conviction (even if transient) and the energy with which she pursued it was at once her greatest strength—and her weakness. Often she would have a few words with Anand before she made her move, but there was absolutely no guarantee that she would change her mind if he thought what she was proposing was unwise. Once she made up her mind, she became a mobile centre of All India Radio, as it were. She would meet all and sundry, brainwash anyone she could trap in a corner—friend or foe. She would sweep through like a hurricane, leaving everything in a shambles.

Whispers started circulating, at once, that Anand was using Aruna's ferocious attack to unsettle Chaudhury. Didn't I tell you that his visit to Pramod Rai's constituency was not just an accident? After all, wasn't Anand close to Mahendranath in the beginning? At any rate, not close to Chaudhury at all in his battles with Mahendranath? . . . Well, every leader commits the costliest blunder of his life at some point—and pays for it for the rest of his life. Chaudhury is no exception. This blunder will cost him very dear. You see, Anand is not a dumb follower. He is basically independent, with a mind of his own. He was the one person to watch, always. Shekhar is a match for him in many ways, but Shekhar is also vulnerable in many other ways. People still call him a bastard in private. He has several skeletons in his cupboard. You can attack him any time on one of those counts. Anand, on the other hand, has only one vulnerable point: Aruna. That story is old hat now. Besides, their erstwhile fire has all but gone out. They quarrel today, join hands tomorrow. That is how he sets her against anyone he wants to destroy. Still, no one can blame him openly, given Aruna's unpredictable nature . . . I always wonder how a shrewd man like Chaudhury could even think of making Anand a minister. You don't raise cobras in your back yard, do you? . . .

Anand thus became a focus of political gossip and speculation. Curiously, Chaudhury's shaky position had shifted the focus to Anand. Shekhar contributed to it, of course, in his attempt to malign him. However, that was not the whole story. The sixth sense of political animals saw him as 'one of the nexts'. Soon, they saw him as 'the next'. This latest rumour swelled and grew. Chaudhury was aware of it, of course. In his own calculating way, he had been instrumental in starting some of the rumours by subtly propelling three or four aspirants into a race for the chief ministership. Each of them felt that Chaudhury wanted him to be the next. This was a contingency measure Chaudhury took, just in case . . . Chaudhury didn't approach Anand, perhaps because he knew he couldn't manipulate him the way he wanted. When he tried to discuss the topic some days after Anand's return from Delhi, Anand said, 'Please don't talk of a change in this state. Let what is to happen happen. As you know I have conveyed my views to Indira Gandhi through the person who met me in Delhi. I have nothing more to add until I know why she wants you out, if she does . . .'

'Your view hasn't stopped the wind blowing or the fire burning,' Chaudhury pointed out. 'Indeed, some of our cabinet colleagues have already entered the succession race.'

'And you don't know a thing about it!' added Anand with a mischievous smile.

Chaudhury became serious. 'Look, Anand,' he said. 'You just can't stop the aspirations of human beings. I didn't initiate anything myself; I merely paved the way to take the credit for whatever happens. They know Indira Gandhi wants me to step down. No one knows, yet everyone knows. So, when there is a change eventually, the next fellow shouldn't think he got it in spite of Chaudhury. Because that's not true and I am opposing no one.

The state needs a chief minister; if it isn't Chaudhury, it has to be someone else. When it comes to a choice, no one goes by merit alone. The result is anybody's guess. So, everyone is in the fray. Why not? The process has started as a frantic general scramble, as it always does. At the moment it looks like a lottery. Then, it will come down to a few. Later, to two, making it a toss of the coin. Finally, the lucky or unlucky one will be drawn from Indira Gandhi's bag.'

Anand was still unwilling to discuss alternatives. He insisted on the need for Chaudhury's continued presence at the helm, for the time being. He found no one else to replace him—in political skill, in understanding, and above all in his liberal approach to ideology. He didn't subscribe to any ideology himself—least of all to socialism. Yet he was not against any ideology, including socialism. His only concern was not to endanger his solidly entrenched, conventional position. And Anand considered this neutrality the best trait that a chief minister could manifest at that crucial time. Chaudhury wanted to remain in power, of course. Yet, when he thought he got a signal from Delhi, Anand found him ready to meet the Delhi demand halfway. Indeed, he sounded eager to do so, although he wasn't, really. It was an intelligent public posture. He articulated it in a way that no one could call insincere. Besides, if he did have to step down, his present stance would entirely be in line with the predicted eventuality. It was a noteworthy exercise in finesse and guile.

Anand was quite clear in his mind that Chaudhury was still the best chief minister visible in the state. And chief ministers simply don't arrive from heaven—or hell—just like that.

Suddenly Chaudhury leaned forward across the table—rather uncharacteristically because his habit was to lean back and stretch his arms whenever he had to make a special point. He now looked straight into Anand's eyes and said, 'You have been dodging the question too long, I see. You know you can't dodge it for ever. I know you are not as blank in the head as you seem on this critical question. So, why not share your thoughts, for once?'

'You are right. I am not blank in the head,' responded Anand. 'I have thought and thought about your possible successor and found no one. So, anyone will do, I suppose, if you must go . . . Clearly, this is not a very positive opinion. Besides, if I say what I think, I shall be raising a bumper crop of enemies. So I am keeping silent . . .'

'I know you're discreet and hold your tongue most of the time,' observed Chaudhury. 'On occasions, however, your silence may lead to serious consequences. Anyway, you are reluctant to speak out, so I don't want to ask you for your views—'

'That's it,' cut in Anand. 'I am reluctant to speak out, but I am willing to speak—to you, for instance.'

'Go on, tell me exactly what you feel,' Chaudhury said.

'I'm of the definite view that if you have to go, your successor should be the one you suggest.'

'I don't think that is possible,' observed Chaudhury, as if he had thought over the matter already and come to a conclusion. 'At least the mood of the people in Delhi doesn't justify your wishful thinking. Besides, when Indira Gandhi doesn't want me as chief minister, I don't see why she should listen to me in the choice of my successor.'

'You mean there is no difference between the two scenarios?'

'Of course there is; but who is going to convince her? And in any event, she doesn't have the time to really take all the details into account and come to a considered decision.'

'Delhi does have the time to take decisions—considered or otherwise. This is a vital matter for the state. Someone should bluntly tell them the implications of the options available. At least someone should make an effort.'

Chaudhury remained unmoved. Anand suspected that the chief's interest was ebbing away, fast. This was contrary to his nature; he was too tough to lose interest so easily. There must be something more to his apathy than meets the eye, Anand surmised. Meanwhile, Chaudhury was lost in deep thought, smoking cigarettes in an unending chain. He puffed vigorously, as if the smoke would act as an antidote for the turbulence churning within him.

'Why don't you have a frank talk with Indira Gandhi?' asked Anand.

'What about?' Chaudhury shot back, a bit surprised.

'There are umpteen issues on which the party Prime Minister and an outgoing party chief minister could usefully exchange views,' Anand said. 'You could talk about your successor, among other things.'

'She doesn't want me—why, I don't know and can't figure out,' Chaudhury mused. Then, suddenly, he blurted out, 'So why should I discuss my successor? Or bother about him?'

Anand fell silent. Not because he didn't want to argue, but because he had heard Chaudhury's position on the issue—loud and clear. There was nothing more to argue about. Within minutes, he rose to leave. A wall had risen, as it were, between him and Chaudhury within those few unforgiving moments.

*

In one sentence, Chaudhury realized, he had revealed himself to Anand. Anyone would do. And no matter who his successor was, Chaudhury's attitude was sure to be the same—hostile in the extreme. Nothing personal, Chaudhury reminded himself. If Indira Gandhi wanted him to step down, it was for her to unfold her plan to him. It was for her to take him into her confidence. It was for her to give him the respect he deserved—and expected. He didn't want to cling to power—or did he? He didn't quite know. Yet, he was not entirely insincere, he told himself as he concentrated on what, according to him, was appropriate for Indira Gandhi to do. Which she had not done and was not likely to do. That gave Chaudhury a peg to hang his anger on. He warmed to the subject among those he considered trustworthy.

'Prime Ministership has now become proprietorship,' he fumed. 'I don't know where we are heading. I have done what I could for the state. Let someone else improve on it, by all means. In any case, no one is permanent . . .'

'Why is she humiliating you?' one in the inner circle asked. 'How can anyone else manage the state without your cooperation? Doesn't she realize even this rudimentary fact?' Chaudhury merely shrugged his shoulders.

His sense of grievance grew as the days went by. Yet, Chaudhury remained calm, letting others mouth his thoughts in public. He did let slip a snide comment, or half a comment, now and then. Barring this, one would have thought that he enjoyed the prospect of quitting the chief ministership.

By now, his exit had become common talk, but no one had asked him to step down—except, of course, the odd newspaper wedded to Mahendranath's faction. The bulk of the press, however, made it appear that the world would come to an end without Chaudhury. Perhaps they meant their own world, since they were so dependent on Chaudhury's 'friendly' treatment of them.

As the weeks passed, Chaudhury made whatever moves he could to safeguard his position. He knew that his lobby in Delhi, though low-key and almost invisible, was dependable. One or two of the Prime Minister's personal assistants were said to be its first rung. Then came middleweight politicians who had umpteen occasions to meet her. They had the liberty to ramble on about anything under the sun, while she heard them out with the indulgence shown to pets. It looked like she was wasting her time—but wasn't, really. From that voluminous raw ore of gossip, rumour and imaginative stories—often mixed with sheer stupidity—Indira Gandhi could sometimes glean some invaluable nuggets of importance. She would store them away in a remote recess of her mind, to retrieve on some future occasion. She could extract oil from sand, some said admiringly, others apprehensively.

Along with these, there were the Intelligence sources to be tapped. Unfortunately most Intelligence operatives were not very intelligent or resourceful; they only paraphrased hearsay into official jargon. The Prime Minister often found their information worthless, yet some precious sparks emerged from these massive reports too. She scrutinized them with razor-sharp concentration.

On the very top of the ladder came Indira Gandhi's close confidantes. Some of them looked like mere hangers-on, but it was said that they were very influential and kept a close watch on everything with a thousand eyes. Some of them had been Panditji's confidantes too, which added to their importance considerably; in fact some of them were close to the family and like family members themselves. It was among these different coteries that the state leaders chose some 'cultivable' individuals whom they took care of assiduously—through a bewildering mesh of quid pro quo. The most valuable lobbyists chief ministers could have were Indira Gandhi's close confidantes, and most chief ministers did everything they could to get into their good graces. However, several of these so-called top men were false pretenders, or corrupt parasites—and the chief ministers knew this perfectly well. Yet, these too flourished; in God's political creation, everyone had a place. The chief ministers obliged them, on the wise principle that you can't expect every bullet to hit the bull's-eye. You have to waste a lot of bullets, just to get one accurate hit. And in any case, the wasted bullets should not matter, so long as the chiefs got them gratis from other sources.

Chaudhury's network covered all these categories effectively. On the top rung, along with several luminaries, was Gopi Kishen, a very exalted public functionary in the Delhi Administration. Everyone in Delhi worth his salt knew Gopi Kishen—or, at the very least, about Gopi Kishen, from experience, personal or observed. Some called him a legend, others branded him a fiend. Be that as it may, there was talk that Indira Gandhi listened to him with respect. It was also believed that Gopi Kishen had some of the Prime Minister's personal assistants in his pocket. This, in effect, was his crowning achievement. The personal staff of the Prime Minister—or of any No.1 for that matter—always ended up taking a great deal of abuse. What is often meant for the No.1 is vicariously administered to them. Many other operators in Delhi claimed that they could, like Gopi Kishen, open their pockets to reveal at least some of the PM's assistants in them. Each such influential leader had his clientele. No one knew anything definite about these claims; they were possibly so much rubbish. However, Chaudhury was wise enough to keep many such functionaries happy, to be on the safe side.

After Anand left, Chaudhury had a long telephonic

consultation with Gopi Kishen. He smoked several cigarettes while the talk lasted, till the overflowing ashtray spilled over the desk cluttered with petitions, supplications and invitations.

# 53

GOPI KISHEN STARTED ON HIS ROUNDS EXACTLY AT 7 A.M. RATHER, it was exactly 7 a.m. when Gopi Kishen started on his rounds. You could set your watch by watching Gopi Kishen step out of his palatial residence on Ashoka Road, New Delhi. It was his unfailing morning routine, be it freezing winter or blazing summer. His reputation was impeccable on this score. Someone had once mentioned this to the Prime Minister herself. To which she had responded with a smile.

That day, he was in high spirits. Chief Minister Chaudhury had called him up the previous night and had a long talk with him. He was always happy when this particular chief phoned, for he had proved a windfall to Gopi Kishen. Indeed, Chaudhury was a permanent milch cow, a *kama dhenu* and a *kalpa vriksha* which bore fruit in all seasons. When it came to maintaining a Delhi lobby, several chief ministers, some even shrewd or influential, had to talk mainly with money. It had to rain from the states on Delhi in a heavy downpour. There was just no other way. Chaudhury was aware of this, of course. Like many other state leaders, he had reason to believe that Gopi Kishen was close to Indira Gandhi. He was not quite in the 'kitchen cabinet', yet was reputed to be one of those who procured provisions for the kitchen. This was good enough for the shrewd Chaudhury. The servant has his own influence, doesn't he? So, at the end of the overnight conversation, he had hinted at a 'suitcase' that he was to send Gopi Kishen—'very soon'. Remembering this, Gopi Kishen felt a rush of pure joy.

As he was about to enter his car, Gopi Kishen saw a bedraggled peasant stumbling towards him. He had a sodden paper in his hand—evidently a petition. Gopi Kishen frowned on the fellow who threatened to delay his fixed, immaculate routine. Heaven knows whom they voted for at the election, but they seemed to think they had bought you up, he reflected bitterly. As if you owed everything to them—your office, your name, your fame—everything. In particular, your continuance in power . . . Before the peasant could get within ten paces of the car, Gopi Kishen shouted, 'Come to the office; no time here!' and banged the door shut.

The moment he reclined in the soft rear seat he forgot the temporary annoyance and began to luxuriate in his euphoric thoughts. Like a cat purring contentedly, rubbing its body against the leg of a chair . . . Many in Delhi cited him as a living example of a successful politician. Successful politician *and* businessman. You couldn't separate the two; they were Siamese twins in Gopi Kishen's case. His late father Lala Harikishen had initiated him into the mysteries of politics-cum-business . . .

It had begun thirty-five years ago . . . It hadn't been easy. Yet, it had been exciting, intoxicating. Both the Siamese twins had flourished. They had become equally hefty in course of time, by the process of mutual reinforcement. Gopi Kishen had courted imprisonment after careful planning by his father—his dear, wise and far-sighted father. Everything Lalaji touched had invariably turned into gold. In particular, business—import, export, transport, bullion, textiles, liquor—you name it . . . He had a magic touch with the British government in those days. That was the secret of his success. His name had been among the probables for a Rai Bahadurship for some time. However, even as he pursued his business vigorously, he had been quick to sense the peculiar unease of a regime on its way out. Maybe it was trying not to seem unstable, but it wasn't quite succeeding . . . On the Indian side, jail-going had acquired high respectability, promising bright prospects for the jail-goer in the near future . . . Lalaji's instinct told him that his young son Gopi Kishen should go to jail at the earliest. Patriotic jail-going by Gandhiji's followers (whether real or feigned) wasn't an option that was always available. The old man had a way of presenting the opportunity and withdrawing it unexpectedly. So, said Lalaji, you had to hurry and grab the chance whenever it was on, if you wanted to build up a record of patriotism for the right day. Lalaji had already begun to see that day's pale red dawn, long before anyone else noticed it . . .

Soon, such an occasion presented itself. Lalaji was in a hurry. After some reluctance, Gopi Kishen decided to sacrifice his life of revelry, so natural to a millionaire's son. It was no mean act of self-abnegation by any standards—or so he thought. Once he was assured that he wouldn't have to drudge in 'C' class like thousands of other satyagrahis he became enthusiastic about his new role; he would at least be 'B', if not 'A'. Thoughtful Lalaji had seen to that. However, the officer whose help he had enlisted for this purpose was himself shocked at the very idea. He couldn't make out what Lalaji was up to. A millionaire's son voluntarily courting arrest along with the riff-raff from the streets, the slogan-shouting good-for-nothings? It was, to say the least, scandalous, he thought.

He said so bluntly to Lalaji.

'This is politics, Lalaji, for heaven's sake!' he remonstrated. 'You have no business here, neither does your son . . . '

'Politics *is* business, my dear sir,' said Lalaji, blowing thick clouds of chillum smoke from his mouth and nostrils. He mused for a minute and added, 'Indeed, I say life itself is all business; nothing but . . .'

'But Lalaji, how can you be so callous to your son? How can you ask him to court imprisonment? This is preposterous. You're committing a blunder!'

'I don't know all that!' said Lalaji testily. 'I only know I'm in good company. Excellent company. My business instinct tells me that when Motilal Nehru, Jawaharlal Nehru, Rajendra Prasad, Abul Kalam Azad and Rajaji are all going to jail, some profit must come out of jail-going sometime, somehow.'

'Lalaji, those others consider jail-going a patriotic duty . . .'

'I don't know about them and I don't care. I see my son's jail-going as a political investment for the family. Good business!'

'Whatever you may say, Lalaji, you are ruining your son. You're doing something you don't understand at all. You're bringing a permanent stigma on your family. You're literally going to the dogs, if you don't mind my saying so . . .'

Lalaji sat still for what appeared a long moment. Should he contradict an officer of the British raj to his face—even if the raj was nearing its end? That would be rather impolitic, he concluded. Besides, the raj could continue for some years, you never could tell . . . Nevertheless, he had to stand his ground. He couldn't afford to miss this grand opportunity of jail-going—possibly the last before the country became free. His family simply had to have a jail-going record; no question whatever about that. He was too shrewd to let slip such an opportunity. The officer's protests exasperated him, even though he made them in good faith. Frankly, Lalaji thought, the dimwit had no business to lecture to a businessman on how to run his business. Besides, Lalaji had to build up his son's character too, before the old club-drink-sex virus infected him and ruined the family's prospects permanently. He decided to end the debate.

'What will happen to Gopi Kishen's health in that rotten jail?' the officer demanded to know.

'I've thought of all that, I assure you,' answered Lalaji. 'Gopi will eat the same food as he eats at home, including . . .'

'That's enough,' cut in the loyal officer, reluctant to allow further elaboration of what all could be 'thought of' and managed, in the prisons of the British raj. 'You know best, Lalaji,' he said resignedly at last. 'I was only being helpful, that's all . . .'

'I know, I know, and I thank you for all you did, sir,' said Lalaji, glad that the discussion was over.

And thus Gopi Kishen had courted imprisonment, as part of a

strategy devised by his astute father. When he was released from jail, he surprised his friends—even his mother—by his radiant health. He had well-rounded cheeks, a new spring in his step and considerable additional weight—while most other satyagrahis came out as slow-moving cadavers . . . There was no one to welcome them at the jail gate with garlands; they had nowhere to go. At least some of them were not sure their own families in the villages would take them back, given the stigma attached to jail-going in a tradition-bound society. In short, for several jail-goers, jail was not a welcome experience. Gopi Kishen, on the other hand, not only gained weight, but was instantly hailed as a 'leader' the moment he mounted the *rath* (chariot) decorated specially for his first triumphant ride in a grand procession. The crowds gathered at the gate were immensely impressed. Some among them, who had also seen the other released prisoners, commented, 'There are jail-goers and jail-goers!'

*

Gopi Kishen's car sped along the streets of New Delhi. There was little traffic; an occasional truck rumbled past. Newspaper vendors with piles of morning papers tied neatly to their bicycles pedalled briskly by. The early sun was so gentle, it could hardly be felt.

The car suddenly screeched to a halt at the kerb and Gopi Kishen jumped out like a nimble teenager. The person walking along the footpath looked up in surprise and stopped too, rather awkwardly, seeing Gopi Kishen almost sprint towards him. 'Namaste, namasteji,' cried Gopi Kishen, with a joy and fervour out of all proportion to the occasion, as also to the state of their acquaintance. If you had read the pedestrian's innermost thoughts, you would have heard him mutter, 'The meddling bastard!' However, Gopi Kishen had already overtaken him, pumped his unoffered hand and crushed him in a big bear-hug. Watching them, you would have thought they were old college friends meeting after twenty years. In fact, they had met casually just a couple of days earlier for the first time. Gopi Kishen had carefully ensured that his route would intersect with the path taken by the other person—a highly-placed official in a permit-giving ministry of the Central government—on his daily morning walk.

Gopi Kishen talked all the time, as if weaving a verbal web to ensnare the officer. The web was reinforced by repeated references to the Prime Minister and one of her trusted assistants. The only exit from the web lay in a pointed reference to 'that file', which Gopi Kishen brought up repeatedly. The officer at last bought his freedom by murmuring something. Gopi Kishen got back into his car triumphantly and shouted, 'PM house *chalo*!' to his driver, loud enough for the escaping officer to hear.

However, the moment the car was out of the officer's sight, Gopi Kishen gave his driver another destination . . . The driver nodded, said '*accha jee*', smiled a bit to himself and swerved into a lane. The lane, in turn, led to a maze of other lanes and by-lanes. A stinking thick crust of rubbish accumulated over several days lay on either side of the small lane. The municipal authorities thought only the main roads needed daily cleaning. You clean up the places you exhibit. Incredible how much filth gets stored elsewhere—in your unexpressed thoughts, for instance . . .

At last, the car stopped in front of a heavily curtained, dismal-looking house in the old part of Delhi. Gopi Kishen found his friend Ashraf waiting for him impatiently. Before Gopi Kishen could say anything, Ashraf said, 'Come, let's hurry; no time even for a cup of tea. Those farmers have been waiting for us since daybreak . . . '

'What's all this hustling for, Ashrafbhai?' queried Gopi Kishen.

'You mean to say you don't know?' asked Ashraf in utter surprise. 'You haven't heard about the flood situation? You don't—'

'Oh, that?' crooned Gopi Kishen, evidently relieved. 'I know all about the flood; it can wait.'

'I'm sorry, it can't wait. The situation is terrible.'

'I'm sorry too, Ashrafbhai, but whatever the situation, I have to complete some visits first . . . They are my first priority.'

'Are you in your senses, Gopi Kishen?' demanded Ashraf

irritably. 'How can you think of anything else when flood waters have entered the villages and thousands are marooned?'

'I know,' snapped Gopi Kishen. 'But my visits are far more imp—'

'Visits to whom, may I ask?' Ashraf queried sarcastically. His half-closed eyes reflected utter contempt.

'You may certainly ask,' replied Gopi Kishen, matching the other's sarcastic style in measured tones. 'I'd be happy to enlighten you, Maulvi sahib! My priorities are—a visit to the Prime Minister's house, then to the lieutenant-governor and then, if you want to know . . .'

'I don't want to know!' exploded Ashraf. 'I never realized you were so callous . . . and . . . and . . . ' He was choking with anger.

'Easy, my dear friend, easy,' said Gopi Kishen, not at all put out by the other's outburst. 'I'm neither callous nor anything else you'd like to call me. I'm businesslike, practical, pragmatic.'

'You're nothing of the kind and I'm dead certain about it!' roared Ashraf. 'Imagine hanging around the PM's house, while whole villages get washed away! . . . I just can't . . . can't . . . '

'Now will you quit this bloody ranting and do as I say?' shouted Gopi Kishen at the top of his voice, shocking the other into silent attention. 'Listen, enough of your moralizing! Please go to the PM's private secretary at once . . . now . . .'

'Now? Whatever for?' asked Ashraf, amazed.

'For this and that—any damn thing or bloody nothing!' Gopi Kishen exclaimed heatedly. 'Go, meet him, say your *adab arz* and whatever else you Maulvis say—say all that and burst into tears. Can you do that? Do you have command over your tears? Can you cry at will . . . ? Do that anyhow and give him a graphic description of the havoc caused by the flood, and the people's miseries . . . How you went to the villages . . . how you saw *ki* only Gopi Kishen, the indefatigable Gopi Kishen, the dynamic Gopi Kishen, was rushing about like a madman. Helping the poor. Consoling them in the PM's name all the time. Conveying her message. Taking no credit for himself. How you and the people were moved to tears by Gopi Kishen's absolute loyalty to Indiraji . . . plus any other thing in a similar vein that occurs to you . . . Understand?'

'But . . . but . . .' stammered Ashraf.

'No time for your buts!' cut in Gopi Kishen. 'Here, take this for expenses. Don't ask questions. Talk less. Better still, don't talk at all. Only do as I've told you. I've to be off now.' And having pushed a wad of currency notes into Ashraf's pocket, Gopi Kishen left.

'Stop!' cried Gopi Kishen, suddenly noticing a crowd on the footpath. The driver stepped hard on the brakes and the car ground to a halt. Gopi Kishen descended with his usual feline spring and plunged straight into the throng of people who were milling around confusedly. His surmise proved correct—these were flood-affected villagers, on their way to the PM's house. To tell her their tales of woe, no doubt.

'Oh! My brothers and sisters!' Gopi Kishen began to weep and beat his breast. 'What an ordeal you've gone through! Which village are you from? Sitapur? Oh! I've just returned from the other end of the district block. I'm going straight to the LG, then to the PM . . . Oh! What incredible damage! What a terrible calamity! . . . Oh . . . Oh . . . Oh . . . Oh!' The whole crowd responded to his infectious lamentation. Their hope had been eroded by sustained official callousness and non-official indifference. Gopi Kishen's caterwauling allowed them to succumb to despair. The leader of the group was a middle-aged peasant. He looked tough and suspicious and would not be taken in by Gopi Kishen's antics—until the latter took him aside and whispered something to him, without seeming to whisper. After which, his reserve dissolved completely into the surrounding flood of tears. At Gopi Kishen's insistence, someone served tea to the whole group from a nearby stall. Meanwhile, the leader and Gopi Kishen had a little talk.

'Remember what I promised? On my word of honour,' Gopi Kishen whispered in the same casual manner. 'Meanwhile, you have to go to the PM's house rightaway. She'll start seeing people in about half an hour. Go tell her about the flood, your losses and all your complaints. Listen, tell her *ki* Lala Gopi Kishen alone ran to the rescue of the sufferers, gave them all possible help, day and night . . . Got it? . . .'

'But . . . But . . .' began the leader, hesitating.

'No time for buts. Add to what I promised a peon's post to any relation or friend you recommend . . . Now I must be moving. Do come in the evening, about seven, alone . . .' And Gopi Kishen disappeared with his usual alacrity. The suffering peasants had swallowed his incredible performance along with the tea they gratefully accepted.


'Ah, Gopi Kishen,' began Ranjan Babu when he encountered him outside the building that housed the food ministry, relishing every word. 'You've been caught on the wrong foot this time! I just don't know how you're going to wriggle out! Too bad . . . Tch . . . Tch . . .'

Ranjan Babu was poison to Gopi Kishen. Each would have given anything to see the other's end—politically, and even in a more final way. Both belonged to the ruling party. Which meant that they were natural, permanent, implacable, irreconcilable rivals. A thirty-year war had raged between them. It promised to continue until God summoned one of them, in a bid to restore peace in this part of the nation.

Gopi Kishen's face fell, but only for a moment. He regained his cheer and poise with the speed of a seasoned politician and countered, 'You've been praying for it too long, Ranjan, but the gods aren't with you at all. Never have been. My feet are still as steady as ever; make no mistake about that. However, do tell me what's up, just to relieve yourself of your tension—you seem to be about to burst! I'm listening.'

'No one's luck holds for ever, Lalaji,' observed Ranjan Babu philosophically. 'Else, they wouldn't call it luck. You want to know the cause of your journey downhill? Very well, perhaps you remember your speech in South Delhi the week before last . . .'

'Which speech? I've been making so many . . .'

'That's the trouble with you, Lalaji,' said Ranjan Babu, 'as you'll no doubt realize now. Even after receiving the command to talk less and work more, you've been talking and talking endlessly.'

'What have I been talking about?'

'I know, I know. In all your speeches you've been asking the people to talk less and work more. In this process, your own talk is flooding the countryside. This has been noted at the highest level, if you don't mind my saying so. Noted again and again . . .'

'No doubt due to your good offices!' snarled Gopi Kishen.

'Well, I don't plead not guilty . . . but that's besides the point. I am specially referring to the speech you made on a common platform with the leaders of the Communist Party . . .'

'What of that?' Gopi Kishen demanded, as if innocently, although he began to see light at once, even as the other spoke.

'Nothing of that,' said Ranjan Babu quizzically. 'If you think there's nothing, there's nothing! Only, when you were honeymooning with the communists all these years, you dubbed me a right-wing reactionary. It so happens, Lalaji, that you have become a fellow traveller now!' And he laughed in sheer contempt.

'So you've been spreading this canard these days, is it?' said Gopi Kishen. 'My dear fellow, how long have you been away from Delhi, may I know?'

'Only once, to Afrozabad a little while ago. What of that?'

'Ha ha ha!' guffawed Gopi Kishen. 'Nothing of that. Nothing at all. Only, my dear Mister Smart, bad old Gopi Kishen has thoroughly outsmarted you. For the umpteenth time, if I may add for the sake of statistics . . .'

'Oh, I know your various bluffs too well,' countered Ranjan Babu, rather meekly. 'We'll see about that!'

'Sure, sure, my dear fellow,' crooned Gopi Kishen. 'We'll certainly see about that. In fact, I've already seen to a few things—about you and me, I mean . . .' He did not elaborate further, but shook his enemy's hand with aplomb, leaving him a bit unnerved. In less than five seconds he was gone in his usual sudden manner.

As his car sped away, his bluster began to slowly dissipate. He was no longer sure of what he had seen to, as he had just told Ranjan Babu rather ominously. True, he had mounted a blistering attack on the Communist Party, the moment he came to know that the Prime Minister had criticized that party. Indeed, he had condemned the communists for their past, present and future, more bitterly than anyone else in Delhi. And he had been the first leader in Delhi to take the initiative—which was itself no mean distinction. However, when a few days later the Prime Minister said something milder about the communists and trained her guns again on the Jana Sangh, Gopi Kishen had hurried to publish a speech of his through a news agency—a speech he had never made, at a meeting that had never taken place. This speech, of course, condemned the Jana Sangh. He didn't give a damn whether the Communist Party was good, bad or indifferent. He didn't bother whether the Jana Sangh was black, white or rainbow-coloured. All he wanted was to be on the right side of the Prime Minister and to defeat the constant attempts of Ranjan Babu and company to malign him in high command circles by any means fair or foul. He tried to accomplish this by making all sorts of statements and speeches, that often made him look absolutely foolish. Yet, Gopi Kishen, who had matured as a politician long ago, was not very worried about the way he was viewed by the world at large. Indeed he had come to find a distinct advantage in looking foolish in politics, at least occasionally. The court jester could get away with much more than any one else in the king's presence. So the more stupid the better, he had concluded, and had remained happy ever since.

Gopi Kishen knew that Ranjan Babu was lobbying for Mahendranath's group, against Chaudhury. He knew of Ranjan's recent visit to the state and his return with a 'briefcase'. The briefcase came from Chaudhury; still, Ranjan opposed him. Gopi Kishen knew Ranjan could not open his mouth in Indira Gandhi's presence. Everywhere else, he opened it as wide as the India Gate. His talk spread far and wide and gave him the reputation of the maker and unmaker of chief ministers. Gopi Kishen and Ranjan Babu were perfect counterfoils to each other in the craft of lobbying. Both were spurious; yet, both had milch cows in the states.

Right then, however, the urgent demands of the flood situation worried Gopi Kishen. Not so much for the affected people, as for himself. How could a person be away from Delhi, helping the flood victims, and at the same time remain in Delhi to counter the vicious propaganda of his rivals? Whenever there is a calamity anywhere, the lobby opposed to the person in power within the ruling party suddenly becomes active. So, concluded Gopi Kishen, his absence from Delhi for flood relief work would certainly cost him dear. In fact, he would become the worst flood victim himself, unless he did something effective to forestall his foes. So, what should he do? He thought over this dilemma and made up his mind. Defending his position against enemy attack was more urgent than running to the rescue of flood victims, which he could do a little later anyway. Victims would remain victims; a few days' delay would not alter their awful condition significantly. So, he should first sort things out in Delhi. He should impress the proper quarters with planted, advance evidence of his yeoman service to the flood victims, without doing that service. When this front was secure, he could concentrate on the flood relief itself, he reasoned. He set to work accordingly.

He was happy with his own adroit handling of the situation. At least so far. Yet, he knew only too well that in such matters there was always some snag somewhere. All of a sudden, the rope becomes a serpent. Vipers emerge from harmless grass. He felt uneasy at these visions; however, when you put your head in the mortar, as they say, how could you avoid the blow of the pestle? . . . He shook off these thoughts and tried to keep his morale up as his car stopped in front of the Prime Minister's house. He jumped out as usual and put on his mask of carefree joviality. It was difficult to say whether the sentries and guards greeted him first or vice versa. It was something of a photo-finish. However, their mutual cordiality showed that Lala Gopi Kishen was a regular visitor to the PM's house—certainly up to the reception room.

Just then, a group of some twenty peasants came out of the gate, having had the Prime Minister's darshan. They were beaming with pleasure. They recognized Gopi Kishen at once and greeted him. Gopi Kishen gave them a broad grin, tried to look important and said, 'You've met her? Good. I'm meeting her just now. You see, she summons me towards the end of the morning interviews, so she can discuss things in detail . . .' Suitably impressed, the rustics straggled away down the road.

Gopi Kishen, trying to look conspicuous and busy, exchanged pleasantries with one and all. Suddenly, he sighted one of the personal assistants of the Prime Minister some fifty yards away. Tearing himself abruptly from the person he was talking to, Gopi Kishen virtually sprinted across to the assistant, greeted him, shook his hand, hugged him, paraded his friendship exuberantly—and then stood back to watch the general effect of these manoeuvres.

Meanwhile, another group of peasants arrived at the reception. They recognized Gopi Kishen too and greeted him. Again, he tried to look lofty and said to them, 'You've come to meet the Prime Minister? Good. I've just met her. You see, she calls me quite early, so I can brief her on important matters before other visitors arrive . . .' Having impressed this group too, he told them about his round-the-clock service to the flood victims in scores of villages and promised to visit their village 'very soon'. Gopi Kishen's beguiling assurances were uppermost in their minds when the visitors went into the Prime Minister's presence. For the rest, reflected Gopi Kishen, one had to leave something to God, to keep Him occupied too!

Gopi Kishen lingered at the Prime Minister's house for almost three hours—without the slightest intention of seeing her. That was the only way of staying as long as he liked. To all new visitors, he said he had just met the PM. If he chanced on some who came out after meeting her, he told them she was just about to call him in. Either way, the technique was perfect. He was not lingering there for nothing, however. He was on the lookout for the vipers in the grass who had positioned themselves to carry on their tirade against him in the Prime Minister's house. Soon, he located one such suspect and demolished him effectively with his bully-cum-banter technique. The man slunk away. Gopi Kishen resumed his vigil.

However, there were undetected snakes too. Despite Gopi Kishen's vigil, they briefed and rebriefed everyone who was anyone in the Prime Minister's house against him. He has done nothing for the flood victims. He lobbies all the time in Delhi. Doesn't even attend office regularly. He is almost unlettered. Corrupt to the core. Has made millions. Has his touts and agents planted everywhere in Delhi. Has a share in all blackmarket operations, which he allows to flourish unhampered. Wheat. Rice. Cloth. Fertilizer. Any damn business is Gopi Kishen's business. Hobnobs with communists too, day in and day out. He is a political liability. Too dangerous in any position of responsibility. Has been around for too long anyway. It's high time he stepped down in favour of a younger, more dynamic and loyal person.

It was about eleven. He could safely relax his vigil now, since the PM would be going to the office. Gopi Kishen left the PM's house and arrived at his own office. There he found some of his followers anxiously waiting for him. 'What's the fuss about now?' he barked. 'My God! Can't a fellow have a few minutes of peace? Must he have his nerves shattered twenty-four hours a day? Come now, what is it?'

One of the sycophants came forward and said, 'Oh, it's nothing, Lalaji. The newspapers say some prominent leader died in Bangalore last night. We thought you'd like to issue a condolence message . . .'

'Of course, of course,' beamed Gopi Kishen, relieved that the matter was, after all, only the death of someone in far-off Bangalore. 'I would certainly like to issue a poignant condolence message. Well then, take it down: Say *ki* I'm shocked at his untimely demise. Recount his invaluable services to the nation. Mention his going to jail—you may add *ki* he and I were in the same jail. Don't say which jail. Say I can't believe *ki* he's dead, I can still remember his handsome figure, tall—no, no, don't say tall or short . . . neat moustache—no no, shave the moustache off, it may turn out to be a howler . . . his resonant voice, dignified bearing, great scholarship—no, no, don't mention scholarship, say wisdom instead, that's less verifiable . . . his loyalty to the Prime Minister, etc. Say *ki* the country in general and the state of Madras in particular has lost a great leader . . .'

'Are you sure it is the state of Madras, Lalaji? The deceased was from Bangalore,' said one of the assembled flatterers.

'Why, I'm quite sure, they're all Madrasis down there in the South, aren't they?' said Gopi Kishen. 'Anyway, don't waste too much time on a dead leader. Write all the usual compliments—it doesn't hurt anyone to praise the dead anyway . . .'

When they were about to take their leave, Gopi Kishen took someone aside and asked him, 'By the way, what was the dead leader's name?'

The man cleared his throat and said softly, 'The leader was a lady called Ranganayakamma . . .' Gopi Kishen's hanging jowls quivered as he realized the monstrous mistake he had made.

Before he could stammer anything, the other man hastened to say, 'Don't worry, Lalaji, we'll change the message to the feminine gender. We'll also alter the description. It'll be all right . . .'

Once the matter of the dead leader was disposed of, Gopi Kishen warmed to the topic of the flood. He harangued his followers for over half an hour, non-stop. At the end of the thunderous oration, one of the followers politely reminded him that he, Gopi Kishen, had not yet paid them the amount he had promised for the last job they had done. Prices may go up or come down, but political prices, called 'expenses', never come down, Gopi Kishen lamented. One of his followers reported that spreading lies wasn't all that easy or cheap. Not because they were lies, but because they had to break through a barrage of counter-lies erected at equally huge expense by the other group. 'Take this very example of flood relief, Lalaji,' he went on to elaborate. 'I assure you it's very difficult to neutralize Ranjan Babu's men. This morning I was brainwashing a small but influential group in a coffee house on how you've been serving the flood victims. Suddenly, that *goonda* Sarjoo Singh barged in and shouted that I was telling a pack of lies. He asserted that he had visited all the affected villages himself, but found no trace or mention of Lala Gopi Kishen. That Lalaji had been hanging around the PM's house all the time and spreading false reports of his wonderful service. That he was, "that very minute", rolling in bed with Munni Bai, the notorious prostitute of Daryaganj. That he took bribes through her, her share being fifty-fifty. That—'

'Stop it!' shouted Gopi Kishen, white with anger. 'You should have broken his neck then and there! The liar!'

'Of course, he is the biggest liar going about Connaught Place,

Lalaji,' agreed the other fellow quickly. 'Still, what could I do? What are we all peddling in, except lies and illusions? Need I tell you, Lalaji? When has truth ever triumphed over falsehood? In Delhi, at any rate? Only a lie cuts a lie, and lie management costs money.'

'Money, money, money!' roared Gopi Kishen. 'It's the same song every time! What did you do with that Sarjoo Singh? Didn't you—?'

'Yes, I did, for sure,' responded the follower. 'I did manage him. Two thousand cash down, tomorrow morning, at the coffee house. Or else, he said . . .'

'Shut up!' snapped Gopi Kishen. 'Stop your wretched threats!' And closing the outer door, he distributed ten thousand rupees among his faithful followers. Whereupon they immediately dispersed, brimming with reinforced loyalty.

This was just one small detachment of the forces Gopi Kishen could muster. Money flowed ceaselessly in this game. However, he didn't have to worry too much, as long as milch cows like Chief Minister Chaudhury needed his lobbying service—which was always. His own money was safe. His lobby remained well oiled and greased with other people's money.

Gopi Kishen slumped in an easy chair, heaving a deep sigh of relief. What a dog's life, he muttered in extreme fatigue. At that moment, he could have strangled his father to death, for the 'business' he had chosen for him decades ago. However, since his father had been safely dead for years, Gopi Kishen's sudden patricidal urge remained a fantasy.

Just then, a head peeped cautiously around the front door, which had been left slightly ajar by Gopi Kishen's departing followers. The body attached to the head inched slowly forward, hesitantly, timidly, but determinedly. The typical stance of the Indian villager on a visit to the city is something that deserves to be watched through a researcher's microscope. Behind the exterior of innocence and simplicity, there is a tough cunning. It serves to magnify those two characteristics and gives the unwary city dweller—with his ridiculous ego—a false impression about the villager. The mask suits the wearer most of the time. However, on the rare occasions when he drops it, his fury and truculence completely overwhelm the city men. An occasion of this kind suddenly arose when Gopi Kishen recognized the watchful head and the wary body as those of the peasant who had accosted him at his residence early that morning.

Well, that was the limit. The last straw. Equally so on both sides, as it turned out. Shouting at the top of his voice Gopi Kishen pounced on the peasant, snatched his petition and tore it up. 'Get out, you pest!' he roared. 'Who let you in here? How dare you barge in like this? Is this your grandfather's property?'

'Is it *your* grandfather's?' the peasant shouted back, in a ferocious outburst that startled Gopi Kishen out of his wits. The sight of his torn petition lying on the floor drove the peasant into a profound rage. It was, no doubt, the pent-up fury of failure and frustration.

'Who are you, Lala?' the peasant yelled. 'Are you God? Are you my master? How dare you tear up my petition? I know now that Sarjoo Singh was telling the truth! That you are a heartless beast! A shameless bribe-taker! That you haven't moved a little finger for the poor flood victims. That you're still bribing people to go and tell lies in your favour! You fat bastard! . . . I'll show you! I'll go to Mataji this minute—this very minute. Ranjan Babu will take me there in his car . . . You verminous dog! . . . I know all about you . . . How you lick that Munni Bai's—'

The torrent continued unabated, continuously embellished by an inexhaustible and fertile vocabulary of earthy obscenities, fresh from the village. Sarjoo Singh . . . Ranjan Babu . . . Munni Bai! Gopi Kishen suddenly felt paralysed. His head began to reel terribly, as if express trains were hurtling inside his skull.

The shouting disturbed the office staff and two or three peons came running to their boss's rescue. When they tried to touch the peasant, he raised his lathi menacingly and hollered, '*Aao, salo!* (Come, you swine!) I'll split your heads and spill your brains on the floor, along with my petition!' The peons, all three of them, rushed out together to call for police help—leaving the boss, the peasant and his lathi clear in the field. That was the bravest gesture they could manage, as civilized citizens of Delhi!

695

The scene, however, changed abruptly even before police help could arrive. Within minutes, a car—which had evidently been waiting at the nearest street corner—appeared and came to a halt. Ranjan Babu, Sarjoo Singh and two others jumped out and rushed to the spot where Gopi Kishen and the peasant stared at each other in panting fury. Ranjan Babu took in the situation immediately and led the peasant away, as if to make peace in an explosive situation. Gopi Kishen's collapse was complete. He would have given all his wealth to get that one moment back—the moment when he had torn the peasant's petition up. He suddenly felt he would suffer a stroke. The stroke did not come. Then, he imagined he was having a heart attack. The attack did not oblige. Finally, he felt he was about to faint. He didn't. He was sadly surprised to find that none of these conditions came to his rescue. He was as healthy as ever to his great disappointment; he cursed his nerves, pursed his lips, shut his eyes, indulged in long sighs and for once didn't have the faintest idea of how to get out of the vexed situation he found himself in. It was the gravest crisis he had ever faced in his entire public life. He knew that at that very moment, Ranjan Babu was presenting the peasant before the Prime Minister.

Meanwhile, he received good news. Not unexpected, but even the expected was so much more welcome in the midst of misfortune. Chief Minister Chaudhury had kept his word. The suitcase had arrived from the state capital. The commissioner of the state guest house in Delhi rang up to say that his chief minister had sent a suitcase (he simply called it a box—*baksa* in Hindi) containing some rare antiques and artefacts of the state. The *baksa* had been delivered at his residence. Besides, one of Chaudhury's ministers, Shri Shekhar, happened to be in Delhi. 'I believe you know him, sir,' said the commissioner. (I don't, but I can always recognize anyone coming on the trail of a *baksa*, Gopi Kishen thought.) 'He would like to pay a courtesy call on you, sir, which he always does whenever he is in Delhi.' (Never did so far, but never mind; Chaudhury sent him, but he is perhaps jockeying for himself here, using his chief's money, speculated Gopi.) . . . He lost no time in taking out the antiques and artefacts—in complete secrecy in his bedroom. They had come not a day too soon. They were so many sticks of dynamite to explode under Ranjan Babu's chair.

Gopi Kishen made scores of telephone calls to alert his friends to Ranjan Babu's plan of action. None responded. A random sampling of the responses—rather non-responses—convinced him that something was seriously wrong. On a normal day, you couldn't have got Gopi Kishen on the phone for hours on end. His line would be continuously busy. His followers would, instead, personally go to him to get things done. But that day, most of his loyal followers preferred to be out of their homes. '*Baher*'—someone in the family said invariably, when Gopi Kishen himself tried to contact the followers. This was no coincidence, he knew. It indicated a definite shift in a politician's career. Sensing this, he swung into action immediately. His car hurtled along highways and byways and the narrowest lanes of Old Delhi. It scraped its sides against jutting walls and broke its springs in pits and potholes. And when the car couldn't proceed further, Gopi Kishen jumped out and raced onwards on foot, in a tremendous effort to band his followers together, to fight his foes. It was the instinct for survival, operating at peak efficiency.

Slowly and steadily, the counter-attack gained momentum. Within a couple of days, several clubs and coffee houses were talking about the commissions and omissions of Ranjan Babu and company. First, corruption—the universal talking point. Haven't you noticed the fourth floor coming up on Ranjan Babu's palatial building in Vasant Vihar? You haven't, really? Then, what have you seen in Delhi? Or have you been moving about with your eyes shut? Well, better open them wide at least now; they are meant to see things of beauty such as Ranjan Babu's four-floor mansion . . . Nepotism—another important talking point. Do you know that every relative of Ranjan Babu's has landed a comfortable job somewhere or the other in Delhi? Well, if you want to know why there is so much unemployment in Delhi, Ranjan Babu should provide the single largest answer. He has hardly left any jobs for others. He's able to corner jobs even before they are created . . . As for womanizing, the less said the better. How can you suffer such a fiend in civilized society? No woman of any age or

appearance dares to seek an interview with him alone. He is a
disgrace to Delhi. The stud-bull at large. And on top of everything,
he takes great pride in his sexual exploits. Never tires of bragging
about them, the shameless profligate. And so on and so forth.

Now, the crux of the matter. Can you believe that this fellow,
Ranjan Babu, is busy spreading canards against good old Gopi
Kishen? He is bribing farmers to go and tell the Prime Minister all
kinds of absurd stories to malign Gopi Kishen. What's the world
coming to, anyway? Most preposterous.

It was simple political logic. If I am bad, you are worse. If both
keep our mouths shut, both of us have a chance of passing off as
tolerably good. If both talk, one's talk cancels the other's out, and
both end up looking awful. Since both sides are seen as equally
bad, each will now have to be assessed on other grounds. This
game can be played in many different ways but its result is usually
the same—the clouding of the real issues at stake.

As the hours ticked by, the spate of mutual vilification
succeeded in swamping the real issue—Gopi Kishen's performance
in the flood relief programme. No one discussed the flood now;
the public debate regarding the good and bad qualities of the actors
in the political drama occupied centre stage instead. Gopi Kishen
congratulated himself. He had released a fairly large amount of
money by way of fresh investment. Several citizens of Delhi, who
had not seen any flood-affected areas, formed into task forces and
moved about. They acted the part of flood victims and described,
with a flood of *Khuda ki kasam!* (By God!) oaths, the great service
rendered by Lala Gopi Kishen. They went round—according to a
carefully drawn up itinerary—to ministers, party leaders,
journalists, functionaries of political parties, newspaper offices,
restaurants, shopping centres, railway waiting rooms, the
Parliament House, Rashtrapati Bhavan and many such crucial
nodes where talking points gain currency. In the space of another
day, Gopi Kishen's popularity-cum-credibility curve had ascended.
His service to the flood victims slowly entered the area of belief,
having successfully crossed the hump of doubt and the plateau of
neutrality.

Still, Gopi Kishen felt uncomfortable. There was something

that wasn't quite right with the situation. He smelled it, but could not locate it. He had planted hundreds of canards and counter-canards in the course of his long innings in politics. The game had its own dynamics and inner momentum. There was nothing to match it; it had become an addiction with him. In a way, he had even come to love Ranjan Babu, his worst adversary, for the political 'kick' the latter gave him—now the joy of winning, now the redoubled spirit of vengeance on losing. Over the years, nothing had come to matter—win, lose or draw—except the excitement of the game. It was vice for vice's sake.

For the first time that day, however, he began to feel a kind of emptiness creeping into the excitement, like water seeping imperceptibly into a boat through a tiny undetected hole somewhere. He tried to think over the new phenomenon, slumped in his favourite easy-chair close to the telephone. Every time the phone rang—it had started ringing by now—he felt a slight nervous spasm somewhere inside himself. This was an unusual sensation, something he had never felt before. On previous occasions, every ring of the phone resonated like a celestial musical note in his political cosmos.

With a determined effort he shook off the new feeling and stood up. It's just fatigue that is playing tricks with me, he concluded. An hour with Munni Bai would perhaps demolish . . . but no, it was too risky now, he thought. Besides, spending time with Munni Bai struck him as rather incongruous in the prevailing context. Like fornicating in front of a funeral procession. Just doesn't fit in, he decided finally and let himself drift into obsessive speculation again.

The day had been full of confusing developments for Gopi Kishen. Every time something threatened to crush him, something else would exhilarate him. Just then, his private secretary announced the arrival of Shri Shekhar, minister. Gopi Kishen had not expected the visitor to turn up so soon after the arrival of the *baksa*.

Shekhar shook hands with Gopi. The minute he had set eyes on the Delhi fixer he had disliked him—it was a case of hate at first sight. Shekhar knew—from his customary thorough homework—that Gopi Kishen's sworn enemy in Delhi was Ranjan Babu whom he had tried to propitiate recently in the state capital. He couldn't quite decide which of the two lobbyists he hated more. Ranjan Babu's snub nose matched perfectly with Gopi Kishen's protruding canines. There was little to choose between them visually, just as there was none, characterwise. Even *I* feel fed up with the dirty work Chaudhury has entrusted to me, mused Shekhar. His core of decency was at a great depth; the common run of evil couldn't ordinarily reach it. Yet, for once, he had to acknowledge that this Gopi-Ranjan duo had penetrated to his core and provoked cries of conscience, which Shekhar didn't even suspect existed within him . . . Then, in a flash, it occurred to him that if he played his cards right, he would be several paces closer to his avowed goal—of destroying the system from the inside and with it, people like Anand. The thought eased the antipathy he felt towards Gopi Kishen.

So, thought Gopi Kishen, this is one of the horses in the race for chief ministership. He has apparently come to plead Chaudhury's case, but wouldn't be averse to being crowned himself, if possible. Should he, Gopi, play on the fellow's ambition? He wasn't quite sure about the ambition, yet thought it a safe bet to assume that it was there. After all, this is a game where each one is out for himself, isn't it? he reasoned. He didn't recall having met Shekhar before; Chaudhury did not like his ministers making trips to Delhi except on official work (which included the 'dirty' work he considered essential for his own political survival).

The first few minutes of the interview were therefore rather formal.

However, the box of 'antiques and artefacts' asserted itself soon, as it was bound to. Shekhar came straight to the point.

'Where do we stand now, Gopi Kishenji?' he asked.

'You mean Chief Minister Chaudhury?' Gopi queried.

'Yes, who else?' Shekhar's voice betrayed a bit of irritation.

'I'm sure it will work out, Shekharji,' Gopi Kishen said casually. Shekhar at once noticed Gopi's lackadaisical attitude. 'How will it work out?' he asked. 'Chaudhury would appreciate some specific details . . .'

THE INSIDER

Gopi Kishen felt himself trapped by this query. He hadn't the foggiest idea of what he could do to help Chaudhury. He couldn't approach Indira Gandhi directly, any more than he could reach the summit of Mount Everest. The sum total of his effort amounted to cornering one of the Prime Minister's private secretaries. Besides, in coping with his own predicament in the flood relief affair, he had been too preoccupied for several days on end. All that he could do for Chaudhury was to take possession of the latter's *baksa*. And here was this Shekhar demanding results . . .

'I have spoken to the concerned persons,' he began vaguely. 'I'm sure Chaudhuryji is safe and no one can disturb him . . .'

'I'm not interested in how anyone else feels,' Shekhar cut in impatiently. 'Please tell me, Gopi Kishenji, what is Indira Gandhi's decision?'

'That's what I'm just about to find out,' Gopi Kishen lied smoothly. 'I am at it, I assure you, Shekharji. And I hope to convince Indira Gandhi not to remove Chaudhury. I must warn you, however, that I find an unfavourable climate here regarding him. Of course, one scoundrel who is working overtime against Chaudhury is Ranjan Babu. But, he is a lightweight, whatever he may say about his clout with the Prime Minister. He won't have any effect, take my word for it, Shekharji . . .'

Gopi Kishen rambled on and on without giving Shekhar the faintest idea of what he proposed to do regarding Chaudhury. The reason was simple: he didn't know it himself. Shekhar felt like knocking Gopi's teeth in, with one blow, just as he had had the urge to punch Ranjan Babu's snub nose the other day. However, he was only Chaudhury's errand boy and had no mandate to apply violence, whatever the provocation. So, he appeared hugely impressed with Gopi's spiel, while mentally witnessing the huge *baksa* of 'antiques and artefacts' tumble into the bottomless pit of Delhi's bogus lobbyism.

Coming out of Gopi Kishen's mansion, he felt relieved, even exhilarated, as if he had emerged from a stinking public urinal. Does Indira Gandhi know, he wondered, what her 'loyal' followers do in her name twenty-four hours a day? In any case, he concluded, she wouldn't care. Unlike Anand, he did not credit Indira Gandhi

701

with any compunction or sincerity; in his view, she was a politician
first and last. She needed the Gopi Kishens and Ranjan Babus as
much as they needed her patronage—real or imaginary. It was a
matter of mutual convenience.

Just as he came out of the compound, there was a heavy
downpour. Within minutes the roads of New Delhi were flooded.
Shekhar's sudden spate of contempt for Gopi Kishen matched that
overflow. When his car entered Ashoka Road, he realized that he
was close to his party headquarters' office. An old college mate of
his was one of the party general secretaries right then. Why not
drop in for a few minutes to pay a surprise call on his friend? A
little gossip with the party functionary would ferret out some
useful insights regarding the state imbroglio, as it was seen from
Delhi. In any event, he had nothing else to do that day, after his
futile visit to Gopi Kishen. He could perhaps bring his anger under
check, if his friend the general secretary could tell him how Delhi
reeked of Gopi Kishens year-round . . . On this impulse, more than
anything else, Shekhar asked his driver to turn into the building
that housed the party headquarters.

Back in the mansion, Gopi Kishen felt immensely relieved at
Shekhar's departure. The latter's demeanour had been
contemptuous, his very stance disdainful. And Gopi Kishen, for
once, could not blame him. After all, Chaudhury had not paid
through his nose only to be consoled with empty promises and
spurious encouragement. Yet, Gopi thought, he ought to know
that what was called 'getting your money's worth' in regular
business practice could not be applied to politics. Politics was a
game in which you staked and staked . . . Only a real idiot could
ever entertain any hope about the result. This gamble was very
different; no one knew what the result would be—and when it
would strike, in the manner of lightning. These fellows from the
states, with all their intelligence, would never understand the
finesse of Delhi lobbies, Gopi reflected. As for himself, now that
the *baksa* was safely in his possession, he could afford to ignore
Shekhar. He wouldn't even recognize him, he resolved. What do
they think lobbying is anyway? Is it like barking orders over the
telephone, like chief ministers and ministers do in the states?

The phone rang suddenly and stabbed him into alertness. He lifted the receiver with disproportionate force, as though it was imperative to cut off the second ring midway. As though he was thereby preventing a collision of two planets. Soon after he emitted a nervous and very loud 'hello', his face showed a mixture of irritation and amusement, for it was a wrong number.

Gopi Kishen began to pace up and down the veranda with unaccountable impatience. He found considerable relief from his solitary misery when five or six of his lieutenants arrived together. They gave him an unusually excited account of their three-day achievement. At that very moment, they assured him triumphantly, a two-hundred-strong lobby was working ceaselessly, with almost computerized precision. They had wormed their way systematically through the labyrinthine channels of political power and leadership. The final assault on the top was well under way—in fact, it must be over by now, they announced gleefully. It had been extremely difficult though, they hastened to add. Ranjan Babu's network being virtually impenetrable, they had had to muster all the ingenuity they possessed, to match Ranjan in every department of the game. And match they did, by God—*goonda* gang for *goonda* gang, leader for leader, money for money, threat for threat, prostitute for prostitute. Well, relax now, boss, they chorused smugly. The ship has reached safe waters.

To Gopi Kishen, each word sounded heavenly. The stream of assurances soothed his nerves, like a beautiful lullaby. It did not, however, put him to sleep; instead, he came alive in a remarkable way. His face lit up and he plunged into a torrential admixture of thought and talk. Briefly, it had to do with an elaborate programme of flood relief. He declared he would undertake it the very next day and never relax. He would do everything that his lobby falsely claimed he had already done. He would compete with his own lobby. Fact would catch up with fiction and surpass it. Food, clothes, medicines, fodder for cattle, cash—he would personally look into every detail of every item. He would pull up the officers; get the lazy ones transferred at once. Corrupt rascals would get the sack forthwith. He would tone up the entire

703

administration within forty-eight hours. And if Ranjan Babu maligned him, to hell with him. He, Gopi Kishen, would not even take notice of what his arch enemy did . . . He blustered and bragged, weaving a perfect plan. His stunned followers listened in complete and incredulous silence.

The telephone rang, angrily and urgently this time. Every telephone owner knows the myriad moods of his phone by the subtle nuances in its ring. Now doleful, now happy. Now melodious, now neurotic. Gopi Kishen, however, was too absorbed in his outpourings to observe anything. He picked up the receiver simply, stopped his expatiation and listened . . . and listened. His followers stood still, trying to listen through Gopi Kishen's face.

'Hello! . . . Gopi Kishenji? PA to PM speaking. How are you, sir? Me? I'm fine, thank you. H'mm . . . I have a message for you, sir, rather urgent. You see, this Ranjan Babu's tirade against you—PM thought it was too much. So, in fairness to you, she got the matter quickly looked into. The field report is now with her: I'm sure it's in your favour, since you have done so much for the flood victims. Will you be good enough to see the party general secretary in this connection? PM positively wants this now. The GS is actually waiting for you. Would you please see him right away? Good. I shall inform the GS at once. Thanks a lot, sir. Namaste . . .'

Gopi Kishen stood dazed, still holding the receiver, ignoring the dial tone. Then dropping the receiver onto its cradle, he retreated into the innermost recesses of his house, walking slowly, like a corpse stalking the burial ground. His followers could not follow where he was going.

*

'What is this, Gopi Kishenji?' demanded the party general secretary, with transparent annoyance.

'What's what, sir?' demanded Gopi Kishen, with a composure remarkably at odds with the turmoil he felt within him. He had come braced up and prepared to meet the party functionary whose face seemed to further redden with every passing minute. Gopi Kishen's counter-question made him furious. To say the least, it sounded impudent.

'I'm sorry, Gopi Kishenji,' he said with considerable restraint. 'Here is a serious complaint that you haven't visited a single flood-affected village . . .'

'Who said that?' queried Gopi Kishen.

'Ranjan Babu and company, of course . . .'

'How do they know? Have they visited any villages themselves?'

'Well, I know they haven't either. But that's neither here nor there. It's you who are in power and answerable . . .'

'Sure, Mr Secretary,' echoed Gopi Kishen. 'I'm answerable, of course. Please tell me, is there no one else answerable besides me, in our great party?'

'It's not that . . . heh . . . heh . . . all are answerable. Yet, being in power . . .' the secretary mumbled.

'Power, power, power!' countered Gopi Kishen, with perceptible heat in his tone. 'So that's what it is all about, is it? You already have the answer there, don't you, Mr Secretary? Am I alone in power? I thought *ki* the party is in power, not an individual. So, if the others in the party start a campaign of vilification against one individual, won't he do the same—to defend himself at least?'

'What about the people—those who elected you to the high office you're holding?'

'That's a myth, Mr Secretary, and you know it,' answered Gopi Kishen. 'The people elected me to the legislative body. After that, whichever office I hold, it is in fact a nomination. While my position as legislator will last five years, my nominated office has no security whatever. Anyone could topple me any minute; so, I have to defend myself every minute. Where is the time for anything else, Mr Secretary?'

The general secretary felt a little mortified, but stood his ground firmly. 'But Gopi Kishenji,' he began, rather vaguely. 'What about your constituency at least . . . ?'

'Sorry, Mr Secretary,' Gopi Kishen interrupted. '*My*

*constituency is the Prime Minister's house. Make no mistake about that.* And please don't reel off the usual political slogans to me, for heaven's sake!'

'Gopi Kishenji, this is outrageous. You haven't visited a single village. Yet your friends have been saying all the time that you've done excellent work. Well, let me tell you, the truth has been found out . . .'

'That's it!' exclaimed Gopi Kishen. 'Found out! In this particular case, yes. Maybe I overreached myself. Maybe time went against me. Things developed too quickly—yes, that's the truth. Yet, there are so many other truths you've never cared to find out. Last year, for instance, there was widespread drought and I worked like a man possessed. No food, no rest. And all the time, Ranjan Babu continued his backbiting, taking advantage of my absence from Delhi. It took four months for me to restore my image—again only by lobbying. For the rest, I'm sure *ki* no one has noticed my work till today. Why didn't you ask us both last year, Mr Secretary? Why can't you get over the lobby syndrome, for once? I'm not the only one at fault, I'm merely a sacrificial goat. The system is rotten, Mr Secretary, and so is the party . . . Where does our great party stand today, Mr Secretary? . . .'

So saying, Gopi Kishen stood up, handed over the letter of resignation he had come armed with to the gaping general secretary and walked out. After he had left, the general secretary walked slowly over to the ante-chamber next to his office where a visitor was waiting. It was his old college friend, Shekhar, whose visit had been interrupted by Gopi Kishen's arrival. Both men looked at each other wordlessly, Gopi Kishen's harangue ringing in their ears—*Where does our great party stand today, Mr Secretary?*

*

Shekhar called Chaudhury in the state capital and reported the Delhi developments briefly. 'You may now forget about your *baksa*,' he added with a venomous chuckle.

Chaudhury heard him out. 'Maybe I'll have to pack my own

suitcase now,' he commented grimly as he stubbed his cigarette in an already-overflowing ashtray.

# 54

GOPI KISHEN'S RESIGNATION—DISMISSAL, TO BE MORE EXACT—
came as a mild surprise. Only mild because, by now, the removal
of high functionaries had ceased to shock or outrage anyone,
including the victims themselves. They could see the end coming
beforehand; so most of them were ready for it when it did come.
They knew that a dismissal was akin to an eclipse. Like all eclipses,
it was temporary. It was a case of Rahus and Ketus in the ruling
party's political firmament. And as every Hindu astrologer will
assure you, you can propitiate every *graha* (planet) including Rahu
and Ketu. You can calm down their wrath by *shanti* rituals and
can indeed make them feel as pleased with the 'subject' as before.

The interest in Gopi Kishen's fall vanished within a few days.
To Chief Minister Chaudhury, however, it was a fairly severe
blow. True, he had not put all his eggs in Gopi's basket alone. He
was too shrewd not to be aware of the snakes and ladders game
of politics, particularly with Indira Gandhi as the sole dispenser of
both the snakes and the ladders. He had continued to cultivate
Ranjan Babu as well, despite the other's treachery, on the

pragmatic principle that you could never tell when he could be useful. At one point, he thought he had the distinction of being the sole common client of Gopi Kishen and Ranjan Babu. It looked as though he would go down in the ruling party's history as the impossible meeting point of the Gopi-Ranjan parallel rails . . . However, that unprecedented distinction did not come his way. Ranjan accepted his *baksas*, but promptly deserted him. He found Chaudhury's proximity to Gopi Kishen intolerable; indeed he found it difficult to accept anything about Chaudhury—barring his money, of course, since it came from the Nasik Printing Press and did not strictly belong to Chaudhury! Aside from Ranjan, Chaudhury found his other sources rather reliable. Yet, after Gopi's ignominious departure, they manifested unease. Chaudhury's star took a sudden dip. He was confident of Indira Gandhi's assured blessing upon his head—until the exact moment when he needed it most. At that moment, he somehow found Indira Gandhi receding into the hazy distance. The phenomenon was as puzzling to him as it was to all those who faced it.

But Chaudhury did not panic. Rather, he let no one see him panic. He had already set up three of his cabinet colleagues as rivals for the post of chief minister in the event of his removal. He then goaded them, separately of course, to try their luck in Delhi. He made each of them think that Choudhury would squarely back him. They fell into his trap and began an all-out tirade against one another. More and more *baksas* made their rounds in Delhi. More and more busybodies posing as Indira Gandhi's conscience-keepers appeared overnight from nowhere. One minister who took the race too seriously happened to be from a poor background. He had remained poor, since Chaudhury was very particular that no minister—other than himself, that is—have anything to do with the handling of money. The minister did exactly what a person inexperienced in the art of bribe-taking ends up doing. In his anxiety to grab a one-time bribe, somehow, (presumably to stop with that and return to his original honest self) he handled the transaction rather amateurishly, and got into deep trouble. Everyone in the state was shocked, including Chaudhury, of course. There was no way out of the scandal. In any event, Chaudhury didn't want to bail his minister out. While trying his luck for the chief's post, if a minister chose to lose his present job, it was his funeral, Chaudhury reasoned. The minister was eased out. Two decades of honest public service came to nought overnight. In a few weeks, he drifted into political oblivion. No one cared, nor expressed any regrets.

It was not clear if news of this incident reached Indira Gandhi. The people saw it as a simple case of an honest minister becoming dishonest for the first time. The moral drawn was not so much that one should condemn corruption, but that one should not be incompetently corrupt.

By now, it was common knowledge that a search had begun for Chaudhury's successor. No one said so, no one knew anything for sure. Yet the news was all over the place. The newspapers, as usual, were full of speculation, projecting a host of likely candidates. These ranged from the most obvious to the most obscure, not to speak of the most absurd. And the media ended up predicting a 'surprise choice'. This equalized everyone's chances, wrapping them all in delightful uncertainty.

'What is this surprise choice going to be?' Shekhar asked Chaudhury, a few days after he returned from Delhi and reported on his aborted mission.

Chaudhury's mood had been inscrutable for some days past, even to his close friends. He was cool and collected—indeed more so than usual. He went about his chores as if he were to stay in his position forever. The pose was perfect. Nevertheless, even that equanimity betrayed traces of panic. The threat of a volcanic eruption and subsequent havoc was unmistakable.

Chaudhury lit the umpteenth cigarette of the day, as if to brace himself for a real performance.

'How do I know?' he said with a shrug. 'It's you who have made trips to Delhi where they make and unmake chief ministers. In any event, one who is on the way out shouldn't bother about the successor.'

'After me, the deluge, you mean?'

'Why not?' queried Chaudhury. 'Look, I know for sure that I am the last chief minister of this state from Indira Gandhi's party who has something called a spine . . . '

'You take that as a qualification for immortality!' Shekhar sneered.

'I have no such illusions, and you know it,' Chaudhury retorted. 'You may laugh in your sleeve, but I do worry about this state, you know. I was the Centre's favourite when Mahendranath was chief here. That was part of politics, mine as well as Indira Gandhi's. She used me against Mahendranath; I got the top post in the state as a reward. Now she finds me either dispensable, or a menace, someone to sideline or humiliate. Either way, I have to go. But I have a will of my own. I don't owe anything to Indira Gandhi except this post of chief minister, which I'm about to quit. Then we are quits, and she will realize that. . . Since no post is permanent, I try to anticipate what people will say after I am out. That is the real test of a politician's worth.'

'What do you think they will say?'

'Damned if I know!' exclaimed Chaudhury. 'They will perhaps say something that falls midway between your view and Anand's . . .'

'What an elucidation!' exclaimed Shekhar. 'Two unknowns to explain a third! But first, why don't you think of a likely successor? Why are you suddenly harping on public opinion, which even you can't claim to have cared about, ever?'

'Neither do I care for it now, if you want to know!' responded Chaudhury. 'Truth is, good old Chaudhury has not, repeat not, reached his political terminus, my dear friend! I still have a long way to go. So some amount of tolerant public opinion when I step down would help, I guess. At least the crowd of journalists whom I have obliged so generously shouldn't jettison me immediately, not all of them at the same time, at any rate. I don't ask them to be grateful; I am realistic enough in that respect. All I ask is that they spare me a little to ensure a better future for themselves. That's all. But I agree that the immediate task is to find a successor, rather to cause him to be found!'

'What's that supposed to mean?' queried Shekhar, marvelling at the convoluted brain operating feverishly under Chaudhury's lily-white, straight-tipped, starched, slightly tilted Gandhi cap.

711

'Simple,' explained Chaudhury. 'You see, right now, I'm *persona non grata*. They're supposed to consult the outgoing chief minister on his successor, but that formality means nothing. In this case, my own nominee will meet with instant rejection. That is an unspoken formula I know so well. I have seen it operate in many other cases.'

'Then why don't you suggest a name—or *the* name?' Shekhar prompted, with a certain amount of simulated eagerness.

Chaudhury burst out laughing. He laughed and laughed in utter delight and said, at last, 'You are a genius, Shekhar, I concede this as I have always done. What a brilliant idea, to get me to suggest Anand's name! Superb stratagem!' And he kept laughing louder and louder.

'Well, I can't refuse your compliment, since you judge me correctly,' admitted Shekhar. 'But isn't it the right name? And whatever may be my view, isn't Anand's name making the rounds already, in its own quiet, mysterious way? I'm sure you know what's going on, here and in New Delhi, especially New Delhi!'

'Do you think Anand is getting his own name touted around here and in Delhi?'

'You and I both know that that bundle of virtue would do nothing of the kind, ever!' Shekhar spat, as if telling a most distasteful truth. 'However, names have a way of making the rounds by themselves. Sometimes they appear by the logic of elimination, sometimes by sheer accident. It's a question of your preference and how you get Indira Gandhi to choose your nominee without suspecting that he is yours!'

'I don't think that is possible, Shekhar. I know her well enough not to expect her to commit such a blunder. She hasn't yet sent me the signal to step down, yet the rumours as well as extraneous indications thicken by the day. This is yet another of her mysteries and I've had enough of the guessing game. I can't possibly quit on my own; that would be ridiculous. Yet she wants me to find the excuse to go, myself—if I have to keep her goodwill. It's a hell of a problem and I don't have a solution!'

They discussed the topic threadbare, covering the same ground over and over. Chaudhury finally gave up, without resolving his dilemma or pinioning Shekhar effectively. While taking his leave, however, Shekhar felt that the old fox couldn't have failed to hatch something, after all. Else, how could he be Chaudhury? He's merely playing it close to his chest, like he always does, he thought, as Chaudhury reached for another cigarette.

\*

'Impossible!' was the near-unanimous verdict in all 'knowledgeable' circles of the state, about the likelihood of a 'good fellow' like Anand becoming chief minister. 'You just don't understand,' one politician took pains to explain to another. 'One of two qualities, ideally both, go to make a successful chief minister. One, he should be ruthless in doing whatever he wants to do, right or wrong; in fact, he should even be more ruthless when he is wrong. Second, he must be an inherently evil person capable of dealing with evil, since he will deal with nothing else. I am merely being realistic, cutting out so many irrelevant platitudes. I have nothing against any chief minister—Mahendranath, Chaudhury or any other. In fact I like Chaudhury, if I have to cite a name . . .'

'Unfortunately, it so happens that right now Indira Gandhi doesn't like him,' was the ready retort. 'So please name someone whom she does . . .'

'As I said, it is not going to be Anand. And if I have to choose, Shekhar is more like it; frankly, he seems to fill the bill better.'

There was a persistent rumour that the landlord lobby in the state had become busy overnight. While the 'lobby' was active and slanderous in the extreme, individual landlords were rather sober and circumspect in their public utterances. This was quite significant; it indicated that nothing, absolutely nothing, could be ruled out. 'For the simple reason,' Balram explained, 'that nothing anyone thinks here in the state has any relevance to the end result. The only person who knows is Indira Gandhi; all else is just noise.'

Curiously, the more 'everyone' thought Anand's choice improbable, the more his name managed to persist 'in the air', as it were. Newspapers squarely called him a non-starter. 'We have nothing against him personally,' one editorial pointed out sedately. 'However, one has to be realistic in a matter of this nature. There is no denying that Anand has acquitted himself exceedingly well in whatever he has had to do as minister. Nevertheless, one cannot help feeling that the controversy on the so-called land ceilings will certainly overshadow his prospects. It is not a question of whether he is right or wrong. The main question is: will he run the state successfully?'

They found several things that were unsatisfactory about him, though there wasn't a grain of conviction in their accusations. Their bizarre reasoning was that Anand was 'too this or too that' to merit consideration. The 'too this, too that' argument did not amount to—at least did not appear to amount to—adverse criticism. Yet it ruled Anand out. 'Don't ask why, but just don't think of him'—this was the gist of current editorial wisdom.

Another factor many politicians objected to, though they did not say so overtly, was Aruna's exuberant support of Anand. While everyone else had the right to oppose Anand, for whatever reason or for no reason at all, she was somehow denied the right to speak in his favour. This attitude made no sense and led to several skirmishes in which Aruna prevailed without any doubt. Of course, these encounters only harmed Anand—assuming that he had any desire to become chief minister. And this no one was sure of, apart from vague general assumptions about human ambition.

The uncertainty seemed interminable. At some point in the long wait, Shekhar ceased to be a mere spectator and became a participant of sorts. For some unaccountable reason, until that point he had never fancied himself in the race. What made up his mind was a long phone call from Shyam Sunder—Anand's schoolmate and friend-turned-enemy. Shyam had failed in his attempt to get Anand defeated in the election, but had not quite abandoned his mission of Anandocide. And now, with Anand's potential elevation as chief minister knocking at the door, he couldn't imagine a worse calamity for the state and a more insufferable affront to himself personally. True, the event was still hypothetical; yet prudence demanded that the landlord class take no chances. And Shyam Sunder's conversation with Shekhar firmed up the resolve on both sides. The plan quickly took concrete shape.

They arranged for the filing of a criminal case over the theft of ten truckloads of top quality timber from the Reserve Forest close to Shyam Sunder's village. The help of a forest department official and of a police officer was secured through appropriate enticements. All the ten or twelve villagers who carted the stuff in the dead of night were chosen from Shyam Sunder's trusted cadre. They swore to the authorities in the name of all the gods and goddesses they could name, that they had felled the timber and were carting it to a truck sent by 'Mantri Anand Sahib' to a nearby roadside point. To further strengthen their case a man purporting to be the truck driver was arrested after a search that lasted two days. A cast iron FIR was lodged, with Anand as the main accused, and the cartmen and the mock truck driver as co-accused.

This smart arrangement satisfied Shyam Sunder. But somewhere in the inner recesses of his mind, he felt a twinge of nervousness. Everyone in his village knew about Shyam's own business of illicit felling of Reserve Forest timber for the black market. For every consignment sent, Anand's name was used to silence the officials. Of late some audacious villagers had started whispering that at this rate, Minister Anand must have built dozens of mansions in the state capital. The elders, however, muzzled them into silence. 'They are friends, our landlord and the minister,' they warned. 'Don't you idiots poke your dirty noses into their private matters. Beware!'

This was before the 1967 election, when Shyam was Anand's closest friend. During that election, however, everything changed. Shyam Sunder used all his energy and well-established authority to get the votes in his village cast against Anand.

And today Shyam Sunder was elated at having pulled off an impossible feat. Anand was accused along with his (Shyam's) own servants in a theft case—and what a case! Shyam imagined his old schoolmate and friend behind bars. Getting disqualified from membership of the assembly for six years!

In this euphoric mood, he hardly noticed Shekhar leisurely

entering his drawing room. Shekhar tapped his shoulder and brought him round. The very next moment, he lost himself again in the delightful mental image of Anand behind bars. Shekhar had to calm him down with some firm handling.

'There is nothing to celebrate, Shyamji. You have misunderstood the thrust of our mission, I see.'

'Why do you say so?' demanded Shyam Sunder, somewhat annoyed. 'Is my dear friend not going straight to jail?'

'Of course he is, provided the allegation is true!'

'What do you mean? I don't know much about your legal intricacies, but didn't you plan it all yourself?'

'I did—and let me tell you I did a wonderful job. But we both know that the case is false. You also know what could happen if the truth came out . . .'

Shyam Sunder was angry—and alarmed. 'So you're threatening me?' he shouted. 'Are you saying I will go to jail?'

'Please calm down, Shyamji, no one goes to jail. The idea was to prevent Anand from becoming chief minister . . . Remember?'

'Yes, I remember, but I had also thought—'

'Then you were thinking of something that no one intended, Shyamji. As matters stand, sending Anand to jail is as much out of the question as preventing him from entering the assembly has been, if you really want to know . . .'

'Then what is the point?'

'There is a big point, Shyamji. The landlords of this state will bless me when we block Anand from becoming the chief minister. Now tell me, are you prepared to loosen your purse-strings really wide, for once?'

'That should be . . . no problem,' replied Shyam Sunder. 'But what are you up to?'

'Please listen. I'm giving you two lists of selected journalists who believe in the great blessings of the quid pro quo system. One list is from the state capital, the other from Delhi. I shall send a reliable subordinate to you tomorrow; he will take care of everything. All newspapers here and in Delhi will have banner headlines on the same day on the theft case against Anand. At least for a week there will be very interesting side stories on how it all happened. That

will cook your schoolmate's goose for all time to come . . .
Understand?'

'That seems good, but will he continue as minister? And what
happens to the case?'

'Its utility will be over in a week's time. It won't see the light of
day after that. That is to save your skin, as you will see. The next
task will be to find a chief minister who will take the land reform
portfolio away from Anand. He may even exchange it for
something very important. After all, there are many vital
departments in the state government crying out for efficient
ministers, such as Anand. And all is well that ends well this way.'

On the third day the banner headlines appeared, as promised,
as planned. The reports were lurid, yet they looked so real. As a
result, no one in his senses, in the state or in Delhi, could think of
supporting Anand in the race for the chief ministership.

There was no reason not to believe the stunning revelations.
Every detail was plausible and could be corroborated. Timber
lifting was a common occurrence in the Reserve Forest areas. The
authorities usually looked the other way. The people didn't mind,
for with timber prices skyrocketing, the flourishing black market
in illicit timber gave considerable relief to house builders and extra
margins of profit to contractors. As a result, the local forest and
police officials prospered.

Given this scenario, it was no surprise to hear news of
large-scale theft of timber. What was surprising was that the
minister involved was Anand. No, said some, it was too wild to be
true. Others demurred. 'How could so much that has come into
print be all false?' they said. In a strange and inscrutable way,
everyone was on the lookout for some kind of repudiation of the
news to prevail over their diminished belief in Anand. Or the other
way round.

For a few days, everyone expected more and more dramatic
developments to clutter the newspapers. The scoop was too big to
taper off at its most compelling stage. For one thing, the landlord
lobby was ready and willing to do anything to take the matter to
its logical—and legal—conclusion. They primed a host of
journalists, particularly tabloid reporters, with all kinds of

inducements. They strained each nerve to decimate Anand, the sole danger to their existence.

Yet the tempo of Anand's attackers could not be maintained for too long. Gradually, a slow backlash started. Ironically, it began in Shyam Sunder's village. One of the elders of the village, who happened to be literate and also antagonistic to Shyam Sunder, was in the tehsil headquarters town. He went to a hotel for lunch and saw a newspaper lying on the table. The villager chanced on the headlines and read on. It was, of course, Anand's story with all sorts of sensational embellishments. The man was so amazed at the lies that had been printed that as soon as he returned home, he told his illiterate wife what he had read. The illiterate sisterhood of the village promptly relayed it among themselves through whispers. The whispers were conveyed, in turn, to the mostly illiterate menfolk. The reaction took shape, again in whispers. And finally, the decade-long truth of Shyam Sunder's illicit felling of Reserve Forest timber trickled back, in bits and pieces, into some circles in the state capital.

Attention at once centred round Anand's 'mansion'. The best of investigative journalists available in the capital could not identify that imaginary structure. They had, perforce, to abandon the search. This deprived them of photographs and other details to continue the story further. In any event, those who were responsible for the original story did not bother about a photograph because they knew the truth. Besides, very few people believed this story about Anand. So the remnants of the fabricated scoop went round and round, losing impact in each frenzied gyre for want of corroboration.

At around this time, Aruna provided another interesting sidelight to this fantastic story. She was boiling with uncontrolled rage at the conspiracy hatched against Anand. One morning, she called on the forest minister—an embodiment of total apathy in the cabinet. The CM had included him in the government solely for his caste. People like Shyam Sunder, who considered the Reserve Forest their private property, were happy with the forest minister. Since he did nothing anyway, there was no danger of his doing anything wrong. However, the minister was otherwise an amiable person, also known to be honest.

He was among the Aruna-fearing ministers and tried, as far as possible, to avoid even talking with her, leave alone confronting her. So, when he saw her walking into his drawing room, as if she were completely familiar with the place—which she wasn't—the minister only uttered a monosyllabic welcome. Then he lapsed into apprehensive silence, resigning himself to whatever was coming. Meanwhile, a hot cup of coffee was presented to her by a servant, presumably to keep her temper cool.

She came straight to the point, cutting short the minister's anticipatory tension. 'Do you know anything about the theft of Reserve Forest timber by your cabinet colleague Anand?'

'Well . . . I'm afraid I don't know much beyond what the newspapers say.'

'How's that? You're the concerned minister and Anand is your cabinet colleague, isn't he? . . .'

'They deal with such matters at the CCF's (Chief Conservator of Forests) level, even lower down . . .'

'Even when it involves a cabinet minister?'

'In that case it is for the chief minister to look into—'

'Look, I am an MLA in my own right. I want to visit the village the timber came from. Why don't you too pay an official visit—maybe a surprise official visit—to the village? It is your duty to know the truth, isn't it?'

By that time the minister had recovered some of his composure. He said, 'Of course it's my duty. But tell me, do you seriously suggest that I probe into Anand's theft case myself, at my level? Are you sure?'

The minister thought this was a very smart question and would catch her on the wrong foot. With Anand involved, how could Aruna . . . She will somehow wriggle out now, he told himself, congratulating himself mentally.

However, Aruna said, 'Why not? Cabinet ministers have no special privilege to steal valuable forest property, have they? So what's the problem? It's only appropriate that the forest minister himself probes into his colleague's blatant offence; why leave it to less important officials?'

719

That cornered the minister. Yet he did not want to get involved in an unwanted tour with this dangerous woman tied to his back. He began going through his diary to check his pre-arranged tour programmes. He confused his private secretary in the process. The secretary was unable to comprehend what the minister really wanted. He could flatly say that no tour slot was available for months and months. He could also say with a beaming face that luckily the following two or three days were absolutely free. With no firm signal from the boss, he went round and round in circles.

Aruna watched the fun for a while, then said to the minister, 'Well, minister, I don't wish to put you to any difficulty. I shall visit that village myself, with some more MLAs and others. Minister Anand has no business to pilfer government property, without telling anyone anything about his huge housing project. Do you happen to know where it is, minister?'

Have they fallen out? Why is she now after Anand's blood? Has the impossible suddenly become possible? The minister kept speculating grimly after Aruna took her leave. She came out of his house with a visible swagger. She also had an intriguing smile on her lips, which the minister's private secretary noticed immediately.

From there she went straight to Shekhar's residence. Everyone knew her so well that there was no question of any private secretary daring to say, '*Sahib bijee hain* (The boss is busy)!' Shekhar promptly came into the reception room, as if he had known of Aruna's arrival through telepathy. He welcomed her affectionately and took her into the drawing room.

'I am on a mission,' she said, without any preamble or pleasantries—which she never exchanged with him anyway. 'Will you help?'

'What is the mission, sister?'

'To expose a serious crime . . .'

'Who is the criminal, by the way?'

'How is that relevant? Haven't you heard that the law is law even for the son-in-law? My mission is to fight corruption in high places; any objections?'

Shekhar understood at once. Aruna went on, 'I want to visit

the place of the crime tomorrow with a group of MLAs. I want you to accompany us, along with a press party. It is your duty as well as a great personal opportunity, if I may point out. Will you come?'

'Sorry, sister,' said Shekhar. 'I can't make it tomorrow; I have some important engagements in the secretariat here. Besides, I would advise you against visiting that place . . .'

'But why?'

'Don't ask me; please read the newspapers for a couple of days. Please, for Anand's sake . . .'

'But he is the corrupt minister I want to expose. Shouldn't you be helping me voluntarily?'

Shekhar looked rather distraught. He said again, in a very earnest tone, 'Look, sister, enough is enough . . . You win; the game is up. There is nothing in the case. I know Anand will make it to the top this time. Now just listen to me and . . . no visit . . . Please, all right?'

Aruna gave a broad grin and agreed.

Within the next three days a very different version of the timber theft was put out. It completely absolved Anand but remained delightfully vague about the 'crime'. The scribes, this time, were necessarily different from the earlier ones; they too took bylines, all of them. Consequently Shyam Sunder had to open his purse-strings wider than before, since he had to salvage his own position, come what may.

Meanwhile, most surprisingly, the announcement of a special visit by the Union home minister to the state capital suddenly dominated the headlines. The avowed purpose was to participate in a literary function that had been planned some months earlier. People generally knew this, but when it actually materialized the literary aspect cut no ice with the local politicians or the media. Instead, the newspapers, with undeniable justification, said that the Union minister would hold 'in-depth' discussions with Chief Minister Chaudhury on the political situation in the state. Some clarified the issue somewhat by mentioning the succession struggle for the yet-to-be-vacated chief minister's post.

The discussion between Chaudhury and the Union home

minister was extremely cordial. The home minister was all praise for Chaudhury for the manner in which the latter had administered the state in a most difficult period. It sounded like a farewell eulogy—or so Chaudhury thought. Towards the end, a very casual mention of 'the requirements of a dynamic situation' was made—and duly noted. Then an assortment of inconsequential subjects were discussed.

As if suddenly reminded of something, the home minister very casually mentioned 'this rather unusual story about one of your ministers'. However, Chaudhury went into the matter in some detail and produced an envelope with a neatly typed report from the IG (CID).

'Oh, this is not really necessary,' the home minister said, but still took the envelope and slipped it into his briefcase.

'It's all right,' Chaudhury answered, composed and amiable. 'It came to me only this morning. I thought I may as well share it with you, since you happen to be here.'

'Thank you, very thoughtful of you,' said the home minister.

Nothing more appeared about the theft case. The headlines simply changed. It was somewhat embarrassing to the correspondents (even though they had been well compensated) who had specially taken bylines when the news had broken out. Now they hoped their readers would forget their sensational reports. The newspapers began to carry bland homilies about corruption in public life. With that, everything returned to normal.

Not that the readers were to be denied dramatic headlines for too long. Chaudhury suddenly sent a one-line letter of resignation to the party president in Delhi. Even this was a doubtful piece of news for there was no confirmation forthcoming. This time, however, the high command announced that the Union home minister and another senior member of the party's working committee would attend the meeting of the ruling legislature party to 'elect' a new leader in place of Chaudhury.

Now, at last, there was no mystery any more.

Through no one knew how many twists and turns between Delhi and the state capital, Anand's name surfaced as the prime contender just a day, even less, before the meeting of the legislature party. However, no editor in the capital expressed any surprise when he was finally made chief minister. They had divined it 'already'. On the whole, they were not too enthusiastic about the choice, nor about the future of the state. One perceptive prognosis made in an important editorial was that unless Anand functioned from then on as chief minister, and reduced his individual zeal for any particular subject (such as, it said casually, land reform) there would be no stability in the state. The editorial categorically stated it held no brief at all for the landlords; nevertheless, it merely wanted to point out the facts. So if the chief minister thought that the rabble, aroused by the promise of free land taken from the landlords, would become his mainstay in running the state, he would be sadly mistaken. Anand, of course, made a quick note of this.

The swearing-in ceremony went off simply, uneventfully. The Union home minister and the senior party leader left for Delhi. They however suggested to the new chief minister that it would be a 'good idea' to complete the list of ministers after first calling on the Prime Minister in Delhi.

'In other words, Mr Chief Minister,' explained Chaudhury casually after the swearing-in, 'as per her instructions—sorry, not exactly her instructions, but of those around her, who will now keep you and your state under their thumb!'

Anand did not reply. He had so much to think about in the wake of this sudden development. It had catapulted him into an unknown seat, full of invisible spikes.

Next morning, he called on Chaudhury, 'for blessings and advice from my illustrious predecessor-in-office', as he put it. It was an encounter with mixed feelings. Goodwill mingled with tension, two strongly-held views clashed at several points. Yet there was evidence of a joint will to look to the future.

'Now for some definite advice about ministers—' began Anand, as if zeroing in on the most important issue in the new context.

'That is the prerogative of the chief minister, isn't it?' queried Chaudhury.

'That's the theory, I know,' agreed Anand. 'But I'd like some practical advice.'

'You know everyone around here, so let us skip things like the caste factor and other group pressures. I assume you will not have a group of your own, unless you want to start one—'

'No,' cut in Anand. 'I can't possibly do that; besides, I don't consider it really necessary.'

'Then what would be your main support?'

'Results first, results last, so help me God!' replied Anand with a touch of solemnity in his voice.

'I'm afraid I don't know much about results, being an old player in the game. I can only wish you well with your ideology and visionary convictions. By the way, what have you decided about Shekhar?'

'Why, I think he should be in the cabinet; else, I could not fill the void.'

'I am no one to advise you; you will have new people to advise you now. Yet for whatever it is worth, let me tell you that Shekhar will be a litmus test for you.'

The meeting ended on a fairly cordial note. It was surprising that so much mutual restraint had entered their relations overnight. Where had their usual friendly and uninhibited banter disappeared to?

Two days later, Anand duly called on the Prime Minister in her South Block office. The meeting was short, though not too short. Anand was to meet the home minister and the party president to work out the details—of ministry-making. The exercise lasted exactly three days. Anand's only important meetings were with the home minister and party president; all the others were courtesy calls. But even within those few days, newspapers in the state capital made it appear that the new chief minister was completely hamstrung due to his very obsequious attitude to the Prime Minister. He was just circling among a host of persons (some in authority, some completely out of it) begging them to form his cabinet for him.

During his stay in Delhi, Anand received an indication that the PM was not in favour of including Shekhar in the cabinet. But of course, it was for him to choose his team; he knew best, said the people who had passed on the message. However, Anand knew that the suggestion could not be ignored; it was in actual fact a command.

Back in the state capital, Shekhar's exclusion caused a sensation. And Chaudhury commented to a journalist friend, 'Didn't I tell you that the state no longer has a spine? We have entered the era of nominated chief ministers.'

# 55

A STEADY STREAM OF VISITORS FLOWED INTO THE CHIEF MINISTER'S
residence and flowed out again. Every type of person you could
imagine was represented: genuine well-wishers, friends, fake
friends, toadies, opportunists, political fixers, hangers-on whose
only aim was to be found somewhere within that compound. The
same chant could be heard everywhere. Congratulations,
Anandbhai! It's wonderful to see you as chief minister. Something
very good has happened to the state, I am sure! You deserved it,
of course; I always said so. But not all deserving persons get what
they deserve. This is the tricky road of politics! Anyway, God bless
you, heaven save you from the evil eye!

Some rejoicing was genuine, since Anand had his supporters
and admirers; but it wasn't spectacular, because there was no
particular political group to celebrate the occasion with pomp and
pageantry. Indeed, a sombre atmosphere prevailed when Anand
assumed his new office. There was serious introspection in many
circles. You could feel an overall sense of restraint—even
foreboding. It was like the arrival of an alien about whom people

know a little, but not enough to respond with anything beyond caution. Besides, it all felt deceptive, as if it was not quite the thing one would ordinarily accept in one's stride. The unexpectedness gave rise to some disbelief. It appeared that even in a democracy where, in theory, anyone could rise to any position, the general public attitude did not quite amount to accepting anyone's rise to any position.

In the first place, what kind of choice was this? It was clear that Indira Gandhi had nominated Anand as chief minister. Why? Did she see something in him that she did not see in anyone else? Was he exceptionally efficient? Was he loyal to *her*, through and through? What was wrong with Chaudhury? Wasn't his exit part of a larger mystery? Finally, who was going to piece together the jigsaw puzzle called Indira Gandhi?

Anand was not the torch-bearer of any single interest in the state. No particular class, no dominant caste, no identifiable section. Could he have reached this position in the normal course, even with luck? Obviously not, except through Indira Gandhi *and* by this absurd method of nominating chief ministers. That was the unanimous verdict. So the moral was: if you had Indira Gandhi's blessings, you didn't have to have anything else—class, standing, influence, long service, or even a powerful caste with access to unlimited money and muscle power. All these somehow became irrelevant. If she approved of you, you were nominated. That was that. But what was this nomination meant for? That was the question of questions. And one answer was as good as the next.

The first theory, which the influential gentry espoused and a large section of the press loudly echoed, was that Indira Gandhi's thirst for absolute power was insatiable and that she would not tolerate anyone whose political standing pre-dated her accession to Prime Ministership. She wanted all chief ministers to be junior, and therefore totally subservient, to herself. So she had eased out all the seasoned leaders who had remained with her after the split in the party. Those who had fought her and set up splinter factions were lucky, since they were spared the humiliation of now being jettisoned unceremoniously, albeit with sweet smiles.

The second theory, equally plausible, had it that Indira Gandhi nominated new chief ministers in order to break the stranglehold of powerful regional bosses who simply would not move out of the power-queue, even after they had outlived their utility. They had founded their groups, like gangs, and knew exactly what needed to be done to win elections. So they won elections and stayed put. When they did not win, they safeguarded their positions of vantage in the party so that only *they* would be the candidates in the next election. Only *they* would either sit in the legislature or wait in the wings. In this jockeying process, it was a case of power for power's sake. Little was done for the people; the status quo continued. The general opinion was that Indira Gandhi had to resort to nomination to keep pace with the dynamics of the time. Anand had subscribed to this view. He had explained it time and again in the past without ever suspecting that the nomination would fall on him. When it did, it was rather embarrassing for him, reflecting as it did, by implication, on the performance of past chief ministers, including Chaudhury.

The first factor that punctured his theory of nomination was his own inability to include Shekhar in his cabinet. No one expected him to do so; however, while the people thought he wouldn't include Shekhar, the fact was he *couldn't*. Only a few knew how this non-inclusion had come about. It was Anand's first taste of the limited power of a nominated chief minister. Shekhar himself had no way of knowing the truth, of course. Even if he was told, there was no way he would believe it. And no one told him, since no one wants to express the unbelievable anyway. It was just as well, because Shekhar himself would not have been too happy to work under Anand's stewardship. He said this bluntly to some of his friends, while still blaming Anand for not including him.

Indira Gandhi was still glowing in the aura of the Bangladesh victory. Many thought that the triumph of Bangladesh would keep her image lustrous for a long time to come, nationally and internationally. This was true, but Anand firmly believed that developing a resplendent image abroad should not be taken to mean that you may relent on solving the internal problems of the country. Indira Gandhi's party was duty bound to convert the *garibi hatao* slogan into direct action against the ubiquitous, pervasive poverty stalking the country in all its menacing starkness. And it was here that she needed the support of her nominated chief ministers.

After the Shekhar fiasco, some friends advised Anand that he would do well to be a bit cautious in choosing ministers. He should also entrust some arduous and time-consuming portfolios to junior ministers and confine himself to general supervision and coordination only—and, of course, to the political management of the state in general and party management in particular. It was a sensible suggestion, based on conventional wisdom handed down from chief minister to chief minister. However, Anand included in his agenda the not-quite-clear task of changing the basic rural agrarian structure, enjoined upon him mandatorily by the party manifesto, as he understood it. He also believed that the starting point of all economic activity in the Indian situation was land relations. He felt that far-reaching change was possible only when the highest authority was totally committed to bringing about a transformation. Everything in land relations moved slowly, if at all. There was a persistent inertia and deep resistance to change. The resistance was not invariably for selfish motives; along with such motives, in a vast number of cases, some sections of people also sincerely believed that change was not desirable at that juncture.

The first few days passed, not exactly in celebration, but in a kind of artificial exuberance. It was just to show that the change of guard had been noted. They held some receptions, some rallies, several meetings—in which everyone said and did everything right. However, in the final analysis, what they said meant nothing—neither to the actors on stage, nor to the audience. All that Anand could do was to rush through the ceremonials, as if to get them over with—without, of course, showing any disrespect or indifference to the organizers. In the process, he became acquainted with a wide variety of individuals whom he had so far known only casually, but would hereafter put to work in a new structure of kaleidoscopic activity.

First came the chief secretary, the kingpin of the state services. Anand had been meeting him off and on since he first became minister, and regularly at cabinet meetings. He was a meticulous person, correct to a fault in everything. Anand had related an interesting anecdote about him many times to his junior colleagues. Years ago, when he was himself first inducted into the government, a dinner had been organized for the members of the cabinet. Being one of the earliest to arrive, Anand had sat in a corner, watching the scene. The chief secretary, as the host, had to receive each minister. To Anand's amusement, he saw the chief secretary make, each time, a modulated movement that showed respect directly proportionate to the rank of each arriving minister. When Anand, a junior then, had arrived, the chief secretary had made almost no movement from his chair. He simply folded his hands and made as though to rise, without actually separating his ample behind from the seat. Then, for the education minister, he did detach his bottom from the chair, but that was all, there was no further movement. But when the home minister appeared, the chief secretary got up and went several paces ahead, as if to catch the minister. And so on, regulating the distance he traversed to meet the incoming minister. And finally when Chief Minister Chaudhury arrived, the chief secretary almost sprinted to meet him. Anand kept marvelling at the methodical nature of the Civil Service. On many other occasions over the years, the chief secretary had given numerous examples of his 'correctness'. Everything about him smacked of the 'establishment'—easy to predict, but very difficult to change.

Anand received the chief secretary with due courtesy. First, they disposed of a few formal items. Then Anand casually asked if anything in the government needed change urgently—such as rules, regulations, laws, protocol, etc. 'None whatever that I can think of, sir,' replied the chief secretary, with supreme confidence.

'You know I have been looking after land reforms for some time. Do you think there is anything to be done about that subject?'

The chief secretary paused a little and said, 'Yes sir, I do, if I may submit . . .'

'Please go ahead . . .'

'Please entrust the portfolio to some other minister, sir. You will hardly find the time to handle it now . . . '

Anand did not reply. A few minutes later, the chief secretary withdrew and Anand found himself in deep thought. He had hardly done anything to turn the land reform slogan into a viable programme. It was still a far cry from implementation. There was a law in the statute book, but it was like an empty shell. There were too many loopholes through which it could become—indeed had already become—a dead letter in practice, either due to deliberate inaction or through extreme negligence. He had to replace the law entirely. And here was the chief secretary asking Anand to throw Indira Gandhi's star programme in some other minister's lap—and perhaps to forget it forever.

The following day, he called the revenue secretary. This individual happened to be much easier to get along with. The new-found mania for land ceilings did not quite impress him, he said frankly. He gave a lucid account of why the idea would never succeed, let alone solve the problem of landlessness. Then, making an about-turn, he concluded, 'But sir, we are here to carry out whatever is the new policy. As it is, I did study your party's manifesto with all its noble ideals.'

The message was clear. The bureaucracy had nothing to suggest. They didn't think they needed any change anywhere. Everything was just fine as it was. But, of course, if the government wanted to do anything new, the officials, down to the lowest rung, would carry out instructions.

The officer in charge of land reforms in the revenue department had nothing new to say, either. Having worked with Anand for some months, he had a fair idea of what his boss wanted. However, Anand had not been the sole boss. Chief Minister Chaudhury had dominated the department by remote control and through many invisible levers. The officer had been walking a tightrope so far. And now he wished and prayed that the land reforms portfolio be handed over to some other minister more ignorant of the subject and less intent on the party's manifesto. When this did not happen, he prayed that the chief minister would find him as mediocre as he really was and shunt him to some other department.

As a party man, Anand shuddered at the scenario. Finally, he took over not only land reforms, but the huge portfolio of land revenue—reforms, ceilings, settlement, record of rights and registration.

Then, for many days, Anand was drawn into a welter of activity in almost every part of the state. It extended from inaugurating a sports meet to attending party rallies to giving away awards to Sanskrit scholars to a conference of district forest officers and many similar functions to which a chief minister *must* devote time. He had to look into his government's public relations meticulously. He had to take special care to avoid the ever-present danger of distortion, exaggeration and downright falsehood in the media. Anand could see the obvious difference between a single-subject minister and the jack-of-all-trades that the chief minister had to be. And the greatest task of all was the giant responsibility of law and order—a perennially problematic area. No wonder, he thought, that commitment to the status quo had become so ingrained in Chaudhury.

Now, at the top of the governmental pyramid, Anand felt very much alone. However, he gained a wider view of ground realities from the top. After a full week of activities unrelated to his portfolio, he thought briefly of land reform. The subject now seemed worse off under him. He felt guilty, but concluded that giving the subject partial but personal attention was preferable to leaving it in the hands of a disinterested minister. The issue, he now realized, was more than just that of taking some land from landholders and giving it to the landless. It involved a re-appraisal of land ownership. Could the state expropriate the landowner from the land merely by passing a law? Would that be an appropriate method to deal with millions of tradition-bound people who had physically and psychologically been identified with their land for ages, for historical reasons? Would they take the reform lying down? And if they didn't, what then?

Some intellectuals in the party had foreseen, even earlier, that the slogan of 'land to the tiller' was not merely about land. By this slogan the party had really mounted the first direct attack on the status quo. Most leaders and activists did not subscribe to this view. They asserted that the manifesto was merely to garner votes. Implementation was, after all, relative. It depended on the attendant circumstances.

Anand and those of his view agreed that no programme could succeed one hundred per cent. However, in the case of land, there was an inherent transparency. No one could conceal land. Whatever the entries in the revenue registers, everyone in a village knew how much land each of the landholders, big or small, owned in the village. And if a ceiling was imposed, as the party promised, people in the village could easily see how accurately or otherwise you were implementing it. From that standpoint, to enforce a land ceiling was simplicity itself. It *could be* correct hundred per cent, no less. But how exactly was one to go about it—that was the main question. Anand explained these factors to the officials of the land reform department—and became engrossed in other urgent matters of state.

This was a golden interval in the country's post-Nehru history, never to return or be repeated. A charismatic leader, a very stable government, everything under control everywhere, the first harvests of the Green Revolution, Indo-Bangladesh *bonhomie*, friendly relations with all neighbours—except Pakistan as usual, regrettably. A precious year and a half without fire-fighting—the time, as many right-thinking persons commented, when the government could have imparted a lasting momentum to any programme of change. And for some time this was what happened. The administration swung into action.

First, the ruling party's working committee held its meeting in New Delhi. It had an elaborate agenda based on the party's manifesto. It gave rise to high hopes among the landless and the other poor throughout the country. The newspapers gave extensive coverage to the event. Did they (not quite they, but their multi-millionaire proprietors) develop an interest in land reform and other egalitarian measures of the ruling party overnight? Or—and some knowledgeable people thought this more likely—were they building up to the anticlimax which they saw coming, given the inner workings of the ruling party, Indira Gandhi notwithstanding?

Along with land ceilings in the villages, the working committee was also to discuss another intricate matter—ceilings on urban land. This was getting to be even more controversial. The entire lobby of the urban rich went into action. It employed all its resources and influence with the government and political parties. The meeting became quite intractable. Indira Gandhi found it difficult even to steer it properly. Those who waxed eloquent about agricultural land ceilings, having absorbed the slogan of 'land to the tiller', suddenly took an about-turn and delivered impassioned speeches at top volume on the impossibility of imposing a ceiling on urban land. There will be chaos bordering on civil war, they warned grimly. Emulating the urban lobby, some intrepid opponents of agricultural land ceilings shouted at the top of *their* voices. They charged the ruling party with unconcealed urban bias; it had become crystal clear at this discussion, they asserted. The rural people would never think of supporting this party from now on, they predicted grimly. They had done so earlier, falling for the party's guiles, but they were wiser now. They asserted that the very idea of a ceiling, urban or rural, was vicious. Why should the government arrogate to itself the right to tell people how much land each of them should have? It was best to go slow, very slow, on this lunatic scheme. Why not concentrate instead on other items of the manifesto?

It was a complete stalemate. They discussed the issue the whole day and decided that the Prime Minister would carry on the discussion with the chief ministers and committee members separately till late evening, and then announce her decision.

What decision, Anand wondered. Once the manifesto had spelt out a promise, it was impossible for the party to go back on it. He wanted to find out from other chief ministers about their individual discussions with the Prime Minister. But they were all equally vague on the subject.

Anand's turn came at around 9 p.m. The discussion zeroed in on what the manifesto enjoined on the party governments. Indiraji sounded quite enthusiastic in the beginning. However, as the topic developed a little more, they touched upon several serious ramifications. It was extremely difficult to make the surplus landholders part with their lands; the very idea of 'surplus' was unacceptable to them. How then can you seize land from the unwilling hands of hostile farmers? After all, they had lived on it for generations. The case of absentee zamindars was entirely different. They did not even know how much land they had. So the abolition of zamindari in the fifties did not overly disturb them. They did carry on litigation for some time, but it was fraudulent, meant mostly for higher compensation, not for land. And in the end they did squeeze whatever they could out of the government. Anyway, they were already settled in the cities, doing business and becoming involved in other lucrative avocations. So the loss of land in some far-off villages did not upset their finances. However, the big farmers living in the villages happened to be the leaders of these villages. And they had always been friends of the ruling party . . .

The arguments were familiar; they had been repeated for many years. Several chief ministers had vigorously stressed them in the day-long discussions of the party's working committee. They were no doubt reiterated in the separate discussions they had had in the evening with Indiraji. She had absorbed, as it were, all the pros and cons of the matter for the nth time, yet almost made it appear that she was listening to them for the first time—every time. At his meeting with her, Anand repeated all his favourite theories on land ceilings. He said there could be no real change in India without giving a new meaning to the ownership of land. Land was, and would be for quite some time to come, the main means of production in rural India. Its ownership should conform to some tenets of social justice, at least until such time as other avenues of employment such as industries or services developed adequately. Imposing land ceilings required careful handling in the beginning. Once this was done, a rural revolution would be ushered in. Ceilings would enable the state to diversify the economy, and bring into its sweep a vast number of village artisans whom the landlords had always kept at subsistence levels. Gradually, a well-balanced economy would emerge.

Indiraji heard him very attentively, without any visible reaction. Anand believed that there had been none to the other chiefs either who had preceded him and expressed contrary views . . . That was her style, as everyone knew.

Then Anand related a story that was circulating in his state. Some couples from the landlord class had taken fake divorces for the purpose of securing separate holdings in the name of the husband and the wife as per the ceiling law. Indiraji began to laugh at this extreme example of avarice, and asked, 'How do you propose to combat this matrimonial fraud for land?'

'We have thought over it, madam,' replied Anand, 'and I still don't know what to do. These are the lengths to which the craze for land could go . . .'

'So you want to become a marriage-wrecker!' exclaimed Indiraji.

'Not really, madam, I only want the land belonging to fake divorcees; I don't intend to meddle with their happy marriages otherwise!'

The meeting ended on that humorous note. The upshot, as Anand understood, was that Indiraji was inclined to go along with the imposition of land ceilings. Her support would be available for the venture. He had no reason to check back on her instructions to other chiefs. It was obvious that they would be the same for all party chief ministers. It could not be otherwise, he assumed.

Accordingly, the state government finalized the new law of ceilings. But what exactly was the strategy of implementing it in thousands of villages? What would be the budgetary provision needed? What time-frame was envisaged for collection of accurate data of holdings? How long would it take to complete the task and then do a thorough follow-up? How long for the distribution of surplus land to the landless? The government promptly referred these very important questions to the revenue department for immediate examination and a complete report in a couple of months. No extension, it said.

The revenue department acted with commendable swiftness. Instead of two months, they completed their task in six weeks. On the first day of the seventh week, their report was on Anand's table, beautifully bound, neatly typed. Very pleased, Anand complimented the chief secretary who had brought the report to present it to him personally.

Anand opened the file and glanced at the executive summary. The very first line made him sit bolt upright in his chair. He stared at the summary in utter disbelief. The final paragraph simply said:

> The total time and expenditure required for completion of the project of implementing the Land Ceilings programme as envisaged in the proposed legislation will thus be three years and four months and Rs 65.78 crores respectively.

Anand quickly calculated that the implementation of the law—*his* law—would be complete midway through the next five-year term of the legislative assembly! In other words, the next government! He could do no more than say 'Thank you' to the chief secretary, who stood beaming on the other side of the table. He was no doubt keen to tell the chief minister about the hard work that had gone into the report. However, seeing Anand's face turn visibly livid, he promised to come back sometime in the afternoon for a detailed discussion.

But news of the report had already got out. The evening editions of newspapers came out with roaring mockeries of the land ceilings programme. Anand was promising results—in other words land to the landless—during the term of the next chief minister! And most probably a chief minister from another party! How generous of him to shower such largesse on the landless poor of the state! Editorials and cartoons in the following weeks broke all records in their levels of contempt and ridicule. There was also a tinge of satisfaction about the fact that after all the fanfare and braggadocio, the government's programme should produce a post-dated cheque on the failing bank of the ruling party.

Anand was crestfallen. They had literally cheated him—the bureaucracy, he thought at first, but corrected himself. Where had the bureaucracy erred? Nowhere, was the answer, no matter how many times you read the report over and over. Genuine effort had indeed gone into the making of the report. It was impeccable.

In a somewhat desperate mood, Anand started on a round of intensive consultations—with MLAs, former MLAs, MPs, former MPs, former ministers, senior bureaucrats, communist intellectuals who swore by land reform—and a host of other interest groups. He also included, for good measure, critics of the programme and, of course, hard-boiled landlords like Balram.

In effect, the implementing machinery of the government had turned round and bluntly declared that it would take three and a half years to complete its task. It had made the government a laughing stock, nothing less! There *must* be some way of doing things quicker and better. Why did the authors of the party manifesto not think of the time-frame while drafting it? It was too late now, anyway.

Uncharacteristically, he picked up the telephone and dialled Shekhar's number. He had never imagined that he would have to call Shekhar at a time of such perplexity. Shekhar, by now MLA *simpliciter*, had not been expecting a call from Anand. He had, to a large extent, understood Anand's predicament. He now gave the question earnest and serious thought. Yet, he could not think of how one could possibly condense a three-and-a-half-year task in order to finish it within a year. On the other hand, you could not leave the programme halfway through the term. If you can't complete it, don't begin it; let things lie, he advised.

Meanwhile, reports came pouring in that in most villages the land ceiling scare had spread. All landholders, irrespective of the extent of their holdings, were in a state of panic. They did not know how much land each family could have, since the government was yet to introduce the Bill in the legislature. So everyone who had any land thought that the government would take his land and distribute it to the landless. The level of discontent was high. Everyone seethed with anger. In many villages, the communists instigated the landless to occupy lands forcibly. After all, the lands would come to them anyway, so why wait for the law?

Anand thought this was the worst crisis of credibility he had ever faced in his life. He began to repent having commissioned that implementation report. In other states, things were allowed to develop, or drift, on their own. Several chief ministers took it easy. They were in no particular hurry. Anand felt he was the odd man out. He had no support except his convictions.

Through all this turmoil, Aruna came to see him occasionally, as if to figure out the shape of things. She was unhappy to find Anand obsessing over his work. She feared this would be his undoing. In any event, she could see neither success nor satisfaction in his undertaking such a thankless task. But she could render no help in solving his problem, for she was as illogical and impulsive a thinker as Anand was a calm and collected one.

The landlord lobby was more than happy at the discomfiture of the overenthusiastic fool of a chief minister, as they openly called him. Serve him right, many of them said with visible glee. They busied themselves in getting their holdings distributed among existent and non-existent members of their families, including the dead and the unborn. Exhausting that list, they brought in the names of pet dogs and cats as real persons owning holdings. In the coastal areas, many landholders bored holes in their agricultural lands and inundated them with sea water. The idea was to get them entered for salt manufacture, exempt from ceiling. The types of fraud improvised within those few weeks defied all imagination.

In a near-comic anticlimax, it was Balram, the confirmed landlord who, in his own way, cast some light upon the situation. He showed up at Anand's house one day, after a long absence on pilgrimage. He described his yatras in detail and gave Anand some of the prasad he had brought from several shrines. Anand thanked him and gradually steered the talk towards the ceilings imbroglio. Balram heard him out patiently and said, as a first salvo, 'Hmm, your perpetual problem again, I see! Why, your revenue chaps will work merrily for three and half years, with all the extra staff which you will no doubt provide. Then they will ask for another three years on some pretext. You can't refuse midway. Finally they will bring you nil returns. Take my word for it . . . '

While they chatted in this strain, Anand's secretary informed him that a large gathering of the state village officers association had come in a procession. A deputation on their behalf wanted to meet the chief minister.

'They're pests,' exclaimed Balram. 'They always ask for more emoluments. They loot the villagers by fudging records all the time! Well, the chief minister has to meet all sorts of characters, I suppose. I shall leave you to them now . . . good luck . . . Goodbye.'

At the door he suddenly stopped and turned round. 'One piece of advice, Anandji,' he said. 'These VO chaps are extremely clever. Each man knows every bit of land in his village like the palm of his hand. They are the authors of all irregular entries. Yet they need to be cultivated. That's what I always do . . . '

The deputation came in and presented a long memorandum of demands—past, present and future. Then they demanded an immediate answer. The implication was that in case no satisfactory response came, they would go on strike. The land revenue collections would begin soon, so it was the ideal time for threats to strike work. The tradition was that there would be a quarrel with the chief minister. Then the village officers would go on strike. A stalemate would follow, each side sticking to its guns. Then there would be some hard bargaining. They would arrive at a compromise. They would call off the strike and all would be well as usual. They were going through these familiar motions. Suddenly Anand thought of something and said to the leader of the deputation, 'Well, Sharmaji, I have a new offer for you this time, instead of the usual bickering.'

'What is that, sir?' asked the sceptical Sharma.

'Will you meet me tomorrow at this time? I would like to study your demands and a few other matters concerning your profession. I assure you, you will like my offer . . . '

There was a murmur from a section of the deputation, but they agreed to come back the next day. Everyone was a bit mystified. Anand himself wasn't quite sure why he had said it; it was only a flash of intuition and needed time to explain itself. Meanwhile, the members of the deputation folded their palms in obsequious namastes and straggled away.

# 56

THE VILLAGE OFFICER IN THE RURAL AREA WAS, AND STILL IS IN many states of India, a multi-purpose functionary. His duties are many and varied. Depending on local conditions, he acts as an unofficial magistrate. His powers are those he enforces, sometimes through goodwill, sometimes through bluff and bluster often accepted unquestioningly due to the ignorance of the illiterate masses in the village. One of these officers is the keeper of land records of the village. On these records stand the various edifices of the state government and the whole gamut of planning and implementation. The village officer also records the rainfall in the village, and the arrival and departure of strangers, vagrants, suspicious-looking individuals, beggars, village theatre troupes, gypsies, pundits and a host of such visitors. The ordinary villager may see such visitors come and go, but does not take note of them. The VO has to maintain several registers, besides sending many reports concerning the events of the day, or the week. In terms of remuneration, he gets what one could call a pittance. It has no relation whatever with the tasks he does for various government departments. But the common belief is that what he gets is not remuneration, but some kind of honorarium. This has been the custom since the days when the post was hereditary (it still is in several states). For the rest, he lives like an earthworm in the earth, or a tiger (jackal may be more like it) in the forest. What village officers earn depends solely on their own capacity, the earth and the forest being completely free! Naturally, their existence seems parasitic, since no one ever sees them work, in the field or in the village. People just see them live, and live well, by village standards. The people in general thus deride the VO; some perhaps hate him. Yet, almost everyone in the village needs his services in some matter or the other, at some time or the other.

When an official of the revenue or police department visits the village, the villagers are able to observe the real worth of the village officer. He talks to the official, explaining things to him the way he wants to (or the way his 'client' pays him to do in case of disputed matters). That is why all wise people keep on the right side of the village officer, insignificant though he may be.

The village officer also forms the base on which the inverted pyramid of corruption normally stands. In the hierarchy of bribe-taking, those at the highest level take the biggest chunk. What the village officer manages to get are the scrapings from the bottom. Yet this is the portion most visible in the village. The recipients of the larger chunks are far from the scene; their booty quietly reaches them, wherever they are.

Thousands of villages lived according to this pattern for generations till it became a part of life. As societies modernized, however, the odium attached to the village officer increased. It was compounded a hundredfold by the nefarious ways adopted by some of these individuals. There were demands for the abolition of the post. But to replace it with regular stipendiary posts would be very expensive and cumbersome. The village officers themselves lost no time in forming formidable trade unions, and exhibited their muscle by resorting to strikes and demonstrations. The confrontation became a regular annual feature. Their infighting constantly aggravated the situation and led to several unions being formed. They vied with one another to increase their demands. Each time, the most impossible demand became the fraternity's minimum one, which was invariably met by a blanket refusal by the government. Protracted negotiation followed. Rivalries among the unions and their leaders made matters worse, while both the government as well as the poorer village officers suffered.

This state of affairs continued for many years, even decades. When Mahendranath was chief minister, the situation began to deteriorate and it continued to do so in Chaudhury's regime too. After Anand was inducted as chief minister, there was a slight improvement, though it meant nothing in concrete terms. The VOs knew that Anand was from a village and that his late father had actually worked as a village officer. That meant some notional familiarity with, and sympathy for, the village officers and their problems. Cynics, of course, said that all this optimism was just so much wishful thinking. They asserted that with this 'insider', the village officers were in for worse treatment. It was then that the unions decided to stop the futile speculation and test the new chief minister. Hence the demonstration and the call on Anand by a high level deputation on behalf of the unions.

The second meeting called by Anand began sullenly and with mutual grousing, as usual. Grievances had mounted for years. But for some temporary palliatives year after year, those in charge had made no attempt to find a lasting solution. So, after a repetition of the old story from both sides, Anand expressed interest in going to the root of the matter, for a final settlement. Even to hear the chief minister say this was a new experience for the deputation. Tension began to ease; the talks became less formal. When Anand told them how he had mastered all their registers in one summer vacation, the atmosphere turned quite cordial. In that mood, Anand said, 'After all, gentlemen, strange as it may sound, I could just as well have been sitting amongst you as a member of your deputation, to plead your case!'

On that very friendly note, Anand invited them to a sumptuous lunch, again for the first time in the history of the state. When the discussion resumed after lunch, there was a perceptible change in the attitude of both sides, particularly the deputation. 'We only want the government to look into our long-standing problems, sir,' said the leader of one union.

Not to be lagging behind in goodwill, another leader quickly added, 'The government may take time, and we understand that perfectly, so long as matters are moving and you take us into confidence.'

Anand finally decided that the revenue department would thoroughly examine the matter, in consultation with the representatives of the village officers' fraternity. It would submit a detailed report ('to me', said Anand with unmistakable emphasis). Then he would call them for a final discussion and the problems that had been nagging them for years would be solved once and for all.

The deputation rose to go, after thanking the chief minister profusely. Even the cynics could not help joining the thanksgiving. However, one of them added, 'We do hope that this government will not repeat the numerous breaches of promise of the past years.'

As they were about to move from their seats, Anand casually said, 'By the way—' and motioned them to sit for a moment. 'Now, if you gentlemen don't mind, I have a small request to make . . .'

The deputation sat down again. Before they could guess why, coffee was served. While the guests wondered if this was the only surprise in the offing, Anand began, 'You see, we have established a friendly relationship today. In view of that, I decided to ask you to do something for me. It is completely outside your duties. Let me also tell you that there is no compulsion from my side and even if you refuse to oblige me, I shall not take it amiss. I shall stick to all the promises I made in the official part of the meeting today.'

The preface was a bit too vague for them to understand. However, Anand's emphasis on the voluntary nature of the task seemed to bind them in an invisible commitment.

An elderly member of the deputation responded, 'We would certainly like to oblige you, sir, in whatever you say. Please go ahead and tell us what you want us to do . . .'

'First, you must answer some general questions,' Anand began. 'Only then can I formulate my task properly. Now, take an average village with say, four thousand survey numbers of agricultural land. Let us assume there are around fifteen hundred *pattadars* (peasant proprietors). Can you tell me approximately, very approximately, how many of them would own thirty acres of double-crop wet land or more or its equivalent in dry land?'

'A question, sir!' A hand went up and a young member asked, 'What is the equivalence between wet land and dry land for our calculation?'

'Well, you know that these factors vary widely according to the fertility of the soils. Let us roughly take one double-crop wet land as equal to two single-crop wet and one single-crop wet as equal to three acres dry . . . '

In about five minutes, the answers poured out. 'I think, sir,' said the elderly member, 'an average village could have around twenty-five to thirty *pattadars* owning holdings of that size . . .'

There was general agreement on the answer, though not without some murmuring among the deputation. When the murmurs ceased, Anand said, 'After all, gentlemen, we are giving only approximate figures. Thank you for the answer. Now, my next question is: How many days, or weeks, would you take to cull out and note down the details of these twenty-five or thirty holdings?'

Anand heard some suppressed but still audible laughter among the deputation. The question, as Anand had formulated it, hurt their professional pride. This time, one of the younger members grinned and said, 'Days . . . and weeks, sir? You must be joking! How can you talk of days and weeks for this work?'

'I don't mean to belittle your efficiency at all, please don't mistake me!' Anand hastened to say. 'Since the work is voluntary . . . '

'Makes no difference to us, sir,' said the elderly member with some passion. 'We will do the work free for you, whatever it is. As for your question, I am sure none of us would take more than a couple of hours to write down the details of such holdings in each village . . . '

There were shouts of approval from all the members. It was a question of their efficiency, and everyone responded spontaneously to the challenge of proving their skill.

'That's splendid,' Anand said. 'Now, let me define the task for you. You have to send, in a given pro forma, the details of the holdings as discussed just now, from each village, to your respective tehsil offices. Starting from a given date, the longest time for this would be seven days . . . . Done?' He looked at all of them with a smile.

'Done, sir!' was the firm answer.

'And lastly, your work will be voluntary, but it will not be free. Please don't get annoyed, as I see from your faces. I am grateful for your goodwill and ready response, but I can't accept it gratis. The government will pay one month's salary, or other corresponding remuneration, to each village officer for doing this work in time.' There was a murmur of mild protest. However, Anand repeated the offer firmly and added, 'Now I have only one stipulation to make. The information you will be sending is extremely important. It will transform our rural society. It will benefit millions of landless people. You belong to a calling which is as old as the village. No government can fully reward you for the service your forefathers have rendered for generations. I do not know what the future of your hereditary office is going to be. They say there are legal and Constitutional ramifications in the matter. But even as a gesture of goodwill and affection for the villages your families have lived in for generations, I want you to give me accurate, hundred per cent accurate, information. Even now I tell you, if you think you cannot perhaps make it accurate, you are free to say so and forget about the job. I shall appreciate a plain reply because the punishment for inaccurate information will be very harsh.'

Now he is questioning our honesty, thought the deputation. There was no question of backing out now. The elderly member replied, almost instantaneously, 'We take up the challenge, sir. Only keep your revenue inspectors off our backs and we assure you hundred per cent accurate information, as you insist . . . '

A day was fixed for the village officers to begin their task. The deputation took leave of Anand in a spirit of goodwill and amity. This was a pleasant change for them. Meanwhile, the chief secretary and others in the adjoining rooms of the secretariat were getting restless. In terms of protocol, it was unthinkable that the chief minister should agree to meet the representatives of the lowest rung of the administration so cordially, even with camaraderie. 'How will tehsildars and other officials be able to control and discipline these thugs after this?' they moaned. 'The fellows will now go back and brag about their clout with the chief minister. How unfortunate! The most abhorrent part of the meeting, of course, is the commitment they have just given. Furnishing all the basic information about land holdings almost free, almost instantly! Why, they have made the department of land revenue redundant at one stroke!'

Once Anand arranged the passage of the voluminous information from the villages to the tehsils, he found it easy to complete the rest of the pyramid: tehsil to district, district to the board of revenue, thence to the revenue secretariat and on to Anand as revenue minister. The total time stipulated came to five weeks. The daunting figures of three years and four months and an expenditure of Rs 65.78 crore estimated earlier by the high level committee loomed before everyone as a huge joke . . . Anand, however, did not discuss that report with any of the high-level dignitaries who had co-authored it. In fact they gave it a silent and decent burial, saving everyone concerned a lot of embarrassment.

To add to the scare among the peasants everywhere, the landlords had been persistently spreading rumours. They asserted that the ceiling law would apply to every farmer—big, medium or small. The media worked overtime to magnify the woes of the farmers. The newspapers said that farmers had never got a fair deal at the hands of Indira Gandhi's party. They received nothing but unmitigated neglect in return for their unstinted support. And now Indira Gandhi was about to take their lands away. You may wager your last naya paisa that Indira Gandhi is sure to introduce collective farming here, in the manner of the Soviet Union. She has always been partial to the communists. Mark my words, she will not rest until she has established collective farms all over the country. Every farmer will become a wage-earning farm servant.

The Central and state governments tried their best to allay these fears, but wild rumours continued to accentuate them. The disinformation was being spread mainly by the landlords. Farmers were fast losing their sleep.

At long last, there appeared a silver lining. The newspapers published the fact that the government was calling only for the particulars of holdings more than thirty acres double-crop wet. The farmers welcomed the news happily. It calmed their earlier apprehensions. This time they discussed the issue in terms of actual size of the holdings. Every farmer understood the extent to which the law would affect him. They could see that it affected very few in most villages. The vast majority of farmers would remain untouched. This prospect carried conviction at once to the peasantry. Millions of small farmers who found themselves 'saved from the ceiling', as they saw it, thanked Anand from the bottom of their hearts. It meant their land was safe and it also saved them a lot of under-the-table payments to the meddling revenue inspectors always on the prowl.

Meanwhile, the spate of fictitious land transfers and fake partitions to make holdings smaller and smaller went on unhindered. Almost everyone in the countryside knew that this had been going on for several years. It began when the leaders first mooted the idea of land ceiling in Nehru's time. And recently, in the few months since Anand had become chief minister, it had attained grotesque proportions. In thousands of villages, the transfers made a large number of surplus landholdings disappear into thin air overnight. Anand clearly saw the unenviable prospect of Indira Gandhi's favourite law being aborted even before its passage by the legislature.

The new Land Ceilings Bill was receiving finishing touches. Everything about it became quickly known, since the media had given the widest possible coverage to all those aspects which could enrage farmers. Each passing day multiplied the number of fake partitions, fake transfers, fake divorces to claim separate ceilings, fake gift deeds, contrived consent decrees of ownership of land, false perpetual leases—in short, every fake legal scheme one could think of.

Anand found himself completely outmanoeuvred by all these devices. Helpless, he watched the blatant violation of the sanctity of law. Legislation was no longer a tool of social change and economic reorganization. Anand remembered the confident forecast of Comrade Bannerjee a few months earlier. He imagined him, at that moment, standing in front of him and smiling, partly with derision and partly with sympathy. 'Anandji, I appreciate your sincerity so much. You spoke the other day, in Chaudhury's house, remember? Your devotion to the cause of land ceilings made me feel that the law, as you have tailored it, may perhaps succeed. I almost pronounced an adverse verdict on the methods of the Naxal comrades. I thought those methods may, after all, turn out to be unnecessary, given missionaries like you struggling in the so-called democratic system. But not now . . . now, both you and I are wiser. We're wiser about landlords, wiser about vested interests, wiser about inadequacy of your implementation and a host of factors. The time is not far when people will indeed be wiser about the democracy itself which you chose for the country . . .'

Comrade Bannerjee's voice—now an insistent boom instead of the restrained but firm tone Anand remembered—reverberated in the chief minister's head and in his whole being, compelling attention. 'You have tried parliamentary democracy for several decades now,' the voice continued. 'Our spurious communists also wriggled out of their more difficult tasks. They somehow zigzagged their way into your indolent and selfish ranks. I have no doubt that their hypocrisy is worse than yours; you at least never embraced communism. But tell me, Anandji, what problems did you solve through parliamentary democracy? Political problems? Social? Economic? In point of fact, you have done much to consolidate the status quo. Well, that could perhaps have been done much more efficiently by the Imperial government. What one really wants is change. And in terms of change, what has democracy achieved? To one like me outside your charmed circle of government, the sum total of change you can legitimately claim to have brought in is very little. I don't say it is nil. Had it been nil the system would have perished long ago. So your leaders brought about just enough change to ensure their survival; some change also came on its own, by the natural processes at work everywhere, in spite of hurdles, I believe. However, the intended beneficiaries received very little from that change. Can you deny this?'

Comrade Bannerjee went on and on. His voice boomed louder and louder. His tone became more and more accusatory. Perhaps I shouldn't have listened to him at all in the first instance, Anand thought. These extremist chaps have a way of assaulting you, once you become their captive audience. And they are all so negative and destructive, with nothing at all to suggest as an alternative . . . But even if Bannerjee was wrong, Anand realized that he himself wasn't proven right! And Bannerjee continued relentlessly, mercilessly, 'I told you, I sympathize with you, Anandji! But when will you wake up to your folly? I am only twenty-six years old, but I can see the complete collapse of the democratic system in India clearly before my eyes. I have found in you a person of brilliance. Many like you have devoted their lives to finding systemic alternatives. No one has succeeded so far. Even when I spoke to you in Chaudhury's house, I thought you were at the wrong place. You belong to that tragic coterie who keep thinking of epochal changes and of new civilizations. They seldom succeed, but they know this well in advance. They do not fear failure, so long as the world can derive some bits and pieces of wisdom and insight from them. But I find you are bent upon wasting your life in plugging the holes in a countrywide sieve. I am sure you will fail, sad though it is to say. They will punish you for robbing their land . . . and their status. They will hang you for your honesty one day, mark my words . . . Run, Anandji, run for your life; do something that makes sense. Do something worthy of a visionary even if it fails, as this land farce also will. No one gives a damn for your genius! Escape, dreamer, save your dreams and your dreaming, before they get you condemned, before they destroy the real you and set the hounds of their suborned public opinion against you—so that you may never rise again! Go, go, go, for heaven's sake, go! Don't be a FOOOOOOL!'

Anand winced under the deafening exhortations and the desperate allegations. He felt his head was about to explode.

The very next moment it was all quiet, all calm after the storm . . . The sea was still, as if it had never known any turbulence. The shore glittered in the rays of the setting sun. Anand saw a lovely young child running towards him. He bent and gathered her in his arms. He felt her blossom in his arms, rapidly, incredibly, exquisitely. A being too resplendent for his gaze . . . Suddenly, he knew . . . This was his Other Half whom he knew so well, had known all his life, all his *feeling* life . . . many lives, he didn't know how many!

Anand lowered his eyes. There was no way he could look at that . . . object or apparition, he couldn't say which. He could only feel the presence, feel it in all his being, and beyond his being . . .

He heard the gentle note of a celestial voice, such as he had never heard before . . . Soothing as a lullaby from heaven, reassuring as a loving mother's song. 'Perplexed?' he heard the sweet query. He didn't know what to say.

Then he heard her whisper, 'You worry too much. It's simple . . . ' He felt something like a touch . . . then he heard the voice again. It was a short, crisp formula that he understood all at once! 'See?' it said reassuringly. Yes, yes, of course, he could see . . . How simple! God! How absolutely simple! 'Thank you, thank you, thank you!' he said, louder each time, still louder . . . to his Other Half! Suddenly he found his eyes open and heard someone say, 'What is it?' It was Veena, who had woken up hearing his fervent thanksgiving. 'A dream?' she asked. 'Yes,' he grunted.

'Can you get me the revenue secretary?' he asked no one in particular in the dark. Veena put on the light and stared at her husband in amazement while he lay back and laughed as if he had *suddenly* found the key to life's mystery. It was 3 a.m.

*

'Are you aware of the fake transactions to escape the ceilings legislation?' Anand asked the revenue secretary, summoning him early next morning.

'Yes sir, the practice is pretty widespread now.'

'Are you getting reports from district collectors?'

'There hasn't been much reporting of late, sir; but we know generally that the last six months or so have seen a spurt in these irregularities.'

'Do you think anything can be done about it?'

The officer paused for a few moments and said slowly, 'Frankly sir, I do not think anything can be done, given the fact that the new law is still to come. And by the time the Bill becomes law, I'm afraid the surplus left for resumption by the government would be rather small.'

Anand did not flinch at this description; he was now a man possessed. He sent the revenue secretary back after thanking him for his advice. Then he called the law secretary who echoed the same sense of helplessness. Nothing can be done, nothing . . . That was the refrain.

'Who is the best legal draftsman in your department? The secretary himself vets the draft at its final stage, I understand. Is that correct?'

'Yes, sir, the drafts come to me in the final form. We have three draftsmen. The best of them is a young assistant secretary called Nagraj. He is very competent, both in legal knowledge and drafting . . . '

'I would like to have a little chat with him,' said Anand.

This came to the secretary as a big shock. 'Very well, sir,' he said. 'But I must submit that he is a very reserved person. If CM approves, I shall bring him over myself.'

'No need for you to bother. Just send him in, I want to see that rare combination of competence and shyness myself.'

The law secretary left reluctantly; he had no choice. He was loath to let a junior under him anywhere near the chief minister, to demonstrate any technical brilliance.

Within a minute, the telephone rang. It was Aruna. Her voice startled him. 'Hello there, dreamer, how are you?'

'In big trouble, I suppose,' Anand replied. 'And how are my opponents?'

'In great spirits, I must say,' Aruna replied. 'Our landlord fraternity are in real celebration, coupled with intense activity. Not a minute to waste. They are now sure to complete the fake redistribution of their lands before you introduce your ill-fated Ceilings Bill . . . My brother of course is in the pink of health and working at peak efficiency. His house is full of lawyers, tehsildars, naib tehsildars, even district collectors and, of course, innumerable revenue inspectors twenty-four hours a day. And yes, a very special feature are the dozens of happily married couples with contrived court decrees of divorce. They're really enjoying themselves, as if they're in a huge drama. They are all there for advice and blessing . . . It's a sight worth seeing.'

'Anything more of interest?'

'Well . . . I may as well tell you all. Bhaiya sometimes becomes moody and feels depressed. He appears very confident to others, but I find him a bit nervous when he is alone. Last night we had dinner together. He never talks of land ceilings or anything about the law to me. However, after dinner last night, he looked at me and said, quite seriously, 'I wish we had not become involved in this wretched confrontation. Anand is not the kind of person one likes to fight against. And worse, he may still successfully torpedo our frantic efforts to conceal our land. You see, he is after all an insider!'

Anand sighed and hung up after some further conversation. Then he heard a gentle knock on the door. He said 'Come in,' and Assistant Secretary Nagraj entered gingerly and announced himself. Anand came round the table, sat on a nearby sofa and made Nagraj sit next to him. This single gesture had the effect of dissipating Nagraj's shyness to a large extent.

Nagraj reported that right then he was finalizing the draft of the new Land Ceilings Bill. It would take three more days to complete it at his level.

'What is the use? All your effort will go waste. I'm sure you know why.'

'I do know . . . a little, sir; too many fake transfers and redistributions.'

'You're right; now can you think of a way to stop them?'

Nagraj remained silent, thinking for a long while. Then he said, shaking his head, 'I'm afraid there is no lawful way of stopping lawful transactions.'

'Do you think they are lawful, Nagraj?'

'Indeed no, sir. But the law presumes any lawful-looking transaction to be lawful until otherwise proved. How can the government review all these thousands and thousands of transactions and prove each one of them *mala fide*?'

'You're right again, Nagraj; no way out that way . . . Now, listen carefully, I want your frank opinion. First, I want to promulgate an ordinance. It will make it compulsory that any transfer which anyone effects, by any means, after midnight *tonight*, of any land from out of any holding over thirty acres of double-crop wet or equivalent, shall require the prior permission of the district collector. Note that I am not banning the transfers outright. Second, the Bill which you are finalizing right now will contain a provision that all transfers effected, divorces decreed, lands converted into salt pans in the coastal areas, partitions of ancestral lands, or any such transaction, made within six months immediately before the commencement of the Ceilings Act, shall not be valid for the purpose of computing holdings under the Act, unless the district collector finds them genuine and not intended as a means of escaping the application of the said Act. The collector shall determine this as per rules to be made under the relevant provisions of the Act.'

'How about divorces, sir? The law disregards them too?'

'Yes, there too we make a simple provision that the law will raise a presumption that any divorce granted within six months preceding the commencement of the Act is for the purpose of inflating the permitted ceiling limit of that family. This, of course, is a rebuttable presumption. The couple in such a case would have to prove that the divorce was genuine and they had no intention of escaping the Land Ceilings Act . . . Like any other fact, this too, I am sure, can and should be proved . . . I am sorry to say this, but since legislation is a weapon of social change and nothing less, how can we let anyone defraud the law blatantly? If the degradation of social values compromises the marriage sacrament too, I think the state *must* act!'

'I have just one doubt, sir,' began Nagraj. 'If we fix six months before the commencement of the Act as the cut-off time, in case the passage of the law takes longer, for any reason, there will be an uncovered gap during which fraudulent deals will again become lawful . . .'

'You're right, Nagraj,' responded Anand. 'So the time-frame you indicate in the draft should leave no scope for such a gap under any circumstances.'

'I understand your intention, sir,' answered Nagraj. 'I shall make the draft accordingly.'

Anand watched Nagraj's face for his opinion. Nagraj's tense lips expanded into a broad grin of complete satisfaction. At last he stammered, 'Now it's perfect, sir, absolutely unassailable. I have no manner of doubt, sir.'

'I don't know how it came to me, or why!' Anand mused, lost in the memory of the glorious presence manifested in his dream. 'I also found, rather was made to find—a name for it. The name suggested was "pre-legislation precaution". I could never have thought of it myself . . . How I wish we could master this technique in the warfare of legislation!'

Nagraj was all admiration.

'Now, there is no time at all to lose, Nagraj,' Anand hastened to say. 'It is six now. I am calling an emergency cabinet meeting exactly at 11 p.m. Before that the ordinance should be complete in all respects. The cabinet will pass it by 11.30 and I shall personally take it to the governor for his signature. This process will not become known to anyone until I have obtained the governor's signature. Under my orders, you will directly submit the file to me, without routing it through any other officer. Is everything clear?'

'Yes, sir,' responded Nagraj, forgetting all the departmental rules that very moment. However, he suddenly remembered something and said, 'But sir, as you know, this is a concurrent subject under the Constitution. The President of India has to give his assent to the ordinance . . . .'

'Yes, yes indeed, I absolutely forgot about that, I must admit!' said Anand, frowning. 'All right, we'll change the plan a little. Once I obtain the governor's signature, the chief secretary and the revenue secretary and you will complete all the necessary communications to the Government of India overnight. The revenue secretary and you will take the first flight to Delhi and set the ball rolling there. You will chase the file from table to table. I shall speak to everyone concerned over the phone, including the Union minister. There will be no need for delay because this ordinance does not seek either to create any new rights or to extinguish any existing rights. So I am sure you will have no difficulty. You will return the day after tomorrow.'

Nagraj, too overwhelmed to say anything, simply bowed and left. He worked in a dedicated frenzy from that moment on.

The following morning, the news of the ordinance hit the state like an earthquake!

# Epilogue

'THIS IS OUTRAGEOUS!' CRIED SHEKHAR. 'A CLEAR DECLARATION OF war against all the landlords, every one of them. A regular war unleashed by the state on a helpless class of useful citizens. How can anyone countenance this . . .?'

He was talking to Balram who had rushed over to his house the moment he heard news of the ordinance.

Balram was hardly able to speak coherently. Very rarely had he found himself so angry and yet so helpless. 'Ordinance? . . . Ordinance?' he muttered again and again, gritting his teeth.

'No party high command ever asked any chief minister to decimate a whole class of citizens so thoroughly and mercilessly. Such warlike offensives have never been heard of in any democratic legislative process. The ministers in the cabinet are absolute nincompoops, I must say. Else, how did they go along with this monstrous decision?'

Shekhar did his best to match Balram's indignation. He had no reason whatsoever to be so enraged, since he neither owned a cent of land nor had a shred of sympathy for the landlords. Yet, his outrage, if anything, seemed to surpass Balram's—so skilfully had he managed to work himself into a frenzy.

'Oh, Shekharji, if only you had been in the cabinet,' Balram moaned, 'you wouldn't have let this calamity happen!'

Balram stood up suddenly. In a voice choking with anger, he brought himself to utter, with a great effort, just three words—three explosive words:

'He must go!'

He shook Shekhar's hand, his own trembling with rage, and left the drawing room.

On the night the ordinance—Chief Minister Anand's

'pre-legislation precaution'—was receiving finishing touches, a recently divorced young landlord and his ex-wife were making love. It was a full moon and though in classical Indian mythology such a night is reputed to kill the base libido (*kaam dahan*), it had the opposite effect on the couple in bed. They had felt an upsurge of desire for each other since their fake divorce. The phantom divorce had blessed them with a whole extra family holding of surplus land in their double-crop wet land area. In the history of matrimonial relations in the world, never had a divorce led to such profound marital joy as it had showered on that couple—and hundreds like them in the state that night.

'God, I'm so happy,' the wife whispered between moans.

'So am I,' responded her partner, who was and wasn't her husband.

They had, with great affection and reverence, hung an exquisitely framed copy of their four-month-old divorce decree on the wall close to the bed they slept in.

But alas! Within twenty-four hours of their frenzied love-making, the unlucky couple were smashing, with uncontrolled anger, the beautiful frame with the heaven-sent divorce decree.

\*

'About eighty per cent of the divorces were decreed within the past six months, sir,' the revenue secretary reported proudly. 'Those surplus holdings will now come to the government.'

'Thank you, the revenue department has done a fine job,' said Anand, in a sincerely appreciative tone.

The revenue secretary didn't quite know how to take this gratuitous compliment; he was not at all sure his department had done anything to deserve it.

'And please send my word of appreciation down the line; there is still so much to do,' Anand added.

He personally spoke to the law secretary, passed on to him the statistics provided by the revenue secretary, thanked him for the prompt work done by the law department and asked him to send a similar message to everyone in the department. 'By the way, I am expecting your draftsman Nagraj to explain to me certain points regarding the draft rules under some important clauses of the Ceilings Bill. We don't have to wait until the Bill is passed to take up the drafting of the rules. We'll keep a full outline ready from now on and quickly give it final shape depending on the provisions that are actually passed. The draft will come to me after you vet it, of course. I only want to understand its underlying principles at this stage . . . '

'Very well, sir, I shall send him at once, sir,' responded the law secretary, inferring (correctly of course) that he himself was not wanted.

When Nagraj arrived, Anand told him, without any preamble, 'Please see that you are ready with all the draft rules as per the first draft bill, from day one. We have to consider both of them together—the Bill in the legislature and the corresponding rules in the law department. Time is of the essence.'

'Yes, sir, most of them are ready; I have brought them for your kind perusal and instructions.' He placed the fat bundle of files respectfully on Anand's table.

\*

After the budget was passed, the budget session was extended by three weeks for the preliminary consideration of the new Land Ceilings Bill. Chaudhury (who was still only an MLA as a result of not having been suitably rehabilitated by Indira Gandhi) and Shekhar came together automatically to delay the passage of the Bill and to sabotage it in a variety of ways. Almost every newspaper in the state, except out-and-out communist organs, tried to find fault with the Bill—indeed, the very idea of land ceilings and the philosophy behind it. This was something Anand had anticipated, because most of them had been against the idea of ceilings even when it was propounded in the ruling party's election manifesto. Their criticism now was of a general nature; they could not direct it particularly at Anand. What they concentrated on, however, was his 'insane, suicidal ordinance'. This, they pointed out very correctly, had neither been considered in the manifesto, nor by any other chief minister, of any party, left or right, in the whole country. This will toll the death-knell of the ruling party, they declared with the supreme confidence which only complete ignorance can generate. The communist papers found it difficult to cope with the piquant situation. In the end, they went to great lengths to find an unprecedented number of blunders on the part of 'this' government, in order to make its stand on land ceilings (which was in consonance with their own outlook) seem of negligible importance. They didn't quite succeed.

Anand undertook an extensive tour of the state, to explain the various provisions of the Land Ceilings Bill and also to gauge the general feeling among the people. When he spoke, he adopted the style of a virtual referendum, consulting the people on every point; in fact he was getting each point endorsed by them. He found, to his pleasant surprise, that the ordinance had been understood and hailed as a great boon by the landless masses. This, however, went unreported in the papers since the media had declared war against it already. Since the provisions of the ordinance which had appeared in the newspapers earlier (this they could not avoid, nor obfuscate) clearly spelt out who they were intended against, the positive response of the poor, as such—regardless of whether or not they actually got land—was tremendous. For the first time, a peaceful law was seen as being used as a weapon of effective attack for a just cause. Fake divorces, in particular, became a matter of great hilarity and ridicule. In hundreds of villages where these were known to have occurred—and nothing was, or could be, hidden from the villagers themselves—the concerned families became the butt of jokes and faced intense, but silent, social humiliation. This added considerably to the animosity the landlord class felt towards Anand. In the final analysis, given the support of the people, it was unthinkable that the ordinance could prove suicidal to the ruling party, as the newspapers had predicted.

*

'There's no way out,' said Shekhar. 'The ordinance is impeccable and unbeatable. Do you know what happened to the writ petitions in the High Court?'

'I got word just a while back,' answered Chaudhury. 'They were dismissed *in limine*, for obvious reasons. Even if any judge wished to look at them, he couldn't have, since there was no violation of any fundamental right.'

'The landlords are engaging famous lawyers to move the Supreme Court . . . '

'Good luck to them. There's no harm in trying. Miracles are known to have happened and much of man's faith derives from them. Yet, in my view, we should lie low, for the time being at least. Those immediately affected will struggle anyhow. Let them. Politicians should bend their heads for the wave to pass over them.'

'But the Bill is being rushed through its legislative stages. The first reading will most probably be over in the current session and the clause-by-clause consideration will also be at least halfway through. I have tried my best to pressurize the Speaker to delay the passage; after all, no important business has ever been completed on time. He is very sympathetic, having been a criminal lawyer whose income swells in direct proportion to the number of murders committed in the landlord-dominated districts. He has tried to delay proceedings, to no great effect. The passage of the Bill threatens to take place ahead of schedule, in fact!'

'That is strange,' Chaudhury commented. 'Delaying government business, I thought, was the easiest of legislative tactics . . . ?'

'Generally, yes,' answered Shekhar. 'But this wretched ordinance has created a wave of euphoria among poor people all over the state. It seems the people themselves are taking part in the deliberations of the legislature. Then, of course, you have Indira Gandhi with her *garibi hatao* slogan, looming large as Anand's guardian angel. I tell you, this Indira Gandhi-Anand combination has the potential to jeopardize the status quo in the state. It is a truly worrisome situation.'

'I haven't been attending the assembly regularly,' Chaudhury said. 'But I think you are exaggerating.'

'Please attend for a few days and see for yourself how virtually every MLA is behaving. They are withdrawing all dilatory motions, even the ones they themselves had initiated, as if paying attention to anything other than the Land Ceilings Bill was a heinous sin. I am sure Anand has somehow managed to bring pressure on the legislators from their constituencies. Even a walking corpse like that Maulana fellow is bellowing against the landlords. I can't believe my own eyes and ears, Chaudhuryji, believe me!'

'Still I say, lie low and let us see. I am not very enamoured of the landlords, Shekhar, but I should have gauged the potential of this issue earlier. How I wish *I* had been chief minister at this moment!'

Shekhar said nothing, but he said to himself, 'How could this hypocrite, this pseudo-socialist, have ever thought of an inspired stroke of genius like the ordinance? God! How I hate Anand! He makes me feel small, with his guts and his conviction!'

After a while, Chaudhury said tentatively, 'I think the Speaker is still the best bet. You must somehow *gherao* him, Shekhar.'

'You think I haven't tried? I moved earth and heaven, I assure you. He did respond, even pretended to be sick to avoid sitting extra hours on some nights. But Anand promptly put the deputy speaker in the chair. That fellow is young, as you know, and dotes on Anand. He is adding his own extra hours to Anand's extra hours! Saturdays have been made working days. No one—no leader of any party or group in the assembly—dares protest against this slave-driving! It's a hopeless situation, Chaudhuryji. The whip of the people is pursuing them relentlessly! There is an invisible mandate from every hamlet in the state that their MLA-slaves shall not show any sign of shirking this time!'

Chaudhury lapsed into deep thought. When he finally spoke, he said, 'You said something about the Indira Gandhi-Anand combination, didn't you?'

'Yes, I said it's invincible.'

'Is there nothing, nothing at all, that can break that combination?'

'I can't think of anything just now.'

\*

Shekhar stayed awake that night plotting and scheming, but when morning came he still hadn't come up with anything that would work. In any event, nothing could be done in Afrozabad, which happened to be Anand's fortress just then. So Shekhar decided to make a trip to the main hive of intrigue—Delhi, where he could, along with Chaudhury, try and make something happen. Another brilliant idea struck him as he was dressing. He was sure that Mahendranath could be involved in the anti-Anand crusade—fully and completely. The reason was simple. Mahendranath hated Chaudhury and would be happy to finish him politically; but a new problem called Anand was threatening to eclipse them both. Mahendranath didn't want, any more then Chaudhury did, someone else to usurp the Afrozabad political throne, through the legend called Indira Gandhi—for the next twenty years. In this common task, Shekhar was sure that Mahendranath wouldn't mind joining hands with Chaudhury—not necessarily directly, given their mutual animosity, but through Shekhar's own very efficient and subtle coordination.

Shekhar, however, was in for more shocks. Anand's methodical approach, using the legislative machinery available to him, had defeated his opponents at every step. When Shekhar casually opened the *Great India Times*, he was flabbergasted to read the following announcement by the State Government of Afrozabad:

GOVERNMENT OF AFROZABAD
Department of Land Reforms

Offers are invited from graduates and double-graduates from any Indian university for the work of village-wise verification of land holdings of a given size and above, for the purpose of computing accurately the extent of surplus lands in the holdings of individual surplus-holders as determined by the survey conducted recently by the state government. Those who volunteer for this work will be grouped in batches of suitable size (to be notified shortly) and taken to visit each village in the state under arrangements made by the state government. The district collector and some responsible non-officials in each district will be in overall charge of the operations in the district. Volunteers will be taken to districts other than their own and provided all necessary facilities to do their work. The entire task is intended to be completed in as brief a time-frame as possible, in view of the urgency of implementing the Land Ceilings Act. The work will be voluntary and with no renumeration. However, the state government will award each participant in the above-mentioned verification programme a social work certificate. Offers may be sent to the Deputy Secretary, Department of Land Reforms (Ceilings), on or before . . .

Reading that announcement, Shekhar rapidly began losing his equanimity along with his appetite for breakfast. His phone rang. It was Chaudhury. 'Another bombshell in the papers, Shekhar,' he said grimly. 'You have read it, I am sure?'

'I certainly have,' Shekhar replied, controlling his anger with a supreme effort. 'Chaudhuryji, this development is so disconcerting that one landlord friend rang me just now to say that he felt like cultivating the Naxalites. I see no other way . . .'

'Don't act in haste, Shekhar,' Chaudhury told him simply.

In a week's time the newspapers reported prominently that in response to the state government's announcement of the scheme, over nine thousand highly educated and highly motivated young men and women had filed applications to serve in the state-wide land verification programme, soon to be initiated. Concealment of surplus land, under the circumstances, became impossible and everyone knew it.

Shekhar was demoralized completely. As a landless politician, rabidly opposed to the feudal class, he was tormented by the excruciating realization that this legislative coup, staged so magnificently by Anand, actually had its genesis in his, Shekhar's, scheming brain. His *vakra buddhi* had finally coiled him in its own festering convolutions.

'What do you think I should do now?' he asked Chaudhury in desperation.

'Break the combination, remember?' Chaudhury replied calmly, deliberately.

*

It looked impossible at first, but when they began to work on it, it turned out to be quite simple. Surprisingly so, thought Shekhar. Analysed coldly and logically, it was easy to ask the question.

Who was Anand to Indira Gandhi? She didn't even know him well. She regarded him as a trustworthy colleague dedicated to the cause he served. But was land ceilings the only cause worth serving in the whole wide world? Suppose, Chaudhury reasoned, Indira Gandhi found her own position endangered because of Anand's effort—found out through her own closest well-wishers that the smoothest way to resolve the situation was to ease Anand out so 'he could concentrate on larger issues which required greater dedication and intellectual prowess' . . . if she felt so and said as much . . .

But who was going to get her to make such a pronouncement?

And how could one get her well-wishers to communicate this to her?

None of this would be easy to manage, especially as the new task assigned to Anand would need to be so challenging and so urgent that it could not wait till Anand had wound up his crusade against the landlords. And he should not feel that he had been tricked into leaving his cause halfway.

Eventually, each one of these tasks was achieved quietly . . . Indira Gandhi was saved from the land relations crisis. Anand was put on an onerous party assignment; if he felt anything about the change of assignments and the reason behind it, he didn't utter a word about it.

He rose to higher positions almost as though he was part of some giant bureaucracy . . . No one asked him what he had done in his last assignment . . . When elections came, the party sank or

765

sailed by the Leader's charisma that was the sole device used to woo the electorate. Election results thus became largely unrelated to performance.

When the country appeared to be on the verge of chaos, a national Emergency was declared—and the democratic institutions of the country received a battering.

Anand remained with Indira Gandhi, through all her trials and triumphs—but with the uneasy feeling that when land (*vishala prithvi*) slipped out of her hands, her hands lost their grip on the country's future. Nothing else her various advisers tried—loan melas, programmes for the landless, housing schemes and a host of other initiatives—could substitute the criticality of the land reform programme to revolutionize the rural scene. And Indira Gandhi herself was defeated, unbelievably.

Then came a government of another party at the Centre, after the confusion of the Emergency. Morarji Desai became Prime Minister—of another party. Indira Gandhi paid for her services by being sent to Tihar Jail by the Lok Sabha. Other cases—dozens of them—did not result in a conviction.

The people welcomed Indira Gandhi on her comeback trail, having become disillusioned with the other party which, in turn, split and collapsed for reasons of internal dissension and utter non-performance. She rode back to power and became Prime Minister again in the midterm poll to the Lok Sabha in 1980. Once again she enhanced India's prestige in world councils. By the time she returned, new generations had taken over throughout the country; there was a radical change in their aspirations. Thanks to the spread of education, the hunger for land began slowly giving way to the hunger for jobs. It took time for this be realized at higher levels.

Then came Operation Blue Star, followed in quick succession by Indira Gandhi's assassination.

Along with other members of the party's parliament board, Anand recommended Rajiv Gandhi's name to the President, to be appointed Prime Minister.

For another event-packed term, Rajiv Gandhi ruled India and Anand assisted and advised him, along with other loyal colleagues.

Then came Rajiv's defeat and another party's government. It fell in nine months. Then came another, for a few months. When elections to the Lok Sabha had to be called again, midway through the campaign Rajiv fell to a human bomb.

Anand, who had decided to retire from active politics and had declined to contest the Lok Sabha election, was called upon to shoulder the Prime Minister's task, suddenly, unexpectedly, in an extraordinary turn of political events. A new phase of his life had begun.